What Goes Bump in the Night

The Council Of Night Chronicles: Book One

By Hellen I Knight

Copyright © 2024 by Hellen I Knight

All rights reserved.

No part of this publication may be reproduced, distributed, or transmitted in any form or by any means, including photocopying, recording, or other electronic or mechanical methods, without the prior written permission of the publisher, except as permitted by U.S. copyright law. For permission requests, contact hellenknightbusiness@gmail.com

Any scanning, uploading, and distribution of this text without permission is theft of the author's intellectual property.

This is a work of fiction. The story and all names, characters, places, and incidents portrayed in this production are products of the author's imagination or are used fictitiously and are not to be construed as real. No identification with actual persons (living or deceased), places, buildings, and products is intended or should be inferred, or is done under fair use claim.

Editing by Gracie Happeny and Clarity Lynn

Book Cover by Hellen I Knight

ISBN 979-8-218-43555-4

1st edition 2024

Table of Contents

Chapter 1.......1

Chapter 2.....13

Chapter 3....27

Chapter 4....44

Chapter 5....66

Chapter 6....90

Chapter 7.....116

Chapter 8....138

Chapter 9....157

Chapter 10....172

Chapter 11....199

Chapter 12...224

Chapter 13...252

Chapter 14...276

Chapter 15....301

Chapter 16....323

Chapter 17...350

Chapter 18....381

Chapter 19....410

Chapter 20...446

Chapter 21....483

Epilogue......523

For anyone still looking for magic
and someplace to belong.

Chapter 1

The trolley rattles and bumps down the street like it always does, but with the new charm he just figured out, his spellbook adjusts for each dip and change, stays perfectly level for Etienne to flick through during the ride. It makes reading on the go *waaaaay* easier, something he's prone to doing as a very dedicated and diligent apprentice, always wants to make sure he's at the *absolute* top of his game no matter what.

He may only be in the middle of his second practicum of apprentice work, but Etienne's already getting trusted with solo assignments, a fact that makes pleased heat bloom in his cheeks and sends his toes curling happily in his boots.

The task he's prepping for now is *extra* special though, because mother specifically requested he take care of it personally, and it's nothing earth shatteringly major, but all the work they do for the parish is important in some aspect or another.

Even if this particular kind of assignment gets on his nerves.

As is practically a weekly occurrence around here, one of the wards is having a specter problem, *again*, and like *always*, it's *'unclear what we could have done to disrupt the spirits'*, which Etienne *knows* means city planning has done something stupid and doesn't want to admit it. Specters can be pesky spirits sure, are fueled by their unfulfilled desires to the point that they sometimes become violent, but if you deal with them early, they generally don't end up murdering anyone.

Honestly, it wouldn't have even *been* a problem in the first place if they'd just listened to mother and hadn't built that shopping center where they did, but *why* would you *ever* wanna listen to your *spirit witch coven* concerning matters of *displacing restless spirits?*

Etienne rolls his dark blue eyes and clicks his tongue, has a passing thought of just leaving the humans to figure it out for themselves. They got into this mess on their own, and since they only want the family's guidance when they *feel like it,* they should have *no problem* getting themselves out of it.

But that would go against the coven's tenets, and Etienne's a good witch, *a good son,* he'll serve the parish as he's supposed to even if it irritates him, lazily waves a finger in the air and the page in his spellbook flips easily at the command. His eyes flick over complicated notes, diagrams of the sigils needed for the appeasement ritual carefully laid out in his precise hand, and it's not a hard spell, just requires a lot of ingredients.

Wiggling his pale fingers at the little folded up section of parchment, the supply list unfolds to its true size, and Etienne skims over everything he'll need, compares it to what he knows he has back at Maisette. There's only a couple things he's missing, *chamomile - phoenix feathers - indigo candles,* but he can get all of those at Madame Élise's, is lucky her shop is right in the Quarter then, so after lunch with mother, Etienne can-

"Woah! Are you a *real* witch?"

Etienne can't help it when his eyes flick up, nor when they narrow at the starry-eyed child staring at him across the trolley, goes back to his spellbook with a huff and hopes that's the end of that. It's not though, *it never is,* and the kid's voice bounces up and down with excitement as they practically beg, "Hey, hey, *hey!* Can you do a trick for me like, um, l-like make my hat purple?"

Mothers of the Night hold my tongue and stay my hand, Etienne thinks waspishly, beckons his spellbook higher and buries his nose behind it, figures that's about as clear a message as he can send nonverbally, doesn't trust himself to speak kindly at the moment.

It doesn't deter the kid in the slightest, and their pleas only grow in volume, pitch, and *irritability,* to the point that Etienne knows

What Goes Bump In The Night

this isn't a local child, has to be a tourist here to *see the sights,* go on those silly little ghosts walks and visit the fake palm readers that set up shop under glowing neon signs. His magic sparks in response to his agitation, maroon particles zinging out of his fingertips, and Etienne has to take a deep breath, reciting the tenets in an effort to calm down.

One, everything exists in a balance we oversee that balance, a foot in the world of the living and one in an open grave, the house of balance and choices, the ones that make sure the delicate gilded scale that is so easily tipped stays level, because at its fulcrum, at its center keeping equilibrium, is *you.*

Two, death is but a marker to change it is not to be feared, all things must come to an end but there's no terror watching the sun set or closing a dear book, and hanging onto things is dangerous and letting go is freeing and remembering is the happy middle ground that keeps something alive for eternity.

Three, we do not exist outside the cycle we are not above it, they are a part of it, they oversee it, impartial observers that help both living and deceased move on, the steady hand that pulls the grieving up and gently nudges the ones at peace forwards, a guiding light at the last fork in the road.

Four, protect those-

"Hey, buddy, pal, *come on,* you wouldn't mind doing *one* little trick for us, would'ya?" That's an *adult* speaking now, and Etienne tries to keep his patience with children because they haven't had a chance to learn, but adults are another matter entirely.

Lowering his spellbook with a downward tip of his hand, Etienne finds the man addressing him, *clearly* a tourist if the shopping bags and *'I ❤ NOLA'* shirt are anything to go on.

The big red heart printed across his chest has Voodoo pins stuck in it.

Etienne feels his eye twitch.

◆✦◆ 3 ◆✦◆

"I have cash, by the way. What do you charge like...twenty... fifteen? For a basic spell?" The guy says, sitting up a little like he's about to pull his wallet out, and Etienne's spellbook snaps shut loudly, the ringing clap of it drawing a few curious observers in the trolley.

Eyebrows flying up his forehead in shock, the man looks like he's about to say something *stupid,* but Etienne cuts him off before he can, "*I* am not a *circus monkey,* an' I don't appreciate you suggestin' as much."

"I- *what?*"

Etienne doesn't deign that with a response, gets to his feet because his stop is coming up anyway, and shakes a loose lock of black hair out of his eyes. He ignores the way the man is gaping at him as his spellbook slips back into its holster, and tipping his chin up, Etienne feels the point of his hat bump into the trolley's ceiling, "I do not *perform tricks* an' I. Don't. *Recite. Spells.* For your *amusement.*"

It's dead silent save for where the gears grind together as the trolley starts to slow down, little bells ringing to announce that a stop is coming up, and black shoulder cape fluttering behind him, Etienne strides past the wide eyed tourist family without a single look back.

He wraps a hand around the pole near the shuttered doors to the car, Decatur Street passing by in slowing blurs, and pulls a face when he hears called snippily at his back, "Hey what's your problem man? You don't have to be-"

"My *problem-*" Etienne whirls around, eyes narrowed and dangerous because how can he just pick *one thing,* grinds his teeth together thinking about neon signs and tacky merchandise and cameras always aimed in his direction, "-is that you *imbésils* come to *my home* an' act like this is all some *fun game.* You think I'm a *performer* here to entertain you, well *I'm not,* I'm a *Boudreaux.*"

Some of the color drains out of the man's face, his partner

✦ 4 ✦

What Goes Bump In The Night

next to him looking equally as alarmed, and it's clear they've heard the name before, but it's likely only ever been under the context of *last of the old ways necromancers and blood sacrifices under new moons dug up graves defiled tombs,* and Etienne's lips pull back in an ugly sneer. He doesn't bother correcting them, they aren't worth his time, *none of them are,* turns his back to the entire car and steps off the trolley as soon as the doors rattle open.

His boots click on uneven paving stones but Etienne's used to it, cuts across the busy street with a huge group of pedestrians, colorful buildings rising around him, trees with gnarled twisted limbs full of Spanish moss waving in the breeze that comes off the Mississippi.

The sidewalks around Jackson Square are always packed with vendors and street performers, but it's extra busy for the lunch hour rush, students hurrying past in between classes and tourists rubbernecking trying to find somewhere to eat.

Etienne only really comes this way to take a shortcut across the square, mother's favorite tea house is further back in the Quarter and this is honestly the fastest way, but otherwise, he avoids this part of the city like the plague.

Unlike most everyone else trying to get through the bustling crowd, Etienne doesn't have any problems, people getting out of his way quickly, and he can always tell who's who, local humans swerve around him and refuse to meet his eyes, while the tourists full on stop and stare and point.

Some of them even bring their phones up to snap a picture before he passes, and Etienne forces his face neutral, won't give them the satisfaction of pointing out an ugly sneer. It honestly wouldn't matter if he smiled at them or not, they'd all go home and say the same things, *look look I saw one I actually saw one of the death witches that haunts New Orleans look at the skulls wears all black to hide the blood creepy disturbing freakshow.*

Humans get one look at Etienne, *at his family,* and let their imaginations run wild, fill in the gaps of their understanding with nonsense drivel perpetuated by popular media. They don't bother learning because it's too hard, they don't bother under-standing because *questioning makes them uncomfortable,* and it's so much easier to be told what to think so you don't actually have to put any effort in.

Every year it seems, there's some new terrible movie that, *'isn't set in New Orleans',* but is filmed here anyway, featuring a grue-some horror plot about blood drinking savages in the bayous, and it's, *'not based on any real covens',* but Etienne would recognize the mark of his house anywhere.

The golden chains on his hat bounce and swing as he holds his head high, breezing past fatally curious onlookers and gawkers, has always taken pride in the name he was given, in the maroon markings under his eyes, just wishes his way of life was offered a *shred* of respect.

In the shops around Jackson Square, nylon witch hats hang in neat rows, pieces of cut glass sit out claiming to be attunement crystals, big, colorful signs promise an understanding of witchcraft in under an hour, and it drives him up *a wall,* but what really sends him over the edge is the fact that it's not just his ways being bas-tardized.

It's all of theirs.

Trumped up tea shops pretend to be rootwork apothecaries, women sit behind wobbly tables waving their hands theatrically over crystal balls, one storefront asks *'Wanna get back at your ex?'* and has bright, garish looking dolls strung up in the window rid-dled with pushpins.

It's horrible and disgusting, but there's nothing they can do about it, *he's tried they've all tried,* but the city council is more interested in turning a profit from tourism rather than protecting their Occult community's traditions.

Etienne has sadly been forced to get used to it, blocks out the chintzy tourist traps as he heads across the square, all of it some-thing like visual white noise at this point. There are some things

What Goes Bump In The Night

that are easier to accept than others, like he doesn't really care if non-witches want to wear the same style of hat or collect crystals, but there are a few traditions that outsiders have *no right to.*

And what really rankles and snarls up his insides are the people he passes that have sloppily drawn on markings under their eyes, made up shapes and lines *that don't mean anything,* patterns they've decided on simply because *they look nice.*

Bearing the markings from a coven house isn't a fashion state-ment, *it's a privilege,* one that Etienne wears with distinction be-cause he was *chosen* by Maisette, selected from birth to be the newest member of the family, *to one day lead it.*

Being a witch takes so much more than knowing basic incanta-tions and wearing a pointed hat, but so many people think they can order a box of crystals and chalk from online, use eyeliner to fake markings, and call it a day.

The bond Etienne shares with Maisette, with mother, with his siblings, goes deeper than blood, it's written in the fabric of the universe, and seeing people treat it so blasé and casual cuts to the quick.

You can either let this eat you alive shéri or you let go, mother's voice washes through his head and Etienne exhales sharply, knows she's right, *hangin' on is not our nature we believe in change an' goodbyes always remember that mô shè,* takes everything he's feeling, *anger frustration resentment,* and sets it free.

Soon though, the hubbub of Jackson Square fades and Etienne ducks down some winding back roads and heads further into the French Quarter, shopfronts going from garish and offensive to more muted colors, signs in gilt lettering hanging above ancient looking doors. The people he passes here are dressed more like him, flowing handspun fabrics decorated with aspects of their sect, slouched hats and vibrant headscarves, heirloom spellbooks hanging off hips.

They incline their heads when he goes by, some even pausing briefly to tip their hats, soft murmurs of *bon jou mishé scion* that

✦ 7 ✦

Etienne always politely responds to, weaves his way down pitted cobblestone roads, dark wrought iron grates arching over him gracefully, lanterns guttering in the shade the buildings provide.

Magic sits thick in the air here like it doesn't in a lot of the more commercial areas of the city, and Etienne inhales deeply, feels it swirl and catch in his lungs, blows out a slow exhale, smiles seeing maroon particles zip and dance in the air.

The tea house they frequent, Amandine's, is a little corner shop on a dark brick red building, shares space with an apothecary and a few antique parlors. Thick baskets of ferns hang off the upper balconies, begonias choked dense in planter baskets under the windowsills, and today, the shutters on the windows and doors are all thrown open to let in the afternoon light.

A small bell chimes when Etienne steps in, coat rack by the door leaning down in offer to take his hat, but he waves the thing off politely and it straightens back up.

"Bonjou!" Yvonne greets on their way back to the kitchen, tray of dirtied dishes hovering over their shoulder as they incline their head, bright blue locs swinging with the motion, "Your mother's at her usual!"

"Mèsi!" Etienne calls, winds around little round tables and intricate chairs, boot heels clicking on the black and white tiled floors, floral scent of tea hanging strongly in the air, undercut by the mouthwatering smell of something stewing in the back kitchens.

Amandine's is always busy, but even then, the chatter from other tables is hushed, regulars calling out gentle greetings to Etienne as he squeezes past.

"Ah, petit Boudreaux, how are you today?" Mister Ambroise asks over the lip of his teacup, silver-streaked braids falling down his back, held in place by a dark blue scarf patterned with starbursts, and Etienne pauses, dips his head respectfully, "I'm good, mishé, how're you? How's your family?"

"They're well, thank you for asking, shè gaçon. Maman really

What Goes Bump In The Night

enjoyed the handmaidens you brought back from the bogs, she sends her gratitude." Ambroise says with a spark in his murky green eyes, and a deep, full bellied laugh echoes in Etienne's ears, gentle pat at his face ghosting by, *mèsi shéri mèsi,* and he beams wide.

"Of course, Mishé Ambroise, an' please, don't hesitate to ask for anythin' else you need." Etienne says and then dips his head again in farewell, spotting mother at her favorite table near the back of the shop. Sunlight streams in through the open window, kept off her face by the wide brim of her hat, and she tips her head up as Etienne goes to her side.

Mother always has an ageless quality about her, dark skin smooth and unblemished, amber eyes sharply intelligent and focused, hair kept in neat braids she's pulled half back today, the rest tumbling loose over her shoulders.

Etienne leans down to kiss her cheek, scent of gardenias and magnolias strong in his nose, "Bonjou, maman."

"Shéri! Perfect timing! Nanette just dropped off the tea." Mother says with a lovely smile stretching her black painted lips, waves a hand and the second chair scoots back for him to drop into, tea-cup and saucer rattling across the table when Etienne beckons them forwards. One look at the serving ware and it's fixing his tea just how he likes it- a bit too much honey, splash of cream -pauses in its proper place off to his right and waits patiently for him to reach for it.

"How are you today, maman? How was your meeting with the other atriarchs?" Etienne asks, taking a sip of his tea and hums in appreciation, the serving ware clinking happily at his approval. Teacup perched delicately in her hands, mother raps her fingers against the porcelain, "Oh it went just fine, Madame Odette sends her love as always an' wanted to know if you could help her with an errand next you're free?"

"I'd be more than happy to." Etienne promises immediately, and mother smiles at him, gentle shape of it crinkling her honied eyes and maroon markings, "Anchante, I'll let her know. Oh! Don't know

✦✦ 9 ✦✦

if you heard, but the Cheneverts just had a new member declared, little girl this time."

Etienne coos an appropriate amount and they drift to talking about what gift the family should present to the new little one. He thinks a three-moon amulet of bronzite would be good, mother is partial to her crow skulls and onyx, and they get into a playful little argument while they wait on lunch.

Nanette swings by to drop off their food while they're in the middle of pelting each other with sugar cubes, arches a thin eyebrow that makes mother laugh and has Etienne flushing embarrassed color high in his pale cheeks.

"Mèsi, Nanette!" Mother sings as the plates set themselves down, wiggles her fingers and sweeps up all the forlorn sugar cubes into a nice pile by her elbow, and sighing long suffering but fond, Nanette cuts a curtsey to her, "Bien sûr, Madame Catherine."

Nanette leaves them with one more amused, scolding look, and still giggling around the rim of her teacup, mother's eyes suddenly go wide as she tips her head back, clinking her nails quickly against porcelain, "Oh *non,* non non non- *Mères-* I just remembered, I have a meetin' with Professor *Pebble Brain* this afternoon."

"Maman." Etienne chides but he's laughing now too, has honestly heard *much worse* from her in regards to the president of Hermes University, picks up part of his sandwich and asks before taking a bite, "What does she want this time?"

"Chancellor Richards didn't say, but I swear to the Mothers if that-t-that- *know-it-all* makes me listen to *one* more lecture on *'the modern benefits to practical alchemy',* I'm gonna turn her into a bullfrog an' fling her out to the bayou." Mother declares loftily, and Etienne nearly chokes on his food he starts laughing so hard.

"You are *impossible.*" He tells her fondly, and mother sputters, waving a hand dramatically, "No! *She's* the impossible one! Bringin' all those little heretics *here, Mères de la Nwit,* I swear, shéri, I'm gettin' them outta our parish mark my words."

What Goes Bump In The Night

"I know, maman, I know." Etienne soothes, reaching across the table to take her hand, their magic curling out and around one another's, *family kin know you know those markings one and the same,* squeezes her fingers reassuringly, "You've already got all the other atriarchs support, all you need now is the chancellor an' city council's."

"Blowhards the lot of them." Mother sighs, but when she smiles, it crinkles her eyes and dimples her cheeks, "Thank you though, shéri, you're such a kind soul."

"Always, maman." Etienne says earnestly, and they detangle their hands, go back to lunch and put aside worries of incessant alchemists and their unnecessary need to change everything, at least until the belltowers ring in the next hour and mother has to go.

Etienne rises out of his chair and goes to pull hers back for her, helps her up with a hand and leans in to kiss her goodbye, brims of their hats knocking into one another a little, "I'm goin' by Élise's before I head home, I'll light a candle for you while I'm there. Do you need me to pick up anythin'?"

"No but tell her I said hello, an' mèsi Etienne, I'll need all the peace I can get." Mother says with a roll of her eyes, cups his face in one of her hands and rubs a thumb across his cheek, "Have a good rest of your day, shéri, I'll see you tonight."

"Yes ma'am." Etienne smiles and moves out of the way so she can sweep past, dark skirt fluttering behind her, inky shine of feathers sticking out of her hat, glittering golden chains and pieces of onyx swinging in time to her steps as she leaves the tea house.

Saying his goodbyes to Yvonne and Nanette, Etienne heads to the door as well, waves to Mister Ambroise and the flickering shape of his mother sitting across from him, the two of them enjoying a nice cup of tea together.

Before Etienne can leave though, he gets caught up in a few more conversations with Voodoo priests and fellow witches, holds the door for an ancient, tottering trio of past coven matriarchs that all gush over him in heavily accented English, one former LeBlanc matriarch insisting he lean down for her.

She pinches his cheek in a wizened set of fingers, rheumy eyes swirling with the knowledge of too many futures and possibilities as she smiles at him with gilded teeth, "Such a good gaçon. Beacon of the communi'y you is, gonna make a *fine* patriarch some'ay."

Etienne can't help the way his chest swells with pride, only thing he's ever wanted to do is serve his coven, *his community his people,* to the best of his ability, knows without a shadow of a doubt this is where he belongs, that this is what he was *made for.*

"Mèsi beaucoup, Madame Bathilde." He beams at her, and she pats his face roughly, lets him go with a hazy, cackling laugh and a confusing, "Don' mind the metal now, chil', it'll grow on'ya."

"Of course." Etienne says politely even though he has no idea what she's talking about.

A lot of older LeBlanc are like that though, they see too much for too long and it starts to slip away from them over time. Madame Bathilde hums a snatch of some winding song and meanders after her friends, and Etienne finally slips free into the late afternoon sun, inhales, feels magic spark in his lungs, at the tips of his fingers, and grins.

Most witches are content in their lives, with their stations, but Etienne knows the other scions are worried about taking over after their parents someday, and while a warranted anxiety, it's something he tries not to feel.

This is his life's *calling,* the only thing he was brought into this world to do, and while overwhelming at times, it *is* a grounding thought, has Etienne stepping down the street confidently, sure in who he is, what he's doing, and where he's going.

Chapter 2

Etienne has almost everything he needs laid out on the storage sigil, but he can't find his accursed stash of wormwood charcoal anywhere, pushes back from his worktable with a groan. "Maisetteeeee, *heeeeelp.*" He whines, leaning his head back in despair and his chair gets jerked around, tips up on its front legs and shakes him out of it.

The floorboards rattle under his feet, shuffle across his room and his bedroom door swings open, boards out in the hall jumping to catch his attention before scuttling off to the right. Etienne pokes his head out of his room, somehow isn't surprised to see the paintings rocking back and forth near a door further down, candelabras twisting to point accusatory candles at his older brother's room.

"Mèsi, Maisette." Etienne calls and the paintings do one last spin, candelabras puffing up happily like they have small chests, flames leaping higher as Etienne goes to stand outside his brother's door, knocking on it loudly, "Éy, Oliver! You home?"

Above his head, the crown molding wiggles letting Etienne know that yes, Oliver *is home,* and he fights the smile back, runs his fingertips down the wood of the door and lets some of his magic slip free, feels Maisette shudder in response.

"You're not supposed to have favorites." He whispers in a chiding tone, and the doorframe bends in something like a shrug, *we know we know but we do,* door suddenly gone out from under his hand as it swings inwards, replaced with the blinding pale shock of Oliver's hair.

"Frèret, what's up?" Oliver asks, leaning against the doorjamb, tan, tattooed arms crossing his chest casually while he reclines.

He's dressed down, simple black slacks and peek of bare toes, white button up patterned with half lidded eyes and Luna moths, hat hanging off one of his bedposts, must not have any work today or just got back from an assignment.

"Oh...nothin' much, just got a mystery I'm trying to get to the bottom of." Etienne sighs, hand coming up to tap a long finger at his chin, tilts his head to the side and makes it out like he's absolutely stumped, "Ya'see, I'm tryna get all my things together for an assignment and just...looks like my supplies up an' grew legs again. Strangest thing I tell you."

Rolling his eyes so his whole body moves with it, Oliver shuffles his arms a little closer and tips his chin up, snorting defensively, "Yeah okay, an' what makes you think *I* have'em?"

"You *always* have'em."

"No I *do not-!*" Oliver is in the middle of snipping when a pillow gets catapulted off his settee and smacks into the back of his head, knocks him forwards just the barest amount, and he glares over his shoulder at where his furniture is all rattling at him, "Alright *alright!* Yeah *bon, whatever-* I...might'a borrowed something or another last week, *hex me Etienne.*"

"See? Now was that so *hard?*" Etienne says with a teasing lilt, grinning as the doorframe over their heads buckles in then out, *Maisette giggling along with him not supposed to have favorites you're not,* and Oliver opens his mouth to argue back when the front door unlatches downstairs.

A familiar rush of magic floods in and brushes along Etienne's mind, *wide devil grins and howling hyena laughter think we'll get caught bright flash in green eyes,* and unbidden he can feel his own magic reaching out, answering the call, *welcome home welcome back welcome family-*

"*Cé koté mo yê!* Come check out this *weird ass* thing I brought back!" Her chipper voice shouts up from the foyer amidst faint scuffling noises, and that's more than enough to intrigue Etienne, and he goes bounding off down the hallway, calling dismissively

What Goes Bump In The Night

over his shoulder, "I want my charcoal back on my desk before the night's over, Oliver!"

He doesn't get a response and isn't expecting one, skids to a stop at the top of the staircase and the banister sway forwards to catch him if need be, but he manages to not trip over his feet for once.

Below him, his sister is still shrugging out of her sheer overcoat, passing it off to a coat rack that's bent down for her, mess of bags dropped at her feet. She takes her hat off and hands that over as well, ruffling her vivid ginger hair, catches sight of him out of the corner of her eye and spins, arms open wide, "Ti martre!"

Floorboards jumping at his heels, Etienne clatters excitedly down the stairs, feels the bottom step lift up to help propel him forwards and his socked feet slide *fast* over the polished wood floors, "Katie!"

She catches him easily despite being so much shorter, spins them in a fast circle, broad grin stretching her green lips wide, "Bon jou! How are you? You ready to see the *weirdest* thing in your *life?*"

"Can't be weirder than that one person who had centi-"

"*Non!* Non mishé- we agreed to *never* speak of them *again.*" Katie declares loftily, tips her head down so she can pretend to glare at him over the rims of her bat-winged sunglasses, "An' *okay,* it's not as weird as *them* but-!"

She lets go of Etienne to fish around in her bags, and he keeps trying to steal peeks over her shoulder, but like she *knows* he'll be looking, she keeps moving to block his view, eventually spins to her feet with something triumphantly held in her hands, *"Behold! A man!"*

"That's a *doll,* Kat." Oliver's voice sighs from behind them, and Etienne spares a quick look back, sees his brother plodding down the staircase with his hands deep in his pockets, sighing again long suffering when Katie snaps at him, "Lamèd to, oliv!"

✦✦ 15 ✦✦

"Well it *is.*" Oliver maintains, coming to a stop beside Etienne and then they both arch eyebrows at Katie and her doll. As far as dolls go, it's not even that creepy of one, just some porcelain monstrosity decked head to toe in frilly lace, eyes blank and vacant, but she rattles it aggressively at them both.

"Nuh *uh.* Get those *damned* looks off your faces, didn't even give me a *chance* to explain, *Mothers-*" She gripes, propping one hand on her hip and using the other to hoist the doll up, showing it off like it's a championship belt she's won, "What you scoff and call a mere *doll just so happens to be* the vessel some murderous revenant has taken up residence in, an' *I'm* the one who caught the bastard!"

That's about the time the doll's head spins around in a quick snap, temperature in the foyer plummeting as it shrieks in a crackling voice, "Damn you *bitch!* As soon as I get outta here I'm cuttin' yer toes off an' makin' a necklace from'em you *stupid-*"

Whatever it's screaming about gets cut off abruptly as bright maroon sigils flare along its body, Katie's magic cracking through the air like a snap of fingers, effectively shutting the horrid thing up. "Yeeaaah." She drawls, taking stock of their surprised faces with obvious glee, "He's got a mouth on him, somethin' of a misogynist too. *An'* I'm pretty sure he's got a thing for feet."

The doll rattles spastically in response, like it violently wants to argue against that accusation, but it's held immobile by the sealing spells inlaid over its surface. Etienne cuts his eyes in between it and Katie, runs through a list of everything he's ever seen and yeah, *okay,* sexist vengeful spirit with a foot fetish possessing a porcelain doll *definitely* makes the top ten.

"Yeah. That's pretty weird." He agrees with a nod, and Katie beams at him like the *sun,* uses her free hand to push her sunglasses up into her hair, green eyes blowing wide in joy, *"Right?* He's been killin' people in the eighth ward for over a week, been hoppin' bodies until me and Louisette cornered him today. Jumped into this lil'merde thinkin' we wouldn't notice."

What Goes Bump In The Night

She holds the doll by one leg and shakes it roughly, crowing loudly, "How you like that huh? *Piece of shit lamèd latèt-* taken down by two *women.*"

"What're you gonna do with it?" Oliver asks, stepping up to poke at the doll speculatively, and tendrils of his own magic leak out to bolster Katie's spells, not like her magic needs it by any means, it's just a subconscious manifestation of his desire to *help.*

"Well me and Louise were gonna do the usual, track down the body, salt'n'burn it. Make sure it's buried proper this time." Katie rattles off while the two of them nod, all very familiar with how to dispose of revenants and other displaced spirits, "But problem is we've got *no clue* who our friend is. Obviously he ain't cooperatin', so Lou's looking for the body the old fashioned way, needed time to scry, and, well, I got stuck babysitting. Which, speakin' of- *Maisette!*"

The floorboards under their feet ruffle, *we're here we're here what do you need daughter,* and motioning Etienne to make room, Katie calls, "Would you mind puttin' the baby down for his nap?"

Katie then drops the doll and kicks it hard, punts it clear across the foyer and into the air vent that snaps open, loud discordant banging fading out as it hurtles off into the basement. "Thank you Maisette, mô shè!" She sings and the vent grate clangs shut, squeak of the metal almost sounding like a kiss being blown across the room.

Out of his two siblings, Etienne wouldn't be hard pressed to say his sister is his favorite. Whereas Oliver is morose and quiet, always seems faintly irritated with Etienne any time they talk these days, Katie is vibrant and fun and *hilarious.* She can make him laugh no matter what, pulls stupid faces at him across the dinner table and is more than willing to engage in some fun pranking, has had him giggling at her antics a million times before just like she's doing now.

"Well! That was my day! What about you boys, huh? How are you? How are my dear frèrets?" Katie coos, clasping her hands over her heart as she flutters her lashes, and swaying a little closer, Etienne is *more* than happy to tell her.

"Good! I spent the morning pullin' information from the archives for Tant Atha, and then I met maman for tea and we discussed the specter assignment out in the second, *which-* once I get my *charcoal back,* I'll have it taken care of in no time." He informs her proudly, shoots Oliver a smug look and gets an eye roll for his troubles, distracted a second later as his hair is mercilessly ruffled.

"Ooo, big man, *huh?* So grown up, doesn't need his sister chasin' him around anymore." Katie sighs dramatically, moves forward as he moves back, keeps her hand firmly glued to his head, "Aw, what's the matter *petit* frèr? I thought you were a grown up witch now, what'cha runnin' from, huh?"

"K-Katie-! Stop!"

"Mmm...*nah."*

They scuffle around the foyer, Katie teasing and poking at him, both of them acting like they're children again as they tumble through doorways and crash into anything that's not nailed down, Oliver sulking off to the side watching them with a narrowed gaze.

The three of them are relatively close despite the six year age gap, but that's just a byproduct of being a smaller coven with less spots to fill, means that there's never more than a few children at a time.

Katie and Oliver were mother's first, came to her when they were no more than four, a fairly standard age for a coven house to lay its mark. Up until then, they'd lived with their human families before being called forwards, and since they arrived at the same time and were relatively the same age, they're often referred to as *the twins,* even though they could not look more different.

Pale and petite, Katie has vibrant ginger hair she keeps in a messy bob, face elfin and mischievous no matter the situation, counterpoint to Oliver who always looks slightly gloomy, dark serious eyebrows looming above black eyes, broad shoulders and prominent nose.

What Goes Bump In The Night

And then there's Etienne, their *little* brother that towers over them both, too long limbs he's always tripping over, delicate, refined features mother tells him make him look distinguished and stately rather than weasely.

If asked, bystanders would not be able to name them as *cousins* let alone siblings, but appearances don't really matter much in their family. None of them look anything like the others, only thing they all have in common are the maroon markings under their eyes, a symbol of how deeply connected they are, more so than any standard blood relations.

That's what humans always fail to understand about coven houses, how it's not simply a case of adoption, or conscription as many misinterpret it, but rather a calling that's so ingrained in them, they couldn't ignore it even if they wanted to. Magic isn't just a system of power that shapes reality, it's a living *breathing* thing, and beats through their veins same as blood, linking them all together in a chain that stretches back eons.

Not everyone has the potential to become a witch. It's a selective process that the individual houses carry out, or rather, it's not something the *members* decide on, but is determined by the entity that thrives at the center of every coven, *the wellspring of their magic their guardian the First Parent the heart.*

Maisette selected each one of its children because it knew they were the *best* suited to receive its gift, that they were *destined* to serve the family Boudreaux and carry on the honored traditions as laid down by the Night Mothers.

That's why Etienne takes his station and position so seriously, and for him, there's extra importance levied on everything considering he was a witch from birth. It's a rare occurrence, but not unheard of, carries a certain prestige with it that he's more than happy to wear proudly. There's distinction in knowing your coven house could sense your potential before you'd even drawn breath, and while not *every* scion is a witch from birth, mother wasn't and she's one of the strongest witches he knows, most of them are.

With that kind of weight on his shoulders, Etienne really tries to live up to all their expectations, and he does, conducts himself as anyone in the community would expect the next Patriarch of House Boudreaux to behave...which at the present moment includes shrieking like a banshee as he's mercilessly noogied to death by the elder sister who stands a good foot and a half shorter than him, and yet, always seems to have the upper hand.

Etienne is trying to slip out of her hold, *to no avail curse her,* when there's a muffled creak behind them and a presence rushes over theirs like the sharp snap of black wings.

In an instant, all the paintings in the foyer start wiggling and edging closer to the opening front door, furniture standing up straighter and candles burning brighter, *everything taking a short excited inhale,* and the three of them spin around, greeting at the same time, "Maman!"

Mother sweeps into the foyer like a proud bank of storm clouds from out over the bayou, thunderous rumblings of power hissing in the space between spaces, and it seems like the entire house tilts towards her, showing deference to its Matriarch. *Hello welcome home missed you daughter our daughter love you hello welcome,* Maisette sings in the way the floorboards ruffle under their feet, rugs straightening out so she won't hook her shoes on anything, the magic of their house thrumming absolutely content to have them all back within its walls now.

The coat rack scuttles closer to mother as she shrugs out of her shawl, takes it and her hat gratefully, and while small actions, there's something stiff and controlled about her movements.

Mother isn't young, but she's not in poor health, hasn't expressed any issues with joint pains or weakening muscles, not like Aunt Atha at least.

Her duties as matriarch also rarely take her out into the field, so this rigidness can't be from a physical hurt, but there are still other aspects of her position as coven leader that could cause great discomfort.

What Goes Bump In The Night

Etienne has a feeling he might know what's behind it, *had that meeting today with the Chancellor and the professor bad news then,* and he can feel his own mood plummeting because bad news from the two of *them* never means well for the covens and other sects.

"Shéries." Mother turns to them with a beautiful smile that's a little strained, and they're all quick to shuffle into line, inclining their heads as she passes after touching them each briefly on the cheek. When she gets to Etienne, she pauses a breath longer and he searches her honied eyes, *exhausted frustrated she won't bend they won't yield something has to give,* and he leans into her hand murmuring, "What's wrong, maman? Did the professor talk your ear off again?"

He knows he's guessed right, or has gotten close at least, because her magic sparks against his skin, smile slipping into something far less warm as she pulls back, demurely declaring with all the pleasantness of a storm about to break, "Well now, you could say that. I...have news children, but first, I need a glass a wine an' I need it *now.*"

Exchanging worried glances with the others, Etienne and his siblings trail along after mother into the parlor where the glassware on the sideboard is already pouring out a glass of her favorite Malbec. She takes it elegantly in hand and goes to stand in front of the floor to ceiling French doors that look out over the back gardens, fireflies winking in the gloom that's steadily falling.

"Believin' in change an' letting go is one of the founding principles of this house." Mother begins in the tone of voice she uses during lessons, when she's addressing the council, spine as straight as a column and head held high, takes a sip of her wine before continuing, "We are *Boudreaux,* we understand the *necessity* of movin' on and we do *not* shy away from endings...nor do we balk at new beginnings."

Katie takes a seat on one of the couches and Etienne drops down next to her, nervously picking at his nails and unsure where this whole thing is going. He catches Katie's eye and makes a *what the hell* gesture, but she only shrugs, uncharacteristically serious tilt to her face, and along all the shelves lining the walls, books rattle back and forth, crowd closer together like they're trading whispers.

As if they're wondering what's happening too.

Mother swirls the wine around in her glass, holds it up to admire the way it runs down the sides and says, "I had a meetin' with Chancellor Richards today and Professor Pe- *Doctor Wöllner.*"

That bleeds apprehensive down Etienne's spine faster than anything, because mother never *ever* refers to the president of Hermes University as *anything* other than Professor Pebble Brain, so whatever's happened, *it's serious it's big something's changed don't spiral don't panic keep it toge-*

"As I'm sure you're aware, there's been discussion for years now over the integration status of the university mergin' with our already well established system." Mother's cadence is even but her tone is bitter, all of them *painfully* aware of what the influx of new age magic users has done to the city, slowly eroding their way of life one practice at a time, "An' there's been...*concerns* it's not going smoothly enough, that there's still too much...*misplaced opposition.*"

Mother pauses to take a *long* sip of wine, nearly drains her glass, and underneath the in-between, her magic flares despite her iron-clad control, skitters and skates over reality like feathers ruffling in agitation, "In an effort to *foster better understandin',* we, and the other covens, have been *asked* to take part in a new program that'll-*forge closer ties* between our...*between our two sects.*"

The energy in the room spikes sharply, Etienne and his siblings losing their heads at hearing *Mother* refer to *alchemy* as a *sect,* like it's anything comparable to the traditional practices that've been a part of the Occult community since the dawn of time.

Maisette reacts violently to the sudden mood shift, frame groaning as all the lights flicker wildly, and mother's quick to look over her shoulder, reprimanding firmly, *"Children.* Control yourselves, you are not younglings anymore."

✦ 22 ✦

What Goes Bump In The Night

Etienne takes a deep breath and forces himself to *let go,* recites the tenets as he folds his arms across his chest, moodily wiggling into the corner of the sofa and flips a hand out, "This is *absurd.* New program? What's that mean *exactly,* like- what *more* do they even want from us? We've already given'em a seat on the council despite them not meeting requirements for membership."

"An' relinquished duties *we've* historically provided for *centuries* across the wards." Oliver adds on, hip stiff where it's cocked against an armrest, and Etienne gestures at him broadly, *see see he gets it,* arguing, "They're as *integrated* as they need to be. What else could they *want?* Majority voting rights? A- *monument* dedicated to'em? Or- o-or *alchemists* studyin' at *coven houses?"*

It goes eerily silent.

It goes eerily silent and Etienne thinks he might be sick, stares desperately at the back of mother's head and keeps waiting for her to refute it *and she doesn't she doesn't move a muscle and no no that can't be it that can't be it but she's saying n o t h i n g and no Mothers of the Night no- not this anything but this not his home not his way of life not his identity-*

Ice crackles through his veins, foreboding kind of dread building up and Etienne regrets shooting his mouth off, knows the superstition about speaking things into being and *damn him and this mouth.* He swallows rough, pulse starting to thunder under his skin, magic ballooning out of control like a thunderhead because no, there's no *way,* they have *no right* to ask something like that the city council would never *allow it-*

But they haven't been on the covens' side in *years interests are shifting modernize and move on the city doesn't have a need for things that can't keep up and no no no they can't take this from you too you won't let them you WON'T-*

"M-Mère! You *can't-!* You- y-you can't let them *do this!"* Etienne begs, flying forwards to clutch at his knees, emotions crashing out of control and making the air crackle like before lightning strikes.

He knows he's behaving inappropriately, but he *can't stop* the

✦ 23 ✦

panic that swallows him, *can't stop spiraling,* imagines a future where *everything* gets taken from him, *his clothes his house his name his way of life,* wets too dry lips and stammers, "We c-can't let this happen! We have to fight them, we- w-we- they can't *do this to us! They can't-!*"

"It has already been done. The vote passed this morning." Mother declares with no room for argument, and the parlor falls into a fragile silence, soft tense hush like a string's about to break. Hunching over, Etienne stares unseeing at the richly patterned rug under his mismatched socks, eyes tracing over skulls and shadowy faces and so many other things the rest of the world deemed *weird* and *off-putting.*

Just like him.

What a freak, the less brazen of them laugh, think it's okay because they're hiding behind their glinting phones and camera lenses, *creepy antiquated unnecessary,* locals whisper nervous but grow louder, start turning away from what's always protected them, and it's not the worst he's ever heard, *grave robbers necromancers child stealers angry voices raising like the fists you're scared are next shaking where she pushed you behind her get away from him,* but none of it is *fair.*

Etienne was born to this life, loves it so very deeply, but *Mothers,* it is such a hard thing to love something and be hated for it, to live in service for the betterment of others and have them resent you anyway.

They're gonna destroy your entire way of life dismantle what they refuse to understand kill anything that tries to resist that includes you and your whole family, and it's such a horribly bleak thought, Etienne has to squeeze his eyes shut fast to stop the furious tears from falling.

"The covens still retain autonomy over our houses and I will *not* let one of those...*heathens* in here, so w-we are not losin' *anything,* we are...gainin' an opportunity to *learn.*" Mother's voice sounds like it's coming from a million miles away, like it's a nightmare he

What Goes Bump In The Night

just needs to figure out how to wake up from, and a blanket slides up over his back quickly, *our son our child do not fret do not fear we are here we are here and you are safe.*

His fingers clench in the material like a lifeline, mind sinking back into the thousand reaching *grasping wiggling hands* that paw at his consciousness, and Etienne gives into it, *lets it take him,* rocks somewhere in that black sea far away from here while mother continues speaking, "Startin' next week, every coven apprentice will be matched with an alchemist student of equal skill level in a partnered exercise. This is not optional an' will be enforced both by the city council...and our own. Each participant is expected to *learn* from this partnership an' *teach* in equal measures-"

What's to learn what's to teach have no right to ask such a thing, Etienne thinks venomously, hung up on that point more than anything else, but then Katie draws attention to the rest of it, *the worst of it,* when she sighs in relief, "Wait. *Wait-* so fully claimed coven members don't get stuck on this exchange thing? It just applies to the...*apprentices...*"

She trails off slowly, clearly having realized that while she and Oliver were in the clear, *performed the Blood Rite under the full moon on their twenty-fifth birthdays were marked with charcoal and given their signet rings,* they aren't the only children of mother's, but they *were* the ones that didn't have to play nice with the *enemy and that just meant that oh Mothers no-*

All the air must be gone out of the parlor because Etienne suddenly can't breathe, *knows* everyone's turned to look at him, *they're always looking at him seeing how he'll measure up if he'll be the witch they all expect him to be,* and he glances up, hoping to find some way out of this.

Mother has shifted to face the rest of the room, shoulders set, spine straight, chin level, appearing like she has full control over the situation, *is the force to be reckoned with he knows her to be,* but when he meets her eyes, he finds the truth of the matter, *I stood I fought I gave it my all...and I lost.*

✦✦ 25 ✦✦

He swallows rough.

There is no other way, the grim set to her mouth says, turned down in the corners and creating faint wrinkles, *we don't have a choice,* her fingers sigh as they grip ashenly around the stem of her wine glass, *you have to do this,* cries the slight bowing of her proud head.

And Etienne is a good son.

He's a good *witch,* will serve his coven and his parish as is his duty as Scion to House Boudreaux, and if mother tells him *this is what needs to be done,* he'll do it no questions asked.

Etienne sucks in a huge gust of air and sits up proper, dons the mantle of heir, *of scion,* takes everything he's feeling, all the anger and resentment and brutal frustrations, *and tries to let it go.*

There's a beat of calm, *he exhales,* and then every single book around them explodes off the shelves in a maddening flutter of pages.

Chapter 3

Someone knocks into the back of his chair *again* and Etienne snippily scoots closer to the gross little plastic table, feels his abdomen bump up against the edge and clicks his tongue. *Figures.* Of course this...*coffee shop*, though he really hates to give it the distinction, doesn't have adequate spacing between its tables, prefers to cram people in without any care *whatsoever* about the comfort of its other patrons.

That's just *so like humans,* maximizing quantity at the detriment of quality, and he wrinkles his nose at how *incredibly* packed it is in here, overcrowding meaning it's super loud too, no one seemingly capable of using an inside voice and you know what, while he's at it listing grievances, everything he touches also seems to be slightly sticky for seemingly no reason?

Etienne keeps rubbing his fingers together because he *swears* there's some nasty tacky film clinging to them, but he can't seem to get it off, huffs and folds his arms across his chest, foot tapping irritatedly against the linoleum tiles. Honestly, the noise and the sticky residue aren't even the half of it, and you'd think this place couldn't get any worse, *but somehow, it manages.*

Along with being disgusting and unreasonably noisy, the service here is also quite frankly, *horrid.* He's been sitting at this table for close to twenty minutes and not a *single* server has been by to take his order or see if he needs anything.

It's not like they're short staffed, Etienne can see all of the employees in their little green aprons running around behind the counter, and there's enough of them that'd you *think* one would've been by before now, but *nope!*

Ugh.

This is why he hates coming into this section of the city, it's too close to the university and overflowing with students and clueless humans, all of whom are not being subtle at all in the way they're staring at him.

Etienne's caught the stray too loud whisper and obvious pointing finger, but thankfully none of them have come up to bother him, though that may have more to do with his outfit and not out of an abundance of manners.

He's dressed more ostentatiously than he normally would if he was simply meeting mother for tea, and sure, it's not really the proper occasion to be wearing the inky black tail coat with golden embroidery, ends of it cut to resemble a Luna moth's wings, but Etienne is not about to let this farce of a program rob every aspect of his identity.

"By the *Four*- I didn't think they still *dressed like that!*" Someone snickers off to the side, and Etienne snaps his head over to glare at the group of gawking students, crescent moon and bloodstone earrings violently swinging as he does. They're quick to break eye contact and move along, but not before stealing a few more furtive glances, whispering things behind raised hands like they think he can't tell they're still talking about him.

Fine. *Whatever.* Let them talk.

He's proud of who he is damnit, and the council isn't going to take that from him. They may think they've got the covens playing along to this stupid little game of theirs, forcing them into some mold the city wants them to fit, but it's not going to last. Once it becomes apparent the alchemist students are useless when it comes to *true* magic, this entire thing is going up in flames, *as it should,* mind you.

The *'Society for Promoting Arcane Diversity'* has no true foundations to stand on, is built off of bureaucratic nonsense and a fear of losing the taxable income the college brings in, not anything substantial. Alchemists may think the little tricks they pull are

What Goes Bump In The Night

magic, but what they do manage barely even grazes the surface of a well of power so deep, it sinks down further than the largest oceans.

That primordial surge of raw energy is something they're never going to have access to, and Etienne's not even being exclusionary here, though he has *every right to be,* it's just a simple fact. If you're not born to magic, nor claimed by a coven house, you're stymied in your ability to practice any arcane work.

Alchemy has been the modern man's solution to this age old dilemma, coming on the heels of demonic blood pacts and stolen arcane artifacts, but comparing the Hermes' students to the coven apprentices isn't even remotely fair. It's like pitting a kitten against a manticore, *absolute lunacy,* because *legacy* magic outpaces *learned* magic any day.

Honestly it just shows pure ignorance on the city council's part.

How could they *possibly* think the students are going to be able to keep up with the apprentices?

Best case scenario feelings will get hurt and egos bruised, but given some of the things the covens deal with, serious injury is definitely a possibility. Etienne has his own collection of scars from past slip ups, and *he's* one of the *better apprentices,* which just goes to show what an unmitigated disaster this is about to become.

As soon as the first student gets wounded, their parents will raise hell and the program will get pulled faster than anything, and even though this whole thing is destined for failure, it's still cause for concern.

This is the most brazen move at forced modernization the city council has made in years, and action must be taken immediately. The covens may not hold as much power as they used to, *stripped and broken down over the years reduced to arcane cleanup crews,* but they still have tremendous sway within the Occult community.

All mother needs is time to rally the other sects, and as soon as the city council is left with a human populace that has too many magical problems and alchemists who are inadequate at solving them, they'll buckle faster than anything.

Finally, him and his peoples' voices will be heard again, their concerns will matter and won't get swept off the table as *'irrational resistance to change'.* Over *two decades* of backsliding will be behind them, and Étienne is personally looking forward to seeing it go, longs for the day he'll be treated with the respect he deserves outside of a few select city blocks.

Which-

Speaking of respect-

Etienne fishes his pocket watch out and clicks it open, groans seeing it's closer to *thirty* minutes now that he's waited, which is *beyond* annoying and incredibly rude, and he snaps it shut harshly.

Five more minutes, he thinks waspishly, fingers drumming an unhappy tune against his arms as he glares out at the hubbub of students shoving past one another, *five more minutes and then I don't care what the council says I'm leaving and filing a formal complaint with the Office of Occulture.*

Before he left this afternoon, mother made him *swear* on their name he would be cordial at the bare minimum, and he promised he would, but didn't tell her that privately, he'd decided it was dependent on this partner of his.

If they came into this arrangement treating him with basic common civilities, he'd do the same, *equivalent exchange and all that you know like the...you think you're funny at least,* but this Nicalos Caldwell is over *half an hour late,* and Etienne snorts derisively, doesn't know what he'd been expecting.

Alchemists are individualists. They don't have the same sense of community the rest of the sects do, only care about themselves and use anyone they can in their pursuit of fame and renown. It doesn't matter who they have to climb over to get there, they'll take any chance they can get at that fleeting, elusive spotlight, and apparently, Etienne isn't even notable enough to be used as a ladder rung.

What Goes Bump In The Night

Which is *ridiculous* considering he is the *scion* of one of the most important covens in *the entire parish,* but *no,* he's very *clearly* not worth their *precious* time, *nor* the consideration of just outright canceling, and that stings about as much as the simple rudeness of blowing off a planned meeting.

He's here he's important he matters, and sure, a lot of people in the parish don't feel that way anymore, see him and his family with their skulls and their markings and the dirt under their nails, call them *freaks* and *antiquated leftovers,* but that's going to change, *it has to.*

Checking his watch one last time, Etienne sees it's three thirty-five on the *dot* and rolls his head in exasperation, pushing back from the gross sticky table as he gets to his feet. Technically he's violating the terms of the program by leaving, but he's not about to sit around and pretend like his time is worth *nothing.*

And if the council has a problem with that, they can take it up with the Office of Occulture *and* mother, which, is perhaps a fate worse than excommunication.

Etienne smirks imagining the earful they'll get for waylaying the *scion* of a coven house, wouldn't wish that on his most bitter enemy. *Maybe that'll teach them to mind their business,* he thinks sardonically as he slings his bag over a shoulder, scoots his chair back in before he leaves *because he's not a heathen.*

The chatter from nearby patrons dies down slightly when they notice him walking by, but Etienne's used to it, ignores all the swiveling heads like they're nothing more important than a few annoying scuttling bugs. His boot heels don't click against linoleum tiles as satisfyingly as they do against ceramic ones, but Etienne still throws his shoulders back as he weaves past tables, refuses to hide even a little under the prying eyes he can feel boring into his back.

If these troglodytes don't have the common courtesy not to stare, he hopes they get an eyeful, see what a *true* witch looks like, hopes they learn there's still some of them left and they're not going anywhere.

⁺✦⁺ 31 ⁺✦⁺

Etienne is just reaching for the door handle, is about to slip out of the coffee shop and bid it a fond *good riddance,* when the glass door flies open, some raucously bright colored figure almost stumbling into him in a blind panic. They pinwheel their arms to stop themself last second and push messy ash blonde hair out of their eyes, mouth running a mile a minute, *"Hoooo shit-! Fuck! Man I-I am so sorry-!* In a hurry- *not paying attent-* but yeah sorry man I just-!"

They glance up mid ramble and the words die in their throat, eyes blowing wide once they see who they nearly ran into, *right eye cloudy blue left one deep hazel both filled with clear shock surprise astonished no way death witch of New Orleans,* and Etienne sighs internally.

Mothers, what he wouldn't give to go a *single day* without someone staring at him like he's a zoo attraction, but given his daily experiences, that's apparently too much to ask for. It's an unfortunate part of his reality that he's gotten used to, and humming in polite acknowledgment at the stranger, *hi yes I know you think I'm weird but please move,* Etienne makes to slip past.

But before he can, they grin hesitantly, showing off this little gap in their front teeth while they stammer way too fast, "H-Hey! Um- *hi,* yeah you must be- sorry I'm late, got held up in lab wasn't watching the clock that's my bad but yeah- *um,* a-anyway it's nice to meet you!"

"Um, *alright?"* Etienne says in confusion, little turned around by the stumbling stream of chatter, curiously eyes this colorful *bizarre* eyesore blocking the door, *shorter than you not a difficult thing to be looks strong but in a soft way broad shoulders sturdy frame thick arms pale complexion odd colored eyes metal hand sleeveless color block windbreaker-*

Wait-

Metal hand?

Etienne double takes because he's not sure he saw that right, but nope, one of the hands that clutches at their backpack straps

What Goes Bump In The Night

is a scuffed silver, intricate looking joints and plating flowing all the way up to their shoulder. It's impossible to miss now that he's noticed, *how...how did you miss this,* and prosthesis aren't really something he deals with ever, but even Etienne can tell this one is different.

That it's something special.

The design is unlike anything he's ever seen, looks like a conglomeration of separate pieces that could have multiple configurations, some kind of interlocking pattern etched into the metal's surface at various spots. Honestly, it's rather beautiful, kinda difficult to look away from, but Etienne's aware he's staring and then wonders if they're self-conscious about it, drags his eyes up in an attempt to be polite.

The stranger doesn't comment on his blatant lapse in manners, so either they *are* used to people staring at their arm or they just don't care, and Etienne can sympathize with that, offers them a small smile as he tries to scoot past.

Emphasis on *tries* though, because they won't move and he's *trying* to be polite and not shove this person out of the way, but they don't seem to be taking the hint despite it being *fairly obvious to Etienne* that he's wanting to leave.

They just stay firmly planted in the doorway as they stare up at him expectantly, and it's almost like they're...*waiting* for something, *what do you want stop looking at me shoo,* but at this point, he's not really sure what that could *even be.*

"Uh- is there somethin' I can *help you with?"* Etienne hedges mostly out of reflex, used to running errands and doing favors for fellow Occult members, but has zero intentions of helping this random human out of pocket. If they've got some sort of problem, they can go through the proper channels to get a case number which they *should* know how to do unless they're from another state or a *tourist or oh no-*

His eyes flick over them again, *day bag and tacky clothing staring at you like you're a weird display hey man how much for a simple*

✦ 33 ✦

spell oh for the love of- Etienne only just *barely* stops himself from rolling his eyes, realizing with a grimace that stranger is probably from out of town and thinks he's a performer or something.

And dressed the way he is, *night black tailcoat lunar cycle embroidered in golden thread crow skull bolo tie jewelry he wears for the solstices,* he's *really* not helping his case.

Mothers help you why did you offer to do anything quick take it back aaaand they're already opening their mouth to respond void take you Etienne you imbecile why can't you ever-

"Yeah! Well I figured we could sit down, get coffee or tea or a smoothie or whatever and just- *talk through all this?* Plan out what we're doing?" They say distracted as they start rummaging around in their bag, and- *okay.*

Not where he thought this was going at all.

No, *hey can get a picture for my blog I can't believe you people are actually real,* or, *yeah I accidentally summoned a poltergeist into my house can you get rid of it no I don't have money to pay,* or something else stupid and mildly annoying. Which it's good it's not any of those things! Etienne isn't complaining!

But it's just...it's sorta weird right? Because it *really* sounds like they know him, or think that they do at the very least, but Etienne is *one hundred* percent sure he's never met this person before, he'd remember the arm if nothing else, and furrows his brows in confusion as he looks them over, "I'm...sorry, you must have me confused for someone else. Do I know you?"

Quitting in their search, stranger glances back up at him and Etienne picks out a few more details of their face, like how they have some light discoloration across the left side and a split in the accompanying eyebrow, right above the hazel colored eye, freckles over the bridge of their nose and dusting their cheeks, but none in those jagged patches of whiter skin.

Taken together it's a unique array of features, but Etienne still can't place them, and the stranger snags their bottom lip with

What Goes Bump In The Night

their teeth, tips their head to the side and nervously fiddles with a lock of hair, "Uh- a-are you not Etienne Boudreaux? I-I really thought that...oh- o-oh! Shit yeah okay *sorry* forgot to introduce myself Nica- *I-I'm* Nica, your Arcane Diversity partner, it's ni-!"

And it's like connecting the ends of a summoning circle, electric charge rolling up his body as everything comes into sharp focus- *sorry I'm late – plan out what we're – I'm Nica I'm your – and you're not worth my time kept you waiting rude inconsiderate looked at you bug eyed freak weirdo archaic leftovers city has no use for things like you anymore* -and Etienne stretches up to his full height, eyes narrowing into dangerous slits as he hisses, *"You!"*

"Uh- h-hi? I-"

"You are over *half an hour late.*" Etienne spits, running over whatever asinine excuse they're trying to give, uses his height advantage to glare down the length of his nose at them, "We were *supposed* to meet at three *exact*, and you've kept me waitin' for close to *forty minutes!*"

"I'm? Sorry?" Nica says like they don't really mean it and it makes Etienne's magic *boil, how dare they be so rude don't even care wasted your time not like you matter footnote at the end of history no one needs you anymore,* and electricity arcs across his back molars, "*Save it!* Now I don't know what the requirements are to get into that ridiculous little school of yours, but unlike *your* administration, *I* don't have time to suffer fools nor slack jawed simpletons that can't even *count!*"

Their mouth drops open, color quickly rising to their cheeks as they sputter, "E-Excuse *me?*"

"You're *excused.* Now get outta my way you *niais.*" Etienne seethes and shoves past them, storms out onto the busy sidewalk and picks a direction, too furious to really know where he's going, just fumes while he starts drafting his letter to the city council.

Summary of that being: *I'm not doing this, shove it up your ass.*

"Hey!" Nica shouts behind him, sounding *royally* pissed off and

✦✦ 35 ✦✦

indignant, but Etienne's *really* good at ignoring people yelling at him on the street, *has had a lifetime of it.*

He keeps his chin up as he walks but feels his mood sour further as humans skitter out of his way, their eyes going wide once they see his face, scared like they're stupidly afraid he's going to hex them or something.

Mothers can't stand them what's wrong with them, he thinks in a furious snit, *why do they look at you like that why do they look so afraid,* magic crackling against his palms, *you're not going to hurt them don't they trust you don't they appreciate what you do for them,* frustrated tears prickling at his eyes, *ungrateful cowards betrayers turned their backs on you protected them for centuries and they turned their backs on-*

And while he may be well practiced at tuning out loud harassment, Etienne is *not* used to being stopped bodily, almost falls over when he's jerked around, feet stumbling to try and keep him upright. "Dude. What the *fuck* is your problem?" Nica snaps, fingers wrapped tight around his arm like a piece of steel, and after Etienne yanks himself free of their grip, he can tell they purposefully let him go.

"*My problem?* My-!" Etienne sputters, fingers rubbing over the wrist they grabbed even though it doesn't hurt, "Do I need to explain it to you again in *simpler terms?* You were *late.* Egregiously late, an' I'm not gonna sit around and have my time wasted by some disrespectful *rude imbe-!*"

"Oh! *Oh* you wanna talk about *rude?* Well look in a mirror *asshole,* because there's a prime example riiiight *there.*" Nica snaps and jabs a finger in his direction, brows drawn down low and angry over their stormy eyes, and Etienne is struck speechless because no human has *ever dared* use that kinda language with him before.

"Did- d-did you jus' call me *an asshole?*" He asks in a disbelieving tone, magic zapping up his vertebrae and curling over his shoulders, arching high above him like a thunderhead.

Losing control of his emotions like this has made so many others

What Goes Bump In The Night

cower back in terror, *you're not going to hurt them you would never hurt any of them,* but Nica isn't deterred by the seething cloud of magic, stalks forwards and cocks their chin back, "Yeah. *I did-* you know what they say, *if the shoe fits dickhead.*"

A score of maroon particles crackle to life around Etienne's clenched fists, zing and pop like firecrackers or spattering oil, and he's *so close* to just letting his control slip completely, loosen his grip on that seething, *writhing* mess of power snarling around his chest and give in. *You could do it you could let it out and let what happens happen say it was provoked valid self-defense no one would question you you're a scion,* and Etienne exhales shaky because it's so *tempting-* but he *can't.*

Their kind of magic is emotive, responds to strong feelings and will lash out if left unchecked, and with how angry he is, there's no telling what the outcome would be if Etienne let it loose right now. He could end up seriously hurting Nica, and that thought stops him dead in his tracks, because no matter how mad he is, *no matter how justified his frustrations,* he's not supposed to hurt people.

Mother's voice washes through him then, *we stand between every innocent in this city an' everythin' that goes bump in the night don't ever forget that,* and the guilt that comes with the memory sucks all the fire right out of him, *we never turn that power on the blameless we do not take lives.*

She's right, *she's always right,* and Etienne forces himself to take a deep breath, lets it out, lets *it go,* and untenses his hands.

He settles back on his heels and his magic dissipates like clouds blowing apart in the sky, Nica blinking at him owlishly as he turns to go without a fight, only flicking his wrist dismissively, "Say whatever you like. We're done here. I'll be filin' a letter with my offices to try an' get out of this farce of a program, I'd suggest you do the same but I really don't care. Have a good day."

Honestly that should be the end of that, *you don't blow their head off they get to live another day annoying someone else nice clean easy break get it over with move on,* so it's *really* unexpected when Nica calls out, "W-Wait!"

And for some reason, Etienne does, looks over his shoulder at where they're alternating pressing thumbs against the opposite palm, metallic joints moving just as fluidly as their flesh and bone kin.

Nica's chewing on their lip again, eyes skittering about nervously like they can't find a comfortable place to rest, and it takes them a while, but eventually they huff out a gust of air as their gaze finally settles on Etienne's.

"Look. I...I-I think we got off on the wrong foot or- *just-* I already said I'm sorry for being late, I didn't mean to keep you waiting I- I get distracted like- absorbed in work really easy and it's hard to-brain can't, but *uh-* yeah. Yeah that's my fault and I'm *sorry.*" Nica stresses in their turned around way of speaking, actually sounds like they mean it this time as their hands worry at one another, "I also didn't um, d-didn't mean to call you an uh- *asshole.* O-Or dickhead. I lost my temper and that really wasn't cool, so yeah that too. S-Sorry about that too I-I mean! *Yeah.*"

Well that's certainly an unexpected streak of self-awareness and humility, *didn't think an alchemist would admit they're wrong so readily,* and turning around slowly, Etienne regards Nica with a critical eye.

They're staring at him hesitantly, a strangely nervous expression from someone who looks like they could crack him in half if they wanted to, not that he'd let them have that chance, *but still,* it's not what he was expecting.

Etienne hasn't interacted with many alchemists, students or otherwise, but the general impression he always got from them was that they assumed they were right no matter what. It's a bit unfair considering he doesn't have much personal experience, *he knows that,* but it's the only reasonable explanation in his mind.

Why *else* would they immediately start trying to change everything in the city after the college opened, ignoring centuries

What Goes Bump In The Night

worth of tradition and precedent, if not in favor of their own selfish interests?

Hermes University was founded a few years before Etienne was born, and it's been a thorn in the Occult community's side ever since its inception. Problems began before the doors even opened, started because the mere *concept* of humans wanting to learn the arcane arts hit every magic user in the parish like a slap to the face.

Sure it might not be the Dark Ages anymore, but they still happened, and the centuries of persecution are not an easy subject to move past. That's not something that should ever be glossed over actually, but that's exactly what the original group of alchemists did, just went straight to the city council without speaking to the other sects first.

There was no proper respect paid to the Council of Night or the Voodoo Priesthood or the Seers Guild, no conversation about the implications of what this all meant, no, *I understand this is a difficult subject but can we please talk about it.*

Nope.

They simply pitched their proposal before the city planning board and didn't even bother to clear it with the arcane members who had been serving New Orleans since its founding.

It was incredibly disrespectful, and the administration at Hermes has done little to try and make amends since then. If anything, they keep adding insult to injury as they wrest more and more control away from the other sects, this program being the latest in a long list of ways they're trying to undermine the existing order.

Things have been tense in the city lately, and disdain and hostility is what Etienne's come to expect from anyone outside of his community, which is why he never thought he'd find himself where he has, standing on a street corner while an *alchemist* sincerely apologizes for calling him a dickhead. That's strange enough on its own, but stranger still considering it's coming from someone that seems to have a fiery temper hiding under that nervous expression.

It's humbling in a way, shows Nica knows something of respect, and Etienne *did* promise to give back what was offered to him, *fairs fair equivalent exchange and all that,* so he inclines his head, finally deciding on, "I accept your apology."

They relax almost immediately, hands stilling in their incessant fiddling and give him a hesitant slip of a smile, *little gap in their front teeth anxious way they brush loose hair behind an ear only for it to fall back strangely endearing kinda want to-* and Etienne has to forcefully blink back to himself, weird prickling under his sternum as he turns to leave, pulling the brim of his hat down, "I- well, good then. *I mean-* g-good day then? Just- *have a good day bye-"*

"Hey wait! Aren't we like- yeah okay maybe you've got somewhere to be so rescheduling? Should we- rescheduling? *A-Are we* rescheduling?" Nica finally manages to get out somewhat coherently, frustrated set to their face when Etienne looks back, and he tenses up again, eyes narrowing as he says purposefully slow, "Uh, no, we are *not.* Like I said the first time, I'm not stickin' 'round for this lunacy."

"But- b-but I apologized!" Nica sputters indignant, hopping a few steps forwards, hands waving emphatically between the two of them, "A-And *you* accepted! I- so we're- we *have to* reschedule! The bylaws *state-!"*

Sighing drawn out and long suffering, Etienne pinches the bridge of his nose and tries to lay it out as simply as he can, doesn't know what's getting lost where, "Look. I don' care about the bylaws, I don' *care about this program.* I am the *scion* of one of the oldest coven houses in this parish and I. Do. Not. Have. *Time* to run around babysittin' *you* for the next however long."

"I- *babysitting?* What're- is...*I-* do you-? S-So *that's it."* Nica cocks their chin back and crosses their arms, metal plating glinting bright in the afternoon light, fingers flexing against the crook of their elbows, eyes narrow and storm wind dangerous, "You feel like this doesn't- won't- *shouldn't* apply to *you* because *you're* a *scion,* t-that you deserve special treatment...you- y-you think you're *better than me."*

What Goes Bump In The Night

I know I am, Etienne thinks but doesn't say, bites his tongue and holds those scathing words in by the tips of his nails, was brought up *better* than that, offers simpering and unflinchingly polite instead, "Well...one has to understand the different...*circumstances* of our skill sets. It's not entirely fair to compare the two mô shè, you have to acknowledge that much *at least.*"

"Oh my God you're just- y-you did not just- ugh! Yeah *sure whatever!* I'll give you our backgrounds are different but *acknowledge this-"* Nica steps right up into Etienne's personal space, a seething tide of crackling static prickling at his senses, makes all his hair stand on end, *like right before lightning strikes ozone sharp in your nose storm on the horizon,* their voice low like the threat of thunder, "I am at the *top of my class,* one of the best alchemists in that school and *none of that* was given to me. I worked my *ass off* to get where I am."

And in a brazen display of heedless *audacity,* Nica reaches up and knocks the brim of Etienne's hat back, eyes lightning bright and lethal, "I *earned my position,* it wasn't handed to me *on a silver platter.*"

Etienne isn't a fool, was raised to navigate high society as flawlessly as any atriarch should, *knows* what Nica's implying, *don't deserve your title your powers didn't have to work for any of it,* and magic sparks against his palms as he hisses, "You're talkin' about things you don't understand, I'd watch your mouth, *zòrdi-"*

"Oh yeah? You think you're such hot shit, *prove it."* Nica snaps, still *way* too close and annoying and not backing down an inch, "Find the hardest assignment you can and *show me* how much better you are. Hell. *I'll bet you.* If I can't keep up, if I'm *waaay* too in over my head and *truly* not an equal to you, I'll get you out of participating in the program-"

Mothers, that would be- *step in the right direction freed from this farce make a point to the council to the college get things moving where you want them to go,* and Etienne can't help it, he perks up, is *actually* considering it until the other half drops, "-*but!* But if I *can* keep up, if I can prove I *am* just as good as you, we do

✦✦ 41 ✦✦

the tenure of the program like everyone else. You. *Participate.* No loopholes. No shortcuts. Deal?"

They stick a hand out, *their left one the one that's still skin and bones,* and it's such a tempting offer because Etienne knows who he is, *what he's capable of the power simmering just at the tips of his fingers the legacy he's responsible for,* knows he's better than half the magic users in this parish and yet he hesitates.

Yes, Etienne was named scion from birth, and sure, *some* may hear that and assume he's done nothing much in particular to earn that title, like he's some spoiled little lordling from ages past, but it couldn't be further from the truth. He's studied *hard,* takes every single assignment seriously no matter how trite it may seem, has proven time and time again he's deserving of his position, *that Maisette placed its faith in the right person.*

Etienne has confidence in his abilities and not unduly so, knows he can handle most things thrown his way, refuses to be a disgrace to his name and family.

But he hesitates still.

Because *Nica* also seems confident in their abilities, and it doesn't come across like empty braggadocio.

Etienne's spent enough time around other apprentices to know the difference between hollow superiority and the real thing, and Nica may be anxious and unsure about a lot of other stuff, but seemingly not this, and it makes Etienne wary.

It's a small chance, *of course it's small they're an alchemist and you're a scion,* but there *is* a chance Nica is going to win this wager, will get by on a technicality or some weird trick of fate, *or is actually as good as they think they are,* and then where does that leave Etienne?

Stuck in a program that's only purpose is to undermine and usurp his entire way of life, forced to spend time with someone he's quickly realizing he dislikes a great deal, all because he agreed to a *stupid bet?*

Don't even bother it's safer just to file your letter with the Office of Occulture don't even entertain the notion, he thinks, knows it's the correct course of action, *what mother would expect him to do,* and is about to say as much when Nica cocks their head, arches an eyebrow and drawls, "*What?* 'fraid you're gonna lose hot shot? Worried you're going to find out you're not as good *as you think you are-*"

And electricity cracks over his skin, zaps between his knuckles, *getting left behind not as important as you think you are no one needs you anymore footnote at the end of history you'll show them you'll show all of them,* and without another thought, he takes Nica's hand.

They shake on it.

Chapter 4

Lamplight flickers over the polished glossy tiles and darkly lacquered walls in the Office of Occulture, throws jumping shadows around the room that skitter across the desk like terrors fleeing in the wake of dawn. Etienne raps long fingers against worn wood, heavy head propped up in a hand while various papers jostle one another overhead, all vying for his attention in some morbid parody of a dance.

There's so many of them and he's losing track of what he has and hasn't read, sourly glares at the mess of empty folders spread out on the desk in front of him. It feels like he's pulled every available assignment file in the office, *an entire mountain of them,* and yet, it doesn't seem like he's any closer to a decision.

Etienne's going to *have to* choose at some point though, it's getting late and the office will be closing for the evening soon and he doesn't want to be rude.

A clerk came by to light the lamps what felt like ages ago, politely asked if he would be much longer, and Etienne said no at the time, but it's been *hours* since then and he still hasn't been able to find a *single* suitable assignment.

Crooking a finger, Etienne pulls a couple fluttering pages into view he hasn't read yet, but waves them back into their folders after getting the gist, would sooner be excommunicated than ever take an outsider to perform *funerary rites.* His lip curls in disgust at the mere *idea,* and he quickly beckons another sheet closer, scanning the contents before huffing and dismissing it as well.

New Orleans is a big city, and it is an old city, and so it has *a lot* of magical problems.

What Goes Bump In The Night

The Office of Occulture receives requests for arcane services in a near constant stream from both the local government and private citizens alike, and a good chunk of them are for House Boudreaux alone.

There's always a lot to sift through, and given the small pile he's amassed, one would then assume that there would also be a lot to pick from, but Etienne's only grown angrier and more irritable as he reads and reads *and reads,* and yet continues to find nothing.

Nica *dared him* to take them on the most challenging assignment Etienne could, insinuated they'd be able to handle *whatever* was thrown at them, but all of these requests are either inappropriate for an outsider, or completely and *utterly asinine.*

Every last one of them is something *petty* and *small,* errands that would take Etienne less than an hour to complete, or assignments so simple, a *first year* apprentice could do it alone. There's not really anything here that'll let him prove his superior skill set like he needs to, nothing that'll win him the bet unequivocally *like he has to,* and it is beyond frustrating.

He doesn't really have a lot of options though.

Despite being twenty and considered a *legal adult* under the laws of the parish, Etienne's still an apprentice until his twenty-fifth birthday, which means he's restricted in the assignments he can take. Technically he can apply for more difficult or dangerous tasks, but with the caveat that a full-fledged coven member go with him and act as lead supervisor.

It's a precautionary thing as he *is* still learning, and while Etienne fully understands and respects the ruling of the Council of Night, it is *mildly annoying.* Dealing with undead and wrathful spirits can be incredibly dangerous, true, but he's a good student, quick to pick things up, and the rest of his family knows it.

Mother never hesitates to take him along when she has field work, nor does Aunt Atha, and the two of them are usually very hands-off, let Etienne more or less run the assignment unless something major comes up.

Sometimes Uncle Gilbert will need a second, but he's more cautious of a teacher, prefers to talk through what he's doing and have Etienne take notes instead.

Since swearing their oaths, Etienne's two elder siblings can technically be supervisors, but neither one really has the experience to be a competent instructor yet. Still, Katie will let him tag along on occasion if Louisette is busy, and then Etienne doesn't particularly like working with Oliver, but mother sends them out together sometimes anyway and there's no arguing with her.

Believe him, he's *tried.*

Regardless of who it is though, they all trust Etienne in the field to a certain degree, give him as much free reign as they deem fit, and usually he doesn't have a problem with their supervising him...key word being *usually.*

Etienne knows he's a talented witch, magic has always come easy to him and he excels in his lessons, but he's not deluded enough to think there's nothing left for him to learn.

Which is why he's really enjoyed joint assignments with his family in the past. Each has something they specialize in, unique experiences and stories, and he truly loves learning from them, but this time around, the idea of asking for supervision makes him grind his teeth together.

An uncharacteristic frustration burns bright in the center of his chest, livid and self-righteous in ways that are a little concerning. Etienne is *supposed* to always have a handle on his emotions, can't let them run wild or so too will his magic, but he's really been struggling this evening to get it under control and it's got to be because of the bet.

There's so much riding on the stupid thing, and over the course of the day, Etienne's realized it's turning into more than just a way for him to get out of that joke of a program.

It's become a matter of...well, not really honor, but maybe competency? He started off rationalizing to himself that winning would prove things are functioning just fine the way they are, that the covens don't have anything to learn from a bunch of charlatans.

But it's also become more than that, *it's gotten personal,* and Etienne's not supposed to hang on to things but he *cannot let it go,* how Nica implied he wasn't deserving of his title or powers.

The whole point of the bet has quickly shifted to asserting *Etienne's* supremacy and position in the community, showing that *no alchemist* has any hope of being able to match him in terms of skill, let alone *Nica,* and the mere thought of bringing anyone else along to prove that makes Etienne's toes curl in his boots.

This is something he needs to do on his *own,* show he's earned what he has and that nothing was simply handed to him, and requesting supervision ruins that. It wouldn't matter if mother, or whoever, kept to the sidelines as an impartial spectator and didn't intervene, because no matter how unobtrusive they were, they'd still be there.

Babysitting.

And *yes,* the irony that Etienne told Nica he wasn't going to babysit them, only to realize *he* also has to be chaperoned to some degree is not lost on him.

He really regrets shooting his mouth off, because by rising to Nica's goading, and engaging similarly, he's gotten himself backed into something of a corner, and as he sees it, there's really only two terrible options going forwards, well...*maybe three?*

One, Etienne picks the best worst assignment he can get by himself and *performs it flawlessly,* only problem being none of it will seem challenging and Nica isn't *that* stupid, might actually be able to keep up, which very well means he could lose the bet.

Two, Etienne swallows his pride and asks one of the others to supervise, gets something actually challenging that'll put his skillset on full display, but Mothers know if Nica would consider that a fair win, so again, *he could lose the bet.*

Three (?), Etienne stops being an *idiot* and letting *one meaningless person* have so much sway over him, could just go ahead and file for an exemption from the program here, but there's no guarantee the courts would grant it and either way...it would mean going back on his promise.

And that thought makes him so violently repulsed, his magic accidently shreds one of the assignment briefs circling overhead.

Little scraps of paper rain down like snow, and Etienne snippily waves them off, frustrated with himself to some degree that he's gotten into this situation, but there's nothing he can do.

As inconsequential as it may seem, he gave Nica *his word* on this, *his bond,* and Etienne was raised to understand that means something.

We promise things because we intend to follow through, mother would tell him over and over again, dark hands brushing across ancient pages, *it's not just somethin' to be given away frivolously,* his own hands so tiny next to hers, copying the same gesture as he traces over the pentagram, *keepin' your word is a measure of who you are, don't let it suffer.*

Etienne knows he shouldn't have agreed to the bet in the first place, *but he did,* and now that he's here, he intends to follow through.

Because he doesn't go back on his promises.

Ever.

Even when he's made stupid deals with *stubborn as anything* alchemists who, *somehow,* know how to push all his buttons despite only having met him once.

Show me how much better you are 'fraid to lose hot shot not as good as you think you are, ghosts through Etienne's ears then, imperious and challenging *and bullheaded,* and he can feel his jaw tick back and forth unbidden.

What Goes Bump In The Night

They barely spoke for longer than twenty minutes, but somehow *everything* about Nica seemed to get right under his skin easier than anything. There was just something about their assertive posture, *strength and arrogance acts so superior,* lazy way they crossed their arms, *not even worth their time their energy the nerve,* the *stupid* demanding look in their mismatched eyes, like *Etienne* had something to prove, *like he wasn't worth anything like he was nothing no one footnote at the end of-* and it just, *makes his magic light up livid.*

Etienne feels it crackling against his bones, responding to the deep-seated hostility thrumming hot under his sternum, and this isn't right, *he knows better,* wads everything up and tries to let it go. He doesn't do a good job of it though, resentment rekindling beneath his skin, and the next time he exhales, maroon particles shoot out with it.

Get a grip pull it together you're better than this why are you letting this get to you, Etienne berates himself as he shoos off another substandard assignment with more force than necessary, *they don't mean anything don't sink to their level,* folds his arms and forces his mind blank, goes back to scanning papers.

There's *got to be* something halfway decent here, he must've just missed it, *he has to have,* but he'll keep looking and he *will* find it, *is going to find it,* the best, most *amazing* assignment there is, and then he'll blow it out of the water and win this bet and never have to think about alchemists ever again.

But even after a second go around, and a third *and a fourth and a fifth,* the best options he's seen have been, *appeasement ritual requested for persistent poltergeist haunting pottery shop,* to- *reports of skeleton raccoon eating all my garbage,* and Etienne massages the bridge of his nose in frustration.

What in the name of the inky beyond is he going to do? Because if- *by some cosmic disaster,* Etienne manages to lose this bet, he's going to be stuck with Nica *'anxious rude hothead'* Caldwell until the end of this program.

And if today was any indication of what that'd look like, Etienne thinks he might implode before the school year ends in May.

Mothers of the Night that's over half a year away, he realizes in mounting dread, *you'd be stuck with them for eight months,* and that's the final nudge that pushes him over the edge completely into the dark crushing maws of *stress.* Absolutely done with this entire situation, Etienne cuts his hands irately through the air, dismissing the entire cloud of circling papers in an explosive fluttering of pages.

Etienne slumps forwards on the desk and digs fingers into his tired eyes. He is beyond drained, exhausted and irritable ~~and worried heart rate picking up Mothers calm down,~~ and the worst part is he doesn't have anything to show for it. It'd be one thing if he came out of his search with something worthwhile, but at this point, it's probably been close to three hours that he's been here, and Etienne hasn't actually accomplished anything productive the entire time.

All he's really managed to do is work himself into worse of a snit, magic popping painfully against his palms as his heart drums behind his ribs like the building notes to a thunderstorm, and since that's beyond unhelpful and the office is closing soon anyway, Etienne figures he might as well head home.

There's always tomorrow you can try to find something then you will find something then, he reminds himself even though a part of him doesn't really believe it.

Either way, he's about to cut his losses, push back from the desk and pack up, when he's startled by an achingly familiar voice drawling right behind him, "Well now, don' know what those assignments did but I'm sure they're *very* sorry."

Twisting around in his chair, Etienne already knows who it is before seeing that Cheshire grin and those indigo markings, clambers hurriedly to his feet as he greets happily, "Sabine!"

"Mon ami, how're you this ev-? Èy, watch your feet, Eti." Sabine laughs, moving before Etienne is even really aware he's tripping, catches him under the arms and helps haul him back up, "Mères de la *Nwit,* how you've made it this long is *beyond* me, you klutz."

What Goes Bump In The Night

Laughing now too as he leans in, Etienne cheek kisses Sabine and declares in a haughty droll, "It's all thanks to my unprecedented prestige and talent, somethin' *you* wouldn't understand."

"You're right, can't understand what doesn't exist." Sabine fires back immediately, and grins delighted at the way Etienne mock glares at him, indigo markings crinkling ever so slightly under his thin, mono-lidded eyes.

"You are a *menace*." Etienne tells him with a long suffering sigh, but his magic is happily coiling around Sabine's own, cool touch of indigo that slides across his consciousness like a friendly breeze, and angling the brim of his cream colored hat up, Sabine simpers, "I am a *delight*."

That may or may not be true depending on who you ask, but Etienne's always enjoyed Sabine's dry wit and scathing humor, has known him basically their entire lives. They're only a couple years apart and grew up seeing one another frequently since their houses are old friends. The two of them have always gotten along famously, which is an added bonus since their position as scions brings them together often for social events and the like.

"Hm. A *delight?* Now that's debatable." Etienne grins and draws another soaring laugh from Sabine that sends his shoulder length dark hair swaying, and moving to clap him on the arm, Etienne asks, "How're you? How's your parent?"

"We're both well, thank you. They actually just closed out the General Appliances case today, got the settlement the Laferriere were lookin' for and everything." Sabine says and holds up a thick, cream colored envelope with bronze filigree, the LeBlanc crest embossed in the front, "An' I volunteered to bring the paperwork on down since I saw you might be here. Glad I was right."

"You usually are." Etienne agrees easily, doesn't mind feeding Sabine's ego every now and again, has firsthand experience with how pinpoint accurate his scrying is. Visionary work is some of the most finicky and unpredictable of magics, and House LeBlanc excels at it, covers a variety of sectors in the parish considering how versatile their skills are.

Chiefly though they function as the primary judicial system for the city, a tremendously dull field that's never interested Etienne much but captivates Sabine like nothing else will. He supposes that's a good thing considering one day Sabine will be heading it as the LeBlanc Patriarch, and while it may put Etienne to sleep, he's glad there's someone out there interested in legal precedence and due diligence.

"Ah what can I say? Bein' perfect is relatively easy, *well*...at least for *me*." Sabine says airily while he flips the envelope and catches it deftly, tucks it under an arm as he inclines his head, "What're you doin' down here so late? I know y'all run assignments after dark but I didn't think you *picked'em* this late."

And just like that, the simple pleasantness of running into a friend is ripped right out from under him, and Etienne is suddenly reminded of everything simmering in his veins. He groans impassionedly and aims a glare over his shoulder at the messy desktop, papers cowering deeper into their folders at his poisonous glare, "We *don't*. I've just been strugglin' to find something that'll work for this...*problem*, I've uh, *recently acquired-*"

"*Ugh-* are you talkin' about the *Society for Promoting Nonsense and Fuckery?* 'Cause ardam and I have *so many thoughts* about that." Sabine grouses, flipping hair over his shoulder, and in the space between spaces, his magic snarls up like branches rattling ominously in high altitude winds, "We were going to file an injunction against the city, but they've covered their bases well. Ardam is workin' on something though, they won't let this stand."

Etienne didn't think they would. Sabine's parent is a formidable atriarch and possibly an even more brilliant judicator, has been one of mother's leading supporters ever since she first began petitioning for the closure of Hermes University a few years ago.

House Boudreaux and House LeBlanc have always had strong ties, were some of the founding families of New Orleans, and even today the atriarchs from both houses still head their local branch

What Goes Bump In The Night

of the Council of Night.

Mother and Atriarch Renee are powerful leaders each in their own right, and the two of them working together is certainly a force to be reckoned with, but the city council has managed to hold their ground in a way that's completely unprecedented.

In the past, they've never fought the Occult community this hard over anything, and Etienne knows they're only doing it now to appease the university's administration. It's sour to admit even in the privacy of his own thoughts, but there's no denying how public opinion and favor has shifted over the years.

Times have changed, and what humans used to accept as part of a life that's shared with the arcane is apparently no longer acceptable. It's been years since tensions bubbled over that violently, but Etienne still doesn't like remembering it, has tried to let it go, but there are some things you can't forget because they scar too deep.

And there is nothing that will ever make him forget the memory of the protests, *of the riots,* of hanging on to mother's skirts terrified while people tried to grab him, too young to really understand why his cousins from Baton Rouge wailed their grief until the whole cemetery shook with it, *scared when people screamed at him so angry the vile words threats that kept him awake at night too frightened to sleep afraid they were next that they would come for his family next-*

Things are better than they used to be, mostly in the sense that society isn't on the verge of complete anarchy, but those rumblings of discontent are still there, and anytime they start to rekindle, it makes Etienne feel like a helpless, scared child all over again.

"What're we gonna do, Sabine?" He murmurs softly, turbulent swell of emotions rising up over his head like building storm clouds, heart stuttering *constricting in his chest scared don't want to be panic stop it get control powerless no you're not,* and jerking at the sudden uptick in frantic energy, Sabine leans forward quick to pull him into a hug.

"Hey hey, Eti, it's okay, it's gonna be *okay*." Sabine soothes, steady palms running comfortingly over his back, the deep blue calming tide of his magic weaving around the snarled erratic ball that Etienne's has become, gently starts to untangle it, "You're okay, it'll be okay, just breathe, yeah? My parent is gonna get this sorted okay? Then it'll be nothin' but a dumb joke we laugh about at solstice, okay? We're...we're gonna be *okay-*"

"But you don't *know that,* not for sure. It could get worse- *w-what if it gets worse?* What do we- what if...w-what *if t-they-" come for us next what if we have to fight them what if we have to kill them,* is what gets stuck down his throat, and Etienne suddenly can't speak, terrified to put it to voice and bring to life every one of his worst nightmares.

"It's *not* coming to that." Sabine insists firmly because he knows without having to be told, understands all of the fears that keep Etienne up at night, "It's *not.* No one in the parish wants war, you *know* that, they're not gonna let it go that far. We'll be okay, we're just...livin' through unprecedented times right now."

Etienne has heard that phrase thrown around so much in the last few years, *one for the history books you'll find it interesting one day just a rough patch it'll pass,* and frankly, he's tired of hearing it, *is tired of living in unprecedented times.* All Etienne wants more than anything is peace, *respect,* wants to feel secure in this city he loves and not constantly like they're one small step away from hurtling back to the Dark Ages.

"They used to burn people like us." He whispers hoarse, anxiety prickling over his skin like bugs crawling out of a nest, and Sabine pulls back just enough so their eyes can meet, knocks the brims of their hats together, "Hey. *Listen to me.* We'll be okay, I *promise.* The covens haven't been this united in ages, they can't take us all down. An' as long as we have each other, we can weather any storm."

One of Sabine's hands drifts up to squeeze at Etienne's shoulder, bright zap of his magic sparking from the contact, and he smiles that rare genuine smile of his, the one that's completely warm and heartfelt and loving, "It'll be okay, Etienne. There's no use worryin'

What Goes Bump In The Night

about a future you can't even see yet, you'll just drive yourself mad, *trust me.*"

He winks then and it drags a wet laugh out of Etienne, and yeah, it catches and rattles around in his chest weird, but it feels good, like the last of his anxieties are blowing apart in the sky from tender winds.

"Oh? S-Speakin' from personal experience then?" Etienne jokes weakly, blinking his eyes fast to make sure he doesn't *actually* cry over this, "Honestly it'd make a lot of sense."

"*Hey!* I'm not *mad,* just eclectic. Not like you'd know personality if it bit you on the nose." Sabine laments with a snide click of his tongue, and *Mothers,* Etienne is so incredibly glad to have him as a friend, slips easily back into their playful rapport, "Ah I see. Is that what you call what happened after Renee dropped you on your head? *Personality?*"

Sabine gasps over-the-top and dramatic, hand coming up to fan out across his chest, looks completely scandalized as he tosses his head, "Well I *never!* Such an insult...Mishé Boudreaux you wound me, *truly* and *deeply!*"

"I didn't think it possible to deeply wound somethin' so shallow." Etienne drawls in his most imperious voice, inspecting black painted nails with a picture perfect expression of extreme boredom, Sabine sputtering loudly in the background.

A lot of people find their relationship odd, hear them sniping at one another and assume they're being serious, and Etienne doesn't really know how many more times he can explain that they're honestly *not.*

It's just...a fun game they play, butting heads and trading playful insults, because they both know they don't mean it, that they think the world of the other, and when it really matters, they drop it. Sabine is a lot sweeter than most people assume, loves his family and cares deeply for his friends, has so much genuine concern for the city and the people within its borders, but he's also a jackass.

And Etienne loves that he's a jackass, knows he can take the teasing just like he dishes it out, and it's such an easy comfort, having a friend that can keep pace with you, who knows you as well as the two of them do.

Sabine is one of very few people who Etienne feels he can be completely open with, shares with him all of his fears and anxieties like he can't with the rest of his family. It's not that Etienne doesn't adore or trust his coven, he does, *so very much,* but they just- have *so many expectations* for him and who he's supposed to be, *how* he's supposed to behave, and he *knows* he can live up to them!

But it's just...*hard* sometimes, to be the perfect witch, *perfect scion perfect son,* and Sabine gets that, faces the exact same pressures at home too. That's one of the reasons they get along so well, because they *understand* what it's like, to have the future of your entire family resting on your shoulders just like Atlas under the world.

Shared experiences like that breed close bonds, and Etienne wouldn't trade it for anything, can't imagine his life without Sabine in it. They call each other best friend, but change the markings under one set of their eyes and it'd be the most natural thing in the world to greet *hello brother.*

Things have grown quiet between them now where they stand in the Office of Occulture, partly because it's late and they're both a little tired, but mostly because they've started making a series of increasingly ridiculous, scathing looks at each other.

Etienne is fighting to keep his composure and losing terribly, honestly didn't know Sabine's eyebrows could *go* that high, bites his lip *hard* to stop a wide smile from curling his lips. They only manage to keep up the arch glares for a few moments more, and it's unclear which one of them caves first, but they quickly dissolve into spastic fits of giggles that warm Etienne better than any drink ever has.

"*Mères*- you're such an oddball." Sabine cackles with nothing short of boundless affection, and kicking at him lightly enough so

What Goes Bump In The Night

it doesn't really hurt, but hard enough it draws out a sharp smile, Etienne rolls his eyes and chuffs fondly, "So're *you*."

Sabine opens his mouth to bite something back but pauses as the wispy voice of the clerk comes on over the speakers, somewhat irately informing anyone left in the office that it'll be closing in the next five minutes. The line cuts with a harsh click and Sabine makes this affronted face that has Etienne snorting, but he doesn't wind up saying anything, just steps back and drops his sheaf of papers into his hands again.

"Well, suppose we should make ourselves scarce, make sure no one pops a blood vessel." Sabine drawls, jerks his head at Etienne's pile of mess and sends all the bronze ornaments hanging off his hat jangling, "You find what you need? Or do you want me to stall for you?"

Kindest jackass ever rudest sweetheart to exist man of many contradictions, Etienne thinks with a bemused smile, flicks his eyes over his shoulder and considers it, but ends up deciding it's better to just go home. He sighs and crooks his fingers to call the folders back, "No...thank you though. I don't think any amount of time will fix this, m'afraid I might've screwed myself no matter what."

"Must be bad if you're on the verge of cursing." Sabine muses as they make their way up to the bank of clerk windows, only one lit given the late hour, and shuffling into line behind him, Etienne digs fingers into his temple, "You have no idea. I might've...made somethin' of a rash decision and am now regretting it *immensely*."

"Oh do tell, I *love* horrible decisions." Sabine leans back against the counter while the clerk is busy filing his paperwork, levity quickly dropping from his face as Etienne starts recounting the whole infuriating tale, doesn't even turn around at first when the clerk asks him to sign something.

Etienne really isn't meaning to go on for as long as he does, but it just keeps spilling out, overflowing like a cup that's been filled past its carrying capacity. He does start to trail off once he notices the clerk repeatedly nudging a paper into Sabine's elbow, goes to

✦✦ 57 ✦✦

point it out and gets waved off before he can say anything.

Wordlessly holding his hand out for a pen so he won't interrupt, Sabine doesn't even bat an eye as the exasperated clerk slaps one into his waiting palm, motions for Etienne to keep going while he twists to read over the form on the counter.

"-and then they called me a hotshot! An' I just- *ugh,* wanted to show them up I guess so I agreed to it! I still can't believe they had the- *nerve* to imply I'm not as good as I think I am! Which is! *Absolutely absurd.* I'm more powerful than they could *ever* hope to be." Etienne rants while Sabine scribbles across the paper in a flourish, whatever form that was rocketing off into the back once he's done.

"What an absolutely *repulsive* little piece of trash. *Mothers,* you really drew the short end of the stick with this one." Sabine murmurs in the tone of voice that never means anything good, eyes dark and dangerous, "See, mine at least knows who his better is, it's all- *mister scion* this, and- *of course sir,* that. But yours? They sound like an *utterly miserable ingrate* who doesn't know their place."

"They *don't.*" Etienne agrees hotly, indignation and furious anger scorching under his ribs just like earlier when Nica flipped his hat up, distorted memory of their voice overlaying others, *I earned my position wasn't handed to me did nothing to earn what you have no one needs you anymore lose you to the annals of history freak child stealer necromancer,* and for a brief second, his magic slips loose.

Electricity crackles through the air, acrid bitter stench of ozone washing through the office, and Etienne frantically tries to reign his emotions back in, can hear the crystal chandeliers whining at the sudden influx of power. He takes a deep breath, recites the tenets, thinks about mother, *about Maisette Katie Atha Gilbert Abel Felix Oliver everyone depending on him an entire city of innocents ~~are they really~~,* exhales snapping maroon particles and strangles the fury burning in his chest.

✦✦ 58 ✦✦

What Goes Bump In The Night

"Sorry." Etienne bites out, shame creeping over him at that public loss of control, and while the clerk has made themself scarce, Sabine doesn't seem too bothered by it, lazily flicking his wrist, "Don't be. I'd be beyond furious in your position so I don't blame you, but Etienne. This is the *simplest* solution."

Unslouching from the counter, Sabine strolls forwards with all the languid grace of a large cat that acts like it's not a predator, "Don't even give this person the time of *day,* you're better than that. Just file for an exemption tonight and I'll make sure it gets before a judge first thing in the morning. I'll even represent your case myself, pro bono of course, it'll take ten minutes *tops."*

Mothers- it sounds too good to be true but it's *Sabine* promising this, so he probably could, *you wish he would...you know you can't if only you'd thought,* but of course Etienne *hadn't* been thinking earlier, had he? He'd gotten so swept up in the thunderstorm rattling through his veins, didn't even spare a single second to have *one* rational thought, and now he's reaping what he's sown.

"I appreciate it Sabine, more than you know, but I can't really-" Etienne is in the middle of explaining, knows that as much as he may want to, he *can't* go back on a promise, but Sabine isn't listening, accidentally cuts him off, "Oh don't start, it's not a big deal at all. I'll just go up there-"

"Sabine, I really do appreciate it *but-"*

"-throw our names around, *oh you cannot possibly expect the scion of House Boudreaux to stoop to this level,* remind them of who they're dealing with, yeah?"

"Yeah I get it but Sabine *you're not lis-"*

"If I play my cards right, and I *always do,* I should end up with Judge Othonos and *she* owes me a favor, which, *that's* a story I need to tell you sometime-"

"That's great Sabine, now if you'd just *listen to-"*

"-but regardless, they should be swayed easy enough. Your house

✦ 59 ✦

really can't afford to be down an active member anyway- honestly, I've *no idea* how y'all've been managing to keep up as long as you-"

"Sabine." Etienne snaps harsher than he normally would, angry heat coloring his cheeks because that was getting a little too close to a very sore spot they *never* talk about, "Listen, I appreciate it, *truly* I do, but I can't just let you loophole me outta this. I...I agreed to the bet an' I've *got* to follow through on it, now if you-"

"Did you sign somethin'?"

It's not what Etienne's expecting *at all* and he stumbles over his words, looks at Sabine with brows arched and an expression that reads, *what does that have to do with anything* ~~did you mean it did you mean it when you implied we couldn't manage~~, and ever the opportunist, Sabine's quick to take advantage of his confused silence.

"Did you sign somethin'?" He repeats, arms crossing elegantly over his chest, fingers picking out a lively beat against his biceps, "Because unless you signed something, it's not legally binding and won't hold up in a court of law. Which! I'm assumin' that alchemist can't provide documentation that the bet was *even made* in the first place, so they've got no grounds to hold you to it. I wouldn't worry."

"I- I-I'm *not a child,* you don't have to- I know the basics of how the legal system works, *Sabine.*" Etienne bites out, *control yourself be an adult what's wrong with you calm down he didn't mean it like that,* and he sucks in air through his teeth, really makes sure to modulate his tone appropriately when he says, "I understand there's nothin' *legally* binding me to the deal, but I promised I'd do it. *I gave them my word.*"

And for Etienne, that's basically the end of the argument. He made a promise and it doesn't matter if he hates that he made it, he's going to follow through, *accept the consequences,* but Sabine just looks at him like he's the biggest idiot who's ever lived, lazily waves a hand in the air as he drawls, *"And?"*

...and?

What Goes Bump In The Night

What does he-

That's-

He seriously just- *and?* And *what,* Etienne goes back on his word? Uses his connections to shimmy out of this problem he's caused himself with next to no consequences, break the bond he gave and prove he has no integrity, that his word means *nothing,* like he's *exactly* the entitled brat that Nica made him out to be?

Goosebumps erupt across his skin at the thought, magic snaps against his palms and Sabine asininely asking him that question doesn't matter, there never would have been another answer.

"I gave them *my word.*" Etienne grinds out carefully soft but dangerously rough, whisper of storm wind on the horizon before the clouds break open, thunder rumbling under his bones watching Sabine roll his eyes as he sighs flippantly, "Look. *Eti.* It would be different if it was one of us, but an *alchemist? Un drigay?* Don't be an idiot."

It feels like the bright flash of lightning streaks past, *ozone sharp in his nose storm on the horizon scared you're gonna lose same look in those mismatched eyes prove it prove you're better,* and it's barely more than a whisper when Etienne says, "What did you just call me?"

"I'm sorry but it's true. You're actin' like a fool and I actually care about you enough to point it out. If it's any consolation you're not normally an idiot." Sabine shrugs easy, voice relaxed and almost smug, like he's done some great favor for him and Etienne should be offering thanks profusely. It makes the air skip in his lungs quick, pressure building up fast, frustration so thick and choking he half fears it's tangible.

Etienne loves Sabine, he really does, but there's just some moments where it feels like they're more suited to being at each other's throats rather than best friends. Those times are usually few and far between, fleeting fits of frustration that plague any close relationship, but *Mothers,* is it aggravating sometimes to be friends with him.

"Alright let's get one thing straight. Me wantin' to keep my word and stand by promises *that I made of my own free will,* doesn't make me an *idiot,* and I don' appreciate you thinkin' of me like that." Etienne snaps, chin cocked back and shoulders leveling, and Sabine opens his mouth to likely try and argue, but Etienne doesn't let him.

"*Secondly,* I'm not gonna say it again. It doesn't matter who it is, if I promised to do something, I am *going to do it.* Period. *End of story.* Do you understand me?" He hopes to the Night Mothers his face isn't as livid as he fears it might be, is really struggling to keep his composure right now, magic cracking under his skin like claps of thunder, "Havin' *integrity* is more important to me than- *weaselin' my way* outta something I don't wanna do. *Got it?*"

Sabine blinks at him owlishly, and for once in his life, seems to be speechless, stares at Etienne like he's not quite sure who he's looking at. That more than anything is the cue that Etienne needs to get a handle on things, and taking a deep breath, he rocks back on his heels and tries to calm down.

There has to be something off about today because his patience and temper aren't usually so hair thin.

He doesn't lose control of his magic, doesn't throw temper tantrums in public and almost blow out light fixtures, *doesn't get mad at his friends knows how to behave how to be the perfect scion the perfect witch the perfect son,* but he's not acting like it.

It's probably just stress.

This entire week has been taxing since finding out about the program, stoking to life old fears and new worries, and Etienne just needs to calm down. That might be easier said than done given how hard his pulse is thundering, thoughts a jumbled mess he's struggling to untangle *can't think straight,* every rough exhale leaving him tinged with glowing specks of maroon.

Thankfully, Sabine isn't completely tone deaf, picks up on the palpable tension in the air and realizes that it might be best for him to back off. He holds his hands up placatingly, posture straight-

What Goes Bump In The Night

ening out, voice less easy but less smarmy, "Alright, alright. I'm not tryin' to step on any toes, just wanted to help you out is all. I'm sorry if I overstepped anywhere."

That's...it that's all not gonna apologize for calling me an idiot for condescending to me for implying my house can't handle our duties ~~that we're on the brink of collapse~~, but Etienne forces it out, tears the snippy ball of hurt and indignation from his subconscious' fingers and does what he's supposed to do, *makes it let go.*

"No...no don't apologize, I'm sorry for seemin' ungrateful. I shouldn't'a lost my head like that." Etienne says like he's reading off a script, and he honestly kind of is, "I've just been stressed all day trying to find some assignment that'll work but it's just-there's *nothin'.*"

Sabine hums lightly in the way he does when he's trying to keep his thoughts to himself, waves a hand at the thick stack of files tucked under Etienne's arm and hedges cautiously, "Doesn't look like nothing to me. You...*really* couldn't find anythin'?"

"No. It's all idiotically simple or somethin' I *can't* take an outsider to, an' I didn't request the higher levels because *then* I'd have to ask mère to supervise and I didn't want- I-I just..." Etienne trails off a little, knows he's being something of a stubborn moron, but he's got to do this on his own.

He's going to be patriarch someday, has to be able to do things under his own power, and sure, that's probably a long way off, but it's always looming present and overshadowing in his mind, how he'll be the one everyone looks to for guidance one day.

"So..." Sabine starts, fingertips of his left hand touching his thumb in rapid succession while he thinks, an old tick he's never really grown out of, "You need an assignment challengin' enough that you'd need your mother's permission...but *won't* ask her 'cause you don't actually want her coming along, but then any assignment less than that isn't satisfactory, effectively meanin' you've hamstrung yourself?"

"I- *yeah...*" Etienne sheepishly rubs at the back of his neck, very

✦ 63 ✦

painfully aware of the oxymoronic nature of the situation. To prove he's capable and powerful, he has to take an assignment that requires parental supervision, *thus* proving he's not really as capable or as powerful as previously boasted in a fit of blind stupidity.

Mothers when will he ever learn to shut his void cursed mouth...

"I might just have to cave on it and ask her, but I really don't wanna. Hence me sayin' I might've screwed myself." Etienne sighs, but instead of agreeing that yes, *you are screwed,* Sabine just snaps his fingers like he's solved the problem, cheeky smile coming back, "Okay, fantastique. *Again.* Eti, this is *beyond* simple."

He pauses for dramatic effect, *true showman till the end,* and Etienne arches an eyebrow in question as Sabine fans his hands, declaring like it's the most obvious thing in the world, "Just take a higher level assignment without asking permission."

Etienne wants to strangle him.

"An' how am I supposed to do that, *génie?* I'm not forgin' anyone's signature and I sure as hell can't recreate their magic imprint, so *how* am I supposed to get the forms to pass?" Etienne asks in annoyance, watches Sabine bounce forwards with excessive pomp and vigor and is half considering whacking him over the head with his stack of files.

Maybe that'd finally get the haughty expression off his *insufferable face-*

"Oh it's quite easy, mon ami. All you need to do is find an assignment that's not in the system yet, and I miiiight know just the one." Sabine angles his head like he does when he's practicing opening statements, *cocky confident know more than you wish you were half as good as me,* a judicator to the very core, "It'll just take a little finaglin'- *hey,* you've already completed your lessons in seal work, correct?"

"I mean, some of them yes, but what does-"

✦✦ 64 ✦✦

What Goes Bump In The Night

"Great! You'll do just fine then. Alright well, we better get goin' before Mishé Marcel turns in for the night." Sabine then scoops the stack of folders from out under Etienne's arm, thuds it onto the counter before he can ask what's going on and makes for the front doors, calling airily over his shoulder, "Allez! We don't have all night to save your pompous ass!"

"Éy! *What're you-?* If anyone's *pompous* it's *you! Imbésil à la recherche de paon!*" Etienne fires back, and yet he's hurrying along after him anyway, hoping beyond measure that he might've finally found some solution to his problem.

Mothers know what Patriarch Marcel is going to be able to do, but Etienne trusts Sabine, *always has always will,* steps out into a dreary rainy night right on his heels. Sabine holds out a crooked arm for him and Etienne takes it without hesitation, his magic slipping along Sabine's just as easily.

It's not quite the same feeling as family, but it's a close thing, and they grin at one another, bootheels clicking in time as they make their way down pitted cobblestone roads, and like this, while they're together, *best friends future patriarchs brothers in everything but name,* it almost seems like they can take on anything.

Chapter 5

"What the hell are you doing here?"

As far as greetings go, that barely even counts as one, but considering it's the first thing out of Nica's mouth, Etienne really has no other choice than to assume that it is.

Nica had been in the process of stepping out of the library just like Sabine foresaw that they would, but froze once they spotted Etienne waiting outside, a tense little moment of unsure awkwardness growing up between the two of them that refuses to pass.

They're still frozen half in the doorway actually, light spilling past them and throwing an aggressively long shadow that edges over the toes of Etienne's boots, and it's really silly and petty and frankly unnecessary, but he purposefully scoots his feet until they're not anywhere close to touching Nica's shadow.

"Ah well, *ya'see,* I've just decided to throw everythin' away and become an alchemist. Was wondering if you got any tips?" Etienne drawls where he's leaning back against a lamp post, messenger bag propped against his leg, and at the deafening silence that follows, he arches an eyebrow, "No? Well if there aren't any more stupid questions, we've got an assignment to get to."

"What the *fuck* is your pro- w-wait- wait *what?* Assignment? That's- I-I didn't...*did I forget,* did we- did we arrange- m-make- plan s-something? And then I...*forgot?*" Nica says all in a stumble, hands flying to pat and dig through pockets, genuine concern on their face while they gnaw at their lip.

Odd, Etienne thinks as he watches from under the brim of his hat, *must have a bad memory must be common for things to slip must cause them stress,* sees them hurriedly go for their backpack and figures he needs to say something, *"Relax.* You didn't forget anything, somethin' just...*came up,* an' I figured it'd be a good opportunity is all."

Nica looks up at him then with a quizzical set to their face, like they're not really sure what he's talking about, so Etienne explains slow in exasperation, "For the bet? Ya'know...the one we made *yesterday?* The one where you promised to get me out of this nonsense once I prove my drastically superior talent? That ring any bells or-"

"I- yeah. *Y-Yeah* I remember." Nica huffs, throwing their backpack over their shoulder with more force than strictly necessary, "I just didn't think you meant like now- like a day later like tomorrow-*today.* Like I thought it'd be next week. Monday? *Ya'know-* when we're supposed to have our *meetings.*"

That would be...a fair assumption to make.

Mondays are their designated meeting times as assigned by the provost in charge of the program, which was a decision based *entirely* off Nica's class schedule and didn't take Etienne's into account at *all.* Sure, his day to day *is* a little trickier to figure out since it's not super consistent anyway, but it would've at least been polite to *ask him* what worked best.

"Well if you'd been listenin' earlier, I *said* something came up and thought it was a good opportunity for our little...wager. Now if we're done with the obvious, we gotta be across town before moonset so let's *go.*" Etienne bends to scoop his bag up, elegantly fits the strap over his shoulder and glances up at the sky quick, clicks his tongue in irritation because they really are burning moonlight.

This ritual is time sensitive and if he misses his window, then he'll have to wait until the moon is back in position, and the Gagnons can't wait until then. It may not be in the system, but this assignment is a high priority request nonetheless, one Patriarch Marcel granted to him in *good faith,* and Etienne is *determined* to not let him down.

✦✦ 67 ✦✦

I expect amazing things from you kabri we've all got our eyes on you, Marcel had jovially told him before Etienne left last night, and while it made his chest warm with pride then, it makes cold spikes of nerves rush down his spine now.

You're going to do fine you're not going to let him down, Etienne thinks firmly, fingers tightening sharply around his bag's strap as he starts to head off down the street, but pulls up short hearing indignant sputtering.

"Wha- *what?* No! You can't just- *show up* and start yelling- *ordering* me around!" Nica snaps, hands flying through the air as they erratically gesture back and forth between them, *"Look.* It's been a long day, I'm going home and- *whatever this is,* can- will- *is going to* wait until next Monday."

"It most certainly will not. The moon won't be in this position again for another synodic *month."* Etienne stresses, but it doesn't look like Nica cares, eyes rolling as they pull their headphones from around their neck, making to leave with a flippant, "That's a *you* problem, buddy."

Etienne bites his tongue on what he wants to say, *implied I'm spoiled look at you think you're too good for me won't hold your end up shows your poor character,* lets them get far enough down the sidewalk to entertain the notion of victory, and then calls loudly, "So I take it to mean you forfeit then?"

He knows Nica heard him because they stop near instantly, stand there with a rigid back and clenched fists, and Etienne counts down from ten in his mind, suppressing the smug smile that's threatening at his lips when they turn around before he gets to *six.*

"Okay what the fuck- *I* am not *forfeiting."* They growl low as they stomp back towards him, finger jabbing angrily in his direction, "You *agreed* to take me along on the toughest mission you could, but I *never* said that I'd just- go along *whenever!* I have shit to do!"

"As do I and yet here we are." Etienne simpers as he straightens up and cocks his shoulders back, makes sure to drop all traces of levity from his tone, "The way I see it, you have two options. One,

What Goes Bump In The Night

come with me now and lose fair and square or *two*- leave an' forfeit the bet in my favor. Either way works for me, but the choice is yours, mô shè."

Nica opens their mouth and then promptly shuts it, brows drawing down in a ferocious glare that would be intimidating to anyone without arcane talents. *"You..."* They hiss all drawn out and slow, *distant crack of far off lightning storm's on the way,* "Are *real* fuckin' annoying."

"Trust me the sentiment is mutual. Now allez, we're gonna be late." Etienne says airily as he spins on his heel and makes for the nearest trolley stop, can't fight the bright surge of triumph he feels listening to the angry footsteps following behind him.

Hermes University is close enough to Jackson Square that the trollies come by pretty consistently during the day, but they're a little less frequent at close to two in the morning. Etienne has the late night schedule memorized though, needs to so he won't miss a ride home after being out until the wee hours of dawn working an assignment.

Thankfully there's one pulling up right as they get there, and Etienne fishes his pass out of his bag, hops onboard and nods at the conductor, "Bonswá, Francoise, how're you?"

"I am well Mishé Boudreaux, how do you find yourself this evening?" Francoise responds in his creaky hollow voice, pointed tips of his ears sticking out past his cap, red eyes glowing in the dark, and sliding his pass through the reader, Etienne says, "I'm well, thanks for askin.'"

The pass reader makes a happy little chiming noise, and Etienne slips his card back into his bag, mentions before moving to find a seat, "Oh, Francoise, don't forget your monthly check-in. I don't believe we've seen you yet an' it's always good to be proactive."

"Of course, mishé. My apologies for any inconvenience, the centuries really wear on the mind." Francoise chuckles and it echoes leaving his throat, wavery and tremulous like wind curving past bare branches, "Is next Tuesday agreeable to your family's schedule?

Tis my next free evening."

"Should be, I'll let maman know." Etienne calls, dropping down into an empty seat and sets his bag next to him, and Francoise turns to smile at him, small enough to be polite but large enough that you can still catch a glimpse of one pointed fang, "Fanmé. I shall see you then, jeune Maître Boudreaux. *Oh-!*"

Belatedly realizing there was someone behind Etienne, Francoise is quick to spin back around and face forwards, voice dropping into distantly formal customer service, "My apologies for the lapse in attentiveness. Good evening and welcome aboard, will that be exact change or-?"

Etienne stops paying attention as Nica gets on and goes through paying their fare, ruffles around in his bag until he fishes his notebook out, slips the gilded pen free of its holder and jots down a quick message to mother.

Mother

<< Just ran into Francoise, he's coming by next Tuesday for his monthly vampirism wellness check. Love you and hope you're having a good evening.

And the ink's barely dried before the message disappears with a soft *fwoom*, afterimage of it glowing grey across the parchment, letting Etienne know it's been delivered but not read yet.

Up at the front of the car, Nica gets done paying and the trolley doors creak shut, a very normal thing that sounds exceptionally loud and jarring tonight. It makes Etienne's heart rate pickup for whatever reason, skittering fast behind his ribs because he's actually a little nervous about this assignment and *you're on the way now less than an hour until you get there and it's fine don't worry stop thinking about it don't make up problems it'll be okay-*

What Goes Bump In The Night

But Etienne *can't* stop thinking about it, mind running in a cyclical cycle like how a hurricane swirls to life, parading around every worst case scenario it can imagine and even though he recognizes what's happening, it doesn't mean he can stop it.

Mothers not now please why tonight, Etienne pleads miserably, tries to be subtle as he takes deep breaths in an effort to stymie the building anxiety attack, starts flipping through pages in his notebook looking for a distraction.

He finds comfort in reading old conversations between him and mother, *lunch dates and I love you's and reminders to get things turned in on time,* gets lost in past messages from Katie, *silly doodles and musical debate and planning for concerts,* looking to remind himself that things are okay and by extension *he* is okay. Etienne runs shaking fingers over dried ink and wishes he wasn't alone right now, hears footsteps coming towards him and remembers *shit he isn't alone right now,* pretends like he's not a *second away* from rattling out of his skin when Nica comes down the aisle.

It's not like it's a state secret that Etienne has anxiety issues.

Anyone that thought about it for longer than a second would be able to tell, *he's not really that good at hiding it,* and he absolutely *loathes* how transparent he is, doesn't like *anyone* knowing, *not his friends not his family especially not random pushy alchemists on the street-*

Which is why he masks it as much as he can, has built up something of an overconfident façade he hides behind, wants to look more sure of himself than he is, because otherwise, it's an absolute disgrace, right? *To have a future patriarch crippled so much by his own mind?*

Etienne just hopes he looks normal at least as Nica draws closer, watches them out of the corner of his eye and trusts they have enough sense to sit somewhere else, and then grimaces as they throw themself into the seat directly across from his.

Go away go away please just go away, he begs desperately while

✦ 71 ✦

there's some quiet shuffling as they sort their stuff, prays they'll leave him be but since the universe apparently hates him, Nica turns and huffs *way* too loud in the quiet of the trolley, "So am I *allowed* to ask where we're going?"

~~No don't wanna think about it don't wanna acknowledge it why would you bring it up GO AWAY~~

"Audubon." Etienne says purposefully short, thinks he did a good job masking the shake threatening at his words and flips to the section in his notebook marked by a teal ribbon, begins scribbling out a snippy complaint to Sabine, only half listening as Nica scoffs, "That's it? You're not- *yeah okay,* whatever. You know, if the situation was reversed- o-opposite- *turned around,* I'd at least give you *something* to work off of."

"You *asked* where we're goin', an' *that's* where we're goin.'" Etienne mutters, pen fussing over paper as he writes, forcefully trying to distract his mind from thinking about the assignment in any way he can.

It's making him irrationally anxious for absolutely no reason, *pre-assignment jitters they all get them it's normal ~~but not like this something's wrong~~,* and thankfully, Nica makes a fine distraction, mostly because do they ever whine about *everything.*

First it was, *I don't wanna go you can't make me,* and now it's, *I want to know everything even though I didn't care earlier tell me immediately,* and it's beyond frustrating. Etienne's got several things in mind he *could tell them,* none of which have anything to do with the assignment, but he won't breathe a word of it. He was raised better than that, knows how to mind his tongue and manners, because mother always taught that if you didn't have anything kind to say, it was best to just not say anything at all.

And Etienne's a good son, tries to take all of her lessons to heart, so he's writing everything out instead.

His gilt navy pen flows seamless and sharp over cream colored parchment, venting a mountain of frustrations out in ink for Sabine to read when he gets up tomorrow. Etienne harps on everything

✦ 72 ✦

What Goes Bump In The Night

he can think of, from how inconsiderate and rude Nica is, to their constant use of vulgar language, just- *anything* that gets under his skin, and at the moment, *there's a lot.*

It's therapeutic in a way, but it starts getting really petty, *complaining about their mannerisms how raucously bright they dress the ugly grimaces they give him,* and Etienne should stop, *he really needs to stop,* but writing is the only thing distracting him from the annoying cadence of their voice ~~and the creeping dread at the back of your mind anytime you think about the assignment what are you doing bad idea can't back out you promised PANIC~~

"-not trying to be difficult but- *look.* I know we agreed to do this- *a-and I am doing it.* I just- dude you gotta- *have to-* give me *something."* Nica huffs overwrought and grumbling, pauses to see if he'll say anything, and when he doesn't, they sigh and keep going, "It just...i-it just doesn't seem *fair.* Like. L-Like- it's like taking a test with *no* prep. I don't even know the *subject,* so *how* am I supposed to do *anything?"*

That makes something squirm around uncomfortable in his gut, ~~hit too close to home that's why no it didn't shut up,~~ and Etienne slows in his scribbling but quickly gets back to it, ~~pen wobblier this time hand shaking bad idea what are you doing get a grip.~~ He's not particularly interested in responding, ~~can't can't CAN'T-~~ and after a few seconds tick by with no response other than pen scratchings, Nica mutters sulky, "You know what? *Forget it.* What'm I even sayin'...it's not like it matters to *you.* You don't give a shit if it's fair."

His pen jerks to a sudden, guttering stop, and Etienne whips his head up to glare across the aisle, "And what is *that* supposed to mean?"

Nica is sitting with one of their legs tucked up under them, backpack in their lap, and in the dimly flickering light from the sconces, the dark circles under their eyes are exceedingly prominent. They shrug, the motion moving the plating in their right arm and it ripples like dragon scales, "I mean what I said. You don't care if you've got an unfair advantage, don't care about making this even- *a-a fair contest.* Because a win is a win for you, right?"

The trolley passes by a streetlamp and it flares orange light out in a halo behind Nica, throws their face into dark shadows as they murmur, "You'd rather not have to work to *actually* earn a victory and it...and it *tracks.*"

Etienne feels his eyebrows fly up, violent thud behind his ribs, *absolutely brazen can't believe they just implied spoiled brat didn't earn anything you have silver platter,* bright electrical crack rushing through his veins and making his voice stutter as he snaps, "I-I'm not *withholdin'* information as a- *a-as a cheap trick* to win!"

"Okay, then tell me what we're doing and where we're going. Since you're not scared of losing to me fair and square." Nica demands, arms folding on top of their backpack, "If you were actually inter-ested- *wanted-* this bet to be fair, you'd give me *something,* because how am I supposed to help- *do anything-* when I-I don't even know what *I'm doing?"*

Oh something about that just hits Etienne *hard, ~~because it's you you're in the same position right now felt confident last night with Sabine at your side but now you're alone and you have no idea what you're doing~~ shut UP.* That's not it *at all,* he's fine, it's just pre-as-signment jitters ~~it's just the storm in his head~~, *they all get them he's got them it'll pass ~~leave nothing in its wake~~,* he can do this, *he's got to do this shook Patriarch Marcel's hand and you promised you can't back out you don't want to ~~you need to~~ you promised ~~you made a mistake~~ you have to do this ~~you can't do this~~ AUGH-*

There's a lot happening inside Etienne's head right now and he's struggling to get ahold of it all, keeps trying to detach himself from the brewing storm of emotions growling to life under his bones. *Breathe get control of yourself breathe you're fine it'll be fine,* Etienne reminds himself, repeats it like a mantra until everything is forcefully still and he can *think again.*

Yes, he hasn't told Nica what the parameters of the assignment are, but not because he was trying to *steal a win,* but because he knew it was going to go right over their head, *~~honestly goes a bit~~*

What Goes Bump In The Night

~~over his not sure this is a good idea~~. The magic involved is fairly complicated and not something they're going to understand, *which is the point,* but *fine.*

If they wanna know, Etienne'll tell them, sucks in air through his teeth, makes sure his voice is measured and controlled when he says, "House Gagnon is movin' a cursed and bound Class A dragon skeleton tonight from Audubon to City Park, an' someone, *me,* has to modify the Lucretius seal on it."

Sharp thud racing ever faster get it together you're a scion you agreed to do this gave your word measure of your character don't let it suffer mistake mistake MISTA-

"That...doesn't seem too hard? I- I-I don't get what the big deal is..." Nica hedges with a crinkled brow, sounds so dismissive, like none of this matters, *like the way he feels doesn't matter,* and it's the wrong thing to say at the wrong time.

Something cracks open and Etienne flings his hands in the air, words pouring out fast and erratic like the way his pulse thunders under his ears, "Oh yes! You're right, *h-how silly of me!* It's just the *simplest* thing to modify a few decades old *Lucretius seal* from grounding to transitional *back to grounding-* w-without releasin' the thing mind you! And then movin' *dragon bones* near across the city *before moonset! You absolute idiot!"*

And it's like a balloon popping, *pressure instantly deflating,* and Etienne feels better for all of about two seconds before reality comes crashing back in.

"Jesus! *Fucking-* don't get your pants all in a knot! I was just asking, man." Nica snaps, twisting sharply to face forwards, messy ash blonde hair falling across their face and hiding their expression, and that...might've been a little harsh. There's a certain level of decorum Etienne is expected to keep, both as a scion and then as a son of Catherine Boudreaux, and he knows he's just violated that pretty resolutely.

His anxiety makes him irrational at the worst times but that's not an excuse, he knows not to let it spiral out of control, but it

✦✦ 75 ✦✦

clearly just did, and that's his mistake.

Etienne shouldn't've let his emotions run wild like that, shouldn't have raised his voice at *all*, and nervously taps his fingers against the pages of his notebook, unsure what to do for a moment.

"I...*I'm sorry*. That was improper of me." He eventually murmurs, guiltily looking across the aisle at Nica and the tensed muscles in their arms, remembering yesterday and their apology to him, "I shouldn't've gotten a tone with you, and...a-and I didn't mean for it to seem like I was keepin' things from you in order to win. That's not my intention at all an' I apologize for that."

Etienne's relatively proud of how it all comes out, thinks it's a good blend of measured yet sincere, and finds he really does mean it, doesn't want a hollow or stolen victory, but instead of doing the mature thing and accepting his apology, Nica tosses their head and without even looking at him, bites out, *"Eat a dick."*

His mouth drops open and maroon electricity sparks between his fingers, sudden quick bursts of leaking power that singes his fingertips, and you know what, *never mind*. Etienne *isn't* sorry for snapping at them actually. They're a jerk and an asshole and he doesn't owe them *anything,* least of all an apology, and yeah, *okay,* he gets that they might still be upset, but there's no reason to respond like that.

It's absolutely immature but hey, they can be a toddler and pout if they want to, *Etienne doesn't care,* has other, *more important* things to be worrying about anyway.

Resolve a little steadier, he reasons it'd be better to spend his remaining time before they get to Audubon studying rather than stewing over Nica, and hastily slips his pen back into its sleeve. Etienne glances down at the mess he'd scrawled out to Sabine before closing his notebook, and is quick to snap it shut, an uncomfortable feeling poking around his chest he thinks might be embarrassment.

That was honestly really childish of him. He's *supposed* to know better, *does know better,* and there's no taking it back but he can make sure it doesn't happen again. *Be the witch your mother expects you to be,* Etienne reminds himself as he tucks his notebook away, *you're her son you're her scion you don't have room to be anything less than perfect,* draws out instead the thick tome on Lucretian seals he *uh, borrowed,* from mother's study.

It's absolutely ancient but still in good condition like all of their books are, front cover a dark, lacquered maroon that shines faintly in the dim lights of the trolley. Colorful strips of ribbon poke out from various spots in the book, mark places Etienne deemed relevant in his hurried read through this morning, and he flips to the first one.

The sections he highlighted with his magic glow softly in the gloom, and Etienne starts reading, brow furrowing not a second later. He usually considers himself a pretty good notetaker, but some of the parts he marked make absolutely no sense until he flips back a few pages and gets the context. He ends up doing that a lot, but in his defense, he hasn't really had the opportunity to be as thorough as he normally is with his studies.

In-between when Etienne got back last night from the Gagnon's, his daily duties today, and then leaving to find Nica, there hadn't been enough time to read the entire tome in uh...*complete detail-*

But he skimmed the whole thing! And read the important passages, made notes where he felt appropriate, *even if some of them are confusing what in the world is this one going on about...a transpositional sigil is equal to the same output as a grounded semi-terrarial sigil and can be used in substitutional settings wherein the caster would normally...Mothers what does that even mean-*

Anxious energy coils sickly hot through his veins again, and Etienne is more than a little frustrated with himself. He was fine last night when Marcel was explaining the assignment, felt like it was something he could handle, so why is it only *now* that he's having such strong reservations?

You're too caught up in it too far in your own head, Etienne thinks, flipping back and forth between the same two pages, tries to imagine what Sabine would tell him if he was awake and here with him. *You're spinning yourself in circles mon ami,* elegant hand waves and eyes dark like the night but warmer than the sun, *don't get lost in this maze you've made,* gentle hand on his shoulder and the soft, clean smell of wide open spaces and playful breezes, *take a second breathe a little you can find your way back out.*

Etienne stops turning pages rapid fire because that's...actually somewhat helpful, and fake Sabine chuffs, rolls his eyes and leaves Etienne with something he really needs to take to heart but struggles with from time to time.

It's going to be okay, trust yourself.

His eyes slip closed briefly, *thank you,* but then they flick back open because it *is* going to be okay. Lucretian seals are just a more advanced version of Octavian seals...*kinda,* and that's something Etienne has a fair bit of experience with. So as long as he takes the trolley ride to brush up on everything, it ~~shouldn't~~ *won't* be a problem at all.

Etienne settles in to get his last little bit of studying done, grateful for the peaceful hush that only comes in the late hours of the night.

Streetlamps cast warm orange light that runs across parchment like a train rushing past, hypnotic and lulling, only sound being the gentle crinkle as pages are flipped and the mechanical squeal of brakes, and it's so easy to get lost between pages and under theories that tangle in your brain like string. Night air slips in through open windows, gentle and sweet, tinged with the smell of summer warmth and the stray night blooming flower, brushes across Etienne's cheeks like a set of doting fingers.

His magic coils lazily along while he's reading, flexing into and out of the patterns it'll have to form for the ritual, guttering slightly whenever he makes an attempt to form the seal. It's a tricky shape to keep and hold in your mind, takes a lot of concentration to even get close, and more times than not, it falls apart like the way water falls out of a sieve.

✦✦ 78 ✦✦

What Goes Bump In The Night

Etienne is determined to get it though and rereads sections continuously, works on coaxing his magic to assume the shapes it needs to. *Come on you can do it just get it together,* he berates, latest attempt fizzing out with crackling pings and pops, but that time he'd gotten past the first ring of glyphs, so he'll count that as a win.

He doesn't know how long it's been, probably only a few minutes but it could be closer to hours and he'd never know, not when he's completely absorbed by work like this. Etienne is focused entirely on the glowing maroon lines spreading and contracting over the practice section of the tome, is really deep in thought, and thus is in turn *really* startled when a palm slaps against his seat unexpectedly.

The smack of flesh against wood is *jarringly* loud, and Etienne jumps on instinct, upending the book out of his lap in a fluttering mess.

Bright, surprised laughter echoes around the near silent trolley, hearty and warm, *honestly kinda nice,* and he snaps his head up, glaring like absolute death at Nica, *"What?"*

They're leaned over a little, arm braced against the back of Etienne's seat, face scrunched up while they spit giggles out, obviously taking *way* too much enjoyment from startling him, "D-Dude? I barely even- *just,* jumpy much? Do you- d-do you need someone to hold your hand or- *ha!* A-A pillow to hide behind?"

"Shut. Up." Etienne hisses, shooting to his feet and tries to regain some semblance of composure, but he knows his face is bright red and that only makes it flush worse, "I- I-I was busy readin' an'- *I just-* would you *stop laughin'-* what do you even *want?"*

"Chill, *chill-* we're here, don't get bent out of shape about it." Nica straightens up with a final rap of their hand against the wooden seat, pauses before leaving and tacks on with a smarmy grin, *"Jumpy."*

"I am *not-! Ugh."* Etienne throws a hand up and then pinches the bridge of his nose, sighs longsuffering but decides this isn't the hill to die on. *Sooner you get this started sooner you get this over with,* he reminds himself while stooping to retrieve his fallen

✦✦ 79 ✦✦

book, smooths the ruffled pages out before he tucks it away in his bag.

Following along behind Nica, Etienne wishes a perplexed looking Francoise a pleasant rest of his evening and a promise to see him next week, tips his hat in farewell as he steps off the trolley and then nearly runs right into Nica. They've barely moved off the last step, and there's an awkward minute or two where Etienne almost falls over, feet snarling together in his haste to *not* hit them.

Somehow, through no help on Etienne's part, he and Nica manage to do a horrific imitation of a pirouette to stay upright, and Etienne is spared from faceplanting against the sidewalk. He stumbles into a more stable stance and knocks the brim of his hat up, about to ask them what in the *world* their problem is, when he sees their face and it clicks.

Audubon is completely deserted at two in the morning, nothing but the wind rustling in the leaves and the low, mournful cries of some of the night creatures echoing from within the nature preserve. It's black as pitch out here, save for where the scant few streetlamps illuminate things in spaced out halos, the whole area entirely eerie and haunting and it bleeds Nica's face whiter than the moon.

Oh you've got to be kidding there's no way are they actually afraid of- a banshee chooses then to shriek horrifically, loud keen of it ripping through the air, and Nica flinches *hard,* shoulders coming up around their ears, and it takes a lot of effort to keep the cocky smirk off his face.

"What's the matter?" Etienne all but purrs, rocking his head to the side, dark of the night enfolding around him like a loving embrace, comforting slide of *other* rolling over his shoulders, *"Afraid of the dark?"*

Jerking their wide, terrified eyes to him, Nica tries to glare and fails spectacularly, voice weak and shaky as they stammer, "S-Shut *up.*"

"Oh bless your heart...you *are.* Well now, no need to worry. I'll

What Goes Bump In The Night

make sure nothin' gets'ya." Etienne drawls, strolling languidly past Nica and then pauses, throwing a considering look over his shoulder at the death grip they have on their backpack, "But I mean... you can always go back if you wanna...*scaredy cat.*"

Nica's gaze had been jumping frantically from shadow to shadow, but it lands on Etienne's after that and something hardens at the core of it. Their hands tighten into fists around their backpack straps but they start walking forwards anyway, shoulder checking Etienne when they stalk past him, muttering darkly under their breath, *"Dick."*

The impact is enough to make Etienne sway dangerously, foot flying out to steady him, and he glares at the back of Nica's head, fingers rubbing the sore spot on his arm.

"Creatin." He mumbles hotly, magic frizzing at the edges from his irritation, but he takes a deep breath and then lets the squirming anger go.

You're so close to being done with this- with them -just a few more hours now, and it's such an uplifting thought, it puts a little bounce in his step. Using his longer stride to catch up with them, Etienne easily passes Nica and then keeps ahead of them, leading the way towards the front of the nature preserve.

With several hundred acres worth of land, Audubon is the largest wildlife sanctuary within city limits and has been managed chiefly by the Gagnon since their house was first built in New Orleans. Historically it served as their training grounds, and while it is still largely used for that, it's also become something of a tourist attraction in modern times.

Humans have always been intrigued by the arcane, sometimes fatalistically so, and touring the Gagnon's menagerie is a safer way to satisfy that curiosity without getting their faces torn off. It also supplies the Gagnon with a little extra income after the government takes their cut, which, *naturally* the city council got involved with administrative duties at the preserve before too long.

Once they realized a profit could be turned from the massive tract of land they previously had no jurisdiction over, the city argued that as long as humans were there, it fell under their purview, and while being under the city's purview meant they now had to pay local taxes, it also meant municipal funding and outreach programs.

So Etienne supposes it's not all bad.

The tours *do* help raise awareness for preserving habitats for arcane creatures, provide *accurate* tips for what to do if you encounter one in the wild and a score of other resources, but any time the city starts poking their nose into things, they start finding problems where previously there were none.

And tonight is a prime example of that.

It doesn't take them long to get to the meetup destination, and even if Etienne couldn't remember where he was supposed to go exactly, it's pretty obvious they're in the right spot.

Unlike any other building they've passed, all the lights are still blazing in the visitor's center, highlighting a small group of people laughing and joking around by the front entrance, rich, brick red hats bobbing up and down as they talk animatedly.

Quickening his pace, Etienne cups his hands around his mouth and shouts to get their attention, *"Swaré!"*

He gets a score of friendly responses in return, knows Jack's voice right off the bat, is pretty sure that's Tanis and then there's Bea waving her arm enthusiastically, other braced on her hip as she calls back, "Coucou, nabot!"

"Éy!" Etienne laughs bounding up to her, gets drug into a one armed hug that crunches nearly all the air out of his lungs but leaves enough so he can wheeze, "I'm *literally* the same height as you."

"Oh yeah? Square up then, *nabot.*" Bea challenges and lets him go, tan arms folding across her chest as she cocks her chin back, dark braid with its froofy white bow slipping over her broad shoulders. Etienne straightens up as much as he can without going up on tiptoe, has in the past and has gotten whacked for it, but

What Goes Bump In The Night

he's absolutely delighted to see his hat brim just *that* little bit higher than Bea's now.

He waggles his eyebrows at her, and she clucks her tongue, socking him on the arm with a grin dragging her lips up. "Yeah *yeah,* rest high on your laurels, torpe. You've won *nothin',* congratulations." Bea snaps sarcastically, and cocking his head to the side, Etienne boasts, "Au contraire, I do believe I've won a great deal... *nabot.*"

Bea's smile broadens as she throws her head back in laughter, great booming sound of it echoing through the night like raucous claps of thunder. Light catches in the dark of her eyes and sparks off the iron charms swinging from her hat when she shakes her head at him, sighing fond, "Aaahh, Eti, you're such a lil'menace. Never change, shéri ."

Etienne opens his mouth to respond, has an *amazing* retort at the tip of his tongue, but Bea glances to his left and her face sobers a bit, mantle of authority settling over her, "Oh, uh, hello. And who might you be?"

"I uh- *hi.* Nica Caldwell, I-I'm *Nica.* I'm a student over a-at Hermes and then um...E-Etienne's Arcane Diversity partner." Nica doesn't sound happy about that fact as they hold a hand out, and for once, Etienne finds he agrees with them on something wholeheartedly. *We won't be for much longer it'll all be done soon,* he thinks wistfully, watches as Bea takes their hand with no hesitation, doing a firm handshake while she introduces herself and the others.

"Pleasure. This's my brother Jackson, he's the dragon expert, and that's our cousin Tanis, they're head of park outreach." She says nodding at them each in turn, and they both raise their hands one at a time in greeting, "And I'm Scion Beatrice, but you can call me Bea."

"H-Hi! It's um, i-it's nice to meet y'all, I'm Nica." Nica says again for some reason, and Etienne turns to give them a weird look, watches color flame up their face as they seem to realize they introduced themself *twice,* hand nervously ruffling through their

✦✦ 83 ✦✦

hair, "A-Aaaaaand I already um- said- mentioned- *t-told you that.* Hah- are we- s-should we um-"

They gesture shakily at the visitor center, arm limply dropping back to their side while they attempt to hide in the collar of their windbreaker, so clearly embarrassed, *Etienne's* starting to feel bad for them. As always, Bea is extra friendly and quickly jumps over the social blunder, claps her hands together loudly to draw everyone's attention, "Yes! Right! No time like now *or whatever-* well, everyone ready? The three of us are good to go, you all set up, Eti?"

"Mm hm, got everythin' I need." He says and gives his messenger bag a soft pat in reply, doing one last run down of the ritual steps in his mind to make sure he remembers them all. Etienne's *pretty sure* he has everything memorized, but loses his train of thought halfway through when Bea spins on her heel, skirts fluttering as she calls, "Great! Let's get goin' then! These bones ain't gonna pick up and move themselves!"

The front doors of the visitor center swing open for Bea, letting all of them into the main reception area, a long, spacious room with high vaulted ceilings crowned in skylights that stream light in during the day, but only loom overhead as black voids at night. Dark cherry wood paneling covers the walls and posts supporting the upper level balcony, makes everything feel warm and close, tiny little coppery tiles spreading out in a looping mosaic under their feet.

Various displays and exhibits lay scattered throughout the entire building, informational signs sitting neatly under taxidermied creatures that stare blank at the world around them, interactive displays for children to engage with that teach, *and warn,* about the animals the Gagnon care for, and soaring above it all is an absolutely massive dragon skeleton.

It's suspended with several faintly glowing levitation charms at strategic points, ancient bones posed in a mimicry of flight so it looks like the beast is swooping past, and even from down here, Etienne can see the bright maroon spark of the Lucretius seal on its skull.

✦✦ 84 ✦✦

What Goes Bump In The Night

His fingers tighten around his bag's strap.

"Holy *shit.*" Nica breathes and he's quick to look over at them, watches their head tip back to really take the entire thing in. They spin in a slow circle as they gape up at the skeleton, an unguarded kind of bright fascination on their face, and Etienne can't help but wonder if they've ever been here before.

Practically every child in the parish comes to the nature preserve at some point, humans and Occult members alike, but given the way Nica's staring at everything wide eyed, Etienne doesn't think they have. Maybe they actually are from out of state like he first thought, not that it should matter in the slightest, but as he watches Nica marvel at the bones over their head, soft little grin tugging their lips up, he just...really wants to know.

And it's weird. It's a weird thought to suddenly have.

Etienne cuts his eyes away fast, rubs distractedly at the tip of one of his ears because it feels strangely warm and checks to see where Bea's gone off to.

Most of the furniture that was in the center of the room has been moved in preparation for the skeleton to come down, and there's really only a few big pieces left. It looks like the others have it under control though, Tanis is just unloading a squishy looking armchair well out of the way and then Bea is helping her brother move the reception desk.

They come trundling past and she must notice the way Nica's still boggling at the dragon as they shimmy by, more than happily grunts over her shoulder, "Yeah, that's ol'Gertie, a Golden Crested Swamp Reaver or draconis mississippiensis. About sixty-two feet, would've been roughly...pbbbfff- seventy...three? *Six?* Around seventy-six tons."

"Jesus..." Nica whistles, finally tips their head back down and makes an aborted gesture to help with the desk, but both Bea and Jack wave them off. Seemingly not knowing what to do now, Nica awkwardly shuffles from foot to foot and stuffs their hands in the front pocket of their windbreaker, clears their throat roughly, "I

✦✦ 85 ✦✦

uh- I-I didn't think there were any dragons still that big?"

"There's not, least 'round here. We manage their population these days to make sure there aren't any more Gerties." Jack explains as he sets the reception desk down with a heave, dusts his hands off and grins crooked, scar through his lips growing real thin, "She really puts it into perspective for what it used to be like, ya'know? Which is why it's a damn shame we gotta take her down."

"Wait...i-if you don't wanna take it- *her* down, why are you?" Nica asks with such naive befuddlement that Etienne can't help snorting, earns himself a sour glare he rolls his eyes at, and almost like they practiced it, all three Gagnon sigh in answer at the exact same time, *"OSHA..."*

Nica blinks, "What."

Bea throws her hands out and then plants them on her hips, striding forwards slow while she stares up at the skeleton forlornly, "Yeah we got audited few weeks back an' apparently havin' her all in one piece like this is a *'workplace safety violation'*, which is- *beyond* stupid. But they argued that since she's not *technically* dead *dead* that-"

"I'm sorry- *WHAT?"* Nica backs up fast out from under Gertie's shadow, keeps snapping their alarmed gaze between the dragon's remains and Bea, "What do you *mean* that thing i-isn't *dead?* It's only- *nothing left-* t-there's just bones!"

"Well. *Yeah.* Some warlock cursed her remains in- *oh what was it,* like the eighteenth century or somethin'? To try an' destroy the city." Bea explains, gets a thoughtful look on her face as she strokes fingers down her long, intricate braid, "So I guess you're right. *Undead* would be a more appropriate term, which is why we're joined by the *lovely* Mishé Boudreaux this evenin'."

She tips her hat in his direction and Etienne jerks to attention, swift prickling rolling over his shoulders because everyone's turned to look at him, *eyes on you all the time how do you measure up,* and affecting a confidence he knows he should feel, Etienne repeats one of the adages of his house, "What's dead should stay dead."

◆✦◆ 86 ✦◆✦

What Goes Bump In The Night

"That it should! Now enough chit chat- I think it's 'bout time we got these old bones movin'!" Bea calls chipperly as she starts for the other side of the hall, and Etienne's heart skips in his chest, nerves licking up his throat he's trying to force back down.

You're fine you'll be okay you can handle this, he exhales shaky and is annoyed to see bright flecks of maroon, keeps getting zapped by more spillover crackling painfully between his flexing fingers, and it feels like a bowstring drawn to the breaking point when he hears Nica snicker at him, "What's wrong with you? Got cold feet, *s-second thoughts* or somethi-?"

Twang! And there it goes.

"Will you *just- mind your own damn business!*" Etienne snaps, whirling to face Nica with his heart thundering in his throat and hands shaking from anxious magic roiling out of control, "You are the *least* qualified person to be here, a-an' have *no right* to be makin' *any assumptions* about *me* o-or *my abilities!*"

Nica freezes where they are, shoulders locking up and spine going stiff, arms held awkwardly at their sides as their expression drops into the vilest thing Etienne has ever seen. He just arches his eyebrows in question, *got something you wanna say,* but they turn away with a huff, moodily stuffing both hands in their front pocket again, and Etienne clicks his tongue, "Yeah, that's what I thou-"

But the words die right in his throat as Nica suddenly whips to face him, light flashing fast in their eyes as they go up on tiptoes, *something lancing into the very core of his chest stops his heart cold where it trembles,* high whine of electricity that underscores their snarling voice, *"What?* WHAT did you *think* y-you POMPOUS *insufferable piece of SHI-!"*

"Éy, éy, éy- come on." Bea chides from across the room, clapping her hands to draw both their attentions, each hit echoing percussively in the silence and banging along to the rapid fast tempo of Etienne's heart, "Come on, none of that. We got a job to do, yeah? Let's try an' remember to be professional."

With a heavy huff, Nica rocks back on their heels and shoves

✦✦ 87 ✦✦

past Etienne, hands locking over the back of their neck as they storm across the reception hall. Etienne turns to watch them go, still struggling to find his breath, chest shaking with how hard his pulse is going because the amount of energy that just skated along his consciousness is *alarming.*

He's used to feeling other witches' magical signatures, casual brushes here and there between family and friends, but even then, it's barely much of anything, just the faintest impression of the power funneling through their bodies.

Whatever the hell Nica just did, it felt like closing your hand on a live wire, *a punch to the gut being clubbed over the head like getting struck by lightning,* completely unmetered energy crackling wild and barely under control as it arced past.

Etienne's *never* felt something like that before, and eyes boring into the back of that garishly colorful windbreaker, he's not really sure he knows what he's dealing with.

Because that much energy all condensed together like that, held in place through what seems like sheer force of will, betrays an incredibly powerful and skilled caster, and for the briefest second, he *doubts- himself this bet his ability to win back the supremacy he thought he had-*

A sharp whistle snaps Etienne out of it and he jerks his head up, sees everyone watching him from across the room, swallows rough and tries to straighten up, but it feels like something insurmountably heavy is pressing down on his shoulders. Bea has her hands on her hips, eyebrow cocked where she stands under the shadow of the colossal skeleton, dark outline of its roaring maw engulfing her like an ill omen, "Well...you ready? We're all waitin' on you."

And something constricts harsh in his chest, *all those eyes on you all the time looking to see how you measure up if you'll be the witch they all expect you to be can't let them down can't fail no room for error can't be anything less than perfect,* and letting out a shaky breath, Etienne nods, forces his anxiety out so he can focus.

✦✦ 88 ✦✦

What Goes Bump In The Night

But it doesn't go.

It doesn't go.

Chapter 6

Etienne has about seven minutes between when the Gagnon start undoing the levitation charms and when Gertie touches the floor to do any last second cramming. He paces back and forth near the front entrance, book in hand as he tries to block out the others loudly coordinating with one another in the background.

It's tricky business getting the skeleton down since it has three separate levitation charms and they all have to be decreased by the same amount, at the same time. If they're not, they run the risk of the skeleton breaking part, which in turn would disrupt the seal keeping the malevolent spirit bound, and for obvious reasons, that would be a *colossal problem*.

Thankfully Bea and her family know what they're doing, have clearly spent a lot of time training together before, so they're making quick work of it, and that's...*great*. It's awesome actually, *really fantastic*, because the sooner they get this over with, the sooner it's done and maybe the nerves that're eating Etienne alive will *kindly knock it the hell off*.

First step set up the fail-safe binds make sure they're connected properly then move on to the transmogrifications, Etienne reminds himself while he absentmindedly chews on a fingernail, has to cut it out a second later when he tastes nail polish flaking off in his mouth, *next unlock primary ring of glyphs might cause a surge that's normal begin modifying secondary ring release the...no wait- DO NOT release the...t-the uh-*

Thumbing quickly back through the book, Etienne scans pages fast hoping to either find the passage he needs or something to jog his memory, sense of urgency inching up the lower Gertie gets to the floor.

✦✧✦ 90 ✦✧✦

What Goes Bump In The Night

Where is it where is it where is it, he thinks, can see the page he's looking for in his mind, the exact layout of the text and everything, but for the life of him, can't really remember what it actually says nor where it is.

Come on come on you know where it is just find it you can find it, except for he really can't, fingers stuttering as a dark shadow passes over them, *okay just think don't release the what you know this just remember trust yourself,* which Etienne tries, wracks his brain for anything he can remember, *what would be logical what makes sense what do you not wanna release the last ring it's probably the third ring right,* and that has to be it.

The last set of glyphs is what's directly connected to the curse's energy, funneling it around in a continuous loop so it doesn't have anywhere else to go while the outer rings keep it contained. If he were to release the core layer, even for the barest second, it stands to reason that Gertie's warped consciousness could resurface and break free.

Something feels like it clicks together in Etienne's mind, *the missing piece to the puzzle,* and a wave of relief rushes through him so strong that he gets a little dizzy. He grins, fingers delightedly tapping against worn pages because he *knew* he'd figure it out. It just took some time and a bit of added pressure, but he got it, *which of course he did,* he *is* a scion after all, and an excellent one at that.

His instincts are *good,* and Sabine was right, he really does need to stop worrying so much and trust himself more.

A dull thud rumbles through the room, and looking up, Etienne happily snaps his book closed as he comes face to face with a snarling maw of massive teeth, feeling genuinely confident for the first time all night.

He steps up to run his hand along a canine that's thicker around than his thigh, fingers jumping next to an incisor, both nestled in the mouth of something that could've swallowed him whole with little to no problem, and really gets an appreciation for how

✦✦ 91 ✦✦

terrifying the beast must've been when it lived.

If he's remembering right, it took his many greats grandmother and then the Gagnon atriarch at the time, along with a dozen fully claimed coven members from each of their houses, to bring the dragon's remains down before it could lay New Orleans to waste.

What a nightmare that must've been, he thinks, dropping his hand from its idle wandering, is glad that the only thing he has to do tonight is modify an already active seal.

Which, speaking of.

Etienne has to stretch a bit up on his toes to see, but there, in between the massive dark hollows that are Gertie's eye sockets, spread out along its nasal ridge like a luminescent growth, is the Lucretius seal. Composed of intricate, delicate lines of glyphs that circle each ring, the seal glows with rich maroon light that dims and brightens in a sort of pattern, pentagram slowly spinning at its center, almost like the thing is breathing softly.

It's a little less daunting of a task now that it's closer, less like it's out of reach and something not so far removed from his comfort zone, because now that he's gotten a better look at it, it really doesn't look that dissimilar to an Octavian seal. Obviously there are differences, *Octavian seals are just for malevolent human spirits are less complicated Lucretius seals are for anything with magic require more safeguards,* but it still looks like something he's pretty familiar with.

Mothers, he's a little embarrassed with how worked up he managed to get himself over this, and Etienne knows he's something of an unnecessary worrier, drives himself mad with cyclical thoughts and constant anxieties, but it's been a little different lately. Things have been extra rough for a while now, and he's not really sure what's causing the spike in anxiety this time around, has been doing everything his old therapist told him would help and it's not doing much.

Which is vaguely concerning and it's enough that Etienne is *almost* convinced to revisit medication, but last time put him

What Goes Bump In The Night

so far out of his own head, he's not eager for a repeat, even if it means his brain will stop gnawing on things.

Still, whatever he wants to do about his mental health is really a debate for later, and dropping down onto his heels, Etienne takes a quick step back from Gertie and slips his messenger bag off his shoulder to set on the floor, nudging it out of the way as he says, "Right. So we only have until moonset to get this done, but that should be plenty of time as long as we don't run into any delays."

"Just tell us where ya need us, nabot." Bea says chipper and having her defer to him is strange, both because she's older and also just her general personality, and it takes Etienne a second to process, slight hesitation tripping his order up, "I um- *okay*. I-I'm gonna need y'all to secure Hawthorne binds- *o-or some equivalent*, in evenly spaced spots along the body, and then I can get started."

Bea and the others all immediately call out the affirmative and get to work, jumping, copper light blazing to life like embers being stoked in the hearth, warm sooty smell of fire tickling his nose as the Gagnons' magic wires its way over old bones. While they're doing that, Etienne cranes his neck to see if he can access the seal from the ground or if he'll need to climb up on Gertie's skull, *looking like the latter,* when he hears soft behind him, "Um...w-what do you want *me* to do?"

He glances over his shoulder, and it's a bit like that victorious feeling you get when you're almost done with a really difficult exam, seeing Nica standing there staring at him hesitantly. Etienne doesn't even bother turning fully to face them, makes a considering expression as he asks already knowing the answer, "Well...are you able to make anythin' remotely resemblin' a Hawthorne bind?"

"I don't...t-think so? B-But I could construct a-!"

"That won't be necessary. Nothin' personal, but *mundane* restraints aren't of much use." Etienne cuts them off quick, in parts to rub it in their face how unneeded they are, but also, *quite frankly,* because it's true. If the curse were to break out of the seal and reanimate Gertie, *which it won't,* but if it *did,* physical restraints

✦✦ 93 ✦✦

aren't going to do much of anything to stop it.

Even without the strength it pulls from the dark magic possessing it, that dragon could easily tear through pretty much anything, save for pure steel perhaps, which would still do jack all against a curse of this magnitude. The warlock that did this really was hellbent on destroying New Orleans, and no *alchemy* done by an *undergrad* is going to put much of a dent in it.

"Alright, if Hawthorne binds are off the table..." Etienne muses, pretending to think it over, starts throwing out a few more suggestions he knows Nica wouldn't be able to do, "Could you perhaps lay down a back sealed containment buffer, just in case any malevolent energy leaks out? Or perform a quick augury to make sure there aren't any unforeseen problems?"

"I- I-I don't know what- I don't think I- *you're just-*" Nica struggles to get out, eyes dropping away fast to bore holes into the floor, and clucking his tongue, Etienne drawls languidly, "So no to that as well, hm? *Oh I know!* Why don't you come up here with me an' help steady my transmogrifying with your own magic- but...oh, *wait,* you can't do that *either.*"

Color is spreading quickly across Nica's cheeks, could be embarrassment could be anger, *Etienne really doesn't care,* twists back around and says triumphant, "Honestly I'm a bit stumped then, mô shè. And it's a shame, really *truly it is,* but since I can't think of anythin' else you could *possibly* help with, it might just be best if you...*stayed out of our way.*"

Nica doesn't respond and Etienne isn't expecting them to, feels the hairs raise along the back of his neck in response to the sudden surge of electricity that spikes through the air though. It catches him off guard for a second, truly overwhelming at first as it crackles to life, but it fades fast and he snorts derisively. The raw energy Nica's apparently capable of harnessing *is* impressive, he'll give them that, but if there's nothing they can do with it, then it's functionally pointless.

It can't be worked into seals or glyphs or sigils, can't form binds

What Goes Bump In The Night

and create tethers, doesn't let them scry into the distant future nor the far flung past. Ritual magic might be possible if they had the right tools, they can at least generate the energy needed for it, but performing the rite would require knowing information that's kept so closely guarded, it might as well be housed behind the cage of a witch's ribs.

In the end, Nica is basically nothing more than a foul mouthed lightning rod, and like most alchemists, isn't good for much else besides the fabrication and redistribution of elements. Etienne had been worrying himself unnecessarily earlier, *kinda does that a lot habit he needs to break,* and more than happily puts the notion that Nica could've ever been a challenge out of his mind.

"Should be all set on my end, Eti!" Bea's voice breaks the relative quiet as she calls from her spot by Gertie's neck, sparking lines of the bind held tightly in her fists while the rest of it loops over and under gaps in the skeleton. She does a few test pulls to make sure it's firmly in place, gives Etienne a thumbs up when both Jack and Tanis shout that they're ready as well, and he cracks his knuckles.

Time to get to work.

Hooking his foot through a gap in Gertie's teeth as a boost, Etienne curls his hands into the nostril cavity and uses it to help haul himself up. He's not the most graceful about it, toes of his boots scrabbling slightly against smooth bone, but he gets up on top of the skull eventually and that's all that really matters.

He wobbles sharply once he stands up though, thrown off by the uneven slope to Gertie's head and the bony ridges that keep his feet from being level. The last thing Etienne wants to do is fall off this damn thing in front of everyone, and given his luck, *he would,* so he makes sure to be extra careful when he inches forwards closer to the seal.

Etienne crouches down as soon as he can and sets his fingers just at the glowing edge of the first ring, and now that he's within range, he can feel the bright snap of electricity that defines his family's spellwork. Each coven has a specific impression their magic

✦✦ 95 ✦✦

leaves behind, *one for each point of the pentagram one for each Mother,* and then each witch has a unique mark as well, and while Etienne can tell this was done by a Boudreaux, *sharp bite and tingle hair raising along your neck ozone in the air storm's on the way,* he isn't familiar with the imprint.

Doesn't mean he doesn't recognize it though, and his hand draws back fast because he's only ever felt the afterimage of this magic, *flickering in wards and chaining massive seals in place bright streaks of it still sparking in the air decades later,* last remaining vestiges of the greatest exorcist the parish has ever seen, the witch he was named for, *the former Patriarch of House Boudreaux-*

His grandfather.

A man Etienne never met but almost feels like he has in a way, can't go anywhere in New Orleans without being reminded of the pillar of strength the Council of Night lost. Éleutaire was renowned amongst the Occult for his mastery of banishings and sealwork, honestly, almost singlehandedly ushered the parish into an era of unprecedented security they're still enjoying to this day.

He laid the groundwork for a safer life for all, was a beacon of the community and a much beloved patriarch, and Etienne mourns the fact he never got the chance to know him, *to learn from him,* but Éleutaire died long before he'd ever been born, before mother was not that much older than he is now.

And he died the way a lot of Etienne's family dies, *protecting others.*

Stretching his hand back out, Etienne actually touches the seal this time and the gentle zing of electricity rushes up his fingertips, what feels like the barest brush of a large hand against his consciousness next.

Hi I'm Etienne...your grandson, he thinks at the nebulous impression drifting past, knows it isn't really anything more than a memory of a memory, but he calls out to it anyway, *we never met but your daughter named me for you she hopes I'll be half the witch you were...and I do too...I just want you all to be proud of me.*

What Goes Bump In The Night

His fingers tense up a little where they touch lightly at the first ring of glyphs, suddenly very aware of where he is and what he's about to do, *the name he's got to uphold.* There's a lot of pressure to get this right, both to ensure the safety of everyone here and not disgrace his house, and it's only for the briefest moment, *the smallest amount of time,* but for a second, Etienne *swears* he can faintly smell cigar smoke, *taste orange bitters on the back of his tongue,* and it's almost like something drops to rest on top of his head.

Etienne looks up fast and sees no one, that feeling going as quickly as it came on, but it leaves his chest warm and tingly, like sitting next to the hearth on a cold day with a good book, and his fingers relax. He exhales slow, *I won't let you down...I'll make our house proud,* finds his center and calls his magic forwards, the seal growing brighter now that he's touching it with *purpose.*

Connecting with another's magic is always a jarring experience at first, *rush of alien power who is this who are you get out- wait... know you family kin settling back down,* but once the sense of *other* ruffles out of him, Etienne is happy to see everything looks like it's still in working order, spellwork contently humming away all these years later.

Lucretius seals are a little notorious for going haywire over time, need routine checkups to make sure they're still functioning as intended. Most of the issues come from how they're laid out. Made up of three concentric rings, Lucretius seals increase in complexity and importance the closer you get to the core, rely on each other to keep whatever it is they're sealing bound, which is why it's such a delicate balance when you go to modify them.

Fatally disrupt one layer, either by overloading it with power or not handling it properly, and the whole thing falls apart.

Hence why Etienne was a nervous wreck earlier because he really only has one shot at this, and he's more confident now, is pretty sure he can handle it, but the margin for error is still practically microscopic.

Pressing down against the skull with his fingertips, Etienne rotates his hand a little, slowly twisting that first ring of glyphs until it dissipates under his command with a sharp crack. The inner two rings spin fast trying to accommodate for the disturbance, bright whine in the air from a surge in power, but they even back out just like the book said they would.

Alright so that's one step down...about three more to go.

Unlocking the first ring was the easy part though, the topmost band of glyphs basically just the lid keeping the rest of the seal secure, and it's on the second where he needs to make his alterations.

Grounded to transitional unlock it from this location get it to draw energy from local ambient sources, he flexes his fingers and his magic responds, curling into the glyphs that'll open the seal to pull the power it needs from a wider area. This part still kinda ties Etienne's brain into knots, knows Lucretius seals have to take energy in from outside sources to remain functional over an extended period of time, but he's still a little unclear on the specifics.

When it's grounded, the seal only pulls energy from what it's immediately tied to, which is more stable but inconvenient if you've got to relocate the cursed object, as it'll move out of range and lose power. So that's why you'd change it to transitional, open its intake channels to draw power from basically everywhere, increasing its instability but making it transportable in the tradeoff.

And that's all fine and good, Etienne understands that, *it's not a hard concept,* but what he doesn't get is how *much* energy it's supposed to be taking in once he makes the change.

The book he borrowed was filled with charts and equations for how to determine that, but half of them he couldn't figure out how to read, and the rest were functionally useless without their accompanying lessons. And Etienne is normally a very dedicated student, but where mother's lectures are always thorough, never leave him with hanging questions, his own little impromptu study session left a lot to be desired.

He's good at thinking on his feet though, just needs to use logic

What Goes Bump In The Night

and what he already knows to make an inference.

If Etienne's increasing the scope of available energy, it makes sense to decrease the rate at which the seal takes power in, keep it from overloading and failing, and figures slowing its intake by half would be a safe bet.

Plan in mind, all Etienne needs to do next is overwrite the second ring of glyphs with his own, seal it back up, affix temporary crux points to the separate skeleton pieces for transportation and then they should be good to go, which sounds fairly easy, right?

Do this, that, one other thing, and be done!

Simple!

Except for he's having trouble getting the glyphs shaped correctly.

"Come on...*come on-*" Etienne mutters under his breath, shaking his hand out a third time after he'd messed up *again,* but he can't settle for anything less than perfect. Magic is finicky and demands *absolute precision.* It's a hugely destructive force that needs careful direction, otherwise you're just leaving a door wide open for all kinds of unstable power to pour through, can end up with outcomes that are so far removed from what you actually wanted to happen.

Which is why he spent the majority of the trolley ride working on this, coaxing his magic to assume the *exact* lines Etienne needed it to, but any progress he made then is completely gone now. His magic is all over the place, squiggly and twisting into shapes randomly, like it's not really sure what it's supposed to be doing, and Etienne waves off his latest attempt in irritation.

He can't help looking at his grandfather's work, the flawless, crisp lines of it, compact and intricate in ways that showcase the absolute control the caster had over their power, and his hands tighten into fists.

Nowhere even close to that to him want to be worthy of your name but are you, Etienne exhales rough and shakes his head,

✦✦ 99 ✦✦

chains on his hat tinkling together softly as he does, *no don't think like that you can do it you can get there you just have to try.*

Arching his fingers over the second ring again, Etienne slips his eyes closed and really focuses on what he's doing, sinks into the power swirling at his core.

It reaches out for him instantly, climbing up his arms and curling over his shoulders, cupping at his face with what feels like scores of hands, each touch of them sending a spark of electricity zapping through his skin.

Hello hello love you know you known you forever hello loved you always, it whispers against the very shell of his being, echoing through time and space as an undeniable bond of existence, *everything you are is us everything we are is you ours is yours always and forevermore,* something oozing out over his bones, catching in his lungs on every inhale, sparking deep in the thundering chambers of his heart, *command us as is taught command us as is known our child our heir our future command us as seen fit-*

And Etienne opens his eyes, electricity crackling down the length of his arm and spreading out between his fingers like a mini lightning storm. The air shifts wildly, blows dark hair into his eyes and kicks up a small breeze, magic coiling elegantly under his fingertips, *feels like a dozen hands laced overtop his snaked through his veins lingering in his blood our heir,* and he slowly draws his fingers together, pulls back, and there, smoking faintly across Gertie's skull, is a new set of maroon glyphs.

They're not quite as precise as grandfather's, slightly crooked here and there, but they're solid and legible, settle in amongst the older magic like they've always been there. Etienne rocks back on his haunches, little lightheaded all of a sudden from the overload of power he just flooded his body with, but otherwise feels relatively okay...*better* than okay, actually.

A deep, all consuming euphoria starts to bubble up through him, like the warmth of summer nights and the rush of night air against his face while riding on broomstick, makes him giggly and

What Goes Bump In The Night

breathless because he did it, *Mothers*...h-he really did it!

Etienne reaches a hand out without calling for his magic this time, just smooths a palm lightly over the seal, feels all his hair stand up on end as *power* races up his arm, and most of it is grandfather's still, *cigar smoke bitter of orange oils warm calloused hands and booming laughter,* but there's parts of him in there now too, *late summer nights floral notes of tea flashing grins and rumble of rainstorms.*

A grandfather and a grandson a progenitor and a successor a patriarch and a scion, he thinks winded, tears stupidly gathering along his lash line that he brushes away quickly.

Magic is tied to emotion, and when witches reach down that far in them to pull it out, touch at the core of what's been passed along from generation to generation, it tends to send their emotions haywire for a little bit.

That overwhelming sensation of *belonging* sweeps and curls through Etienne like wraiths out above the bogs under a full moon, has him sniffling for no particular reason as he affixes a new outer layer of glyphs into place, trying to be subtle about wiping his eyes against his shoulder. Thankfully this set isn't as complicated as the last, and he gets it after one or two tries, that intense, emotional feeling mostly gone by the time he's done, and he exhales wet.

With an elegant flick of his wrist, Etienne spins the top ring so it locks into place, entire seal glowing once brightly before going back to its rhythmic pulsing, though it...*does* look like it's going a tad faster now. He waits with bated breath to see if anything starts unraveling, *Mothers please don't please please please,* but when it doesn't, Etienne just chalks it up to his mind playing tricks on him.

Still, he keeps an eye on it as he gets to his feet, and *willing* it to behave, climbs down off Gertie's skull with way less grace than he originally climbed up. Etienne hits the floor in an almost trip and goes stumbling forwards trying not to fall, manages to right himself, hopping between feet to regain his balance.

✦✦ 101 ✦✦

He twists to survey the skeleton, knocks the brim of his hat up and can't help smiling pleased, and it may not look like much, but that's the trickiest bit of magic he's ever done, *and he did it all by himself.* Pride is almost as intoxicating a substance as alcohol, and Etienne thinks he might be a little drunk off it when he hears Bea lazily call next to him, "Well? How's it lookin' up there, nabot? Todo bien or nah?"

"It's good, *great even!* I-It's done- I mean, *I'm done* b-but it is done too I just- yeah!" Etienne says all in a rush, laughs giddy at the way Bea arches an eyebrow at him, the phoenix feathers poking from her hat glimmering iridescent in the copper light the Hawthorne bind is putting out, and she draws out slow and fake annoyed, "Awesome. Soooo can I release this thing yet or not? My arms are gettin' tired."

"Oh no they are not." Etienne rolls his eyes and Bea winks at him, flexing one of her muscular biceps for show and he laughs again, shaking his head in fond amusement, "But yes, *vantè,* you can drop the bind now."

"Sweet! You can let'er go boys!" She crows loud, opening her hands and letting go of the bind completely, and it goes whizzing off through the air, fizzing like a sparkler as it dissipates. Tanis and Jack follow suit, and the last of the Hawthorne binds unloop quick from the skeleton, warmth from their magic still tingling in the air when Etienne strolls past Bea towards the dragon's ribcage.

He's still got to affix crux points before they can break the skeleton down into its separate parts, and meanders along until he finds a good spot to spread his palm over a massive rib for the first one. Etienne goes to copy the seal's signature, something that isn't supposed to be hard or overly complicated, basically like a copy-paste, but magic sparks against his palm *painfully,* loud cracking rumble of displaced air as his hand is blown back.

"Woah shit! You good?" Bea shouts, rushing to his side and grabbing for his hand, clucking her tongue at whatever she finds.

It feels singed, skin growing warmer and tighter as the pain sets

What Goes Bump In The Night

in, but Etienne literally couldn't care less right now, eyes locked on the spattering crux point he just tried to make.

All it's supposed to be is a simple locus that draws the magic of the seal to it, temporarily extending the influence for a few hours before it dissipates at moonset. It's not supposed to be anything more than a slowly spinning ring and pentagram, but this one keeps jerking around spastically, going too fast one way and then doubling back, glowing lines of it mutated in ways Etienne hadn't intentionally shaped.

It looks...broken, *incorrect,* almost as if there's some larger problem somewhere that's preventing it from forming like it's supposed to, and all the moisture dries up out of his mouth in an instant.

Something's wrong.

Something is really wrong, and Etienne rips his smarting hand out of Bea's hold, goes darting back towards Gertie's skull and hoists himself up as fast as possible.

His heart is going so fast it makes him even wobblier than normal, *it's fine it's fine it HAS to be fine,* and he trips forwards, cracks his knees harshly against unrelenting bone, comes face to face with the Lucretius seal, hands splayed out to either side of it and-

Oh no...

No...no no no nonoNONONO- this can't be happening, he- h-he did everything he was supposed to! Or at least...Etienne *thought* he did, but this doesn't look right, *it's not right it's not it's not IT'S NOT,* something must have broken- *messed up somewhere don't know what's wrong Mothers don't know what HAPPENED,* and the entire time he's panicking, the inner ring spins ever faster and faster, putting out enough light it's almost blinding.

"Fucking hell-" Etienne hisses sharp through his teeth, scrabbles back onto his heels and knows he needs to do *something,* but it's like his entire mind has completely blinked out of existence.

This is bad this is really bad, his heart jackhammers under his

✦✦ 103 ✦✦

ribs, smoke starting to curl off the seal, *what do I do what happened don't know have to do something,* presses his shaking fingers to the first ring and then stalls with indecision, *what do I do what DO I DO can't think need help need mother need someone but there's NO ONE you're the only one here you're the one that's supposed to KNOW-*

And it just hits Etienne hard and fast and all at once, the understanding that *he is the only one here that can fix this,* that the lives and safety of *everyone* in this room are on his shoulders, *are dependent on his abilities,* and he suddenly can't breathe because he honestly has no true understanding of this magic and it might get them all killed.

"B-Bea! BEA! Something's- *s-something's wrong!* Put the binds back- *p-put them back NOW!"* Etienne shouts, hand trembling over the glyphs, terrified to open it *terrified to leave it as it is,* has no idea what the best course of action is but every second he wastes, the more dangerous it gets. *Have to stabilize it have to cool it off have to reopen it,* he thinks with a jolt, teeth sinking painfully into his lower lip as he presses out with his magic, the bright, whip crack of binds snapping into place making him jump a little.

"Etienne! What's goin' on, what's wrong?" Bea yells but her voice sounds so distant, barely a low murmur against the rushing in his ears, "Come on, talk to me! Stay calm, okay? We'll get this all sorted if you just *stay calm."*

He can't though, unlocks that first ring and it feels like getting electrocuted, *so much* energy racing back up his arm his nerve endings go dead.

That shouldn't happen, *it shouldn't be storing that much power,* and there's no longer a shadow of a doubt that he did something wrong, *don't know what happened bad idea not ready should have listened shut UP we don't have TIME,* and now the seal is failing catastrophically because of it.

"Etienne! Talk to me!" Bea screams again, but he *can't,* tongue a dead useless thing in his mouth, struck down by skyrocketing

What Goes Bump In The Night

anxiety and a paralyzing kind of forced concentration. If he doesn't get this thing back under control, it's breaking apart and Etienne *cannot* reseal it, *knows he can't,* means he'll have unleashed a cursed monstrosity he has no hope of stopping right in the heart of the city.

He never should have agreed to this, *should have listened and trusted himself when it mattered most wishes so violently for a do over NO TIME FOCUS,* but it's too late for that, and it's about to be too late for all of them *unless he stops twiddling his thumbs and figures something out.*

The only thing he can think to do is to change it back to grounded, hopes that slows whatever reaction is happening to destabilize it so much, presses shaking fingers against the second ring of glyphs and takes a deep breath. *You can do this you don't have a choice,* Etienne nods his head once, sharp and jerky, pictures the grounded set of glyphs in his mind, *exhales you can do this you have to do this.*

He calls his magic up to execute, *electricity at his fingertips storm in his veins know you know us,* but the second he presses out, the entire seal lights up *like the sun,* whole thing rending away like wet tissue paper under his fingers as a massive shockwave blows him back.

Etienne slams into the ground *hard,* goes sliding across the floor disoriented and aching, hands numb and unhelpful where they try to push him up. The entire room swims, ears ringing from the explosive clap of power that went off right in his face.

Nothing seems real, *everything is so hazy,* but it is entirely too clear, *and entirely too real,* when eerie white blue light starts to flood Gertie's eye sockets, that massive head shifting ever so slightly.

Get up get up GET UP YOU HAVE TO GET UP, his mind screams at him but his body is borderline unresponsive, jerking slightly from aftershocks of electricity, and all Etienne can do is watch in horror as the skeleton lifts its head, bones scraping against one another like low rumblings of thunder.

The long line of the dragon's neck arches up almost to the ceiling,

✦✦ 105 ✦✦

and Gertie works its jaw, grinding the joints together until they snap into place with a sickening crack. Someone's yelling something but Etienne can't parse it, sits there like he's frozen in a nightmare as the thing bows its head forwards, jaw gaping open and exposing rows and rows of swordlike teeth, sharp intake of air like a bellows and then it *roars.*

It rattles all the windows in the visitor's center, feels like the force of it physically clambers inside Etienne's skull and vibrates his bone marrow, *stops his heart jerks it back to life,* all the destructive power of an earthquake but it's living under his skin now. In one slow, *agonizing* movement, the skeleton shifts its weight up onto its legs to stand, enormous talons flexing and splintering the tiles below it, and the floor shakes a concerning amount as Gertie takes a single step forwards.

Fiery bands of copper light come shooting from the darkness like bolts of lightning, snarl over the dragon's maw and chain its legs together, pull taught and force the monster back to the ground with a thunderous crash. Gertie thrashes like a mad thing in response, but Bea and the others hold strong, send out more lines of snapping light that are thicker and almost look barbed, dig into ancient bone like fishhooks.

The smell of soot and smoke hangs heavy in the air, temperature increasing drastically the more magic the Gagnon call forwards, sigils that glow like forge fires spiraling to life across the floor, all in an effort to try and contain this monstrosity. Bea and the others are doing everything they can, but before they can secure them, Gertie's colossal skeletal wings flare open and crash into the walls, somehow kicking up wind despite being only bone, sharp tips of them stretching far enough to smash the skylights above.

Glass rains down sharp and vicious, thankfully kept out of Etienne's eyes by the brim of his hat, but he feels it slice his palms open as he plants them on the floor, pushing himself up on wildly shaking arms. The Gagnon might have Gertie pinned down for now, but they won't be able to keep it that way.

Their magic is really only effective on living creatures, and seeing

What Goes Bump In The Night

as how Gertie is an undead monstrosity possessed by dark evils, that means dealing with her falls solely under the purview of him, *of House Boudreaux.*

And if he's going to do what he was born to do, he has to get up *now.*

It's a struggle to get his legs under him, Etienne's knees are still wobbly and threaten to drop him back on his ass at any given moment, but he grits his teeth and *forces them to work.* Vertigo cracks him upside the head, world undulating like a seething ocean, and he whips around drunkenly trying to find his bag.

Need...the thing- pages and papers and book need the book have to...get it have to figure out, Etienne spins in a circle, squinting blearily at a dark shape he thinks might be it and staggers in that direction. His coordination isn't the best even under normal circumstances, but freshly electrocuted and with a good knock to the head, he's not in the best shape, feels his feet looping over one another almost instantly and *wow that didn't take long-*

But there's hands catching him under the armpits before he can fall on his face, and someone hauls him backwards, dragging Etienne away from spastically flapping wings that could club him to death, which is coincidentally where he's also mostly sure his bag is and the exact *opposite* direction he's getting pulled.

"S'op it!" He slurs, digging his heels in but whoever's got him is *strong,* wraps arms over his torso and yanks hard, sends Etienne crashing back into their hold like a ragdoll, "Stop! I gotta...I-I gotta get the thing you- y-you *bèt pitit gason femèl!*"

"*Fuckin'-! Christ!* I am tryin' save yer stupid ass!" Whoever is carting him yells, and *oh,* oh Etienne knows *that voice* all right, thuds his head back against a broad, soft chest and glares livid at Nica's upside down face, demanding harshly, "Lemme go this *instant!*"

They mutter something too indistinct for him to hear, but he sees their bloodstained lips move and can hedge a guess at it, swings one of his legs back to kick at them, "I said- *let me go!* You-y-you *stupid deaf niais-!* You're stupid you're- y-you're so, you're gonna get us all *killed if you don't lemme-!*"

✦✦ 107 ✦✦

H.Knight

"FINE!" Nica shouts, dropping him unceremoniously and Etienne falls back with a grunt, presses a hand to his aching head. He doesn't think he has a concussion but *Mothers* does it hurt, throbbing pain under his eyes like a migraine, makes nausea spike through him anytime he tries to focus on something.

Breathe in one two out one two breathe in...breathe out, Etienne works through as slowly as he dares, and the second his vision stops spinning even a little, he's pushing himself up again on shaking legs.

Your fault this is all your fault, undulates around in his mind like coiling banks of fog, sounds of Gertie struggling and Bea shouting orders a terrible symphony that makes guilt slide freezing up his spine, and he grinds his teeth together because he knows, okay?

Etienne fucked up majorly and *he knows he did,* but all he can do now is fix his mistake, put things right, *make sure no one loses their life we don't take lives shéri you know the tenets you know our way protect those who cannot protect themselves protect them from-*

"-everythin' that goes bump in the night." Etienne murmurs under his breath and takes a stuttering step forwards, teeth clacking together as his boots slip over tiles, send him careening into a pillar and he wraps his arms around it for support, feels it shudder through him when one of Gertie's wings slams into the walls above.

Flickering binds cover nearly every inch of the skeleton, thread through gaps in the bones like needlework, but with a sharp jerk, a back leg punches free, snapping a dozen lines in the process. They fizzle out immediately, providing enough give for Gertie to plant her foot, driving forwards with so much force, Etienne hears Bea scream in alarm, and more binds spark away into nothing.

This is getting out of hand rapidly, and he's got minutes, *maybe even seconds,* until that thing breaks loose and remembers how to use its fire and then there'll be no stopping it.

No time there's no time go- go NOW, Etienne snarls at himself, pushes off the pillar and hasn't even set a foot into the main atrium

What Goes Bump In The Night

before he's jerked back, cold press of metal over his wrist.

"W-What do you *think you're doin'?*" Nica hollers, eyes blown wide in alarm, split lip bleeding a trickle of red down their chin, and Etienne tries to tug his hand free, but just like last time, *he can't,* voice going sharp as he snarls, *"For the love of-!* Let. Me. *GO!* I'm tryin' to keep that *thing from killin' us!* B-But I can' do *shit* i-if I don't get my bag so *if you'll just-!"*

"Do you even know what you're doing?"

Etienne's body locks up in a telling way, frustrated infuriated ~~terrified~~ emotions swelling up his throat and choking him into silence. He opens his mouth but nothing comes out, fire bright stinging in his nose and eyes because *they're right they're right you don't know even if you get the book you're not gonna know all your fault it's all your fault,* and Nica's face hardens like they can hear every one of his panicked thoughts.

"You don't, do you? *Christ...*" Nica exhales rough, fingers tightening where they're still wrapped around Etienne's wrist, and he swallows past the lump in his throat, *how do you measure up not good enough never good enough prove it prove how good you are prove it to them to everyone ~~to yourself~~,* croaking, "I-I can *do this. I can!* I-I'm a *Boudreaux,* I...I *have to do this."*

"You've done enough." Nica says not unkindly and it's somehow worse, the sympathy, *the pity* Etienne can see in their eyes instead of sharp scorn, *don't look at me like that stop looking at me eyes on you all the time stop it can't take it can't take it caN'T TAKE IT STOP PITYING ME-*

"Look, I think I got a plan that'll work but I *need you* to stay *here."* Nica squeezes his wrist for emphasis, and a fuzzy tingle runs up Etienne's arm he almost recognizes. It's almost like...*i-it's almost like- something sparking in the thundering chambers of your heart all the hair raising along the back of your neck storm's here storm's on the way ~~know you~~,* and he chokes on the air in his lungs, stammering fast, "W-What? *N-No!* I won't- *I-I'm not-!* Why can't y-you get it through your head? There's nothin'

✦✦ 109 ✦✦

you can do to help! Y-You're just *an alchemist!*"

So much complicated pain and frustration passes over Nica's face, brows drawing low as they open their mouth to respond, but whatever they were gonna say gets forgotten entirely when an explosion erupts behind them.

Etienne whips around and squints his eyes against the searing heat, flames jumping high from a sigil that just failed, magic roiling across the floor uninhibited and his heart jackhammers out of control because he can hear screaming and can't find Bea and Gertie is now entirely loose.

The skeleton ruffles its vertebrae, wings flaring open completely and swirling the fires up ever higher, neck arching like a snake about to strike, thunderous roar that shakes everything in the room *knocks your eyes around in your skull echoes down to your bones terrible thing unstoppable power can't do it your fault gonna get them all killed failed your line got people hurt supposed to protect them you're supposed to protect them-*

And Etienne doesn't think, sparks electricity all down his arm until he hears Nica let go with a yelp and then he's gone, sprinting out across the reception hall.

Smoke and ash fill the air, *burn* in his lungs but he can't slow down, can't take the time to gasp and cough for a clean breath like his body demands he do. Everyone is counting on him, *their lives are in danger because of him,* and Etienne may be a lot of things, *neurotic and bitchy and overconfident,* but he doesn't lose people, won't *ever* be the reason bodies have to be buried.

All the hairs raise along the back of his neck and he ducks on instinct, feels a massive gust of wind pass over his head, catches the barest glimpse of off-white coming back around and dives to the side, barely getting out of the way as that wing hurtles past again. It kicks up a slurry of soot laden clouds, has Etienne coughing violently into the crook of his elbow, but once the air clears a little, *there,* across the hall laying under a pile of shattered glass-

His bag.

What Goes Bump In The Night

Etienne has never moved so fast in his entire life, toes of his boots pressing into the slick tile and launching him forwards, muscles bunching and contracting, *lungs on fire ashy heavy against his tongue*, mind eerily blank, only focused on one thing. *Get the bag get the book get the bag get the book save them you can still save them,* pounds in his head like a manic set of war drums, propels him forwards, and nothing has ever mattered more than that collection of dusty pages bound up in crumbling leather.

It hits like a drunken punch of relief to finally feel the bag's cloth strap in his scorched black fingers, and Etienne's hands shake like crazy as he works on freeing the book, but it's okay, *it's going to be okay he's got the book he can do this he can fix this they'll be okay no one will die he'll save them it'll be okay he can do th-*

"ETIENNE!"

He jerks his head up, eyes going wide, *whip fast blur racing towards you move move MOVE,* can't make his feet respond fast enough and a rock hard force slams into his ribs, *crack feel a crack crunching pain bad that's bad,* wind whistling past as he goes flying through the air. Etienne smashes into something unyielding, scream punched violently out of his lungs along with whatever air remained and drops to the floor like deadweight.

He must blackout for a second, comes back around to *everything* wailing in hurt, gasps for air on instinct and then chokes ragged. Red hot pain flares up Etienne's chest, cinches tight over his lungs and demands he stop breathing, but his head is spinning and *he needs air,* but every inhale drags new tongues of fiery agony higher *and he can't breathe needs to breathe everything hurts gonna pass out no you CAN'T-*

Because there's smoke and ash and burning things, people are screaming, *a dragon a beast an undead monster is roaring whistle sharp inhale like a bellows,* and he's the only one that can fix this, *you did this your fault it's all your fault get up you have to get up.*

Etienne shifts his weight onto an arm but it drags on his ribs and he *can't he falls he's weak and maybe what they say is true,* guttural

✦ 111 ✦

grinding noise of fire snarling to life, *maybe it's time for all of them to move on,* look up and see those blue flames growing at the back of a skeletal maw, *maybe they're right maybe you're not good for anything anymore-*

A charged sensation rushes over him, goosebumps erupting across his skin, dizzying swoop in his head as the pressure in the room drops sharp and fast, *ozone bright and electric all your hair stands on end storm's on the way storm's here know you family kin know you.* Etienne darts his eyes towards that feeling in confused desperation, doesn't know how it'd be possible, *couldn't get here that fast how would they know can't be has to be,* but there's no way that's anything other than his house's imprint.

He's expecting mother naturally, maybe Katie, *Atha Gilbert Oliver Ulyssia Great Grandmother someone anyone of his family,* but somehow it's none of them actually, and he knows then he has to have a concussion, must be hallucinating, and that there's no way for what he's seeing to be the truth.

Because it's Nica.

It's *Nica* standing there with white blue fingers of lightning crawling over their body and feet planted surely, the runes carved into their metal arm shining brighter than the sun.

They bring their hands up, fingertips meeting and arching, electricity crackling to life between them and it kicks up a ferocious wind, blonde hair whipping about, so *much* light glowing in their eyes it doesn't seem real.

There is a monumental amount of energy building up in one space, *in one person how is that even possible absolute raw power storm unhinged,* increasing exponentially every second and it sears white hot in Etienne's mind, a glaring sign that *here* is a force not to be trifled with.

Here is something that can hold its own, *something that's powerful.*

And he isn't the only one to notice.

What Goes Bump In The Night

Gertie loses interest in him fast, *not a threat how could he possibly be a threat,* and whips towards that sparking pillar of energy. The monster's dimmed flames surge anew, throwing crazy jumping shadows everywhere and Nica doesn't even flinch, just glares up at the towering skeleton in open defiance.

That moron, *that complete idiot they won't make it they're gonna die you are going to watch them die,* and Etienne frantically shoves himself up with a howl, can't let that happen, *isn't going to,* but it's too late. Neck arching deadly and beautiful, Gertie roars like everything that haunts nightmares, goes to exhale, Etienne ignores the burning pain in his chest and screams *run,* Nica doesn't listen, *of course they don't listen,* stands there and rips their hands apart and *energy* erupts in a massive spitting shockwave.

White blue lightning suddenly arcs between every vertebrae and joint on the skeleton, scorches the bones black from the sheer amount of heat it generates, and Gertie shrieks, fire choking off in its maw as it writhes. Smoke starts rising in hissing columns from its body, nothing like the ashy clouds drifting off the fires that are still burning, and Etienne almost gags as the *foulest stench* permeates the air.

And he's bore witness to many horrifying sights, *missing limbs bodies torn open rot and decay and depravity,* and it is still one of the most disturbing things he's ever seen as Gertie starts to *melt,* what has to be acid eating it away one chunk at a time, dissolving all its bones into sludgy piles of goo that plop wetly to the floor.

Thrashing wildly in an attempt to get the burning substance off, Gertie tries to take a step forward and crumbles, legs collapsing out from under it, their surface riddled with holes and no longer able to support its weight.

The dragon shrieks like the damned, flailing talons clawing futilely at the floor, but its movements become weaker, bones falling prone with thunderous booms.

Etienne wets his lips, staring wide eyed as the partially melted skull slams into the floor, cavernous cracks and welts opening up along the cranial plating. Gertie screeches pitifully, warbling cries of distress that start to choke off as the acid burns through its jaw, top half of the skull coming loose and sliding sickly off center.

It's unnerving watching the creature struggle to remain together, but in the end, its efforts are ultimately pointless, and with a few flickering, sputtering flashes, the demonic light in its eye sockets finally dims. Without the curse to keep it together, the skeleton falls apart completely and quickly erodes in the acid that now puddles against the floor, melting away into nothing more than oozing mineral deposits.

The ensuing silence is deafening.

What...the *hell just happened?*

Etienne is still having trouble thinking past the pounding in his head and the screaming from his almost certainly broken ribs, but there are two things he is absolutely sure of.

One, none of that should have been possible.

Two, and yet, *somehow,* despite defying everything he thought he knew, *shaking his very concept of self to the core,* it was.

It was possible, *it did happen,* and Etienne is struggling to understand that.

Because cursed objects are hard enough to destroy on their own, take entire teams of Laferriere to get it done, but cursed *remains* are another beast entirely. They will defend themselves violently until the threat is dealt with, but that was over so fast, the curse didn't even have time to react.

It was almost like every single molecule of bone had been covered with acid in a split second, *completely eradicated in twenty destroyed before you could even blink,* there *was* no time to counter.

And that level of skill and power is unbelievable, goes beyond anything he ever thought an alchemist was capable of, *only good for manufacturing too slow too weak can't stand a chance,* and

What Goes Bump In The Night

so when that chilling spike of power comes again, Etienne woodenly turns his head. Wind swirls around Nica in a small cyclone, blowing frizzy, static riddled hair out of their eyes, the very air displaced by the heat and energy that jumps off them in small bolts of lightning.

Electricity catches and fractals apart between the joints of their metal hand, dances elegantly across their fingers as they bring them back together, and somehow Nica must feel his eyes on them, rolls their head to the side and grins.

It's wild and *triumphant, blood staining their teeth an entire storm in their eyes earned what I have reaped what is sown none of it was handed to me,* low, sonorous boom of thunder echoing through the room as they break their hands apart.

The hissing that was coming from the acid eating at the floor is gone instantly, transmuted back into whatever Nica pulled it from, *the air the earth the building itself,* somehow did it faster than Etienne could think, with no array and no additional supplies.

He swallows rough, *like nothing you've ever seen like nothing you've ever known what are you dealing with don't know not sure you ever did-*

And as if it wasn't obvious enough, *as if Etienne had any sort of delusions to the contrary,* Nica cocks their chin back, electrical field dimming around them but not in their eyes, pupils still glowing like a lightning storm as they pin him in place, *power so similar to your own know you different source same energy know you how do I know you,* slick red of their bloodstained lips mouthing, *I win.*

Chapter 7

The walk home is, as the kids say, *not fun*.

It took a healing draught and a half to get Etienne back on his feet, which is way more than he'd normally take but he didn't really have a lot of options there. Standing was not a thing that was going to happen without considerable intervention, so he downed one bottle of the stinging potion and then half of another, an almost concerning amount, but that was apparently the bare minimum so he could stand on his own without falling over.

And it didn't even heal him entirely.

The draughts worked fast like they always did, returned feeling to his singed nerves but left the skin blistered, wiped the small cuts and lacerations away easy, and only lessened what were going to be *stellar* bruises along his side, a quick patch job for the most immediate concerns.

Some of his ribs had definitively been broken earlier and the feeling of them snapping back into place was almost worse than when they got broken originally, had Etienne hissing sharp through his teeth as they moved grotesquely under his skin. Closest thing he could compare it to would be earthworms writhing in the dirt, unnatural jerk and *twist* as the bone righted itself, left him hunched over and trying to take small sips of air.

Breathing still hurt even after the draught worked through what it could, muscles and tissues protesting lividly at all the abuse, both from the initial damage and then the rapid fast healing. His skin was raw and tender in a way that meant it was probably going to be fifty shades of dark purple tomorrow, and Etienne had to bite his lip hard as he was hauled up, swaying unsteadily on his

What Goes Bump In The Night

feet for longer than he was particularly comfortable with.

Thankfully, no one else was too badly hurt.

Nica was...*fine*, few cuts and scrapes here and there but they'd live, and once Etienne made sure of that, he tried to forget they existed in general.

All the Gagnons had burns across their palms from where they had been hanging onto their binds, but they weren't super serious, nothing worse than you'd get from a pan on the stove. Specifically though, Tanis had an ugly gash sheeting blood down their face that was mostly superficial, Jack was somehow *completely* fine besides the burns, and then the worst Bea had was a broken wrist.

She took the bones righting themselves like a champ, shot a hard gust of smoke out of her nose and rotated her wrist quick before striding off to do damage control and there was...*a lot* of damage to control.

Fires still weakly smoldered here and there, had gone from magical to mundane as the surfaces around them started to burn and feed the flames, but they had mostly put themselves out by the time Gertie was uh, *dealt with*. Unfortunately, most everything else had sustained massive amounts of damage, was going to require extensive efforts to repair and Etienne looked around him with a growing sense of frantic helplessness.

All the skylights were smashed, glass scattered across the floor and still clinging to the dented metal framework in some spots, thick iron bars bent out of place by the sheer force of the dragon's wings. Most of the first floor pillars had been broken, upper walkway sagging dangerously, looked about one second away from coming down as well, and then there was the small sea of milky white calcium deposits now growing across the tiles like a creepy nest of stalagmites.

It was an absolute mess, but they were lucky it had ended at *an absolute mess*, because it truthfully had been seconds away from becoming an *unmitigated disaster*. Sure they'd gotten hurt, property and things had been damaged, but all of them could

✦✦ 117 ✦✦

have lost their lives, *almost did,* and if Gertie had escaped, *who knows* how many people would've wound up dead, and the only reason *any of that* happened was *because of Etienne.*

"I'm sorry...I'm *s-so sorry.*" He hoarsely whispered after he hobbled up to Bea's side, the crunch of her boot nudging at the mess that was once Gertie slowing, but she didn't say anything and he wet his lips nervously at her silence, "Bea...I- I-I don't think I can *tell you* how sorry I am, I-"

"We're mortal, mistakes happen." Bea murmured hollow, and for a second, Etienne was relieved she wasn't disappointed with him, but then she turned her head and it felt like getting his ribs broken all over again.

"But there's a difference in a *mistake,* an' endangerin' the lives of yourself and others." Her eyes were hard yet so miserably soft, *poor thing just a child feel bad for you stop looking at me like THAT,* mouth pulled to the side in an unhappy grimace, "Don't even *think* about lyin' to me. I *know* you weren't prepared to deal with somethin' like this, *you knew you weren't,* but you...*took the assignment anyway...*"

Bea sighed exhausted and shook her head, little iron charms on her hat clinking together softly, and Etienne was trying to keep a handle on his emotions, but anxiety was crawling up his throat like a deranged thing. Spillover magic sparked and charged the air around them, and he felt color flame in his cheeks when Bea looked back at him, disappointed cast to her face as she reached out to place a hand on his shoulder.

"Etienne, confidence can be a good thing. Means you're sure of yourself and trust you can get the job done, but empty confidence is like a poison, it kills whatever it touches." Bea told him, squeezing his shoulder once, the heat of her palm burning like a fire against the icy chill that'd spread through his body, "You're a *scion,* you're gonna be leading your house one day, *you gotta do better.*"

Hearing that hurt worse than the broken ribs, hurt more than anything else ever had actually because it was like confirmation,

What Goes Bump In The Night

proof that the vile thoughts scuttling around at the edges of his mind were *right.* All the nasty voices that whispered that Etienne *isn't capable,* that he's a disgrace to his name, *to his house to his people all those eyes staring at you all the time watch them fill with contempt are you surprised,* and his mouth was drier than a desert when he stammered, "I-I'm so sorry! *Please,* I-I didn't mean- I just-w-what can I do? *What can I do to help fix th-?"*

"Don't take this the wrong way...but I think you should just go home." Bea said with a wince, withdrew her hand slow and he chased after it desperate, heart thundering up somewhere by his tonsils, "But I-!"

"You're still injured. *Bad.* You need rest. Go get some sleep and just...try an' make better decisions next time, m'kay? *Learn* from this." Bea urged him gently, reaching over to knock knuckles against the underside of his hat, "I know you probably will anyway, but try an' not give yourself an ulcer. Yeah you messed up but you're still one of my favorites, Etito."

There were tears brimming in his eyes before she had even walked off, and Etienne hated that Bea probably saw them, tucked his chin down close to his chest and attempted to will them away. *Stop it stop it be an adult be mature don't cry over this,* Etienne thought, sniffling miserably, *let it go move on ~~ignore the gaping pit in the center of your chest the one slowly dragging you in you're not worth anything~~ STOP IT-*

And he was barely keeping it together as is, was holding onto his composure by his teeth, but it all came crashing down the second he heard Bea go, "Hey- Nica, was it? What you did was *absolutely* incredible, no- *seriously!* You saved all of us, dude! I can't thank you enough...an' I hate to ask, but would you mind stickin' around and helping with-"

Etienne didn't hang around long enough to hear what Bea needed, felt the hot slide of tears down his cheeks and was *gone,* disappeared out into the dark press of the night where there wasn't anyone nearby to hear the way his breath hitched.

Walking home alone in the wee hours of the morning, battered and bruised and trying to muffle his crying, was probably one of the saddest things he's ever done, and not like, *depressing miserable sad*, but more like *sad* as in *pathetic*. It's honestly really embarrassing, and Etienne tries *forever* to wrangle his unruly emotions back in line, but every time he thinks he's calmed down, he just starts thinking about that whole fiasco again and it shatters his heart back apart.

Feeling the seal come apart under your hands being completely helpless to stop the mess you'd caused the way Bea grimaced just go home how Nica smiled I win floor dropping out from under you let them all down good for nothing, and something tickles down the side of his nose and *Mothers of the Night not again thought he'd gotten it under control-*

"F-Fuck me-" Etienne groans wetly, stops on the sidewalk to angrily wipe this new round of tears from his face, thought he'd finished crying a while ago but apparently not.

Mothers get over yourself stop crying no one cares, Etienne reminds himself, fingers digging in harsh like maybe the pain will put his mind back in order, *you messed up you made a mistake stop the pity party and get over it you know how to act you know better.*

And yet that reminder does absolutely nothing to help. If anything, it actually just makes him feel worse because he *can't* get his emotions back under control, whole nasty cocktail of them snarling around his chest. Guilt crawls over Etienne's skin like beetles breaking down a stump, and despite knowing he's supposed to be better than this, he can't stop the unchecked electricity that snaps against his palms over and *over again.*

It's a lonely mope-fest for one tonight, er- *tomorrow...today whatever,* with Etienne as the shining star, abject misery hanging off him heavy as he trudges home, and he wants to be an adult about all of this, but it honestly feels like he's one more thing away from just sitting down on the curb and bawling his eyes out.

There's too much happening internally to really process, and *besides* the choking, *crushing agonizing* disappointment with himself, Etienne is also in a lot of pain from his half healed injuries, which isn't helping his mood in the slightest. Exhaustion sinks all the way down to the hollows of his bones, and some rational part of his brain keeps saying he just needs to sleep, *that he'll feel better after he sleeps,* but he doesn't think he's going to be able to.

His mind is spinning *fast,* keeps *agonizing* over every single mistake, *there're so many of them see them all over and over and over again make it stop please make it stop,* speculations running wild with how things could've been different, *if you'd done this gone there weren't so incompetent but you didn't you weren't you failed everyone Mothers stop please,* and it's in the past and *he can't change it,* but he can't make himself let go either, ~~never been able to you hang on too strong first rule of your house letting go and goodbyes can't even do that unfit mistake they never should've chosen you~~ *stop stop stop please S T O P-*

It feels like something massive is brewing as his thoughts just keep recirculating, and it's winding all the anxious energy Etienne has up tight and tighter, which is *bad,* and he knows it is, *but he can't stop it.*

That's the worst kind of torture, to know something is a problem and that you need to stop, but being unable to.

It's like sitting helpless at the eye of a hurricane, deceptive stability that's rapidly deteriorating, and you can see the waves are rising, the wind is picking up, and that backwall is coming roaring right at you and there's nothing you can do.

Everything that happened tonight was your fault let your stupid pride get to your head how are you supposed to be a patriarch when you act like this when you don't think- he didn't mean *to,* honestly thought everything would be okay, but that just shows his naivety, *his incompetence,* how unfit he is to *lead-*

Wasn't just a simple mistake deep violation of the very core of your beliefs mistake you're a mistake Maisette never should've chosen you it made a mistake- can't breathe for a second, the nightmare that keeps Etienne up all night and all day, choking squeezing *grasping dread* that he isn't meant to be where *he is-*

Going to lead your house into ruin all on your shoulders and its crumbling ends here ends with you going to drive your way of life into the ground, h-he won't though, *he won't ~~he will~~,* knows how he's supposed to act, *supposed to behave,* knows everything that's riding on his shoulders ~~*feels like it's crushing you out of existence,*~~ and yet he still keeps failing anyway can't do anything right *and it's all your fault good for nothing no one ever wanted you can't take it back stuck with you your fault your fauLT YOUR FAULT AND FUCKING HELL HE GETS IT OKAY-*

Etienne *is a mess,* a child playing pretend, and *by the Mothers,* he is *beyond* frustrated with himself because of it! He's mad that he agreed to this assignment in the first place, *what in the world had he been thinking moron idiot incoMPETENT SIMPLETON,* is practically beside himself with fury that he put everyone in danger like that, *not just stupid but dangerous reckless SELFISH could've gotten so many people killed.*

And that's the worst part of all of this, because Etienne is a *Boudreaux,* and his first priority is always supposed to be protecting the people of this parish from the horrible things that slither out of the dark, *not purposefully endangering them.*

He's supposed to lay down his life if need be, *is fully prepared to do that would do it in a heartbeat,* but tonight, he accidentally set one of those horrors free instead and the shame he feels is near crippling.

Etienne thinks he's experiencing misery to the full extent of the word, feels horrible bodily, emotionally, *mentally,* but isn't about to complain because he knows he deserves it.

Honestly he deserves so much worse, got off light with a few bruised ribs and some minor burns, and then the talking to Bea gave him that could *hardly* be counted as a punishment. It was barely a slap on the wrist, ~~*you're a scion do better fist right through your gut is she right are you,*~~ but none of that even comes *close* to

What Goes Bump In The Night

making up for almost destroying half the city.

*Mothers...*he...h-he could've destroyed New Orleans, and it really just kinda hits Etienne then, the gravity of the situation he caused. Everything seems to rush into him all at once, and it's most likely the adrenalin and shock wearing off, but the tidal wave of emotions that crashes over his head feels like it kicks the air from his lungs.

What in *the beyond* had he been *thinking?* Etienne is only halfway through his apprenticeship, *has five more years* before he's a full-fledged witch, and he *was such an idiot* for thinking he could just- *jump ahead like that!* None of this is a *game,* there are real, *terrible* consequences for mistakes and it's not something you take shortcuts with, but that's exactly what he was trying to do, *find a loophole and skip past his problems.*

That's just like him though, isn't it? Etienne's not a hard worker, he's just tricked himself into thinking he is, slacks off with his studies and uses his position as scion to bullshit through the rest.

It was a mistake naming you heir, something whispers to him ugly, icy slide of claws curling over the edges of his mind, a thing with too many teeth that knows him too well grinning from the dark, *Maisette made a mistake and it can't even undo it they're all stuck with you and they wish they weren't.*

Etienne curls his hands into fists, breaths coming in ragged pants and that's not true, *it's not,* he's just spiraling, *he needs to get a grip remember to ground yourself remember to off yourself,* but he's so upset with himself and *so frustrated,* it just keeps feeding back around in a loop, a hurricane of seething self-hatred that only picks up more and more steam.

He hates that he broke the seal, *something his grandfather put in place never going to be anything like the witch he was-*

He hates that the skeleton was destroyed, *a part of the past don't have many things like that left wonder how much longer till they're all gone till you are-*

✦✦ 123 ✦✦

Hates that he endangered the entire city, *you're supposed to be what protects them* ~~you're not fit to lead not fit to be a witch~~-

Hates that Nica did what he couldn't, *said they were nothing what does that make you then* ~~less than nothing couldn't do what you were supposed to do couldn't protect anyone don't deserve what you have don't deserve anything~~-

And Etienne *hates* beyond *imagine* that he was the cause of it all.

He just...*he thinks he just hates himself.*

"Get. Over. It." Etienne grits out through his teeth, arms wrapped crushingly around his chest in a way that's more punishment than comfort. Why is he acting like this, *why is he acting like this,* it's not the end of the world, the way he's feeling is so stupid and *he's stupid he's an idiot not good for anything mothers just shut UP-*

Fucking hell, he's so melodramatic, blows things out of proportion and Etienne hates that he does that ~~he hates that he's himself~~ stop IT! Be an adult! Grow up, *move on,* let this go and act like a normal person *for once in your life,* but his brain is all souped up in a mess of feeling sorry for himself and also wanting someone else to feel sorry for him and then angry with everything for *wanting that in the first place.*

You did this to yourself you don't get pity can't change what happened stop obsessing over it, but that's all his mind will do, unhelpfully rerolling the entire disaster until Etienne wants to scream. Not for the first time he wishes there was an *eject* button in his head, something he could hit that'd get him *the fuck out of here,* but he's trapped, chained to this thing that hates and loves him in confusingly equal measures.

There is no way out though, it's like this all the time, spinning and spinning *and spinning,* and there's no end, *there's no escape or there is but not one he'd ever take,* and Etienne is...*so tired actually,* feels like the entire world was just unceremoniously dumped on his shoulders.

With a sigh, he makes his arms unlatch and stop squeezing him

What Goes Bump In The Night

near to death, remembers what he's supposed to do when he gets like this, and traces around his right hand with his left. *I like... my fingers...I like the way they bend and curl,* he thinks, fingertips bumping over knobby knuckles and the pale crescents of old scars, *I like how I can do things with them I like how they can feel,* runs his wandering hand up to the soft cotton of a black shirt sleeve, faint grain of the texture brushing against sensitive skin.

I like feeling things cloth and bone and the warm slide of gold, fingers skating higher to his neck, running up the side and stopping where his pulse beats, *I like feeling this,* palm spreading out and eyes slipping shut, absentmindedly counting the steady thuds against his skin, *I like this I like knowing I'm alive.*

And at the core of it, Etienne does, *he really does like being here,* it's just his anxiety that makes him doomsday spiral like it's the end of the world when it's really not. It hasn't been this bad in a while, and while it's never been *super great* or even *practically pleasant,* lately it's been bordering on *unmanageable* and that's a problem.

He should probably talk to mother about that, *heart rate spiking imagine the look on her face the worry the concern ~~the judgment what if that's it what if after that she'll sit you down look you in the eyes tell you she has to pick someone else~~,* but m-maybe he shouldn't be worrying about that *just yet,* leave it to be a headache ~~nightmare~~ for another day.

What Etienne's pretty sure he needs right now more than anything is sleep, because it's getting close to the twenty four hour mark of being awake and that *never* helps. He also thinks he's starting to feel the backlog from those healing draughts, body slowly growing stiffer and seemingly more like it's filled with lead by the second.

Accelerated healing has its benefits but *Mothers above,* getting hit with all that energy loss at once is like getting the flu two times over *and* getting trampled to death by a herd of pegasus.

It's an unfortunate side effect from those kinda potions, which

♦✦♦ 125 ♦✦♦

only *expedite* the body's ability to heal, and don't magically vanish the injury with no consequences.

Simply put, it means you still feel *every* aspect of the healing process, but now all at once!

It is a bad time.

Or it's especially bad when you've broken a few ribs and have been mildly electrocuted, should probably go see a proper healer but you're too embarrassed to admit what you did so you chug a draught and a half, *generally not recommended,* and then because you're too ashamed to have anyone see you crying to yourself, you *walk* the few miles home, *really specifically not recommended,* only aggravating your still healing injuries all while having something of an emotional breakdown.

...

Thankfully Etienne isn't *that* much of an idiot...only enough of one to release a cursed malevolent skeleton in a fit of blinding ego, *endangering himself his friends and the whole city in the process idiot what were you thinking,* and he sighs at himself, pinching the bridge of his nose. *Okay just...stop thinking for the next half hour turn yourself off or something please for the love of the night be quiet for once,* he begs his mind, knows it probably won't listen but it's the thought that counts or whatever.

Rolling his stiff shoulders and resettling his bag, Etienne resumes the long slog home, what's supposed to not be much more than a half hour walk nearly doubling because of how crotchety his body is getting. A smart decision would've been to wait for the trolley, but he's a little short on sense tonight and practically overflowing with idiot stubbornness, and besides, he's almost home the next time he sees it go past anyway.

Home for him is the Garden District, one of the oldest sections in the city *and* one of the last wards that is still primarily inhabited by members of the Occult community, and it shows. Houses here are hundreds of years old but look practically brand new in the morning light, glimmer with protective magic that dances and

What Goes Bump In The Night

sways like tree leaves in the wind, characterizing marks of each sect worked into wrought iron fences or waving proudly on colorful banners.

Etienne passes the homes of Seers and Voodoo priests, other coven houses that light up in his mind like spinning sigils, all with ancient trees gracing their front lawns, weighed down by massive branches that drape near to the ground and have whole forests of ferns growing along them.

There's broomsticks cluttering front porches and ceremonial garb hanging out to dry, odd creatures scuttling back under roots that watch him stumble past with too many eyes that see far too much, drawn here because of the thick press of magic that settles in against the very heart of the earth.

Life here is different, it's richer in a way, more connected to the flow of energy that thrums through every single thing, and Etienne finds that he can finally breathe a little easier now that he's home.

Now that he's where he belongs.

To say Maisette is a sight for sore eyes is an understatement, creamy white of its siding almost glowing softly in the warm light of dawn, elegant porch railings and filigree unfurling like moon-flower blooms, its dark, steeply peaked roofline slightly reminiscent of the hats they all wear. Some of its curtains are still drawn shut but there's lights glowing in several windows, means people are either just getting up for the day, or more likely, haven't gone to bed yet.

A family of insomniacs, Etienne thinks with a jaw cracking yawn, and shuffles through the front gates that obligingly swing open for him. The protective sigils burned into the flagstone flare gentle as he passes over them, *welcome back missed you welcome hello son missed you welcome home,* and he sends an answering curl of magic back at Maisette, feels its unknowable multitude rumbling happily almost like how a housecat purrs.

This early in the day, the front courtyard is filled with bright birdsong and the soft burbling from the fountain at its center, water trickling out of the jug held in the half skeletal half flesh hands of the statue.

Etienne limps past it, eyes raking over the woman's carved face, *soft placid smile on one half wide macabre grin on the other,* thinks both sides have a different kind of serenity about them.

There's a simple contentment with life on the right, in the part that's alive, *not overwhelming exuberance because life isn't always ups its downs too it's supposed to be level...balanced,* and then calm understanding on the left, *in the skeleton,* gentle knowledge that life isn't meant to last forever, *there's peace in a skull there's rest in bones things finish things end its time to start anew.*

And to him, they're both beautiful.

All things must die but all life must be protected, Etienne recites internally and tips his head at the statue, shuffling towards the porch steps with single minded determination, only thing he can focus on right now being falling face first into his bed and sleeping for the next hundred years. If he's lucky, it's still early enough most people will still be in their rooms and he won't bump into any of them, knows he's due for the *chewing out of a lifetime,* but would at least like to get some sleep first.

Unfortunately, as is the continuing narrative of the night- *day- whatever,* it doesn't look like Etienne's going to get what he wants, and it's something like dread watching the front door fly open.

Etienne hears them both before he sees either one of them, and thank the *beyond it's not mother,* but their loud lilting voices make him exhausted just listening to them chatter. Where the two of them find so much energy *this* early in the morning, he doesn't know. *Maybe you're just getting old,* Etienne muses, knows Abel would agree with him and snorts tired, tries to straighten up as much as he can when he hears excited voices crowing, *"Etienne!"*

Felix somehow gets to him first, slams into Etienne's middle and nearly takes him down, either headbutting or nuzzling him with his mop of brown curls, it's always hard to tell.

What Goes Bump In The Night

"B-Bonjou, Felix." Etienne wheezes, slaps a hand on his head to ruffle at his hair and also to try and pry him off, but he's a stubborn thing, stays attached like a limpet while his sibling bounds up.

"Matin, Eti...*damn,* you look like *shit.*" Abel whistles, orangey -yellow beads bobbing at the ends of their short, thick braids, and grimacing so hard he's afraid he pulled something, Etienne grouses, "First off, don't let your father hear you talkin' like that *an'* second. I just got in. What's *your* excuse?"

It's a little meaner than you'd normally get with a cousin, but Abel is fourteen almost fifteen and is a little mean by definition, *likes to make it everyone else's problem,* and they just prove Etienne right as their dark cheeks crinkle in a big grin, "Well if I look bad, I figure it's just 'cause I'm related to *you, cul de intello.*"

Oh for the love of, *nerd ass?* That's just- *why-* do you...*do you see his point-*

Etienne sighs again, the sound going all whistly when Felix chooses that moment to squeeze harder, clearly did it on purpose if the spitting giggles Etienne can hear are anything to go off of. At some point in the last year or so, both of his little cousins grew up enough and decided that the *new* coolest thing wasn't *Etienne,* but was rather *making fun of Etienne,* and every day he wishes they'd go back to staring at him googly eyed in awe.

"Ah, Etienne, bonjou." A lilting, airy voice greets him, and he looks up quick, sees Uncle Gilbert making his way down the front steps, leaning heavily on his cane as he navigates the narrow treads. A distinguished yet bookish man, Gilbert is long and lanky the same way Etienne is, always dresses sharp in soft sweater vests and long trailing coats, thick glasses perched on his nose that make him look a lot older than he actually is.

He's only barely fifty but has the air of someone who's lived for centuries, keeps his dark hair messy and short, beard trimmed neatly, silver streaks running through both that his sisters like to tease him about but he takes it all in good stride, says his partner enjoys it at the least.

✦✦ 129 ✦✦

"Bonjou, nonk." Etienne calls nervously as Gilbert strides across the courtyard, sharp rap of his cane accenting his slightly uneven footsteps, and when he draws closer, the smile he gives Etienne curls up sly, "My, my...looks like someone had *quite* the evening. Anything I need to worry about?"

"I- *uh- no.* I-I...I took care of it." Etienne stammers unconvincingly, winces at the obvious lack of confidence in his own voice, and hives break out across his skin watching Gilbert fold his hands on top of his cane, voice deceptively light as he asks, "Are you sure?"

Abel snorts none too discreetly, knows that tone *they all know that tone,* because while Gilbert may be relatively laidback and calm, soft spoken to the point it's easy to forget who he is, *the position he had what he's capable of,* he still has a very intimidating presence that rears its head from time to time.

The simple *command* he can radiate is absolutely stifling, and it's there in his dark eyes now as they narrow behind the lenses of his glasses, brim of his hat angled low and casting shadows across his tan face. One of his eyebrows cocks and it's the smallest of gestures, but there's so much in it, *skepticism and doubt and you wanna try that again,* and it's enough to let Etienne know that *Gilbert knows,* and he dry swallows rough because if Gilbert knows, *it means mother knows.*

Heart rate skyrocketing magic exploding to life crackling through your bones like lightning out of control hard way her face gets set pressure building like a storm over the bayou mother second Matriarch first broke her rules broke the Council's unforgivable Mothers of the Night help you-

"N-Nonk I-!" Etienne tries desperately, mouth clicking shut to cut himself off when Gilbert holds a hand up, his tone kind yet firm, "Some advice? Don't try and talk your way out of this one. The best thing you can do at this point is sit down, own up to what you did, an' apologize."

Gilbert is a very gentle man. He is patient and forgiving by nature, doesn't hold grudge filled resentment, treats everyone, *his*

What Goes Bump In The Night

niece and nephews his children, with an understanding hand, but there's still something pinching the corners of his eyes, *dragging his lips down,* and it's obvious to Etienne then that his uncle is disappointed with him.

It's somehow worse than if he was simply angry because it means trust was broken, a promise wasn't kept, *expectations weren't met let them down you let them all down,* and it makes Etienne incredibly lightheaded. His knees start shaking like crazy, which is embarrassing enough on its own, but Felix is still attached to him and pulls back, big dark eyes staring up at him curiously.

"You okay, Eti? You're shiverin' real bad." Felix murmurs, and Etienne can't think of what to say, stares down at Felix's inquisitive, freckled face and wonders if he'd be disappointed in him too if he knew, if that's what it'd take to finally put an end to the hero worship once and for all.

Because Etienne isn't a hero furthest thing from it deluding yourself they're deluded to have chosen you mistake disaster nothing good will ever come from you spark of ozone crack of lightning rumble of thunder know you how do I know you blood stained lips and glowing eyes and I win mouthed across what could've been your tomb and you're not needed anymore were you ever-

"Etienne?" Felix prods again after feeling the sharp spike of his magic, small furrow appearing between his brows and that's when Abel steps up, gently tugs at their little brother and gets him to reluctantly let go with a quiet, "Come on, bub, give'em a sec', yeah?"

"What? But I just..." Felix whines as Abel pulls him away, gets steered towards the front gates but not before throwing one last lingering look over his shoulder, waves a little to Etienne who can't find the energy to return the gesture.

Without his little cousins around to diffuse some of the tension, the atmosphere between him and Gilbert grows *stifling,* like the weight of all the consequences from the entire night are pressing down on the two of them.

"How mad is she?" Etienne barely manages to whisper, nervously

✦✦ 131 ✦✦

peeking out from under his hat at where Gilbert kinda hems and haws, eventually deciding on, "Well...no one died so you've got that going for you, but you've put Catherine in a rather tough spot. Marcel is furious about the whole mess, you're lucky you weren't here earlier."

Etienne winces and ducks his head fast, is *very* aware of Marcel's infamous fiery temper and sharp tongue, knows he doesn't take any slight or threat to his house well. Tonight was a whole fiasco on its own, and naively, Etienne had assumed its negative impact would stay where he left it smoldering in the visitor's center, but it could honestly end up causing a major problem between their two houses.

Intercoven relations are a lot more delicate and finicky than most outsiders assume, and while there's never been open warfare per say, disputes between arguing houses leaves the entire community uncomfortable and tense. They're all united as Witches of the Night, would never seek to cause serious harm or actively move against the other covens, but that doesn't mean they have to *like* one another. In recent years, mother has worked so tirelessly to unify them all into a single front, knew they had a better chance of standing up to the city council if they were together, but it's a tenuous situation.

A feud breaking out is the last thing any of them need right now, could threaten their entire position, and cold sweat trickles down the back of Etienne's neck because with the way things went last night, he may have inadvertently started one.

Likely guessing where his thoughts have gone, Gilbert sighs and steps up, warm palm dropping to rest on his shoulder, "I won't ever lie to you, névé. You caused a lot of trouble for us last night, but nobody's out flingin' hexes just yet. Marcel is rightfully upset, and *Mères*, is that an unpleasant thing to see, but he can be reasoned with, so don't fret just yet."

Nodding his head jerkily, Etienne blinks his eyes quick trying to dispel the tears he can feel gathering at their corners, jumps a little at the press of fingers under his chin coaxing his head up.

What Goes Bump In The Night

Gilbert smiles at him softly, eyes warm and deep, like the quiet hush of the night and the comfort of darkness, fingers like stoking coals against his frozen skin, "It'll be okay, Etienne, this is a bump in the road, nothin' more. Besides, if anyone can talk their way outta this, it's your mother. She's the best atriarch I've ever known, she'll get it sorted."

"O-Okay..." Etienne mumbles wetly, doesn't doubt that in the slightest, has looked up to and respected his mother for as long as he can remember, which is why he's so terrified to talk to her. At the end of the day, he knows she loves him wholly and completely, but there's a difference in loving someone and being proud of them, and Etienne so *desperately* wants her to be proud of him.

He's her heir, *he's* the person she's expecting to take over after her one day, and he wants her to feel total confidence in that, to look at him and see what he's capable of and feel secure leaving their line in his hands, *trusting* him to be the man she's raised him to be, and when Etienne fails her like this, it's nothing but an insult to her.

His mistakes call into question mother's ability to train apprentices, throws doubt on how much control she actually has over her coven, makes their entire house look like a joke when they're supposed to be one of the leading pillars of the community. There's no doubt that his mother is an amazing witch, deserves all of the praise and accolades and respect she gets from the city, but stuff like this makes people *whisper*, and it's not fair for her to be undermined like that just because she has a failure of a son like him.

And something kinda breaks in Etienne's chest at the thought, composure slipping away along with a few wayward tears that race down his face, must collide against Gilbert's hand because he swipes a thumb up, brushing them away.

"Oh, Eti, don't let this eat you alive. You've done wrong but it's not *unfixable*." Gilbert stresses, hand moving to cup the side of his face firmly, fingers flexing out and zinging faintly with the reassuring touch of his magic, "I know it's hard, but go talk with Catherine, make your apologies *make your amends*, and then put this behind you. Let your guilt *go,* move *on* from your mistakes."

Mothers, would that he could, but Etienne's bad at letting go, is bad at so many other things he's supposed to be good at, and no matter what he does, he knows this won't ever leave him, *not really.*

It'll just come back to haunt him when it's dark in his mind and he's alone and scared, something stalking him from the shadowy recess where light doesn't reach and suddenly the night isn't so inviting anymore.

And Etienne's not the best witch, *but he's trying so hard to be,* and he's not that great of a son either, *sky high expectations and he's struck a thousand feet in the ground,* but he'll make himself do whatever they ask him to do, *will mold himself to be whatever they want him to be,* doesn't care as long as they smile at him with warmth in their eyes and admiration in their voices, *telling him he did good telling him he did well,* that they're all *proud of him.*

That's all he's ever wanted, to have his family look up to him like Etienne does to them, wants so very badly to know that when they hang his portrait alongside the other past atriarchs one day, that the generations following after will be able to point to him and feel proud naming him as their own.

Etienne wants to be like his grandfather, *he wants to be like his mother,* he wants to be what inspires future Boudreaux children to carry on the mantle of their family, but right now, there's just not that much inspiring about him, *and he worries there never will be.* He's decent in his studies, and he does a lot for the community but he could always be doing more, and it's so incredibly frustrating to feel like he's still not anywhere close to where he wants to be even after all that.

Sometimes Etienne thinks he's made progress, *has improved is better than he was before,* but then something will happen and he'll be reminded of how nothing's really changed, will see how he's still so far from the goal that was set for him the day he was born.

It's a lot of pressure, ~~too much pressure~~ *you can do this ~~you can't,~~* and on occasion, it feels like it'll bow his shoulders *break his back,*

What Goes Bump In The Night

but Etienne bulls through it because what other choice does he have. This is his *life,* this is what he was *born* to do, and there's no other path for him to take.

N-Not that he'd *want to,* he's perfectly content where he is but it just...it gets to be too *much* sometimes, *screaming howling spitting panic gonna drive your house into ruin last of your line spinning out of control which way is up which is down* ~~help can't do this HELP,~~ but he can handle it, *he has to.*

Sniffling miserably as he tries to pull himself back together, Etienne takes everything he's feeling, *disappointment fear stress doubt guilt exhaustion,* and locks it up in a box far away, slides it under the bed to collect dust and straightens his thoughts, *brings order back to his mind plays the role he's supposed to know how to fill,* croaking dutiful but a little hoarse, "Y-Yes sir."

Gilbert's dark eyes roam over his face, but for once, Etienne must've finally got everything under control like he's supposed to because Gilbert just pats him once on the cheek, saying way too gentle and affectionate before he pulls back, "Don't mistake my advice for criticism. You still have so much to learn but you're a good witch, Etienne, and you're on the way to becomin' a *great* one. I know you're gonna do amazing things, my boy."

Are you though still said you had so much to learn are you ever gonna get there or are you just destined to always disappoint, the thing with too many teeth that hates him whispers, and an unpleasant shiver runs down Etienne's spine, but he smiles politely, nods his head at Gilbert as he takes a step back as well, "Thank you, nonk, I appreciate it, *truly.* An' I'll...make sure I do better next time."

"Atta boy, that's the spirit! Always strive to be better than the day before." Gilbert merrily raps his cane into the cobblestone a few times, each hit of it slamming into Etienne like Gertie's tale did, deep, percussive pain that strums through his whole body, *better than before not good enough you're never good enough,* and he hears himself murmur distantly, "Of course, nonk."

Clapping him once on the arm in farewell that hurts more than

✦✦ 135 ✦✦

it should, Gilbert steps away, going to join his two children loitering by the front gates who're *valiantly* pretending like they haven't been listening in, tips his head to the side and looks at Etienne over the rim of his glasses, "Well, we best be off! I've got to get these two down to the academy for mornin' lessons, but if I were you, I wouldn't keep your mother waitin' that much longer."

If you were me you'd sooner go lay facedown in the bogs for a thousand years rather than do that, is what jumps first to Etienne's mind, but what comes out of his mouth is a genial, "Yes sir of course. I'm on my way in right now."

"Excellent! Bon chans, névé! I'll see you this afternoon, but do try an' get some rest in. You look like you could use it!" Gilbert teases lightly with a wink, and he means well but it only serves as a grim reminder to Etienne how *much* everything hurts. Those draughts have really, *really* hit and it's almost crippling. His body feels impossibly weighed down, chest achy like there's a vice squeezing his ribs, eyes itchy and sore, and he's so exhausted, Etienne really does believe he could sleep for a thousand years no problem.

Standing on his feet is suddenly the hardest thing he's ever had to do, but he can't rest, not yet at least. There's still that conversation he has to have with mother that he'd rather do anything else to avoid, but Etienne knows he can't, *knows he has to be something like a good son a good witch,* so instead, he woodenly raises a hand in farewell, listlessly watching the other three exit Maisette's grounds.

None of them are really paying attention to him anymore.

Abel's nattering about something they're learning while Felix jumps around at Gilbert's side, *so happy so excited for the day to begin for everything that life's gonna bring them when's the last time you felt like that,* Gilbert smiling at the two of them like they're the center of his world and the gate clangs shut behind them loud like thunder.

Etienne lets his arm drop once they're out of sight, bones grinding together with the motion and everything crackles around him like monochrome static. The courtyard seems impossibly still now,

What Goes Bump In The Night

almost like it's trapped outside the flow of time despite the bright light streaming down and the chipper call of birds darting through branches, like the space under reality where his magic lives is collectively holding its breath, *waiting for the storm to break.*

Turning slowly, Etienne looks back at Maisette, at its steep roof that now looks uninviting and ominous, at the dark windows that all stare at him like a dozen bottomless eyes, *growing feeling of dread in the pit of his stomach,* and can't help but feel like he's at the center of a massive hurricane, knows what comes after the eye has passed by.

He swallows rough, pulse jumping up into something fast that pelts like rain, and there is no part of him that *wants* to do this, but what other choice does Etienne have. He can't run from this, *can't outpace it can't escape it,* so he doesn't, accepts his fate and drags his stiff, protesting legs up the front porch steps one clattering step at a time, takes a deep breath and gets ready for that back wall to come rushing at him like an unforgiving train.

Chapter 8

The metal of the front door handle is freezing against his clammy skin, and for half a second, Etienne is scared to depress the lever, afraid the entire thing is going to crack apart in his hands like brittle ice, but once he musters up the courage to try, it doesn't, swings open smoothly like always, letting him into the empty foyer without a sound.

It's almost too serene, light pouring in through the huge windows flanking the door, highlighting the swirling dust motes that get whipped into a frenzy upon his arrival, gentle calm of the morning a flimsy façade that's barely hiding the palpable tension in the air.

Etienne can feel the electric crack against his skin once he steps inside, but there's no one waiting for him, and he can't tell if that's a good or bad thing, anxiety zapping along his nerves uncomfortably as the coat rack comes scuttling up.

It bends down in offer to take his hat, and Etienne tiredly slips the thing off and sets it on a prong, only then seeing all the sooty white ash staining the black wool, grimaces because that's gonna be a real pain to clean later. The coat rack must sense his displeasure and misinterprets, stands bolt upright and nervously clacks two of its prongs together, looking guiltier than any piece of furniture honestly should, and Etienne waves the poor thing off, murmuring gently, "No no, you're okay, m'just tired. But I promise you're doin' a great job *uh-* holding hats and everythin'?"

Not his finest bit of social interaction, but his brain feels like it's been fried and this is a *coat rack* anyway so why is he worrying at all. For its part, the coat rack doesn't seem to care the slightest bit about his social ineptitude, wiggles happy from the praise and does a little salute before skittering back into its designated spot.

What Goes Bump In The Night

It settles down into inanimacy once more but the pure contentment rolling off it is practically tangible, and Etienne shakes his head at it fondly, wishes everything in life was as easy as appeasing your furniture was.

Now hatless, Etienne rakes a hand through his gritty hair and makes a face, knows he probably stinks of brimstone and blood and unpleasantly burnt things, *desperately* wants a long hot shower and then a nice long nap in his super soft bed, *needs* it like you need air in your lungs, and like it knows his thoughts, the study room door creaks open off to the left, hanging wide in a gesture that reads, *oh no you don't.*

Etienne feels his stomach flop over unhappily, prickling tension erupting across his skin and raising goosebumps, and he's stuck in place for a second, knows what he *needs to do knows what he doesn't want to do knows what's gonna happen either way,* and growing impatient with him, the door waggles back and forth.

I'm not gonna ask again, ripples under his feet and it's Maisette but it's also not, because while Maisette is its own sorta consciousness, *gleaned and gathered from generations,* it's at the same time an extension of all of them, *their minds their desires their thoughts,* but there's only one witch in this house that can sway the multitude to her beck and call.

And Uncle Gilbert was right before he left, *it's best not to keep her waiting.*

Slowly moving down the hall, Etienne scrambles to get what he's gonna say in order, *apologize accept responsibility make amends promise to do better beg her to forgive you,* and Etienne's good with people, knows what to say and how to say it to get the outcome he wants, but whatever concise thing he was building falls apart completely the second he steps into the doorway and sees mother sitting behind her desk.

Bright daylight streams in through the floor to ceiling window at her back, warms the dark emerald of the walls into a softer green, catches off the gilt edges of the books lining the numerous

❖✦❖ 139 ❖✦❖

bookshelves, an extensive collection that houses some of the oldest and most valuable tomes the family owns.

Etienne tries not to stare at the obvious hole along one shelf, bag hanging off his shoulder growing exponentially heavier as he shuffles into the room, keeps his eyes instead on the parquet flooring and rich rugs under his feet.

There's two highbacked cream velvet chairs in front of mother's desk, and he pauses behind one, fingers curling over the ornate wood at the top of it, prickling sensation between his shoulder blades because it feels like he's being watched and judged by the score of taxidermized mounts lining the walls, but whenever he nervously glances at one, it's as lifeless as always.

The scritching from mother's pen is the only sound, silence pressing in and seeming to amplify Etienne's pulse, which thunders and echoes in his ears like a storm out of control. *Do something say something get this over with,* he barks at himself, but it's like all of him is frozen solid, held completely immobile while he's drowned alive by his own heartbeat, paralyzed waiting for mother to make a move.

Her head is angled down while she writes, river of thin box braids spilling over her shoulders and past her profile, partially obscuring her face so Etienne can't really get a read on her, which has him incredibly anxious. He doesn't even feel anything when he hesitantly reaches out and pokes his magic against hers, no backlog of emotion or flickering sensation of thoughts, *absolutely nothing but an electrical wall of static,* but the contact does make her stop writing, pen stilling as she orders evenly, "Sit *down.*"

And Etienne does, scrambles around to the front of the chair and drops back into it, leaves his ash stained bag on the ground so it won't dirty anything up, and waits. He's not really sure what he's expecting. Mother doesn't yell, but she can project like the grandest of orators, voice loud and commanding in the way that makes people stop and listen, swayed by the simple *authority* she's able to stoke in her words.

What Goes Bump In The Night

It's a tone she hardly ever uses with her children, instead, prefers to course correct with gentle yet firm reprimands, but this isn't anything like getting caught swiping cookies before dinner or loosing a jar of spiders in someone's room.

This is a big deal.

It's sneaking around behind her back and messing with magic you don't know how to control, endangering lives when you're supposed to be the one that protects them, destroying another coven's property and breaking faith with that house's atriarch, levying so grievous of an insult, it could be enough to spark a feud between their families.

In short, Etienne has royally fucked up, has won for himself quite possibly the *worst* outcome of the whole situation as instigated by his blind pride and suffocating ego.

He's caused enough trouble to last a lifetime, which is bad enough on its own but is amplified by his position as *scion*. What holds him above everyone else also means the margin for error is smaller, greater expectations and responsibilities leading to greater downfalls, and mother never yells, but if there was one instance where she'd break that pattern, it'd be now.

So, on pins and needles he waits, body tensed like it's bracing for attack, won't flinch when it comes swinging at him because Etienne knows he's earned it, but it never comes. The silence just stretches on and on, skitter and scratch of the pen like a fast ill-paced metronome, starting and stopping at random intervals same as Etienne's heart, every pause lasting a thousand years while he waits for her to let loose.

But mother never does, starts writing again *he starts breathing again*, and the light dances with the wind in the tree branches outside, little dappled pattern racing over silky dark walls and deep toned wood and Etienne starts to realize that while *he's* waiting on *her* to start, *she's waiting on him.*

Understanding that makes it so much more daunting of a task, because now it's all on Etienne, and he doesn't want to miss anything, *doesn't want to get it wrong,* but he doesn't know where to begin. He would much rather mother lay it all out, *this is what you did wrong this is how you messed up this is what you need to do,* XYZ and ABC, then he could just agree, apologize, and move on.

That would be treating Etienne like a child though, and mother has never once done that, has afforded him the same respect and consideration she gives her peers his whole life. *Coddling* was never a term used in their household, and it's not that she isn't an affectionate mother, *held them when they were scared of the monsters under the bed and the things lurking out in the night,* but she would also explain what the monsters were, would teach them how to get rid of them.

You are strong enough to stand on your own an' fight your own battles, she told each of them over and over again, wiping away tears and helping tiny hands clear sniffly noses, and it's a little different now because the only monster Etienne's facing down is the one he made himself, but the sentiment is the same.

He has to stand and face this thing, admit to his mistakes and accept the consequences, which is quite possibly the worst fight to win, because there's no feelings of victory at the end, only ones of grim defeat. Etienne did it to himself though, can't whine can't complain *can't dodge it,* snarls his fingers up together until they're bleeding white and tries to remember the five proper steps to an apology.

Express regret accept responsibility make amends promise change ~~request~~ *beg forgiveness,* and that's easy enough, he can do that, knows he's in the wrong in the first place and regrets what happened *with every fiber of his being,* but then why *is it so hard to get the words out.* A few seconds drag on laboriously as Etienne opens and closes his mouth uselessly, inexplicably mute the one time he needs his voice more than ever, held prisoner by the crippling paranoia that's started to creep up his throat.

A storm's brewing to life in his mind and it whispers that if Etienne admits his faults to mother, it'd just be more incentive to replace him as scion, which, *no,* that's *never* happened before *anywhere* but there's a first time for everything and if it was gonna be anyone-

Makes sense that it'd be you can't measure up to your forbearers would lead your house into ruin too anxious too indecisive too much wrong inside your head it was a mistake picking you no one wants you here you were a mistake and they can't get rid of you let them all down that's all you do you LET PEOPLE DOWN-

Etienne knows what's happening and Mother's, *he's trying to stop it,* wants to prove he can be an adult and regain some faith by admitting to his wrongs, but the more he attempts to wrest his mind back in order, the more it spirals out of control, and he's panicking and it's been silent for too long and the disappointment is *thick* in mother's voice as she sighs, "Nothin' to say for yourself then?"

And like a punch to the gut, it all comes vomiting up.

"I-I'm sorry! I am- s-so sorry! I shouldn't've done- I-I didn't mean to do it! I thought I c-could- *I wasn't t-thinkin' I-* I don't know, *I don't know what happened.* B-But I am so incredibly sorry a-an' it'll *never* happen again, maman, *p-promise.*" Etienne pleads as he leans over his lap, every word that's falling out of his mouth getting tripped up and tangled on one another, a mishmash of desperate begging nonsense he hurls at mother's feet, "Please b-believe me. I never intended for any of that to happen an' I- I-I don't know what I was thinkin' but it won't happen ever again, y-you have my *word.*"

She looks up at him once, amber eyes flat like a stone wall, *give nothing away,* before going back to whatever she's working on, and it's so obvious a dismissal, the room around Etienne *spins.*

Not good enough you're never good enough, choruses in his mind as that feeling of lightheadedness sweeps through him, and Etienne scrambles for purchase against it, *for coherency,* works on talking past where his heart thunders in his throat.

"I messed up, *I-I know I messed up,* and please believe me when I say I *regret* everythin' that happened. *So much.* I never shoulda done it...*b-but I did.*" Etienne says as evenly as he can, winces when his voice still stutters and spikes, ducks his head in embarrassment and watches where the light gutters over worn floorboards, "I'm sorry for goin' behind your back, I'm...*sorry* for messin' with magic I-I don't understand, I'm sorry for causin' you trouble with Patriarch Gagnon and I...I-I'm sorry I-"

This one is the hardest to say but it's also the most important, *really* makes hives breakout across his skin because it goes against everything Etienne's been taught since the day he was brought here. It still makes him sick thinking about it, *the smoke the fires the unholy terror knowing you could've killed them all that you would've been to blame,* but he licks his lips and forces himself to whisper, *to admit,* "I-I'm sorry I endangered the lives of o-others. I never meant to, b-but I still did, an' I'm so sorry mère...*m'so sorry...*"

And somewhere in the study, a clock ticks, that pen continues to scratch against paper, there's his own too loud breathing and the wind rushing by outside, faint creaking as Maisette shudders and shifts around them, but otherwise, it's silent.

"I...I-I accept *full* responsibility for what happened- *a-and the consequences.* I'll serve whatever punishment you see fit. I-I'll do whatever I *h-have to do* to make it *right.*" Etienne stammers, hopes it's the correct thing to say, and his fingers clench hard around one another, bright sting of nails against the soft flesh of his palms, "I promise you, *nothing* like this will *ever* happen again. I don't know what I was thinkin', *why* I thought this was a good idea, but there won't be any repeats, I give you *my word.*"

He'll even swear on the Night Codex if she asks, would sooner risk excommunication than disappoint her again, *hates that he already has you let her down you made her feel ashamed to have you as a son ~~didn't she always,~~* something twisting up ugly and painful in his chest like bramble vines as he hushes, "I know I've d-disappointed you...I know I've embarrassed the coven, an' I am so unbelievably sorry. I never shoulda done what I did. It was wrong an' there's no excuses...I-I hope you can forgive me."

The sounds of writing stop and so does Etienne's heart. He's too

✦✦ 144 ✦✦

What Goes Bump In The Night

much of a coward to pick his head up, keeps it bowed and listens to the quiet *snick* as the pen is set back in its stand, the softest of preludes to the rumble of words that come rolling across the desk.

"I find myself curious, Etienne-" Mother starts, slow cadence to her tone that does nothing to mask the backlog of serious emotions she's suppressing, "-because you acknowledge you '*messed up*' and that you, '*never should've done this*', which implies a certain level of understandin' that you *knew* what you were doin' was *wrong*, an' yet you did it *anyway*. So. I am...*curious*."

Her chair scraping back cracks through the air like the screaming jolt of lightning, sets his nerves on fire and makes him shrink down into his collar, rich, deep timbre of her voice intoning in low grumbles of thunder, "I am curious to know what lead you to this choice. I am *curious to know* what *excuses* you told yourself until you decided it was okay. I am *curious*, because for *the life of me*, I cannot *possibly fathom* why *you* would do somethin' like this!"

Oh this is mother angry like he's never seen her before.

Or at least- has never seen this level of furious emotions directed back at *him*, a foreign experience Etienne *really* isn't liking. It's making him wish a hole would open up under him right now so he could escape from it, but unfortunately, Maisette isn't taking pity on him and neither is mother.

"Mère-" He tries once, taking a cautious peek at her, but the look she levels at him has Etienne snapping his mouth shut so fast, he accidentally cracks his teeth together, ducks his head again with shame flaring hot across the back of his neck.

"No, *please- tell me*, Etienne. Tell me *what* was goin' through your mind when you *lied* and told Marcel you could handle this? Or when you snuck in here and *took one of my books* without asking?" Mother demands, still not yelling but that power is in her voice, the one that sounds like it could tear the world asunder, "Or how about when you didn't tell anyone where you were goin' or what you were doin' or *when you broke the seal on an infested terror-!*"

"It was an *accident!*" Etienne bleats suddenly, snaps his head up

✦✦ 145 ✦✦

and sees mother standing with her hands braced on the desktop, face more livid than he can ever remember as she leans across it, "Of course it was an accident! You wouldn't be sittin' in this house if it *wasn't an accident!*"

Etienne bites his tongue harshly, cold sweat running down the back of his neck, hadn't even *thought* about that, about how if mother didn't have as much faith in him as she apparently does, what he did could be grounds for excommunication. *They'd brand you an apostate and hunt you down like a wild animal without hesitation,* whispers icy through his ears and he swallows rough, thinks he might *actually* be sick across the carpet as mother's hawklike eyes bore into him.

We were a lawless people before the Mothers, he remembers her saying, fingers tensing into rigid claws under that stare and he's-*standing in front of five towering statues so old any discerning facial features are long gone feel like they're watching you anyway bow your head grab the knife affirm your duty,* and he can't forget that, *will never forget,* the promises he made under a new moon, *the ones signed in blood bound forever vow you can never break know what happens if you do They didn't maintain order with leniency-*

Tension is mounting up steep, thick in the air like the smoke from the fires earlier, *makes it hard to breathe hard to think and they wouldn't they can't- but you broke their rules Mothers you can't do this all you have everything you are they can't take this from you but they could and you think you might just-* but mother sighs and it starts to ease off.

She straightens back up and sinks down into her chair, looks exceptionally older and more exhausted while she kneads at her forehead, "Gaçon...please, *please* explain to me *what in the hell were you thinkin'?* I just...I am truly at a loss shéri. This isn't like you at *all,* you *know better.*"

You're a scion you gotta do better – don't break Their rules don't break her rules know what'll happen – still have so much to learn – bloody palm pressing into the alter no turning back – do you even know what you're doing, echoes in a painful mixed-up clamor from

What Goes Bump In The Night

his memories and Etienne winces, digs his toes into the soles of his boots trying desperately to ground his spinning mind.

"I'm sorry *I-I'm sorry-*" He wheezes, heart beating behind his ribs like a wild thing, would send his magic crackling erratically if he wasn't already so drained from last night, "I- I don't know, I thought it was a-a *bad idea* before I- b-but I'd already promised Marcel a-an' I didn't know *what to do* and I couldn't go back on the bet either and by then i-it was too *late and I just-*"

"Bet? What're you- *Mères de la Nwit.* Do *not* tell me all this was because *someone dared you to-*" Mother snaps and Etienne stares at her frozen and helpless, never meant to admit to that but he can't take it back now, and mother scoffs appalled, "I'm sorry, are you *a child?* That's the most *idiotic, stupide insensé- where* did you even *get* an idea like that? Who's head is *empty enough that they would-!*"

Understanding dawns on mother's face before he can defend himself, quick sprig of crackling electricity that jumps between her clenching fingers as she hisses, "It was *Sabine* wasn't it? *Pour l'amour de-* I keep *tellin'* you *an' Renee* that boy is *nothin' but trouble* but neither of you *will listen- nwit aidez-moi, je vais étrangler cet-!*"

"What? *No!* I-It wasn't him, mère! He didn't have anythin' to do with the bet." Etienne insists frantic, and it's generally a bad idea to lie to her, but this is *technically* true and also conveniently leaves out the part where Sabine suggested this assignment. A lie by omission should be fine as long as mother never finds out, but that means Etienne's gonna have to tweak some facts and shift some blame to keep Sabine out of trouble.

It'll direct a little more of her ire at Etienne, and while he *loathes* upsetting her, he cares about protecting his friend more.

Pressing his shaking palms against one another in his lap, Etienne leans forwards and pleads, "I know you think he's...*uh,* brash and headstrong, b-but Sabine's a good friend, and he wouldn't put me in danger like that. This wasn't his idea *at all,* I-I *promise.*"

"Given the amount of times it *'wasn't Sabine's idea',* I don't think

◆✦◆ 147 ◆✦◆

that boy has ever had a thought a day in his life." Mother declares with all the severity of a class five storm, arms elegantly folding across her chest as she cocks her chin back, demanding, "Alright. Well if it wasn't Renee's reckless son, who was it? Because I know you Etienne an' you didn't come up with this on your own."

She'd be right about that. Etienne may have his moments where he can be goaded into bad ideas, but he doesn't instigate them, *thanks for something anxiety,* plays it pretty safe all things considered. So if he tries to convince mother this all stemmed from him, she won't believe it for a *second,* but there's pieces and parts she'll buy, knows the man her son is and the vices that plague him.

And there's one thing in particular he always struggles with.

"I um...w-when I had my meeting this week with Nic- *uh,* t-that alchemist, we got into a...*heated argument,* o-over the value of the diversity program." Etienne begins slowly, tapping his thumbs together and apart in an anxious tick he gets from time to time, "I-tensions ran high I don't...b-but they told me they'd um, g-get me out of doin' the program if I could prove I was better than them? So I wanted to find an assignment where I could show off- *s-show my skills* I mean, and where they'd basically be useless..."

He shrugs, can feel the tips of his ears growing hot, is aware he's digging his own grave but if it keeps Sabine out of trouble, Etienne'll keep digging further and further down, "And then I remembered Bea mentionin' the OSHA complaint, about how they needed to move the skeleton soon an' I...a-an' I thought it was a good idea, that it was...the *perfect* opportunity to show how outmatched that alchemist was-"

Sharp bright smell of ozone metal fingers arching like the elegant curling struts of stained glass never felt anything like this electricity sparking in eyes and in the air jumping to life in your heart 'fraid you're gonna lose hotshot, and there's color bleeding across Etienne's entire face now, hot and sick with humiliation the same way a high fever is, "I-I thought I could do it, I thought I had everythin' under control but I was um...I-I was wrong...*obviously.*"

What Goes Bump In The Night

"Obviously..." Mother echoes soft, draws a hand down her face and partially covers her mouth, only moving her fingers to murmur incredulously, "So this was all so you could...*prove* you were *better* than *some alchemist?*"

Etienne shrugs again and snarls his fingers around one another, knows he doesn't have to say anything more to sell her on what the underlying cause of this entire mess was, and even though he's expecting it, it still feels like a shot straight through the heart when mother sighs exhausted, *"Foolish boy...*your pride is going to be your downfall."

Chest swelling with euphoric elation you did it you did it you're the best chasing that feeling always chasing after it jubilant with victory and stupid with pride so much better to feel this than the other things you feel hate what you are with it despise what you are without it want it need it it's k i l l i n g y o u-

"I know." Etienne more or less just mouths the words, toes curling painfully in his boots as mother leans across the desk, dark fingers pressing firmly into the lacquered wood, "You listen to me, I do not like the alchemists and I do not trust them. I want them out of our parish same as you, I want that college abolished, *same as you,* and I want back what's rightfully ours, same. As. *You.*"

She raps her fingers into the desk on each word for emphasis, brows furrowing and corners of her mouth pinching displeased while she chides, "But I do not put this city, innocent people- *our charges,* in dangerous, *compromising situations,* all in an attempt to prove myself. I don't have to prove anythin' to anyone, I know my worth. So should you."

Say it like it's the easiest thing in the world don't know anything nothing worthwhile in me never gonna be as good as you never amount to anything disgrace disappointment mistake why do you even bother with me, Etienne thinks miserably and slips his eyes shut, ignores the burning in their corners and whispers the only thing he thinks he's capable of saying evenly, "Yes ma'am."

Void below, it feels like his ribcage is crunching inwards, gro-

✦✦ 149 ✦✦

tesquely folding back in on itself and rending out a gross, fleshy monstrosity that makes even the simple act of breathing torturous. Etienne knew this was going to be a hard conversation, thought he was prepared for it, and it is so unbelievably frustrating to once again find himself back in the same looping spiral of crippling doubts.

No matter what he does, he can never seem to break out of it, and yeah he tried the whole anxiety meds thing once, which helped to an extent, but they didn't really *stop* anything, just kinda dulled his reaction to it. In the end, they hadn't been worth it to Etienne, but unless he can find a different way out, he's left trapped in the heinous prison of his mind, tortured with cycling thoughts and the way his body makes negative emotions manifest as physical pain.

That's the worst part about all of this, the deep, stinging ache that trickles down his arms and settles throbbing at the center of his palms, constricting force under his ribs, head alternating between pounding and spinning dizzy fast, but ever so slowly, like the drip of an IV or the roll of condensation down a glass, it all starts to grow fuzzy, *get greyed out,* almost as if a wall is creeping down in between him and the rest of the world.

"Given your actions last night, I assume you understand you're grounded?" Mother inquires from what sounds like underwater, and it takes a good long minute to figure out what she's saying, but once Etienne woodenly nods his head, she continues, "Until further notice, I will assign you whatever assignment I see fit to. You're no longer allowed to pick your own nor are you to be goin' anywhere I don't know about first, got it?"

His tongue might as well be made of lead for how useful it is at the moment, and Etienne can only manage another nod, somehow must be an adequate response because mother doesn't pause, "Also before the afternoon is over, I'll be needin' a formal written apology to House Gagnon *and* a personal one for *everyone* that was affected by last night. An' don't even *think* about reusin' the same format, make each of'em sincere *and* unique."

Fizzling crackling pop broken radio static in one ear out the other who even cares not him he's not anyone he's not anything, and that's not a good thought to have, *that's not a good thing to be,* but Etienne can't find the energy to feel his extremities let alone care about the way his mind is hazing out into rainclouds.

There's been times before when something like this has happened, *lose focus lose feeling lose yourself,* and it'll go away eventually, *it always has in the past,* but like a lot of things, it doesn't seem to stay gone for long so maybe it *never* really leaves him.

Maybe it just recedes.

A chair sounds like it's being pushed back a few rooms over, soft creak of footsteps filtering through from another dimension, and there's a dark shape at the edge of reality and muffled words hushing into someone else's ear he overhears on accident, "Etienne? Are you listenin' to me...? What're you...a-are you- look at me, baby, *look at me.*"

And he does because what else is he to do, ratchets his head up like a rusted out set of cogs, looks at her since she asked him to but he's not really seeing anything. Mother is little more than a fragmented collection of shapes by his chair, something Etienne's supposed to recognize as a person and yet hardly does, wonders if he might've fallen asleep at some point and this is the terrible confused limbo of lucid dreams.

"I love you, shè, don't ever think I don't." She tells him and he doesn't know if she should, squeezes his fingers together until it should hurt and feels *nothing,* "I have loved you completely an' utterly since the moment I first held you in my arms, and nothin' will ever change that. *Nothing.* You hear me, Etienne?"

"Yes ma'am." Something says with his voice and his mouth, thick rubbery feeling coating a tongue that swipes at too dry teeth, and maybe he's the only one who notices how wrong it sounds, because mother doesn't say anything, just leans forward and brushes fingers along his cheek. The sensation is dulled, comes to him muted and barely there, the spark of her magic like a distant dream he's struggling to recall.

✦✦ 151 ✦✦

"Are you alright? They told me you'd been injured." She murmurs and swipes at something on his cheek, *could be soot could be blood doesn't matter,* and it doesn't matter either that his bones grind together when he shrugs stiff, that his ribs groan like old wood when he takes in breath to hush, "Nothin' worth worrying about."

"You are *always* worth worryin' about, mô dou gaçon." Mother counters with a gentle smile, fingers possibly squeezing against his skin if the warm curl of static is anything to go off of, but he can't really tell, "I'm sorry I didn't say this earlier, but I'm glad you're alright, I *really am*. And I'm not tryin' to be mean with you this morning, I know you're tired an' hurt but it's serious, baby. You coulda died last night, you know that?"

That was honestly the furthest thing from Etienne's mind but he doesn't think he can tell her that, nods slow and feels her hand slip up the side of his face, elegant fingers carding through his snarled hair. "I was so worried when I heard what'd happened. I knew you were alive but I-" Mother sighs, being oh so careful as she detangles some of the knots in his hair, "This life we live is a dangerous one, and I know you're capable, but I still *hate* when you take unnecessary risks like that Etienne."

"Sorry..." He hushes and ducks his head to the side ashamed, but she turns it back with a few gentle fingers under his chin, eyes glittering like sunset on the river, "I'm *not* askin' you to be sorry, just careful."

Etienne nods and her hand drifts back up to petting through his hair, accidently brushing over a tender spot along his skull that makes a sharp jolt of pain flare out from the spot. "Ya'know...and I *can't* believe I'm sayin' this..." Mother begins in a rueful tone, tongue clucking lightly while she picks debris and ash free from his inky locks, "But I'm...glad actually, that that alchemist was there last night. They saved your life shéri , an' that's not a debt that can be easily forgotten."

"Of course, mère." Etienne mutters sour, keeps having snippets of last night replay in his mind and thinks he's gonna be haunted by that memory for the rest of his life. Will be seeing Nica stand-

What Goes Bump In The Night

ing at the center of a miniature cyclone with their lightning eyes and their bloodied teeth bared in a violent, jubilant grin, until the day he dies, and what an utter travesty that is.

Mothers of the Night you've made such a mess of things, he thinks, consequences trundling on past in his mind's eye like a macabre circus, because *naturally,* not only did Etienne lose the bet in the most horrendous manner he could've, landing himself in a world of trouble the likes of which he's never been in before but *then,* on top of *all that,* now he owes Nica an unpayable debt too.

Mothers when it rains, *does it sure pour.*

This is by the far the most embarrassing thing that's ever happened to him, and Etienne would probably be more stressed about it if he still had the energy for feeling things, but that well's run dry, clanging echoes rattling up from an empty wellspring.

There always comes a point after a very long, very exhausting, *very shit day,* when there is no more patience to be had and emotional maturity takes a steep nosedive, where an executive decision is made by the brain that you are done, physically incapable of dealing with one more damn thing.

Etienne is done.

He think's he's been done for a while now, ever since the seal exploded and Gertie got to its feet, breathing to unlife once more, sealing his fate far more effectively than he was ever capable of sealing the curse.

Okay, that bit of ribbing actually kinda hurt thank you brain *you horrible piece of soggy meat,* and with that new chink in his self-esteem, Etienne thinks it's high time he passed out. His eyes slip closed briefly in utter exhaustion before he looks up at mother, struggling to find words in the fog that's engulfed his mind, "I...I think I might go lay for a bit- *g-go lay down for a bit-* I won't forget the letters, promise maman, b-but I just- if it's okay with you *I-I just need-*"

Etienne loses what he's trying to find and drops his eyes defeated,

✦✦ 153 ✦✦

and *Mothers of the Night,* he can't keep doing this for much longer, can feel that wall of apathy start to crack, claws of something dark curling wicked over the top. *Not yet not yet please anything that's listening not yet,* he begs desperately, leg bouncing in an effort to distract from the way his eyes sting and his nose burns, and small mercy that it is, mother smiles at him soft.

"Of course, shéri , you've had a long night. Go on up to bed an' we can talk some more later." She commands gently, pulls back with an affectionate pat to his head that jars the beginnings of a migraine loose. Getting up is more of a struggle than Etienne tries to make it look like it is, legs and back stiff from the tension of holding still for so long, and he sways embarrassingly a few times.

Mother offers him a hand, but he waves her off, subtly uses the back of the chair to push himself upright instead. He stumbles for a second as black spots crowd his vision, but everyone that knows Etienne knows he's something of a klutz, so that's likely all mother assumes it is when she laughs, briefly touching him on the cheek again.

Her eyes are warm and tender in the morning light, but there's still something shrouded in heavy darkness at the edges, a deep disappointment that Etienne sees, and it closes his throat up with unshed tears.

Let her down you let her down memory of this will taint her view of you forever, that thing peering at him over the wall gleefully cackles, and Etienne sucks in air fast through his teeth, trying to keep it together as mother moves back behind her desk, black beaked skulls of her familiars, Noxhale and Griezzdl, clacking against her hip as she goes.

"I got a mornin' meeting with the city planning committee and then a guest lecture at the academy, but I'll be home after that." Mother says, most of which is directed more at the air than *him,* "Maisette, make sure he doesn't sleep past two if you would. I'll need time to get those letters out before nightfall."

The chandelier in the center of the room swings a bit like a

◆✦◆ 154 ◆✦◆

What Goes Bump In The Night

nodding head, a few of its arms snapping out and up into a quick salute. *Understand understand got it daughter we understand,* the curtains whisper as they ripple back and forth, books rustling along the shelves in soft agreement, and mother's desk chair so graciously pulls itself out for her, attending to her like she's its reigning sovereign.

As far as he's ever seen, mother doesn't struggle with anything, is as poised and confident and sure of herself as a person could be. It's such a far cry from the child she's raised, and Etienne often used to wonder what the problem was, if it was her methods for parenting or something fundamentally wrong with him, but as time's worn on, he's pretty sure he's got his answer and it has nothing to do with her.

Awkwardly reaching down for his bag, Etienne can feel what control he has left slipping and the tears gathering, needs to get out of here before he breaks down, but freezes instantly when mother drawls, "Aren't you forgettin' something?"

Probably, he's kinda a fuckup that way, and Etienne stares at her helplessly, fingers knotting themselves into the strap of his bag. He has no idea what else she could possibly want, *what step he missed what else he failed to do,* and his throat is choking up so fast *eyes watering nose stinging can't do this he can't good for nothing can't do anything right-* and it takes a few rounds of mother looking at him, at his bag, and then the shelves until he gets it.

"O-Oh-!" He stammers wet, shakily flips open the flap of his bag and rears back as the book on Lucretius seals comes rocketing out. It's still covered in soot and ash, violently shakes loose glass from its pages and flips around to snap at him a few times like a disgruntled dog, doesn't waste any more time shooting off to its rightful spot, happily nestling back in amongst the other tomes.

"Well now, suppose I don't have to worry 'bout you *borrowin'* that one again. I think it'd take your hand off if you tried." Mother muses with a bright laugh and that shouldn't be what does it, *but it is,* and Etienne spins fast on his heel as the first tears fall, mutters one last *'sorry'* before hightailing it out of there.

✦✦ 155 ✦✦

He takes the stairs two at a time to the second floor, biting his lip hard to keep quiet while he scrubs at his eyes, feeling so tired and pathetic and *sad and stupid and humiliated and just- every* awful thing you can think of all at once.

Etienne wants to fall face first into his bed and forget this whole week ever existed, *maybe forget he ever existed crawl under a rotting log out in the bogs sleep for a thousand years,* and of course, the *one* time he wants to be alone more than anything, he bumps into his older brother.

"W-Whoa, Eti! *Hey-* where's the *fire,* huh, *golden boy?*" Oliver jokes with a sly grin after they've nearly run into one another, and it's too on the nose, means Oliver *for sure* knows about what happened last night and is intentionally being a jerk about it anyway. Things have been tense between them lately, but this just hits at such a horrible time, and words hitching embarrassingly on the sobs he's trying to muffle, Etienne roughly shoves past him snapping, "O-Oh *shut up, Oliver!*"

He stumbles into his room before Oliver can snipe anything back, doorknob flying out of his hand as he slams the door shut behind him with a percussive rattle.

Etienne stands there breathing heavy for a minute, maybe two, back braced against the trembling wood while he waits, hanging on for dear life as hot tear after hot tear spills over his lash line.

And it's only once he hears the floorboards creak, *once he hears Oliver move off hears the things he mutters darkly under his breath* ~~spoiled brat entitled jackass can't stand him bitch of a brother~~ *pretends like he didn't hear pretends like he dIDN'T PRETENDS LIKE HE-* that Etienne's shaking knees buckle, *that he finally gives up gives in the thing with claws that hates him welcoming him home,* and he sinks to the floor sobbing his eyes out.

Chapter 9

Three weeks creep by with all the unhurried plodding of a five legged swamp walker.

Etienne sleeps about twenty hours collectively that first day, gets pitched out of bed by his mattress halfway through his attempt at hibernation so he'll write those apology letters, and he does it bleary eyed while mostly still asleep. He doesn't think he makes much sense in a single one, but hey, that's unique or whatever, falls back into bed after sloppily signing his last signature and is out within seconds.

But after that, time slows to a grueling crawl.

Being grounded sucks. He can only go where and do what mother tells him to, can't see his friends *can't do as he pleases,* has lost all the freedom he'd won over the years by being a dependable son. It's just temporary, *he knows that,* but it might as well be an eternity, stretches on ahead of him indefinitely like a life sentence, and melodramatic though it may be, he *really* does feel like he's in prison.

If Etienne gets finished with his errands early, then he has to go home immediately, and he spends enough time there as is, so he really, *really* tries to stretch them out. Otherwise he'll get stuck with the worst chores of the household, spends *hours* transcribing notes and doing research for everyone else, a task he used to do for fun every once in a while, but now kills him a little slower every time.

"Dude you're *still in here?* Man you fucked up *bad.*" Abel whistles the next time they're both in the library working on something for Gilbert, and after *days* of dealing with their teenage bullshit, Etienne doesn't bother saying anything, just flips them the bird and gets whacked upside the head by a displeased curtain tie for his troubles.

Thankfully mother left him his notebook, so he can at least still talk with Sabine, scribbles quick messages to him in between flipping through dusty tomes and getting bullied by his younger cousin.

For the most part, Sabine is sympathetic to his situation, but he's not exactly apologetic and it starts to get under Etienne's skin, because the way he sees it, this whole mess is at least *half* his fault.

Etienne isn't trying to shift the blame or anything, knows a ton of it falls on his shoulders *as it should,* but Sabine honestly shouldn't have been goading him on in the first place. There's a line between giving your friend a peptalk and actively encouraging them to do something that'll put their life and the lives of others on the line. Sabine's guilt lies in the fact that he was being an enabler, ignored Etienne's concerns in favor for hyping him up, and no, he wasn't doing it for malicious purposes, but it was still an irresponsible thing to do.

And he just acts like he doesn't care at all.

Sabine

>> *Bonjou Éti! A bunch of us are going to Five n Tin later for Luce's birthday, you coming or what?*

<< *yesh I would love to but I'm still grounded Sabine*

>> *What?*
>> *Still???*

>> *That is some unfortunate luck you have mon ami!*

<< *yeah*
<< *unfortunate luck*

>> *Well you will be missed! I'll give your best to Lucinda, she's been asking about you, you know. So.*

>> *Things to think about* :-

>> *Anyway let me know whenever you're released and we can go celebrate!*

It's a kneejerk reaction when Etienne drops his pen and in a fit of utter frustration, sweeps everything off his desk in one go.

Papers flutter everywhere, notebook thudding loudly as it hits the floor, and he hunches over, fists his hands in his hair while electricity sparks up and down his spine. Ugh- what a, *completely rude inconsiderate boneheaded move,* inviting him out when Sabine should know *full well* Etienne's still grounded, and then to add *insult to injury* by mentioning stupid thrice damned *Lucinda Laferriere-*

Who is a *perfectly* fine witch besides the *massively* obvious crush she has on Etienne, which just makes every one of their interactions super stilted and awkward because Etienne's not interested and he's *never* been interested.

Not in her, not in Jayson Chenevert from the academy, *not in anyone,* and it's really not a big deal, *shouldn't* be a big deal at least. He's always been like this, loves having people in his life that he's close with but doesn't understand the need for a relationship where you kiss and hold hands and want to have sex.

It's completely alien to him, *and Sabine knows this!* They've talked about it over and *over again,* because while Sabine is very understanding and respectful of the fact that Etienne's not interested in a sexual relationship, he seems completely baffled by the fact that Etienne doesn't really care about having any *other* kind of relationship.

"Like- *none at all?* Ki a la moun, how can you not want *anythin'?"* Etienne remembers Sabine asking him bewildered years ago, the two of them laying crossways on his bed studying for finals, and no one had ever *questioned* Etienne before, he didn't know what to do, shrunk down into his shoulders and mumbled, "I just *don't.* It...i-it seems silly to me, I dunno-"

Which then sparked a very impassioned monologue from Sabine acclaiming the virtues of having close interpersonal relationships, stressing the importance of caring about others, and Etienne valiantly tried to defend his position, explained it wasn't disinterest in being close with someone. He *liked* feeling loved by his family and friends, loved loving them in return, but it was more like he didn't get that silly fluttery feeling books and movies loved to portray, didn't understand why he should care about having someone to hold his hand or share his life with.

As far as Etienne was concerned, his life was full enough as is, and he couldn't see what a partner would add to it that he didn't already have.

"I...it just doesn't make sense to me. I don't think I've *ever* felt like that." He stressed, thinking back to the times when he'd been asked to coffee or if he was seeing anyone, remembered being irritated more than flattered, and like the cacophonous first note to a symphony of utter disaster, Sabine had just scoffed, "Don't be dramatic, Eti, you just haven't met the right person yet."

Etienne can't remember everything that came after, but he remembers how it ended, with a small hurricane at the center of Sabine's room, after which he was promptly dumped on his ass outside the LeBlanc estate by their displeased house. It was one of the worst fights they've had to date, although tonight could be bordering on a close second given how pissed off he is, but Etienne violently kicks his notebook under the bed so he won't say something he regrets.

"Stupid stupid *stupid inconsiderate fort en gueule connard-!*" He seethes, waving his hands erratically as he stomps around his room, pent up frustrations sparking maroon cracks of electricity across his skin, "Can't believe he'd-! With Luce *again- ugh!* What a- *w-what an impossibly rude-!* 'Oh you just need to unwind and then you'll find someone, *Etienne-* s-stop being so uptight all the time *Etienne!* Don't you *wanna have a partner Eti-?*' AGH! SHUT UP!"

This goes on for some time until there's a firm, yet cheerful set of knocks against his door that cuts through his tirade. Normally, Etienne would be really embarrassed at getting caught out by someone in the house while he's throwing a temper tantrum, but he's so aggravated and mad, he just doesn't care, rakes a hand through his messy hair as he storms over.

He has every intention of telling whoever it is to *fuck off and leave him alone,* will literally say that verbatim if they can't take a hint otherwise, and then he yanks the door open and sees Katie standing there with a knowing look and her viola.

They play *loud,* saw through every furious heart pumping song they know, bows flying like fire across the strings and drawing out high pitched screaming notes that tear at the air in the most satisfying way. The memory of drums rolls through his mind like the low bass of thunder, fill in the gaps their instruments just can't reach, and Etienne plays hard, coaxes the same skin tingling hair raising riffs from his violin that he's used to hearing from wailing guitars.

Playing with Katie is electric, sets his pulse racing and his magic humming to life, narrows his entire world down to his bow and the way his fingers fly across the strings, and like this, there are no pushy best friends or parents that ground you, there aren't expec-

✦✦ 161 ✦✦

tations for you to be something you're not or punishments you wish you could get out of.

It's just him and his sister and the music they jolt to life, bright sharp snap of the tempo like lightning arcing between the clouds, flares of light branching out into a web of pure energy every time their bows drag across chorusing strings, and its utter magic. It's standing in a packed stadium screaming yourself hoarse with the band on stage, it's flying blind through a storm chasing something that's only revealed in bursts of light, it's taking each other's hand and having your power crack together like two parts of the same whole, a sigil flaring to life beneath your feet larger than you've ever seen.

They play the way lighting falls out of the sky, all destructive power and searing intensity encased in pure elegance, like the kind of majesty that can only be found howling at the eyes of storms or rumbling up from far below, something terrible and beautiful in equal measures.

Just like us just like this thing we are, Etienne thinks, eyes slipping closed as he sinks into the knot of energy at his core, the one that pulls on him with a thousand grasping hands, *not human not pure energy something in between a storm given flesh,* shivers as that feeling rushes over him, spectral fingers sliding over his shoulder his arms *his wrists tangling with his own pulling tugging urging him somewhere,* but he's not scared, *he's never been scared-*

Etienne tears his bow across the strings for the last chord and his violin yowls like something out of the wild, *like peals of laughter peals of thunder one of us one of ours always and forevermore child,* vibrating aftershocks trembling in his fingertips as it falls quiet, only thing breaking the silence their heavy breathing and the quick drumming of rain.

Which, *that's new wasn't raining earlier coincidence or did you-*

Thunder booms lowly overhead and his eyes slide open, catch the next flash of lighting that throws the whole world into sharp relief, and next to him, Katie grins slow and lethal, bow held in her fingers

What Goes Bump In The Night

like a weapon as she huffs, "Look...we made it storm again."

Playing with that much energy is incredible, *sets his pulse flying sends his heart racing makes him feel alive,* but it also leaves Etienne loose limbed and a little sleepy, so, they dim the lights while the storm thunders on past, squish onto the settee in his room. There's plenty of room for them both but they sit close anyway, lean up on one another and watch terrible old black and white horror movies, passing between them a pint of lime sherbet Maisette obligingly brings up along with two spoons.

Etienne contentedly licks sherbet off his spoon watching some guy get eaten alive by black goo on screen, snorts at the over the top screams of terror set to dramatic music, and has already stuck the whole spoon in his mouth when he feels a pointy chin dig into his shoulder, "M'hey. You know you shouldn't feel bad about who you are, yeah?"

He makes a garbled noise of confusion in response, not really sure what she's talking about, and Katie tilts her head back towards the TV, says idly while a cheap looking skeleton flops out of a pile of sludge, "Earlier. You were sayin' stuff about people wanting you to have a partner an' date an' you just sounded so...you *know* you don't have to be somethin' you're not...right?"

"Yeah I know...I...*I know.*" Etienne says softly after pulling the spoon free, keeps his eyes glued on the screen and ignores the way his pulse skips and jumps, starts before cutting himself off almost immediately, "I just-"

"Yeah?" Katie prompts gently, but he can't say it. There aren't many things he's ashamed of about his identity, least of all this, but anxious discomfort flares under his skin anyway.

Because while Etienne may be confident in who he is, the frantic need to not let anyone down is stronger, and it's always felt like he's been letting Sabine down in this way.

If Etienne dated and liked people, a lot of things would smooth over real quickly. He'd get what Sabine and so many others always spoke of, would understand all the shuffling feet and twirling hair

✦✦ 163 ✦✦

and shy looks, maybe he'd appreciate Sabine trying to set him up with Lucinda, maybe it'd ease out some of that tension in their friendship he can't tell if it's actually there or not.

But dating and kissing and the uncomfortable concept of doing anything more...*none of that* is what he wants though, and that's the crazy thing right, how Etienne doesn't want this for himself and yet he daydreams about what it would be like if he could feel butterflies in his stomach, wonders what it'd be like to see a random person and want them closer than family ever got.

Fantasizes about what it feels like to be normal.

Which- Etienne *knows* there's nothing wrong with the way he feels, *knows* it's okay to not be interested and just live his life the way he wants, but there's still this part of him that's so desperate to be what everyone wants him to be, *to be the perfect version of himself,* and it keeps making him feel guilty for not fitting into a box he was never meant for.

It's embarrassing to be so dependent on the approval of others, but for as long as he can remember, Etienne's always been chasing after it, can't bear the thought of not meeting every expectation set before him. Realistically, that's not a goal that can be met, but he tries for it anyway, obsessed with being so flawless, he won't ever disappoint anyone, like a perfectly tuned symphony violin playing in exact harmony with all the other ones around it.

Something that never misses a beat never drops a chord, *never is anything less than perfect,* and he sighs, idly clacking the spoon against his back molars.

"I...it's complicated. Like- I don't feel like I'm missin' out or gettin' left behind or anything, but...b-but at the same time I do." Etienne murmurs, doesn't know why there're times he just can't be proud and own who he is, *where he doubts himself,* because as insane as it sounds, he'll often find himself missing this thing he doesn't even *want,* "I am happy bein' by myself an' I'm happy other people can find happiness together, I just...don't think it's for *me.*"

"And that's perfectly okay. You know maman's the same way, and

What Goes Bump In The Night

so's like half the rest of witches in New Orleans." Katie says, long black acrylic nails scratching up into the back of his hair, and Etienne leans into it, sighing, "I know, which is why it's so...I-I just-I don't know *why* Sabine can't get it, s'not a hard concept, but he pressures me *all the time* an' I just- w-why can't he just-!"

His fingers make frustrated, strangling motions at the air, small jolts of maroon lightning jumping in between their tips before he drops his hands, and still scratching lightly across his scalp, Katie offers sweetly, "Want me to hex'im for'ya?"

It's not like he actually considers the offer, but Etienne lets it hang in the air for a minute, blissfully and *meanly* imaging Sabine with purple stripes or an alligator snout the next time he starts on about finding Etienne a date he doesn't want.

The thought makes him laugh at the very least, which was likely Katie's whole goal, and he drops his head to rest on hers, nosing at coppery curls that're richly perfumed by the scent of candied apples and strangely enough, burnt sugar.

"Hmm, I appreciate the offer but no thanks. I'd just get stuck listenin' to him *whine* about it, an' that's more a punishment for *me*." Etienne mumbles with an eye roll, can feel Katie do the same as she groans, *"Ugh, right?* Sorry- and no offense, but I'd literally go insane spendin' extended periods of time with him. I have no idea how you or Louisette does it."

"Lots of patience and an ability to only listen to every other word." Etienne jokes and Katie laughs bright and sharp, *finger snap of lightning dancing past engine backfiring bare feet rushing down the hall empty jar of spiders in your hands hurry don't let him see,* her magic popping and crackling against his happily as she giggles, "Oh ho ho! *Selective hearin',* I like that ti martre, remind me of it next time I got some old codger yappin' at me he ain't gotta follow protocols."

"Will do." Etienne chuckles, and things grow quiet between them while they watch the rest of their movie, both of them sighing at the inaccuracies of how the filmmakers depicted desiccating swamp oozes, but overall laughing at the general campiness of it, melting lime sherbet quickly disappearing along with the clueless protagonists.

It's at some point around the end that Etienne starts to feel a thread of regret, guiltily watches the scene where the few remaining characters are making their last stand and taps his fingers together in a jumpy staccato while the two best friends defend one another.

"It's...he's not a-a *bad* person." Etienne says quietly, wincing as the ooze gets one to the horror of the other, *grab my hand I can't it'll get you don't give up forget me save yourself run,* "He's pompous an' a bit full of himself b-but he really is a good friend. He's kind, supportive, *loving*...he honestly cares about me a lot, Katie."

A few memories flicker past, *hunched over being so stressed you can't breathe hand on your back on your face just listen to me Eti it'll be okay* and *giggling so hard your sides hurt as you nitpick dancers from across the ballroom floor grinning impish over wine glasses* and *studying side by side working back to back passing things without having to ask one of you can move and the other is already there hand outstretched.*

"Sabine has been there for me, a l-lot of the time when no one else has...he's helped me with- *just,* so *m-much."* Etienne's voice shakes a little even on just that, and he won't ever tell Katie more, but that's the closest he'll ever get to admitting to the fears and doubts and *crippling what ifs* that plague him constantly, "I- I can't imagine not havin' him in my life...I-I don't know where I'd be, *who I'd be,* without him."

And that's the truth. So much of who Etienne understands himself to be was helped defined by Sabine, that wicked sharp sense of humor and the confidence he was taught to wear like a cloak, self-worth he can't find unless someone else is already pointing the way, intense caring he thinks he always would've had but knows is brought forward even stronger by Sabine's own.

That's what so many people miss about Sabine, take him and his cocksureness at face value and completely overlook the compassion

What Goes Bump In The Night

he leaks like a cracked well. Not every LeBlanc is a judicator but every judicator is something of a bleeding heart, and it's there in the way they care so very much about upholding justice and separating right from wrong, returning fairness to those it was taken from.

Sabine is by every definition a civil servant, may not seem like it, but he is, fights with everything he has to protect peoples' rights just like how Etienne and his family fight to protect them from the undead.

Sure the situations are different, but their desire to protect is the same, and Etienne feels that's what's always drawn the two of them together, that shared devotion to serving the greater good.

They make a good team, *a good pair a good partnership,* and no, it's not without its problems, but what relationship isn't. What it boils down to though, the real heart of the matter, is whether or not those problems are something they can work past, and if it's worth it to even try. Etienne thinks it is, has known Sabine practically his whole life, has been allowed past shields and masks and fronts other people probably aren't even aware exist, and knows that at his core, there's a genuinely good person.

It's just hard with him sometimes, *hands snarling in your hair frustration snapping lighting to life never been so angry never felt so betrayed,* but...*standing shoulder to shoulder got your back you got mine never laughed so hard never smiled so much Cheshire grins and shining dark eyes fingers locked together friends forever Eti,* it's worth it.

Sabine will always be worth it.

"He means a lot to me, a-and I *know* I mean a lot to him. I...I don't like the way he acts with me about dating an' junk, but he just- h-he's not...he *thinks* he's helping?" Etienne ends unsurely, is aware of how weak it sounds and feels Katie's wandering nails halt tellingly, tacks on quick before she can lose it, "B-But I'll talk to him about it! It's probably just a misunderstandin' or something- *I mean-* I don't like labels or anythin' s-so he's probably just confused o-or doesn't understand how he's bein' rude or-!"

◆✦◆ 167 ◆✦◆

"Etienne, pou ede Mères de la Nwit, if you make one more exc-"

"I'll *talk to him.*" Etienne stresses and presses his nose into her hair, breathes in deep the smell of spice and sugar and...*burning things?* It's not a bad smell, not like sulfur or brimstone or overflowing cauldrons, but something more homey, like campfires or crackling brush.

Which is *odd* for his sister, but he doesn't get time to question it as she pulls back, fixing him in place with her sharp green eyes, "You better, *an' it better go well.* 'cause if I find out he said whatever kinda nonsense to you again, he'll be right sorry he ever crossed *my* little brother."

"He hasn't *crossed* me, Katie." Etienne says around a small smile, loves her and that fiery protectiveness she radiates that's always kept him warm, but he's an adult now and can stand up for himself on the playground, "Yeah m'little frustrated, but it'll pass, it always does. I don't think there's anythin' he *could* do that'd make me mad forever. Honest."

"Well I'm mad *now. Honest.*" Katie grumps, tips to the side and flops back across the settee in a dramatic sprawling of limbs, declaring, "Who does he think he is? Talkin' to you like that- what does *he* even know, huh? Not like *his cul bèt* has ever had a relationship longer than a few months. Datin' is *stupid anyway!* Romance is overrated! *People are annnooooying!*"

"*Mothers what're you-* you have *literally* been in relationships before-!"

"*Which!* Is how I know they are *dumb,* even if I do enjoy them *immensely.*" Katie kicks her stockinged legs over the side of the settee and bounces to her feet, hands ruffling her bob back into something more *artfully* tousled instead of *manic bedhead.* She pads closer to Etienne and reaches over to push lightly at his forehead, tipping his head back to look *up* at her for a change, a rather odd experience if he's being honest.

Her hand sweeps up through his hair, brushing wayward dark strands out of his eyes before dropping down quick to bap at his

What Goes Bump In The Night

nose, and Etienne scrunches his face up in a smile at her.

Katie's answering smile brings out a dimple in her cheek, corners going mischievous as both her hands drift to either side of his face, a seemingly gentle gesture unless you know her but by the time Etienne realizes what she's about to do, it's too late.

"You are one of the loveliest people I've ever known." Katie murmurs softly, sweetness of her words tempered a bit with the way she squishes his face in between her palms, won't let go no matter how much he whines in protest, "You are so kind and gentle, my most *dear* tallest *littlest* brother, you deserve the *world.* You deserve the moon an' the stars an' the- *did you just LICK me-?"*

"M'no-" Etienne lies muffled, poking his tongue fast back in his mouth before she notices but Katie has eyes like a hawk, catches him out in an instant.

Howling in mock disgust, she finally let's go of his face to ruffle at his hair and they get into something of a slap fight, batting hands at one another that quickly escalates into them lunging for ticklish spots without mercy.

Etienne falls off the settee at some point and then it's just open season, and they end up breathless and stupidly chasing each other around his room, shrieking in delight as they jump over furniture like they're children again. It settles parts of him he didn't know were all bent out of alignment, and for the first time in a week or so, Etienne actually sleeps like the dead that night, drifts off with Katie breathing softly on the other side of the bed.

What more could you ever need than this, he thinks when he wakes up in the morning, feeling very loved and safe and cared for, dreamily watches the bright light streaming in through the windows and breathes in deep. All of them don't share beds that often, but sometimes Katie will crash in his or he in hers after they get back late from a concert, and then Etienne's been woken up a few times by both Abel and Felix wiggling into his bed, sniffling over nightmares Gilbert isn't home to soothe.

It's nice sometimes, sharing a bed with another person, satisfies

✦✧ 169 ✧✦

a tender, personal part of him that craves simple intimacies like that, and Etienne rolls over, smiles a little seeing how Katie has stolen most of the blankets in her sleep, wrapping herself up tight like a burrito with a fluffy shock of orange hair sticking out the top.

He loves her, *so much,* and moving slowly, Etienne brings his legs up, being careful not to shift the mattress too much as he plants his feet somewhere in the small of her back, feels her stretch once as she starts to wake up and doesn't hesitate, shoves her off the bed in a squawking tangle of limbs and pilfered covers.

Katie curses him every name *under the sun,* is batting off flying bars of soap with one hand and using the other to beat him with his own pillow, leaving Etienne sprawled across the bed giggling until he can't breathe.

There's so much happiness and affection pushing at his ribs, it's making golden light pool off his fingertips, each little drop falling away into glittering constellations once it leaves his skin, and that feeling races up his arms, comes to settle warm and tingling under his eyes. It's absolute joy, like long summer nights and the sweet wind blowing back in his face from out over the river, *like starshine,* like full moons and nighttime flights and an entire sparkling city unfurling below the handle of his broomstick.

It's magic it's quicksilver it's maroon lines and a place you're always meant to be, and he laughs loud and unrestrained, knows his markings have got to be glowing brighter than the noonday sun.

Etienne eventually drags Katie down with him, wraps his shimmering hands over her wrists next time she hits him with the pillow, *doesn't have to yank hard never has to try hard with her,* and down she comes. The two of them lay there giggling and tired as Maisette gives up on washing her mouth out for all the cursing, crown moldings creaking unhappily over their heads while the bars of soap dejectedly bob back to the bathroom.

"Y-You're such an *idiot.*" Katie huffs at him, absolute adoration skipping off every word, and the morning is good and warm and

✦✦ 170 ✦✦

What Goes Bump In The Night

kind, their pinkies laced together across his rumpled bed sheets, glow in Etienne's skin fading slow but not the feeling it leaves behind. No, that nestles contentedly under his bones, solid and comforting like a dragon with its hoard, and he smiles broad, feels it stretch his face and crinkle his eyes and can't imagine there's any other kinda love out there that means more than this.

Chapter 10

And things kinda drift into a rhythm Etienne can deal with.

He gets up, he goes on errands for mother and does the assignments he's approved for, spends afternoons with Abel in the family library trying not to fall asleep and most evenings playing violin with Katie, and then in any time he has left over, he ruefully blocks out entire hours of it to meet up with Nica.

He doesn't want to be doing it, but he does it anyway, because there's no arguing that he lost the bet unequivocally, even if it wasn't obvious the Gagnon were suspiciously down an entire cursed dragon skeleton. Etienne is a man of his word to the bitter end though, will hold up his part of the bargain and see this program through, but there are literally so many other things he'd rather be doing with his time than tromping around New Orleans with *Nicalos Caldwell.*

Which happens at a much greater frequency than Etienne was prepared for.

To be perfectly honest, he hadn't really read over what the requirements of this *'diversity program'* were before they made the bet, and since losing said bet, he's had to learn what it is he's *actually* supposed to be doing, and *that's* where Etienne found out the program was a much bigger time commitment than he originally assumed.

Nica was surprisingly patient when they explained it to him that next Monday after the nature center debacle, wasn't mocking or scornful as they walked him through it piece by piece, and Etienne got the impression that they'd done something like this before.

What Goes Bump In The Night

For whatever reason, it just brought more useless questions about them squirming to life in his brain, like, *are they an older sibling or maybe a tutor or work with community centers or were they a camp counselor,* and Etienne always tried to tune the niggling things out, kept having to remind his fatally inquisitive nature that *it didn't matter.*

That he didn't care.

Outside of that though, the general air between them that Monday remained *incredibly* awkward and *incredibly* stilted. Etienne was still beyond embarrassed about what'd happened, knew he'd made a fool of himself and had given Nica all sorts of impressions about his skill level that were only half true.

But small mercy that it was, Nica didn't seem inclined to gloat or rub it in like he expected, was relatively professional the entire duration of the meeting, and Etienne was begrudgingly grateful for it.

"Okay so like- to make our lives easier- *less complicated m-more streamlined-* I um, we should uh, switch numbers- *e-exchange* phone numbers I mean." Nica said while distractedly tapping at their phone, metal thumb clacking against the screen in a way that was super annoying at first but had kinda faded into the background after a while, "It'll be easier to plan stuff a-and keep up with one another? *J-Just for the program I mean!* You don't- *I-I don't-* it's not like I want-"

"I *get it.*" Etienne bit out, was already almost a week into being grounded and had just found out he'd now be spending upwards to *twelve hours a week on this dumb idiot program with this dumb idiot alchemist,* and his patience wasn't what it normally was, "Unfortunately, *I* don't have a *phone* an' I'm assumin' *you* don't have a-"

"H-How do you *NOT have a phone?*" Nica yelped, cutting him off, and eye twitching in irritation, Etienne had to take a few deep breaths before explaining the *very simple basic principle that he thought everyone knew but oh well guess not-* that magic and electronics didn't historically mix well.

✦✦ 173 ✦✦

Which, *apparently,* was the first time Nica had ever heard of it, and it sparked a litany of questions that lead to Etienne reluctantly pulling out his notebook in an attempt to get them to *shut up,* whole thing somehow ending with them at the closest stationary shop buying a charmed notebook for Nica.

"Do not. Touch. *Anythin'.*" He hissed, knew the Laferriere branch member that ran this shop and already didn't wanna think about what they'd be whispering about *Etienne Boudreaux* being seen with an *alchemist.* It was mortifying enough on its own, and Etienne just wanted to get in and get out, not draw any more attention than he already was, but that was apparently *too much to ask for.*

Looking him directly in the eyes with a blank expression, Nica began touching and running their hands over everything they could reach in blatant disregard for what he'd *just* asked them not to do. Etienne swatted a hand at them but they easily sidestepped his attempts to *get them to stop cut it out you're embarrassing me,* and together, they stumbled, accidentally knocking over a wobbly display of quick notes pens that descended on them with the fury of any wrongfully abused stationary.

In the end, Etienne couldn't decide what was worse, being associated with Nica in any capacity or having to stand at the shop counter completely stone faced and pretend like, *clumsy oaf* and *bumbling goon,* weren't written all over his face in a myriad of ink colors.

Nica had eventually decided on a small, dark blue notebook with clusters of pixie dragon scales here and there to mimic constellations, and Etienne sat with them outside the shop as he got his own book out, gilded geometric designs on the black cover glinting in the afternoon sun. Flipping curiously through their blank notebook, Nica seemed to realize it had an enchantment on it so that it'd have an infinite number of pages, and this little grin started tugging their lips up as they kept thumbing through it faster and faster.

"Hey, knock it off, you're gonna confuse it and we're *not* goin' back in there to get you a new one." Etienne huffed and chose to

What Goes Bump In The Night

ignore the overly dramatic eye roll he got in response, held his own notebook out and instructed curtly, "Here. Go to the first couple pages an' put your finger in any empty box, it'll assign your contact for you."

The two of them swapped books without any more preamble, and Etienne flipped to Nica's absolutely blank contact sheet, pressed his thumb to the first empty square and felt the sharp prick as the enchantment drew his blood. It wasn't much, deep red smudge disappearing down into the paper like a vanishing stain, and then in the slow even flicks of his own handwriting, Etienne watched his name scrawl itself in the box.

His penmanship was *flawless* as usual, elegant lines flowing together in graceful cursive swirls, and a second later, his customary dark emerald ribbon came crawling out from between a few pages, marking his spot in Nica's notebook. He picked at it idly, didn't like how this little part of him was now here *forever*.

An odd feeling swirled through his gut at the thought, like this whole thing was something larger than it seemed, *like it was something much more permanent than a simple government assigned program,* and it made him let go quick when he heard Nica's uncertain question, "H-Hey um, i-it's not working? *I think?*"

Etienne rolled his eyes, and perhaps he was still a little miffed over the whole quick notes pen situation, *or maybe he was just worried about how lasting this seemed like the consequences were all sinking in,* but either way, he was *just* irritated enough that it seemed like a good idea to snip as he turned his head, "Are you *serious?* What is complicated about *put finger in box,* for you? Or is it because your hand is outta *blood someho-*"

And then he actually looked over and saw Nica with their metal thumb pressed to the page and every word that was still in his mouth died a gruesome and horrible death.

"You know what...I *think* you *might* be on to something. I think it *is* outta blood." Nica said in a frighteningly even tone, face blank and unimpressed in a way that was alarmingly hard to read, and they held their hand up, *the metal one the one you keep forgetting they have the one that likely wasn't always there oh what have you done,* fingers fanning out in a *what can'ya do* gesture, "Though I *really* have *no idea* why *that could be.*"

Whatever social aptitude Etienne actually had disappeared in the blink of an eye, guilt sweeping through him like a violent tumble of wind, shame crawling hot and fiery up the back of his neck because *what in the fuck is wrong with you can't mind your tongue to save your life Mothers of the Night curse your stupid ass.*

Somewhere, something was screaming at him that he should've known Nica was right handed, that he should've realized they would *still* use their dominant hand unless *instructed otherwise,* and that *he should've been considerate of the fact that said hand was a prosthesis.*

Etienne wanted to crawl into a hole *immediately, wanted to cram the words back in but he couldn't,* and his heart rate skyrocketed as he clawed his fingers around the edges of the notebook in his lap, voice going all shivery and jumping while embarrassed color bled across his face like a stain, "I-I-! I am s-so *sorry!* I didn't- *I wasn't-!* That was entirely inappropriate a-and I sincerely apologize but *I never intended to be insensi-!*"

"*Holy shi-* dude, *d-dude- DUDE!* C-Chill, *it's okay.* M'just fuckin' with'ya." Nica laughed awkwardly, red tinting their cheeks too as they quickly snapped their head away, metal hand wrapping over the back of their neck and digging in harsh, "I uh- *s-sorry,* yeah I- I think stuff like that- *ya'know,* funny amusing *e-entertaining a joke-* but it is uh, *n-not* always. I-I'm weird, *sorry,* so just *yeah...* yeah s-so- so you were, uh- sayin' I need to like- um, just use my *real-* o-other hand?"

It took Etienne a second to parse all that, blinking in confusion trying to make sense of Nica's turned around stream of nervous chatter, but more or less what he got out of it was that A, they weren't angry, *messing with you they're...teasing you just like- wicked sharp grins affectionate insults you're such a klutz mon ami it's okay you're okay,* and B, that they'd asked him a question

What Goes Bump In The Night

he needed to try and answer intelligently.

Which was a tall order considering he was still reeling from the fear he'd just been *massively* insensitive and insulting, but Etienne scraped together what sense remained in his empty skull and did his best, "H-Huh? Oh-! Ah, y-yeah that's not- you're um...you're gonna have to use your o-other hand? I-It uh, it needs blood to work. Sorry I...I should've said that earlier."

"No no! You're okay! It's- *yeah.* Y-Yeah I forget a lot too sometimes and it's like- *on me."* The laugh Nica forced out was doing its best to be light and airy, but it couldn't fool Etienne, he recognized nervous induced levity when he heard it. And he didn't know Nica super well, but he didn't need to to figure out they must also have issues with anxiety, understood it in the way they fidgeted and broke eye contact often and spoke in circles.

It was a rotten thing to deal with, Etienne knew that all too well and hated it more than that, and he decided the kind thing to do would be to cut both of them some slack, made an agreeing noise in the back of his throat but otherwise, let the conversation go.

Unlatching their hand, Nica's arm slowly dropped from their neck and they didn't say anything else, but they did glance at him real quick for a moment. There was something sorta appreciative in their eyes, or maybe it was a thing closer to relief, *honestly didn't matter either way it was something that wasn't hostile that wasn't warry,* and then those mismatched irises were darting back down to look at the contact sheet just as fast.

Nica only hesitated briefly before reaching out with their left hand, hissing softly through their teeth as the enchantment bit into the flesh of their thumb. *Oops probably should've warned them oh well too late now,* Etienne thought with a wince, felt a little bad watching the way they jerked their hand away reflexively and shook it out, their nose scrunching up while they inspected the pad of their thumb.

They clucked their tongue once they saw the small prick against their skin, fingers rubbing against one another like they were try-

❖✦ 177 ❖✦

ing to soothe an ache much worse than a simple finger prick, gaze dropping back to the notebook in their lap and then strangely, their entire body locked up. Etienne blinked in confusion, saw how tense their shoulders got, metal fingers tightening into a squealing fist and flesh ones halting in their fiddling, and his eyes jumped curiously back up to their face.

Half of Nica's hair was pulled back today, held in place by a colorful scrunchie and it left their profile unprotected, meant Etienne saw the way their eyebrows knit together sharply, horrible discomfort on their face as they watched their name spell itself out in the little box.

It was an odd reaction, *so much about Nica was odd he was coming to find,* and Etienne couldn't help himself, was fatally inquisitive by nature. He leaned over ever so slightly, just so he could read the chicken scratch Nica called handwriting, and it took a second to understand what he was looking at, in part because *Mothers how do they even read this what a mess* and also because he didn't recognize the name.

Etienne blinked, eyes tracing over the shape again and again, sure he was just reading it wrong, but nope, that was a first name completely different than the one he knew them as, and it took a second of *what's the big deal so they have a nickname,* before it clicked and then it wasn't such an odd reaction anymore.

Oh...oh not a nickname but a dead one, he remembered thinking and a few things fell into place as Nica sighed in something like expected defeat, *like they were used to it used to reading this thing they weren't anymore,* went to reluctantly pass the notebook back but Etienne stopped them with a firm hand.

Nica glanced over at him unsure, deeply vulnerable look in their eyes and he may not like them, thought they were rude and bullheaded and annoying as anything, but everyone deserved the simple decency of being called by the name they wanted.

"You can change it." Etienne murmured, gently forcing his notebook back into their lap but didn't reach for their left wrist to drag

What Goes Bump In The Night

their hand into place, knew that was too intimate a gesture for two people who could barely stand one another, "Just touch it again an' picture what you wanna change it to."

Hardly looking like they were breathing, Nica brushed trembling fingers over what they weren't and in a few quick swipes, it was gone, and they relaxed a fraction, but Etienne didn't think they started breathing again until *Nicalos* was scribbling itself across the paper. They let out a shaky exhale once it was done, closed the oil black cover slowly and their flesh fingertips lingered on the slick surface, running along the grooves of filigree with a delicate sort of consideration.

Nica opened their mouth briefly like they were gonna say something, but clicked it shut not a second later, simply passed the notebook back in a trembling hand without saying *thank you,* and Etienne took it without saying *you're welcome.* Their eyes met on accident as they traded off the book, and for such a small moment, it still felt like it meant something more, because even though neither had said a word, it was like they'd both heard and understood one another anyway.

They weren't suddenly the best of friends or even friends in general after that, but there's less hostile tension in the air as they sit across from each other in that sticky gross coffee shop on Monday afternoons, filling out assignment logs and discussing their upcoming schedules. Now that he's grounded indefinitely, Etienne's is easier to work with, so they mostly just dodge around everything Nica does, carve out enough time to meet the program requirements.

Which, *like mentioned previously,* is a *lot* more than Etienne was initially expecting.

Besides their assigned Mondays, they also have to meet at least *two other times* a week to shadow the other on an assignment, *one for him one for them,* which takes them all over the city and only prolongs the amount of time they're stuck together.

It's...not the most enjoyable experience, and not just because

Etienne is assigned to nothing but low level apprentice work and looks like a fool, *if he has to chase down one more rodent adjacent terror-* but it's mostly awful because the more time they spend together, the less he can argue that him and Nica aren't entirely... *dissimilar.*

A-As people! *Not casters!*

Because as people, they are *both* dedicated and driven and obsessed with performing flawlessly, traits Etienne has no other choice than to begrudgingly respect, but as *casters-* and Nica is *not* a caster Etienne just can't think of a *better word* -but as casters they're still wildly different. Comparing their abilities remains hardly fair, *and yes,* the power the two of them draw on *happens* to be similar in a weird trick of fate, *storm clouds and sizzling ozone and all your hairs standing on end,* but how they access it is worlds apart.

Etienne relies on the gift he was given and the door that was opened for him, funnels up torrents of energy from the seething ocean of it that churns beneath reality, and then Nica uses math and chemistry and the small current of electricity their body produces, rends into being whatever they've calculated for.

It's different, *they're different,* but at the same time it's eerily the same, touch of sparking electricity that sings to Etienne like a siren's song from the very depths of his consciousness and he hates it, hates the shivers that run down his spine whenever Nica completes an array, like the brush of fingers he thinks he knows but doesn't.

I know you think we know you, whispers through his mind, spectral hands curling over his shoulders and reaching out towards Nica curious, *do we know you not sure I do thought we did,* and Etienne can't think straight whenever his magic wraps inquisitively around Nica's electrical current, lost entirely in the alien yet abstractly familiar sensation that rushes through him, *not the same but close enough not us but not entirely not who are you.*

Nica catches him staring a lot but thankfully never asks, just cocks an eyebrow and Etienne will whip away embarrassed, can't

What Goes Bump In The Night

figure out *why* his magic is so fatally intrigued by whatever the hell Nica's doing.

A lot of how it's reacting is outside of his control, because while it is in parts just a source of power Etienne manipulates, it's at the same time something of its own entity, and often acts without his conscious decision.

And by the *Mothers*, is it ever fixated on Nicalos Caldwell, keeps poking and prodding at the energy Nica whips into being, has grown more incessant the longer it goes without getting a response and Etienne's pretty sure that's the problem. If Nica could just reach out, *reach back touch at it let it touch them*, it'd drop this fixation immediately, and it is the most *disheartening* thing to realize that's *never* going to happen because Nica *can't do that*.

Whereas Etienne's magic is a semi-sentient collection of impressions from everyone that's ever carried it before, Nica just has themself and the power they generate on their own, and it's not the same, lacks all the depth of legacy magic. Alchemists are skilled at matter manipulation, he can't discount that, can rearrange atoms and pull complicated elements from thin air, but the energy they bend to their will doesn't think and live and *breathe* the way magic does.

That's what's always set witches apart from the rest of humanity, how the power they wield is so much more than a blunt instrument or a clever tool, but is rather almost an entity all on its own, one that feels and moves along with them. A witch's magic is interwoven into practically every fiber of their being, so much a part of them, most can't distinguish where they end and *it* begins, and for Etienne personally, he doesn't really see a point in making that distinction.

He is his magic and his magic is him, they work in tandem like any other part of his body and mind, a perfectly orchestrated symphony that's been playing ever since the day he was born.

Etienne doesn't just think of his magic like a source of power, it's also how he understands and interacts with the world around him, and used to be, that's how he'd distinguish one of them from the rest of *everyone else,* but now with the advent of alchemy, the waters have apparently become somewhat...*muddied.*

Witches often greet one another by brushing magical signatures together, come to know and recognize each other through this connection, and for whatever reason, he thinks his magic is confusing *Nica* for another witch.

It sounds absolutely ludicrous, but Etienne can't come up with any other logical reason for why his magic keeps attempting to connect with Nica, like it's desperately trying to place this source of power it otherwise has no context for.

More than anything, Etienne wishes it'd give up, is so tired of hives breaking out across his skin and shivers running down his back anytime Nica claps their hands together, has to fight the instinctive urge to turn in their direction, this core part of him hopelessly reaching out to something that stonewalls it every time, leaves such a horribly empty feeling in the pit of his heart.

Etienne doesn't know if it's an isolated phenomenon he's experiencing because of his house, the close connection he has to electricity and raw energy making some wires cross, or if it's something other witches have noticed.

Nothing like this has ever happened before in recorded history though, so there's no texts for him to read, and then Etienne can't *ask* anyone else because in case he's wrong, and this *is* just a him thing, he doesn't want anyone to know how embarrassingly fixated his magic is on this one random alchemist.

And it becomes increasingly obvious over the span of a few weeks *how* focused it is, and it's *got to be* some combination of the fatally curious nature of magic and then how much time they're forced to spend together, but Etienne realizes he's started learning all sorts of things about Nica he's not intentionally trying to.

For starters, Nica actually talks a lot less than he initially assumed, and unless they're actively discussing something for the program, their meetings tend to be relatively silent. Etienne truthfully doesn't

What Goes Bump In The Night

mind, prefers silence over meaningless small talk any day, but what really begins to drive him up a wall is how much Nica starts to fidget about an hour or so into their meetings.

He eventually picks a pattern out to it, notices they're more still if the café is quiet and relatively empty, and that it's worse if it gets crowded, leg jiggling like crazy while they clack their nails against the plastic ear covers of their headphones.

A few times Etienne's seen them act like they're gonna slip the things on, but they always stop for some reason, and he usually just puts it out of his mind, figures they have their reasons and the two of them aren't even friends anyway, so it's really not his problem.

But then one day the café is *absolutely* packed, is way too loud and noisy even for *him*, but Nica looks about two seconds away from losing it, has reached for their headphones on four separate occasions and has stopped every single time, and the *only reason* Etienne says anything is because they are *literally* shaking the table with how hard they're bouncing their leg and it's either that or he electrocutes them both.

"Will you just- *put those damn things on already.*" Etienne grinds out, gestures emphatically to the bronze headphones slung around Nica's neck when they look up confused, and flesh hand flying up to wrap above one earpiece, they stammer, "I- wha-? You- *I,* but I-I-I know that's not- *it's-* uh- i-ill tempered? B-Bad mannered! It's *rude,* I-I'm trying to say *it's rude I-*"

"You could literally call me every slur you can think of an' I wouldn't care so long as you. *Calm. Down.*" Etienne stresses, doesn't force eye contact again after Nica breaks it, has learned by now that's another thing that sends them crawling out of their skin, "Look. I'm almost done with my part, so just put the damn things on until then. If I need your attention, I'll get it."

Nica hesitates, and the *why* is absolutely beyond Etienne, but they keep stealing glances at him like they're expecting him to take it back, *to change his mind to tell them not to.* He doesn't though, *he's not going to why would he when they're clearly miserable,* and once

✦✦ 183 ✦✦

Nica seems to realize this, they cautiously slip their headphones on.

The difference is immediate.

They relax so fast, broad shoulders dropping as they tap away at their phone, sinking a bit further down in their chair and Etienne unwinds as well, goes back to writing while Nica starts to hum a little, head bobbing back and forth.

After that, the headphones are a much more regular thing. Nica will slide them on if things get too much and it does wonders for the both of them, mostly in the sense that Etienne is saved his blood pressure spiking and Nica looks less like they wanna crawl into a dirt hole under the earth. Sometimes though, they'll start swinging their foot wildly under the table in time to the music, accidentally knock into Etienne's leg every now and again, and he never says anything because the alternative of them taking their headphones off is so much worse.

Besides, he's used to it as a chronic sufferer of someone with long legs and nowhere to put them, tunes out those little *nudge nudge tap nudges* easily enough, fills out his paperwork and listens idly to soft humming and forgets how he's getting lightly kicked in the shin every few minutes.

The two of them meet up every Monday, but it's hardly ever at the same time, which, luckily or not, the café keeps long hours for the students that frequent it, so they at least have somewhere to go, but that's the other thing Etienne learns pretty fast.

Nica is always busy.

Like, *obnoxiously busy,* is either running late to their meetings because lab ran over or is in danger of missing a study session because the assignment they're on is taking longer than expected. Their class schedule is absolutely maxed out, has them juggling regular classwork with lab reports and then whatever program nonsense they get up to with Etienne, and that's not even covering what they do *outside* of schoolwork.

On the *short* list of things Etienne knows, there's the tutoring

What Goes Bump In The Night

for chemistry and math Nica does for other undergrads, something the school pays them for but honestly doesn't seem worth the trouble, and of course you can't forget the various clubs with alphabet soup acronyms they're involved with and are always running late to, and then, somehow, *in between all of this,* Nica finds time to go to the gym pretty regularly for boxing.

The perpetual dark circles under their eyes suddenly make a lot more sense, and Etienne asked them once why didn't they just do less as they were frantically shoving their laptop back into their bag, late *again* for something else, and Nica had simply stared at him like they didn't understand the question.

And that's another thing, Nica can never seem to be on time to anything, will come shooting up from the table and bang their knees against the underside once they remember they have somewhere else to be, and Etienne stops yelling at them for it about the same time he understands that's not a fight he's going to win.

Colorful sticky notes spill out of pockets in their backpack, litter study guides and day planners, their phone goes off like a chiming clock every other hour, peppered with reminders and things they're trying to remember, and yet most of it seems to come as a surprise to Nica anyway. Etienne doesn't ask because he knows it's not his business, but he's pretty certain whatever's going on goes past an intensely absent mind or wandering thoughts, and that's when he stops fussing at them, knows there's just some things out of everyone's control.

Also it's really not that big a deal to write them the night before the two of them are supposed to meet up, confirming where and when and *that Nica'll be there don't forget again or I'll fry your headphones mark my words,* and it's rare, but sometimes Etienne will scribble a reminder across one of their garishly colored sticky notes as a backup, slap it into their day planner amidst a sea of others, his elegant cursive standing out so starkly against Nica's messy script.

And somehow, they're making it work, and no, it's not really what either one of them *wants* to be doing, but it's...less miserable

✦✦ 185 ✦✦

than Etienne was originally thinking it'd be, *but only marginally.*

There are some things about Nica that Etienne is totally fine with. Like their fierce dedication to school and overall begrudgingly impressive intelligence, *their soft absentminded humming,* but there are many of their character traits he becomes acquainted with over their weeks together and subsequentially comes to hate a great deal, feels like he's gonna tear his hair out if he has to spend one more second in their general vicinity.

Nica is so stubborn, won't bend or backdown and has a tendency to argue over anything they even remotely disagree with, and even though they're not super talkative, when they do speak, it's always *way too loud* and *impossible to ignore.*

Entire hours are lost to the two of them stalemated in the most *pointless* arguments over completely *inconsequential* stuff. Etienne prefers to take the trollies but Nica insists the bus is faster, they can't agree which part of the sidewalk to walk down and end up getting separated frequently, Nica is prepared to die on the hill that the beignets at Café Du Monde are the best in the city when *anyone* with a *single braincell* to their name knows it's Loretta's.

Specifically their crab stuffed ones.

Obviously.

The argument *that* one sparks though is absolutely bizarre for multiple reasons, *who argues about fried bread in the first place for the love of-* but what really throws Etienne for a loop is when Nica rounds on him snapping, "Oh *shut up!* You don't like sweets anyway so your opinion is biased an' *therefore less impactful-!"*

"Mères de la Nwit! That is *not* how *points of debate work you niais an'-!* I- wait...w-wait how do you know I don't like *sweets?"* Etienne stammers perplexed, is pretty sure he's never mentioned it because *why* would he be making small talk with *Nica,* but they just snort, roll their eyes like it's obvious, "Oh *please.* All you ever order is that bitter ass minty green tea and you never ask for sugar. S'not exactly rocket since, bud."

What Goes Bump In The Night

Insulted at the dig to his tea preference, Etienne already has a counter argument ready, *well that's because everything else at that overly commercialized shop is actual trash,* but then he registers what Nica's saying, *realizes what it means,* and his mouth clicks shut. Nica...knows his tea preference. Nica knows he doesn't like sweets, *Nica's been paying attention to him,* and Etienne is struck dumb wondering what else Nica knows about him.

Do you think they know how obsessive you are with your stuff, he self-consciously scoots the bag sitting between his feet under the table a little closer, always needs to know *exactly* where it is at all times, *do you think they know what kinda music you like,* and Etienne doesn't wear band shirts out of the house, but the few pins he has on his bag are all sharp letters and cracked skulls and pointy lightning bolts, *do you think they know what a mess you are,* dry swallow against a constricting throat, *everything you're trying to keep hidden do you think they know can they see it what a wreck your mind can be do they know dO THEY-*

That's the only one that really scares him, the fear that Nica somehow *knows,* that they've seen through the front he wears like armor, and it terrifies Etienne near to death because no one can *ever* know all of the doubts and anxieties that eat him away on the inside. He's a *scion,* he's not supposed to be questioning whether or not he's fit for the role.

He was *born to be this, he has to be this,* and Etienne starts trying to mind how he acts around Nica after the beignet debate, doesn't want to let anything slip and show that he's not in perfect control.

And because it's *Etienne,* king of fuckups and overthinking, he slips up anyway.

They're out one night around dinner and he's *this close* to catching the raccoon terror he's been trying to get for the last *two nights.* Which is *beyond embarrassing,* but the thing is smarter than he gave it credit for despite not having a brain anymore but *he's so close just needs to snap the banishment sigil down and he'll have the little shit-* and that's when Nica's phone alarm goes off.

✦✦ 187 ✦✦

Etienne lunges for the skeleton on instinct, but it howls like the damned and has clawed its way up a drainpipe before he even gets close, and since the universe hates him, Etienne falls in a clanging mess against all the trashcans it was rummaging through. He hauls himself up spitting vile swears, smacking loose bits of detritus from his clothes and reeking worse than the bogs, rounds on Nica with lighting jumping between his fingers and a *whole lot to say to them about them and their damn phone,* and then settles back on his heels once he sees what they have in their hands.

"Sorry..." Nica murmurs sheepishly after swallowing, tucking the rattling orange bottle of pills and a sticker covered water bottle back in their backpack, "I know- b-bad timing but I forgot how close- t-the time, and I uh- I-I really can't miss those so...*sorry.*"

"It's...*fine.*" Etienne huffs out, maroon particles shooting from his mouth on his next exhale, and he's still annoyed Nica made him lose that squirmy little *rat bastard terror,* but he's trying not to be because it doesn't feel justified anymore. He remembers that, keeping up with the time and tiny glass bottles, the fear that came from missing a round and the self-induced panic attack that always followed, doesn't want to make them feel bad for something out of their control.

And given how guilty Nica looks at him as he walks back over, they *do* truly feel bad about forgetting their alarm, so with a sigh, Etienne rights his hat and slips a suspender that'd fallen off his shoulder back into place, says without thinking, "Don't worry 'bout it, stuff like this happens an' I've been there before so...*I get it.*"

"O-Oh!" Nica breathes, seems surprised, and Etienne hadn't really meant to say that, *doesn't know why he said that,* but it's too late to take it back and he just valiantly hopes Nica will drop it, will read his body language and see how fast he whips his head away *and will take a hint,* and it is an actual nightmare when he hears Nica ask all peppy and interested instead, like it's something *normal to ask,* "What were you on meds for?"

Electricity crackles up his spine instantly, jolt of it fluffing his hair as his shoulders go back, color rising to his cheeks because this isn't something he normally talks about with *anyone* besides mother, and even then he avoids the topic completely unless he *can't.*

It's his embarrassment to keep buried, *his responsibility,* and Etienne is ashamed beyond belief anytime it comes up, knows he's supposed to have all this control over his emotions and yet has none.

What a disgrace you are, something from the recesses in his mind hisses, *can't even control yourself how are you supposed to be a leader how do you expect to govern anything,* pulse fluttering like a caged bird *like a guttering flame, disappointment that's all you are a second rate no good failure they see it they all can see it and now even that idiot alchemist knows,* and his heart stops and he panics and electricity sparks painfully against his palms as he whirls on Nica.

"That- is really *none* of your *business, drigay."* Etienne snaps archly, chin up shoulders back, *ignore the way his hands shake pretend you don't hear the way his heart stumbles act like you see someone else,* and he storms past Nica without a second look back. They scramble after his bootheels, stammering an apology or something that Etienne doesn't really care to listen to, and when he won't respond, when he won't wait up, *when he won't look at them,* Nica's voice starts to peter off until it's not there at all.

They spend the rest of their required time in a tense silence.

Later, after the moon has risen and Nica's gone home for the night, Etienne actually ends up catching that raccoon terror and a few others, finds them eating someone else's garbage and cracks a banishment sigil into being under their boney paws faster than they can move.

They flap their loose jaws open at him, shriek and claw at the sparking walls of the sigil like that's going to do anything, but it'd take more than they're capable of doing to disrupt it. Terrors like this are hardly worth the time for anyone above the age of fifteen, so it's the easiest thing in the world to supersede his will over their own, tearing their souls from the mortal plane once more with a violent jerk of his hand.

Etienne rends them out of existence so forcefully, their disembodied bones clack to the ground covered in electrical burn marks, and he sighs seeing it, has to stop and breathe for a minute to try and calm down.

Once he takes that precious second to clear his head though, *to lose his frustrations to recenter his mind,* he can admit that how he reacted earlier might have...*been a touch too harsh.*

He knows he has a bad habit of letting inconsequential things affect him more than they should, *takes too much too deeply to heart,* and while he'll maintain that Nica shouldn't have asked something so prying, *so personal,* he also gets that they really didn't mean anything by it. Annoyingly, Etienne knows them well enough at this point to understand that it was simply honest curiosity that made them ask, and not anything based in malicious intent, Nica's desire to *know* overriding whatever social graces they *actually* have.

By nature, they like to pick things apart, *they're a scientist after all,* kinda look at the world like it's one big puzzle to solve, whereas Etienne is something closer to a politician, *looks underneath every word and reads in between every line,* never taking anything at face value. His tendency to do that is both a necessity and a curse, and he often has to remind himself that sometimes, people really just-*say what they mean,* a truly baffling concept he's not sure he's ever gonna be able to wrap his head around completely.

So Nica asking him about medication like they did...*while impolite,* was not a hidden attempt at undermining him, nor an attack on his hopefully not too obvious insecurities. It was just a stupid, *honest* inquiry that popped out of their mouth because they're curious to a fault and apparently, don't *think* about asking graceless questions they really shouldn't.

Still, how deep their comment struck into him, like marrow burrowers out in the bogs looking for his spinal column, *diving right for the most vulnerable part of him,* gives Etienne pause, scuffed toe of his boot nudging idly at lifeless bones.

What Goes Bump In The Night

Never before has such a genially innocuous question from a stranger driven such a reaction from him, and usually, he's better at keeping his temper under control, *can smile fake like mother be politely scathing like Atha turn the barb back on whoever threw it,* but for whatever reason, Nica's comment just hit him hard and left him reeling. There are seldom few things that can do that to him, *bold faced bigotry slurs casually slung at his face snide questions about his family,* and honestly, Etienne is a little surprised with how negatively his emotions flared up, like he'd been dealt some sort of grievous insult rather than asked a tactless question.

"What's wrong with you...why do you even *care?*" Etienne murmurs to the charred bone he's rolling under the sole of his boot, struggling to understand himself and the way his heart seemed to drop when Nica asked earlier, like he was *worried* about them thinking less of him than they probably already did.

And he generally hates the idea of anybody looking down on him, *seeing him as something lesser,* but as much as it stings, it shouldn't matter in Nica's case because Etienne's already made himself out to be an utter fool in their eyes.

Mothers what they must think of you after everything, Etienne grimaces, working his jaw back and forth while he presses down on the bone, *at best you're an incompetent goon and at worst a useless coddled child,* and hot shame flares across his face considering which option is better, *it's neither,* and he tries in vain to remind himself *he doesn't care what Nica thinks of him.*

Or he shouldn't at least, but the longer he spends rolling that tiny femur bone under his boot, its quiet clacking against the cobblestones parroting back the same metronomic question he just asked it, *why do you care why do you care I think you know,* the more he understands that the embarrassment nervously squiggling around his chest isn't tied to whatever impression he holds about himself, but rather the very real, likely *very negative* impression *Nica* holds of *him.*

And the second he puts it together, the *second* he realizes he wants Nica to think highly of him, *just like he does with mother with*

✦✦ 191 ✦✦

the other scions like with his community, the bone shatters under his heel into a thousand razor sharp splinters.

At this point, Etienne has gotten pretty good at cramming unwanted thoughts in little boxes and kicking them under the bed, does so now as he robotically salts and finishes burning the raccoon bones, leaving nothing but a small pile of ash and some soot black marks across the pavers, *trying to leave his thoughts with them.*

Which-

Whatever.

The neighbors will probably complain about the mess, but Etienne's worn out and frustrated enough *having something of an internal crisis* and he just doesn't care. Let them complain, *he doesn't give a shit.* What's mother gonna do?

Ground him harder?

He catches the late night trolley home and tiredly says hi to Francoise, chats lacklusterly with him until some more vampires get on and gladly takes the chance to excuse himself from that nowhere conversation. Etienne pulls his notebook out to try and distract his thoughts while the three of them fall into speaking the rapid, sibilant words of ancient Gaulish, chews on his lip as he flips through the pages looking for that familiar teal ribbon, *for some stability.*

It's not too late that Sabine shouldn't still be up, and *Mothers of the Night,* has Etienne ever missed him while being grounded, but he stops short before getting to Sabine's section, distracted by the soft glowing coming from the newest ribbon in his book. It's a dark gold color, *like ripe wheat like early evening sun sharp bright smell of ozone hair falling out from behind an ear little gap in their teeth I win hotshot sends your blood boiling every time what do you think of me could you ever think me great I wish you would,* and he thumbs to that part with narrowing eyes and a hiccupping heart.

What Goes Bump In The Night

Nicolas Caldwell

> hey I ~~just~~ just wanted to apologize again for what I ~~asked~~ asked earlier

> it was really out of line and im sorry if I made you ~~uncomfortable~~ uncomfortable or anything

> I say stuff alot without really thinking about it and

> I dont know

> I shouldnt have said it. thats your personal buisness and I was way out of line for prying

> prying?? not prying. Lol sorry I cant spell worth shit

Mothers of the Night...this...really is the *worst* handwriting he has *ever* seen in his whole *life,* and Etienne squints, has to bring the book closer to his face to try and read parts of Nica's writing.

It's like the bastard lovechild between cursive and script, some letters looping back around for no reason and conjoined in the weirdest ways, but he gets the hang of it after a beat.

Etienne's eyes flick over the messy scrawl, snorts at the misspellings and crossed out words, the lack of punctuation, how some parts look like they were written out fast, *more errors sloppier lines rushing nervous oh God what did you do,* and then there's bits that're neater, *slowing down calming down sorry I'm real sorry,* little doodles peppered here and there Nica likely didn't intend to send, ones that came in between the text blocks, chaotic flowers and structured chemical compounds and eyes, just-

So many disembodied eyes.

The whole thing is very honest, *very genuine,* and it's not like

Etienne thinks the apology they were trying to give him earlier was a lie, but he was ~~nervous embarrassed ashamed~~ *mad* at the time, and now he's...tired maybe? Just that little bit sleepy that makes the whole world seem softer and more unreal, and maybe he's less inclined to be harsh when he's like this, ~~or maybe he's just getting less inclined to hate them Mothers don't even think that why not,~~ but it means he's reading Nica's messages with something like rueful fondness pushing up against his bones.

Etienne's fingertips wander over dark ink eyes unthinkingly, brushing at smooth parchment, and he traces a pointer finger along the sharp snapping lines of some chemical structure he doesn't know the name for, *wonders what it is what it means ~~if Nica would teach you,~~* jerks his hand back like he's been burned and hastily slips his own pen free, begins writing.

<u>Nicolas Caldwell</u>

<< *I accept your apology.*

<< *I'm a relatively private person, and I'd appreciate if you refrained from asking me those kind of questions in the future.*

<< *They're very prying and make me uncomfortable because—*

Because we're strangers because I don't know you, are both things Etienne almost writes and then stops, pen nib quivering in midair while he stalls with lies he can't call truths anymore, blinks hard and realizes *they're not true anymore, blinks harder and realizes they're gonna be lies from here on out can't go back can only go forwards took their hand called it a deal took their hand and said fairs fair ~~already reached back twice what if there's a third time what else would you take their hand for~~*

◆✦◆ 194 ◆✦◆

Nicolas Caldwell

>> hey!

>> yeah no totally like I said Im reel sorry

>> and you dont need to explain I get it no worries

>> thats all on me anyway

>> wont happen again promise

<< *Right. Okay. Good then*

Etienne rolls his pen back and forth between his fingers, still a little disarmed with how quick Nica is to admit to their faults, *like they're not ashamed or anything like they have nothing to hide,* and he wonders if he could do that, very nearly brings pen to paper to admit his own, to apologize for the way he snapped, ~~for the thoughts circling in his mind hey do you think you could ever see me as something good as something great do you think we'll always kinda sorta hate each other or do you think we could ever be fri-~~

But before he can lay down a single stroke, *bring to life all these true untruths* ~~voice something that scares him with how much his heart jumps in excitement,~~ he's interrupted by a whole slew of messages that pop up one right after the other almost like divine intervention.

Nicolas Caldwell

>> so maybe awkward time to but we still good for our thing thursday?

>> MY thing!

>> well I mean not my thing but like

>> the thing we said we were going to do thrsday for the program thats the thing I ma talking about

>> construction site

<< I'm still available if that's what you mean.

<< Just let me know what time, and the address, and I'll meet you there.

There, *conscience professional...devoid of any feeling or warmth,* clean crisp lines that are elegant and perfect and what he's supposed to say, but something twists up uncomfortable under Etienne's breastbone *because that's not what he meant,* and his pen finds its way back to blank hollow lines, ink spilling out unrefined and saying things he's not really thinking about.

<< And I'm sorry too

<< For snapping at you. That wasn't very kind of me and I'm sorry

<< I suppose I need to work better on that

>> I

>> thank you for apollogizing I really mean it

>> I did kinda deserve to get told off, Im not great with

What Goes Bump In The Night

> knowing social boundaries and sometimes it helps when I get told explicitly what they are
>
> ⁊⁊ but yeah if you could maybe say it a lil uh, softer next time? Id appreciate it
>
> ⁊⁊ oh and I do forgive you btw so dw

B T W, Etienne mouths confused, has no idea what that typo could even *be*, *'but'* maybe? *'but so...do?'*... he honestly has no idea, shakes his head in fond amusement, lips quirking up in a little half smile as he makes sure to write *extra* clear and *extra* neat, like Nica's own handwriting might be cowed somehow into actually achieving legibility if his is extra nice.

> ≪ *Thank you, and I'll keep that in mind.*
>
> ≪ *Which, speaking of keeping things in mind, don't forget to send me that address before Thursday. I'm not spending the whole day hunting you down across New Orleans, lost bets be damned.*
>
> ⁊⁊ lol fair enough
>
> ⁊⁊ but yeah ill need to find that tomorow it is late and I think I have a test tomorrow but yeah ill
>
> ⁊⁊ ill see you then

There's enough of a pause Etienne assumes that's the end of the conversation, goes to slip the cap back on the end of his pen and close his notebook when a new line of ink bleeds across the creamy paper. *Night Etienne,* it reads, and he stops, stares at those two little words as orange light sweeps in waves over the page.

It's like the ebbing flow of the tide, like the soft breathing of a low fire, something so oddly and deeply personal about seeing his name spelled out in someone else's hand like that.

He does close his notebook then, knows it's rude not to respond but he just- *can't.* Something sour and prickly is snaking around in his gut, coiling up his throat and down through his fingers, hurts and burns almost the same way anxiety does when it gets out of control, but this makes him less sick in a way.

It's not entirely painful, but it's not entirely pleasant either, kinda ticklish actually, like insects crawling over the lining of his stomach and it sends his pulse jumping weird in the staccato beat of falling rain. Whatever it is, Etienne doesn't like it, hugs his notebook to his chest as he slides down the bench seat, old wood creaking under him in protest, watches all the little ribbons sticking out from the pages like they're going to bite him, but none of them light up again.

And he doesn't understand it, but Etienne finds it's easier to breathe after that.

Chapter 11

Thursday, for all intents and purposes, seems like it's going to be a good day.

It's the beginning of October and the temperature is finally cooling down in the most vague of ways like usual, means Etienne isn't constantly rolling his shirt sleeves up while he's out running errands downtown. There's a nice breeze blowing back in off the Mississippi, and he pauses along the waterfront, hangs his hands over the metal railing and grins as the cool wind ruffles through his bangs, golden chains hanging from his hat clinking together softly.

Fall is generally a little drier, which isn't saying much down here, but the sky is impossibly blue today, thin wispy clouds stretched far overhead and Etienne grins up at them. Those have always been his favorite type, loves the way they look like rising steam or thin swipes of paint, and he just takes a second to stay and watch them blow past, enjoying this small moment of existence he's found.

Honestly, the wonderful weather is just gilding the edges of what Etienne's already considering to be a pretty fantastic afternoon.

Thursdays are normally when he swings by Madame Élise's for a candle making lesson, and today's had actually gone relatively well for once. He didn't get hot wax all over himself for starters, and in the end, managed to make something that didn't look like an absolute mess for the first time since she started giving him lessons.

His designs were still nowhere near as elegant and clean as hers, *watching enraptured over her shoulder as the quick flick of her wrist creates looping coils and delicate flowers and graceful arches exposing layers and layers of beautiful colors Mothers how does she do it,* but Etienne could at least be happy with his simplistic pattern of stars.

"You're definitely improvin', shug." Madame Élise commented in her soft voice, dark, wrinkled hands quickly wrapping his lumpy navy candle up in some paper, twine tying itself around the parcel in a neat bow while she held everything in place, "I can feel the intent in this one an' it's a good one. Very focused."

"Thank you, I was really tryin' to draw on ambient energies like you said." Etienne took the wrapped candle when she held it out to him, her family's symbol shining brightly from the dark material of the wrapping paper, and dipped his head towards her in respect, "Though I'm nowhere near as good as you, madame."

The Voodoo priestess laughed lightly, one arm folding across the counter as she leaned over to tweak lightly at his cheek, fingers warm against his skin, "I got years of practice, honey, but you're gettin' there! Keep coming on by an' you'll be a proper chandler before too long."

It was such a simple little bit of praise, but Etienne still felt like he was floating on cloud nine as he thanked Madame Élise again, promised to see her next week and then stumbled blissfully out the front door.

After he left her shop, he was planning on just grabbing a quick bite to eat somewhere nearby before heading home when, by sheer happenstance, he ran into Sabine over on Toulouse Street. They hadn't really seen each other in almost three weeks besides in passing, and one round of exuberant greetings and a very tight hug later, Sabine more than happily derailed his trip to the courthouse so they could go get lunch together.

Etienne was so excited to catch up, he kinda forgot he was still technically grounded until after they'd already sat down and ordered, scribbled out a hasty note to mother explaining and hoped he hadn't just extended his sentence.

He chewed on his fingernails waiting for her response, bicker-

What Goes Bump In The Night

ing amicably with Sabine about the habit, *you're going to get nail polish in your mouth again no I am not oh sorry didn't know you could see the future too imbécile,* was picking flecks of black paint off his tongue while Sabine laughed at him when her reply bleed across the paper.

Mother

›› *Take your time, sheri, and enjoy your lunch. I'll see you before you head out tonight.*

Which was the *best* possible response he could've gotten, meant an end to his previously indefinite grounding might finally be here, and as promised, Sabine offered to take the two of them out that night in celebration.

Etienne was wholly on board for that, wanted a night out with friends *so bad,* needed a chance to goof off and get away from the house for a few hours, *no responsibilities no chores no assignments nothing hanging over his head just a chance to relax and unwind and not scrounge around a dirty construction site with...ah fuck-*

And then he remembered what day it was.

"Oh *lamèd-* wait I don't think I can tonight, I forgot I have a thing later." Etienne sighs as he sips at his drink, a lightly refreshing cocktail Sabine had ordered for them both in pre-celebration, and snorting while he crunches through the cucumber on the edge of his, Sabine rolls his eyes, "How do you have a *thing later?* I thought you were still potentially grounded."

"I am, *I think,* but if it's on official coven business, maman allows it, an' this is for the diversity program so it...*technically* counts," Etienne says with a shrug, and speaking of, while it's on his mind he should probably remind Nica they have an assignment later, *just in case you know how they are,* sets his glass down to send

✦✦ 201 ✦✦

them a quick message.

"Are you seriously *still* doin' that? I got out of it like- *last week.* The idiot I was shackled to already bombed two tests an' I argued the program was negatively impacting his time to study and *yada yada yada,* I got rid of him." Sabine reclines back in his seat, peacock feathers sticking out of the band on his hat catching in the light as he nods his head lazily, "I could do the same for you. Do you know if yours is doin' badly in anythin'?"

Etienne snorts involuntarily at the mere thought, can't imagine a world where *Nica Caldwell* would ever willingly let themself fall behind in a class, but before he can tell Sabine as much, there's an entire mess of incomprehensible gibberish leaking across the page of his notebook under his message. It's all jumpy and erratic, written in a bonkers frantic hand so Etienne can only read bits and pieces, but he gets the gist of it, *holy shit oh my God thank you totally didn't remember forgot sorry,* rolls his eyes and pens back a short, *you're welcome.*

"-doesn't have to be much honest, I can really spin anythin' the way we need it to and...éy, Eti, you listenin' to me?"

"Huh? Yeah sorry, I am...an' I...appreciate the offer Sabine, but you know I can't. I gave them my word so...I gotta uphold it now." He says absentmindedly, clucking his tongue in fond amusement when a bunch of exclamation points spring up in reply to his message and nothing else.

That's another strange habit of Nica's he's still struggling to parse, they'll just send punctuation for seemingly no discernable reason, and spinning his pen in a circle, Etienne drops it to the page and ends up sending them a lone question mark back, "Besides, m'pretty sure Nica's gettin' straight A's...though I don't know *how* they're managin' to do that. They've got so much they do, m'surprised they got the time to *think* let alone *study...*"

While he's talking, a whole platoon of exclamation points starts hopping across the page under his question mark, each iteration growing sloppier until the last one trails off in a sharp jerk, and

What Goes Bump In The Night

Etienne finds himself grinning a little, wonders if Nica got caught not paying attention in class. That'd be hysterical if true, and he starts trying to fill as much space as he can with question marks, makes sure to pick his pen up after each one so it'll send on its own, effectively spamming them with dozens of unread messages.

It's something silly he and Sabine used to do back in the academy to annoy one another, except they used words instead of punction marks, *pages upon pages full of nerd and dork and idiot spelled out in crisp cursive lines snickering with your head bowed hoping no one hears,* and the method might be different but the idea is the same.

Etienne doesn't really know what possesses him to do it now.

It might be the good mood he's in, spirits lifted by the nice weather and a pleasant lunch, or maybe it's the thought of Nica's face watching his ribbon flash softly but being unable to check it, knows how fatally curious they are and how the *not knowing* will drive them up a wall, only to open their book later and find four pages of nothing but question marks.

And the mental image *that* brings up almost makes Etienne laugh out loud, and he has to bite his lip hard to keep it in, but there's nothing he can do to stop the wide smile that spreads across his face, light crackling of electricity sparking around in his chest, makes him all giggly and stupid and it's like *rushing down the hall trying not to slip spitting laughter don't let him see* and *hiding behind the curtains of a party you're not supposed to be at with champaign you're not supposed to have clink your glasses together cheers mon ami* and *yelling at one another about the dumbest things something that's not anger clawing up your throat tugging at your lips pushing at your ribs think it might be-*

"Who're you writing?"

Etienne snaps his head up startled, pen stopping as his hand lolls to the side, sees Sabine staring at him with an impressively cocked eyebrow and an expression that's hard to read, honestly forgot he was still there until he'd said something. Embarrassment sweeps through Etienne hard and fast at his lack of manners, tints his face a brilliant red as he quickly shuts his notebook, capping his pen and sliding them both off to the side, "S-Sorry! I- i-it's *nothing, I just-* that was really rude of me. I'm payin' attention now, *promise.*"

"You're fine, don't worry about it. If there's somethin' else more important you need to be doing, then by all means." Sabine says far too fast with a cool flick of his wrist, looking very unbothered and slightly bored, but Etienne knows him and knows that's one of the masks he wears.

The LeBlanc family is way bigger than Etienne's own, countless children and cousins and aunts and uncles all branching off into a sprawling mess of houses that take up an entire city block, and Sabine may be their scion, but that's still so much to stand out against, even for him.

The need to compete and win is practically a part of his bones, means he's hyper aware of the attention given to him, absolutely *loathes* it when he feels like he's being ignored or dismissed, *forgotten amongst the crush of bodies and indigo markings I'm here I'm here don't forget me I'm right here,* and by ignoring him in favor of pestering Nica, Etienne's really hurt his feelings.

He's hit at a spot he should know not to as his best friend, and kicking himself internally, Etienne leans across the table towards Sabine, "Hey. I *mean it.* I really am sorry for bein' distracted while we're hanging out, that's not bein' fair to you. I wasn't tryin' to ignore you, *promise,* but I was anyways, and I'm *sorry.*"

Sabine clicks his tongue like this is a minor annoyance, arms folded across his chest in picture perfect indifference, *brushes things off always brushing things off don't make it out to be something bigger than it is don't let them know how much it actually hurt,* but his eyes have always been his tell, inky depths vulnerable in a way Etienne has often wondered if he's the only one allowed to see.

"I *have* missed you an' I *do* want to spend time with you, and I'm

What Goes Bump In The Night

really sorry if I made it seem like I didn't..." Etienne assures softly, and he holds one of his hands out then, pointer finger extended, asking gently without trying to pressure, "Do you forgive me?"

Appearing to mull it over for a second when he's probably already made his decision, Sabine works his mouth side to side before he leans forwards as well, hooking his finger around Etienne's own. "You know if you're lyin' I get to keep this." Sabine tells him all prim and proper, lightly wagging their linked hands back and forth in lieu of an actual answer, but Etienne knows what he means, snorts as he shakes his head, "Yeah sure, you know what-? If you really want my dismembered finger, s'all yours."

"Thank you, I'll add it to my collection." Sabine unhooks their fingers and reclines back, picking his drink up once again to elegantly swirl the contents in the glass, and the pure nonchalance he's exuding does make Etienne laugh, arms folding across the table while he cocks his head to the side, "Okay now I'm curious, is that just a collection of *my* dismembered fingers? Or is it less exclusive than that? Whose fingers do you even *have?*"

And grinning from under the brim of his cream hat, Sabine murmurs all haughty and jovial around the rim of his glass, "A man never steals fingers and tells, ducon."

They slip back into familiar, easy banter after that, get into something of a mock trial about the alleged finger theft Sabine's supposed to have been perpetrating, but move on from that once they notice their waiter giving them weird looks, work on getting something planned for tomorrow night instead.

Since it'll be a Friday, it's easier to get people together, and as Sabine is rattling off names of who to invite, he does mention Lucinda Laferriere offhandedly, and Etienne thinks about saying something, *she's been asking about you things to think about not interested never been Etienne if you don't tell him I'll talk to him promise,* but...he doesn't.

Not inviting her when they're planning on asking the rest of their friends seems a little mean, and before all this crush nonsense, the two of them used to get along just fine so Etienne feels bad excluding her. Besides, it's not like it's her fault she's got a crush on him, and then it's not *his* fault he's not interested, but it puts them both in a shitty awkward situation that Sabine is unintentionally fueling by encouraging this ill-fated clusterfuck.

You need to tell him to leave off, a part of his mind that sounds suspiciously like his sister harrumphs, and Etienne wrings his hands in his lap, *knows* he really needs to say something, stop this train of disaster before it gets too much further down the tracks, but every time he goes to open his mouth, *he can't.*

He hasn't seen Sabine in *weeks* and he knows they've both missed each other, plus they're having such a good time right now, and Etienne doesn't want to ruin that by starting a fight, and this for sure will start a fight. It always does to some degree, because Sabine will *insist* he knows and then Etienne counters with the fact that he *clearly doesn't,* and their friendly bickering turns decidedly less so and the next thing you know, either one or the other is storming off before they accidentally make a hurricane.

Again.

They really probably should have a conversation about it for the health of their relationship though, that would be the responsible adult thing to do, and he *will* do it at some point but just...*not right now.* Etienne will find a better time, *eventually,* so he shelves everything brewing in his head and tries to get back into the conversation, laughs and smiles and talks excitedly about which bar they should meet up at, ignores the way his fingers are twisting into knots in his lap.

But despite his best efforts to let go and move on, *chill out watch the clouds,* he does end up falling back into thinking about it on the trolley ride home, head leaned up on the window frame while St. Charles Avenue rolls past, mind building for him scenario after scenario for how that conversation could go.

Which is marginally helpful only up until the point where they all end in colossal disaster, and not like, *oh no we disagreed and*

What Goes Bump In The Night

now we're not talking for a while, but more like, *oh no we disagreed and now Sabine puts forth such a compelling argument for why you're wrong about your feelings and have you been gaslighting yourself this entire time and now you're not friends anymore and you both hate each other forever yippee!*

And that's not even remotely logical but his brain insists it is anyway, so like- *thanks for that anxiety.*

It doesn't stop there either, *why would it,* mutates like a cancerous growth, and suddenly each imagined, ruinous situation between him and Sabine catapults Etienne into an even worse one, and it gets to the point where he's half convinced he's gonna get home, and for some reason, be disowned on the spot.

"Stop it stop it stop it-" Etienne hisses under his breath, lightly beating his knuckles into his forehead like *that's* gonna get his mind to shut up, tugs his hat down to hide his face when he notices other people staring and just tries to forget he's capable of conscious thought for, *preferably,* forever.

Maisette can tell he's still overthinking when he gets back, consciousness worriedly poking at his own as a thousand whispered concerns echo in his ears after he steps through the front doors, and Etienne runs his hand idly down a wall in the foyer, murmuring gently, "M'okay, just bein' me. Nothing much to worry about."

Worry worry worry of course we worry foolish boy course we worry, it grumbles at him, floorboards ruffling off towards the kitchen in almost an insulted, stuck up way, and he smiles softly hearing cupboards start being loudly opened and shut.

Etienne drops his hat on an empty prong when the coat rack leans down for him, entire thing bereft of any others besides his, means he's the first one back for the day but that doesn't mean he has the house to himself.

Tinny old scratchy music pours out of the parlor, crackling with so much static it's next to impossible to understand what the lyrics even are, but they've all tried replacing her records in the past with newer versions, and she always demands the old ones back.

✦✦ 207 ✦✦

Checking his hair quick in a mirror, Etienne combs down flyaways and straightens his crow skull bolo tie, retucks his shirt, generally tries to make himself look as presentable as possible before poking his head into the parlor.

The Boudreaux may not be as big a coven as the LeBlanc, and *despite what some think,* that doesn't mean they're *'utterly decimated'* or *'on the brink of collapse'.* Sure, perhaps they *have* been a little stretched thin in recent years, but they have enough active members to fulfill their duties to the city and Etienne *dares* anyone to say otherwise.

Him and the others *are* managing without Gran Tant Ulyssia or Gran Mémé, and even if they weren't, none of them would ever think of raising a complaint. It's honestly rare for witches like them to hit an age where they can step down from their responsibilities, and so they'll never begrudge either woman for enjoying her hard won, and *much deserved*, retirement.

Most spirit witches don't have that luxury, which is the reason Etienne gets so heated whenever people try to question why everyone in his family isn't *pulling their weight equally.* His elders have done their job without protest for decades, have given so much and have experienced so much loss in equal measure, and yet outsiders still have the gall to ask them for more.

Etienne won't stand for it and doesn't, has gotten into very intense arguments on the subject, a few of which have nearly escalated to trading physical blows, and the only thing stopping him from slapping some loose lipped idiot is knowing what mother would do to him when she found out. Just thinking about it now makes electricity crackle against his palm, bright pops of maroon that he hides in fast clenched fists, works on tamping his emotions down because he doesn't want Gran Mémé to feel it but thankfully, she doesn't even look up as he walks over.

She's sitting in one of the squishy armchairs by the French doors that look out into the back garden, sunlight draped over her lap along with an inky black afghan, phonograph on a nearby table wheezing out the most godawful Big Band music Etienne's ever

What Goes Bump In The Night

heard. The volume is cranked all the way up, honestly makes the static worse, but she can't hear it otherwise, and he winces as he crouches down by her chair, lightly rests his hand on her arm to try and get her attention.

"Bon jou, Gran Mémé!" Etienne all but shouts, watching her deeply tanned, heavily lined face for any sign of having heard him, and his mouth pushes to the side when she just slowly blinks her dark, rheumy eyes.

He wiggles a little closer, bouncing up on his toes as he squeezes fingers around her wrist gently, and this time, flares his magic out to brush along hers while he tries again, "I said, *bon jou Gran Mémé!* How are you?"

Another slow blink, but something sparks in the depths of her eyes now, and Etienne shivers at the slow building pressure of magic against his own, like the low booms of far off distant thunder that still manage to rattle the teeth in your skull, her power swelling languorously to regard him like how a massively ancient creature might inspect a mouse scuttlinsg by.

"Oooh! Mô dou gaçon!" Gran Mémé exclaims in her creaky voice, wisps of snow white hair falling across her wrinkled face as she leans closer to him, adjusting her half moon spectacles, "I didn't think you were comin' home...you've been gone so long, shéri ."

"I've only been out the morning, Mémé." Etienne says loudly and has to hold very still as she reaches a hand towards him, tremoring fingers poking at various spots around his face before landing on his cheek, current under her skin snapping against him like an electrical fence.

"Hmmm? S'that all it's been? It's felt like years to me..." She chuckles, thumb sweeping in a stinging arc under his eye, touching at where his markings dip down by the side of his nose, "Oh how I've missed you..."

"Really? It's only been a few hours." Etienne resists the urge to cock his head to the side, afraid she'll accidentally poke his eye out with one of her gnarled fingers, and she hums absentmindedly,

✦✦ 209 ✦✦

doesn't sound like she heard him as she keeps murmuring, "My... s'it been a while, shéri...you've grown into such a handsome young man, mô gaçon, so strong too...you'll do just fine, gaçon, *just fine,* s'no need to worry...*no need to worry,* you'll make a fine patriarch my Éleutaire..."

Etienne has never felt his stomach drop out of him so fast, mouth going dry at the tender look Gran Mémé is giving him, knows now it's not for him, *that it's for the son she lost almost thirty years ago,* and swallows rough. He's frozen with indecision on what to do, is aware like they're all aware of how badly her mind has deteriorated, remembers the healer saying it was better to gently correct her when she's confused, but to be careful not to upset her further, which is a problem considering what she just called him.

They never talk about Éleutaire with her if they can help it.

His death has haunted their family for decades, but it affected Gran Mémé worst of all, acts as the key that unlocks a bottomless well of sorrow her dementia trips her into every now and again.

It's not just his death she mourns when she gets like that, *it's her brothers, long dead in the line of duty – her cousins, their minds and bodies torn to pieces – her grandchildren, taken too quickly too soon,* everything piling on top of her and dragging her under.

The deep suffering she feels is excruciating, palpable to everyone else in the house, a maelstrom of agony that drives liquid hot spikes of despair into the base of their skulls and fillets their chests wide open. Mother says she used to be better at controlling her emotions, but the ability to restrain them has slipped away along with her mind, and they all try to be cognizant of that.

Which is why no one brings up Éleutaire around her, even if it's to reminisce about happier times, because Mémé always inevitably asks when he's coming home and they don't wanna lie, *not to her not to their matriarch deserves better than that,* but they also don't wanna tell her the truth, can't bring themselves to cause any more harm to someone who has already suffered so unduly.

So they dance around it, avoiding the harsh but inescapable

What Goes Bump In The Night

reality that comes from their line of work, a truth all of them know and understand, one Mémé used to know as well but is now lost to her, gone somewhere down at the bottom of that well, hidden by the murky waters of time and a mind slowly coming undone.

And it's something Etienne has to be mindful of to tiptoe past as he rocks up on the balls of his feet.

"Thank you, Mémé, but um- I'm not- I-I'm not *him*. I'm Etienne, your great-grandson?" He offers kindly, makes sure to keep his tone as light and judgment free as possible, but he can tell she doesn't really understand him, eyes growing unfocused once more while she pats his cheek with a sweet smile, "Of course, mô gaçon, of course. Would you sit with me for a bit? It's been so long since we've sat togethero...maybe you could play somethin' for your old maman?"

"But *I'm not Éle-* I...of course, Mémé. Lemme go grab my violin an' I'll be right back." Etienne murmurs and gets soundlessly to his feet, Mémé's hand sliding slowly off his face as he straightens up, like she can't bear the thought of letting him go, *like she's afraid he won't be coming back.*

Death is something their family deals with every day, working to keep balance between life and its inevitable conclusion, and while Etienne grew up with it all around him, understands it's nothing to be afraid of, he can still feel the aches it leaves behind. Everyone mourns, both the living and the dead, and as Boudreaux, they're supposed to be the keepers of those goodbyes, to sit with the grieving and help them see all the new hellos waiting for them, to understand that for something to begin, something else has to end.

It doesn't stop it from hurting though, Etienne doesn't think there's anything that will ever make people stop aching for their loved ones, but that pain is a part of life and the best thing you can do is accept it.

Healing hurts, and so often people forget that, will shy away and try to avoid it, let things fester instead of accepting that pain, lock everything they're feeling far away because it's easier and it rots

✦✦ 211 ✦✦

them from the inside out every time.

Etienne gets why they do it, nobody wants to hurt, and it's scary to think that sometimes, the pain never really goes away, will linger in the memories you can't bear to forget, and that fear of loss makes people hold onto things they shouldn't. Gilbert told him once when he was younger that there was a difference between remembering someone and hanging on to them, and Etienne hadn't understood, asked for an explanation while his small hands fiddled with the evergreen branches they were hanging around portrait frames.

"Well...*how should I put it*...rememberin' someone is...when you can find solace in what they left behind, but still acknowledge that they're gone. You miss them, and that hurts, but it doesn't stop you from livin'." Gilbert grunted, boosting Etienne higher on his shoulders so he could reach a painting of some long dead great-grand far above his head, "An' holdin' on is the opposite. You *can't* let them go, their memory hurts you to the point that life becomes unbearable...death is no longer understood to be an inevitable acceptance, it's a punishment."

Which was kinda a lot for an eight year old to take in and process, but the sentiment must have reached him anyway because Etienne doesn't remember asking any more questions, just quietly helped Gilbert keep putting up branches.

More than half the wall was covered by the time they were done, wreathes of rosemary and holly circling each portrait of a Boudreaux that had lived, served, and died in the name of the Night Mothers, some of them ages before he'd ever been born and some only a few years back.

"Death touches our house with a heavy hand, névé, but don't let that frighten you." Gilbert murmured, long spindly fingers combing through Etienne's hair while he stared up at the portraits above them, sad little smile on his face as his dark eyes darted from one to the next, "Life is still worth livin', love is still worth feelin', just understand our existence isn't something that's meant to last forever."

What Goes Bump In The Night

Lessons like that were common growing up, and while other witches might've considered the topic too heavy to discuss with children, Etienne sincerely appreciated it, feels like it helped him learn to cherish life and the people in it a lot more. His house has always had close associations with death and the beyond, something that gets twisted and warped into dark horrible things, made out to be like they're the source of all nightmares, and it's often forgotten how much the Boudreaux are also tied to life.

They're the house of balance, the steady hand that helps lead the dead on and helps the living stand back up, theirs is the arm that gets flung in between every innocent and everything decidedly less so, the bridge between worlds *the thankless guardians of the night,* and the toll it takes on them is immense.

There's empty seats at their dining room table that Maisette still puts out place settings for, rooms no one's lived in for years but that are always kept clean, doors left ajar, like they're simply just waiting for whoever lived there to come back home, everyone making space for people that aren't here anymore and never will be.

Well...*physically* at least.

Etienne bounds into his room and is quick to grab his violin off its stand, knows scores of Boudreaux have played it before him and can feel their electrical imprint lingering in the wood, phantom memory of fingers joining his sometimes when he plays. These residual touches don't scare him, *they've never scared him,* and maybe it's because their family is more acquainted with loss than some of the other covens, but for them, death has never meant the complete end to someone.

How can a person really be gone when they live on in stories and memories, in the odd, personal little traditions that get carried over from them to someone that loves them so, in this magic of theirs that's run from one generation to the next like an unending river, picking up bits and pieces of its forbearers along the way, and yeah, some people may be gone now, but they've never truly been lost.

✦✦ 213 ✦✦

They're still here, kept alive through the simple act of *remembering to,* and it's not forcing them to stay, *it's not ignoring that they're gone,* it's finding acceptance with the fact that they did what they were put on this earth to do.

They lived.

They died.

And life moves on.

The phonograph has stopped by the time Etienne sets foot back in the parlor, and in the soft silence, he can feel *them,* watching from the walls with their painted eyes and curling like jumping static below his bones, their hands overlaying his as he fits his violin into place against the crook of his neck. *We're with you...we are always with you,* they whisper against the edge of his being, a deep, resonating susurration that echoes across all of time itself to reach him now where he stands, *what you are is us what we were is you electricity for blood a storm eternal our son our child our evermore.*

Etienne has always known that what he is, in essence, is an amalgamation of everyone that's come before him, a distillation of their hopes and dreams, *their living memory,* and that as long as he draws breath, as long as he stands and lives and does his duty, none of them ever really died, or at least, never died in vain.

Because their house survived, *the line is unbroken,* everything they were and are passed on to him, and that's why Etienne's always known it's never just been his fingers wrapping over the fingerboard.

He tucks his head and draws the bow across the strings, and in his mind, *in the snapping undercurrent of his magic he hears it,* the same movement done by different hands staggered decades apart, a perfect chorusing that doesn't quite pitch or warble the same every time, but swells together into an entire symphony orchestra that's been centuries in the making.

And at its center, at the front, *at the pulsating quaking heart of*

What Goes Bump In The Night

it all keeping it going keeping it alive, stands him, *their heir their scion their future,* and he plays for them like it was the only thing he was born to do.

When Etienne finishes, when his bow hangs trembling in the air, pulsating in time to the frantic steady drumming of his own pulse, he feels like the sunshine is brighter somehow, *the room lighter voices laughing something brushing against his arm,* and curiously turns to look over his shoulder. Gran Mémé is smiling at him, markings under her eyes glowing vibrantly and reflecting back in her spectacles, the light streaming in through the windows warping over her shoulders like a shawl, like she's a blackhole and it has no other choice than to bend to her desires.

"Mèsi, shéri ." She murmurs, looking right at him, and for the first time all afternoon, Etienne knows she really is seeing *him* this time, holds his violin to his chest as he sweeps into a bow for her, "Plézi mô, Gran Mémé."

Her chair heaves to its feet and clacks back a few steps, making room for the other armchair to come waddling closer, and she gestures at it as it settles with a heavy huff of cushions, "Come, *sit.* Tell me 'bout what you've been up to, I feel like we haven't talked in *ages.*"

And Etienne does, props his violin up against the leg of the chair and hits on the highlights of the last few weeks, which, *there haven't been a lot for him,* so he finds himself telling more mundane little stories instead. He talks about chasing down raccoon terrors and shooing poltergeists out of attics, about being bored to death at construction sites, how Nica loses anything unless it's already *physically* attached to them, a lot of unimportant events that come spilling out like they matter anyway.

Etienne gets so wrapped in one retelling of the night Nica lost their wallet, then their backpack, *then their wallet again* in rapid succession, he forgets this is probably all incredibly droll to her, a former Boudreaux Matriarch, but Gran Mémé seems to be enjoying it anyway, sips idly on the tea Maisette brings them and nibbles on a small plate of these tiny apricot tarts Etienne could, *and has,* eaten by the fistful before.

They're still chatting by the time mother gets home, and the delight she feels upon seeing Mémé so aware and talkative rocks along Etienne's consciousness like a gentle summer breeze. Mother leans down to kiss her grandmother on a wizened cheek, the two of them sharing a few quiet words together that Etienne doesn't want to eavesdrop on, is quick to collect his violin and head back up to his room.

With fall on the way, the sun has been dipping below the horizon earlier and earlier, and while not quite on its way to setting yet, the lamps have already all come on around Etienne's room, casting warm light over the dark teal walls. He sets his violin back in its stand by the bay window, ruffles a hand absentmindedly through his hair and fiddles with the stuff at his desk, trying to think if he's gonna need anything in particular for tonight that'll keep him busy while Nica is busy doing boring Nica things.

To be honest, most of what Nica does on these *'assignments'* is beyond boring, *running labs or pulling research or going out to collect samples,* but Etienne has a particular hatred for when they visit construction sites. There's never anything for him to do really, save trail along behind Nica and the site foreman, basically spends several hours trying not to fall asleep on his feet, nodding off despite his best efforts anyway as he listens to them discuss what building materials can and can't be salvaged.

It's good that the city is making a push to recycle supplies where they can, but *Mothers,* why does *Etienne* have to be there for it?

He's not an alchemist, only has the barest grasp of chemistry and can think of like, *six other things* off the top of his head he could be doing instead that'd be more productive. Ya'know...*actual* tasks that'd help the populace of New Orleans, and not him wasting four hours being an unwilling attendee to a dual lecture *about concrete and its many transmutable uses.*

A gentle knock at his door has him snapping his head up, and he grins seeing mother leaning against the doorframe, sleek black

What Goes Bump In The Night

skirt dusting at her knees and moon white blouse glowing next to her dark umber skin, gold glittering at her neck and wrists. Her hair is out of its braids for the time being, and she's slicked her coils back into a low, poofy bun that rests against the nape of her neck, something that's effortlessly elegant and still easy to wear out even with her hat.

She mustn't have had any important meetings today, casual attire and lax posture cluing Etienne in to the relaxed nature of her day, which is good because unless otherwise forced, mother won't take breaks.

"Bonjou, baby." She greets as he comes up, pushing off the door-jamb to wrap him in a tight hug, and he's not too terribly much taller than her, but when she tilts her head to the side, Etienne can see a bunch of tiny flowers tucked in the knot of her bun.

"Bonjou, maman, you have tea with Miss Lessie?" He guesses, hand darting up to pluck the small bouquet free, and with a click of her tongue that's entirely too fond to be called chiding, mother sighs, *"That woman...she leave plants in my hair again?"*

"Mm hm, primrose this time, I think." Etienne holds the little bundle of flowers up for mother to see, petals pale yellow and centers a dark ocher, and she takes it with a shake of her head, tucking it behind her ear this time, "I swear...she's been doin' this ever since I was a little girl, loved pokin'em up in popa's pockets too. Grew a whole garden in there once while they were havin' lunch, you know. He had geraniums spillin' all over the place for the rest of the day."

Etienne can't help snickering at the mental image, *grandfather with his serious eyes and stately moustache attending council meetings with pastel petals overflowing out of his suit pockets,* and mother laughs as well, but it's touched by a soft kinda sadness, "He could never be mad at her though, would huff and puff about it all he liked, swear he'd get her to stop, an' yet he'd come home next day trailin' honeysuckle with the stupidest grin on his face."

"That's love for'ya." Etienne snorts, can't *count* how many stories he's heard about his grandfather acting like a goofy, lovestruck

✦✧✦ 217 ✦✧✦

fool for one Miss Celestia Chenevert, former coven matriarch and now full time menace. The two of them were never married in accordance with human customs, but they were bound in the ways that matter, a difficult thing for atriarchs to be when your house comes first above anything else, but they quite famously made it work.

"It was *somethin'* I'll tell you that. I don't think I've *ever* seen another man so gone for his wife." Mother says and takes a small step back, eyes squinting at something before she reaches up to start fussing needlessly with his hair like all mothers are prone to do, "How was your day, shéri ? Your lesson with Élise go okay this morning?"

"Mm hm! I really think I'm actually improvin' a bit on sensing ambient energy, but my candles still *uh...leave a lot to be desired.*" Etienne scratches at the side of his face awkwardly, lets her fiddle with his bangs how she likes because last time he told her to leave off she moped about it for a solid hour.

"Aw, you'll get there honey, don't you worry. Élise is a fantastic teacher and you've always been so quick to pick things up." Mother coos, finally satisfied with whatever she's done to his hair and drops her hand to thumb at his cheek, energy under her palm tingling against his skin like a warm current, "Just keep trying your best an' I'm sure you'll get it eventually."

And she probably didn't mean for it to sound this way, but that stings like a nettled barb against his heart, embarrassed heat flooding up the back of his neck because Etienne can't tell if she's disappointed in him or not for being so slow to get this, *thought you'd be better get it quicker taking too long need to push yourself not making her proud,* and he swallows past the new dryness in his mouth, forces himself to say evenly, "Yes ma'am."

"That's my boy." Mother smiles and pats him once or twice before letting go of him entirely, feet shifting under her like she's almost done with the conversation, *like she's almost done with him who needs a failure like you anyway disappointment get a grip shut UP-* head cocking to the side inquisitively, "You're goin' out on an

What Goes Bump In The Night

assignment tonight, right? With that alchemist? Do you know when you'll be back?"

"I um- yes ma'am! *I mean-* yes I-I am goin' but I don't really know when I'll be back, these run late sometimes o-or get cut short an' I don't really have a lot of control." Etienne rushes, fingers digging and pulling at one another while a chorus of whispers tell him he's an *idiot, a worthless buffoon an embarrassment to your name to your entire line who would ever want a nothing like you-* and he's stammering fast to try and drown it out, "B-But I can stay home if you need me too! It's construction site work so it doesn't really matter if I'm there or not an' I can try and reschedule with-!"

But mother just holds up a hand, halting him in his tracks as she says, "It's okay, honey, *really.* I don't need you to do anythin' for me, I was just wonderin' when to expect you home s'all."

"O-Oh..." Etienne breathes, wind completely taken out of the sails to his anxious spiral, and he rocks back on his heels, feeling a little unmoored now and also incredibly foolish. *Oh you've really done it now,* he worries, knows that was too overblown of a reaction for a few simple questions, but he couldn't *help it,* rationale ripped away from him the *second* he thought she was disappointed with him.

Fuck shit you idiot you moron can't keep your head about you for five seconds just had to go be a literal freak over nothing and you know she's gonna ask because what the fuck was that and uuuuugg gggGGHHHHAAAAAHRRRRGGGGG-

This is not particularly a conversation he wants to be having at the moment, but mother isn't an idiot and she *knows him,* knows how he gets, and Etienne's eyes slip shut very briefly, *fuck what're you gonna do can't blame this one on lack of sleep,* and sighs exhausted, *"Maman listen-"*

"Don't you start your bullshit with me Etienne Christophe Boudreaux." Mother commands and he wearily opens his eyes, sees her hawklike gaze flitting over him, *assessing remembering worrying,* and he grimaces preemptively, already knows what she's gonna

✦✦ 219 ✦✦

say before the whole thing is really out of her mouth, "Look. I've been tryin' to let you sort this yourself- *don't make that face at me, yes* I've noticed, *I'm your mother-* but I can tell it's gettin' bad again and I think it might be time to go back an' see-"

"While I understand your concern, mére, let me assure you that I'm *fine.*" Etienne interrupts in a calm, but firm tone, projecting *I'm okay I've got it together I'm in one piece* even if he's not, because that's the only way out of this mess, and after the botched Lucretius seal mission, he really can't give her any more reasons to question his ability to manage himself, "Yes, I have been more...*stressed* lately, but it's just from tryin' to fit all this *diversity program* nonsense in, and I feel like I've finally caught my stride with it."

Which isn't...*entirely* a lie and also neatly assigns an identifier to what's been causing the increase in his anxiety levels, when in reality, Etienne doesn't actually know *what's* wrong.

The first time around they did all this, *doctors and medication and short lived therapy,* it was apparently a fairly obvious source according to the therapist, *puberty in combination with repressed childhood trauma,* which sounds worse than it was but Etienne has always had a bad habit of blowing things out of proportion.

And what was bothering him then isn't even what's bothering him now!

Recently, it's just been sourceless wave after sourceless wave of sick, prickling paranoia that gnaws at his bone marrow and leaves him shaking, body jittery with how hard his heart is pounding, but no matter how much searching he's done, Etienne can't figure out what's causing it.

Which is *why* he doesn't want to go back to see his doctor or his therapist, because they're going to have questions for him that he can't answer, and the last time that happened, they both prescribed him a couple small glass bottles of off-white pills that did nothing but fill his head with cotton.

The meds worked in theory, but Etienne hated the way they made him feel and he'd sooner lose a limb than go back to that

What Goes Bump In The Night

hazy lull, so for now, he just grits his teeth and hopes whatever the hell is bothering him will pass. He *has* been entertaining the thought of telling mother about what's going on, as laboriously painful a task as it'd be, but every time he goes to do it, he loses his words entirely.

How is he supposed to explain the hot, sticky, *nebulous swamp* in his head when he can't even articulate himself past, *I don't feel right?* When he spends actual hours thinking himself in circles, to the point that he can't even figure out what he wants the conversation to be *about* anymore? And *why* would he risk *everything,* and throw even *more doubt* on his ability to be *patriarch,* something he already worries is being called into question behind his back, by revealing what a neurotic mess he really is?

So, no *thank you,* he's plagued by anxiety, *not an idiot.*

At the end of the day, his brain may be absolutely exhausting to live with, but it *is his,* and Etienne will keep making the choices he considers are in their best interests, and until he either has a concrete problem he thinks needs help solving, or this goes away on its own, he doesn't see why anyone else should have to know the whole truth of the matter.

And nothing's going to change his mind, not even whatever difficult time mother is promising to give him in response to his counterargument, the prelude to which is slowly drawing across her face like an ill omen.

"Mm hm- you literally just had a small panic attack because I asked you what time you'd be home. So explain to me how that means *you're fine?"* Mother points out snidely, arms folding across her chest in a move that really used to intimidate him as a child and...does...*l-less so now,* eyebrow cocked in an accusatory manner, *daring him* to try and talk his way out of this one.

Which, she knows him well, he is absolutely getting ready to do, but whereas she assumes he's going to fail, ~~don't read into that ignore it don't read into it,~~ he at least has some confidence he's gonna get the outcome he wants.

✦✦ 221 ✦✦

You can't be friends with Sabine LeBlanc for over ten years and *not* learn how to make words work for you.

"That...is true." Etienne relents, knows he needs to be strategic in surrendering some ground if he's going to win this battle, "But-*to be fair!* I've been a little keyed up all afternoon because Gran Mémé called me Éleutaire again an' that was an utter nightmare to navigate, so then when you asked me what I was doin' later, I panicked a bit-"

"A bit?"

"-which was an overreaction on my part, I'll admit that, but I was worried you were still upset about me goin' out to lunch earlier. I thought you were gettin' ready to ground me further, which I obviously wanna avoid at all costs, an' it caused a huge influx of stress."

"Why would I *ground you* for stopping to *get lunch?*" Both of mother's eyebrows shoot up and then drop into a confused furrow, tone of her voice clearly indicating that she believes this is another point in favor for Etienne going back to see Cynin, but he anticipated this, launches smoothly into his next rebuttal.

"Because I'm still technically grounded an' I'm not supposed to be spendin' time with my friends, *which*- not tryin' to argue I shouldn't've been punished because I absolutely did, but I *do* think the lack of social interaction has made my anxiety flare up worse." Etienne sways forwards on his toes a bit, hands clasped behind his back while he talks, and if he's subconsciously mirroring the way Sabine presents opening arguments in court, it's entirely unintentional, "Oh- and speakin' of, a couple people are goin' out tomorrow night an' I thought it might help things if I went, but of course, I'll abide by whatever your decision is on the matter, maman."

The following silence doesn't ring with absolute victory, but it's not completely suffocated by defeat either, and Etienne settles back on his heels, heart in his throat while mother goes through a whole range of facial expressions, *mouth opening mouth shutting tired blink of her eyes brows scrunching together mouth opening,* hand coming up to pinch the bridge of her nose as she finally

What Goes Bump In The Night

lands on an exhausted, *"You spend too much time with Sabine..."*

And that's how he knows he's won.

By the time Etienne's leaving that night, broomstick in hand and already running late to meet Nica, he's sworn about eleven different times to schedule an appointment with Cynin if he really feels like he needs to. He has *absolutely* no plans to do so, but mother doesn't need to know that, and in exchange, he manages to extract a verbal confirmation from her that he is, in fact, *no longer grounded,* something that tastes even sweeter than the early fall wind in his face as he flies over rooflines.

The sun has just dipped below the horizon, dark of the night starting to crowd out the fiery bands leftover from sunset, deep, purple black creeping down from overhead like a mourning shroud, and he grins like a fool at the sight, banking hard as he heads towards downtown. All of New Orleans spreads out before Etienne like a massive glittering net, twinkling lights glowing brightly in the encroaching night, and his heart flips wildly inside his chest, wonders how long this thing with Nica is supposed to last, because if it's not too late, he might be able to goad Sabine into going out with him tonight as well.

Fuck, and if that isn't a fantastic thought to have, the realization that he has *the freedom to do as he pleases again,* and he whoops with an excitement that's all light and giddy *and practically over the moon,* dips sharply to skim the tops of some trees for the hell of it, scaring the absolute shit out of a family of swallows in the process.

Etienne laughs overjoyed and delighted as they flutter past, tips his head back into the chilly wind that skates along his skin, threads of it brushing over his face like freezing fingers, ruffling through his hair *pulling at his jewelry,* and he smiles, cannot believe what an absolutely *fucking* wonderful day today has been, can't help but feel that tonight is also gonna be even *better*.

Chapter 12

It's unusual for Etienne to be the one running behind for an assignment, and even after opting to fly instead of waiting on the trolley, he's a good twenty minutes late, comes skidding to a quick stop on the street out in front of the construction project, a flurry of swirling leaves kicking up behind his heels as he lands.

Like all the sites Nica's dragged him to, this one hasn't been demolished yet either, *even though it really needs to be,* old brick building still standing but looking beyond past its prime, narrow windows boarded up and most of the other entrances sealed over with plywood as well. There might've been a wooden sign above the double front doors at one point, but the splintering thing is beyond illegible now, whole area sectioned off by a wobbly chain link fence Etienne doesn't think would really deter anyone determined enough to trespass.

Nica's actually already beaten him there, is leaning up against a lamppost near the curb playing on their phone, blue light glowing softly over the slope of their face, but they look up immediately when they hear him land.

Etienne can just *tell* they were getting ready to make some sort of snide remark about him being late, *nose wrinkled lips pulling up in a smirk eyebrows arched check your watch much,* and then their whole expression melts away into unbridled excitement as they blink, "Woah! *Holy shit!* You *actually* have like- *a-a magic broomstick?* That is the coolest fucking thing, dude! Is it new or somethin'?"

"Uh, not particularly?" Etienne drawls, looking down at his ash broom handle and the spiderweb of electrical burn marks he's left in it on accident over the years, and after making the *most* con-

What Goes Bump In The Night

founded noise Etienne has *ever* heard, Nica demands in a series of hand flails, *"What?* If it's not- you're telling me this whole time you've- *why* the *fuck* do you always take the trolley *then?"*

"Hello? Do you have *any idea* how hot it gets in the summer down here, *especially* when you're wearin' *all black?"* Etienne arches both his eyebrows as he steps up on the curb beside them, finds a bit of silly pleasure in the fact that Nica has to inch back a little to keep looking at him, "It's *miserable,* like gettin' baked alive, and flyin' doesn't help that. Honestly, it's kinda worse up there since there's no shade."

Nica opens their mouth really quick to respond and then shuts it just as fast, seems to think something over as they nod their head back and forth, mismatched eyes flicking over Etienne briefly, "Yeah okay, I guess that makes sense. But like...if it sucks so much, why keep up the goth aesthetic then? Could you not just compromise and-?"

"Woah woah *woah,* hang on a sec- *back up,* I'm not goth. *Why do you think I'm goth?"* Etienne asks, absolutely *beyond* confused on where Nica even got that from, cocks his head to the side and tries to think if he's ever said or done anything that'd give them that impression. He doesn't talk about himself much, hasn't seen a point in it ~~maybe you should change that~~, but as he's learned, Nica is wicked perceptive, so maybe they've seen the pins on his bag and made some incorrect assumptions.

Which is *moronic* because the bands he listens to aren't even *close to being goth,* and sure, Etienne respects goth rock as a *genre,* but it's just not his personal preference. If anything, he supposes it would be more accurate to refer to him as a metalhead over a *goth,* but a lot of uh...*regular people,* get the two music genres confused regardless.

And, *just a hunch,* but Nica- *'everything I own is either luridly colorful or soft pastels'* -Caldwell doesn't particularly strike him as the type to know the difference.

Etienne *could* be wrong...but he doesn't think he is.

✦✦ 225 ✦✦

"Ha! That's funny!" Nica crows, tipping their head back in wild laughter, but their jovial cackles start to peter out when Etienne doesn't join in, just keeps staring at them perplexed like he's out of the loop on what's so funny, and their jaw drops open a little, "You're...joking right? Like you're- *you're fuckin' with me right*- no? Dude! *Come on!* How are you *not* goth? You wear *nothin'* but black *literally* every day, like. *Every day.*"

"It's practical." Etienne retorts with a sniff, rolling his eyes when Nica huffs, *it's practical,* in a skeptical tone, clearly still thinking about him complaining over the summer heat, "Yes, *it is,* so *shut up.* Black is the easiest color to keep lookin' nice when you've got corpses bleedin' dead man's blood all over ya. Have *you* ever tried gettin' that stuff out of fabric? No? Well here's a hint. *You can't.*"

Scoffing scandalized, Nica folds their arms across their chest and shifts their weight from foot to foot, eyebrow cocking ridiculously high as their lips twitch up into a sly grin, "Laundry? You're seriously telling me this all boils down to doin' *laundry?* That's... okay Mister Spookypants, then explain all the uh...t-the morbid uh...stuff- d-decorations- *paraphernalia?*"

"*What* morbid paraphernalia?" Etienne sighs exhausted, choosing to ignore the nickname ~~insult?~~ as he flips a hand at them, long fingers curling dismissively, "This is perfectly normal everyday attire."

"You honest to God have a bird skull at your throat-"

"My mother is a *fell raven summoner!*" Etienne defends hotly, touching at his bolo tie self-consciously while Nica starts to laugh heartily, fingers absentmindedly dipping into its empty eye sockets *and okay they might have a point,* but he refuses to concede, inclines his chin sharply in their general direction and snaps, "Well you dress like a- *l-like a pack of highlighters* threw up on you! What's even the point of *that?*"

"Hey man, don't diss the windbreaker, it's *retro-rific.*" Nica grins at him big, showing off the little gap in their front teeth and a dimple he's never noticed before pops into being, and it's weird, but Etienne's heart kinda kicks up, pulse shivering under his skin

What Goes Bump In The Night

as what has to be irritated heat floods his cheeks.

He snaps his head away with a tongue click, suddenly can't think up any sufficient retorts so he begrudgingly gives this one to Nica, wonders how they're always so good at getting completely under his skin and mutters waspishly, "That's the *stupidest* word I've ever heard..."

"Yeah, well it's got more spice than *stupidest.*" Nica quips back, and Etienne will deny to anyone that questions him whether or not he has to bite a smile back, fiddles with the ends of his bolo tie and rolls his head to the side, snarking, "Oh, s'that not good enough for ya? *Well how 'bout this-* your wordplay is *absolutely absurd* an' witless, completely ridiculous as it is farcical, a weak willed attempt that's lackin' in ingenuity an' utterly *gormless-"*

"Nah nah- *hold up- gormless?* No *way* that's- now *you're* just makin' words up you hypocrite!" Nica laughs brightly from deep in their chest, something that's full bellied and nose crinkling, and it's so absolutely infectious, Etienne can't fight the smile off his face any longer, sways forwards on his toes while he insists, "No it's real! I swear! It has roots in Middle English an' Old Norse, though it's kinda up for debate which language family takes more of the creditin' influence considering *gaumr* is the original Norse spellin' and-"

Nica just laughs again, though it's softer this time, *crinkles their nose all the same forget what you were saying doesn't matter hey there's that dimple again,* and shakes their head, accidentally knocking hair into their eyes, metal hand pushing it out of the way as they snort with no bite whatsoever, *"Christ.* You're such a fuckin' *nerd."*

Squiggly feeling suddenly rushing through his veins heat rolling across his face jumping staccato in his chest what is that has to be pride right probably just his ego getting fed ~~doesn't feel the same feels weird feels nice make it happen again,~~ and Etienne has to clear his throat, doesn't think that was a compliment but chooses to take it as one anyway.

✦✦ 227 ✦✦

"I- *thank you*. I do pride myself on my intelligence." He preens, mostly sticking his nose in the air for the effect, and he doesn't quite get another full laugh, but Nica kinda hums one, tipping their whole body to the side before jerking their chin at the construction site, "Yeah, *I can tell,* but if you're done with your vocab lesson *Merriam-Webster,* we should probably get rollin'...these resource surveys don't do themselves and we're already a *liiiiiittle late.*"

They say that last part with a smarmy grin, eyebrows waggling, *wanting* Etienne to rise to the bait, but he won't.

Instead, he feigns complete innocence, spins his broom around in a hand and strides towards the chain link fence, throwing airily over his shoulder, "Well why didn't you *say so?* Honestly Caldwell, your time management skills aren't really up to snuff, what with all your *pertinent* questions concernin' *my* wardrobe preferences an' the like. Lucky for you then that *I'm* here to keep things movin'.'"

"I-! But you *just-!* You were the one that- *ASS!*" Nica shouts at his back, but it's not spiteful, isn't filled with anger or vitriolic irritation, and as Etienne slips through a gap in the fence like how a specter passes through solid walls, there's really no other way around it. Their tone is *fond,* pitched up with good humor and practically singsong in teasing delight, and his arm swings back almost unbidden, catching the edge of the fence.

Etienne spins on the balls of his feet and uses the momentum to drag the fence open wider, holding it like it's a ballroom door and Nica is another esteemed colleague entering on his heels. They shimmy past with a surprised light in their eyes and a soft *thanks,* tucking persistently in the way loose hair back behind an ear, and watching the keychains on their backpack bounce while they walk by, Etienne wonders if there could be something to this.

He's been ignoring it, *trying to at least,* but that box is back out from under the bed and he has no idea where the lid's even gone, can't stop thinking about how mean smiles have turned into genuine ones, the way insults have backslid into sharp tongued teasing. Etienne was kinda hoping it'd go away if he just never acknowledged it, *crammed it deep into the recess of his mind and forgot,*

What Goes Bump In The Night

but staring after Nica, he can't deny the urge he has to catch up with them, to keep teasing *keep having fun.*

Suddenly, he wants to try and find ways to make them laugh, to get them to *rib him back,* thinks a bit breathlessly that if things were different, that if there was a pointed hat on their head and colorful markings under their eyes, the two of them might already be friends.

And if *that* isn't a thought that'd put him straight on his ass, Etienne isn't sure what is, can't believe he's standing here and *actually* allowing himself to contemplate being friends with *Nica Caldwell,* but the idea of it doesn't sound like the grueling death sentence he once figured it'd be.

Nica is actually pretty funny, is learning how to make him laugh and is getting really *scary* good at it, has almost had him bursting out in unrestrained giggles on multiple instances now. Arguing with them is exciting and *lively* every time, in parts because Nica is so stubborn, and it's something of a challenge trying to win against that, and Etienne has always loved a good challenge. They're also wicked sharp and pick things up fast, ask a thousand questions but never repeat a single one, love breaking things apart and understanding every facet and he *gets that.*

It's haunting in a way, but when you really get right down to it, the two of them are fundamentally more alike than they are different, and for all intents and purposes, sound like they would make stellar friends.

Which in of itself is *completely mindboggling.*

Who would've ever thought, Etienne thinks in a daze, *me...friends with an alchemist,* and it still makes something central in him balk at the idea, *no no never not them how could you ever enemy usurper insurrectionist,* but if he takes the alchemy out of it, just considers what it'd be like if Nica was anyone else, warmth unfurls under his bones like moonflowers twisting open on summer nights.

That...wouldn't be too bad actually, *he doesn't think he'd hate that Mothers of the Night you wouldn't hate that,* and excitement

◆✦ 229 ✦◆

makes Etienne's heart jump once picturing the places he could show them, all the hidden spots around the city you'd only ever find if you'd lived there your whole life, wonders if Nica would like them, if they'd ever wanna maybe go get lunch sometime, conversation flowing lively and sharp, peppered with snappy comebacks and wide grins and not a single mention of the program *once.*

And that sounds *nice, that really sounds nice but is that an okay thing to want why not you have friends outside the coven you have friends that are human none that are alchemists but maybe this is how you do it maybe this how you change things start with one person start here start now ask if they'd like to ask if they'd want to ask them to be your-*

There is suddenly- *so much happening in his head,* mind practically tripping over itself spinning up possible scenarios and whole conversations, and he can't *stop* thinking about it, wonders what Nica likes to do for fun, *if they'd ever take him along.*

Etienne wants to ask about their hobbies, where they're from *why they're here,* just sit and listen and talk and share, loves to learn loves to *know,* wonders if they're the same, *if they've wanted that too knows about your tea preference your aversion to sweets knows enough about you to still ask more,* wonders if they'd wanna hang out *if maybe after this they'd wanna go get drinks together with you-*

Mothers, what is he even *thinking, this is beyond stupid why do you care who says they'd even want to,* but Etienne can't shake it, feels a bit like he's had all of his internal organs removed without prior approval and shuffled back into the wrong spots, trails along behind Nica as they hop up the front stairs two at a time and just tries to set his mind right.

Tries to forget the way you want to sit together and share a meal share drinks share laughter forget about how you want them to look at you like you're something amazing forget the question bubbling up your throat pressing against your lips hey after this would you want to maybe go-

✦✦ 230 ✦✦

What Goes Bump In The Night

On second thought, you know what's more interesting than whatever the fuck his brain is doing?

These stairs.

The cement covering them is cracked and lumpy under his boots, completely broken off in some spots and showing the much older brick lying underneath, whole crumbling thing rising above what looks like a partially recessed first floor. Little half moon windows dot the bottom level of the building, rusted out but still strong looking iron bars caged over them, glass panes dusty and dark and giving no indication to what's behind them.

Squinting at one of them, Etienne tries to get a better look for curiosity's sake, almost feels like he sees something shiver past, but before he can decide if it was just his eyes playing tricks on him or not, a throat is cleared up ahead of them. He swings his head over, noticing a pair of construction workers he hadn't seen before taking a smoke break near the top tread of the staircase.

They're both big guys, thick arms draped lazily across paint stained jeans, sticker covered helmets at their feet, and they eye the two of them with something like annoyance as Nica comes to a stuttering halt a few steps down.

"Uh, *h-hi!* I'm-!" Nica starts, friendly greeting dwindling away into nothing when one of them tucks his cigarette into the side of his mouth, hand flicking at them in a sort of shooing motion, "Hey. Beat it *kid.* This is a closed worksite, an' I don't care what bullshit excuse you got, but y'ain't supposed to be here so get lost."

Etienne is immediately irritated.

He already hates it when one person speaks over another, finds it *incredibly rude,* but the dismissive hand wave is really what does it for him.

What a prick, he thinks, eyes narrowing, steps up right behind Nica and is more than willing to take over the situation if need be, *hi we're here to do you a favor so maybe lose the entitlement buddy do you have any idea who I am,* but Nica starts talking before he can.

✦✦ 231 ✦✦

"Ah! I um, sorry- *y-yeah I just-"* They kinda jump up and down on their heels in front of him, nervously fumbling for their phone, and he can't see their face, but from body language alone, he can tell they're staring at anything other than the man addressing them, "M-My advisor was supposed to- *said he emailed-* I'm from the college- *Hermes,* I'm uh, I-I'm supposed to be doing y'all's resource reclamation survey?"

That seems to spark something in the workers' eyes, and they both loosen a little, not exactly like untensing because they were never really all that wound up to begin with, but it's like that slow sit back people do when addressing an equal, *a show of respect.*

"Oh...alchemist, huh? Yeah, Carter did mention one of you was gonna be comin' by to help out." The second guy says appraisingly, inhaling off his cigarette until the end glows red hot, eyeing Nica with a friendly kind of regard now, and then his eyes flick to where Etienne is minding his business looking over Nica's shoulder, and the corners of his mouth suddenly tighten as he shoots smoke out his nose, "What's with the stiff though?"

And everything stops- *he did not just say that he totally did is he out of his mind ungrateful bastard hands reaching for you people shouting weirdo freakshow stiff corpse get out of our city* -before coming back into sharp relief.

It's such a small word, and yet it hits like such a slap to the face, *harsh and stinging,* sends angry electricity zapping up Etienne's spine, teeth grinding together at the casual slur, and he stands bolt upright, *sets his shoulders,* brings mother's imperious, *icy* command into his voice and snaps, "I am Scion Etienne Boudreaux, first of my name and *heir to my line,* and if you know what's good for you, you will *show me some respect."*

Both the workers' brows fly up in shock, clearly weren't expecting to get such strong backlash for their bigotry, and taking a second look at one of their helmets, Etienne isn't surprised to see an ANTISO sticker proudly slapped on the side.

His lip curls.

What Goes Bump In The Night

"While I'm here, you'll either address me as *'Master Boudreaux'* or *'Master Scion'* if, *for whatever reason,* you *have* to speak to me. Otherwise, *I don't wanna hear a peep from you.* Is that under-stood?" He seethes, eyes narrowing into dangerous slits where he glares at the two men from under the brim of his hat, *"Or do I need to dumb it down further?"*

"Dude!" Nica exclaims sharply, swinging a metal elbow back at him that Etienne deftly avoids, turns to gape over their shoulder and whispers dismayed, "What the *hell's* gotten into you?"

"They started it-!" He spits back, catches movement out of the corner of his eye and sees the workers standing now, one of them mouthing the tail end of something to the other, *look'it corpse breath's mad uppity little jinxfli-* control snapping completely before the word is even out of the man's mouth, lightning arcing across his back molars as he snarls, "You wanna run that by me again, *zòrdi manjè-!"*

Etienne had already been about ready to step out from behind Nica, but he surges forwards now, or he would if it wasn't for the sudden bar of *actual* iron that rams into his gut, draws him up short as he wheezes pathetically for air.

"Knock it the fuck off." Nica hisses right in his ear, and Etienne seethes, but he can't get enough breath to tell them to *get out of his way,* scrabbles ineffectively at the metal hand fisting itself in his shirtfront.

Ignoring his struggling for the most part, Nica's arm twists so they can wrap fingers around the dark material of his shirt like a vice, effectively keeping him pinned in place while they turn back to the men with an assuaging, "S-Sorry 'bout that! He didn't mean it, he's uh...h-he's a little *high strung.* If um, i-if you wouldn't mind though, can y'all let your boss know we're here? We'll be ready to start i-in *just a sec! T-Thanks!"*

There's a pause, and then some vague scuffling implying the workers have done as asked, dull thud of a door swinging shut, but Etienne stopped really being aware of things after *he's a little*

✦✦ 233 ✦✦

high strung knock it off sorry 'bout that about him you two are okay though it's okay what you said, drops his broom to wrap both hands around Nica's arm and doesn't care if this is going to hurt.

He normally really tries to keep a lid on the amount of spillover magic he leaks, but he's so angry ~~hurt~~ furious ~~betrayed~~ he couldn't give less of a shit, intentionally reaches for his power, *intentionally calls it forwards,* lets the entire writhing tide of it crackle through where his fingers are digging into sleek metal plating.

Nica yowls as the blowback lances up their arm, maroon lightning fractaling apart between the separate joints and briefly sparking arrays to life, bolt of energy coming to a crashing halt against a thick band of rune etched metal that's approximately where the ridge of their shoulder would be. A high whine precedes the low booming rumble as his power dissipates with a cacophonous crack, runes left a deep cherry red and steaming faintly in the autumn evening, and Nica staggers back with a groan, clutching at their twitching arm.

"*OW!* W-What the *FUCK WAS THAT FOR?* That really hurt you shithe-!"

"*HIGH STRUNG?*" Etienne yells over them, cuts his hand through the air and leaves a snapping lacework of electricity in its wake, "Those *shit heels* call me a *stiff* an' a *JINXFLINGER* and *you* have the *gall* to say *I'm high strung-* to apologize on my behalf, to *speak OVER* me, t-to put your *HANDS ON ME?* How *DARE* you! Where do you *GET OFF?*"

"Jesus, j-just-! *Calm down!* They were *fuckin' jokin'!* All construction guys are like that!" Nica shouts right back, pulls themself upright and squares off against him, feet braced like they're expecting an attack, and Etienne scoffs, but his heart is beating like mad under his sternum, "Oh so that makes it okay then! People can just say whatever *offensive shit they want* so long as *they're takin' the piss?* Don't tell me you *honestly* believe that!"

Please don't please don't please don't, thunders back and forth in his mind, a metronome of outrage that makes him sick to his

What Goes Bump In The Night

stomach each time it ticks past, *thought we could be kinda wanted to didn't know you were,* and violence bangs demanding from under his esophagus.

Every conversation Etienne's had with Nica is suddenly running past, forced into this new possible light and he wants to throw up, doubts every laugh every smile *every time things eased out between them,* thoughts growing blacker and angrier as they snarl over his shoulders, howling like the damned, *lied to me tricked me didn't mean any of it hateful just like the rest closeminded don't listen won't learn B I G O T-*

"It's not like that!" Nica insists, but their shoulders are still set, feet braced, entire posture combative and angry *and defensive,* and all of Etienne's hackles rise, and he wonders, *wonders wonders wonders where Nica's from what they know who they believe,* and there are so many pins and things hanging off their backpack, he's never really paid attention, but he suddenly can't shake the fear that there's one with an angry red line struck through a hat just like his.

"Then *what is it like?* 'cause it don't look real comfortin' from where I'm standin'!" Etienne demands hot and fiery, thinks about mother pushing him behind her while the crowd screamed for blood, *remembers standing in the looming silence of Gerome's tomb worried his family was next,* knows what gets whispered behind his back and can't accept for a *second* he's been spending time with someone who sees him the same way.

As something lesser.

And for the briefest second, *he has hope that's not the case,* because Nica falters, toes of their shoes shuffling closer together, eyes dropping away in surrender as the bravado drains out of them, and he dares to believe he's wrong.

He's an idiot.

"O-Of course I don't agree with shit like that! It's not like- *I-I'm not like-"* They stammer, left hand flying up to dig into the back of their neck, right hanging limply at their side, and it's a *misun-*

derstanding of course they're not really like it's okay you're okay, but then Nica wets their lips and the rest of it falls out of their mouth like the blade of a guillotine dropping, "I-I just...look, I'm sorry they hurt your feelin's b-but like- *you don't have to get so mad about it.* I promise they didn't mean nothin' bad by it, they were just...messin' around, ya'know? So like...m-maybe just...*calm down a-a little?*"

Etienne rears back like he's been struck, pressure dropping suddenly as wind swoops past, and it's too cold out for a thunderstorm to form, but it's a near thing, electricity jumping off his body in great crackling bursts. He stares at Nica like he's never seen them before, watches as they stumble away from him in a panic, eyes wide and glued on where his power is snapping barely under control, and he's seen that look *he knows that look jerking back from you on the street parents pulling their children out of the way fiend monster freak not safe not normal evil thing wretched creature something of the night kill it BURN IT-*

And something fissures apart in his chest.

"Y-You *listen to me-*" He orders, takes a step forwards and Nica takes another back and the storm brewing over his shoulders snarls brokenly, "You do not get to tell me how to feel, *you* do not get to decide what *I* find offensive or not, and you most *certainly DO NOT* get to *apologize* on my *BEHALF to the people calling me SLURS!*"

"*I-I don't think they meant-*"

Thunder growls overhead like a warning, tide of something he's really not supposed to be feeling lapping at his ankles, and in that instant, Etienne knows why people call them monsters, hears it in his voice as he draws out slow and dangerous, *"Shut. Up.* I *cannot* impress upon you how *little* I care what you *think."*

Nica shuts their mouth with an audible click, eyes glassy in the orange light from the streetlamps, and he doesn't want it to, but it pulls at his heart and Etienne hates that it does, something much more complicated than anger sinking its teeth into the softest parts

What Goes Bump In The Night

of him. The once livid flames licking at his insides start to die back, putrefy into the smoldering burn of anguish and it *hurts,* aches in his hands and crawls painfully up his arms, settling like a vice across his chest as he watches the first few tears fall.

They're clear like rain, *flash like stars,* drip out of eyes he's used to seeing pinched in mirth, trail down soft cheeks that're usually bunched up by a big smile, *heartache and frantic pain in someone he thought was a friend,* and it's all manageable until that voice he's only ever heard be strong and lively whispers in a broken hollow, *"E-Etienne- I- I-I didn't mean-"*

"Hey. We got a problem out here?"

The tone is gruff, *sounds faintly like an order,* and slowly ratcheting his head to the side, Étienne sees who he guesses is the site foreman, *can you let your boss know yeah Carter said you'd be stopping by-* leaning out the front door.

His dark brows are drawn down over darker eyes, skin around his mouth pulled into an unhappy frown that really mars whatever positive features he might have, whole countenance twisted by ugly hatred. The hand he has braced against the door is clenched into a fist, other hanging at his side but looks seconds away from going for something at his toolbelt, *wrenches and pliers and hammers all tools but could be used as weapons,* and *apprehension* crawls up Etienne's spine.

He rocks back on his heels, suddenly *very aware* of where he is and what he *isn't,* power slinking back into the confines of his chest like flood waters begrudgingly returning to their river, and says through his teeth, *"No.* We're *fine."*

"Oh yeah?" Carter cocks an eyebrow, but there's nothing friendly about the gesture as he tips his head to the side a little, never taking his eyes off Etienne...nor his hand away from idly fingering at his toolbelt, "You sure about that? 'cause I don't think I need to tell ya how much I really do *hate* havin' problems around my site, since, as foreman, *I'm* the one that's gotta *solve them."*

The threat implied is really so obvious, it's almost comical, *mind*

✦✦ 237 ✦✦

your business or I'll mind it for you, but Etienne isn't necessarily intimidated by it. He can feel his magic still roiling just beneath the surface of his skin, knows that if it came down to it, there is nothing on this earth that would stop it from protecting him with fang and claw. This one human wouldn't *stand a chance,* would be ripped apart in seconds, but a lone angry man isn't where the real threat comes in.

No, what the real danger to Etienne is, *to all of them is,* is how there's way more of *them* than there are of *him.*

It's how fast humans will jump to defending one of their own against a common foe, *how little they stop to think for themselves,* and given the attitude of the workers he's already met, no one here tonight considers him a friend. And that's what makes hives breakout across the back of his neck, the thought of others coming, *of mobs forming,* wrenches being traded in for guns, *barrels with their inky pinhole eye aimed at your chest one click one hit and you're done just like ~~giving a speech he was giving a speech and they shot him on stage mid-sentence dead before he hit the ground at a rally for unity and they shot him could be you he was a patriarch IT COULD BE YOU~~*

But he knows better than to throw gasoline on a spitting nest of embers.

And it rankles and catches painfully at his pride, but Etienne recognizes he needs to *let this go,* isn't supposed to take lives, and while he can't be faulted for protecting his own, he can be for driving a conflict to its breaking point.

Remember who you are and what you're not, he reminds himself, breathing out slow and sending a cascade of snapping maroon particles into the night, *you're a protector not a killer you came from humans but you're more than them don't sink back to their level,* inhales and straightens up under the mantle he's been wearing since birth.

"Well. Lucky for you then there's nothin' that needs solvin.'" Etienne says mildly, and electricity only sparks between his fingers

What Goes Bump In The Night

once, an angry little hiss that spits its own threat, *just try me see how it goes think you're faster than lightning ~~am I faster than a bullet~~,* and Carter catches it, eyes narrowing as he repeats in a murmur, "Yeah...lucky for me then."

Things fold into a stifling silence after that, tense with the threats still looming in the air like displeased spirits, and for the briefest moment, Etienne considers washing his hands of this entire nonsense and heading home. He's balking at the thought almost immediately, can't stomach the idea of walking down these stairs and giving Carter any sort of notion that he's *won* somehow. In part it's a pride thing, *your eternal vice the monkey on your back,* but a lot of it is also who Etienne understands himself to be, *the integrity of his character,* and he knows not to let that suffer.

Yes, he is still angry and hurt and upset, doesn't think *anyone* here is worth his time, but even if he leaves for those reasons and those reasons alone, to him, it's still like he's turning tail, *like admitting they got to him.*

Don't give them anything let them keep thinking you're completely above reproach, Aunt Atha told him the first time he really understood what it meant when people muttered *stiff* under their breath as he went past, *as soon as you give them a reaction they know they've got you never give them one,* her thin lips puckering as she swiped dark color over them, inky eyes flitting to his in the mirror when she heard him sniffle, *don't let them win mô poule always remember you're better than whatever they call you.*

And Etienne knows that ~~do you~~, but it's still hard to hear all those things, and it gets under his skin like you wouldn't believe. That's always been one of his buttons since practically forever, having disrespect thrown at him, and he really tries to not let it affect him, *temper you can't dare to break power you can never release feelings buried but never forgotten,* emphasis being on *tries.*

Etienne would be the first to admit he's an emotional person.

He's a witch for starters and being in tune with his emotions has been a core principle since he was a child, but he also kinda thinks

✦✦ 239 ✦✦

that's just who he is as a person. Take away the magic and the markings and you'd still be left with an Etienne that has a too big heart, someone who takes everything to it, who seems to feel everything twice as hard as everyone around him, and that's really the reason he always has troubling distancing himself like he should.

He feels *so much all the time,* can't let go when he's reeling with physical pain from an emotional wound, can't move on when his mind plays everything back for him on near perfect loop, *can't detach when he holds on so strong.* Working to not be like that is difficult, is a constant uphill battle *a fight against himself,* but if Etienne is going to be patriarch someday, he's got to master it, has got to learn to separate who he is from the duty he's supposed to perform.

Tonight is a good test of that. Etienne is angry, but he can't act on it, he's hurt but he can't let any of them know, kinda wants to cry thinking about how this all started, *foot knocking into your shin gap toothed grins hand over your heart over your mouth sorry about that about him stopped me defended them thought you were my,* but he'll never let the tears fall.

Instead, he'll be the patriarch, *the one he's destined to be,* will do his duty, pay his respects, hold his head high and *never give them an inch.* His palms still ache and *burn* with hurt though, something that settles deep under the meat of his flesh and yet, at the same time, feels like it exists outside of it altogether. Etienne is subtle about curling his fingers up and rubbing at his skin, attempting to soothe that persistent ache, and doesn't dare turn his head to where Nica is standing next to him, messily wiping tears off their face and avoiding him the same.

~~*Giggling snort pushing hair behind their ear excited jumping in your veins do you could we think I'd like to following up the stairs behind them trying to forget the question bubbling up his throat pressing against his lips hey after this would you want to-*~~

No.

No, he...thinks he's done with that now, *knew it was a stupid idea*

What Goes Bump In The Night

~~no you didn't,~~ rock solid conviction settling heavy in his chest, knowing with a fair bit of certainty that this is the last night he's going to be seeing them.

Etienne may be a man of his word, hates to break it, but there are some lines that just *cannot* be crossed, and continuing to spend time with a person that makes excuses for bigotry is something he really can't force himself to keep doing, past promises or not.

It does hurt in a bitter way to think *this* is how it ends, somehow so much worse than it started, and his mouth turns sour knowing he's going to have to go and take Sabine up on his offer, will have to ask him to now loophole *Etienne* out of the program like he just did for himself. And even though Etienne has refused his help a couple times now, there's no question in his mind that Sabine will do it without hesitation when he asks, though his snide ass will probably be thinking, *I told you so,* the entire time.

Etienne feels his face flame hot with embarrassment at the thought, hates to be made to look the fool, but what other choice does he have? He can't keep doing this, not with Nica, *not after he has a better idea of who they are stinging prickle under your sternum against the corners of your eyes can't you calm down a little,* but he finds something like vengeful comfort in knowing he just needs to get through tonight and then it's done.

One more assignment and that's it, Etienne slowly relaxes his fingers, forces them out long and straight and then lets them rest where they will, *just a few hours show them who you are what you're made of don't let them think you can buckle,* and he won't, lifts his chin and is nothing except a scion when he asks, "So, are you gonna let us in or did I fly out here for nothin'?"

"Depends. There gonna be any more funny business?" Carter snipes back, but he's relaxed considerably, gone from the promise of violence to the assurance of only nasty comments and Etienne can handle that, narrows his eyes and draws out dark, *"Depends.* Keep your clowns in their circus tent an' there won't be."

Carter rolls his eyes and mutters something under his breath too

✦✦ 241 ✦✦

faint to hear, but it wouldn't take a genius to guess what he says. He unslouches from the crumbling doorframe without further comment, stepping out into the black of the night with a grand sweep of his arm back towards inside, "Well by all means then, *please,* come grace us with your presence, *sire.*"

Biting his tongue on the retort that comes bubbling up, Etienne snaps a hand out to the side, calling his broom back into his waiting palm and the sharp smack of polished wood against flesh makes the two humans jump. He spins it once as he strides forwards, coming about level with Carter and finds with dark amusement that he *is* taller than the other man, means Etienne can dip his head to address him when he props his broom in a corner by the door.

"I wouldn't touch that if I were you. *Might electrocute ya.*" Etienne warns from under the brim of his hat, knows it throws his face into absolute pitch shadows when it's as dark as it is out, and a needlework of lightning jumps off his tongue on the last word, whole effect probably making him look like something out of unholy nightmares.

Or Etienne hopes so at least, because if people are going to act like he's a creature of the night, he might as well help them remember that was once something they feared.

Grew soft with us coddling them, he thinks meanly as he pushes his way inside, *don't remember what it was like when they used to be afraid of the dark,* both front doors knobless and flying open alarmingly easy when he tugs at them, like they're loose on their hinges or something, *maybe that's a fear they should learn again.*

He sighs as soon as he thinks it, doesn't mean it *knows he doesn't mean it,* but he's hurt and sad, giving in to the temptation of being cruel right back. *Hanging on to resentment like this is poison,* Etienne reminds himself, rolling his head and trying to drive some of the stiffness out of his shoulders, *it'll kill you if you're not careful.*

And he gets that, *he knows that,* so with a last frustrated exhale, he mentally cuts the lines that are all snared up around the

What Goes Bump In The Night

indignation and *fury* from back outside, sets it free *lets it go,* feels marginally better once he does. The only thing Etienne should be focusing on tonight is just getting through it with a level head, can stew later when he's back home or better yet, when he sees Sabine tomorrow and has the most understanding ear he's ever known listen to all his grievances.

That puts a little more pep in his step, front door swinging shut behind him with a groaning clatter, and now that Etienne is inside the entrance, he's greeted by a plastic curtain quarantining the worksite off from the rest of the world. The edges of it are already smeared thick with grime that clings chalky to his skin as he holds it open for himself, tiny flecks of dust drifting loose and making him almost sneeze, and he rubs distractedly at his nose while finally stepping into the building proper.

It's old to no one's surprise, air stagnant with age and wet rot, metal scaffolding here and there trying to support the sagging floor above, work lights harsh on his eyes after being outside where things were much dimmer for so long.

Etienne has to blink a few times to get them to adjust, squints at his surroundings while they do and is a little surprised to see so much furniture left behind. There's stuff everywhere, moldering bookcases practically collapsed in a heap along one wall, his heart twinging painfully at all the books rotting along with them, desks upon desks stacked up in branching hallways that disappear off in each cardinal direction, what looks like old sports equipment and toys rusting in big metal trashcans by a boarded up backdoor.

Papers are still tacked to the walls and a few bulletin boards, though some have fallen off their rusting screws, spill a colorful mess of pages that turn black muddy brown the closer they are to the floor where detritus collects.

Some of the sheets higher up from the sludge are still legible, show messy scribblings of sunshines and flowers and little stick people smiling, *completely anachronistic to everything else,* each depiction way too cheerful for the mildewing ruin they've found themselves in.

✦✦ 243 ✦✦

The city must've used this place as a school once upon a time, not uncommon around here where building space is limited by what was already there, but as Etienne wanders further in, boots squelching into decomposing drifts of leaves, he can't help but feel a deep sense of *unease.*

Contrary to being easily startled, Etienne doesn't get unnerved by things that often, has seen all manner and form of rot and decay and knows what can lay lurking in the shadows, and there is something about this crumbling old school building that makes all his hair stand on end.

He sends his magic out in a great flexing roll, tendrils of it creeping across the space between spaces like branching lightning, curling under the fabric of reality, *poking and prodding,* trying to pinpoint the source of that feeling, and ice suddenly nettles at his fingertips, starts crawling up the length of his arms. Chasing after that sensation, Etienne looks for the root of it amongst all the collected ambient energy, *plants living animals breathing the arcane resonating,* ice climbing higher every second, but it slips away from him every time he gets close, almost like it's shy and doesn't want to be found.

Yeah...there's really only *one* thing that could be, and as if on cue, the back of his neck starts prickling and Etienne spins on his heel, looking down one shadowed hallway, half expecting to see some drooping face staring back.

There's nothing there as far as he can tell, but the feeling of eyes on him won't leave and he sighs exhausted, because of course, *it just figures,* the *one* night he's not expecting to have to do any actual work, and he winds up at a bigot run construction site that is also, *naturally,* haunted.

"Fantastic..." Etienne mutters under his breath, massaging at the bridge of his nose, lets out another aggrieved gust of air and plants his hands on his hips, figures there's nothing to do besides come up with a game plan.

Annoyingly, he's a bit short on supplies already, hadn't even both-

What Goes Bump In The Night

ered to bring his bag since he didn't think he'd be *doing* anything, means he's limited to whatever the storage sigils in his spellbook contain, but he should be able to scrape together whatever he needs to shoo the pesky spirit off.

Etienne isn't sure yet what it is *exactly,* needs to do a little more digging, but it's definitely apparitional, might be a few ghosts given the age of the building or maybe even a poltergeist, knows how much they love cluttered, old abandoned buildings. Either way, he doesn't think it's anything major.

From the looks of things, *scaffolding up sections of plaster removed furniture collected in one place,* it seems like the construction crew has been working here for a few weeks, and if there was a serious problem, they would've reported it already.

Still though, if there's *any* hauntings going on, no matter how benign, workers really shouldn't be here until one of the family certifies the property as officially cleansed. The fact that they're still on site is mildly aggravating because it means they likely haven't noticed anything, and of course they wouldn't *the absolute boneheads,* but it means the first they're gonna be hearing about it is from him, *Etienne,* the- *witch the stiff the freak the jinxflinger-*

He's gotta be the one to tell them what's going on, somehow explain why they need to shut down and vacate the site for the next day or so, just to make sure everything's clear. *You are the most unlucky bastard in all of New Orleans,* Etienne thinks morosely, blowing a lock of black hair out of his eyes.

He knows he's not gonna have an easy time convincing these morons to listen to him, and like he was summoned at the mere thought of idiocy, a construction guy comes ambling out of a nearby hallway whistling a peppy tune.

It's at least not one of the guys from earlier, *slimmer set of shoulders not as impressive of a frame,* but Etienne still distrustfully eyes the man's hardhat while warily drawing closer, reminding himself to be professional, *informative,* but still assertive when he says, "Excuse me sir, I know you probably have work to be doin'

✦✦ 245 ✦✦

but you're unfortunately gonna need to-"

"Huh-? *Woah-* hey! Lookit *you!*" The man interrupts in what sounds like excitement, thick eyebrows disappearing up behind the line of his helmet, and a genuine smile appears from somewhere amidst the bushy scruff of his beard, "Hey I'm really diggin' the getup, Casper, but didn't anyone tell'ya Halloween was at the *end* of the month? *Not the beginnin'?*"

To punctuate this apparently *hysterical* display of wit and humor, the man slaps his thigh and lets out a loud laugh, tools jingling together while his shoulders jump, and Etienne wonders if the plaster on the walls is rotten enough for him to smash his own head through it.

Unluckiest bastard in all of New Orleans, plays through his mind a few times like a clanging circus monkey, and exhaling hard out of his nose, Etienne makes to go find someone else when the guy starts waving his hands profusely.

"Hey, *no,* don't go, m'just yankin' your chain, buddy. Come on, *c'mere,* what can ol'Reggie help ya out with, huh?" He says cheerfully, looks like he's about to reach over and clap Etienne on the shoulder, but Etienne steps out of the way *fast* and Reggie drops his arm with a sheepish look.

Settling back on his heels, Etienne's eyes dart up to the man's neon yellow hardhat, can't immediately find any Anti-Sorcière propaganda, which doesn't necessarily *prove* anything, but the apparent lack of any serious ill will drains some of the hostility out of him.

Maybe this one isn't as bad as the others, Etienne relents somewhat, shoulders untensing the barest amount, *maybe he is actually just teasing,* and knocking the brim of his hat up so his face isn't entirely hidden in shadows, he warily starts his shpiel over, "My name is Etienne Boudreaux. I'm the scion of the local spirit witch chapter, an' I have reasonable cause to believe this property is haunted, so if you wouldn't mind-"

"Oh come on-! *Still?*" Reggie interjects *again* and Etienne feels

What Goes Bump In The Night

his eye twitch, both at being interrupted once more *and* the fact that *apparently,* they *know the place is haunted and have been working here anyway Mothers help you,* but it doesn't look like Reggie notices his growing irritation, tipping his head back with a chuckling groan, *"Man.* These things are *persistent,* I tell you *what.* We've been tryin' to get rid of'em for like a *week* now, and Carter was so *sure* he'd *finally* gotten it, did all that research and everythin' ...I just- you *sure* it's still haunted?"

"Pretty sure." Etienne says in deadpan, mind boggled a little bit wondering what other authority this guy could want rather than an *actual Boudreaux* telling him a place is haunted.

"Damn, that sucks..." Reggie sighs and nods his head a few times, looking very downtrodden about the whole thing, but then the hands he has planted on his hips suddenly shoot up, gesturing emphatically in Etienne's direction, "B-But *hey! You're* here now! And bein' a ghost *uh,* what'd you say...*siphon?* But yeah bein' a ghost siphon an' all, I'm sure you know *exactly* how to kill these things for good, yeah?"

There is...*so much blatantly wrong with that statement,* but Etienne isn't sure he has the patience to unpack it all, opens his mouth, shuts it, *shakes his head,* lets it go and settles on, "I- *sure.* Now- you said *things,* right? As in *multiple* apparitions? Do you know 'bout how many, or even just a rough estimation?"

Blowing air hard out his lips so that they vibrate together, Reggie scratches at the back of his head, knocking his hardhat back and forth while he thinks, "Shoot...that's a toughie, I'm really not too sure 'cause I've never actually *seen any-* I think a couple of the guys have but like, it can't all be the same one, r-right? There's *way* too many voices for it to be one, *oh,* unless it's like a *ventriloquist ghost.* Is that a thing? *I feel like that could be a thing-"*

"It's not a thing. *Er-* well it technically is but not like you're thinkin', okay so you've heard them then...do you remember anything they've said? Doesn't have to be much, could just be one word or a sound even." Etienne is leaning more towards ghosts now in his assessment considering poltergeists often don't speak,

✦✦ 247 ✦✦

are more inclined to throwing things and giggling manically, but ghosts often try to communicate with the living.

They're typically very shy spirits, are prone to hiding and are reluctant to show themselves, whisper things out of sight because they lack the energy to manifest properly. In pretty much every case, they're completely harmless, bear no ill will and are simply confused and scared as to what's going on, most of them not even realizing they're actually dead.

Dealing with ghosts is kinda like dealing with Gran Mémé, *lots of patience lots of care lots of gentleness,* and sending them back to the aether is one of the beginner tasks first year apprentices accomplish on their own. So for a moment, Etienne is pretty confident this is gonna be a walk in the park, just needs to find where all of them are hiding, coax them out, console them before sending them back, *chew out Carter for disturbing restless spirits,* but then Reggie actually answers his question and things get more complicated.

"Ah...*ya'know,* it's just typical horror movie stuff. Crying and moaning, sometimes clickin', *m-mostly crying.* Uh, I've heard *'help'* and, *'can't leave',* a lot, which is super spooky not gonna lie. Oh! And then one of my buddies *swears* he heard one say *'I can't breathe'* which- *don't like that."* Reggie finishes with an uneasy laugh, clear he's trying to bring levity into a situation that's actually unnerved him greatly, and apprehension picks its way up Etienne's spine like a horribly slow set of doting fingers.

Oh you've got to be joking, draws unhappily through his brain, new idea starting to take shape in its wake, *way less pleasant way more concerning,* but it might *not be that,* he might *not* truly be the most unfortunate bastard in all of New Orleans, and with something like a sigh, Etienne hates to ask because he already feels like he knows the answer, "When you said cryin'...can you describe it? Like was it more soft, sad crying or like...angry crying? *Like screaming?"*

And the distinction really is important because ghosts are never angry, they don't torment people, but other things do, and from

What Goes Bump In The Night

the way Reggie shrugs, rubbing at the side of his nose, *other things have been,* "I- I-I guess more upset? Like...it's loud...it's *r-real loud,* and I swear but like, l-like it sounds like they're bein' ki...*Jesus,* I got chills just thinkin' about it. S-Sorry man, I know I'm not bein' much help but *shit- I-I really hate talkin' about this-*"

"No no, I understand. It's very unsettling to deal with this kinda thing, you have every right to be afraid, but don't worry, I'm here now. I'll take care of it, you don't have to be scared anymore." Etienne soothes and unfortunately, thinks he has a better idea of what's haunting this place, but he wants to be certain, "Okay now this is very important you answer me honest, but has anythin' violent or harmful occurred here? Like since y'all started working, has anything been damaged? Have any of you been hurt?"

"I mean...n-not really? It- the ghosts throw things sometimes but we- w-we just thought they were like...messin' around, ya'know? *Playing,* b-but yeah, no one's been hurt besides the usual stubbed... thumb..." Reggie trails off, seemingly like he's realized something, face bleeding ashen, "Wait- *wait,* are you sayin' these things *could* hurt us? Like *they're dangerous-* c-could they *kill us?* Are we in d-danger *right now-?*"

Yes possibly maybe depends, is what almost leaps off Etienne's tongue but he turns it fast into a considering hum, can see Reggie starting to freak out and needs to calm him back down, "Any serious harm is...*highly unlikely,* so I wouldn't worry about that, but these spirits *are* dangerous, an' I think it'd be best if all y'all suspended work until the issue is resolved."

"*Jesus fuck-* don't have to tell *me* twice. *Fuck* this creepy ass dump, man." Reggie says with extreme vitriol, a sentiment Etienne shares and finds great amusement in, barest hint of a smile creeping up his lips as he asks, "Do you know who's all workin' tonight? I need to make sure everyone is out of the building before I start anythin'. The spirits might get a little riled up and I'd rather y'all not get caught in the crossfire."

"Yeah...y-yeah no I'll radio the rest of the guys, don't worry 'bout it, but...do um, do you need anythin' though? Like I don't really know what I can do to *help*, but like, just let me know if there's somethin' you need, m'kay?" Reggie offers, tugging on his beard, and it's crazy how such a small gesture of aid completely and resoundingly flips Etienne's opinion of the man.

Good person, curls warmly through his head, chest growing light, heartened any time he's reminded that *yes,* there are still people out there who respect who he is and what he does, and he smiles kindly, "Thank you, but just make sure everyone's out- *oh!* And do you know if there's a certain place that's been more active? It'll help save me some time."

"You got it boss." Reggie flicks him a lazy salute, starts unclipping the radio at his belt and then uses it to gesture down the hallway across from them, "Honestly, whole place has been kinda buggy, but it was worse in the art room. Head down that way, staircase is at the end of the hallway, take it up to the second floor, hang a right, you won't be able to miss it."

With everything seemingly sorted down here, Etienne thanks him again, offers one last reminder not to linger in the building too long and Reggie waves him off, already speaking over the radio. The reply that comes back is garbled and lost to static, whatever Reggie says in response fading out as Etienne heads down the hallway, being more mindful to the shifts in ambient energy now that he's pretty sure he knows what he's squaring off against.

"Why is it *always* specters..." Etienne grumbles, finding the debris strewn stairwell and carefully picking his way up it, bit of dark amusement kicking around in his chest thinking about how often city projects are beset by the spiteful pests. It's honestly comical at this point, not a single thing can get done without someone *somehow* disturbing a nest of the vengeful spirits, but a specter infestation really is no laughing matter.

They're angry violent spirits that died angry, violent, *painful* deaths, seek a release from their own personal torment that typically has them turning those anguished emotions back on the living, meaning they pose significantly more of a threat than a common ghost. People can and *have died* at their spectral hands

✦✦ 250 ✦✦

What Goes Bump In The Night

before, *bodies ripped apart blood splattering the walls never even saw them coming,* but despite the danger level ramping up significantly, Etienne still isn't too worried.

From the sounds of things, the haunting hasn't gotten out of hand yet, sounds more like it's really just getting started, what with the whispering and manipulation of physical objects, and as long as he deals with it tonight, there isn't much cause for concern. Because the threat to life specters pose only really becomes a problem when they've been left unchecked, *antagonized further,* their festering emotions growing more and more sinister as they decay into nothing resembling the human beings they once were.

But Etienne won't let it get to that point, will slow down the haunt until everyone's out of the building and then he'll cleanse the whole thing proper, might have to make a midnight supply run in order to do that, but there's no rush.

The situation is under control.

✦✦ 251 ✦✦

Chapter 13

Water is dripping overhead from somewhere, a soft little metronome that underscores the click and slide of his boots up the stairs, soles slipping a bit on the grime covered treads. Etienne flails out blindly for a handrail on instinct, only coming to regret it once he feels the moldering wood stick to his palm, lets go fast and unhappily rubs his fingers together.

That's one of the things he's routinely disliked about New Orleans, how warm and damp it always is, leads things to fall into the stickiness of molding rot that squelches any time you touch it, and this building is a horrible showcasing of it. It must have sat abandoned through at least a *decade* of storm seasons, no one around to repair any damaging leaks before they began their ruinous campaign, slowly but steadily destroying everything that was once safe inside one drip at a time.

Etienne comes to a small landing and a boarded up window that probably used to look out over the back half of the property, peeks through the slats and can't make out much of anything through the filmy old glass.

Bet that's where the school yard was, he thinks idly, heading up the last flight of stairs before coming to the second floor proper, notes that the stairs keep climbing to a third floor which, if his memory serves him right, should be in the attic of the building.

He glances curiously up the darkened stairwell, can't see much of anything since there's no lights up that way, and when he reaches out with his magic, Etienne doesn't feel much of anything either. It's still just that pervasive, faint chill lingering in the air everywhere he reaches, breaking hives out along the back of his neck, but it doesn't seem like it's coming from anywhere in particular, which is

What Goes Bump In The Night

incredibly odd.

Usually hunting down spirits is like playing a game of *hot'n'cold,* feeling out where their icy essence leads until you get to the source and can deal with it from there. And sure, sometimes it's not super apparent, can be the *biggest* pain in the ass tracking down where each trail leads, but this is the fuzziest Etienne has ever felt it.

The way the energy is filtering back to him, it's almost like it's diffused or something, *a misty freezing cloud that curls through his fingers, his toes doesn't seem to come from anywhere can't come from nowhere,* and he shakes his head, sets the golden chains on his hat swinging.

Weird...*weird weird weird weird,* everything about this is just, *so- off.*

Specters are generally fairly obvious to find, *they like to be known they like to be heard,* so maybe it is ghosts after all, could account for the hazy trails and initially shy nature, but then it wouldn't explain the interaction with physical objects, something Reggie was *very* adamant about having happened. It might actually be multiple things, ghosts *and* a poltergeist maybe, which is a pretty rare combination but not *entirely* unheard of, and the building's old enough to have borne witness to several eras of spirits.

Etienne doesn't have an exact age on the place, but given its general construction, the cemented over old bricks outside, and the fact that nothing in the city is ever just used for one thing, he's willing to bet it's been here since the turn of the nineteenth century at *least.* Which leaves a lot of time for ghosts to have settled in amongst the cracks and crevices, perhaps even starting to diffuse themselves as their energy naturally fades, and while not a great answer to the fuzzy readings he's getting, Etienne isn't really sure what else to think.

Something unusual is going on that's for sure, which is quite the statement coming from *him,* and the most productive thing he can do about it is find the art room, *find where it all started,* and hope there's some more answers there. Hanging a right as per

✦✦ 253 ✦✦

Reggie's directions, Etienne heads down a dimly lit hallway, this one lined with banks of wooden lockers set into the wall, some of them with their doors hanging wide open and listless.

Papers flood out, a soggy mess that hits the floor and muddles in with the other pieces of debris, most of it looking like crumbling chunks of the ceiling that have rotted out from water damage, likely coming from the floor above.

Etienne glances up in trepidation and sees rings of black stained plaster, spots where it's swelled outwards from collecting moisture but hasn't yet collapsed, and sticks his tongue out in disgust, has never been more grateful for his hat.

There's a smattering of construction supplies up on this floor too, *sets of tools joints and beams of scaffolding ropes of electrical wires,* but even with his nonexistent experience, Etienne can tell they weren't finished setting up yet, passes half put together sections of scaffolding that look like one stiff gust of wind would knock them over.

Whatever's been happening here must've gotten to the construction guys pretty bad to leave work like this unfinished, and at one point down the hall, it gets dark enough that Etienne has to wave a guide light into being, the little silvery white ball coming to float just above his head.

It throws long shadows out before him, like moonlight cutting down through bare branches, his shadow monstrous and looming, and it's in that half darkness when he feels the first one. It's very brief, but it hits him hard, and Etienne suddenly gets a very cramped, claustrophobic sensation, halts in his tracks because it feels like there's something in front of him that'd trip him, but when he looks down at the floor, there's nothing there.

An echo, he realizes, nudging the toe of his boot forwards and naturally, meets no resistance, but it still crawls prickling over his skin that *something is there something is right in front of you don't step on it.* He focuses harder on the sensation, trying to draw out more of what it is and gets the impression of something heavy, *something slumped over,* feels like it's a sack of grain or maybe a bale of cotton, has the sense that there's more lining the way up ahead.

Etienne had been wondering if maybe this place used to be a mill warehouse, could've even been a cotton exchange if it's old enough, and that brief flash of an echo feels like it lends credence to his speculations. This being a former industrial building would explain the presence of specters way more than a generically typical decommissioned school would, because safety regulations are really only a modern advent and warehouse accidents are still all too common.

And nothing breeds anger and resentment like dying on the job, could actually account for why the specters only got riled up into activity by the presence of the construction crew.

Maybe they feel a sort of kinship, Etienne thinks, stepping through whatever is on the ground, feels a jolt of icy energy snap up his leg but ignores it, continues making his way down the hall, *maybe that's why they're harassing them...maybe they're resentful because these guys live...maybe they're planning on changing that maybe-*

Something creaks behind him and Etienne looks over his shoulder, doesn't see anything but it feels like something is seeing him, atmosphere compressing together like a crush of bodies leaning in, and he clucks his tongue, "What? Got somethin' you wanna say?"

Ideally, he'd get a reply of some kind, spirits are always more drawn to him and typically have an easier time interacting, but the only thing he gets is that same intense silence. It's not oppressive or choking, isn't like hands wrapping over his ears or fists stuffing down his throat, but it is present, *purposeful,* a heavy weight that settles uncomfortably over Etienne's shoulders, letting him know he's not alone up here walking these halls.

Come out I know you're there you're not slick there's no use hiding not from me, he wants to shout, won't though because specters often do the exact *opposite* of what you ask of them, seek to cause aggravation and torment in any way they can. His eyes flick from shadow to shadow, magic fizzing off him like the waving arms of a sea anemone, trying to catch a glimpse of *anything,* and it's so weird that there's still nothing when any other time he's been after specters, they've made their presence known long before now.

"Fine...suit yourself." Etienne informs the air, turns back around and is half expecting to see something, can't *count* the number of times he's been jumpscared by some asshole spirit, but the hallway is empty *and also not,* that same sensation of heavy objects cluttering the floor along his path.

Again, he walks forward unbothered, acting like there's nothing there *which there's not,* and again, *ice eats at his shins nettles at his calves you're stepping on something ~~stop it,~~* but he doesn't stop this time as he sighs, "You know, if you don't want me up here you should say somethin', 'cause otherwise I'm not leavin'..."

Addressing spirits directly is generally not advised as it draws their attention to you, which is obviously a *very* bad idea unless you happen to be a member of House Boudreaux, in which case, it is often incredibly necessary.

Intentionally antagonizing spirits can be extremely dangerous, because if you're not careful about it, the situation can rapidly spiral out of control, *fatally so,* and yet, it is still an approved tactic that gets taught to all young apprentices.

Sometimes there really *is* no other option to draw out particularly stubborn spirits than to become the object of their own ire, and yes, pissed off spirits may be one of the leading contributors to the numerous scars littering Etienne's body, but he's also been able to keep a lot of people safe that way.

"If you don't like me up here, you need to let me know." He repeats, hoping it does *something,* but the only thing that protests is the floor under his feet, soft groans and creaks that come from age and not lingering spirits. Ugh, he knows he's being too vague with his nettling, and that to really get under their skin, he needs to get *personal,* but he doesn't have enough of an idea yet to really

What Goes Bump In The Night

take a guess at what would set them off besides generic issues.

"They're probably gonna tear down this building...but I'm assumin' you already knew that. Is that why you're upset? Because they're disturbin' the place where you died?" Etienne tries goading, hits a particularly squeaky part of the floor, and for a second, it sounds like metal wheels on some cart squealing past, "Or maybe do you see the people workin' here and think of yourself? Do you miss the way you used to be...*when you were alive?*"

It's hard to describe the way the atmosphere shifts, but the best way he can think of is to say it's *thickening,* growing more muffled and heavier the further he walks, and Etienne wets his lips, knows he's got *something's* attention, "Are you jealous that they live an' you don't? Or is it not really jealousy, but more like *envy?* You *want* to be alive but you're not, and you despise that these people get to live while *you* don't...does that make you angry? Does it *piss you off* to know you'll never get a second chan-?"

He jumps when there's a loud crash behind him, spins on his heels with his heart in his throat and electricity building at his fingertips, eyes straining against the gloom as metal pings and rattles, sounding like one of the sections of scaffolding just collapsed.

Now, could be the thing just came down on its own, *saw how shoddily it was put together how many supports were missing could've just buckled,* but the timing seems a little too convenient, and paying attention to the small things like that is what sets a good exorcist apart from a dead one.

"Didn't like that did you..." He mutters under his breath, nudges the brim of his hat up and waits on pins and needles to see if that was enough to stir some of them up, feels all the hair raise on the back of his neck and is turning before he even really registers the sound. It's the faintest thing, *the softest scuffle slide,* like a smooth shoe sole being drug across the floor, way daintier than he'd think any warehouse worker would walk, but the oddity of it is forgotten the instant he catches a glimpse of white.

✦✦ 257 ✦✦

It ripples like water, dancing at the edge of his vision like how moonlight shakes down through black tree leaves, and he's after it like a shot, skidding down the hall where it disappeared until he comes to another branching four way split. Etienne spins to glance down each darkened offshoot, sees more pale bars of light from boarded up windows, more gaping empty hollows of rotted open lockers, *not a single fluttering piece of fabric or soft leather boot trailing white lines like long curling fingers follow me,* stops though when he comes to face the hallway that leads towards the back of the building.

*Mothers of the Night what in the...*well, Reggie *did* say it would be obvious...

Maybe at one point it was supposed to look whimsical and inviting, *artwork taped to the walls little sculptures and colorful streamers hanging from the ceiling cheery handprints dipped in paint splashed across pale plaster,* but now, with the muted lighting that leaches all the color out of everything, the murky floors and dripping strips of moldering streamers, *muddy handprints seemingly trying to claw their way free,* the hallway leading to the art room looks like it'd be more at home out in the Au Delà bogs than here in this old school building.

There's caution tape crisscrossing the mouth of the hallway, Etienne can see more draped loosely over the double doors ahead, and since he doesn't know where that apparition went, he figures the art room is probably the best place to start looking. He doesn't hesitate ducking under the first set of tape, hopes it's there because of the hauntings and not because the floor is structurally unsound, supposes he's about to find out one way or another. The old wood creaks threateningly on his first step, but it holds, and he tries to keep his ensuing steps light as he draws closer, guide light reflecting back harshly in the glass panes set into the doors once he's right in front of them.

He waves the thing further up, but still can't really see inside of the room because of it, goes for a door handle and halts, brows drawing together seeing the thick line of crumbly white *something* stretched out in front of the doorway. Etienne crouches down and

✦✦ 258 ✦✦

What Goes Bump In The Night

touches at it lightly, rubbing the gritty texture between his fingers, is pretty sure he knows what it is even before bringing some up for his tongue to taste.

Saliva floods his mouth instantly, *salt* clinging heavily to every surface as he tries to spit the residue out, and Etienne rocks back on his haunches, baffled as to why the construction crew were trying to keep the specters *out* of the art room.

Well- *okay*, he gets *why* they'd wanna keep them out, most normal people don't want vengeful spirits hanging around while they're trying to do demo work, but from the looks of things, they have this entire area quarantined off and have had it like this for quite some time.

It doesn't seem like they've been doing work up here in *weeks*, so Etienne is a bit confused on why they'd want to keep the specters *out* of someplace they're not even working in. *Maybe there's something in there they didn't want them getting into*, his brain suggests, but it's a weak theory and Etienne knows it, slowly gets back up to his feet and can't shake the feeling he's not been told everything, or that he's misinterpreted something important.

Something about this place isn't sitting right with him, and as he's standing up, his eyes land on the murky glass again and his pulse jumps seeing *something there this time*, and it's not the blurry form of his own reflection.

It hovers just over his shoulder, *moves with him as he leans in means it's on this side means it's right behind him*, and goosebumps erupt across his skin, next exhale hissing out in a cloud of fog. Etienne can hear breathing now that's not his own, *deep and grating*, sounds like it's struggling for each inhale, a desperate fight he doesn't think it won in the end, and never taking his eyes off the distorted image, he murmurs, "What do you want?"

The old glass warps the reflection into something almost unrecognizable, streaky lines of their face bleeding into one another and seeming to drip out of existence, like loose flesh hanging limp off a dented skull, and the reflection never moves, but the gurgling wheezing gets louder.

A freezing presence colder than any winter drags itself into the space over Etienne's shoulder, never touches him but he doesn't dare move so that it might, can hear a throat working right at his ear, clicking and swallowing repeatedly.

"I said- *what* do you *want?*" Etienne asks again, can hardly hear himself think past his own thundering heart and the frantic swallowing that has escalated into outright choking, gasping, *panicked breaths* shot right into his ear, scent of copper and sour bile washing over him *spilling down his shirtfront coughing and coughing and hacking and HACKING but it never comes up nothing ever clears something in your throat in your c h e s t get it out get it out GET IT OUT CLAW IT OUT GET I T O U T-* and it is the barest puff of breath but crashes into his mind like the explosive clap of cymbals as the specter begs frantic, *"A I R-"*

A whisper of pressure ghosts across the thin skin of his jugular before it's vaporized in an instant, his magic reacting before Etienne can even fully register what's happening, current of electricity rolling down his body and discharging threateningly into the air around him.

Get back get bACK GET BACK, it tremors unhappily like grumbling thunder, slinking back under his bones satisfied when nothing tries to reach for him again, but Etienne brings a hand up to wrap protectively over the column of his throat, swallows once and still feels the slick fingertips pressing into each side of his trachea.

That was...a lot more *physical* of a response than he was expecting to get, is more than a little unnerved with how violent that felt, *almost to the point of possibly being fatal,* and will eternally be grateful to the guarding nature of his magic.

He doesn't want to think about what would've happened to him without it, worries starting to gnaw at his mind because things seem to be deteriorating far more rapidly than he had initially calculated for, and the implications for what is to come drastically

What Goes Bump In The Night

ratchets up his level of concern.

"I hate specters." Etienne hisses solely for the sake of hearing something else besides his own staggered breathing. He rubs comfortingly at his throat to reassure himself that, *there's nothing there you're fine,* but understands he really can't waste any more time in slowing down the haunt. The onset of physical violence is always the harbinger to things spiraling out of control, and while his magic will protect him from as much as it can, it won't be able to do a lot to, *say,* stop one of the numerous screwdrivers he's seen laying around from being launched brutally into his eye socket.

And with *that* lovely image in mind, Etienne lets go of his neck to take hold of one of the door handles, pulling the tape apart as he pushes into the darkened art room, being mindful to not disrupt the salt line while he steps across the threshold. *At least that'll come in handy for something,* he thinks with a shake of his head. He's wary of letting go of the door just yet, doesn't want it slamming shut behind him and trapping him inside, and scans the floor quickly for a suitable doorstop.

Thankfully there's an old chair within reach, rusted out metal legs screeching against the floor as he drags it over, getting it good and wedged in the doorway, leaving enough of a gap for him to wiggle out if necessary.

Emergency exit secured, Etienne turns then to face the dilapidated art room, noting how it runs almost the full length of the back wall of the building, huge bank of grimy windows that he's sure used to let in wonderful amounts of sunlight when this place was still an operational school.

There's nothing immediately off about the space, though he is very cautious about moving forwards, still hyper aware and fixated on where the specter almost grabbed him earlier, feels like a red hot brand where its fingers only barely grazed him.

He keeps moving his neck funny to try and dispel the sensation, skirting past long tables that are haphazardly shoved into one another and bumper up next to the walls, chairs scattered about

✦✦ 261 ✦✦

like destitute refugees. Old art projects pepper the walls and windows, rotting supplies stored on half collapsed shelves, what has to be unused paint leaking out of bottles and spilling dark down onto the floor, a river of ominous sludge that sticks tacky to the soles of his boots, looking like it could almost be blood in the moonlight.

Etienne accidentally tracks it across the cluttered floor, tries to mind where he steps after that, but ends up leaving behind the dark print of his boots anyway. Each mark glistens wetly where the light manages to hit it, a trail of foreboding that follows him into the center of the room. Around him, the wind shooshes through the trees outside and sends little faded coins of shadows skittering across the floor, making it seem as if an entire swarm of insects are crawling over the toes of Etienne's boots.

He shakes one of his feet instinctually, can almost *feel* the tiny legs against hSis skin, and hops out of the stream of moonlight as quickly as he can, only feeling silly once he's done so.

There's nothing there calm down don't let your eyes play tricks on you, he berates his consciousness, knows he has a bad habit of falling for illusions, *has always been one of the things he struggles with the most,* and brings his eyes back up to the rest of the room. He can't see much, *it's not very well lit in here shadows thick like ink,* meager glow from his guide light barely penetrating to every corner, but Etienne supposes it doesn't really matter if he can see everything or not.

At this point, he has enough information to be sure that, *yes, unfortunately it really is specters,* and while he'll need to figure out later what the emotional anchor is that's keeping them bound here, he should be fine to go ahead and cast a Sommerset conciliatory spell.

Thankfully that type of sigil doesn't require knowing what the anchoring event is, and even though the later appeasement ritual *will,* Etienne decides for the sake of expediting safety, it's not important to focus on the- *'why is this place haunted'* question, right now.

What Goes Bump In The Night

He'll have to do some more poking around once things have calmed down a bit, but that'll be a little tricky considering that whatever this place used to be, back when these people lost their lives, has been completely scrubbed clean. There are no clues for Etienne to figure out what happened to them hiding in the grimy cabinets or painted across that darkened back wall, or at least, none that he can *see*, and while he really needs to be concentrated on the conciliatory sigil, he can't help the way his wandering thoughts pick over everything.

Soft step of shoes out in the hallway flickering of white trailing ribbons curling lines like a bow like a knot like the strings of an apron doesn't sound like warehouse work, Etienne thinks while unholstering his spellbook, sturdy leather of its cover humming warm and alive under his fingertips, *hacking and hacking and coughing and choking doesn't sound like warehouse injury crushed bones fractured skulls arteries severed blood everywhere not this soft suffocating death,* pages fluttering under his thumb as he sifts through to where he stores his sigils, *doesn't make sense does it have to parts don't match like the wrong pieces for the wrong puzzle something in it something to it something wrong about how you asked what it wanted and it begged you for-*

Chairs go screeching across the floor all of a sudden, and Etienne turns fast, free hand alive with electricity as he cuts it through the air, trying to forestall whatever attack is coming, but nothing lands.

His eyes scan the gloom, *body on edge,* can't tell which chairs moved and finds his gaze darting over the old art tables as well, squinting at the way moonlight spills across them, pale gleam of it almost looking like taught white bedsheets pulled into militant perfection.

Shadows dance over their tops, ruining the illusion, but something is tugging at Etienne, that same kinda prickling sensation he felt out in the hallway, an echo, *an indication that things here are trying to remember what they used to be.* And it may be a stupid idea, but *he's curious,* can't fight it, *leans into it,* sends creeping feelers of his magic out to brush along what's shivering beneath the swell of reality and in between one blink and the next, clusters of neatly made beds stand at attention.

He blinks and the image doesn't dispel, blinks again and it looks like something dark is spreading across those pristine white sheets, *creeping mold spreading rot growing stain of murky water* ~~help~~, *blink* and it looks like something is moving *writhing beneath the covers* ~~help me God please can't breathe~~, *BLINK* and there's that rattling again, *from people from metal carts desperate wheezing of and the tick tick tack of take a corner too hard something rolls out from under the sheet lax fingers stretched out like a Michelangelo but beckoning towards the floor not heaven* ~~don't leave me here can't leave me like this have to help me God please help me help me heLP ME I DON'T WANNA~~

A forceful blink and Etienne *makes* them be just tables again.

But he can hear the rustling of sheets under his eardrum, *sharp rap of heels running past violent squeal of ungreased metal wheels* ~~can't fit anymore in can't fit don't have the~~, feels something wet catch in his throat and inhales deep, *thinks he's choking,* reminding himself *you can still breathe* ~~take deep breaths you have to try and sir or I'll have to~~, pinprick of white hot pain over the bump of his windpipe that sends his head *reeling.*

Ozone burns sharp in his nose even though the tendrils of his lightning have long since flickered away, and electricity always smells faintly like bleach and searing heat, but this goes aggressively antiseptic, acrid and astringent in the way true cleaning chemicals are *get them out of here clogging up the nowhere to put them just throw them in the thud thud as bodies hit the floor like sacks of grains like piles of trash like things forgotten*

Etienne stumbles a bit, unexpectedly lightheaded from fumes that didn't used to be poisoning the air, stutters back on his heels to try and regain his balance and nearly falls on his ass, something rolling under the sole of his boot and unbalancing him further. He flings a hand up thinking he'll be able to catch himself on a bar above him, but there's nothing, and he falls back against a table with a clatter, can't shake the feeling that he sinks into it more

What Goes Bump In The Night

than a wooden surface should allow.

Head swimming, Etienne blearily looks up for the thing he thought he could reach, thinks he sees fluttering white and follows the flowing line of it back down, now finding himself in an entire field of them gently waving in the breeze like curtains, *like ship sails like mourning shrouds.*

Footsteps go rushing past, *echoing through the walls on the ceiling clamoring back from an unplace outside of existence,* arctic snarl of wind coming with it, *makes all your hairs stand on end ~~there's too many don't have enough beds check the soles of their too far gone take them to the basement,~~* repugnant stench of antiseptic and sour metallic copper washing over him.

He has to drop his spellbook to clap a hand over his nose and mouth, *trying not to vomit,* legs growing shaky and *weak* as a tidal wave of sensation crashes into him.

Oh there is so much *agony* hidden here and it bleeds from everywhere, slowly rolling down the walls and soaking free from deep within the plaster, puddling up from the floor, oozing out between cracks in the linoleum from where it lay dormant in the old wooden floorboards, the ones that used to have *every single tragedy borne overtop them clattering pans spilling fluids red spraying free from the front of your-*

Etienne hisses air out through his teeth, hands coming up to dig fingers against his temples, *trying to make it stop,* but it's like a malaise, *spreads through his mind like a rot,* and it- *claws at you threatening to pull you under pull you in hear the crying smell the death rattling breaths and rattling carts taking them in taking them out taking them IN taking them OUT bang slap of the door over and over and over and OVER AND IT NEVER STOPS-*

No, it's not real what he's seeing *isn't real but Mothers it feels so real and it needs to stop you need to stop,* pull yourself together *pull yourself OUT focus get a grip don't get lost don't let them-*

-keep coming mORE KEEP COMING feel the desperation the panic empty glass shattering against the floor not enough there iSN'T

✦✦ 265 ✦✦

ENOUGH keep piling up a mountain of FAILURE and ILLNESS that drips black and bloody and miserable into everything around it help us-

Oh void beyond, the way *that echoes in the hollow chambers of his mind, panicked terrified desperate HELP,* and he's *trying, ~~it's not enough,~~* Mothers he wants to help *is going to help, ~~no you're not said the same thing and now look at us,~~* but he has to get free from this first *but it won't let him go ~~no escape not for us not for you~~ like a thousand void cold hands are trying to drag him down like a myriad of drowning victims are trying to pull themselves up and they're begging desperately for-*

-a chance please give us a chance help us SAVE US don't leave us here holes in our throats it hurts sludge in our lungs it HURTS can't breathe IT HURTS you're supposed to know what to do you're supposed to fix this FIX US please help uS HELP US HELP US H E L P HEL HE LP H ELP H E L P-

Etienne pulls all his magic back in with a shout, can feel his consciousness, *his knowledge of who he is,* being overrun with memories and thoughts and sensations *~~and anger and resentment and VIOLENCE,~~* that aren't his, and his power slams shut its connection to the aether like a clam snapping its shell closed. Everything flooding into him is cut off instantly and he can *breathe* he can *think,* he's not dying, *he's not dead he knows who he is,* and he slumps back against the table to try and catch his breath for a brief moment.

You're fine you're fine you're fine, he repeats to himself while shaking hands rub up and down his arms, *looking for warmth looking for life,* and Etienne's aware that he is more vulnerable closed off like this, but if he let himself stay connected to *all of that-* he isn't sure he would've made it out in one piece. Parts of him are actually still lost *back there, struggling under the sheets legs kicking weakly compressive force in your lungs can't get it OUT,* but Etienne ignores them, *has to,* now *finally* understanding where exactly he's gone and bumbled his way into and it's bad.

It's really bad.

What Goes Bump In The Night

Dropping to his knees before his head has entirely stopped spinning, Étienne pats around the floor with jittering hands looking for his spellbook, needs to get the Sommerset sigil down and secured so he can *get the fuck out of here* as soon as possible. He feels like an idiot for being so slow to put the pieces together, and maybe it should've been obvious from the onset, *the age the presence of specters the foreboding energy lingering in the air can't BREATHE,* but he hadn't thought to look for something he didn't consider a possibility.

Because what this place used to be isn't actually a former grain warehouse with a few disgruntled employees who died on the job, nor was it ever an old administrative building that might've seen an unfortunate murder or two, no, Etienne *wishes* he was that lucky, because the real answer is a million times worse than either of those combined.

Because this place was a hospital.

One that stood for service during one of the worst global disease outbreaks in the record of modern medicine, and the amount of people that likely died within these walls is now only known by the spirits that haunt them still.

Influenza hospital drips through his brain like tarry poisonous sap, a dangerous identifier that he is all too familiar with, knows full well that they're notorious breeding grounds for specters and other malignant entities. So many people died so quickly from what they assumed was a mild case of the flu, that the shock of dying completely and utterly unexpectedly chained them here forever, but Etienne thought his family had gotten all the bad ones already.

Ever since the early seventies, they've made a point to try and scrub all these sites of mass death and suffering clean, but there were so *many* unofficial hospitals and medical centers that opened for the emergency, many went undocumented, *slipped through the cracks,* only becoming apparent what they are when the spirits lingering in the foundations get disturbed.

As part of his training, Etienne has actually been to a handful of former hospitals already, observing mother while she performs the appeasement ritual with stunning grace, sometimes tagging along with Uncle Gilbert as his second if Gilbert's leg isn't bothering him, but no place he's ever visited has been as sinister as this.

The spirits he's encountered have always been agitated, the indignation and helplessness they felt upon their deaths giving them a new restless unlife, and yeah it caused them to lash out on occasion, but Etienne can't remember a single site where he was grabbed like he was earlier.

That's what's different here, there's something undeniably malevolent suffusing the air, and yes, specters are typically very troubled spirits, but there's a difference between, *oh I'm going to get your attention by touching your neck,* and, *I'm going to wring it until it snaps,* and the way that one was trying to wrap its hands around his throat earlier...it was done with *intent, it had a purpose.*

And it sends anxious bands coiling through Etienne's gut because he can't pretend the specter wasn't *trying* to hurt him, and it's unnerving to know that if it hadn't been for his magic startling the thing off, he's not sure how far things would've gone. He might've lived, *come away with bruises and sore pride but his life,* or he could've ended up clawing and digging frantically at his throat, trying to get any faint gasps of air in through the invisible force choking the life out of him.

Which is what's bothering him so much, because that thing full well could have killed him, *possibly was even attempting to,* but most regular people don't have the capacity for murder, nor would they want to, and that's what you have to remember about specters.

They may be shadows of whoever they used to be, are plagued by harsh pain and seething anguish, but they're still human, *they're still people.* They likely wouldn't have hurt anyone while they lived, shouldn't possess that much murderous intent in death, and so Etienne can't shake the idea that something's happened that's driven them to this point.

What Goes Bump In The Night

His fingers brush at a supple leather cover as soon as he considers it, and Etienne breathes out a soft sigh of relief feeling that familiar hum of energy against his skin again, *almost like it's infused with a live current hi know you,* but then all the hairs raise along the back of his neck watching the way his breath fogs visibly in front of his nose.

The ~~bed~~ *table* behind him creaks, *like a body shifting sensation of something damp drawing closer feel the moisture as it leaks into the air I want it,* and not waiting to find out *what it wants,* Etienne scrabbles forwards on hands and knees hopefully out of its reach.

A faint gust of air tickles the back of his neck, *thing just took a swipe at you going for the throat again,* and once more, he's absolutely unnerved by the violent and malignant nature of the spirits trapped here, doesn't understand *why* they're so aggressive so soon.

Maybe all the electrical fields from the construction tools are stressing them out, his mind suggests halfheartedly while he's pushing himself to his feet, free hand crunching against something he thinks is just a wad of old leaves until it rolls a bit under his palm, burnt, earthy scent of singed herbs drifting into his nose.

Etienne knows what it is instantly, has smelled it a million times before, *during rituals wafting around alters smoldering smoke from incense sticks that clings to his clothes,* instinctually doesn't find it odd for there to be a sage bundle here until the little pieces click together in his head that, oh, *right, there are a fuckton of specters here,* and oh, *fuck, burning sage can actually increase spiritual activity.*

Something trickles into his brain then like the slow drip of unseen water from the floors above, *been trying to get rid of them for weeks Carter did all that research what do you mean they're still here hands going to choke you anger freezing like a winter's night eyes burning a hole in your back GET OUT,* and a cold sweat breaks out along the nape of Etienne's neck thinking about the salt line at the door, the burnt sage here in his hand, things that in the right hands *can* be used to deter and mitigate the dangers spirits pose but in the *wrong hands-*

Etienne spins to his feet faster than anything, hands arched fingers splayed, twists a score of guide lights into being and they zip to the ceiling, flood the old hospital wing turned decaying art room with their silvery glow, leaving nothing hiding in the shadows.

And for a second immediately after, *he almost wishes he hadn't.*

"Mothers of the Night-" Etienne tries to say but thinks he just mouths, too horrified by what he's seeing to actually put any force behind it, rendered completely aghast at all the muddy paint cutting sloppy lines along the walls and floor. There are crosses and other religious symbols, *Hamsa hands Dharma wheels Triskele spirals,* shit that looks entirely decorative, *swirls and dashes and interlocking triangles,* collections of pictograms he's never even *seen* before and might possibly be made up, and all of it is done up in thick, gloopy paint that is haphazardly drawn across crumbling plaster in wavering sweeps.

It is a mess, *it is a catastrophe,* worse than any of those tacky little shops selling bastardized *'spells'* at Jackson Square, and from this gallery of disaster, Etienne feels his stomach drop out of him when he recognizes at least a *dozen* of his coven's spells.

He finds conciliatory sigils and containment seals plastered *everywhere,* or, *attempts of them* at least, because no spirit witch in their right mind would *ever* use spellwork this sloppy in the field, *wouldn't even let it leave the confines of their house's property,* intention for the spell completely lost and misdirected.

And these obviously have no magic in them, *no purposeful energy,* but the shapes *mean* something, *the lines mean something,* it's not just an empty pattern, and they can still exact an effect on the environment around them simply by virtue of *what they are.*

What you do matters everything you do has purpose, some memory of mother or Atha or Gilbert *or who fucking cares* whispers through Etienne's ears, and he wants to shout back *now is so not the time,* because in the span of a few seconds, the situation has gone from *dicey* to downright *treacherous.*

His hand tightens into a fist around the sage bundle, *around the*

✦✦ 270 ✦✦

thing that's been drawing the specters' attention here, to this room, where nearly every surface is inscribed with things that are urging them to calm down in the most insensitive way. The spells must be working to some extent, *have kept things from outright exploding,* but they're not doing it *correctly,* are basically the equivalent of plastering a band aid on a cut before ripping it back off, and then doing this over and over *and over again,* tearing open an already fragile wound until it is gaping and bloody *and raw.*

There is no attempt at communication, *only one way sigils telling them to settle down and useless seals trying to bind them after the fact what an insult,* no effort at reconciling or connecting with the spirits, just a rather brusque way of *telling them to get over it.*

What an utter travesty.

Any *'good'* intentions the construction workers may have had by doing this have completely missed the mark, and it's led to them basically having built a glaring neon sign that's impossible to ignore, making these aggrieved spirits feel that none of the pain they're experiencing matters.

No wonder they're violent, *no wonder they're murderous,* Etienne knows he would be after *weeks* with this kind of callousness in his face, and the *only reason* no one's been killed yet are those misshapen seals crammed in between Hamsa hands.

Those are the paper thin lid keeping this volatile and fatal explosion at bay, and all the moisture leaves Etienne's mouth in an instant. His arm curls his spellbook closer, anxiety spiking just thinking about how *close* he was to laying down a conciliatory sigil, which, now that he knows the true state of things, he'd *never* even consider doing. It'd be like handing a lollipop to a torturously injured person instead of providing any actual aid, a, *here you go buck up champ,* kind of energy.

That probably would've sent the specters *right* over the edge, blowing this entire thing wide open and pushing them all further down the path of depravity, corrupting them to the point that, *best case scenario,* they'd kill a bunch of people before quieting back down but that was the *best case scenario,* because the *worst case* was something he *didn't even want to consider.*

Because it was the one where they'd collapse together and form a *tordu* instead.

Hives break out across his skin at the thought.

Etienne has only ever read about tordu, the cursed amalgamation of pure spite and malice that mutates into being during the bleakest of circumstances, a force of woe that gives even experienced exorcists pause. He's never seen one in person and never thought he would because his family is good at what they do, would never let a situation deteriorate to the point where conditions would be likely for one to form.

Stretched thin though House Boudreaux may be, none of them shirk their duties nor shy away from what needs to be done, have always been on top of cleansing any hauntings that get reported, but that's the problem with this place, this *hasn't* been reported, Etienne *knows* it hasn't.

He's been stuck going through assignment briefs and pulling research for the family for a *month now,* and he knows for a *fact* that there hasn't been a *single* report of a rediscovered influenza hospital. Meaning this place has just sat and festered for *weeks,* people working in here with *no idea* of the danger existing right out of their line of sight, and with each fumbling, *idiotic* attempt to fix it themselves, they only pushed the specters closer to the brink of complete apparitional collapse.

Fucking- void beyond-

One wrong move, and they might very well have a tordu on their hands, and while Etienne doesn't think it's gotten to that point, *not yet anyway you're still alive for starters,* things here are still way more concerning than he originally thought, and unlike last time when shit was getting dicey and he was on his own, he's not going to be an idiot about it.

Etienne can't quite remember who's free tonight, *might be Atha*

What Goes Bump In The Night

could be Oliver no pretty sure he had a funeral earlier Katie maybe, but he shakes his head, knows he can figure it out once he's certain there aren't any more civilians wandering around the construction site. *Need to get back downstairs and find that Reggie guy,* he thinks, clipping his spellbook back into place, and maybe he let his guard down too much, shouldn't have pulled all his magic back into his core like he did, but as Etienne gets ready to leave, goes to take a step towards the door, he...*can't.*

It immediately feels like a bucket of ice water gets dumped over him, icy rivulets of *panic* cutting sharp lines down the knobs of his spine because he keeps trying to move and it's like struggling through molasses.

Freezing molasses, that sticks against his limbs and almost seems to drag him back, and the more Etienne thrashes, the *colder he gets the more he realizes he can't move,* teeth chattering from nerves and panic as claustrophobia sets in, *can't get out can't get away crowding you back angry voices shouting over your head hands reaching fingers brushing against the back of your shirt going to grab you trying to rip you away from her bright sharp crack of ozone don't TOUCH HIM-*

Etienne manages to wrangle himself back under control before he has a complete meltdown, panting harshly out of his mouth to try and slow his hammering pulse.

You're not there you're not there you're okay you're not there, he has to remind his spinning mind, but attempting to ground himself in the moment, *where he can't move and his fingers are growing colder by the second,* is not exactly the greatest of comforts either.

He flexes his magic back out like a cracking whip, doesn't know what's happening but is wary of pressing too hard against the veil again, isn't sure his mind will survive another round in the relentless stream of echoes the specters are generating.

Being careful, Etienne just barely touches against the aether, *the softest grazing of his consciousness along its unknowable u n k n o w n,* but even that little nudge of contact sends an uncomfort-

✦✦ 273 ✦✦

able ripple through his skin, that familiar prickling kind of anxiety starting to crawl over him again.

The one he only ever feels when he's stuck pressed between people in a crowd.

And it is the most unnerving thing to be trying to move but *unable to* because there's the sensation of *not-there bodies* compressing you from every side, and he shudders when it feels like they just *crowd closer,* a *hundred eyes* all trained directly on him that obsessively track each quickening exhale that leaves his chest.

It has all the hair on his body standing on end, *heart skipping every other beat,* and each time he reluctantly blinks, Etienne fears the next time he opens his eyes, it'll be to a sea of gaunt faces and sunken eyes, all hollowly staring at him with the kind of intensity only true desperation breeds.

"Let me go, I-I mean you no harm." He entreats in as even a voice as he can muster, is scared to lash out with his magic considering how fragile the situation is, worried that'll be the final push that warps the specters into an abomination of pure nightmare, "I wanna *help you.* I can't imagine what it's been like, sufferin' like you have, b-but I'm here now an' I'll make it better. I *promise.*"

To his immense disappointment, there is no immediate let up, and Etienne squirms as *air* ghosts across the bared skin of his neck, coming dangerously close to hitting the thick artery that's pumping blood like *mad,* undeniable proof in that frantic tempo that *he* lives, *he* breathes, *he has everything they want.*

"*Please.* I know you don' wanna hurt me, *not really,* let me go an' I'll fix it-" Etienne winces at the poor turn of phrase because there is no *fixing this.*

They're dead.

They died and they'll stay that way.

But he can offer them peace, *rest,* a chance to let go and move on, and wetting his dry lips, he keeps attempting to appeal to

What Goes Bump In The Night

their better nature, *their humanity,* "I am a Boudreaux, a *son of the night,* I can and *will* help you but you have to let me go first... you have to *trust me.* Can you do that? *Will you let me help you?"*

Etienne puts everything he has in that plea.

He lets his emotions soak into every one of his words and leach tellingly into the air, so there is no doubt that he means every single thing he's said, his great bleeding heart offered up on a silver platter as a sanguinary olive branch, and for a second, he thinks he's done it.

The pressure eases off, the atmosphere seems to settle, but before he can even sigh a breath of relief, there's a great screaming clatter as the metal legs of a chair are ripped across the floor, entire thing smashing and denting against one of the tables and Etienne can only watch terrified as the door slams shut, trapping him inside what is probably about to become his tomb.

There are hands on him everywhere in an instant, pulling themselves up from the floor along his legs, clawing against the gaps of his ribs, snarled over his shoulders and pulling his arms back, *sickeningly twining through his fingers,* holding him steady as chattering teeth clack threatening at his ears, *at his jugular icy tongue darting out to taste at his pulse,* a hundred voices all garbling brokenly together as one in a deranged howl, *"N O"*

Chapter 14

It's interesting the things that suddenly come to mind right when you're about to lose your life.

"You keep forgetting to hold the basis for illusionary magic true in your mind's eye, which- *counterintuitive I know,* but the foundation for any passable illusion is essentially *a lie.*" Etienne remembers Sabine drawling languidly, long legs kicking idly where he was reclined in an oak tree on the edges of the LeBlanc estate. He'd *said* he'd climbed up there to better see the *terrible excuse for an illusionary sigil,* Etienne was working on, but really, Etienne knew the only reason his friend had climbed up there was to show off.

Dick, Etienne thought like he so often did when around Sabine, pushed sweaty bangs off his forehead and then ran the hand back through the rest of his hair, dark strands practically scorching from where the sun was beating down on him. Granbleu's back courtyard was open to the sky just like Maisette's was, but unlike his coven house, the LeBlanc's property had a distinct scarcity of trees, which helped wind flow through the area much easier, but also meant Etienne currently felt like he was being roasted alive.

"Èy, did you hear me, Eti? It's important to keep that dichotomy in mind, this won't work much unless you listen." Sabine said in a way that had Etienne wondering if his parent had often reminded *him* of that, and snippily shoving his shirt sleeves back up above his elbows, Etienne huffed back, "I heard you, *I heard you.* Just- *give me a sec,* okay?"

Refocusing on the practice area in front of him, Etienne tracked his eyes over the darker lines of sand Sabine had laid out in a template, the general shape of the sigil familiar but most of the interior structure completely alien to him.

What Goes Bump In The Night

Each coven had their own branch of magic they practiced and excelled at, but fundamentally, it all derived from the same source, and while there was no rule *against* learning another branch's specialty, it was generally a lot harder unless you were claimed to that sign.

Etienne had never practiced illusionary magic before today, *never had a reason to,* and unsurprisingly, it wasn't really working like he was used to his coven's spells working. Best way he could describe it was like trying to cram a square peg into a round hole, futilely fighting against something that *really* wasn't wanting to happen, and the lack of progress was driving him slowly insane. *Maybe that was his plan all along,* Etienne thought irately, calling his magic up again and trying to coax it to assume and hold the pattern it kept bucking, *maybe Sabine wants you to lose your mind so you won't beat his exiting score at the academy.*

And best friends though they may be, *Etienne wouldn't put it past him.*

For some- *unfathomable reason,* Sabine had actually been very insistent that he try this little exercise they're attempting, *allegedly* because he's curious to see if Etienne can do it, but *realistically* it was probably because he'd just learned something cool and wanted to show off. That was kinda the throughline for most of their friendship, *Sabine was older Sabine was cooler Sabine knew how to do everything,* and then there was Etienne tagging along at his heels, often feeling like such an idiot little kid even though they're just barely two years apart.

"Any day now, mô shè! I think my hair's goin' grey." Sabine sang all lilting and smug from his tree branch, and resisting the urge to flip him off, Etienne stopped dallying and *pushed* his magic to execute, fingers crooked and bent in an imitation of the gestures Sabine had showed him over an hour ago.

His magic crackled out through the sand at his command, maroon light glowing brightly in place of where there was usually the deep pulse of indigo. It started off okay, craggily following along the lines laid out for it, but all too soon, *like every other time*

✦✦ 277 ✦✦

before now, the moment it got to the first ring of glyphs, it failed, *crumpling inwards,* the entire thing collapsing and exploding in a shower of sand.

"Mothers-!" Etienne swore, throwing his hands in the air as he paced away from the training area, hot and irritated and ready to just throw the towel in over this whole mess.

He kneaded at the bridge of his nose, frustrated defeat bitter on his tongue in the way that always made his thoughts turn back against him, wicked and dark and *angry,* though his shoulders untensed the barest amount as a flicker of breeze danced past.

It toyed with his sweaty hair, wrapped over his arms and seemed to linger on the newest scar sliced through his skin, the one he got because he wasn't fast enough and that revenant was a little too good with a knife. Etienne absentmindedly turned a hand against it, little surprised when the wind seemed to twine through his outstretched fingers, slight more purpose and intelligence in something he was used to just blowing by like a passing car.

A low thud and the crunching of leaves behind him distracted him from the wind though, and Etienne looked over his shoulder, frustrated frown softening into something more like a plaintive pout as he saw Sabine making his way over.

"You're still too tense." Sabine remarked, lazily slipping his hat from his head and tossing it artfully to land next to Etienne's own dark one, their brims overlapping as he came to stand on the other side of the practice area from him, "Your fingers are bent all wrong. They're still too peaked and uh, *what's the word-* craggily. Think more smooth an' soft, like *wind.* Not lightnin'."

"I'm *tryin'.* But it's hard fightin' what I *am."* Etienne grumbled, fully intending on telling Sabine he was done for the day, *that he didn't think this was gonna work,* but then those full lips twitched up into a Cheshire grin, *long finger crooking come here come give it another go come show me what you got,* and despite his better judgment, Etienne turned back around with a sigh.

Sabine just laughed loud and soaring in response, *like birdsong*

What Goes Bump In The Night

like cumulus clouds like a gale, and Etienne couldn't help but find himself smiling back.

"That's the spirit! Now- follow me, watch what I'm doin' and do it exact." Sabine then ran through the hand signs again, making Etienne start over every time he bent his fingers too sharply, so accustomed to the quick fast jerk of spirit magic that came stinging out of his hands and not this ethereal elegance.

That was a good word for it, *elegant,* because the way Sabine moved his hands was like streamers caught up in a lively breeze, absolutely weightless, *effortless,* and Etienne tried his damndest to copy those mercurial movements.

It was hard, not what he was used to in the slightest, but after a few more rounds, Etienne felt like he might be getting it somewhat, following along in a not entirely terrible parody. When Sabine determined he was suitable enough for another try, he took a step back and dipped into a playful bow, hand waving in a, *the floor is yours,* gesture that had Etienne snorting in affectionate amusement.

"Remember, the illusion will only work if you believe it will. That's honestly the trickiest part about it, you *know* it's a lie but you gotta make yourself believe it isn't." Sabine coached as he twirled his fingers in a circle, obedient little cyclone of wind breathing to life and reshaping the dark guidelines in the sand once more, "If you understand it to be the truth, *to be reality,* then *I* will as well."

"Yeah okay, but how am I supposed to believe in a lie when I *know* it is one? How am I supposed to make myself forget what's true?" Etienne complained but dutifully called his magic to him anyway, and over the low hum of hissing electricity, he nearly lost Sabine's uncharacteristically subdued reply, "You'd be surprised how easy it is."

Glancing up before he made his attempt, Etienne felt his brows furrow at the way Sabine was staring at the sigil drawn in the sand, oddly blank expression on his face that melted away as soon as he noticed Etienne looking at him, cocky smirk sliding back into place, "Well? Gonna make me wait forever, Mishé Boudreaux?"

"...of course not, Mishé LeBlanc." Etienne quipped back slower than usual, thought about opening his mouth again for a moment but ultimately, decided against it.

Instead, he made a mental note to ask Sabine if there was something bothering him later, once they were done here and back in his room of course. Honestly, he didn't really need to ask, already knew there was, *knew Sabine perhaps better than he knew anyone*, but now wasn't really the time nor the place to press it.

It might seem like there's not anyone besides them out in Granbleu's courtyard at the moment, but with a coven as big as Sabine's was, it was all too likely someone would accidentally overhear, *too many eyes too many ears too many possibilities for judgment to be cast*, and there was nothing Sabine hated more than people knowing his business.

So, Etienne dropped it for the time being, poured all his attention into trying to get this spell right, hoped that might bring some delighted light into Sabine's shadowed, angular eyes.

He drew in a deep breath, once more held it in his lungs and forced his mind still and glassy with it, did as instructed and cast upon it the lie he was intending to tell, *Granbleu's main ballroom choked with flowering vines for Sabine's recent nineteenth birthday.* It was an easy enough untruth to sell because Etienne had been there and knew the scene well, *clinking of crystal glasses balloons of shimmering light drifting by in a charmed breeze music lively and fast and irresistible*, but it was a difficult fabrication at the same time because so had *Sabine*.

And if anyone was gonna immediately poke holes in something, it would be him, the LeBlanc who had an inner eye that could see through *everything*.

You always did love a challenge though, Etienne's brain nudged in his direction, but he brushed the wandering thought off, had to wait until the waters of his mind smoothed back out into mirror perfection before he could make his attempt, hands coming up to begin shaping the spell. By nature, his magic was static

What Goes Bump In The Night

riddled and electric, jumped and sparked from one thing to the next in a fractaling web of branching energy, but this kinda spell-work required a certain type of fluidity, something with no set path that could curve past anything and still retain its direction.

Lightning always had a target, might meander a bit on the way to it, but once those charges connected, it was like magnets snapping together, *nothing could stop it,* and don't get him wrong, the wind was an absolutely powerful force in its own right, but it wasn't drawn like an arrow from a bowstring. That was what was honestly giving Etienne the most trouble. He *needed* a clear path, a, *go here go there point A to point B,* and yeah, he had a goal he was trying to execute but it wasn't a clear one, was hazy and obfuscated and shrouded in misdirection, needed magic that could curl and change along with it, but that wasn't what his magic was.

It was direct, it was unfaltering, *it was a bullet from a gun,* leapt from his hands and immediately lanced straight for the heart of the matter, which, *in this case,* was an unsteady tower of lies, and it took it to the ground each time it made contact, this attempt being no different than any of the others.

Etienne actually shouted wordlessly in inarticulate frustration when the spell failed, kicked away from the practice area and planted his hands on his hips, spillover crackling agitatedly against his palms.

"That's it-! I'm done." He called, head hunching down between his shoulders when the expected protests started up at his back, "No- *no!* I don't wanna hear it! It's not gonna work, it *never* woulda worked! An' I've had enough of you yankin' my chain around when it's *ninety eight out with a humidity index of eighty-!"*

"Hey, *come on,* don't be like that! I think you almost had it that time!" Sabine coaxed like the little liar he was, and Etienne scoffed meanly, tossing his head in a frustrated arc, didn't even get a single step away from him before Sabine was goading, "What? That's it? *You're* really gonna give up *that* easily? Wow, who would've thought it, *Etienne Boudreaux a quitter-"*

✦✦ 281 ✦✦

It felt like he'd been punched in the gut, *horrible* sense of guilt shooting through his veins demanding he *try again do it again keep doing it until you get it perfect run yourself ragged bleed your fingers dry make sure no one doubts your abilities,* and Etienne swallowed rough.

He knew what was happening, *what Sabine was trying to do knew he said what he did on purpose trying to get a reaction trying to get a rise out of you,* and angry betrayal shot up his spine, electricity cracking between his back molars as he spit to the cobblestones at his feet, *"Oh you did not just-* lamèd to! Don't bait me like that! I'm your *friend,* I tell you stuff like that *because I trust you!* Not so you can *use it against me-!"*

"Wha-? I am *not!* You're just- w-wait! *Eti-!* You've got it wrong- I didn't mean- *I-I wasn't trying to-!"*

"Mothers of the Night- save it Sabine." Etienne sighed exhausted, rocked his tight shoulders and tried to let go of the unhappy way his heart was constricting, hurt thinking this was all some *joke to him,* "I don't know what game you're playin', but I came over here to *study,* not so you could manipulate me and make me look like *an idiot!"*

"I'm not trying to make you look like an idiot!" Sabine fired back, more forthright emotion in his voice than he normally allowed, and it was enough that Etienne actually felt compelled to look back over his shoulder.

Sabine hadn't really moved from where he'd planted his feet earlier, but he'd twisted to face Etienne while he attempted to storm off, watching him with a strained, unpleasant expression, though curiously enough, his eyes weren't focused on Etienne's face. They were looking somewhere off to the side, and following his line of sight, Etienne glanced unsurely down at the gravel strewn ground, naturally didn't see anything worth staring at and brought his eyes back up in confusion, accidentally dancing over his right forearm on the way.

And like magnets clacking together, his eyes were drawn instantly

What Goes Bump In The Night

to the newest line of puckered pink flesh that curved through his skin like an angry river.

Scars were not really a big deal in his house, everyone had them, *everyone expected to get them.*

Their work was dangerous and oftentimes lethal, and it was very much accepted that either you overcame and had a new mark to show for it, or you succumbed and then it didn't really matter much what marks you had on your body.

Etienne ran a forefinger over this newest one, considering, felt the craggy edges and the new shiny skin stretched taut between each raised ridge, didn't think anything of it besides a reminder that he *needed to be better,* glanced up though when he heard a sharp intake of air through tensed teeth.

"I...I'm not tryin' to *manipulate you,* I just...*I wanted to-* j-just thought if you could *do it,* it...i-it might, *I dunno,* give you a leg up against...*a-against everything that's out there."* Sabine entreated hoarsely, dark eyes fixed firmly on where Etienne was touching at the scar, like he was seeing how deep the original cut had been, *like he knew how much blood had come sheeting out,* like he understood that Etienne would've died if he'd been even a *second later* in bringing his arm up to block that knife swing.

And given the way his magic worked, *he probably had,* had likely seen a *thousand* futures where Etienne *wasn't* fast enough, a dozen more where mother *hadn't* been there to save him, countless where the revenant had gotten his throat instead *like it'd intended,* so many chances for things to go poorly, *for Etienne to turn too fast react too slow for mother to be late for her not to get there fast enough for him to bleed out for him to die.*

Each one unspooling out in front of Sabine's inner eye like a demented set of snuff films he couldn't get to stop, the true cacophony of hell that lived unending inside the prison of his own mind, all while he frantically searched for the precious few futures where he could have the outcome he wanted.

Where Etienne lived.

✦✦ 283 ✦✦

Oh...oh Sabine, Etienne thought sadly, thumbing at the scar, knew foresight was an amazing gift and yet an incredibly difficult burden to be saddled with at the same time, that each terrible off-shoot of a possible reality brought Sabine a great amount of distress even though he liked to pretend it didn't.

I can handle it it's not a stressor I can bear it, he'd say over and over again, wiping the blood trickling down from his nose or spitting it free from where it pooled in his mouth, eyes glazed over and glassy, worryingly looking like they'd be lost in the winding confusion of *everything that could be* for eternity.

And the terrifying thing was he really could be, could overload and break his mind like so many LeBlanc had before him, and while Sabine dreamt of all the ways Etienne could die, Etienne dreamt of all the ways Sabine could drown in his own mind.

And neither one of them slept much.

"I don't know why I...*I-I don't know*- I just- *I wanted to keep...*I just w-wanted to *help.*" Sabine murmured whisper soft and incomplete, the words he wanted to say but didn't standing in between them like looming figures.

I just wanted to keep you safe if I could, the silence betrayed tellingly, a want he needed so desperately he cut it off abruptly before he could even ask for it, almost like he realized he actually *couldn't do it, couldn't actually keep you safe.*

The look he got on his face when you'd come back a few days later telling stories with a new line through your skin and a new lesson learned but each scar you showed him seemed to carve a twin of itself around his mouth when it pulled tense or under his eyes when they pinched together or against his own smooth skin when his fingers dug in hard like maybe he could pull it from you if he tried hard enough wipe that mark away and keep it so there would never be any others...

There was a lot Sabine never spoke about because he wasn't allowed, *exactly what his visions were how your fate was dealt couldn't say a word could alter the flow of time irreparably,* but

What Goes Bump In The Night

there was even more than that he'd never even think of giving breath to *because he was scared,* of being seen of being known *of being right,* kept so much locked away behind the façade of a smug curling grin, all with an attitude of certainty he'd probably never felt.

Etienne heard him anyway, *always did,* saw it in his averted eyes and tense stance, the way he could speak and not say anything and then move the barest amount *and say it all,* heart doing an odd little flip that bled painful warmth throughout his chest at the way Sabine was doing it now.

How many times have you watched me die, suddenly came bubbling up in his mind, and he wanted to ask out of morbid curiosity, but bit his tongue on actually saying it, didn't think it'd be the best thing to ask when Sabine had gone so pale under his naturally tanned skin.

It was rare for Etienne to be reminded that this life he lived wasn't the norm, and that even amongst the other covens, most of them didn't start their days with a pretty solid expectation that they might not be coming back home at the end of the night. For them though, *his family,* death wasn't anything to be afraid of, *was expected sooner rather than later,* but he never really thought about if it was gonna be the last time he saw someone when they walked out Maisette's front doors.

They understood their role, they knew for what purpose they lived, *they had accepted the risks,* but they also didn't come stumbling free from visions where they'd watched each other be killed over and over *and over again,* each death more gruesome than the last, and Etienne couldn't *imagine* the kind of paranoia that'd breed, *the debilitating fear,* but he could see it howling like a banshee in the too transparent eyes of his best friend right across from him.

"I think...I-I think I could help you get it, I think I *see- k-know how,* but you *have to- w-*would *you...*give it another go?" Sabine all but begged, tone soaked with supplication like he wasn't just pleading with Etienne to try again, but was attempting to convince

✦✦ 285 ✦✦

an amoral universe the virtues of keeping this *one* person alive no matter the cost, "Please? I know you're tired, *I-I know it's hard,* but w-would you try *for your sake?"*

For you, is what he said, *for me,* is what he meant, *so I never have to feel the pain of knowing you as a corpse,* is everything that he couldn't bring himself to voice.

And Etienne is mortal, *all too achingly aware he is but flesh and bone,* but he stepped back up to the practice area anyway, knew he was being asked, *will you please stay alive,* and understood it was wrong to promise what he did but promising it anyway, "Of course."

This time, when Etienne brought his hands up to begin the signs, Sabine did as well, but it wasn't the vacant demonstration from earlier. There was intention in his fingertips, power between his joints, *magic under his skin,* and as maroon sparked craggily across the sand, indigo swept out to join it, gracefully arcs of buffeting energy that enveloped Etienne's like a guiding hand.

It made goosebumps break out along the backs of his arms, the touch of Sabine's magic against his own like the cooling caress of a breeze against his flushed face on a hot day, and around them, the wind began to stir.

It curled up from the ground, licking dead leaves from the courtyard and twirling them through the air, shook the branches in the trees overhead, would dip and flare out into the wider sky on occasion but came looping back around each time, like it's anchor was here, *was them,* rippling by Etienne in an undulating stream of casual power.

Hello, Etienne thought he heard it coo as it coiled past, *hello recognize you,* tiny flicks of curious air that skated over his skin and tugged giddy at the suspenders hanging lax by his hips, *hello know you dear one hello,* liquid brush of wind gliding past his outstretched fingers when he turned a hand against it, the playful swell of it bouncing past in a bubble of laughter like a friend bidding him a fond farewell.

What Goes Bump In The Night

There was something familiar about the sound of its laughter as it snaked through his ears, *head tipped back in gales of giggles dark hair spilling over toned shoulders angular eyes crinkling in a devious smirk long finger crooking,* and he met Sabine's eyes across the way, watched the light from both their magic flicker and waiver in their inky depths.

Hi, Etienne felt like he said but knew he didn't voice a thing, *hi know you too,* foot shifting seemingly of its own accord across the ground and unsurprised to see Sabine's doing the same, *hi know you in this in the wind in the breeze in the curling air know you anywhere,* the two of them beginning to move like mirror images.

The spell was being held in stasis for the moment, Sabine's magic keeping Etienne's from completely crumpling this ump-teenth attempt, wind whipping about while indigo and maroon chased each other around and around that first ring of glyphs, and leaving one hand flat, palm facing towards the earth, Sabine held the other one out in offer, fingers beckoning.

Come here come give it another go come take a chance come dance with me

Etienne had seen that same sight so many times on ballroom floors and in sparkling dancehalls, never was much a gifted dancer on his own, but he could follow where his partner led him, and it clicked in his brain what Sabine was wanting to try. He smiled a bit as he slipped his eyes shut, appreciated the clever thinking, and did something he'd only ever do with a handful of witches, brought down the mental barrier that was keeping the curious cyclone of Sabine's magic *out.*

And the second it was gone, the *second* the innermost parts of who he was were bared and vulnerable, *an entire gale came rushing in.*

It felt like it lifted him up off his feet, swept through his veins in long strokes, nothing like the fizzy popping of the power he was used to, wove in between the gaps of bones and swelled his lungs fit to bursting, started to braid itself up tight with his own magic.

✦✦ 287 ✦✦

Hello hi who're you hello hi hello, his magic sang, Sabine's echoing it back, both curling against and past one another like opposing banks of clouds, touching excitedly at this seemingly alien presence that was more a reflection of the same power than anyone could ever really understand.

Come follow me watch what I do let me show you how to play, the wind trilled, steps bouncing and weightless, *hand outstretched form billowing eyes wild,* and like the smart snap of light through a thunderous sky, the lightning took ahold, response sharp and direct and *fanged, point the way I'll carve a path show me where to go I'll beat you there lead the way and I will follow.*

And so their dance began.

Know you know you know you, drummed through Etienne's mind in double time, the frenetic beating of it sharp like thunder in the night sky and deeply percussive like a racing heart, *know me know me know me,* sang high and lilting in overture, a chorusing of woodwinds that swelled with the same kinda immense power it took to move weather systems across the globe, *know us know us know us,* an entire song that rattled through his bones and coated every inch of his veins, a duet that felt more natural to sing than any that could ever be composed by mortal hands.

Their magic dipped and surged together, Sabine's leading the way as Etienne's came streaking along behind it, lance sharp edges of it curling and softening, not moving like it'd been taught, *moving like it was being shown.* Rings of glyphs he'd never even been able to make it to earlier were suddenly breezing by, and the more Etienne was moved along by Sabine's magic, *graceful steps and trailing arms the wind in the leaves in his hair touching at his face,* the more he *understood.*

Being mercurial wasn't wholly about lying or trying to hide what you were. It was a willingness to *change,* to not be so set in your ways that only one path seemed viable, considering each option that came before you as just as likely to happen as any others, and electricity may be keen to jump from point to point, *wanted a set path,* but Etienne understood the necessity of *change.*

What Goes Bump In The Night

It was the foundation of his house, *hellos and goodbyes mournful sunsets and hopeful dawns,* something that was borne into his blood, *his gift his rite his inheritance one door shut another opened,* and he'd been raised to know the greatest form of it as just any other chapter to life. Death wasn't the only aspect of change a Boudreaux knew though, *it was the entire walk of life really like a spinning circle,* and Etienne knew that like he knew himself, *like he knew his markings his family his magic...like he knew Sabine,* and the wind shifted direction sharply, spiraling more towards *Etienne,* because at the end of the day, what really was an illusion but a suggested change to someone's reality?

Everything clicked in an instant, *felt like getting struck by lightning like getting slapped in the face by a sudden gust of wind like taking the hand held out for you and being led across the ballroom,* and without being told, Etienne unthinkingly stepped up to the sigil, foot sliding along the side of it in mirror perfection to Sabine's own.

Both sets of their fingers swooped and coiled elegantly, calling forward the illusion in a beckoning hand, and even though he'd never done it before, it was such an instinctual movement that Etienne felt like he'd been doing it for *years,* for his entire *lifetime.*

Like he'd wake up the next day and the marks under his eyes would be indigo not maroon and the hat you pulled onto your head would be cream and you'd be meeting for lunch the best friend who wore all black and had too many scars on his arms and ~~whom you loved more than~~

And in a bright snap of connecting power, the soaring windowed walls of Granbleu's main ballroom rose around them, perfume of gardenias and magnolias thick in the air while their greenery dripped off glittering chandeliers, and the dancers that were suddenly twirling past him weren't real *but they could've been,* and the music the band played was beautiful just like it had been that night, *but it was nothing compared to the symphony echoing lovingly from his very veins.*

And in that moment of heady triumph, Etienne remembered looking breathless across what was once a courtyard and was now

✦✦ 289 ✦✦

a bustling dancefloor, to the person standing across from him, *his best friend* ~~this split off part of himself~~, saw the mirrored shine of *victory* echoed back in night black eyes looking right at him, *through him,* and for a second, *thought they were his own.*

After that afternoon in late August dying on the LeBlanc estate under the summer sun, Etienne had never had much need for the illusionary magic that'd settled in like a gentle sigh against his own crackling spirit magic, but that didn't mean he'd forgotten it, body shifting into position the *second* he feels freezing cold fingers latch onto his skin now, where he's about to be dying in some old abandoned influenza hospital under an autumn moon.

It's an instinctual decision, one he can't take the time to second guess or even to really question why he's doing it, and Etienne yanks his arms free from the specters through sheer force of will. They snarl unhappily, but he ignores them, angles his fingers towards the floor, *ideally where an illusion sigil would be,* and even though there isn't one, he can still see it in excruciating detail, *like he's seen it at least once a day for the last seven years* ~~he has but just through different eyes~~.

Sigilless casting is incredibly advanced and *incredibly difficult to master,* nature of magic wild and untamed unless it has rules to follow, but Etienne doesn't really have a lot of options, feels crushing pressure against his windpipe and then his next panicked inhale can't reach his lungs.

Time's up, *gotta act.*

Forcing his mind still and mirror smooth is a true feat Etienne isn't sure how he accomplishes given what's happening, *adrenaline is one hell of a drug makes the mind sharp as a blade,* and even though his magic pops and seethes threateningly, *wants to attack,* he forces it back.

The situation's delicate enough, he's afraid that letting loose with his lightning would be the spark of aggression that tips the specters into true violent bloodshed, ending his life brutally and sealing the fate of anyone else still trapped inside the building.

What Goes Bump In The Night

Etienne might not be able to scare them away like he did earlier, *electricity arcing off him in a deadly protective net GET BACK,* but he might be able to *trick* them into backing off, *motivate them to retreat...change their perception of reality,* and maybe it's cruel to conjure their absolute worst memory, *their never ending nightmare,* but at the moment, he'd honestly prefer a chance at life over sparing their feelings.

And so Etienne brings to his mind's eye every grainy photograph and flickering echo he's ever seen, *ignores the teeth cracking right at his ears the fingernails trying to pull apart the skin over his trachea,* curls his fingers as elegantly as a summer breeze while white hot freezing hands dig under his skin, *under his muscles going straight for bone,* slides his feet even though it feels like cinderblocks are attached to his legs, *remember your foundations what you're trying to accomplish the deception you need to sell ~~the lie you promised like you shouldn't have will you stay alive for you anything,~~* takes a deep breath even though it goes nowhere, remembers *wind in his hair touching at your face twining through your fingers dark eyes sharp grins dance with me-*

And even though he has no sigil to guide him, hasn't practiced this spell in *years,* is being strangled to death by enraged spirits and isn't even sure this *is going to work,* he sets in mind what he wants to do and orders his magic to execute.

The room lights up like lightning's struck it, air going tight and charged as maroon lines streak out from where he stands like arrows from a bow, arcing and curling together, searing a path through the old linoleum tiles to form a fully complete and *fully stable* illusionary sigil.

Elegant clusters of pictograms in its center spin to life in the blink of an eye, whirring fast in a complicated orbit that pulls the illusion into being, and the second before it fully slides into place, while the edges of his vision are going dark from lack of air, Etienne hopes a bit belatedly that he didn't get the scene wrong.

He won't have a chance to redo it if he did, feels the horrifying touch of *something cold and wriggling* starting to dig into the musculature of his heart, and understands that either this ploy works, or he's dying at the abyssal hands of these tormented spirits.

Thankfully, in a practically seamless transition, *color* and *light* suddenly bleed back into the world, smell of rot and damp decay *gone,* replaced with the bite of antiseptic and the sour tinge of slick copper. He can't hear much over the ringing in his ears, head swaying forward woozy and heavy, but he sees the blurry yet *solid* form of nurses rushing past, can hear their muted shouting, *move them to – don't have the – need a scalpel over,* and a dozen pairs of hands jump off him with a spastic flinch.

Including the ones at his throat.

Etienne sucks in a greedy gulp of air as more of his spectral restraints drop away, can feel the ripples of their panic and confusion lapping against the shores of his mind, an endless current of, *no no no not again God please not again not here can't do this didn't wanna for the love of take me back let me OUT NO NO NO,* and can't waste time regretting what he's done.

Without the specters holding him in place, Etienne nearly collapses to his knees lightheaded, body wracked with adrenaline fueled spasms, but he can't buckle, *not yet,* pushes himself back up and forces his shaky knees to bear his weight.

Around him, what looks like a swamped influenza hospital hurtles on unaware to his presence, exhausted medical staff rushing about with dirtied smocks and old blood splashed across some of their fronts.

They're shouting orders, soothing their patients, *trying to offer comfort to the dying,* a frantic cacophony that's all underscored by the guttural hacking and desperate moaning drifting up from the *sea* of occupied beds.

It's horrible.

There is so much death and despair contained in this one illusion, *so much helplessness,* Etienne can't imagine what it must've been like to live it, *to die in it,* and even though this is his first attempt

What Goes Bump In The Night

at an illusion in *years,* he's confident he's done it right. Because it looks very real, sounds real, feels *real can smell the antiseptic hear the desperation taste the black cloud of illness,* and with one terrified shriek after another, the specters that'd manifested begin folding out of the physical plane.

It's like the soft shooshing rush of displaced water, air whipping about as the electrical field in the room shifts *violently,* spirits not quite returning to the aether but more so collapsing their consciousness back in on themselves to hide from this, their darkest nightmare. They won't be fooled by it forever, will eventually realize nothing in the illusion is actually real, *isn't really happening,* and Etienne's willing to bet they're not going to be too happy about that once they put two and two together.

He's given himself some breathing room though, *work your throat feel pain starting to blossom can still tell where each freezing digit was,* but not much, and as the pressure in the room eases off, it finally feels like the way forward is cleared and Etienne thinks he can get to the door without running into any lingering specters.

There are some that continue to persist, blurry forms sputtering and jerking as they stumble away in a blind panic, drifting through the air like a cloud of dangerous jellyfish.

Those ones still pose something of a risk to him, could immobilize Etienne with their freezing chill if he hits one or the collision could even upend the entire illusion, that little nudge from something *real* showing them how nothing else is, but this isn't the time for hesitation.

We don't have the luxury of assessing every choice we make neve, Gilbert's voice comes to him, *we only have mere seconds to decide between life and death because hesitating gets you killed...or worse,* distant rapping echo of his cane tapping lightly against the metal brace supporting his decayed leg, *you find your opening and don't question it trust yourself make your split second choice and know in your heart it's the right one-*

And Etienne nods at nothing in response, *the memory the senti-*

✦✦ 293 ✦✦

ment maybe himself, digs his toes into the soles of his boots, pushing them down against slick linoleum tile, waits with his heart in his throat *shivering breath in his lungs,* watches as two specters collide and drift apart, sees an opening, *takes his chance,* and then he's *off.*

He weaves past hospital constructs like they're really there, can't afford to crash through one and risk unbalancing the illusion, which is nothing more than a delicate fabrication that sits atop reality like a lightly spun sheet. Any disruption to it could cause the entire thing to come crumbling down, and Etienne tries to remember the original layout of the room as he runs, plotting out where all the mildewed furniture that's *actually* in here lies in the real world.

It's not really gone even though it looks like it is, and the last thing he needs to do is hook his foot on something and go tumbling to the ground, shattering apart the scene with his perpetual clumsiness. Etienne does clip a table on accident where all he saw was nothing but empty space, stumbles to the side on his mad flight to the doors with pain flaring up from his hip, and only manages to stay upright because of the sheer amount of experience he's had doing so.

Use your head or lose your head you idiot, Etienne berates, a less official adage of their house courtesy of Aunt Atha, vaults over where he's pretty sure a twisted nest of chairs is and must make it, doesn't end up tripping once his boots are back on the ground. Etienne all but slams into the doors once he gets to them, concerned when they don't immediately fly open, and rattles incessantly at the doorknobs but they won't budge, won't even turn, *almost like they're welded in place,* and he shouts a vile swear.

"Mothers damn you all-!" He seethes, ramming his shoulder against the seam between the two magically sealed doors, thick wood barely moving let alone *giving,* and Etienne despairs until he hears something clinking delicately. Snapping his head up, his eyes go wide seeing the glass windows set into the doors, the *old, single paned glass windows.* He moves fast, drops his hands to pull the thin material of his shoulder cape around his front, wrapping

What Goes Bump In The Night

it sloppily over his elbow as some additional buffer and padding before ramming his elbow into the glass as hard as he can.

Pain lances up Etienne's arm on the contact, but it doesn't stop him from swinging again and again, each subsequent hit driving a branching spiderweb of cracks through the glass until gratifyingly, the window breaks in a shower of glittering shards. Sharp heat slices through the thin skin covering the bony spire of his elbow, glass cutting him where the cloth of his cape had shifted, and Etienne winces, knows he's about to be feeling more of that as he drives a fist through the broken chunk of the window next.

More glass flies loose, tinkling pretty as it hits the ground and cuts the skin of his knuckles into ribbons, but enough of it is gone now so that Etienne can haul himself up and through the gap.

His hands get cut open on the ragged pieces still embedded in the wooden sill, punch up through the meat of his palms like knives and draw out slow and terrible as he basically throws himself out of the hospital ward, tearing open jagged wounds that leave bloody handprints where he falls against the floor.

"Fuck fuck fuck-!" Etienne hisses, turning one of his shaking palms over and grimaces at the dark wells of blood leaching out of the ragged slash. He flexes his fingers to ensure they still work, that he didn't slice through anything important, and it hurts like a bitch, makes his cuts sting and *throb,* but he can still feel each one of his digits and he deems that *good enough,* scrabbles to get back on his feet.

Unlike the fake crisp brightness of the room behind him, out here is still its rancid dark *grimy true self,* false light from the sunny hospital ward spilling past Etienne and throwing his shadow out into a long black line before him.

The illusion he cast has a pretty limited capacity and range, doesn't extend out to the hallway because Etienne's barely a novice when it comes to illusionary magic like this, and what he managed is *nothing* compared to what's possible in the hands of a skilled caster.

✦✦ 295 ✦✦

It's passable for an emergency situation, *just like Sabine hoped it would be,* but it's not going to hold forever. Some part of his mind has to stay constantly fixated on the spell, making sure his inner eye stays open enough that he can maintain the illusion, and while a LeBlanc would have no problem with that, could probably multitask other spells or duties, Etienne is basically having to *physically* prop his inner eye open by simply continuing to make the conscious effort to do so.

This kinda magic isn't his birthright, doesn't come naturally to him, and while Sabine was able to help him loophole his way into being able to cast it, it's still a tenuous connection. He is on borrowed time and is quickly running out of it, needs to get the hell out of this building before either the specters find out they've been duped, or his fragile connection snaps like dry tender.

Fisting his hands in the shredded ends of his shoulder cape to staunch the bleeding, Etienne hurries down the hall, can feel the mental lines linking him to the sigil waiver and jump, and while they *do* hold, every step he takes feels like it's going to be the one that jostles the entire thing loose. *It'll be okay it'll be fine just have to keep it together for a little while longer,* he repeats over and over again like a mantra, trying to be quick as he rushes past banks of lockers that flicker at the corners of his eyes.

They move like a mirage, cycle in between the gaping rotted form of now, to back when they were new and sleek and had little names cheerfully written on their placards, and then he blinks and it goes further still, back to before they were even installed. When the walls were blank and where creamy white cabinets stood, rows of bottles and supplies neatly stacked behind their glass paned doors, *another blink and another century further,* now the interior walls are all gone, rough brick at the very edges of his vision and filmy light suffused around bales and bales of cotton piled near to the ceiling.

Sharp inhale another blink and it's back to the rot.

And then it begins again, cycling past over and over like a deranged reel of film.

What Goes Bump In The Night

Without even trying, he's seeing brief glimpses into the past, snapshots of times that have been and never again will be, and Etienne rubs at his eyes with his upper arm, trying to clear the film of hindsight that's settled across them. It works to an extent, reminding his brain that he's *here* that he's *now,* but reality still bends like a funhouse mirror.

In each jump, the silence is prevalent and unsettling, each era devoid of life or movement in a way that makes Etienne think he's only seeing the first layer of it, has a gut feeling there are a dozen more he could probably see if he just pushed a little harder, *forced his inner eye open a little further,* but he wouldn't even dare consider it.

First off it'd be incredibly dangerous given how untrained he is in the art of *seeing,* and secondly, from what little that's trickling through the veil of time, *battering his consciousness with a stream of what has been,* Etienne can already feel his head start to pound, overload of information stoking a headache to life. *Mothers...how the fuck does Sabine do this,* he grimaces, squinting painfully against the bright construction lights once he gets close to the staircase again, *feels like your head is gonna split in two and this is just seeing what's already happened isn't even sorting through a thousand futures,* nasty metallic taste flooding his mouth he hopes is just bile but worries could be blood.

He has to disentangle one of his hands to steady himself on the handrail as he starts down towards the main floor, drying blood leaving a sticky smear behind him as he goes. His unbalanced footsteps echo loudly through the stairwell, oddly reverberate and loop back around, and Etienne is afraid to look over his shoulder, in part because he's scared he's going to trip, but mostly because he's worried he's going to see a never ending recursive loop of *himself,* walking down these stairs for an eternity.

Just a little further, he reminds himself, picking up the pace and feels a shiver run down his spine when the clatter of his bootheels echoes back in quadruplicate, *just a little further and then you don't have to touch illusionary magic ever again.*

✦✦ 297 ✦✦

The dilapidated classrooms of the first floor have never been a more welcome sight, and sighing with something like relief, Etienne starts to loosen the frantic mental grip he has on the illusion. He doesn't drop it completely, *isn't suicidal wants to wait until he's safely out the front doors,* but he lets his concentration slip a bit, *inner eye drooping a little further shut,* and it's like downing an inflammation tincture.

Etienne tips his head back in relief, still has the lingering grumbles of a mild headache, but the squeezing tension that was causing it is gone along with the flashes of the past. Which, he'll gladly take all the migraines and trippy visions in the world if it means his life will be spared, but he's honestly not sure how much longer he could keep it up, is glad then that this whole night is almost over.

"Blessed be...*what a mess...*" Etienne mumbles under his breath, kicking down the hall as he runs through a mental list of everything he's got left to get done.

There's not much honestly, mostly just double checking that Reggie got everyone out and then calling mother down here stat. He feels marginally guilty for dropping such a huge problem in her lap with no prior warning, *don't be it's not your fault don't take this guilt,* but he knows it would be *beyond* idiotic to try and handle this himself.

There's only one space on his bingo card of life for, *'trying to deal with supernatural forces way above your paygrade and nearly getting yourself and a bunch of innocent people killed',* and he's already got that spot stamped thank you very much.

Not that Etienne's proud about it, *not by a long shot,* but he has *very* thoroughly learned his lesson and has *no* intention of repeating it.

The only thing he plans on doing once he leaves this place is sitting his ass down on the curb and dealing with his cuts, biding the time while he waits patiently for mother to arrive with backup. Most likely it'll be Katie, *only other full fledged exorcist in the parish,* but hell, it's bad enough here mother might ask Gilbert to

What Goes Bump In The Night

come too, *decayed leg and wasting curse be damned,* and together, they should be able to end this.

Though, his heart does squeeze painfully when Etienne considers that, even with the four of them working side by side, it might not be enough to *save* the specters.

He doesn't have a single doubt in his mind that his family can stop the haunt, *knows they have the sheer power to tear a rift between the planes of reality itself,* but he worries if it'll be too late to offer the spirits peace. The specters were already violent and angry *before* Etienne launched them back to the moment of their demises, and now, once they're freed from the illusion, they'll likely become so hostile, the others won't be able to reason with them either.

They're going to have to raze this place to the ground, he realizes, and it hits like a blow to the gut, because while he did what he had to do to survive, he really can't see any other outcome than a tordu forming as soon as the illusion drops.

And once that happens, the specters' fates are all but sealed, and maybe a different spirit coven could spare the manpower to try and yank that twisted ball of malice back apart, but it would definitely incur losses, and Etienne knows his family *really* can't handle another blow to their ranks right now.

That means, to preserve their line, mother is going to have to make one of the hardest calls a spirit atriarch can make, and order that the specters' apparitional signatures be wiped from the face of the earth permanently.

It's a drastic, last ditch method she rarely likes to employ, but *the needs of the many outweigh the needs of the few gaçon,* and Etienne *has* to remember he is also responsible for keeping the rest of New Orleans safe, not just these few wayward souls.

As much as it twists his heart to consider destroying spirits, there really isn't another choice, and it weighs on him heavily while he trudges down the hallway.

Lost in thought and distracted by the way his cuts are throbbing,

✦✦ 299 ✦✦

ouch ouch ouch why didn't you think to cover your hands before diving out a window, Etienne isn't paying much mind to his surroundings, so when he first hears the faint echo of voices, his senses snap to high alert, electricity building off him like a lightning rod.

Naturally he assumes it's the specters, *heart punching up into your throat fingers trying to tear into your neck CAN'T BREATHE,* but when his magic searches the veil, it doesn't find anything besides the freezing pulsating heartache upstairs, skitters back from it before Etienne can get frostbite.

"What in the..." He starts muttering in confusion, because if it's not the specters, and it's *really* not given how they're still very much unhappily occupied, then he's a bit stumped, didn't think this building would have any other spirits kicking around.

Cautiously slinking down the hall towards the noise, ears straining trying to pick out anything specific, Etienne listens carefully and the more he does so, the less it sounds like the abyssal mumbling of displaced spirits and more like...far off distant human speaking.

There's a distinct pitch and warble to spectral vocalizations that this just doesn't have, *comes through even comes through grounded ...comes through like there's a living mouth saying it,* and it *can't be*...but *dread* begins to gnaw up his spine as his cautious footsteps turn into panicked ones turn into a jog into a run into *a sprint oh Mothers please no please not this anything else but that please don't let them be-*

And Etienne comes skidding to a stop in the main atrium with only the white noise of his heartbeat thundering in his head, feels like the entire floor just dropped out from under him as his eyes go wide, and can't decide if he wants to cry or scream seeing all of the construction workers standing in a loose circle arguing, *absolutely clueless to the danger seething right above their heads.*

Like sheep huddling together right before they're about to get slaughtered.

Chapter 15

There are a lot of things Etienne could say. Smart sounding, *professional sounding things*, that would convey the true danger of the situation that's only worsening while these people squabble pointlessly. It'd be something that would accurately and resolutely outline what everyone needs to do, *assert his authority*, but he is so floored, so absolutely and completely dumfounded and terrified and all too aware of the illusion's weakening hold, that he shouts incredulous, "Are you *out of your fucking MINDS?*"

Heads swivel in his direction and he's thinking about sheep again, comes striding up to their huddle while his mind is frantically grappling for a better hold on the illusion, but it's finicky, like grabbing for the string on a balloon after you've already let go. *"What* are you even *doing in here?* This place is infested with *hostile spirits! Do you have a death wish or somethin'?"* Etienne fumes panicked, glares at each person in turn like he's scolding a bunch of truant schoolchildren and finds a pair of eyes trying to duck his in the crowd, zeros in on them as he snaps, *"You!"*

For his part, Reggie at least looks properly guilty, tugging awkwardly on his beard while Etienne sets his shoulders back and lays into the man, "What the *hell* is *wrong with you? You told* me you were gonna get everyone out! Did you think I was *kidding?* I trusted you! You asked me what you could do to help an' I *trusted you to do this one SIMPLE THING-!"*

"I'm *s-sorry* man, I tried, *really,* b-but I-" Reggie stammers, falling silent as a large hand spreads across his shoulder, patting him a few times before going to move him out of the way, and Etienne grinds his teeth together watching Carter shoulder his way to the front of the group like an ill omen.

"Well well, if it isn't the little corpse *prince* himself, deigning to grace us all with his *wraithly appearance once more.*" Carter mocks in a posh accent, thick, muscled arms crossing over his chest as he rocks back on his heels, entire stance loose but ready, *like he's expecting Etienne to attack him nasty grin like he's wishing you would,* "What doth thou requirest *my liege?* Some more spooky bats? A blood offering? Perhaps a good scrubbing in the tub to remove thine *stench* of coffin rot-?"

"Is this a fuckin' *joke to you?*" Etienne snarls and can feel his pulse picking up, forgets for a second he's supposed to be focusing on regaining the illusion, too caught up in thinking about burnt smudge sticks and abused magic and tormented spirits, and at the back of his mind, *there's a whisper ~~let us out~~,* "You're all in serious danger an' you're treatin' it like it's a damn *game!* I'm not playin' around! I'm trying to *protect you! An' you're mocking me for it!*"

To Etienne's absolute frustration, Carter doesn't immediately sober after that, and uncharacteristic though it would be, he doesn't apologize either. Instead, he just rolls his eyes, flipping a hand at Etienne in casual dismissal *and something slithers through his mind like a ~~wet palm slapping against a plaster wall let us OUT~~,* "Oh don't get your bloomers in a twist. I know *you* think we're all *in grave peril,* pun intended -but we've been here for *weeks.* Shit's fine. *Calm down.* You're stressin' everyone out for *no reason-*"

"I'm sorry are you *kidding me?*" Etienne fires back on impulse, cannot *believe* the audacity this man has to stand here and insinuate Etienne's blowing the situation out of proportion, not when it's his literal purpose in life to know about these kinds of things. Not when it's *his* job to risk his neck to keep *boneheads* like Carter safe. Etienne grinds his teeth together ~~fingers dragging down polished wood flickering to mold let uS GO,~~ aggravated to the point his jaw is starting to hurt from how tense it is, but he can't help *but* be angry.

This is everything he was raised to *do.* He's the one that's been trained to deal with situations like this, *he's* the one that has the skillset and powers to handle aggressive spirits, *he's the one* that when he had spectral hands wrapped around his throat earlier,

What Goes Bump In The Night

was literally being strangled to death while another spirit tried to claw his heart out, *still managed to escape with his life.*

Etienne knows what he's doing *for the love of the night,* but this human is acting like he's just another *idiot pretender,* like he drew his markings on himself and wears this hat for fun and learned all his spells online.

And it *digs* and *crawls* and *buries its way under his skin ~~fingers fitting into cracks slowly worming their way deeper can't keep us in here~~-* like marrow burrowers from out in Au Delà but instead of vermin it's an indignant fury, *one that's infested deep down in his bones,* and he shakes from it, *heart pumping ~~walls rattling YANK and PULL and TEAR OUR WAY OUT CAN'T KEEP US IN HERE~~-*

"Y-You've got some nerve talkin' to me like that after what you did. Do you have *any idea* of what a mess you've made *you cretin?"* Etienne snarls, shifts his weight forwards and then immediately has to try and not fall, unexpectedly woozy as a sharp pain shoots across his temple ~~doctors and chlorine and couGHING and CHOKING and it never STOPS make it stop make it stop MAKE IT STOP let us out MAKE IT STOP~~, "I- y-you're *lucky* no one's died yet! *Shit is not fine-* I saw that clusterfuck upstairs! What the *hell* possessed you to *think that was a good idea-?"*

"Whoah whoah *woah, I'm sorry-* hold up- you went *in there?"* Carter interrupts, and his shell of nonchalance cracks the barest amount, *brows drawing together confident stance flagging f e a r crawling into his eyes ~~take it USE IT GET US OUT OF HERE~~,* "Are you *crazy?* We cleansed that place an' taped it up for a *reason-* a-and you're tellin' me your stupid *lanky ass* went up there to go play *Ghostbusters?* You *stupid or somethin'?"*

Oh that makes Etienne see red like nothing else, mind hazing over with anger and it's impossible to pay attention to anything that's not the way his blood is boiling ~~writhing against these constraints stop it stop it MAKE IT STOP LET US GO WE'LL TEAR YOU APART~~, and he hisses through his teeth, drops a hand from his cape to press fingers against his suddenly throbbing forehead. It feels like something is pressing against the walls of his skull,

✦✦ 303 ✦✦

like hands pushing at an elastic surface stretching it to its limits trying to get out ~~let us out let us out GET US OUT OF HERE~~, and he stumbles back on his heels under a wave of nauseating vertigo.

Etienne breathes hard out of his nose, snaps his mouth shut and tries to will the bile back down his throat, room undulating so violently, he closes his eyes in a reflexive attempt to get ahold of himself.

Digging shaking fingertips into his pounding temple, Etienne struggles to think past the pulsating headache that keeps growing in intensity ~~hands banging on the inside of his skull LET US OUT LET US OUT LET US OUT~~, a frenetic kind of steady drumming that echoes through him like fists rhythmically beating against a locked door.

Bam bam baM BAM BAM BAM B A M ~~GET US OUT OF HERE~~ growing louder and more incessant, ~~rATTLING dOORkNOBS fIN-GERS gOUGED BLOODY FIST SMASHING THROUGH GLASS FREE US~~, each hit *each wave,* feeling like it's knocking something loose, *like something is crumbling apart* ~~hOWLING sCREECH aT tHE bASE oF yOUR sKULL LET US GO,~~ and it only takes a second, but he can feel his concentration on the spell slip completely.

The waters of his mind churn *violent,* sending distorting ripples through the illusion that disrupts the entire thing, and Etienne panics, grabs for the spiraling ends of it, knows he has to regain his hold or the illusion will drop and the specters will run free *and then they'll all die,* and only *barely* manages to refocus his inner eye. It wobbles precariously, *like mirage lines wiggling in the distance,* threatening a full collapse, but *miracle of miracles,* the illusion does settle back into place- ~~UNHOLY WAIL NO NO NO NO NO SO CLOSE LET U S O U T~~ though it's not as stable as before.

And he may not be an expert at illusionary magic, *only knows what he was taught only knows what he was shown only knows what he's known,* but even he can tell his connection to the spell has deteriorated to a critical point.

Pieces and parts are flaking away under his inner eye, binds that

What Goes Bump In The Night

were never really all that sure crumbling apart, and Etienne tries to keep his mind as steady as he can, but the ripples quaking across his consciousness *won't stop*. The specters have ravaged the illusion, might not be aware it isn't real, but they sure as hell know that whatever the spell is doing, it's what's prolonging their suffering, and they're determined to *end it*.

And they will, if things keep up the way they have been, *if Etienne can't keep a handle on his fucking temper.*

The specters got too close to breaking free on this first attempt and they're likely to try again, bolstered now by an almost success and Etienne's negative emotions. He's an idiot for feeding them, *knows* how they thrive off resentment and anger, but he honestly didn't think they'd be able to feel what's happening outside the illusion.

Clearly he was wrong, his slow smoldering fury calling to theirs like a siren's song, and unless he can keep a firm handle on his concentration, any more emotional upheaval is going to shatter the spell apart like bone china hitting the bricks.

It has never been more apparent to Etienne that he has to get these people out of here. Needs to either convince them of the danger or scare them off, but there's a dark depressing part of him he's trying to ignore that keeps asking *what if that doesn't work?*

Either option.

What if he *can't* get them to leave? What if they *refuse? Try to fight back?* Will he have to stand outside while the illusion collapses and listen to them screaming and begging for their lives, knowing he's once again failed to do the *one singular thing* he was born to do?

The thought makes him sick to his stomach, and he can see the newspaper headlines now, *Local Scion Responsible For Entire Crew's Death,* completely glossing over how he did his best, did everything he could think to do, ignoring the parts where these people ridiculed him, *where they fought him,* refused to trust him, how, no matter what he did, it wasn't enough and *it's never enough-*

✦✦ 305 ✦✦

*when have you ever been enough been what you're supposed to be
when have you ever protected anyone only make things worse only
put people in danger maybe they're all right about you-*

There's a hesitant touch against his forearm then and it startles
Etienne into opening his eyes, head snapping up, *vision swimming,* and he blinks in absolute confusion seeing *Nica* of all people
standing in front of him.

Their mismatched eyes are trained on a spot just to the side of
his face as they drop their left arm fast, hold the other out in offer
with something that sloshes a bit in their shaking grip, "I- *h-here.*
You look like- *appear to- seem like you're gonna-* i-it's just water
don't- pass out- *faint,* y-you look *faint* s-so- *here.*"

Mothers, it takes Etienne longer than it should to figure out what
the fuck they're saying, and in the interim of him squinting at Nica
in woozy bewilderment, they must get impatient, push their water
bottle forward when he doesn't immediately take it. Since they're
refusing to make eye contact, Nica must only have a vague idea of
where he's standing, and in a fumbling guess at where his hands
are, they end up accidentally bumping the bottom of their bottle
against his cutup elbow.

Etienne hisses short in discomfort, jerks his arm back as his
wounds throb unhappily, and it prompts Nica to actually look at
him, eyes flitting up to his face before halting and blowing wide.

"H-Hey are you okay? You've- y-you've got-" They gesture at
their temple in mirror to his own, likely seeing where he smudged
blood on accident earlier, and Etienne can practically see the split
second it occurs to them to look down, Nica's eyes dropping fast
to his hand which is steadily dripping dark red blood down his
long fingers.

"What the fu- o-oh my God! *OH MY GOD- h-holy shit-* what the
f-fuck happened?" They stammer frantic, flesh hand jumping for
his injured one and Etienne's still hazy enough, he doesn't think
to move back until Nica's already touched him, his shredded palm
coming to be cradled in their own, *"Jesus fucking Christ!* Y-You

What Goes Bump In The Night

need stitches- *s-sutures!* Whatever magical s-shit you took last time! Just-! *Something-* J-Jesus H Christ *what-"*

"I-I'm *fine*. Let it alone." Etienne insists as he tugs his hand free from theirs, vision pulsing sickly when he sees the smear of his blood staining the pale skin of Nica's fingers ~~red running down the walls pooling on the floors gashes rent open in necks hands hanging limp fists banging on a door didn't help them didn't save them DOOMED THEM ALL JUST LIKE US~~, and grimaces through another wave of aching nausea, *"Listen to me-* we *n-need* to get out of here, *it's not safe.* It's not *gonna hold,* they're gonna break free *a-any minute-* I...I-I can't keep this up for *much longer."*

"Can't keep *what* up? W-Who's *they? What's-* Etienne *w-what* happened?" Nica is demanding in rapid fire succession, and it's hard enough just focusing on staying upright *and* holding the melting illusion together, *like sand crumbling out from between his fingers rising tide lapping at his ankles* ~~LET US OUT LET US OUT LETUSOUTWE'LLKILLYOUALL PROMISE PESTILENCE PROMISE MISERY PROMISE WRATH~~ *promise a flood of* ~~untOLD SUFFERING~~, but then trying to come up with concise answers to their questions on top of everything else *screaming insIDE HIS SKULL from under hIS SKIN* ~~LET US OUT-~~ is basically impossible.

Etienne wets his dry lips, splintered mind darting from one thing to the next, attempting to find the correct combination of words that would impress upon everyone how they need to leave *now, how much danger they're in,* when a way less gentle touch wraps around his wrist, forcefully turning his hand over.

"Awww *fuckin' hell-* what the shit is this?" Carter complains and lets go of Etienne pretty much as soon as he'd grabbed him, throwing his hand back like it's something disgusting or dangerous, "Nah man, I'm *not* takin' responsibility for that. *You're* the one that went past our caution tape- *twice,* so whatever the fuck you did, the liability for that falls *squarely on you.* You can't just blame it on make believe shit."

Out of everything he could've said, this comes so far out of left field, Etienne is left gaping at the man, tongue thick and heavy in

✦✦ 307 ✦✦

his mouth as he eventually puts it together, what Carter's suggesting, and stammers baffled, "A-Are you...*are you s-seriously* implyin' I'm making all this up to try an' *sue you for safety violations-?"*

Which- is an absolutely ludicrous accusation to make given the situation, and while Etienne *technically could* get them in legal trouble, why in the name of the Night Mothers *would he lie about it?*

There's enough upstairs to get Carter and his employer slapped with several fines already, *possibly even shut down permanently their licenses revoked,* but the thought hadn't even crossed his mind, *wouldn't,* actually, not while lives were still at stake.

At the moment, there are more important things to be worrying about than broken *OSHA codes,* but Carter seems inclined to think differently, rolls his eyes and takes a step back, angrily jabbing a finger in Etienne's direction, "Oh, *please-* don't act all dumb, *I know how this works.* You get your ickle feelings hurt, storm off, somehow get- *'injured'* -on my site before runnin' home cryin' to mommy or daddy *or whoever-"*

"For the love *of-* you think I did *this* on *PURPOSE?"* Etienne demands as he flaps both his bloodied palms open, and at the sight, he gets a few groans and whistles from their audience of other construction workers.

It doesn't seem to deter Carter in the slightest though, and if anything, seems to motivate him to continue ranting with vigor, "-which then you'd start making up some bullshit on how *we're* not doin' what we're supposed to here, *how WE'RE in the wrong-* an' then next thing *I know!* That thousand eyed *bitch* an' their nepotism joke of *a legal system is closin' down my damn WORK SITE!"*

"Mothers of the Night! Do you *hear* yourself right now? You sound like a *lunatic!"* Etienne barks, anger making his heart rate spike again, *makes the illusion gutter and fail again* ~~FREE US BOY WON'T ASK ANOTHER TI~~-

And he has to curl fingers into his throbbing palms to regain

What Goes Bump In The Night

control, breathing hard out his nose, "I-I'm not *lying*. This...t-this place is infested with specters. *Infested.* They've tried to kill me *twice already*, a-an' they're literally *minutes* away from comin' down here and *tearin' us all to shreds* unless we go *now*."

That seems to finally shake some of the confidence the others have in Carter, guys turning to shoot each other nervous looks, *whispering amongst themselves do you think he's for real I dunno look at the blood why would he*, but their foreman doesn't waiver this time, seems to double down into his own seething anger.

Chuffing under his breath like he couldn't care less, Carter rolls his shoulders and a wicked sort of hatred seems to come across his face, dark brown eyes about as inviting as an open grave, *"Christ*, you're a real piece of work, huh? I mean, I *figured* you'd be an asshole, got that *pretentious fuckin' title an' everything*, but damn son, you're really goin' above and beyond-"

"Unbelievable! I'm trying to *help you!* Can you not let go of your own personal bias for *ten seconds* an' see reason? You're in horrible danger an' *I'm not the enemy.* Please just- *listen to me."* Etienne stresses, pressing fingers lightly against his chest, *right over where his heart beats like mad*, and in this instance, he's grateful for all the emotions that aways come welling up out of him.

Because it's undeniably right there in his voice, *in his words,* the desperation the *pleading the fear,* the terrible feelings that betray how scared he is and how earnestly he needs *them to believe him to trust him,* and like it did earlier upstairs, *the atmosphere is shifting,* but this time it isn't into one of freezing cold murderous rage.

Workers are looking at him now, and not like he's a cockroach scuttling out from a damp pile of rot, but rather with a hesitant sort of consideration, like they're hearing what he's saying, *like they're starting to believe him.* Etienne doesn't want to get his hopes up, *has learned to be wary,* but over the top of the crowd, he finds Reggie's eyes trying to catch his.

He's a bit hesitant to meet them, worried because he knows he was unkind earlier but when Etienne finally does glance at him,

✦✧ 309 ✧✦

the man only gives him an encouraging smile and two thumbs up.

Good person, rocks through his mind as Reggie makes a *keep going* gesture that swells Etienne's heart and he nods once, pictures mother addressing the city, thinks about how Sabine wins his court cases, *tells himself he can do this,* and lets out a quiet puff of air.

"Think whatever you want about *me* or my people, but y'all know this place is haunted." He starts and blessedly, no one argues with him, *not even Carter,* though he rolls his eyes again as Etienne continues, "You *know* there's somethin' unpleasant here that makes you uncomfortable...*that makes you afraid*...you wouldn't have done all that mess upstairs if there wasn't, but...it's still not right. Even after you did all that...it didn't get rid of it, *did it? You know it's still here.*"

Every one of the humans looks distinctly perturbed now, and Etienne only really talked to Reggie about this, but he knows then and there that they *all* must have been getting scared by the specters, uses that when he says, "Whatever you're thinkin' about right now, the whispers, the freezing touches, *the malignant aura,* know it's only gonna get *worse.* These spirits are incredibly dangerous, 'specially after bein' left untreated for as long as they have, so why stay here? *Why risk your lives like that?*"

Etienne fans his hands out then, in part because he naturally uses them to talk with and also because it draws attention back to his cuts, *nasty and bloodied and painful,* a small glimpse of what they all have in store if they *won't listen,* "The entire reason I'm here- *why my family is,* is to take that risk instead. Let us handle this, you've trusted us in the past to keep you safe, so *trust me now* when I say you need to *go.* Stayin' only gets you hurt or worse, an' what *point* is there to make out of that?"

It's very quiet after he's done, a tense sort of contemplation that Etienne hopes is gonna tip in his favor, *prays it tips in his favor,* legs starting to jitter thinking about how much time has already passed since he came down here and at what point is he gonna have to just cut his losses ~~sick jerk in his chest fists banging on a door you can't open guttural voices screaming for help but you can't~~

What Goes Bump In The Night

~~you CAN'T you-~~

"You're askin' *what the point is?* Well the *point* is that we don't take *orders* from *you, stiff.*"

And, *of course,* it's Carter that's the first to speak.

His arms are crossed defensively over his chest, eyes narrowed and mean like a basilisk's while he enunciates cold and crisp, "Newsflash. *Shithead.* But it ain't the eighteen hundreds anymore, we don't gotta listen to whatever you tell us to do, so get it through your worm rotted skull- *you're not in charge anymore."*

It hurts because it was *supposed* to hurt, and Etienne ticks his jaw back and forth in anger, but otherwise, doesn't react, won't give Carter the satisfaction of an outburst. By now he knows a taunt when he hears one, and isn't going to rise to meet it even though it somehow expertly digs into each one of his most tender insecurities. Though, he will admit, there is a bit of gratification in seeing that, despite its effectiveness, Carter's comment doesn't seem to get him the reaction he was aiming for.

Both from Etienne, who *refuses* to give him anything, and then more startlingly- *also from his crew,* who're tighter lipped than a bed of clams.

Carter had paused with a smug grin on his face after his goad, looking like he was expecting chuckles or backup heckling, but nothing ever comes and he glances over his shoulder shocked, hands tightening into fists by his side at what he sees. Etienne understands why, because instead of sneering and cheering him on, his men won't even meet his probing gaze, shuffle their feet and scratch awkwardly under their hardhats while they whisper questions and start to hush dissent *hey maybe the kid's right what's the harm what's the foul better safe than sorry right-*

"*Guys.* Come on. You can't *honestly* be buyin' this?" Carter gestures back and forth between him and Etienne, but he's losing ground and he must be able to tell, slaps a palm on his chest and demands way harsher this time, "Seriously? *Seriously-* that's the way you're gonna be? After *everythin'* those freaks have done,

✦✦ 311 ✦✦

you're not gonna believe *me* over some- *rude, pompous, e-entitled JINXFLINGER-!"*

Electricity sparks uncontrollably around Etienne's fingers hearing that *fucking word* used at him *again,* but before he can say *anything, shut your mouth don't you dare call me that I'll give you something to be afraid of,* another voice is hushing soft but firm into the tense silence, "...don't call him *that."*

And Etienne *knows that voice, has heard it snippy and rude has heard it giggly and fond has heard it crying and desperate,* twitches his head in disbelief to where Nica is still kinda standing near him, staring resolutely at the floor while their fingers pick at one another.

For half a second, he thinks he's imagined it, can't stop remembering the front stoop, *sorry little high strung didn't mean it doesn't matter calm down,* and clicks his tongue watching the way their shoulders hunch as Carter growls, "What'd you just *say to me?"*

Of course they flinch of course they shrink of course they back down gonna make excuses again they're not on your side they're not your friend they're not gonna- but Nica's metal hand squeals into a fist and their shoulders go back and all the hairs on the back of Etienne's neck prickle as ozone fills the air, *feeling under your skin like before lightning strikes think you're faster than me wanna make a bet hotshot-*

"I said- *you shouldn't call him that!"* They repeat in a louder voice, and there's something in it that Etienne thinks he recognizes, but he can't quite place what it is until Nica shoots a short gust of air out of their nose, picks their head up and says hard and spiking and broking no arguments, "It's rude and it's demeanin' *an' you know that!* Don't fuckin' *say it!* Etienne deserves more respect than whatever *piss shit you've been given'im!* He knows what he's talkin' about, so stop pretending like *you do!"*

Oh, *oh* Etienne remembers what it is now that he can clearly see their face, sucks in a sharp breath between his teeth and gets torn back through time to a different night, *a different danger,* once again finds himself staring across a debris littered atrium at where

✦✦ 312 ✦✦

a storm brews to life, sees that steely expression those flashing eyes like right before lightning strikes current thick in the air cauterizing your skin think you can take me staring defiant right up into that maw of seething blue flames thunderheads on the horizon like to see you fucking try-

Nica is a very expressive person, face betraying whatever emotion they're feeling every single time, and so it's been easy for Etienne to get a read on them, *to better come to understand who they are as a person,* and there's only been one other time he's seen them like this and it kinda stalls the air in his lungs.

Because this isn't the Nica that's too timid to put their headphones on in crowded cafes, this isn't the Nica that stumbles over their words and seems to second guess every one they say, no, *this* is the Nica that created enough sulfuric acid to completely melt a cursed dragon skeleton in under thirty seconds, the one that *glared* right up at the *death doom despair* looming above them and didn't even flinch *once.*

The one that looked at Etienne with lightninging in their eyes and blood in their teeth and smiled like victory like triumph like something out of the night I win-

"He wouldn't make up shit like this an' if he's sayin' get out, *you better believe yer ass I'm listenin' to him.*" Nica declares with a sharp jerk of their chin, and Etienne is so stunned by their vehement defense of him, *the way they look,* he almost stammers out, *since when have you ever listened to me,* but *can't,* too blown away by the assuredness in their voice, "He's a good witch an' *he's not a liar,* so if y'all know what's good for you, you'll listen to *him* instead of bein' told what to think by your *shithead boss!*"

There's a beat of silence and in it, Nica's mismatched eyes dart to him for a second, almost like they're wanting to make sure he's still there.

Etienne meets their gaze head on and half expects to find their eyes alight with the fire of their alchemy, and they're not, but they might as well be, *resolute determined unwavering spitting embers,*

✦✦ 313 ✦✦

though that confident sheen dims a bit when Nica sees Etienne staring back. He wants to say something but can't figure out what he wants it to be, *thank you I'm still upset with you what changed I don't need your help is this an apology,* uncomfortable tension crackling between them and unsurprisingly, Nica looks away first, tucking hair behind their ear in that nervous habit of theirs.

A groan from Carter draws both of their attentions, and Etienne watches him angrily throw his hands out, sees Nica visibly try and stop themself from flinching as he lays into *them* now, and something thorny grows up under Etienne's bones.

"God of fucking *course!* I shoulda known you were a broomlicker given the way you were cryin' earlier!" Carter snaps and color starts pooling across Nica's cheeks, tips of their ears burning red as he gestures violently in Etienne's direction next, seething, "You just gonna throw your lot in with...*with- THAT,* let it *threaten* you and push you around *an' then stick up for it?* Where's your spine? *Where's your sense of humanity-?"*

"Where's *YOURS!"* Nica fires back and it cracks through the room like *thunder,* leaves Carter gaping as Nica draws themself fully upright, somehow the most commanding presence here despite being the shortest, "You don't get to treat people like this! I don' give a *shit* what your problem is, w-whatever it is you think the witches *did to you!* They ain't done shit to *no one* the entire time I've been here an' I-!"

"Oh shut the fuck up you redneck hick! You don't know *me!* You don't know what I've been THROUGH! *Y-You don't know fuckin' ANYTHIN'-!"*

"Yeah well I think I know *more than you!* I'm not an *idiot, I-I'm not a child!* An' I might be country but least I know this ain't how you're supposed to treat people-!"

"He's not a person! He's not- *GOD-* you really don't know *shit!* You have- *N-NO IDEA* what it's like livin' here with t-these- *things!* Infestin' *OUR city a-and preying on OUR-!"*

"What did he do to you! *Tell me what HE DID!"* Nica interrupts

✦✦ 314 ✦✦

What Goes Bump In The Night

belligerent, pointing a shaking finger at Etienne and he thinks for a second they're trembling because they're scared, *avoids people avoids conflict is faced now with both,* but after seeing the *violent carmine* spreading across their face, how focused their eyes are, *wincing* at the sharp thud against the inside of his skull, pain trickling after it like fingers dragging down a wall, *he realizes they're shaking because they're angry.*

~~fi...nally...~~

"I- it's not like- he didn't- *h-he's* a *part* of the problem! It's a *system* you moron!" Carter yells and the sound goes *weird,* all drawn out and echoey and long, like it's coming from underwater or way in the distant past and another bolt of aching pain slams across Etienne's temples, "They act like we're *lesser!* Like they have the *right* to take our money, *our* rights, *o-our children-* a-an' then they *silence us when we say we're not gonna take it anymore!* Which *you'd know* if you weren't so far up in his *jinxflinger cun-!*"

~~let us...~~

"I said *stop callin' HIM THAT-!"* Nica hollers vicious and Etienne almost drops to his knees, head clamoring like a church bell on Sundays with the reverberations, can hardly think past the way everything rings and *throbs,* an incessant pounding making his entire field of vision strobe and *what in the beyond is happening is he tired is he ill is he dying Mothers he thinks he's gonna be sick again-*

~~out...let us~~

"Don't tell me what to do! I'll do *whatever the fuck I want!* Why should I give *him ANY respect,* when *WE* don't get any *back!* When *they* come into *our* homes- *Human. Homes-* a-and *take whatever they fuckin' want!* A-And we have to let them- *WE HAVE TO LET THEM-!"* Oh Mothers, Etienne really thinks he's about to throw up, the increasing volume of Carter's voice hammering against his head like fists pounding on a locked door, *like decayed fingers digging into rotted wood pulling splinters and shards loose chip chip chIP,* and it feels like ice water suddenly pours down his spine when the realization hits and *oh Mothers of the Night no-*

✦✦ 315 ✦✦

out let us out let us out let US-

"I- w-what the *fuck* are you talkin' about? They're- this *isn't an oligarchy!* They don't *own you-* witches aren't *evil!* They're *good* people- *people,* by the way! *H-Humans!* NOT, *things!* T-They are *good people* an' they do what they have to to protect *us* from *monsters-!"* No no no no no, *this can't be happening it's too soon not now thought you had more time,* and whatever the hell Nica's yelling about fades away into the background while Etienne panics because what he's feeling isn't a headache, *it's not a migraine,* and he tries grabbing for the illusion to reinforce it before it collapses, but it's like it gets *ripped out of his hands.*

LET US OUT LET US OUT LETUSOUTLETUSOUT-

"Are you fucking *stupid?* There's *NOTHING* human about them! They're freaks! *A-Abominations-* blood drinkers a-and devil *worshippers AND C-CHILD STEALERS-!* They don't protect us from *monsters!* THEY *ARE* THE MONSTERS!" A disorienting wave of pain and nausea blasts through Etienne, *feels like a fist goes straight through a pane of glass daggers under your skin hot slide of blood down your arm gapping ragged hole...t-there's...a hole... T-THEY MADE A HOLE,* and he hisses through his teeth, keeps trying to fumble for control but he can't *get it illusion being ripped to pieces can't paste it back together why the fuck are they so much stronger-*

LET US OUT LETUSOU T L E T US O UT LE T U S-

"N-No- *NO!* You're- *y-you're makin' shit up!* They don't s-steal *children-* it's- *y-you're* not understandin' it or whatever! You have it twisted because it's not...t-they wouldn't do that! *They're the good guys!* Witches k-keep people *safe,* you just...you have it wrong- *you have i-it WRONG!" Mothers of the Night,* it feels like Etienne's head is being ripped apart, burning line right down the center of it almost as if the specters are about to come crawling free from his forehead, and he doesn't *understand,* can't figure out why they're impossible to subdue when he's been keeping a handle on his emotions, *made sure he wasn't feeding them-*

What Goes Bump In The Night

~~L E T U S O U T L E T US O U T LETUS~~

"Oh *I HAVE IT WRONG?* That's- tell that to my *FUCKING SISTER THEN!* She just h-had her three year old taken- her. *THREE YEAR OLD. Her baby girl,* just! *Gone! POOF!* Woke her up from a nap to find *bullshit whatever* under her eyes an' next *thing you know-* she's got a *pack* of *jinxes at her door demandin' SHE GIVE THEM HER KID!"* Something freezing rakes a burning trail down his spine, *fingers digging into the edges and p u l l i n g huge chunk ripping free dozens of rotting bloodied limbs smashing through paper thin glass LET US OUT,* and Etienne shoves them back with everything he has *but they won't go buck him off GET US OUT OF HERE,* and this isn't making sense, *how're they stronger he's not even angry-*

~~OUTLETUSOUTLETUS OUT LE T US O U T WE'LLKILL YOUALL~~

"SHUT UP! *T-That's not-!* You-! You're L-LYIN'! You...*y-you have to be lyin'!* They always...they w-wanna *go-* t-they *told us* the kids *wanna go-!* That *you're h-happy- that it's an honor-"* The illusion is cracking apart at the seams, like a dam about to burst and he keeps slapping his hands over leaks, *but water still pours out past his fingers runs down your wrists turns rED LIKE BLOOD-* and the specters *have* to be feeding off something negative, *Etienne knows they are,* and if he could *just figure out what it was,* maybe he could *stop this slow it down,* but it's so hard to *think-* especially with Nica and Carter screaming at each other in the background and *Mothers of the Night can't they just shut UP-*

~~PAIN FOR PAIN FLESH FOR FLESH SUFFERED FOR SO LONG ITS OVER ITS DONE~~

And it's like getting struck by lightning, *disorienting illuminating earth shattering,* because it's suddenly very obvious *shut the fuck up don't tell me what you're a liar say that to my fucking face again hate you hate you HATE YOU-* and it's not *his* anger the specters are feeding off of *IT'S NOT HIS ANGER THEY'RE FEEDING OFF OF-*

~~LET US OUT LETUS O U T HATE YOU HATEYOUHATEYOU HA TE EVERT Y H IN G~~

✦✦ 317 ✦✦

Etienne cries out as something *slams* into his mental wards, reels back, *and strikes again,* each hit physically making him shake as a rioting sea of *anger and vengeance and bloodlust* pounds against his consciousness, swelling after each contact into a wave of un-imaginable r a g e that threatens to drown him in its undertow. Everything is coming down around him, inner waters of his mind whipped up into a frothing, stormy sea that distorts the illusion into unusable nonsense, *swirling wall of a hurricane barreling towards him from just offshore CAN'T STOP US,* and this time, Etienne knows there's no saving it.

His head sinks down in between his shoulders, breath coming in sharp pants because his mind is tearing itself apart trying to main-tain the spell, and he doesn't have much longer until it buckles, *but he has some time,* and he's gonna use every second of it. "S...s-stop-*N-Nica-* you...you h-have to *stop-*" Etienne begs weakly, picks his head up with great effort and swings it laboriously in their direc-tion, can already taste copper running thick down the back of his throat, "It's- t-time's up... s'you gotta go, *you gotta go now-*"

But it doesn't look like they heard him, still red across the cheeks while they try and talk over Carter, and gritting his teeth, Etienne stumbles in their direction, grabbing Nica on the shoulder as he spins them to face him, momentarily forgetting about the blood on his hand, *"Hey-* I *said,* get- *outta here.* Time's up, *it's over.* T-Take who'll go an' get out *now!"*

"I- what? I-I don't- are you oka-?" Nica's trying to say, but the room's started pulsating in time to the rhythmic banging crashing inside his mind, and Etienne groans, claps his hand on their other shoulder and demands, *"Listen to me.* You *said* you would! So go. *P-Please.* Get the fuck outta here with whoever else will go a-an' call 911, tell them what's happenin'. They'll get my mother down here an' she'll take care of it but you have to go *now.* I'll keep the rest alive until then."

Nodding their head quick in agreement, Nica goes to step back from him and Etienne has a brief moment of relief, though it's shattered fast when Nica suddenly stops, staring at him wide eyed, "W-Wait- *wait-* you're not...*y-you can't stay in here!* It's too- you

What Goes Bump In The Night

said we were in- I- you can't *stay in h-here-!*"

"I don't have a *choice-*" Etienne is in the middle of saying, but he gets overrun by another spasm, fingers tensing and sparking around Nica's shoulders as Carter takes advantage of the brief interruption to snap, "Like hell *you don't.* I fucking hate the two of you, but I do gotta agree with white trash on this one- *the both of you can't stay in here.* Get the hell out of this building, stay the *fuck* away from my construction site, *an' never fucking speak to me again-!*"

His words spike hard with dark fury and the mental blow that cracks through Etienne's skull at that makes his vision go black around the edges, legs unsteady under him as the specters *inhale that anger.*

Their forms swell using Carter's hostile emotion as fuel, grow more nebulous and less recognizably *human,* warped limbs trying to claw their way free from the splintering mess they've made of the illusion, howling unintelligibly when it doesn't immediately give, and overhead, the lights all flicker in response.

Some of the construction workers look up unsure, start shuffling around like they're considering making for the door, and they should they should *they should they need to go before it's too late,* but they're slow about it, still hesitating, *void beyond they're still hesitating what more do they need are they gonna wait until someone gets killed is a corpse proof enough you're not lying damnit flee you morons do they want you to beg there go the lights again-*

"Mothers of the Night- just *go! Please!* F-For the *love* of whatever you *believe in just go!"* Etienne pleads, and he doesn't have time to feel embarrassed over how desperate he sounds, let's go of Nica and flings his hands out, entreating to them on the verge of tears, "I-I'm *not lyin'!* I'm not making this up, I don't wanna hurt you, I just *want to help you!* I...*I-I don't wanna watch you die-* please *don't make me watch you die-!"*

"Aight. That's enough melodrama out of you. *Come on stiff,* grab your toady an' let's go." Carter acts like he's gonna woosh them

✦✦ 319 ✦✦

H.Knight

towards the door with big sweeps of his arms, but his movements grind to a stuttering halt when he sees some of his men actually following suit, "Woah woah *woah*- hang on- where do you think *you're* goin'? I didn't mean *you guys*. We still got shit to close out before we can head home, you can't leave *now*."

There's a tense pause, atrium swelling with uncomfortable tension and Etienne digs fingers into his temples.

It feels like something is expanding within the confines of his *skull dozens of hands pressing hard against a too thin surface any second it's gonna snap,* and after a beat, it's Reggie's reluctant voice that speaks up, "I- look man, I get where you're comin' from, *really I do,* a-and don't think I'm like- *downplayin' what your family's been through* b-but I just-"

He takes a short inhale, *seems to steel his nerves,* before saying a lot more sure, "But I think we need to listen to the kid- *t-the scion,* I mean. It's- Carter, I know it ain't perfect, but the witches are here for a *reason.* They know their shit, an' I know you're mad 'bout what happened with Shyann, *believe me I understand...*but is it... worth *losin'* your *l-life* over, man?"

"I-" Carter starts in automatic protest and then immediately stops, broad chest heaving as a handful more guys quietly echo Reggie's sentiment, and it's clear he's fighting whatever he's been struggling with, *the anger the resentment the injustice,* but like so many other times tonight, *his eyes narrow his chin comes up he gives in to it,* and his hatred wins out in the end.

"I-I. Am NOT gonna *l-lose MY life.* 'cuase there's *nothin' dangerous here in the first place!*" Carter snaps, cutting his hands violently through the air and the lights flicker again and blood drips down the back of Etienne's throat and a bright line of searing energy starts to split down the sigil in his mind, "It's just an *old fuckin' building* with some *old fuckin' ghosts!* There is nothin' to be afraid of- 'sides whatever *cockamamie bullshit* these *freaks put in our heads!*"

That crack glows like fire, *grows like lightning,* spiderwebbing

What Goes Bump In The Night

out into a terrible mosaic of promised doom that Etienne can't save anymore, feels the sigil shudder as it's struck over and over *and over,* Carter yelling unrepentant and blindly in time to those thunderous hits, "Ya ever notice how they *tell us* what we're *supposed* to be *scared of? Ever notice how THEY'RE never one of the THINGS we're supposed to be scared OF!* Well if you're wantin' a monster to be afraid of boys, stop lookin' around, *there's one standing RIGHT. THERE!"*

With a creaking groan, the sigil bows out, *like a bulkhead about to rupture like a dam ready to burst,* and the lights go *haywire,* flickering spastically at the surge in energy and one last time, Etienne desperately tries to tell all of them *to run,* but no words make it out, everything lost as he chokes violently on the blood leaking down his throat.

Someone shouts his name and there's hands gripping around the crooks of his elbows while he coughs, *holding him steady,* and he looks down into one terrified hazel eye and one petrified blue one, can't find the air to speak so he mouths at Nica to *run,* blood dribbling down his lips, and ever so slowly, their grip tightens on him, and they shake their head *no.*

Etienne wants to yell at them, wants to grab them by the shoulders again and shake them this time, shouting that *you said you'd listen to me you why aren't you listening to me why won't you go,* and Nica stares up at him like it should be obvious, takes the brunt of his weight the next time he sways and the determined cant to their lips says it all, *because you need help because you're scared too because I won't leave you here alone.*

And he's once again struck with the realization that he's going to watch them die.

"D-Don't-" Is all Etienne manages before more mucusy blood gets caught in his windpipe, before the mounting pressure inside his head goes from painful to *excruciating,* brain feeling like it's getting ready to implode and he has to let go of the spell, *he has to he has to hE HAS TO,* but he *can't,* he won't ~~he's not good at letting go of anything,~~ holding out deluded hope that *he can stop this that*

✦✦ 321 ✦✦

he can save them that he didn't fail that he's strong.

And Etienne's an exorcist right, *or- he wants to be one,* knows there's nothing more fundamental or important to that specialization than maintaining an iron resolve, having the wherewithal to supersede your will over any malignant force's, that sometimes, hanging on to your convictions is the only thing that'll keep you alive when things get hard and your life's on the line but then at the same time-

"I'm *tired* of everyone actin' like witches are some untouchable *GODS* come to save the rest of us! Like humanity wasn't *fine before them* and like we *won't be fine AFTER THEM!*" Carter shouts like a madman amidst a sea of strobing lights, blind to everything that isn't his crippling hatred and the black pointed hat in front of him, and Etienne drinks the blood trailing down his throat, *tries to keep the tears from trailing down his face,* "Can't you take a hint- c-can't you take A FUCKING HINT? No one wants you anymore- NO ONE NEEDS YOU A-ANYMORE! You're a *fucking RELIC from a barbaric time!* S-So why don't you go do us all a BIG favor- *and go crawl back out into the night where you FUCKING BELONG!*"

-but then at the same time, Etienne's only flesh and bone, *still only has a great bleeding painful heart,* and he breathes in, *tastes blood on his tongue,* feels heat gathering along his lash line constricting pain in his chest *can't do this – don't let him get to you – can't dO THIS – you're stronger than this – CAN'T DO THIS – yes you can – CAN'T DO THIS WHY ARE YOU EVEN DOING THIS* ~~they all hate you what's the point what's the point whAT'S THE POINT~~, something warm rolls down his cheek *he breathes out shaky,* and with a sound like shattering glass, the seal breaks.

Chapter 16

All the lights blow out at once, bulbs exploding into a thousand glittering splinters as their coils get overloaded with the surging energy that blasts through the room like a shockwave.

Etienne staggers under the sudden pressure change, head feeling a *million* times better and also *a million times more woozy,* and with the way his heels rock back, he's pretty sure he would've fallen straight on his ass if not for Nica already hanging onto him.

"H-Holy *shit-! Etienne!"* They shout above the din of everyone else yelling, an indistinct buzz of worry and scuffling feet and *oh my God oh holy fuck shit what do we,* that spikes sharply in pitch when an icy wind swirls through the atrium. People panic instantly, and it got dark so fast, Etienne can't *see anything,* shadows all encompassing and deeper than death, but he thinks he can pick out shapes of workers as they stumble about, blind themselves while they frantically try and search for the front doors.

Etienne paws at his side with stiff, uncooperative fingers, trying to undo the buckles on his spellbook holster so he can get the accursed thing *free,* but before he can, someone finally thinks to pull their phone out, cold light from it jerking spastically around while she swings it in an unsteady arc, calling with trembling relief, "G-Guys! *Guys!* Over here! H-Hey- the door's o-over *here!* We can get out, *we c-can get out-* come on let's get the *fuck out of her-arACK!"*

Nica lets go of Etienne with a shriek, several other screams piercing the air as they watch it happen too, the woman's face contorting in terrible surprise when the bloody shaft of a screwdriver emerges from the center of her throat, punching clean through skin and cartilage with ease.

She brings a hand up to feel at the piece of metal protruding from her body, thin rivers of blood starting to run down the column of her throat, and the muscles in her neck work, like she's trying to swallow past it like she's trying to talk *trying to scream,* phone falling out of her slack hand as she collapses backwards with a rattling gurgle.

Everything explodes into chaos after that.

The weak cone of light from her phone bounces around the ceiling, revealing snatches of decayed, blackened plaster and catching on horrified faces, everyone's breath fogging while they shout in panic, most of their voices going chocked off and ragged as they start coughing.

There is no visible sign of the specters, but a man digs at his throat like he's trying to pry fingers off, eyes wide and bulging in their sockets while another hunches over hacking desperately, something dark flying from his lips as he wheezes, *"H-Help-! Argh-c-can't breathe- c-c-can't- i-in my lungs, somethin' in my-!"*

Etienne had already been reaching for his spellbook, but it's with a new sense of frantic urgency that he yanks it free from the straps, fumbling it into his bloodied hands. He goes thumbing through the pages fast until his book picks up on his intent, flying quickly past notes and recipes, only stopping once it comes to where all his sigils are stored, each lighting up softly beneath his trembling fingertips. There's one in particular he's looking for, doesn't care about pissing the specters off worse since they're kinda already past that point, and skims his fingers over a repulsion sigil, imbuing it with his magic before swiping it easily from the page and flicking it at the floor.

The sigil cracks into being with a bang, lines incredibly precise and already glowing vibrantly, pentagram at its center whirring to life and discharging waves of delicate, lacework electricity that unfurl from its core like petals on a moonflower.

Almost immediately, specters start shrieking in anger, jittering forms forced into being as they're knocked back from the center

What Goes Bump In The Night

of the sigil, each buffeting wave of energy making their twisted bodies jerk spastically. They keep trying to press forwards against the current though, and it's haunting, watching them act like a pack of feral beasts, fighting to get at where most of the crew is sheltered by the pulsating maroon glow of Etienne's magic.

A few of the spirits almost get lucky, their attempts landing a little *too* close for comfort, *gnarled fingers almost grazing shoulders or about to close vice tight around an ankle,* and motioning violently with one hand, Etienne calls, *"Closer!* Get c-closer to the center! It might feel weird but it's not gonna hurt you!"

And blessedly most of the humans listen, come stumbling up on their feet or scrabble forwards on hands and knees if they can't manage to stand, but a few don't move. They stand there frozen with their chests heaving in rattling breathes, looking at the two bodies prone on the ground, *the ones who weren't as lucky the ones with blood leaking out of their slack mouths expressions petrified into masks of horror,* and it's clear on their faces, that these people have never seen death before, *have never watched someone die.*

And it shouldn't come as a surprise then, when one of the surviving workers *bolts.*

"NO!" Etienne shouts, lurching after the man, but he's on the other side of the room, is already passing outside of the repulsion sigil's radius before Etienne even gets *close.*

"F-Fuck you *dumbass!* I ain't stayin' in here!" The guy yells over his shoulder and it's one of the men from earlier, *from the front stoop the one with the ANTISO sticker look'it corpse breath's mad uppity little jinxflinger trash under your bootheel,* and Etienne falters but he doesn't stop, chasing after him as he makes a beeline for the front doors.

The man goes crashing through the sheet of plastic covering the front entrance before Etienne can reach him, must make it to the door though because something starts rattling violently...and *keeps* rattling violently.

The doors won't budge.

✦✦ 325 ✦✦

Of course they won't, *of course you've been sealed in here too,* and the distant, *futile* sounds of the man trying to get out are replaced by his frantic, fear riddled voice shouting, "I-It...*i-it won't open!* It won't-! *Why w-won't it-? Fucking! OPEN! WHY WON'T...* what- oh my G-God...*o-oh my God what THE FUCK-! G-Get AWAY FROM ME GET AWAAAAY-ARAGUH-!"*

There's the sound of a struggle.

It doesn't last long.

The sickeningly wet crunch comes first, *the garbled animalistic scream comes next,* and blood splashes dark across the plastic sheets as the guy comes flailing back out, collapsing to his knees with a piece of rebar speared through his throat, dull thud of his body hitting the floor halting Etienne in his tracks.

"Mères de la Nwit-" He swears violently under his breath, can already tell the man's most likely dead given the dark pool of blood spreading out under him, *artery must've been hit explains that spray,* and he grinds his teeth together, angry with himself. The whole point of him existing is not to *add* on to the list of casualties, *you're supposed to protect them you're supposed to be the arm that gets flung out the one that takes the blow,* but he didn't, *he wasn't,* and now someone else is dead because of *his* failure.

Etienne doesn't get the chance to dwell on his ineptitude though, as something freezing claws at his trachea and makes like it's going to *rip it out,* effectively snapping him out of his self-deprecation spiral faster than any medication ever has. He throws himself back on instinct, *throat twinging painfully remembering last time how freezing digits tried to crunch your windpipe like a tin can,* and stumbles further under the protection of the repulsion sigil, magic coiling off his arm like a striking snake when the specter forms for the briefest moment.

It's almost unrecognizable as a human, so warped and twisted by its anger and resentment, it is little more than a melted, *deformed maw* that bleeds black sludge and twitches out of reality spastically, as if it's losing the ability to maintain a coherent form.

✦✦ 326 ✦✦

What Goes Bump In The Night

Face hole gaping further open, the thing howls at him like a banshee ~~no way out NO WAY OUT not for US not FOR YOU NOT FOR US NOT FOR YOU NOT FOR YOU N O T F O R Y O U~~, long lines starting to drag off its body like it's being pulled out of this dimension or like it's...*trying to merge into something else,* and Etienne feels his heart stop for a moment.

Oh no...

He always knew this was a pretty sure inevitability, especially once he slapped that illusion sigil down, and while he never planned on sticking around to find out how good of a fight he'd put up, Etienne is now stuck with the reality that *he's going to have to.*

The worst part is that he is no more prepared to deal with a tordu *now* than he was *twenty minutes ago,* back when he decided the best course of action was getting the fuck out of here and calling his mother to come take care of it.

And now, *here he is,* only a few minutes since the seal's broken and already three bodies down, *with the rest injured but there's at least five still standing* ~~for now for now FOR NOW~~, the sole thing standing between these people and their most certain deaths, with no backup and whatever meager supplies he's got in his storage sigils, versus a collapsing nest of righteous fury and resentment that's been brewing for the last *eighty or so years,* something that has enough vicious energy *and* the full intention of killing every breathing thing in this room before luring others to a similar grizzly fate.

Which- *wow-*

Etienne's not a quitter, he doesn't back down *he doesn't give in,* he does his job like he's supposed to and will keep doing everything he can until he *no longer can,* but even still, *he doesn't like these odds.*

"Oh lamèd mò..." Etienne mutters, skipping backwards closer to the center of the sigil where everyone still alive is clustered together, maroon light painting their faces an ominous and sanguine color, knows they're all watching like he is as the specters start drifting

✦✦ 327 ✦✦

closer to one another. Unlike him though, they don't have any idea of what it really means besides *not good,* and for a second, he's not sure if it's better or worse to not have a complete understanding of all the ways you're about to horrifically be killed.

He ends up deciding it's probably for the better to not know, mostly because of how constricted Nica's pupils already are when they come stumbling up to him, each a tiny black pinprick of *fear* in the center of their irises despite the low light, "H-Hey you got, have, *a-are in possession of-* a p-plan, *right?* 'cause like- I-I *don't- I can't- I- J-Jesus Christ- p-please* tell me you got *somethin'-*"

Well Etienne *had* something, but then no one decided to listen to him, so he's kinda back at square one.

His options are limited.

Tordu occupy that section of his texts that are always preceded by the disclaimer, *to be dealt with by a team of seasoned exorcists only,* so he's really not too sure if he'd even be able to *contain* the thing at his current skill level let alone *destroy it.* He understands the base principles behind dealing with trapped spirits like this, *the appeasement the detaching the sending off,* but he doesn't have the *supplies* to perform even the most basic version of the ritual, let alone whatever kind of *Hail Mary* it'd take to properly send *this thing* off.

Honestly, the best chance of survival they got is still his mother getting down here sooner rather than later, and that means Etienne, *for lack of a better term,* has got to *stall* until then. He doesn't really like those odds either, isn't confident enough that he has the magic to ward off a tordu for an extended period of time, not when his mind has already taken such a brutal beating and he's lost a fair bit of blood, but what other choice does he have?

They're not going to be able to escape from here, at least, *not with their lives,* because as they have already made *abundantly clear,* the specters aren't going to let anyone out without a serious fight. Which, staying inside this hellhole is obviously less than ideal, but with the doors all magically sealed and guarded, escaping

What Goes Bump In The Night

becomes a much more risky option than he's willing to take.

Theoretically, Etienne supposes they could try and bust out through a window like he did upstairs, when the specters trapped him in their old medical ward, but unlike then, the spirits are now significantly less distracted and are also *significantly* more enraged.

Not a good thing!

And *yeah,* none of this is good actually nor does it bode particularly well, and in the privacy of his own mind, Etienne does have to admit how bleak the situation is. He can't *say that out loud* though, is struggling for words of reassurance when Nica shuffles closer, arms wrapped tight around their chest as they whisper ragged, "Dude. *S-Say somethin'.* I...I-I'm really freakin' out an' I dunno what *to do.* Please tell me you can get us out of here, *like-* today- i-immediately- *now.* I don't w-wanna die *here- God fucking Christ- I don't wanna die here-"*

"You're not gonna die, and I know you're scared, but it's gonna be okay. I'll take care of it." Etienne soothes despite not knowing if any of that's true or not, and even though his voice is even and he sounds confident, he should've known Nica would see through it anyway, *they always do,* eyes narrowing in anger as they croak, "Don't *l-lie* to me, Etienne."

He's surprised for a moment when he really shouldn't be at this point, because Nica has always been sharp, *has always been clever,* and they've never had any patience for bullshit unless they're the one spewing it. *Damn can't get anything by them they're almost as bad as Sabine,* Etienne thinks with a huff, spares one more look at the shrieking mass that's slowly collapsing in on itself and then turns back to Nica, leaning in closer and angling his hat so the others can't see his lips move.

"Alright. *Fine.* I won't lie to you...it's not lookin' too good." Etienne murmurs lowly, hears a sharp intake of breath and darts his eyes up, and he's closer than he's ever been to Nica, can easily make out all their freckles and the flecks of gold in their irises, can feel

✦✦ 329 ✦✦

the heat they radiate as he says absentmindedly, "Things are 'bout to get a lot worse, an' I'm not sure how much I can do on my own, so I think the best course of action is find a room to hole up in an' wait it out unt-"

"Wait, wait- *w-what? Are you out of YOUR MIND?* W-We *can't-* you can't *seriously* be *thinkin' that's a good idea!*" Nica barks way too loud, drawing the concerned attention of the construction crew, and Etienne hushes them sharply, would clap a hand over their mouth if it wasn't for the way his palms are still sluggishly leaking blood, "Would you- *please try an' keep it down!* I don't need them panickin'! *Look-* I know it's less than ideal but I really can't see a better *option-!*"

"Well try *lookin' harder* 'cause there's *three motherfuckin' bodies o'er there-* " Nica snaps, country drawl *really* coming through now like Etienne has honestly never heard before tonight, "There has to be *somethin'* you can do like- you're a-a *ghost witch!* C-Can't you like- banish'em o-or *trap them or somethin'?* Just- *anythin'* so we can make a run for it? We *can't* stay in *here-* t-those things are gonna KILL us-! T-The rest of us..."

"*Mères-* do you think I *don't know that!*" Etienne fires back, also getting a little bit of a tone because he's starting to get irritated again, can't shake the feeling that Nica is blaming *him* for this situation, like it's *his fault* shit hit the fan so hard, "I'm doin' the best I can with the *crap hand I've been dealt!* And *no- you're right,* it's *not fuckin' perfect,* but- *in an ideal world,* y'all would've listened to me *fifteen minutes ago* an' gotten the hell out of here *like I repeatedly told you to!* Not hung arou-!*"

He cuts himself off then because the most oppressively sinister and *vile* sensation washes over him like a breaking wave, goosebumps erupting along the back of his neck, *down the slope of his arms,* and there's really only one thing it could be.

Nothing he read could've prepared him for the feeling of it, nor the earsplitting, drawn out moaning scream that cracks through the air and makes him jump, and Etienne jerks his head up, coming face to face with an actual nightmare writhing outside the barrier

What Goes Bump In The Night

of the repulsion sigil.

It lays half collapsed on the ground and heaves in stuttering gasps, clusters of gaping mouths scattered over its body, each bared wide open like they're frozen in an eternal wail of pure anguish, rotting teeth poking out of blackened gums. Spectral flesh hangs loose in long ribbons, a mottled mess of combined body parts that flow and blend in a way that is less intentional cohesion and more like they've been *melted together,* faces smashed flat, *limbs warped,* everything wrapped around one another to form a pair of arms, two broken looking hands, *a collapsed ribcage that rattles with each shallow breath cAn'T bReAtHe-*

Etienne feels his feet shift back on instinct, all the hair along his body standing straight up as the tordu struggles to push itself upright, a seething mess of candlewax bodies that groans wheezing cries the entire time it moves.

"Alright..." Etienne hears himself murmur distantly, watching as the amalgamated tendons in the tordu's arms snap grotesquely, sending it back to the floor with a wet thud and a shriek, "...time to go."

"Y-Yeah, *it is-*" Nica says wavering but strangely sure, and Etienne thinks for a second it's odd how they've changed their tune so abruptly, but he's quickly distracted by the tordu attempting to claw its way forwards. One massive, twisted hand slams against the floor, fingers digging into old wooden boards, and with a guttural cough, the tordu drags itself closer, electrical bands from the repulsion sigil washing over it like water off a duck's back.

Oh that is really *not good,* it shouldn't be able to move through the barrier like that *at all,* but the tordu heaves forward again like it isn't even *bothered* by the spell, and breath hitching in his lungs, Etienne shouts strained, *"Time to go!* Grab the wounded an' get ready *to move-!"*

There aren't many of them left, *there aren't many of them who aren't hurt,* but the ones that are in better shape dutifully help their wheezing counterparts to their feet. Etienne doesn't have time to really look and see who's made it, has his own quiet wishes and selfish desires to that outcome he's ignoring, and motions the remaining crew aside, hand falling again to his spellbook while the tordu heaves itself closer with increased vigor.

It must sense them trying to flee, broken and cracked wrong looking fingers sending up a shower of splinters as it *really* digs into the floorboards, trying to propel itself towards them faster.

Etienne hastily flips through his sigils without taking his eyes off the creature, can see in his mind the pages he's thumbing past and debates over his options. He's struggling to decide between another repulsion sigil, *maybe that'll be enough to force the thing back,* or a warding charm, *would only work until it phased through something can't seal off this area too open,* and neither are perfect or a permanent solution, but he needs to choose, *has* get everyone to an easily barricadable spot so he can perform first aid.

Before he can make a decision though, the dark cavities in the tordu's misshapen, *lumpy head,* the ones that are little more than sunken pits in a grotesque approximation of where eyes would be, wrinkle closed as a massive maw splits open along the lower part of its face, and then a howl that freezes his blood and stops his heart blasts through the room.

Unwillingly, his body locks up around him, hand petrified hovering over his spellbook, and Etienne thrashes against the paralyzing effect, keeps telling himself he can move, *knows he can just twitch your fingers let me use my hand for the love of the night MOVE,* but his body remains unconvinced.

Don't be afraid don't let it hold power over you, Etienne repeats desperately like a mantra, *the more you give it the more it takes from you,* but that's the problem, *he's already let it in deep,* fed it with his fear and his anger and his resentment.

And that's a magic in its own right, because words have purpose and intent has power and *feelings carry energy,* and now this thing is stronger than him because he's *made it to be,* and you can't take back what's already been taken, at least not easily.

What Goes Bump In The Night

Time slows to something like a crawl and all the while the tordu draws ever nearer, moaning creaky with each jerk of its twisted limbs, a writhing monstrosity of Cronenberged bodies that fold back over one another like a tangle of vines, and Etienne is at a loss for what to do, knows to sever this bond he's unwittingly forged he needs something stronger than it to break it, but nothing he thinks of seems to work.

He reminds himself of the duty he'd be failing and the promises he'd be breaking by succumbing, about how his house would suffer the loss of another member, *their scion no less,* and how they might never recover from it. He tells himself how he would be dooming and letting down *so many people* who're counting on *him* to make things right, ending up with more bodies dead than alive, *and what kind of spirit witch would you even be then.* He thinks about simply not wanting to die, how there's still so much he needs to do, *a legacy he's responsible for upholding,* and that this can't be his time yet, *not when he never even accomplished anything he was supposed to.*

And none of it works.

None of it works, pushes lackluster and limp against the thing constraining him, not strong enough motivations to actually shatter through the paralyzing grip on his mind. A grip that only grows tighter as Etienne begins to feel the *doubts* soak in. The ones he's always been haunted by but have gotten worse since that night, *in August,* when he stood like an idiot in the Audubon visitor's center after nearly getting another group of people killed, *learned nothing history repeating itself,* when lightning crackled through the room and there was blood in his mouth and ozone in the air *and he realized he wasn't as good as he thought he was,* and that's dangerous.

That's bad.

Because the first rule of being any sort of competent exorcist is *never waiver,* and yet here he is, resolve turned to weak jello and with no belief he can actually do this, and it's like already signing his death certificate, *like waving a white flag I surrender I give up I*

◆◆ 333 ◆◆

couldn't hold my own-

Etienne would grind his teeth together if he could, *force himself to move to act,* but he can't, *he's weak,* and it's somehow even more disheartening that not even his *anger* and *outrage* are strong enough to shatter the bond.

The tordu howls almost delighted sounding then, *like it knows like it's reveling in it,* and he despairs, not sure if there even *is* actually anything that can take back the power he's given this thing over him.

And about that moment is when Etienne sees *light* out of the corner of his eye, *jumping crackling bright white electric blue same color glowing in the depths of their pupils blood in their mouth lightning sharp grin I win,* that grows brighter and harder to look at as Nica steps partially into view, hands up, *fingers drawing together,* and for one insane second, Etienne thinks they're gonna try and use *alchemy* on *the tordu.*

Get away get BACK it's not like that not like last time, he wants to yell, muscles in his jaw *burning* from the effort of trying to warn them, *you can't affect it with chemical reactions it's not a physical construction step BACK you're TOO CLOSE,* and swallows painfully when he still can't force the words out. Looking at Nica's face is difficult, *they're just that little bit out of his field of vision,* but Etienne manages, thinks maybe he can convey with his eyes what he can't with his mouth, and confusion starts to grow in his mind because it doesn't seem like they're...looking at the tordu?

It's kinda hard to tell, but he thinks Nica's actually staring straight ahead, *towards the front wall,* and the why of that is absolutely lost on Etienne until a few things happen in quick succession.

Nica arches their fingers together to start whatever reaction they're planning on, the ambient energy that's coalesced in the room spikes *dramatically,* skates along Etienne's nerves and maybe for the first time since he's known them, he actually gets a *taste* of some intent from Nica's alchemy, a crumbling kind of falling sand *disintegration pulling it apart breaking down molecular structures*

What Goes Bump In The Night

back into base elements a calculated sized hole of loose components space unoccupied-

Etienne understands then what they're trying to do, *we can't stay in here time to go yeah it is please tell me you have something anything not waiting on you they're gonna try to break their way out they want to escape,* and panic sets his mind alight with fire.

Mothers of the Night, they don't know, *they don't know they haven't put it together,* think they can just smash their way free but it's not gonna be that easy and he wants to scream- *don't you see don't you get it that thing's not gonna let us out they're not gonna let us leave killed that man when he tried they'll kill you when you try-*

And something lurches horrible under his breastbone, can see in his mind then the spray of blood the fingers scrabbling at whatever's sunk into their throat *the way that brilliant light would fade so fast from those mismatched eyes-*

Sick terror rolls through him as Etienne's fingers twitch spastically, and he can't stop the images barreling through his mind, *that grinning mouth going slack blonde head lolling to the side the way they laugh bunching up their entire face pale skin smattered with their own blood Christ you're such a nerd-*

-and he has to do something, *he has to do something,* he can't let them *die not them not them can't bear any more death ~~especially not theirs~~,* but the tordu is almost within striking range-

-hands tucking hair behind big ears grins so wide dimples pop up please I don't know what to do I'm so scared looking at you like you'll have an answer have an option have the key to their survival knees buckling as their body goes limp-

-and the wind is picking up *and his pulse is thundering and not here not now,* this can't be how it ends, *didn't want this to be how it ended,* was lying to himself outside when he said it was fine if he never saw them again, *it wasn't true that's not what you wanted,* he wanted to-

-red red too red blood rushing in a waterfall down their front soaking into cotton slipping off old nylon mudding up those vibrant colors hey it's retro-rific nervous dance their hands do content swing their foot does quick fast smart way they talk and you want to ask Mother's do you ever want to-

-the mangled arm that'd been clawing towards them both rears back, distorted tendons bunching as a dozen gaping mouths flap open to *shriek like something from the seventh ring of hell,* only thing understandable in that howl a promise of agony and *blood and fatal ruination-*

-*hey after this would you maybe wanna go grab but you never got the chance to ask and now you never will dead at your feet pooling blood into old boards friendly smile they give you little wave night Etienne-*

-and the tordu must feel it too, *what they're trying to do the escape they're attempting to make,* and it has no intention of letting them out, *will end it here will end it now,* but the second before those tendons snap out, *the second before those broken fingers gouge open deep troughs in the fragile skin covering their throat ripping their trachea free no way out not for us NOT FOR YOU its gonna kill them ~~your friend~~-*

Etienne jolts like he's been struck by lightning, *everything comes into startling focus,* and he doesn't think about moving, *he just does,* goes darting forwards with a hand outstretched and his heart in his throat and manages to get fingers wrapped around Nica's flesh wrist.

He doesn't hesitate. Jerks their hands apart to break the reaction and a flurry of blue electricity crackles around him angry, but Etienne doesn't even care, uses the confusion to drag Nica backwards behind him as he steps forward, *taking their place,* left arm coming up involuntarily to shield him as much as it can.

It's weird, how long sensation truly takes to trickle in.

The first thing that registers though is the strength the tordu hits him with, enough so that he's almost forced back, *enough so it*

What Goes Bump In The Night

might've cracked his radius arm going numb and tingly in spurts, but that's quickly overridden by the *blinding cold* that comes next, a touch so freezing it feels like it's burning the flesh from his arm with its intensity. Etienne grits his teeth against the pain, and he's been hurt many different ways before but even now, he thinks this one might be the worst, knows he's bleeding and bleeding bad despite the fact that he can't feel it yet through the adrenalin.

Immediately, he tastes something sour in his mouth, *feels zipper fast crackles and zings weaving through his molars low bass snarl like a building storm,* and all his hair stands up on end as a massive wave of electricity cracks from his skin like a whip. *Get back get bACK GET BACK GET BACK G E T B A C K,* his magic screams from where it seethes free deep inside him, *crawling out from under his bones from the trembling interior chambers of his heart alighting from the very depths of his being,* a ferocious tempest that slams against the monster and *demands* its warning be respected or it'll learn they're not too different after all.

Wanna go wanna try wanna understand why they named us demons helLSPAWN STORMBRINGER why they hunted us why they killed us en masse WHY THEY BURNED US ALIVE AT THE STAKE wanna learn why they didn't wipe us out why they COULDN'T WHY WE'RE STILL HERE-

The tordu howls in torment, tries to jerk away from the blistering cloud of electricity boiling off Etienne, and before it can get far, Etienne takes the chance to shove it back with a strength he doesn't normally have. His magic coils liquid over his shoulders once before launching forwards as well, responding smoothly to his intent like a well-honed blade.

It pummels into the tordu, *a crashing sea of pure fury,* each bolt of lightning heating up the space around it forge hot until the air blows back with a *crack,* thunder a never-ending rumble that makes his ears ring and his teeth clatter together and his heart race fast like every arc of searing light streaking by.

Each hit punches a new crackling hole through the spectral form of the tordu, quickly riddles the monster down to something that

✦✦ 337 ✦✦

looks more like Swiss cheese, and it's struggling to stay upright, *mouths flapping open hands grasping reaching claws,* but Etienne can see that it's fighting a losing battle. In the end, it's too much of a barrage for the tordu, and there is so much that is gratifying about watching that *abomination* go flying backwards, helplessly shrieking as it hits the floor and then skids a little further.

Odd echoing moans wheeze out of its dozens of mouths where it lands, glitchy form phasing spastically as it settles in a heaving mass against and *through* the floorboards.

It twitches like it's being electrocuted, a mess of writhing melted limbs and static riddled flesh, and its bonds were never all that stable to begin with, *didn't want to be this was forced into being this,* but how it's unraveling now is in large part due to Etienne's magic and *Etienne's magic alone.*

And not even from something well-constructed or purposeful like a *spell,* but instead the raw, *unrefined* force of his magic in its most base form, an energy that has so much boundless potential but generally doesn't pack much of a punch when its unworked like that, *but not his not his his just did,* and a very familiar warmth blooms under his sternum.

Chest swelling with euphoric elation heady glee you did it you did it you can do it you're strong you're powerful you're the best you can do anything, and it is such a sweet temptation to want to fall into it, *to get stupid to get lost to forget himself,* but Etienne shakes his head like he's trying to knock the thoughts out.

It's not over you're not done don't get to celebrate a victory when you haven't won it, he reminds himself, and it's true that he shouldn't take much pleasure in it yet, because despite looking worse for the wear, the tordu doesn't stay down for long.

The crackling holes Etienne blew through its form start to weave themselves together again, wet sucking sound like when your feet get stuck in bog muck making something coil sick in his gut, and Etienne flips his spellbook back open, ignores the way his left arm almost gives out as he shouts for everyone to, *"RUN!"*

What Goes Bump In The Night

And he's worried at first that they still won't listen, *that they don't trust him,* but *finally,* people *heed his warnings,* rush of uneven footsteps and panicked breaths at his back as they race down the hallway behind him without direction. They need to get to a room where he can easily seal them off from the intangible grasp of the tordu, but Etienne doesn't have *the time* to explain that, and then he feels a twitch against his palm and remembers Nica's wrist is still caught up in his other hand.

He's pretty sure he hastily explained enough of his plan to them earlier, *not like they were interested in listening to him,* but it's better than nothing, and without looking over his shoulder, Etienne squeezes his fingers around their wrist once before going to drop it, ordering, "Get them somewhere safe! A-Any room that still has four walls an' a door that can shut! *Go!* I'm right behind you."

Blessedly, Nica doesn't argue with him for once, but they also don't immediately take off like he thought they would, and in the second before his fingers slip off their wrist, Nica flips their hand, wrapping trembling fingers around his own arm. They squeeze once and then hang on, harder than Etienne had grabbed them, and it's mumbled so quietly, he's not even sure he really hears it correctly, but he thinks Nica begs him soft, *"Y-You better be-"*

Then they're letting go and the scuffing noise from their tennis shoes is somehow the loudest thing in the room, even drowning out the cacophonous storm of thoughts that swirl to life in his mind.

Are you...did you really say that did...do you mean it do you really worry about me are you really gonna be waiting up for me, and Etienne has to fight *so hard* not to look over his shoulder, wanting desperately to find those mismatched eyes and ask them if they mean it, *if they really do care for him in some way.*

He almost does on impulse, *can't lie to himself knows how he feels has to know if they could feel the same ~~am I your friend I want to be,~~* but the tordu has heaved itself back up, legless torso hovering above the floor now as it suspends its weight on its two front arms. Pure malice bleeds off the thing in waves that brush vile up against

✦✦ 339 ✦✦

Etienne's magic, and he's already dragging another repulsion sigil off the page when the monstrosity roars and comes charging at him like a rampaging bull.

The sigil strikes the ground in front of the tordu and combines with the one already going, battering it back a little, but not enough, and it pushes through, lashing out again in a whip fast move that he just *barely* misses dodging. Shit that thing is *fast,* and even though Etienne danced back in the nick of time, he still ends up wincing, sharp pain along his cheek that continues to throb and sting as something warm trickles down his skin.

Not good, he thinks with a curl of his lip, and it can't be a huge cut, *probably barely more than a deep scratch,* but he really doesn't need to be losing any more blood, can already feel a telltale light-headedness that never bodes well.

And unfortunately for Etienne, while he might be starting to flag a bit, it doesn't look like the tordu has at all. Speed not wavering in the slightest, it pivots fast to launch another attack at him that he counters with a hastily flung up ward, sparking net of it arcing over his head in a flash. The tordu's broken, claw like fingers scream across the shimmering maroon surface and Etienne feels a twinge in his heart as the ward is tested, his magic pulling painfully much like it did earlier when the illusion was being taxed and strained upstairs.

It hurts in nearly the same fashion, but instead of his head killing him, it's in his heart now, a more familiar pain that will haunt him for the rest of his life just like how Sabine will always be plagued by migraines and bloody noses. Their power comes with a cost, *a price,* and at the moment, this isn't one he begrudges having to pay, nor is it really unbearable, won't stop Etienne from doing what he needs to do.

He twists his hand and the ward rotates, new layer unlocking and pushing outwards, creating a thicker barrier between him and the tordu that is put to the test not a moment later.

Alternating fists, the tordu pounds against the crackling surface

What Goes Bump In The Night

of the ward, keeps trying to get fingers under the raised edge of the second layer and rip it free, but it can't really seem to find much of a grip.

Each hit sends a sharp stinging jolt of electricity through Etienne's chest though, but to his credit, the ward holds and doesn't crumble inwards...at least for now. It's not meant to be a permanent solution, is one of the smaller ones he'd typically use to protect against less dangerous entities, and crinkles like the way glass does when it's about to break as the tordu slams both its warped fists against it.

Time has not been his friend tonight, and thinking fast, Etienne flips through his spellbook. He knows the nebulous steps to taking care of a tordu, *remembers studying it last winter for exams,* but it's been almost a *year* since he's read anything on it. Etienne might not recall everything in picture perfect detail, but he remembers enough to understand he is in no way equipped to deal with one, *lacks the supplies the prep the backup,* so right now, it's not about finding the absolute perfect option, but rather about being creative with the best worst option he has.

And there are a lot of *really bad options,* things that could blow up in his face or just be a waste of the magic that's already taxing his body, but his hand does come to a stop, stilling over a particular page. This...*could work* actually, and no, this sigil is *not meant* for what he's about to do with it, but it should at least snare up the tordu long enough for Etienne to make an escape and get his much stronger, *and much more resilient,* Artuas wards secured wherever the others are taking shelter.

Hopefully.

Or, alternatively, this idiot idea he has will fail catastrophically and do literally nothing and then they'll all die and he won't have to worry about it anymore.

So...*a win-win?*

Morbid humor aside, it's his best chance at buying back some time, and plan set, Etienne tucks a bloody thumb in between the pages to mark his spot, grimacing as another dart of pain zaps up his chest. That one had some bite to it, *felt like bright sharp splintering glass digging into his ventricles,* and just so happens to coincide perfectly with the white hot crack the tordu split the center of his ward with. It must sense him glaring at it, likely knows it's also about to break through the ward entirely, and unhinges its main jaw, bellowing out another grating horrific scream right in Etienne's face that's cold like winter and smells like grave rot.

That rank breath swirls past him, sets the chains on his hat swinging and knocks loose hair out of his eyes, but it doesn't immobilize him like last time, and Etienne's brows draw low, a fierce kind of conviction burning under his sternum. He's found his footing now, isn't going to let that abomination have *any more* power over him, *broke their bond with the one seared around his wrist like a brand I'm right behind you tight grip don't wanna let go you better be,* and when it rears back to crush the ward once and for all, Etienne readies himself.

For his idea to work, he needs to put some distance between the two of them first, and it's reckless and dangerous and probably not advised by literally *anyone,* but the second after the tordu's fists make contact with the shield, *right before it shatters entirely,* Etienne twists his hand lightning fast and releases the last layer of the ward.

It's a move that requires absolutely *perfect* timing, and thank the *Mothers,* but Etienne nails it just right, explosive shockwave erupting out from where the ward fails and tries to expand at the same time, nearly knocks his hat off his head with the windstorm it kicks up.

And like he was banking on, it hits the tordu *hard,* blasting it back across the room because Etienne's magic is predispositioned to not turn back on him, and with nowhere else to go, the full force of the ruptured ward ends up slamming the tordu into a pile of scaffolding.

The entire structure screams shrilly before coming down in a clanging heap, metal supports knocking and pinging against the floor, and before the tordu can phase through it and crawl free,

What Goes Bump In The Night

Etienne quickly flips his spellbook open.

He tries to bring it up so it's easier to get at the sigils but his left arm dips wildly, finally giving out, but that's okay, *he can manage,* wedges his numb fingers into the pages to hold it open as he drags the Pieuvre sigil off the page. Its spindly edges curl over his other hand delicately before he slings it at where the tordu is sprawled, half-dollar sized disc going whizzing through the air until it skims the floor and then expands fully, good sized chunk of space getting swallowed up by vibrant maroon lines.

A dozen waving arms of glyphs unfurl from the spell's spinning center, snap and curl inquisitively like macabre dancers, are technically looking for a poltergeist to snag out of the aether but the second one of them skims the tordu, the rest immediately dive for it.

There is no hesitation in the way they wrap around that abomination, securing it up tight like a nest of strangle vines from out in Au Delà, and once they're firmly in place, they start laboriously dragging the tordu towards the center of the sigil. Poltergeists are a fair bit smaller than literally any tordu though, so the spell is struggling already, but especially when this amalgamation gets enough strength back to try and fight it.

Thrashing like *mad,* the tordu howls savagely, multiple mouths biting and digging into the tendrils, seems like it's *trying to chew its way free,* but the coiling arms of the spell will just shift out of its reach if it gets close, absolutely *refusing* to let go. Which is what Etienne was hoping for, knows Pieuvre sigils to be very determined in how they trap their resistant quarry, but this is very much a task it was never designed nor intended for, and he's nervous to turn his back on it just yet.

Afraid when he does he'll wind up with a spectral hand punched clean through his chest cavity.

Etienne can't let his fear control him now though. He has to go, *needs* to find the others and see who all's still alive, but he's so slow when he starts edging backwards, worried still about taking his eyes off the tordu, wants to make sure this terrible arrangement will hold out for at least a little bit. On the bright side, it looks like the spell is making *some* grounds, *keeps tugging the tordu closer and closer tendrils secured tight,* but...then again, *on the downside,* the tordu is *also* making progress freeing itself.

One of its arms is almost loose, lumpy shoulder heaving up and down as it tests the bonds over and over again, and eventually, the tordu's gonna win out, will only continue to regain strength while the spell will only continue to lose it.

And the perfectionist part of him is demanding Etienne stay and make sure it is *absolutely faultlessly secured,* reinforce what he can and do it *right,* but the self-preservation half knows there is no *right* or *perfect* at the moment, that *'good enough'* will have to be what tides him over and keeps him alive.

No one is taking marks for this it'll have to do, Etienne reminds himself and it is such a hard, bitter thing to swallow, *mediocrity,* but he forces himself to do it and finally spins on his heel to go, only wobbling marginally as the room undulates violently.

Void cursed blood loss, he thinks petulantly as he stumbles towards the hallway the others fled down, the stress and strain of the night really hitting him now. His body feels leaden, *slow,* encumbered by fatigue and the earliest stages of arcane burnout, which manifests as a faint tickling at the tips of his fingers, but it isn't the time yet to sit down.

He can't afford to lose precious ground while he works on catching his breath.

Etienne rubs absentmindedly at his chest, right over his stinging heart, and swings his heavy head from side to side, trying to figure out where everyone went when he spots a familiar freckled face peeking out from a nearby doorframe. "Oh thank f-fuckin' *Christ-*" Nica hisses, and darts out to loop a stabilizing arm under his shoulders that Etienne is ruefully grateful for, using it to then help lead him into the musty room, "I-Is it over? *Like,* is it- dead, *d-deader, re-dead?* I heard that screamin' an' I- are w-we safe now or-?"

What Goes Bump In The Night

And before Etienne can unstick his tongue to attempt an answer, there's a haunting howling *wail* from the front of the building that echoes all the way back here, screams of anger and torment and *everything unholy* and he figures that works as answer enough, leans against Nica when they shudder, *"F-Fuck-* o-okay, *okay,* so um...w-what now? I- I did what I could- *f-for the men,* guys- *p-peo-ple-* but d-do you have any of those health thingies? Some of them are hurt bad an' I-I tried callin' 911 *b-but I can't get signal-"*

"Won't be able to, t-too much electromagnetic interference-" Etienne grits out, left arm really burning now as Nica tries to lead him over to a wall, but he digs his heels in, steering them towards a nearby table instead, "I'll- *ah,* I-I'll deal with the wounded *i-in a sec,* but we need to get this place secured. Can you- I-I need you to make salt, don' think I have enough...*but just-* d-draw a line all 'round the room with it while I...*w-while I...uh-"*

Etienne kinda finds himself trailing off, forgets what he was saying and everything smudges out of existence for a minute, replaced by a dizzy calm black fog he roughly pushes from his mind.

Not yet not yet can't pass out just yet, circles around his mind like a turbine slowly powering down, and thank the Mothers, but it kicks back on briefly, and when he comes to, he's hunched over the table, propped up by his shaking right arm while his left still hangs like burning deadweight against his side.

There's some kind of pressure flitting around his back, checking him over it seems and then pressing featherlight against his sides next, and it's probably Nica and they're *definitely* saying words at him, *distant nervous chattering can't make sense no matter how hard he squints,* but Etienne doesn't have the energy to listen, heaves his spellbook up onto the tabletop with great effort and barks, *"Salt!* D-Did you not *hear what I said?* Don' worry 'bout me, *m-m'fine,* but I need...*s-salt,* g-go *make salt-"*

"-okay first off you are *not fine,* an' secondly, I just told you, *I. Can't.* I don't have any of what I need, an' there's not enough re-sidual sodium or chlorine in *anythin'* to try and transmute it back out! I-I'm not a fuckin'- *miracle manufacturin' plant!"* Nica snaps

✦✦ 345 ✦✦

back and Etienne groans loud and impassioned, muttering snippily under his breath in French about the uselessness of alchemy as he sloppily paws through his spellbook, looking for his supply cache.

He groans again when he hits that section and remembers what a mess it is, knows he should *really* probably reorganize all his storage sigils, *seriously why is mimwart root with the minerals,* but that's a problem for future Etienne if he lives long enough. By some divine blessing, the sigil he uses for salt is at least on the first page, and he immediately places two fingers on it, drawing the tips of them down together in a V-shape until it splits open.

A bright flash of maroon light, a soft crackle, and suddenly there's a five-ish pound sack of rock salt sitting slumped over on his spellbook easy as you please.

It's most likely not enough to help ward the entire room, but if used efficiently, it should make a decent sized circle, and he pushes it gracelessly towards Nica, muttering, *"Here.* Cover what you can. O-One line. Un- *broken.* Preferably symmetrical. Make sure everyone's inside it an' I'll...be over in a sec to uh...do the t-thing...the um, *m-medical thing...? First aide!* S'just...need to get these wards fixed down first, m'kay? *You got it?"*

But it doesn't look like Nica's *got it,* and he has to nudge the sack a few more times before they take it cautiously.

Nica twiddles it in their hands like it's a bomb that has a chance of going off in their face, *unsureness bleeding off them in eddying curls,* and they're hesitating again and Etienne is starting to lose what little patience he has. Both of them understand the danger present. They know what the tordu is capable of, can *hear* it struggling and fighting its restraints, *he can feel in his heart the way those binds are failing,* but still Nica pauses for a moment by his side, bag of salt creaking between metal and flesh fingers.

And Etienne does what he said he'd stop doing and loses his temper a bit.

"What? What're you waitin' on? For that *thing* to c-come in here *an' kill us?"* He snaps, exhaustion and pain making his tone un-

What Goes Bump In The Night

kind and *nasty,* though he does manage to successfully bite back all the other ugly things brewing at his lips, shit he wants to say out of frustration and not because he actually means it.

Be kind be kind be kind you promised you'd be kind, beats from his heart and Etienne hangs his head, so very tired and so very unable to rest. He sighs, knows this isn't just hard and terrible for him, *they just watched people be killed have probably never seen that before now they'll never be able to unsee it,* and he needs to be more understanding of that.

"Nica...listen, I-" He tries, wanting to be something reassuring *they* can lean on, but the world gets spinny again and his train of thought completely derails off the side of a mountain, leaves him staring at his spellbook in abject befuddlement while the pages fade into and out of focus, creating a tense silence that Nica's quiet voice unsurely fills, "No, *n-no-* it's- I'll go, *I-I'm going-* I just wanted- *I-I* didn't mean to earlier, *y-you* didn't *have to-* I just...m'sorry... f-for *me-* for what I-I did, *for your arm,* I mean. I...I-I- *oh G-God-* m'really sorry, Etienne...m-m'so so sorry-"

Everything they're saying kinda crumples in at that point, gone tight and drawn like the way tears always force voices to be, and by the time Etienne scrapes enough sense together to lift his head, Nica isn't there, nothing but empty space where there should be a colorful blur he needs to reassure that it's okay. Injuries and being a Boudreaux are more or less synonymous, he wouldn't hold any wound he got against anyone, *especially for ones received in the service of protecting others,* and besides, as long as he lives, it'll heal anyway so he doesn't really get the big deal.

What's one more scar added to the collection already crisscrossing his arms? Etienne isn't vain or shallow enough to think they detract from him personally in any way, isn't bothered by their presence, and how could he be?

When they're the ones he's gotten from saving *lives?*

That's a trade Etienne would gladly make any day, would much rather be the one hurt and bleeding over knowing his failure to act

✦✦ 347 ✦✦

caused someone's death.

So it's always been odd to him, how people see the scars him and his family wear and treat them with pity instead of recognizing them as the badges of honor they all consider them to be. Each pale line drawn across his flesh is testament to a lesson learned and a duty fulfilled, and not once has he ever looked at them and felt regret for taking the hit, and he knows he'll feel the same about this new one too.

Etienne shakes his head, surmising it's just a cultural difference as he activates the stabilization charm on his spellbook and pushes back one handed from the table, leaving a bloody handprint behind that smears when he drags his fingers away. He beckons his book to follow him and steps backwards into the center of the room, legs wobbling but they hold his weight and he locks his knees to make sure they will continue to do so.

Obligingly, his spellbook has already flipped to the pages where he has a pair of Artuas wards, and there's only the two of them, so he'll have to get creative on his placement, starts to pull one from the parchment before he realizes he needs both hands.

It's actual torture getting his left arm to obey, nerves on fire and tendons shot, but Etienne grits his teeth and drags it up anyway. He can feel the blood trailing warm and sluggish down his skin now, every instinct he has telling him to drop it, to give in *to let go*, but he won't.

Etienne can do this, *he knows he can,* knows he has no other choice than to do what has to be done, *that everyone is looking to him to save them,* and maybe it'd be too much for another witch to handle, *Mothers of the Night-* it should probably be too much for *him,* but he goes to grab an Artuas ward anyway.

Because even though it might hurt and Etienne's hands might shake the entire time he's trying to set the wards right, hoping perhaps vainly it'll be enough to protect against the amalgamation of pure torment he can hear screaming just beyond a few scant feet of wall, he's still a *Boudreaux,* the son of Matriarch Catherine

What Goes Bump In The Night

Amélie, and that means he doesn't go down without giving it his all.

And as the Artuas wards settle into place in opposing corners, their solid bulk spreading distorted out across the floor and over the walls and stretching up to the ceiling, smartly managing to cover the whole room while their innermost pentagrams are clunking happily away like two big waterwheels, Étienne clenches his hands into bloody fists and knows this is really only the beginning.

He has more he can give, *and he's willing to give it.*

Chapter 17

To be completely honest though, despite Etienne's assuredness that he is *fine*, the next however long chunk of time passes in something like a blur. Blood loss is hitting him hard and makes reality stop and start in weird spurts, and even though the general rule of first aid is *'make sure you're stable before offering help to others'*, he still feels incredibly guilty being the first person to drink a swig of healing draught.

He doesn't take much, only found three bottles in his emergency sigil and he's got two people badly wounded and the rest spitting blood out of their mouths, so he limits himself to a few partly mouthfuls, just until the gash sheeting blood down his arm shallows out. It's still an ugly wound even after it closes up some, starts near his wrist and runs in a long line that curves around the slope of his arm, ending by his elbow, and Etienne rolls his shirt sleeve the rest of the way down so no one else has to look at it.

He's not sure how much good it'll do.

The damn thing keeps bleeding, and it's certainly much slower than it was earlier, dribbles out of the wound sluggishly instead of rushing in thick spurts, but he can feel the dark material of his shirt sleeve growing wet and cold. Hopefully it'll start clotting on its own soon so Etienne can quit worrying about it, but it's honestly the least of his concerns right now. He's trying to stay focused though, keep his brain task oriented, but it keeps cycling through his growing concerns like a demented slideshow.

First slide: Fun fact, even with the distance between them and the walls of separation, you can still faintly hear the tordu's echoing screams and wails as it attempts to free itself, *and funner fact,* going off the increasingly annoying pain in his chest, *it's getting close.* The Pieuvre sigil will probably hold for another fifteen minutes give or take, and then the Artuas wards should last about twice as long, so Etienne has *time,* but the question is will it be long enough to see them all safely through this, because a lot of that rides on him and his ability to *maintain* said spells and uh, *well-*

Second slide: Etienne's pretty fucked up. He's weak and his body is barely responding and his magic has more or less gone dormant. It's not gone. Just...*kinda took a step back.* He can still feel it, low lulling hum of it deep beneath his breastbone, but it's not going to jump to his defense quite as quickly now. It won't take the chance of overloading his system and risk killing him when he's already this fatigued, so if he's gonna have to use it, he's *really* gonna have to force it, and Etienne's not sure how much good he's going to be able to even *do* once push comes to shove, *and oh it's going to be shoving real soon-*

Third slide: There are five- *six* people he needs to try and keep alive, and while most of them have a better chance at surviving, *excluding the threat the tordu poses and how Etienne is almost functionally useless,* there are two that he's...*not optimistic about.* He should be able to stabilize them if he gets them healing draught *now,* but with the state of things, part of him wonders if perhaps it'd be kinder to let the ones that are dying *just continue to do so...*

Fourth slide: ...but that feels like a betrayal of the *highest degree,* so Etienne *is* going to have to stabilize them and see to everyone else *and* come up with a plan to better shield them in this shoddy sanctuary he's built, at least until he gets a second to get word out to his mother, but even then, it'll take her time to get prepped and *get down here,* and somehow *Etienne* is going to have to hold out for however long that takes and *Mothers of the Night this is stupid this is so stupid can't do this not gonna work* ~~you're all gonna die-~~

Deep inhale in, *shuddering exhale out,* and Etienne puts mental blinders on, shutting out everything that's not the most pressing, *and accomplishable,* task at hand.

You've stabilized yourself now go help the others you've taken care of yourself now go take care of them, he repeats like a warding spell,

✦✦ 351 ✦✦

ignoring the pain coming from his arm, his ever rising worries and concerns and *fears, the distorted howling he can still hear at the edges of his mind,* and just focuses on the *task at hand,* starting with the two construction workers that are the worst off.

One woman is barely conscious, can hardly breathe with all the blood gurgling around in her lungs, and Etienne helps her sit up enough to take small sips of draught.

"C'mon, I know it tastes odd but *c'mon.* You'll feel better soon." He urges, being gentle as he trickles the pungent liquid down her throat, and then bears her weight with a grunt once the potion starts working and she has to pitch to the side, hacking up the leftover gunk still caught in her throat.

It's a nasty, guttural coughing motion, dredges up phlegm and bloody clots of mucus that she weakly spits free, are indicators that her lungs were punctured when the specters attacked, their non-corporeal hands slipping right past muscle and bone and slicing delicate tissue to ribbons. Etienne's no true medic, but considering the fact she's made it this long, he can assume her injuries weren't as extensive as the man he saw spitting blood earlier while he begged for help, *the one that died face down on the floor the second life you lost,* drowning on his *own blood* pooling in his lungs.

Won't happen again, Etienne thinks with a vicious kick to the heart, wrapping his arm more securely around the lady's shuddering back, *none of them are getting hurt again none of them are gonna die* ~~you sure about that~~ *you'll save them all won't lose another one,* and that's a *promise,* a vow he writes to himself in the simmering electric tide of the magic that was bound to him from the moment he first drew breath.

And no matter how dire of straights they're in, *he has no intentions of breaking it.*

After another minute or two of sputtering, the woman's coughing fit subsides, and her breathing seems to even out considerably, growing a lot more clear and unpained sounding. Etienne dares to

What Goes Bump In The Night

hope maybe she'll pull through despite the blood loss, helps get her comfortable while a weak *thanks* pushes past her lips, and he shakes his head, "You don' need to thank me, it's the least I could do. You shoulda never been in this situation in the first place an' I'm sorry you were."

Her eyebrows kinda draw together while he's talking, almost like she doesn't understand what he's saying, and she might not honestly. There's a concerned, *confused* pinch to her face that smacks of fatigued disorientation, and literally right in front of his eyes, Etienne watches that expression grow slack as exhaustion starts to take hold.

She really should rest.

Her body has been through the absolute wringer, and she'll have a better chance at surviving if she gives it time to recoup and process, but it looks like she's fighting the pull of sleep for some reason, keeps knocking her head back and forth in increasingly sloppy arcs.

"*Rest.* It'll be okay. I won't let anythin' happen to you." Etienne reassures softly and much to the woman's apparent displeasure, in the battle of consciousness versus unconsciousness, the latter finally wins out, and her eyelids flutter shut as she drifts into an uneasy sleep. Being careful not to wake her back up, Etienne takes the chance to lean forward and check her pulse, wants to make sure her system hasn't gone into shock from the draught or the rapid healing of her lungs.

Humans are much more susceptible to getting arcane poisoning than witches or other Occult members, and can literally *burn up* from it, insides destroyed by the magic they're not used to having that's now coursing through them like a wildfire. It's safe for them to have *some* potions, *in measured amounts of course,* but it means Etienne has to be careful on what he's dosing out, can't treat them like he would another witch.

That's why he only gave the lady a *fraction* of what he would've given himself, *this most recent instance of low self-dosing notwith-*

✦✦ 353 ✦✦

standing, and why he only moves on to the other sprawled out form once he's sure the woman is stable and seems to be handling the healing draught okay, chest rising soft and even with each easy breath.

The next person Etienne sees to is in much of a similar state as she used to be, looks half dead laying akimbo on the floor, scent of iron thick in the air, and generically going off the build, Etienne thinks it might be a man. He can't get a good look at the guy's face since someone else is already crouched over him, but he can hear the blood gargling around in the man's slack mouth, each exhale sounding more labored than the last.

Punctured lungs again, Etienne catalogs with a grimace, and then his eyebrows knit together when he also spots the long stripe of maroon running down the front of the man's once white shirt. Nothing about a blood stain that large bodes well, *means most likely his throat has been cut too,* and Etienne's own tendons twinge in sympathy pain.

Thankfully though, the figure kneeling at the man's side has already got a bloodied rag pressed against the front of his neck, trying to staunch the bleeding, and after a beat, Etienne's hazy brain connects for him that it's *Reggie* holding the rag, attempts to look confident when the other man turns terrified eyes on him as Etienne sits down next to him.

"H-Hey, C- *C-Casper,* I'm doin' w-what Blondie said but I...I-I don't think I'm um- *I-I think he might already be-"* Reggie can't finish his sentence, either from nerves or because his voice is so raspy and strained, it's at a point where speaking sounds painful.

He tries clearing his throat, a few hard swallows that make Etienne wince and then shakes his head in defeat, hands tensing around the rag, look like they're hanging on to the blood soaked piece of cloth for dear life.

"Lemme see." Etienne prompts quietly and has to help Reggie pull his shaking hands up, craning his neck to get a good look at the wound slashed across the man's throat. It's thin, *doesn't*

✦✦✦ 354 ✦✦✦

What Goes Bump In The Night

look too deep can't see the trachea, and pulses a slow glug of fresh blood once the compression is taken off that makes Reggie curse despairingly. Despite what he's assuming, that wound still bleeding is actually a *good* sign, means the poor bastard's heart hasn't stopped yet, and Etienne makes a pleased sound in the back of his throat as he sits up on his knees, shuffling closer to the guy's head, "He's not dead, Reggie. *Look,* see the way that thing's bleedin'? Means his heart's still pumpin'. I should be able to help him but I can't make any guaran...*tees-*"

The words coming out of his mouth slow to a crawl and so do Etienne's reaching hands, because in the rush and confusion of everything, Etienne hadn't seen what'd become of every crew member, *had his own wishes and wants but they spoke poorly of him and he won't repeat them,* and it really shouldn't matter who it is that's laying here, *Mothers of the Night he knows it doesn't matter that it doesn't change his duty,* but still, it feels like the entire world turns upside down once he realizes *who's* bleeding out right in front of him.

Because it's Carter.

And Etienne hesitates.

Etienne is not supposed to hesitate.

He's supposed to be a good witch *a good scion, he's supposed to help,* but all that's in his head right now are words and words *and words,* and none of them are nice, *and most of them are mean,* make him angry make him hurt *make him want to scream,* and there's this whisper of a murmur he refuses to listen to that softly entreats *do you really have to does it really matter why bother why care why try at all what's one more down what's this one lost would it really be such a shame if you just said there's nothing you can do if you say he's already de-*

And then an eye slides open a sliver in the gloom and it finds Etienne and Etienne finds it and a very complicated reaction snaps between them both.

Morbid though it may be, Etienne has witnessed countless deaths

✦✦ 355 ✦✦

before now, has seen people in all kinds of states at the end- afraid, sad, peaceful, *defiant* -and he's seen the way they look at him when they're dying and don't want to be.

There's always a certain kind of frantic helplessness burning in their eyes, a desperation that cuts to the quick and leaves raw bone in its wake, and it comes in many different forms, but the core of it is the same every time.

Help me help me God please help me don't leave me don't wanna go God help me please, they're able to beg all without uttering a single word, and sometimes Etienne can and sometimes he can't, *sometimes he lies and says he will so the last thing they know is peace,* but he's familiar with it, the way people's eyes plead with him for more time.

Carter doesn't look at him like that. Carter doesn't look like he wants to ask, *let alone beg,* for a single. *Fucking. Thing.* He looks at Etienne like he's *furious,* like he's angry he's wound up in this position and like he already knows the outcome, *already knows nothing good will come of it,* dark steely gaze defiant in a way that, strangely, isn't directed at the closing maw of death, *but rather at Etienne himself.*

What's it to ya stop looking mind your business, his eye seems to challenge, and it's not that he's not scared, Etienne can read that clear as day in his trembling lips and shaking iris, but Carter appears determined to bull through it. Which could be seen as admirable if he wasn't so hostile about it, expression obvious that he's not doing it for anyone's benefit but instead his own detriment, and Etienne is utterly baffled by the sentiment.

Not even his *own* pride is that bad where he'd refuse the help he so obviously needed, *even from someone he despised,* and it doesn't make a single lick of sense until he sees the other thing all twined up and around the *fear* and the *defiance* in that dark eye.

It's faint, but it's there, hiding in their shadows, an emotion that's hollower than anger. A feeling flatter than peace. Something that lives solely in the hearts and minds of people who have everything

What Goes Bump In The Night

to lose and finally understand that they've just lost it all. *It's resignation,* plain as anything, the begrudging surrender of a fight that in this case, isn't even technically lost yet, *a complete acceptance of utter, pointless defeat,* and it just- *doesn't make any sense.*

Why give in now when help is sitting literally within arm's reach? Shouldn't Carter at least have some chagrined hope smoking in the eye that's glaring at Etienne so waspishly? Because, *surely,* the man can't be that much of a moron, one where he'd willingly choose *to die* over accepting help from a *witch?*

Doesn't he have *any* self-preservation instincts?

But looking at him, Etienne can't find a want to live.

All he can see is that terrified defiant refusal Carter's drowning in, the bleak, suffocating press of resignation like a weighted blanket, *a hopelessness he's assured himself of that nothing can save him when salvation is right at his fingertips yet he refuses to reach for it like he doesn't see a point,* and that's about when it clicks, and Etienne realizes that Carter isn't asking him for help *because he assumes he's not going to get it.*

And you wouldn't think there'd be much left to wound Etienne after everything yelled in his face earlier, all the horrible taunts and cruel jabs, but this digs in deep just like the rest, a fishhook of pain pulling tight in all the soft parts of his heart.

He doesn't even know how to react at first, just stares blankly at Carter, someone who has obviously given up completely on the idea that Etienne could have even a *shred* of human decency left in him. Carter made it clear earlier that he held no love for witches, *freak stiff jinxflinger nobody needs you anymore nobody wants you anymore just crawl back out into the night where you belong,* which was loud and fiery and explosive with emotion, but it's in the quiet moments like this where you really come to understand how far that hatred runs, and somehow, it's worse than outright being called a monster.

People say a lot of things they don't mean when they're overwhelmed and on edge, but apparently, this *really* is the truth of

✦✦ 357 ✦✦

the matter, that Carter can more readily believe that Etienne- *that the creature from his nightmares,* would sooner leave him to bleed to death, *would let him suffer and writhe and wither away in agony while it looked on placidly bored,* rather than offer him any aid, and that?

Oh that cuts deep.

Curling tight fingers into his blood stained palms, Etienne rocks back on his haunches and ignores the solid lump of *hurt* tangling up in his throat, tries to think instead about how he's supposed to handle this.

He knows without a shadow of a doubt that he needs to heal Carter, even if he has to force the draught down the man's damn stupid throat, but needing and wanting to do something are two very different things. And what Etienne *wants* is a far cry from what he knows he *needs* to do. Don't mistake him, Etienne may not be a saint, has intrusive thoughts and dark wishes like any other thing burdened with consciousness, but he'd damn himself sooner than he'd ever act on them.

Which, doesn't change the fact that those malicious fantasies are still there, and in the privacy of his own thoughts, he can admit that, yes, *sure,* right now there is an unfetteringly cruel part of his mind that *does* want Carter to suffer.

Wants him to beg and grovel and feel small, regretting that he ever made Etienne feel the same way, but understanding it's wrong to feel that way, *that it's wrong to indulge those desires,* is half the battle of winning empathy for an enemy.

And that's what this is really, making the *choice* to share care and compassion with someone who will likely never return the same kindness to him, and *Mothers of the Night* it's hard.

It is so hard.

Etienne has learned many harsh truths on his journey to being worthy of the title *Patriarch,* and as of yet, this might be the most difficult one he's had to perform. Because knowing he's supposed

What Goes Bump In The Night

to continue to love even if he's hated, that his duty comes without conditions, *that his oath will always be more important than him as an individual ever will,* is an easy thing to think but a harder thing to practice, but there is no turning away from it.

He knew what he was doing when he more than willingly cut his palm and bled before the Mother of his house, promised to follow Her ways and never forsake the tenets She left for them, and if there's one thing Etienne will always be before any other, it's a man of his word.

"I'm going to help you." Etienne murmurs lowly and Carter's thick brows draw down sharp over his eyes, suspicion and mistrust clear in them as Etienne scoots closer, hands bloodied but reaching out slow, the long fingers attached able to bend and weave the archaic strength of magic together true enough, but at the end of the day, are ultimately no different than Carter's own, *"I'm not the monster you think I am."*

It takes the rest of the first bottle and half of the second to close the gashes that're bleeding Carter to death, both across his throat and then in his lungs, but he doesn't fight it like Etienne half expected him to.

He still lies there and glares like a fiend as Etienne helps him take careful sips, face screwing up further at the astringent burn of the fireweed, and Etienne feels no sympathy for him so he offers no apology. Pulling the bottle from his lips after a few well measured minutes, Etienne hopes Carter will take to the potion as well as the woman had earlier, but his mouth pushes to the side seeing a small wisp of smoke curl out from between Carter's burgundy flecked lips on his next rattling exhale.

Careful there he may glare like a fiend but I don't think he is actually one, Etienne chastises internally, reaching out begrudgingly to feel along the blood slicked column of Carter's throat.

He's looking for a pulse, and at his touch, the man's glower goes from irritated to *boiling.* It's truly an impressively ugly face, nose all scrunched up and eyes bugging out wide, and Etienne can't help

✦✦ 359 ✦✦

but snort meanly while he's counting the drumming beats of Carter's heart.

"Easy now...your mama never tell you not to make faces like that? Could get stuck that way forever an' wouldn't *that* be a cryin' shame..." Etienne grumbles without thinking, a little loopier and more loose lipped than normal thanks to the blood loss, something healing draughts never quite manage to reduce the effects of all too much.

If possible, Carter somehow just worsens his sneer.

He opens his mouth like he's gonna spit some barb back, but the second he lets air out, it staggers free as a grating cough that grows nastier and wetter until it gets to the point where Etienne knows what's coming next. He swoops forwards and grabs Carter about the shoulders, twisting him to the side as a guttering font of old blood and mushy dissolving lung tissue vomits out of his mouth, a disgusting pungent mess that poisons the air even further with its stench of *iron.*

Somewhere off to the side, Reggie yelps and swears again, starts frantically muttering prayers, but Etienne isn't too worried about it, hears Carter hack a few more times before his breathing runs much, *much* smoother, and finds himself humming halfway pleased, "There, that wasn't too bad, was it?"

"G-Get your- *ack! F-Fuckin' hands off me-!*" Carter spits like the ungrateful asshole he is, and for once, Etienne is more than happy to listen to the sniveling idiot.

He does check one last time to make sure the man's pulse is something acceptable, ignoring the valiant, *but ultimately in vain,* wiggling Carter is doing trying to escape his hold. Lightly pressing his fingers against a carotid artery, Etienne counts under his breath, loses his train of thought halfway through to a wave of dizziness and has to start over, and then isn't super pleased with the state of it anyway.

Even though it's been a minute, Carter's heart rate is still going much too fast for Etienne's liking and doesn't seem like it's wind-

What Goes Bump In The Night

ing back down, which, could honestly be due to any number of reasons.

Etienne has a pretty solid understanding of basic first aid, has to as a Boudreaux, knows how to clean and dress wounds and can recognize when something is fatal, but as soon as it comes to all the futzy stuff on the inside, he's way less sure, especially once draughts are involved. The art of making potions falls mostly under the purview of House Chenevert, and somewhere buried beneath all their complicated jargon and charts and diagrams, lie the mysteries of the body and its inner workings.

For all that Etienne's able to understand it, it might as well be contained in a forbidden lexicon of divine origin, something so far beyond what his mortal mind can comprehend that it's housed in a realm completely outside his grasp.

He loves learning though, but *Mothers of the Night,* none of their magic ever seems to stick with him despite how often his good friend, *and even better potions master don't forget that epitaph Eti,* attempts to explain it to him.

Still, regardless of his inability to truly grasp pharmaceutical magic, Etienne *has* managed to pick up a thing or two from Morris through sheer osmosis, and runs through it now while he's attending to Carter.

Okay resting heart rate should be in the seventies-ish but could be elevated due to stress, Etienne starts over counting again just to triple check, *nature of the healing draught would also raise it I think since body would react like it has a fever,* and after fifteen seconds and a little quick math, he gets something close to two hundred. Which again, *isn't great* under normal circumstances, but given everything that's going on, *getting attacked by specters having part of his lung torn out throat sliced near open watching a tordu form,* it is his unprofessional opinion that Carter could be doing a *lot* worse.

Besides, even if Etienne can't quite remember the exact RHR chart for when potion consumption gets dangerous for humans,

✦✦ 361 ✦✦

he's pretty sure one ninety beats per minute is nowhere near incendiary levels. *Probably.* This is further supported by the fact that the asshole's skin seems more cool rather than *burning hot,* which continues to add points to the column of *'most likely not going to be immolated',* so Etienne is hopeful that things will even out once the potion runs its course and Carter gets some rest.

"You should try an' sleep if you can. You'll feel better after this works its way outta you." Etienne instructs coolly, finally sitting back on his heels and putting some much needed space between the two of them.

He idly shakes the potion bottle still in his hand, roughly calculating how much draught he has left versus wounded, feels a stabbing wince from his arm and wonders if there'll be enough left to sneak some more for himself.

It'll be close, Etienne thinks with a sigh and then sees Carter struggling to lay down, reflexively reaches out to help, but the man hisses and jerks away from him and Etienne sighs again, "Your body is still injured an' it needs time to recover. It'll do that faster if you don't push yourself, okay?"

"S'fuckin' *w- w-whatever-* m'kinda shitty magic's this *anyway?* D-Doesn't- *hck,* f-fix fucking *shit.* G-Good for nothin' *stiff.*" Carter grouses as he lowers himself shakily to the floor, and that's honestly the last straw.

Etienne has had it up to *here* with his bullshit, feels his face draw closed in anger and hears his voice go cold and deadly like a winter's storm when he snaps back, "It's the *shitty magic* that just saved your life, *so maybe instead of complainin' about it,* you shut the fuck up an' act somethin' like a decent human being for *once in your life.*"

Carter freezes where he is, half propped up on his tremoring arms with most of his back to Etienne, head turned to the side so Etienne can't see his expression, but it doesn't matter really what face he's making, *whatever he may be thinking,* because this time, it's Etienne that has shit he desperately wants to say.

What Goes Bump In The Night

It's *his* heart that's furiously pounding now.

And in his case, *it's not from potion overconsumption.*

"You are *singularly* the absolute most *annoyin'* and *infuriatin'* person I have ever had the *utter displeasure* of interacting with. And that includes every fucking bonehead on the city council tryin' to eradicate my way of *life.*" Etienne hisses like vile venom and no words have ever tasted more righteous or honied coming off his tongue, "What the *hell* is your problem? Like- *sincerely?* You are...so ungrateful an' *disrespectful* to someone that just saved your life, *miserable though it may be,* an' I get it, you- *hate the big bad witches,* but *Mothers of the Night,* are you fuckin' braindead?"

Etienne's shaking a bit he's so angry, field of vision strobing with the frantic drumming of his heart, and the only reason lightning isn't gathering at his fingertips is because his body's too exhausted to call it forwards, "Do you understand the only reason you're alive is 'cause of *me? The witch?* The- *person,* by the way. *Not. Thing-* but the *person* you've been nothin' but cruel an' nasty to this entire night, when all *I've* done is try an' save your stupid thankless *ass? Have-* saved your stupid *thankless ass?*"

It feels so good to say it, to finally unload like he's been dying too since that first man called him a *jinxflinger,* and the fact that Carter isn't arguing with him, has finally listened and shut his mouth, fuels Etienne ever on and on.

"You keep calling me a monster but I want you to understand why I saved you. An' it's not 'cause I felt like I had to or was tryin' to spite you by proving you wrong. *I saved you* because it was the right thing to do." Etienne says even and firm, not unkind, but not benevolent either, wants to make sure Carter understands it was not a choice he made without effort.

"I saved you because I couldn't sit idly by while you suffered and *died.* Do you understand me? It wasn't because of guilt or *duty,* but because even *you,* even after the way *you've treated me,* still deserve that most base level of kindness." Etienne enunciates, and slowly but steadily, Carter's head sinks down in between his

✦✦ 363 ✦✦

shoulders, and Etienne watches as it bobs sharply, can see that it's guilt and regret weighing on the man now instead of hatred, but doesn't gentle his tone at all when he leaves it at, "So next time you call me a monster? Think about what that fucking makes *you*."

Etienne pushes roughly to his feet and sways violently as his eyes fill with black spots, room spinning from a combination of blood loss and fatigue.

Thankfully though, he's generally used to being unsteady on his feet, knows how to counterbalance and stay upright as he drunkenly staggers over to where Reggie had moved, apparently in a vain attempt to try and give him and Carter some privacy. Crouching down next to the coughing man is a struggle, but Etienne manages to not fall on his face as he holds out what's quickly becoming the communal potion bottle, instructing, "Drink deeply for five seconds an' then no more...also be prepared to throw up some bodily fluid."

And so it goes, Etienne sees to the last three construction workers, most of whom have either small pinprick punctures in their lungs or a bruised larynx, all of which the healing draught is more than capable of mending fully, and it leaves him with three very grateful men and a little under half a portion of draught left.

Which Etienne had every intention of taking for himself, can feel how wet his shirt sleeve is and knows he *really* needs to get that damned gash closed properly, but then he passes where Nica is huddled up against the side of an old desk. At first, he doesn't think twice about not offering them any, knew they'd been standing closest to him when the attack started and that alone would've been a decent deterrent for the specters, but his eyes happen to catch on something and he draws up short.

Nica is sitting with their knees pulled up close to their chest, some kinda notebook propped against their bent legs like a makeshift table as they scribble away, and where their phone is set off to the side, it casts dim white light that catches along the gentle slopes of their face. None of that is what snags Etienne's attention though. No, what yanks on his mind like a stuck fishhook is the

What Goes Bump In The Night

way their flesh arm awkwardly hangs in the space over their bent knees, dangling as far away from their body as Nica can seem to comfortably get it, and in the soft glow from their phone screen, Etienne understands why.

Blistered over their freckled skin is a nasty, dark red burn, the shape of it wrapped and coiled around their wrist in a particular way, and even if the outline of long fingers- *his, long fingers* -weren't so clearly and bone chillingly obvious, it wouldn't take a rocket scientist to figure out where they got the burn from.

Who, they got the burn from.

An icy swoop steals his lungs right out from under his ribcage, feels like it socks him in the gut too for good measure as it ruffles down his spine, and logically he understands it's not that bad of an injury, Nica won't *die* from it, but *Mothers of the Night,* does it ever make him feel like shit anyway. *Must've happened when the tordu hit you when your magic triggered automatically,* Etienne numbly thinks, staring at the charred flesh that's shiny and bloodied in a few places, *where your palm was pressed entirely against them full brunt of your magic discharging across their body,* remembers grabbing on to them but can't think of why he didn't immediately let go, *you idiot you imbecile you cooked them alive like raw meat-*

And fuck.

Fuck.

He hadn't even heard them scream or make any noise of distress, doesn't think they did, actually, because he would've noticed right?

If they'd shouted, Etienne would've let go *instantly*- he wouldn't have just completely blocked out the fact that someone was hurt on *his* account, *right?* Etienne's not that kind of person, *he'd never cause someone pain intentionally,* so if Nica yelled it just...p-probably got lost in the shock and adrenalin of it all, but that doesn't mean he was *ignoring it*- he wasn't *he wasn't but he grabbed them around the wrist didn't let go squeezed them for good measure after would've lit their skin up in agony oh fuck what have you done-*

✦✦ 365 ✦✦

Etienne feels his heart drop when he remembers how he thoughtlessly pressed his fingers into their skin, touching at what is clearly a very painful injury given the strain he can see on Nica's face now, and before he can stop it, his mind spirals off thinking about all the other ways he might've hurt them.

That was a lot of electrical current to suddenly be hit with out of nowhere, and if Etienne's lucky, that burn is the worst extent of the damage, but more likely than not, *this entire night standing in stunning example,* he *isn't* all that lucky.

Nica could have nerve damage or internal bleeding, *a shock that big could've knocked their heart out of rhythm they could go into cardiac arrest,* and he drops to his knees faster than anything, startling them as he holds out what remains of the last healing draught, "Here. T-Take it. Drink all of it unless you feel any chest pains."

"I...*w-what?*" Nica stammers, shuffling their limbs closer into themself, eyes darting from his face to his outstretched hand before understanding seems to click, and a defiant sort of exasperation pinches their mouth to the side, "No, absolutely not. I'm managin' just fine over here, so I'm not about to go and take something I *don't need* from someone else who *does need-*"

"Everyone's already been seen to. You're the last one, and you *do* need it, so just take it." Etienne insists where he bounces forward on his toes, waggling the potion bottle invitingly but still, Nica won't reach out for it. Instead, their eyes skitter off to the side, linger for a moment on something before jumping back to his face with a pointedly flat look, and when he makes a noise of confused inquiry, Nica rolls their eyes and jerks their chin a few times towards his side.

Etienne is already in the process of looking down when he understands what they're getting at, woodenly flexes the fingers of his left hand and feels an answering fiery numbness shoot down his arm as the half healed tendons pull.

What...this old thing, he wants to joke, but given the unimpressed

What Goes Bump In The Night

way Nica is looking at him, he's not sure it'd go over all too well right now. It's not that funny of a situation anyway. Etienne knows he's still bleeding to some degree, can feel it in the way sticky cotton fabric adheres to his skin in places, but the blood shouldn't be showing through. Black *is* practical after all, and yet, Nica just stares at him like they can see it regardless, eyebrow arched like he's been caught out as the biggest of idiots.

And maybe he *is* the biggest of idiots, because without thinking too much about it, Etienne just reflexively defends with, "I don't need it, I'm f-"

"So help me God, if you say you're fine I'm gonna run you over with *a car.*"

His mouth clicks shut audibly, surprised into silence because that's one of the more unusual threats he's ever gotten, and Nica takes the opportunity to lean forwards, wincing like they just bumped their injured wrist on accident, "Listen. I know you didn't take near enough of what you needed to earlier, and I *know* that thing is still bleedin' like a bitch, and yeah, *okay,* I'll admit, my wrist hurts like hell, but m'not gonna *bleed out from it.*"

They give him another pointed look and this time, it's Etienne that rolls his eyes in exasperation, huffing, "It's *mostly* closed..."

"Oh great! So you'll only be mostly *dead.*" Nica says overly chipper, grim set returning to their face immediately after, and when they start speaking again, a soft kind of timidness has crept into their voice, "I appreciate you worryin' about me, really, *I do,* b-but *I'm* really worried about *you too.* I know you've lost too much blood. You can barely walk without fallin' over an' I...a-an' I don't wanna- I-I can't- I- you- y-you're already hurt so *b-bad* and I can't- I...I c-can't make myself be okay with *hurtin' you a-agai-*"

"Hey. No. *Stop.* Listen to me, okay?" Etienne urges as he leans forwards out of habit, has to brace his unoccupied hand against the floor to stop him from faceplanting into Nica's lap, but it's suddenly the most important thing in the entire world, that he makes sure they *hear him,* "I don't blame you for what happened, *not at all.* You didn't hurt me, Nica, the tordu- *that monster did.* You were doin' what you thought was best, trying to save these people's *lives,* an' you couldn't've known that was gonna happen."

But Nica just cuts their eyes away from his fast, and in the light from their phone, Etienne can see how glassy they're getting, burgeoning threat of tears that are preluded by a sharp sniffle and a waivering, "B-But it wouldn't've worked, *w-would it?* My- *m-my stupid* idea t-to *bust us out of here?* S'why you didn' s-suggest it- but I thought *I-I knew so much better,* and then you ended up gettin' *hurt* 'cause of *me.* Because my *b-big- DUMB, fat ass* was in the way a-an' *causin' problems* an' not listenin' to a *single fuckin' thing you told me-!"*

"Hey hey *hey,* c'est bon c'est- *it's okay.* You were scared and actin' on impulse. I'd never fault you for that Nica, *promise,* an' besides, it's really not a big deal. I get injured all the time- part of the job description, ya'know? B-But it wasn't your fault, okay? I don't blame you, *not one bit-"*

"Well you s-should!" Nica spits and it's like a cork popping off, tearful hiccups spilling out of their mouth they immediately try and muffle with their metal palm, "You're hurt, *s-so bad,* a-an' I know you keep tryin'a play it off *but I'm not an idiot!* C-Christ alive, Etienne- y-you nearly g-got- *w-were going to- had-* your *f-fuckin' arm torn off* by that *thing! That's not okay!* An' it w-was *my FAULT!* If I'd listened to *you, i-if I hadn't been here-* but I just- *fucked everythin' up!"*

Both their hands fly up to dig harshly at their scalp, fingers snarling deep into messy ash blonde waves and Nica tugs at their hair despairingly, "Y-You *told me* to listen an' I *didn't.* You told me to get people out a-an' I *didn't.* You t-told me to- *to f-find a room to hide in,* a-an' I *didn't! I didn't d-do shit!* But y-you're out there- *riskin' your neck tryin'a save us,* a-an' all *I did* was get you hurt- b-because I wouldn't *listen,* an' now- *n-now* p- p-people are d- *I-* the workers, *those guys, that l-lady- t-they all were kil-* because of- *b-because o-of-!"*

Etienne's already halfway there, so it isn't much of an effort to

What Goes Bump In The Night

drop the potion and lean in the rest of the way. In the moment, he doesn't question it, just lets his body move how it wants and lurches forward to wrap Nica in a hug. It's awkward for multiple reasons, *the position they're both in the injuries they're trying not to aggravate how they've never touched like this before,* but it's an instinctual reaction, one that has Etienne looping arms across Nica's broad back while he tucks his chin over their shoulder. He feels them tense up and then relax into the contact almost immediately, arms falling to encircle him just as tentatively.

"It wasn't your fault." Etienne mumbles and hears Nica let out a wet sound somewhere in between a laugh and a sob, *"It wasn't.* You did everythin' you could, but you weren't prepared for something like this to happen, an' that's *okay.* That's why I'm here, *that's what I'm supposed to be for,* but I couldn't get anyone to leave either an' do you blame *me* for *that?"*

"W-What? N-No! No of- o-of course not, why would I-?"

"Yeah, *exactly.* So how are you at fault for something that wasn't even *your* responsibility?" Etienne nudges gently and with a staggering exhale, Nica's head knocks heavy against his own, "Those people's deaths are not on your hands, an' all those things you say you didn't do? Well, I guess you're not half as smart as you think you are Caldwell, because you *did* do them."

It's kinda odd hearing *and* feeling the grumbly protest Nica makes, the sound rattling up through his chest where he's hanging tight around Nica's own, but it's not a bad sensation, makes Etienne think of the quiet rumbles of far off distant thunder as he huffs, "Don't start with me. *You did.* You did listen to me, you *did* find somewhere for us to hole up. You tried to get us all out of here and no, it didn't really go the way you wanted, but you got people somewhere safe, drew a near perfect salt line just like I asked...and I know you did your best tryin' to get people to leave, but Nica... you *can't* blame yourself for them not listenin' to you. You just *can't."*

"S-Sure I can." Nica mumbles like the little contrarian, argumentative asshole they are, but there's an upward lilt to their voice

✦✧✦ 369 ✦✧✦

now that has Etienne believing they don't really mean it.

"Mothers of the Night- do you *always* have to argue with me? Like...s'that a requirement for bein' an alchemist? Or s'that jus' a requirement for bein' *you?"* Etienne says with his own rueful grin tugging his voice up, words slurring together a bit under the sleepy haze that's settling unbidden over his mind like a weighted blanket. He's suddenly very aware of how tired he is, and maybe the adrenalin is fading, because he's actually starting to nod off ever so slightly, lured into the welcoming arms of unconsciousness, helped in part by the comforting heat Nica radiates.

It curls through his aching body like summertime sunshine, coaxing his heavy eyelids lower and lower, and Etienne has to force them back open, yank his head up from where it'd been trying to drift into the crook of Nica's neck. *Night Mothers,* they're so *warm,* and it's so hard to want to leave that, but Etienne keeps almost falling asleep because of it. He always forgets he kinda runs chilly until someone dumps a blanket in his lap or snuggles up next to him, and it's honestly a headier intoxication than any alcohol has ever been. Etienne really can't afford to give in to it though, not here, not now, *not with them,* knows he needs to pull back *goes to pull back,* and finds he can't, strong arms locked over his shoulders like steel rebar.

Before he can even protest, ~~doesn't want to not really~~ *you have to can't fall asleep on them* ~~oh but it's tempting maybe for just a moment~~ *you can't,* Nica seems to realize he's trying to move and squeezes him once so fleetingly, he's not even sure it actually happened, and Etienne's brain is addled enough at the moment he could've just imagined it, *suspects he might've,* because next thing he knows, their arms are slipping away liquid quick as they whisper, *"S-Sorry..."*

"Oh don't start up again, we jus' got done with all that mess. I already told'ya...I don't blame you, *m'not mad at you*...you don't have anythin' to be sorry for, not for my *arm,* not for not people not listenin'- *wait,* that didn' make sense *give me a sec-"*

"No, *I-I know-* I mean...I still feel real guilty 'bout all that but

What Goes Bump In The Night

I just-" Nica sighs and shifts their head away from his own, and the absence of that pressure helps remind Etienne that despite the fact that Nica let go of him, *he's* still hanging on to *them,* "I didn't say it before, the uh- *t-the apology? I mean-* like, I never said sorry earlier, *I should'a said it earlier,* at the door stoop- *f-front door stoop,* where the- w-with the- y-you know when the...before Carter? *Y-Yeah I just...*"

And Etienne does pull back then, but he's slow about doing so, hands falling away and settling in his lap while he turns a critical eye on Nica's ghostly illuminated face.

At first, he's just looking for duplicity, *cagey and suspicious until the end,* but then when he can't find it, *he looks for sincerity instead,* and oh does he ever find the latter in spades, sees it dragging weary on a usually cheerful face and watches it roll fluid through glassy eyes, hears it in their voice when they murmur, "It wasn't okay... what they said to you- w-what *I* said to you, an' I...wanna say it now- *apologize, I mean!* N-Not-! *Like I don't-! UGH.* I-I'm tryin'a say *I'm sorry-* for what I said, f-for how it *hurt you,* an' I wanna make sure you *know* 'cause I- I-I'd never forgive myself if I didn't- if I n-never got *the chance to-*"

"Don't." Etienne suddenly interrupts with and for the second time tonight, he watches Nica's mouth click shut with tears threatening at the corners of their eyes, and guilt flickers meanly through his chest but he couldn't let them say it, couldn't let them apologize and resolve their grievances like they're on their death bed.

Because that's where Nica clearly thinks they all are, *toeing over the line one foot already in the grave,* and they might not understand like Etienne understands, *don't know all the ins and outs and the shit hand they've been dealt,* but they're not stupid.

They're smarter than he's ever given them credit for actually, and can read the signs *can come to a conclusion on their own,* and have realized through the bleak but honest lens of pragmatism that the odds are not stacked in their favor.

And...they're not wrong in that regard.

✦✦ 371 ✦✦

Statistically, a lot of things are against them, *the tordu Etienne's lack of experience how badly people are already wounded how badly he's wounded.*

It's not a promising set of cards, and Etienne hadn't lied earlier when he said it wasn't looking too good, *and it's still not,* but he also didn't lie when he said he was gonna take care of it, *which he will.* The *how* of that answer might remain a tremulous solution until mother can get here, but he *has to manage,* and in the time between, he can't have Nica doubting, not when he's still so unsure *himself.*

Etienne can't sit here and listen to them talk like they've gone and accepted defeat *now,* not when he's afraid of losing his resolve again, *of freezing up again,* thinks he might need their support or risk collapsing if he had to do this on his own.

~~Not when he knows he will, that he can't do this without a shoulder to lean on.~~

He can't handle the thought that they've lost hope, not when what he needs more than anything is a friend to say, *it's okay you got this I believe in you,* unwavering reassurance and a hand wrapped back around his wrist squeezing tight, telling him, *I won't leave you to face this alone.*

~~Not when he knows he wants Nica to be that person, that their strength and their courage help steady his own.~~

And he dry swallows rough, remembers a time and a place and a night where he cruelly told them to get out of his way, *that it didn't matter if they were there that he didn't need them,* and irony usually tastes bitter but this is nothing short of a relief.

Not exactly sweet, not at all sour, but somehow welcoming in its own way, and really, *at this point,* there are no more hoops to jump through. His spine is sore from how far he's been bending over backwards. That seemingly bottomless well of excuses has run dry, and at its base, the truth unfurls from the dark of his mind like the first moonflower bloom twisting open in the night air.

What Goes Bump In The Night

He likes Nica Caldwell.

Genuinely. As a person, *as a friend,* and he can't deal with the fact that tonight could be it, that one or the other *or both of them* could die here and he'd never get a chance to ask all his questions, to show them around to the places he's found, to actually take a stab at this tentative friendship they've begrudgingly built.

And he wants to, *Mothers of the Night does he ever want to,* and Etienne's entire job centers around trusting his gut and not second guessing his instincts, *making split second decisions and trusting they're the right ones,* so he stops thinking and overanalyzing *and worrying* and he just does.

He opens his mouth and *jumps.*

"*Don't...*don't act like we're never gonna talk again. Don't act like you're not gonna see me again." Etienne murmurs and his heart thuds fast because he knows the old wives' tale about speaking things into being, and this, *more than anything,* is such a true admission of his feelings, *of what he knows Nica is to him,* and it scares him to think that now they'll know too, "*We're getting out of here,* so keep your apology, y-you can give it to me later. Tell me you're sorry over coffee or tea *o-or whatever,* but not now...not because you think we're gonna die."

For a second, he worries Nica didn't get it.

They just stare at him, mouth slightly parted with an unreadable expression dancing across their face, and Etienne's *sure* they've misunderstood, *that they're gonna start crying,* and they do a bit, but it's around lips that crumple into a hesitant smile, damp little not laugh pushing out in disbelief while they nod their head, "Y-Yeah? Yeah...*yeah o-okay.* We can do that. I-I'd like to get that- *g-get coffee,* I mean, b-but yeah, that'd be...*t-that'd work great.*"

"We're not goin' back to that place on your campus ever again though. *It's abominable.*" Etienne quips snooty, and he is being halfway serious, *he'd burn that place to the ground if he got a chance,* but he's rewarded with a breathy chuckle anyway, nervous not all the way smile pushing at his own lips too when he suggests kinda

✦✦ 373 ✦✦

shy, "I could...take you to the café I go to instead, it's local. They make the best muffaletta in the Quarter if that's your thing, but I...I think you'd like it?"

He's struck vividly then with an image of Nica sitting in Amandine's, can picture exactly how they'd be staring starry eyed and open mouthed at all the moving serving ware and décor, *earnest wonderment so clear on their face,* and suddenly needs it to be reality, nearly misses it when Nica giggles again, wiping at their cheeks with their flesh palm, "G- Gryphonbucks ain't that *bad,* but I'd love to go to your place- y-your *coffee place!* I just-! *I mean-!* Going to get coffee at this place you like would be great *I eat sandwiches and would like that very much-*"

Etienne finds himself laughing a bit at the robotic sounding voice they end their sentence with, each word slow and measured out like Nica's checking to make sure it's the right one before they speak it. He thinks that is partially the reason they do it, but he's also pretty sure they do it to make him laugh, and his suspicions are proven correct when Nica smiles self-satisfied and cheeky, little dimple popping up in their right cheek.

A warm feeling kinda curls through his chest at that, weaves through his bones and makes his fingers vibrate, and there's still a lot that needs to be said, *he wants to hear those apologies he knows he needs to give some of his own,* but he's sure in this decision.

Nica means more to him than the average bystander typically does, and, as unthinkable as he once imagined it to be, Etienne really has come to enjoy their company over the last month or so. They're funny, they're smart, *they care about him too,* and to finally quit beating around the bush, *to put a name to what they are,* seems like a breath of fresh air and a nervous inhale all at the same time.

Because they're friends.

They are the start of friends at least, and another bubble of warmth pushes up through Etienne's chest, makes his skin heat and his nerve endings all tingly, and he can't know for certain that Nica's feeling the same way, but they look at him all hesitant and

What Goes Bump In The Night

soft *and real,* and he thinks that they are.

Etienne has a lot he wants to say, but he'd gotten so caught up in the excitement of something *new* and *pleasant* that he forgot, *perhaps a bit willingly,* about *where* they actually are, and it shouldn't come as a surprise then, that this nice moment they've managed to steal from an objectively terrible situation, it isn't destined to last long.

Whatever illusion of peace the two of them had is shattered the second Etienne winces, fingers flying up to dig into the skin over where his heart twists and stings, an eerie roar accompanying the sensation that has all the quiet chatter in the room grinding to a halt.

Shit- right...okay time to stop fucking around I get it, Etienne thinks while his heart rate picks up, and he quickly expands his senses out to poke at the trembling line connecting him to the Pieuvre sigil. It waivers and jumps under his touch, and while it's not broken *yet,* he can feel in his mind how frayed the connection is, knows it doesn't have much longer.

Alright, *get back on task Boudreaux,* now that everyone's been seen to, the next step is getting in touch with mother, *and to stop daydreaming about hanging out with Nica pull your head out of the clouds do your damn job you're all still in terrible danger,* he berates as he comes tumbling back into his head, blinks to refocus his eyes and then sees the concerned way Nica is currently looking at him.

Their teeth are gnawing worriedly at their lower lip, *deep furrow between their brows,* clearly fallen again into thinking about *final goodbye's* and *not gonna have another chance's,* and to keep them from *both* sliding back into that pit they just crawled out of, Etienne aims for lighthearted and reassuring, "Hey. We can go Monday, to that place I was talkin' about? We'll have our check-in meetin' just like we always do, okay? Right after your O-Chem lab gets out. Sound good?"

And Nica opens their mouth to respond but the tordu howls

✦✦ 375 ✦✦

louder this time, interrupting them, and they choke on whatever their reply was gonna be, *worry* and *doubt* eating away at their mismatched eyes again, so Etienne leans forward, more insistent this time when he asks, *"Hey.* Does that *sound good?* You're not gonna leave me sittin' all by myself for another *hour,* are ya? You can't do that to a man twice, Caldwell, that's just plain disrespectful."

Nica's gaze skitters away as they weakly shake their head and Etienne doesn't know what they're disagreeing with: how it wasn't disrespectful to be almost an hour late for that first meeting, the suggestion that they'd do it again, *the implication that they'll both be getting out of here alive,* and his heart twists painfully at the latter, "Well *I-I'll* be there. I'll be there an' waitin' on you so don't be late, o-okay? Monday the seventh, three-thirty sharp at Amandine's, got it? You gonna make it, Caldwell? Can I count on you to be there?"

"I-" Nica wheezes and then they squeeze their eyes closed, muttering quietly under their breath like a nervous tic, "Y-Yeah okay... *yeah okay, yeah o-okay-"*

They seem like they're trying to collect themself, *filtering things out and working to prioritize,* like what Etienne had to make himself do earlier, and if *he* was scared, *overwhelmed at their minuscule odds the insurmountable task at hand,* he can't imagine what this must all be like for *Nica,* who was never trained for anything like this, *who got flung headfirst into this,* but the next time their eyes flick open, they meet his dead on.

Oh, but that change is ever so stark, and Etienne may never know what it is about Nica that makes their gaze this arresting, but there it is, that electrifying look that has all his hair standing on end.

It's not quite as ferocious as the one they gave Gertie, *hurled at Carter,* but it has strength, *it has resolve,* and so does Nica's voice when they say, "Okay. Yeah, *fine-* I'll be there. Monday, three-thirty sharp, *Amandine's.* And by the way, *f-for the record,* it wasn't an hour that one time. It was only thirty seven minutes. So get your facts straight, spooks."

What Goes Bump In The Night

"An hour, *half an hour-* who cares. It's semantics." Etienne huffs, and then because he thinks he'll have a better chance of it this time, gathers the healing draught back into his hands and extends the faintly sizzling bottle towards Nica, and after a beat, they do take it, sniffing around the lip of it with a cocked brow, *"I care. Sixty minutes versus thirty seven? That's* accuracy...this thing smells like Fireball, you taking any?"

Etienne had just hauled his spellbook into his lap, was about to go find the sigil that he kept his messaging notebook in when he didn't have his bag on him, but he pauses, fingers curled under the front cover as he looks back up, "Wasn't plannin' on it. I know it doesn't seem like much left, but I promise it'll do you more good to take than it would me."

"So this amount wouldn't help heal your arm at *all?* Like- *not even a little bit?"* Nica challenges like they already have a good idea of what the answer is, and Etienne feels his face heat at being caught out but he just rolls his eyes, *won't give them the satisfaction,* flips the cover of his spellbook open and mutters under his breath instead, "Why do you always have to be so damned *difficult?"*

"Uh- hello? *Seriously* dude, pot kettle much?" Nica shoots back and humming noncommittally, Etienne turns past a few pages of his earliest, *sloppiest* notes, more than easily finding the sigil he keeps his notebook in, and goes to place two fingers against the spell while Nica continues arguing without any input from him, "You keep sayin' *I'm* argumentative, but have *you* ever had a conversation with yourself? I swear you're contrary half the time *just for the fun of it-* at least I have a *reason* that's not, *oh look at me I'm big mister important scion an' I can never be wrong ever or I'll-"*

But Etienne stops paying attention, because in what seems like a split second, all the noise around him immediately cuts out, replaced by a high pitched whining that rattles the very backs of his teeth, and he just stares and *stares,* fingers hovering trembling over a sigil that is supposed to house his notebook but is instead *open* and *empty.*

He can't process what that means for a minute, presses two fin-

✦✦ 377 ✦✦

gers against it anyway and drags them down together, thinking maybe he's just hallucinating or seeing things wrong, but nothing happens. And he's deluded enough- *scared enough* -to try again...

And again and again *and again,* but each time is the same as the first and it feels like being stuck in a nightmare and knowing that you are, everything hazy sick prickling that turns your stomach faster than anything, and bile floods his mouth.

Etienne forces himself to swallow it back, starts uselessly flipping through pages and tries to breathe, *tries to remember,* anywhere else he might've stashed his notebook, but he knows like a plague at the center of his being that there is no other place.

Come on come on come on, builds in slow rolls of thunder through his mind, *no no no no no no Mothers please no,* the flashing bolts of lightning that set his nerves *alight,* and Etienne combs through his memories, has to know where it is, *always has to know where his stuff is you have to have it it's here somewhere where else could it be where else could it-*

Standing at his desk, fingers idly trailing over what he needed to bring, the knock at his door, *black pencil skirt brilliant smile bonjou baby I'm fine mére that look she gave you don't lie to me Etienne-* the argument that followed, *you need help no I don't you need to go see your therapist no I dON'T you need to be back on meds NO I DON'T-* trying to get out of there as soon as he could, dodging her, *dodging her questions leave off maman I'm late I'm busy I have to go I don't have time to talk about this with you-* rushing and hurrying and *not thinking about anything but the cool night wind on your face what you were gonna do later completely forgetting that you left your-*

A clammy shiver runs up his entire body and if his arms weren't suddenly made of lead, Etienne might raise one to check and see if his head hadn't just popped off his neck, because with how light-weight and floaty he's feeling, *he wonders if maybe he forgot that at home too.*

Oh Mothers of the Night, blessed we Your children are, so as to

What Goes Bump In The Night

watch over this world of mortal men, guide us with Your hands and steer our hearts true, deliver us from depravity, for Your will is the tenet and Your providence is our-

There's a soft, questioning noise, and Etienne woodenly turns towards it like a set of gears that badly need oil, crackling static boiling up behind his eyes and drowning out his lungs, the same thought lazily circulating in his mind now that his prayer has been interrupted, *what's the use you're gonna die what's the use you're gonna die what's the use you're gonna-*

"Hey uh...e-everything okay?" Nica asks hesitantly, and he just stares at them, at their nervous smile that's trying so hard to be brave and those emotion heavy eyes, the ones that look right at him, *right through him,* and Etienne doesn't know what to say to them anymore because he's suddenly not sure that one *or* the other is gonna make it to Amandine's next Monday after all.

And that thought takes something from him, like someone's come and dumped a bucket of ice water on a fire that was struggling so hard to breathe itself back to life, completely sapping the life right out of it *draining its will killing its resolve* and he doesn't know what to say.

He has no void cursed idea what to say, can only stare at Nica like a *stupid* landed fish out of water, *mouth slightly parted chest heaving eyes bugged wide,* and even though he doesn't utter a *word, what could he say what could he possibly fucking say I've doomed us all you're gonna die slowly painfully sorry I lied I didn't build us a sanctuary I've built us a tomb I'm not good for anything,* he can tell by the way Nica's face breaks that it's answer enough.

Etienne doesn't know how they always know.

How they can read him so well, and he supposes he never will, closes his spellbook with a resolute thump and almost like the universe is getting a kick out of it, that's when the Pieuvre sigil breaks.

Like all great disasters, it's silent at first, everyone behind the salt ring holding their breath at the eerie calm they've seemingly

✦✦ 379 ✦✦

found themselves in, *naively hoping that something's gone right,* and then the entire room shakes as the tordu slams up against one of the Artuas wards. Its once muffled wails are much louder now as it frantically digs and claws at the spell, and Etienne knows people are looking at him, *always are,* but he can't meet any of their eyes, *doesn't have any answers for them doesn't have any solutions for them* ~~doesn't have any hope left for them,~~ and so he bows his head in defeat.

Chapter 18

"O-Okay- easy fix. I brought my notebook, so y-you can just use *mine*-"

It's kind of them to offer, *morbidly hysterical that they remembered to bring theirs when you, the witch, didn't*, but the messaging notebooks don't work like human phones, you can't just use it to write someone when you don't have their imprint, and Nica's notebook still only has that one little useless green ribbon poking out past its blank pages.

"Alright, t-that's *fine*- maybe...l-lemme just try my phone again real quick-"

Still not gonna work. Didn't work when the tordu was a good thirty feet away putting out enough electromagnetic interference to jam the cellular frequency, and so it's *really* not gonna work when the damned thing is howling right on the other side of that wall.

"*Fuck*- o-okay, we'll just...do like you said an' wait it out then. I mean, someone will come looking for you eventually, right-?"

Wrong.

Or, not entirely, because while mother does keep tabs on them and worries when they're not back on time, she isn't going to be concerned if Etienne is gone until well past daybreak, is used to the odd hours the family keeps and by the time she grows suspicious of his absence or someone alerts her, *everyone here will be long dead.*

"*Jesus f-fucking Christ*- okay so we're on our *own*. Okay, okay, okay okay okay...how much time are we working with here? Like-how long do those spells last-?"

As per his probably shit calculations, about twenty to twenty five minutes when they're put under high duress.

Which they are currently being put under.

"Okay and can you make more before those break?"

The fastest Etienne has ever drawn a ward that size is two hours, but that was in the quiet of the abjuration tower with all their instruments at his disposal and not here, in this dirty old classroom, with little to no light, maybe a stick and a half of chalk, and *oh yeah,* an impossibly pissed rage monster trying to claw its way inside.

"Fine, *fine-! I get it...you don't gotta get an attitude with me-* alright. It's still made outta brick in here, so I'll be able to destructure the compounds in the bricks and can get it broken down super fast, create a decent enough sized hole an' then we can just, *make a break for it-"*

No. *Absolutely not.* If any of the walls or floors in here sustain damage to the point that they are no longer a single *continuous* surface, the Artuas wards will come grinding to a halt and the *second* they do, there is nothing keeping the tordu from getting in here and you may think you're faster than it, but nothing beats out an almost century of accumulated agony and spite.

"Well then *what- fuckin' Christ alive, dude! You* suggest somethin' then since *I'm* apparently *such an idiot!* Just- tell me whatever it is you wanna do an' I'll help get it done but we can't do *nothin',* we can't- t-there has to be *something-* an answer a plan *a-a solution, somewhere-"*

But honestly, Etienne doesn't think there is, was already grasping for straws when the best idea he could come up with was *'wall yourself away and wait for someone more competent to come save you'* and now that that plan is shot to pieces, he has no fucking clue where to go from here, has been sitting with his hands in his hair and his head in his knees but he picks it up now, snapping, "There's *not!* Don't you *get it?* I-I have no idea what to do! I can't

What Goes Bump In The Night

call for help, w-we can't get out of here alive, *I can't make* more wards- *m-my magic is almost completely shot as is-!* I don't know what to do, *I have no idea what I'm supposed to do! STOP ASKIN' ME WHAT TO DO-"*

Yelling relieves some of the pressure that'd been building up behind his throat, but it leaves a horribly empty hollow feeling behind, and Etienne struggles to breathe around it, presses his clammy forehead to his knees.

For their part, Nica sits through his blowup with a judgment free if not unimpressed look on their face, and when he moodily settles back into the nest of his folded arms, they just cock an eyebrow, "You done?"

Etienne flips them off and Nica clucks their tongue, leans forwards over their bent knees and ducks their head to catch his eye, makes direct eye contact as they say, "Hey. *I get it.* You don't know what to do, can't find a *single* solution that you think would work, but that doesn't mean there isn't an answer out there. We just have to put our heads together and find it, m'kay?"

"What the hell do *you* know, you're not a witch, what can you even *do...*" Etienne mutters sulkily and then immediately regrets it, knows Nica hasn't done anything to warrant his ire, *that they're just trying to help* futile though it may be, and twists his head to better face them, brows scrunching together in apology, "Sorry, I just..."

"I know." Nica responds with more grace than a lot of people would, blue and hazel eyes far kinder than he likely deserves, "And I know I'm not a witch, but I *am* a scientist, and coming up with solutions to problems people say have none is kinda our whole thing."

Etienne sighs heavily, shaking his head, understands what they're getting at but he just doesn't think blind optimism is ever much of a help, tries to be gentle when he says, "Not every problem has a solution though, Caldwell. Don't your experiments ever fail? Haven't you ever had a theory proven incorrect? Sometimes the

✦✦ 383 ✦✦

simplest answer is just that...*there isn't one.*"

"So that means I can't look? *That means I can't try?*" Nica insists as they curl closer, hands flexing against their legs before their left one hesitantly creeps up, skin and bone fingers wrapping carefully over Etienne's forearm, "Humor me, Etienne. Walk me through it. Start with what you know how to do and then move into what you know in theory, but don't tell me what you can't do, okay? We're not interested in the *can't's* right now."

Their fingers squeeze gently and Etienne's focus immediately snaps to them, to the warm comforting weight of them, getting caught on how nice that simple touch makes him feel, how it grounds him, *centers him,* lets him know he's not alone.

Everything else kinda fades out, *the pain in his arm the tordu's screams in his ears the fear in his heart,* and his eyes drift across the stark contrast of Nica's hand against his black shirt sleeve, tracing over the pale slivers of old scars and the rougher, slightly red skin of calloused knuckles.

He remembers uselessly that Nica mentioned they boxed once, wonders then if that's what the scars and busted up knuckles are from, finds such a controlled kind of violence coming from these hands odd considering all they've ever done is touch him gentle, and their voice is a distant thing the next time they speak, "Hey... did'ya hear me, Etienne? You still all the way in there...? Come on, tell me about ghosts...help me figure out what we gotta do."

"Yeah...*okay.*" Etienne says slow and dumb, forcing his eyes away from Nica's hand because he's starting to think he doesn't want them to move it even though he knows they'll have to, and instead focuses on their face, caught off guard by how close they are, "I... I...I-I don't know where to start, *I don't know what to do,* this isn't somethin' that my apprenticeship's covered yet-"

"That's okay, just tell me what you have covered." Nica has disarmingly attentive eyes this close up, the kind that seem to bore straight through to the core of your being, and for maybe the first time since they've known each other, *Etienne's* the one that has to

What Goes Bump In The Night

look away, can't seem to get his thoughts in order.

And if that's the state of his brain, he doesn't know what good it'll do them, *verbally working through this,* but there's a warm hand wrapped around his arm and Nica wanted him to, so he starts talking anyway.

"I uuuh- *um,* w-well...we've covered basic apparitional disturbances an' I've helped with appeasement rituals in the past, even done a few on my own, b-but this goes *so* beyond what a typical spectral appeasement entails." Etienne stresses, fingers rubbing distractedly at his achy, cut up palms, "This thing- the uh, the t-tordu? It's a...compressed amalgamation of every specter in this building. All of their hurt and pain *and sorrow,* combined into one being of malice, an' it can't be appeased like a normal apparition... *it can only be destroyed.*"

"Alright, and I'm assuming you...can't do that on your own?" There's nothing *inherently* judgmental about Nica's tone, but Etienne shrinks back from it anyway.

An awkward embarrassed *ashamed heat* floods across his face as his fingers pick abusively at torn skin, "I- *ah- y-yeah.* Even if I wasn't drained near dry, I couldn't *um-* i-it'd be next to impossible to do on your own. You need a whole *team* of spirit witches an' not just one *uh-*"

Idiot moron incompetent waste of space, jump lightning fast and giddy with manic glee to the tip of his tongue, and it's a real struggle to force them back, *shut up shut up sHUT UP not right now not in front of people get a hold of yourself,* entire awkward moment ending with a lot of willpower and a too long pause and Etienne finishing his sentence lamely, *"-apprentice."*

Nica is quiet for a moment, thumb tapping an absentminded rhythm over Etienne's forearm while they think, only stuttering and losing its tempo when the tordu slams up against a different side of the Aratus ward.

From the sound of it, the creature has been methodically testing each angle of the room, *looking for a weak point,* and if Etienne

✦✦ 385 ✦✦

could feel even a sliver of pride past the crushing despair plaguing him, it'd be over how the tordu hasn't *found one,* keeps ineffectively circling the room like a shark.

Won't be for too much longer though...it'll get what it wants soon enough, Etienne thinks despondently, leaning over to smoosh his cheek against his bicep, watching bored and with a flicker of fondness at where Nica keeps tapping at him.

There's a definitive pattern to it, and he's trying to figure out the time signature of whatever piece it's from when Nica starts speaking slow, carefully laying their words out like they're testing each theory one at a time in their mind, "So if we're stuck with it bein' here...an' have limited manpower...you can't make any more of those big shield thingies and the little ones earlier didn't seem to work much- *oh, wait-* do you have any more of those prepared?"

"I should have a few repulsion sigils left an' like maybe *one or two* more Pieuvres, but like you said, they don't do much." Etienne mumbles only half paying attention, is pretty sure now that the tune Nica's drumming is in common time, which isn't all that interesting but the tempo and frequency they're tapping at him with *is,* and it's hardly anything to go off but he can't help but think *percussionist.*

"Okay, *awesome.* What if you like- *mashed them all together.* Just made like a uh, super sigil or somethin' and combine every one." Nica says, sounding overly enthusiastic about the idea, and Etienne doesn't mean to be a condescending wet blanket, but he can't help the tired laugh that shoots out of his mouth, "That's not how magic works. Each spell is its own self-contained set of rules an' intentions, and sometimes you can get them to harmonize together, kinda like how gears in a clock work, but I can't just squish them into one overpowered thing."

Nica makes a disappointed noise and their thumb stops twiddling but it's only still for a moment, because all too soon, it's jumping right back into a new piece and then a new idea is puddling from Nica's lips, "Like gears, huh? Is there...a way to chain them all together then? Just so they can work in combination and

What Goes Bump In The Night

offer stronger protection? Like, supporting one another like a net or something ya'know, snaring up the todo- *uh,* topo? Tor...*peee-doooo-?"*

"Tordu."

"Yes right *thanks-* but if we could just, an' I know it wouldn't hold it forever or even really all that good, but if we could just stop the tordu for long enough to evacuate, I can get us outta here lickety -split." Nica snaps their fingers with their metal hand and the sound is oddly hollow and resonant, like a cymbal, "Because it's stuck in here, right? Like it can't leave the building? An' I know you said those big uh, *waaards?* Will fail if we break a wall but if we can use the smaller ones to buy us even five minutes, I think we can get everyone out of here safely."

Etienne does think about it for a moment because he doesn't want to keep shooting down their ideas, but ultimately, he can't see it working.

The tordu has been fused together for long enough now that it's likely stabilized somewhat, meaning even if he chains together all the wards and sigils he's got left, it's going to tear through them like tissue paper in a matter of seconds, and he tries to be gentle when he lets Nica down, "It's not a *bad* idea but I...don't think what I have left could hold the tordu for any meaningful amount of time. It gets stronger the longer it's all bound together, the spirits keep feedin' off each other's combined agony an' it creates an incredibly powerful feedback loop. S'part of the reason it's such a dangerous entity."

Things grow quiet between them for a moment, and then it lasts a little longer than a moment because Nica doesn't immediately pipe back up with a new idea. Which shouldn't be as demoral-izing as Etienne suddenly feels like it is, but without their voice distracting him, he's all too aware of the howling and scrabbling echoing through the room, *the deep terrified clenches in his heart,* and Mothers of the Night, he doesn't think he's ever wanted to fold out of existence more.

✦✦ 387 ✦✦

Not in like a, *'he wants to die'* way, but rather more like, *'fuck he wishes this was just a nightmare he could wake up from',* a sentiment he hears echoed in Nica's weak but passionate, *"Fuck...*o-okay what if we- I could...um, the- *t-the wards,* they're still active, what if we just...l-like we could maybe redirect their, *uh-* fuck...*fuck- fuckiety fucking fuck FUCK!"*

Etienne couldn't agree more.

"God fucking damnit- so we've got a thing buildin' power uncontrollably with no real way to stop it an' we're trapped in an enclosed space with it. Great. Wonderful. *Awesome."* Nica grouses and Etienne hums bleakly in agreement, twists to bury his face back in the crook of his shoulder while Nica just keeps muttering under their breath, "Why can't this be chemistry- *I'm good at chemistry.* I *know* what to do when it's a *reaction* that's boilin' out of control, but that's not how ghosts work. You can't just throw an inhibitor on a ghost, you can't neutralize it, *can't dilute it can't pull a-"*

Etienne picks his head up so fast he gives himself headrush, has to blink a few times to clear his eyes but once he does, he sees Nica staring at him wide eyed, light from their phone casting bright rectangles across their glassy surface, and in a stumble of words he demands, "W-What'd you just say? You just- *say that again-"*

"Uh, I said 'you can't pull a ghost off a Bunsen burner'?"

"No not-! *The other thing.* About diluting. You said we can't *dilute the ghost-* but we *can- I* can, *I could,* it's possible, it's-" Etienne is aware he's not making much sense, but his brain is currently going too fast to really make a good effort at constructing comprehensible thoughts, "But what if I *could-* it's not entirely, *kinda hard to explain,* but like I could stretch the tordu out, *er-* maybe more like pushin' it further away, not physically of course, though I guess it kind of is as long as you count movin' through the inhabitable planes as-"

"Etienne. What the *fuck* are you talkin' about? You're not making any-"

"I can dilute the tordu."

What Goes Bump In The Night

Which still sounds *absolutely batshit insane* leaving his mouth, but it makes the most *beautiful* sense in his head, parts all falling into alignment like he's finally found the pattern of the puzzle, "There's this class of rituals my family uses to guide wayward spirits on, an' it won't get rid of it permanently, the tether binding it to this place is too strong, but if I can push it far enough back into the *aether...*"

Etienne pauses with his brows arched, mostly out of a habit from typically only conversing with other witches, instinctually giving his companion time to jump in with the answer, but Nica just stares at him helplessly and shrugs.

What do they not...oh right- alchemist, he has to remind himself, and already moving to tug his spellbook free, he finishes the thought in their stead, *"So-* it means the distance between the physical plane an' the very far reaches of the aether would act like a...*cushion,* of sorts, making it so the tordu won't be able to harm us as easily. It'd have to expend a considerable amount of energy an' time remanifesting to do any real damage, maybe ten-ish minutes, and in that interim-"

"-we...blow a hole in the side of *the buildin'!"* Nica says slowly and then increasingly faster, end of their sentence punctuated by a loud bark of laughter.

The sound turns a few miserable heads, but Etienne only has eyes for Nica as they lean in, grinning like mad, "Hell yeah! I *knew* you'd get somethin'! Your head's *way* too big to be completely empty of anythin' 'cept hot air."

"Éy- ducon, cut the cockiness. Try an' remember *who's* savin' *who's* ass here." Etienne snarks back but he's smiling a bit manic too, can't help feeling irrationally giddy, thinks it's warranted when he was so sure there weren't any chances left for them but now he might've stumbled into one, "Look, this isn't really gonna be a walk in the park, m'kay? We're gonna have to time shit absolutely perfect an' then I gotta *brute force* an execution that's *not* gonna want to go through- but m'pretty sure it'll work, I just need your help with somethin'."

✦ 389 ✦

"Yes. Of course. *Anything*. Just tell me what to do an' it'll get done." Nica promises without hesitation, and Etienne's smile runs a touch gentler at how ready they are to help, even when they don't know what he's asking for. Which, what he was gonna ask of them isn't anything too outlandish. Etienne has seen what Nica's capable of and he's fairly confident this is well within their realm of expertise, but still, it warms him from the inside out seeing how freely they give of themself.

Kind person, he thinks, turning his eyes back down to his spellbook as he busies himself with pulling taper candles free from storage sigils, dark maroon and creamy white of their wax smooth against his fingers, "I don't have enough magic left to fuel the spell on my own like it'll require, so I need bloodstone, *a lot of it.* I figure if there's a large quantity of it around to help resonate my magic, it'll generate enough power to push the tordu as far back in the aether as we need. But we're gonna need a good sized portion of it, so if you could just start makin' some, that'd be great."

But instead of a super immediate, *super enthusiastic response,* there is a pause.

There is, quite frankly, *too long of a pause.*

His hands woodenly set the candles down before they can break them, thinks he can hear someone else ask in his voice for him, "Is that...*a problem?*"

"Yeeeeaaaaaah...right...*okay, see*- now I get that- *I-I mean,* I *don't* get it *get it* because *um*- not a witch. B-But like, I understand what you're sayin' I just-" Nica answers in a nervous tumble and Etienne looks up slowly, gnawing new worried truth at the back of his mind remembering earlier, *when he asked them to make salt don't have what I need can't make something out of nothing can only use what I have understanding again they're not the miracle worker you assumed they were no such thing as infinite creation-*

"Please tell me you can make bloodstone." Etienne says monotone and hollow, and laughing again, *way higher pitched way less sure entirely more afraid,* Nica darts their eyes away and snaps

What Goes Bump In The Night

shakily, pointing both their hands in finger guns at him, "Y-Yeah so, *about that-* in theory, *practice- o-on paper- hypothetically-* I-I *could, probably,* but i-in *reality?* I have n-no idea- *not a clue-* what bloodstone...is?"

Fuck-

Okay. *Okay.* Don't panic. They just said they didn't know what it was, but that doesn't mean they can't make it. It's possible they could know it by a different name, or perhaps just seeing it is enough, so maybe they need a visual cue? *Can they even recreate something based off visualization alone fuck you don't know how alchemy works...*

Twisting his head to the side, Etienne points up at his hatband where a bloodstone brooch sits clipping a few crow feathers in place, desperately trying, *"This.* It's not very rare, y-you sure you've never seen it? It's super common 'round here, people use it for all kinds of rituals...no? M-Maybe you know it by its scientific name, *heliotrope,* it's a type of quartz mixed with uh- jasper? *I think?"*

He's grasping at straws, and in a perfect world, Nica's eyes would've instantly lit up with recognition at that. Their grin would've been confident and sure as they laughed, *oh right that old thing I can make that easy,* but this is not that world.

This is the world where their eyes dart away again after looking and looking *and looking* and yet, still only came up with *nothing.* Where their face grows shadowed and haunted, brow wrinkling as they sheepishly mutter a dejected, *sorry.* Where their fingers twist together in their lap before quickly jumping apart, *like the action hurt them.*

"I-! *Sorry,* I just- I-I'm not real familiar with gemstones? They're uh, not really used in alchemy? Like- I understand the common elements they're made up of, *silicon calcium aluminum,* b-but we'd sooner use the raw element and not the um- *the r-rock,* which would be the main problem really b-because I've never worked with it so I have...*no idea what its chemical structure even is..."*

"Is there any way for you to find out?" Etienne asks on the edge

✦✦ 391 ✦✦

of *begging,* and Nica taps their first three fingers together on their metal a hand to their thumb, a well known tic that betrays their fraying nerves, "W-Well- I'd normally use my *phone but uh-* a-and I can check in my pocket guide but I don't think- *c-can't remember-* where my backpack. *Issss?* A-An' I don't even know if it covers gemstones or not and um, I- I'm not *real* confident it has *specific ones-*"

What the fuck is it about tonight.

Every time Etienne thinks he's got a handle on things, he quickly finds out he's just as fucked, *if not more so,* than he was previously, and he's two seconds away from burying his face in his spellbook and screaming his head off when Nica looks up at him all nervous and shy and says, "Or if um- *I mean,* I could figure it out if I *uh-h-had a good sized sample-*"

Etienne has literally never moved faster in his life, all but rips the brooch from his hat as he onehanded fumbles the clasp open, tossing it at Nica with a harried, *"Here."*

They nearly miss catching it, awkwardly bounce it between their hands and every time it strikes Nica's metal palm, the gilt edge of the brooch makes little plinking noises against pieces of silvery plating. Etienne is worried for a second that they're gonna lose it, and honestly, it *would* just be his luck if the thing struck at a weird angle and went rocketing off to some unknown darkened corner of the room. Thankfully though, Nica manages to get their flesh hand closed around the brooch, brings it in a clasped fist up to their chest and looks at him in concern.

"I- *a-are you sure-?* It's just, *it's-* i-it's gonna get *destroyed...*I-I don't know if you want me to use this." Nica says like that fucking matters at the moment, and Etienne may like them, *may consider them a friend,* but that doesn't mean he can't arch his eyebrows and look at them like they're being an *idiot* as he drawls, "We're all gonna *fuckin' die* if you *don't.* So. *No.* I don't really give a shit what you do to it."

"R-Right, *yeah,* okay- *right yeah okay-"* Nica mutters a few times

What Goes Bump In The Night

in rapid succession, eyes dropping away, but they unclench their hand and in a move that has Etienne's mouth actually falling open, they flip the brooch over, hanging onto the stone with their flesh fingers while their prosthetic ones effortlessly peel the gold setting away like it's nothing more than tissue paper.

Mothers of the Night and Everything Beyond what in the ever loving flying fuck, Etienne thinks, eyes blinking in absolute astonishment, is in turn very impressed and also a little intimidated.

He is suddenly very concerned for whoever it is that Nica boxes against, doesn't think they would ever intentionally hurt someone to the point of hospitalization, but now it is ever so apparent that they *could actually hurt someone to the point of hospitalization.*

*Damn...*that metal arm really is *something wonder what else it can do how it was made who built it,* but Etienne has to put his curiosity out of mind for the moment. There will be other times and places to ask Nica about the ingenious device that serves as their right arm, and as much as it disappoints him, that instance is not now. Instead, he watches the unsure way Nica hesitates with the newly crunched piece of scrap gold, seemingly like they can't decide what to do with it, and Etienne simply holds out a hand in offer.

Nica awkwardly places the bent setting in the middle of his palm, looking at him one more time with apologetic eyes before dropping them back down to their lap. They scoot backwards on their knees a few paces, putting some space between the two of them, and then they switch the piece of bloodstone from their flesh hand to their metal one.

So many intricate joints and carefully curved plating make up this part of their prosthesis, which is just as heavily rune filled as any other area, though it's difficult to get a good look in the low lighting, and Etienne finds himself craning his neck as Nica closes their hand into a fist.

"Don't look. It's gonna get real bright." They warn, and he rolls his eyes, skin prickling at the crackling *crunch* that emanates from

✦✦ 393 ✦✦

Nica's hand as they flex their fingers, all but effectively crushing the bloodstone into small chunks. A few of the runes around their knuckles pulse dimly, and snorting, Etienne looks up at their face, about to snark *oh is that it,* when Nica rotates their hand open in one smooth move and the entire room lights up like the fucking sun just came up from the floor.

Etienne instinctually throws an arm up to shield his eyes, hears the surprised yelp from the others as they're bombarded with the same searing white light, and fatally curious until the end, Etienne tries to peek through his lashes despite being explicitly told not to.

Thankfully for the sake of his cornea, it seems like whatever reaction Nica just started is already tapering off, harsh glow fading to a less blinding teal that still makes his eyes water and sting as he squints in their general direction. It's blurry, but he can just barely see Nica's blonde hair blowing around them in a frizzy halo like a nascent storm cell, more than easily picks out how forge bright their pupils are, *like twin microscopic suns,* white hot circles of them trained adamantly on their slowly flexing fingers.

Small little licks of electricity crawl and skitter over the metal plating of their arm, runes up and down the length of it shining brightly in select groupings, and they must pertain to whatever reaction it is that Nica's set up, but damn if Etienne knows what any of it means.

His eyes drift back down the length of their arm, following the river of glowing symbols to their hand once more, and now that the light is less intense, Etienne's able to see this miniature cyclone coiling up from the center of their palm.

There's crushed chunks of bloodstone flying around in it, but as he watches painfully wide eyed, they crumble away one at a time, dissolving into a fine powder that seems to spark and glow like embers before disappearing entirely.

Each *pop* of disassembling rock feels like it pokes him sharply in the side, and tiredly, his magic comes winding back up to the surface of his skin, reaching out futilely once more for this power

What Goes Bump In The Night

it wants to know but honestly never will.

Hi hello know you don't we know you hello can you hear us hello are you there feel you why don't you ever say it back hello, whispers in a forlorn hush through his mind, spectral fingers fiddling and picking unhappily around the edges of Etienne's consciousness, and he wishes he could run a consoling hand down along the length of his magic, just wants it to understand and accept that it's never going to get the connection it craves.

What *his magic* wants though, is for it to be like how it is with other witches, a living conscious bond that it can recognize and that can recognize it, something that has enough thought and sentience on its own to reach back out for those curious touches, *a dance partner of sorts.*

But what it's struggling to grasp is that this is never going to be like anything it knows.

They're headed into uncharted waters and there is not going to be any easy way to *do this,* to have the kind of connection they're used to having, and it's a disconcerting thought, to understand that he's willingly signing himself up for an unfulfilling relationship, one where part of him will always be pining over an intimacy it can never have.

And some seed of a sour truth feels like it plants itself in his mind.

"Al...*right-* that should about...*do it.*" Nica says absentmindedly, and that's not much of a warning before the light fades out entirely, plunging them back into pitch blackness that is all the more sinister now, shadows pressing close and seemingly toeing tauntingly across the salt line.

In the dark, the tordu's huffing and wailing goes from mildly discomforting to *truly alarming* once more, and Etienne shivers at the slimy sensation that *drags* down his spine, all too aware of the amalgamation's efforts to breach his wards again.

Mothers of the Night, he hopes this little gamble of theirs paid off, can feel the Aratus wards starting to buckle ever so slightly, and without delving too deep into what *that* implies for their future, wets his lips nervously as he asks, "Did you get it? The uh- *formula,* or composition, *o-or whatever it is* you needed? Because if you didn't, I-I'm really not sure *what to-*"

"Cryptocrystalline quartz with a majority percentage of silicon dioxide, with smaller concentrations of localized ferric oxide that make up roughly thirty-seven to twenty percent of the total mass, all arranged in a triagonal atomic structure." Nica rattles off in seeming gibberish as they shake leftover debris from their hand, and when they glance up at Etienne quick, it might not be a triumphantly confident look, but it is at the very least *sure,* "So, yeah, *I got it.* I can probably source materials from the construction supplies nearby, but like- *how much* bloodstone do you need *exactly?*"

Ooooooh, bad question to ask him.

Etienne doesn't really have a head for numbers, always has to take careful notes and double check his calculations *constantly* before starting any ritual, and in this case, where there is no real precedence to work off of and he's flying by the seat of his pants, *he honestly has no idea.*

"Hah- that's a good...I don't know? *Exactly?* Like- a lot? Like, *pffb,* probably a few *uuuuh* dozen...*hundred*...l-like a large amount, ya'know? Enough to fill a room." Etienne awkwardly scratches at the back of his neck unsure, worried he's saying something stupid, *knows* he must've said something stupid when Nica's eyes blow wide as they squawk, *"An entire room's worth?"*

Okay that does seem a bit excessive now that he thinks about it, and flapping his hands around, Etienne tries to amend his own idiocy, "Not like-! N-Not like to the ceiling! *Just-* enough to cover the floor an' stuff! Like- *okay.* If you were walkin' through a room this size, you'd be kickin' against bloodstone the entire time, make sense? Like *that* much."

Nica just blinks at him a few times, opens their mouth, *shuts it,* and then tiredly shakes their head, *"Right.* Okay so probably at least

What Goes Bump In The Night

a hundred cubic feet, *possibly more,* which is doable in theory I guess, but there is uh- *gonna be one slight problem with materials-"*

A vein ticks to life in Etienne's temple.

"Are. You. *Kidding me? Mères de la Nwit, baise-mò dans cul-la! Ça isit putain de merde totale! To ariyin dòt ke-* I-! Y-You just told me *that you could-!"*

"Hey, hey, *hey! Alright,* chill out! You didn't let me finish, so don't go gettin' your spooky goth bloomers in a twist before I'm even done *talkin'."* Nica huffs, easily cutting through his impassioned swearing, and Etienne quiets down, but he continues grumbling unhappily to himself until they shoot him *a look* and he makes a big show of shutting his mouth, *"Thank you.* Now if you'd let *me finish-* first off, *so you'll calm the fuck down,* yes, *I can fabricate bloodstone.* There's more than enough iron and silicon around or laced through things in here that I can pull it out easy, but the problem lies in the *quantity."*

Etienne instinctually opens his mouth to argue, but Nica tilts their head and arches their brows in deadly incredulity, something eerily similar to an expression mother often makes when he won't shut his damn mouth, and just like with her, it makes him shut his damn mouth.

"Don't start." Nica warns and then brings their hands together, fingers forming a small oval that they slowly stretch apart while they talk, "The problem is in the amount you think you need. If it was just a few rocks? I could have that done in like five minutes, but for basically *an entire floor's worth?"*

Their hands get far enough apart that they throw them up in seeming defeat, metal and flesh palms plopping back heavily to their lap afterwards, "I don't think there's enough raw material here to *make* that much. The iron isn't a problem, it's such a small percentage of the stone and it's in fucking everything, like the chairs an' table legs, but the silicon? I mean...don't get me wrong there's silicon aggregate all over the place, but it's in the bricks and the mortar and if I pull it...I'm not sure the building will *uh,*

✦✦ 397 ✦✦

stay in one piece. Which I'm assumin' is not what we're goin' for long term."

Nica laughs awkwardly then to try and break the growing tension, but halfway through it turns into a painful sounding cough, "A-Anyway- everywhere else that has silicon...it's in such small concentrations that it's *not enough* to pull for a *hundred* cubic feet of bloodstone. So I'm... *k-kinda in a bind here.* Either I make an amount that's safe to, and we do our best with that, *or uh,* I make what you asked for but I'm not sure it'll end up matterin' much... because of um...structural...*failuuure...*"

"Oh..." Etienne breathes out in a short little puff of air, finally feels like he understands a bit more about how alchemy works besides, *infinite matter production,* and is disliking the fact that it's *not* the case. He must make some displeased face about it and Nica must catch it, because they quickly break eye contact, nervously tapping both sets of fingers together, "I can still make as much as I'm able, b-but I...*don't. Know.* If your plan will work with...*less.*"

"How *much* less?" Etienne hates to ask but knows he needs to, and Nica peeks back at him guiltily, like they hate to answer but know they have no other choice, "M-Maybe only a few cubic feet? I could um, try p-pulling some silicon from the bricks b-but uh, with an imprecise reaction I've never practiced before? It could get away from me and...kinda sorta *possibly potentially-* destroy the whole building..."

*Only a couple cubic feet huh...*Etienne's having trouble picturing what that would even look like, tries to imagine a few rulers and then assemble them into a cube, but his mind will not build the image for him. He goes to use his forearm next, remembers something about it roughly equating to a foot, but it just seems like such a tiny amount, he doesn't trust it.

Whether that's right or whether that's wrong, he doesn't think it'll end up mattering much, not when Nica's original projected estimation was around *one hundred* feet, and Etienne is admittedly not a numbers guy, but he *is* an *eyeball it guy,* and if one

What Goes Bump In The Night

hundred cubic feet is what it takes to cover the floor in here with a few inches of rocks, then that's what they really *do need*.

But if Nica says the only way to do that *also* involves bringing the roof down on their heads, that the best chance they have is at the same time the *worst chance,* and ends with them being buried alive? Etienne has to begrudgingly trust that they're right. This is one of those situations where if they can't trust one another, if they fight and argue and *doubt,* then they have no hope of making it out of here alive.

So, he'll have to take their word for it, that a couple cubic feet is all they can safely do, because there's *no point* in locking the tordu away in the aether only to then have an entire building collapse right on them.Which is not the answer he was wanting to the solution he desperately needed to work, but when, in this life of his, are things ever easy.

Tonight sure as hell hasn't *been,* has once more put Etienne in a shit awful position where he's skeptical of his ability to succeed, and he morosely stares at the debris strewn floor thinking about what happens next. And it's bleak. He's injured, *he's drained,* he was counting on a massive influx of bloodstone to help resonate whatever weak trickle of magic he can manage, but now, all the heavy lifting for the spell falls back on him and his heart jumps nervously.

He knows what arcane burnout is.

He *knows* how dangerous it is to keep funneling energy up when his body is already at its limit.

How, *at the end of the day,* his flesh is mortal but this power he wields is not, and that the former will succumb to the latter if he pushes it too far, but if anyone here is going to have a chance he's going to have to, *he's going to have to.*

He doesn't know if he can.

This is dangerous this is stupid you know better you know where this leads only one place this leads ~~you're going to get yourself killed,~~

clamors through Etienne's mind like a struck bell, dries his mouth out makes his palms *sweat sends his heart racing a hundred miles an hour,* and while each ringing warning might be true, there really is no other way forwards besides pretending like they aren't.

His whole life has been lived with the understanding that it is forfeit in the service of protecting others, but now faced with *actively* making that decision...it is much more difficult than Etienne imagined it'd be.

If he doesn't do this, everyone in here is going to die, *end of the story case in point,* but if he *does* manage to successfully trap the tordu, only one of them is really put at risk, so it seems like it should be such a simple choice at that point. *Do the right thing – sacrifice yourself – save the rest,* easy peasy, exactly what he was taught to do- but then *why* does the thought make his hands shake, why are his ears roaring louder than the monster outside, why is every single cell of his *fight or flight* response screaming at him to *run?*

Get a grip get a grip you know what you're supposed to do, Etienne thinks, hands fisting harshly around his biceps, *be the witch you're supposed to be the son your mother counts on you to be,* and maybe he's having this reaction because it's not a for sure thing that anyone will be saved ~~or maybe it's just because he doesn't want to die~~, but he keeps having to ask himself *does it even really matter?* He dies if he does nothing, he'll also likely die if he does something, and if he's doomed no matter what, why not take the option that gives the others a shot at survival?

And yeah the odds of that still aren't *perfect,* but Etienne will just...*have to make it work,* will take this fear and bury it, accept whatever he's given and do what he has to do, and if he burns himself out in the process? *Well...*Nica knows how to get everyone out and once the tordu is dealt with, his family can come collect his body later.

Something squirms in disquiet under his sternum at the thought, at the imagining of his suggested demise, and the sensation unhappily coils around his bones like a guarding snake, a possessive

✦✦ 400 ✦✦

What Goes Bump In The Night

tangle of- *furious indignant scared desperate* -outrage that echoes harshly behind his eyes, *no no nO NO can't give in can't give up you're ours our pride our future our scion need you have to have you can't let you go won't let you go refuse don't make it don't do it leave them all to-*

Enough, Etienne thinks sternly back at the snarled knot of his magic, finding a new resolve in its adamant refusal, *if there is no other way if it's the only choice...it's the one I have to make,* and one popping stretch at a time, he begins to uncoil his legs from the tense cramped position he'd forced them into.

But you, a dozen whispers argue back, twining tighter, *but us,* and Etienne knows it can feel his anxiety and fear and is reacting to that, *can't let it feed off that,* so he's firm when he corrects it.

No but's- prioritizing *personal safety over the safety of others isn't our way...it isn't what was taught it's not the path we should be walking,* and in a rare moment of true self-discipline, he manages to do what mother always tells him to do and lets those feelings poisoning him *go.*

There are seldom few times that Etienne has had to scold his magic back into line like that, reminding it of the greater duty he is called to perform, because while this power did originate from Maisette, *from some wider unknown plane of unfathomable energy,* it is now *of him,* and if he let it, it could grow to be just as selfish and sinister as only mortal man can achieve.

Etienne would never allow things to deteriorate that far though, *waivers,* but ultimately keeps strong in his convictions, and it shows in the way his magic lowers its hackles at the reprimand.

It still writhes agitatedly, displeased and worried for him, *for both of them,* but it drips back down through his ligaments and tendons, pooling under the skin of his hands.

We are yours, it sighs with the echo of a hundred lives, so many eyes and hands and pursed mouths made of shadowy memories and half-forgotten histories, words warped and distorted by how far through time they call back to him, *we are always yours...command*

✦✦ 401 ✦✦

us as seen fit command us as is known...we are yours...

Their voices start to fade out, his magic receding like the tide as it draws away into him once more, and Etienne rubs a thumb across the back of one of his hands, thinks he can almost feel an answering touch mirror his own but from the underside, a barely there sweep of, *we're here we'll stay not alone.*

He tries not to get choked up as the thought draws past, *can't think of what it betrays of his innermost fears,* pushes clumsily to his feet and holds a shaking hand out for Nica who just stares up at him with too big eyes.

"C'mon," Etienne urges, watching as they start to reach for him with their metal hand before they seemingly think twice, and snatch it back fast, choosing to push themself up on their own instead, "we don't have long. Make what you can make without destroyin' the place an' I'll handle the rest. Just be ready to break that wall when I tell you to, okay?"

"But- *wait, I just-* a-are you sure? That's a pretty big discrepancy to...*t-to-* to *overlook,* all of a sudden. You sure it'll be fine? I...I-I know you're runnin' low on magic an' I don't wanna put you in a bad spot, Etienne." Nica eyes him suspiciously and praying to the Mother of his house, Etienne hopes they don't immediately see right through him like they've made a very bad habit of doing.

"It'll be fine." He lies, tries to keep his posture open and relaxed and the resolve for what he plans to do off his face, "It would've been nice to have the extra layer of comfort, but I can manage without it, *promise.* Whatever you can get me will be perfect, so don't worry about me- *I'll make it work.* I've been in worse binds than this an' I've come out all right."

A complete and utter baldfaced lie.

But Nica doesn't know that and Etienne needs them to continue *not knowing that,* smiles reassuringly as they come to stand before him, still with that skeptical light in their eyes when he says, "I'll take what bloodstone you can make an' start on my ritual, which, it might take a minute, but I'll get the tordu pushed back enough

What Goes Bump In The Night

so you can focus on gettin' everyone else out. You'll probably have to make a few trips since they're all so hard up, but that shouldn't be a problem, right?"

"No...no I can handle that." Nica answers slowly but they sound confident enough, which Etienne had assumed they'd be.

They may be shorter than him, but he's under no illusion that they're stronger than him, can easily recognize the strength in Nica's shoulders and the swell of their biceps, something they unintentionally flex now when they cross their arms, head cocked to the side, "But what about *you?* I don't...this would be less material than you said you needed *plus* more effort on your part. You're low on blood, you said your magic's near run out, you've never done anythin' like this before but you're gonna...*I just-* t-the math isn't *adding up* for me, Etienne."

Every time, he thinks, blinking stupidly at their dead set serious face, spiraling bewilderment under his breastbone that's quickly tightening back into raw panic, *every fucking time how do they-*

"I- Nica...*listen-*" Etienne tries only once before they cut him off, fingers flexing in the crooks of their elbows, *eyes on fire,* "Stop lying to me. You told me you would an' I don't know *why* you've gone back on it now, but I can tell yer blowin' smoke up my ass. S-So, I'll ask you again- *what about you?* How do you get out? Did'ya even *plan f-for that?* Because what happens to you when you enact this cockamamy scheme? When you put more than what you have into a reaction that needs *something* to fuel it?"

He opens his mouth helplessly, *shuts it just as uselessly,* and Nica doesn't wait for an answer, steps right up into his personal space, a tide of eucalyptus and raindrops washing over Etienne's senses, makes his heart twist uncomfortably, *like the moment before a storm hits sky grey and swollen and burdened by deep grief,* their voice low and jumpy like the drumming of heavy rain, "M'not an *idiot.* I'm a chemist, *a-an alchemist-* I know something can't come from *nothin'.* Reactions need energy, *spells n-need power,* so what do you give it, Etienne? *What do you give it-*"

✦✦ 403 ✦✦

Etienne swallows rough, can't think up anything fast enough with those *eyes* boring into him, *like twin bolts of lightning dual storm cells don't lie to me I won't I can't I'm sorry,* and Nica hisses air out through their teeth, his silence more of an admission than any words would've been.

"God damnit! You're *n-not- just, no. NO-!* If it doesn't work it *doesn't work, Etienne,* we'll figure something else out but not at the cost of- *n-not at the expense sacrifice f-f-forfeit of-"* Nica struggles to get out, and seemingly with no other way to convey what they want, they lift their flesh hand and lightly press trembling fingers against his sternum, finishing in a hollow murmur, *"...you know what I mean-"*

And he does, feels the heat leaching from their skin and into his own, *wonders if they can feel how fast his heart is going ~~if they're also thinking about when it'll stop too,~~* and whispers in a croak, "There's nothin' else to be done, there's really *not.* This is it Nica, *t-this is what we got-* but it's okay. *I-I'm* gonna be okay. Protecting people s'what I'm supposed to do...I'm a *Boudreaux,* this is what *I'm supposed to do."*

For him, that's all that really needs to be said, the sole justification, *the lone comfort,* but it doesn't seem like it's enough of anything for Nica, frustrated heat bleeding up their cheeks and really making the pale discoloration on the right side of their face *pop.*

"Y-Yeah? Well *whoop-de-fuckin'-do,* because *I'm* a *Caldwell."* Nica snarls, fingers tightening ever so slightly in the front of his shirt, one eye glaring at him with all the ferocity of the sea, the other, the foreboding heather of an unclaimed wild, both taken together the deadliest thing he's ever seen, "An' we *don't lose people. We don't leave'em behind.* So you better put that *stupid thought* out of your head *right the fuck now.* I'm not leavin' you here to *die."*

There's something in that, *something to it,* like hurricane winds and storm surge and standing back to back with all the odds against you, but it's also the hand that helps you up *the one that ushers you on,* the arm you shelter under when the night is too much and the one you grab when the day is too bright and you

What Goes Bump In The Night

can't find your way and he's just- *he's just-*

Etienne doesn't know what it is, *about this night about this moment,* but something changes violently in between one furious pump of his heart and another.

It's almost like the whole of reality lurches around him before reorienting in a slightly different direction, and it happens so fast, *he's not even sure it did.* Etienne wants to bring a hand up and check the rhythm of his heart, thinks it stuttered out of time too in that little blip and needs to make sure it's back on tempo, but Nica's hand is still *right there, burning him,* and his entire body is arrested by the thought.

He can't understand why.

"-somethin' else. *T-There's gotta be something else,* somethin' we're just not *seein'."* Nica's apparently been rambling on, but Etienne hasn't heard a single fucking word, forces himself to listen now and *comprehend* instead of focusing solely in on the five little sunspots burning against his chest, "Like- l-like maybe we take the glass from the windows or would that be the- *one continuous surface.* Maybe there's stuff somewhere, *like,* bricks n' shit *o-or bags of cement,* an' I just need to get to it, *I-I just have to get to it an' then I can get you what you need-"*

"Nica...*there's no time,* don't make things harder-"

"S-Shut the *fuck up! Just-!"* Nica draws most of their fingers into a shaking fist but leaves one pressing harshly against his sternum, "You're bein' difficult- *impossible s-stupid ar- ar- argu-* you're the one that's- just give me a-a second to *think.* I can do this, *I-I can do this I can do this-* can figure it out just need a- *second minute moment* -just need a- *I can do this I can figure it out I can f-fix it,* j-just need a minute b-but I'm not leavin' you, *m'not leavin' either one of you-"*

They make a noise of discomfort all of a sudden and duck their head, finally taking their hand back as they start rubbing aggressively at their right eye, *the hazel one,* like it's bothering them or something.

✦✦ 405 ✦✦

Etienne uses their distraction to collect himself, hopefully is more compelling this time when he argues gently, "I understand an' appreciate your concern, *I really do,* but we're outta time an' options. This is the best chance any of you got an' I...*I-I don't want it to be in vain.* Please just trust me. *Please just go.*"

"N-No- *no,* I c-can get it *I had it thought I-I did where did it-* just need *t-time, just needed m-more time- shouldn't'a done it-* I can *do it* I just need to *think- God fuck,* why's it *so bright-?*"

"Nica? Everythin's gonna be okay, alright? I...I think you're just havin' a panic attack. Try an' focus on your breathing, okay? Can you do that for me?" Etienne urges as calmly as he can, really needs them to snap themself out of this if they're going to have a shot at their plan, but he out of anyone understands how hard that can be, "You're gonna be okay. Just- *think about your home.* You're from Georgia, right? *Er,* South Carolina maybe? S-Sorry can't remember but just, think about where you grew up. *About your family.* Do you have siblings? I bet you have younger ones, you kinda seem like the protective older sibling type-"

He laughs in a friendly way but Nica only whimpers in response, and Etienne would be more concerned if the tordu didn't land a particularly strong blow then, making one of the Aratus wards rattle ominously like a struck gong.

The vibrations lance through his chest, *a shot through the heart,* and he winces, hunching over slightly, tone growing less gentle as the pain and fear redouble, *"Ack-* listen, I know you're struggling right now, but *I need you to pull yourself together.* I can try an' do this without your help but I'll have a better chance with you, and that's what you wanted, isn't it? For me to be safe?"

But still, Nica doesn't respond, just digs at their eye and mutters frantically under their breath, and Etienne is starting to get desperate, *starting to freakout himself what's wrong what's wrong with you,* and maybe, *he ends up pushing more than he should,* "Do you want me to live? Because the only way that's gonna happen is if you do this for me. Just one little alchemical reaction Nica, *you can do that,* you can make it, I know you can, so will you do that

What Goes Bump In The Night

for me, Nica? *Will you please help me?"*

"I-I'm trying...I'm tryin'...b-but it's not workin' w-why won't it work?
I-I keep tryin' but it *won't go-"* They stammer in a hush, metal hand
flexing and moving in a spastic twitch at their side where it hangs
like a deadweight, *"What's w-wrong, what d-does it need-* what do
y-you need-? Y-You can have it, all of i-it, a- a-anthin' you want,
j-just *tell me! 'cause I'm tryin' so hard,* but i-it won't go *it won't
go- don't know what I'm doing* know I shouldn't'a- didn't mean to
*I didn't- i-it was so cold so b-bright I didn't see my fault n-never got
to m'so sorry Syd-"*

Their voice chokes off in a strangled noise and now Etienne *is*
actually worried. It sounds like they're close to hyperventilating,
words quiet and rushed and *panicked,* and given the way they're
talking, he thinks they might be having a dissociative episode instead. Etienne may be well versed at dealing with panic attacks,
but he's less sure when it comes to other forms of neurological
distress, and he has no idea what he's supposed to do.

He doesn't know Nica well enough to know how to pull them out
of it, isn't sure if touch would help them or hurt them or what
could potentially make it worse, and he's toeing the edge of his
own nervous breakdown, *can't take one more thing can't live with
this choice too much longer can feel that weak resolve cracking,*
when the most unwanted voice in the world speaks up, "Hey *uh-*
am I...i-interruptin' something?"

What the fuck do you think, is the first thing that springs to Etienne's mind but thankfully, doesn't make it out, and it feels like all
the air rushes from his body as he sighs exhausted, "What do you
want, *we're busy...*an' you're *supposed* to be resting."

For once, Carter doesn't have some dumbass comment or sarcastic remark to make back, winces with how Reggie is trying to help
prop him up but otherwise, generally ignores the fact that he's not
supposed to be on his feet. His eyes do flick from where Etienne's
standing to where Nica is though, narrowing as he watches them
pinch and pull at the skin around their right eye, at how they
gibber to themself under their breath.

✦✦ 407 ✦✦

Etienne feels his hackles rise at the judging look, steps in between the two of them snapping, *"Carter.* What do you want? We're in the middle of tryin' to get all y'all out of here, so if you're gonna call me another slur or a child snatching demon or *whatever,* can you at least wait until-"

"O-Oh shut the fuck up you d- dam-" Carter starts in that familiar vitriolic, now cough riddled tone, but he stops himself, blows out a hard gust of air and begins again, *"Look.* M'not here to a-argue. I've been out of it, but the boys tell m-me it ain't looking too good, alright? A-An' you're both loud as fuck so I've heard you two freaking out over some shit y-you don't have, but I-"

"We've got it figured out, *thank you,* but in the future, we'll endeavor to keep it down while we're trying to-"

"Would y-you *shut up,* and let me finish my damn thought?" Carter snaps, and Etienne seriously debates it, but with a sarcastic *'the floor is yours'* sweep of his hands, he motions the man to continue, "L-Lord's tits...*you're such a bitch,* but- *whatever.* That's besides the point. *Anyway.* What I-I was *gonna say* before you started getting all smart, was we just poured a new slab an' footings last week, so that's your damn problem solved, *a-asshole."*

Carter looks at him all smug then, like Etienne should be fawning over him and thanking him for this piece of *boundless wisdom,* but Etienne has no idea what he's talking about, doesn't see how pouring something solves *any* problem, and stammers out a bewildered, "O-Okay?"

That seems to take some of the wind out of Carter's sails.

"Uuuh, *hello?* W-What do you mean- *do you not...? Concrete!* We just poured a new *concrete slab* for the foundation! There's literally h-hundreds of yards of it right below your stupid pointy boots." Carter gestures angrily at his feet and like an idiot, Etienne looks down, still not understanding what this great revelation's supposed to be, and groaning impassionedly, Carter coughs, "Un-*fucking*-believable- *there's sand in concrete, dipshit!* I-It's like twenty five percent of its total composition which yeah, is a

What Goes Bump In The Night

smaller percentage, but with as much as we poured, it should be m-more than enough to do whatever it is you need to do."

Looking back up, Etienne squints his eyes in confusion, still not getting it, "We don't...*need* sand though? Nica said they needed iron and uh...*silicon-?*"

"Okay first off it's, *silica,* and secondly- *that's what sand is you dense motherfucker!*" Carter roars, stamping a foot into the floor and nearly tumbling himself out of Reggie's hold, but Etienne barely pays him any mind, snapping his head back to the scuffed-up toes of his boots. There's something spreading through his chest like flashfire, a feeling that's close to watching the sun rise for the first time in *years* throttling him alive, *flooding his veins with pure euphoria,* and he can't stop thinking that, just below those worn floorboards, lies a *chance.*

Lies salvation.

Hope.

"S-Sint lamèd-" He swears in a shaky breath that tastes like relief and sounds half like a prayer, and in the moment where everything seems nothing short of divine, Etienne can't stop himself from feeling drunk off optimism and fresh conviction, not even when the tordu roars and slams into his wards and Carter mutters all grim, "You just gotta get to it first."

✦ 409 ✦

Chapter 19

Etienne narrows his eyes and tilts his head, disliking the section he just drew and takes his white smudged sleeve to erase it. He spins the thin chalk pencil in his fingers as he goes to redo it, careful to be slow and purposeful, uses his other hand to bolster his writing wrist and flicks his fingers up to create a much more delicate swirl this time.

The sigil he's working on is simple enough, just something quick he threw together on the fly, but it still demands absolute perfection, each line and glyph needing to be drawn with the utmost immaculate care. Thankfully though, he's already satisfied with his changes when he hears the heavy creak of footsteps behind him, because he glances back briefly and then his concentration gets broken entirely.

"H-Hey." Etienne stammers and quickly gets to his feet, watching Nica slow to a stop with their arms folded tight across their chest, shoulders drooped, seemingly trying to make themself take up less space than they do, "How are uh...h-how are you doing?"

He hasn't seen them in a bit, has been attempting to give them some privacy after they disappeared behind an upturned desk to presumably get a hold of themself, and they seem like they've calmed down a little, deep steady breath leaving Nica's chest as they scuff a shoe sole against the floor.

"Better. *Fine. G-Great.*" They mumble to the tops of their sneakers, and he's not so sure of that, because even in the low lighting, Etienne can see how pale their face still is, only exception being the abused skin around their right eye which throbs an irritated pink.

Overall though, he supposes Nica does look *way* better than

What Goes Bump In The Night

they did a moment ago, *hunched over eyes unseeing skin and bone fingers digging into their flesh metal and rivet fingers writhing like a dying insect grasping at something that's not there,* more coherency and recognition in their body language that Etienne is immediately very grateful for.

"That's good, *t-that's good,* glad to uh, hear it?" He rambles nervously, fiddling the pencil between both sets of fingers, struggles with where to go from here and knows he needs to ascertain Nica's mental state despite how much he *doesn't want to,* and it lands him on a stilted, "So do you um...do you wanna maybe tal-?"

"No." Nica mutters dark and warning, metal fingers flexing against their skin in a way that looks painful, "Just- pretend, *i-ignore, act like-* it never happened. I don't wanna- *can't- p-please-"*

Which, that's a request Etienne would be more than willing to acquiesce to under normal circumstances, *doesn't like to pry doesn't like to dig into fresh wounds,* but here, *now,* with everything they have riding on this thin line that only succeeds if the two of them each pull their respective weight?

He has some doubts and worries.

And it's kinda terrible timing, but they don't really *have* a lot of time to be delicate about things like he'd like, and so it's pretty awkward trying to figure out how to ask Nica if they're mentally well enough to even be *doing* alchemy in the first place.

It sounds cold hearted, like, *how can he not trust them hasn't he been in the same boat,* and that's almost the whole problem in its entirety.

It is *because* Etienne understands that he feels so unsure about trusting their judgment.

He *knows* what it's like in the aftermath of those mental storms, *has been there himself sifting through the rubble,* knows how shaky and disorienting and cracked apart everything feels afterwards, how raw and split open your mind becomes. Rationale and judgment calling aren't necessarily the first things you're worried about

✦✦ 411 ✦✦

when you can barely remember who you even *are,* after all.

Etienne wouldn't trust *himself* with a life or death situation on the heels of a panic attack, *barely finds the courage to trust himself as is,* and it seems mean, but he's not really sure he can trust Nica right now either.

This plan hinges on him pulling an absorbed amount of weight just as much as it's hinged on *them* doing the same, and if they can't do their part, *crack under the pressure make one slip up,* all this will be for nothing.

So.

Etienne has got to ask if they're able to bear it, *needs to make sure they can.* He doesn't want to, but wanting and needing are two *vastly* different things, and he doesn't really have a choice in the matter right now. Somehow, he has to navigate this tricky situation and find the words that continue to elude him, ask questions he doesn't have the right to be asking, and all of it is so hard *because* he understands.

He's *had* that firsthand experience of losing yourself and struggling to put the pieces back together. He's *had* to make difficult decisions under pressure and knows now he made the wrong call. *He's been asked the same fucking question he needs to ask, are you okay can you do this you sure you can handle it,* knows how much it *sucks* to feel like you're being put under scrutiny or treated like your head isn't screwed on right, *still feeling like that no matter what anyone else says to you doubt in their eyes seeds doubt in your heart looking at your shaking hands were you ever even capable of anything in the first place know the answer and so do they-*

But options are limited and time is short and he *has to do this the needs of the many outweigh the needs of the few garçon,* tries to not be a complete monster at least as he flips the pencil between his hands and hates every word that leaves his mouth, "So is uh, is everythin', *um, alright?* Like do you feel more clearheaded? An' it's fine if you don't! I was just worried 'cause you seemed pretty scattered an' I wasn't sure if you'd be able- *t-that is to say,* didn't

What Goes Bump In The Night

know if you'd be *uh- confident* doing the reac-"

"I said I was *fine."* Nica snaps, arms drawing tighter, *head ducking lower don't look at me don't look at me why is everyone always looking at,* deep red spilling across their face that's either from anger or embarrassment or *both,* "Just because I- *j-just because I-I'm-* I'm *not a-an invalid.* I'm not a- *I-I'm not- I can do it...*I *can-* I said I was f-fine- *a-an' I am fine...*m'just as fucking capable as *you."*

They spit those last few words at him like it's a vile poison coating the inside of their mouth, but the taste seems familiar to them, *how many times have they said it how many times have people looked at them how many times have they been questioned.*

And Etienne immediately regrets and quits with his fiddling, scrambling instead for an explanation that isn't invalidating, *that doesn't reveal too much of himself,* "No! No that wasn't, *t-that wasn't my intention at all,* I wasn't-!"

"Then what *was, your intention?"* Nica hisses at the ground and Etienne whines low in the back of his throat, wants to look them in the eyes so they can tell he's being sincere, but they won't meet his and he won't force them to, has to put it all into his voice then, "I'm not callin' you incapable, *I'm not.* You *are* just as capable as me, often times more so...but I...*b-but I need to know you can do this. I mean-* y-you totally could under normal circumstances but this is, *this is a lot, Nica,* more than I'd ever normally ask of a human an' I don't know if you can...just...*ya'know? Handle it."*

Etienne cringes as he says it, can hear how weak it sounds, and if it's bad for him, it must be doubly so for Nica, who huffs un-happily in response. They toss their head with a careless, *angry* motion, knocking hair across their face, but he can still see peeks and glimpses of that *furious* color staining their cheeks, knows he's not doing it right, *that he's still not giving them enough.*

His heart jumps into triple time at the thought, about laying his own insecurities and shortcomings bare, *admitting to them that he understands that he's been there too that he's on their side,* and Etienne nearly gets sick just thinking about it, has held onto these

✦✦ 413 ✦✦

things for so long, not just anyone can pry them from his cold corpse hands.

But...Nica isn't just *anyone*, he's very much aware of that at this point, and he might still be figuring out exactly what it is that they mean to him, but it isn't *nothing*, and that alone is enough to force Etienne's mouth back open, "T-That didn't come out right, none of that did an' you're right to be upset. *I'm sorry*. I never wanted to...*m-make you feel like I do*, an' I know I don't know much about alchemy, s-so it might not sound like it means anything, but I-I know you're good. *I know you're really good at what you do, Nica.* You're incredible, o-one of the most talented people I know, *I just...*"

He trails off, chalk pencil clenched tight in one fist, thumb pressing against it like it's going to snap the brittle thing in half, and there are a lot of words he could say and a lot of them are ones he's only willingly told Sabine and then unwillingly told his therapist, *makes him weak in the knees dizzy in the head don't do it*, but... *f-fairs fair.*

Nica just had a very personal, *very raw*, moment forcefully drug out of them, is standing there trying to shield their bloody heart in their hands, and Etienne can't give them quite that much, *can't hand his own over isn't sure he'd survive it*, but he can give them *something*.

Not exactly an equivalent exchange, *but not exactly nothing either.*

"I just...I-I just know what it's *like*. When your head's not your own. When everything's spiralin' an' you can't tell up from down. *When you're lost with no way out.*" Etienne murmurs softly, angling his thumb so he can rake his black painted nail along the side of the pencil up to the tip, wonders how hard he'll have to press before he splinters the wood, "S-So...*I get it.* I-I've been there. An' I know how...*difficult*, it is, to think clearly, *to be yourself- t-to trust yourself-* when things get like that, but I'm not judging you for it. *Mothers of the Night*, I'd never judge you for it."

And how could he?

❖❖❖ 414 ❖❖❖

What Goes Bump In The Night

Not when he also knows the sensation of being drowned, *of his head slipping under,* and with a sigh, he flips the pencil quick so the point is facing back down again and offers advice he's always been given but struggles beyond measure to take, "And admittin' you need...*help,* i-is *not* a failing, but good *fuck-* do I understand how *hard* it is to ask for it anyway...how much it makes you feel like a failure anyway..."

Standing in mother's office can't meet her eyes standing before the wall of family portraits can't meet theirs wondering if they'd ever been where you are forced into squishy soft chairs pills forced into your hands don't think they did don't think they were ~~don't know what that says about you,~~ dry swallows rough and thinks he tastes that poison of his own, the one that leaks down from his brain and tries to kill him one drop at a time.

Not good enough not good enough never good enough a disgrace of a son a disgrace of a witch a letdown of a generation-

"I know you said you didn't wanna talk about it though, so I'll leave it alone, but just know that...*you're* not alone." Etienne murmurs awkwardly, works to clear his throat and ignore the way the room is spinning, *the way his heart is hammering why did you do that why did you Mothers what possessed you to tell them that-* "A-And if you ever *uh,* change your mind about that? *The talking about it-* I'm here, f-for whatever that's worth."

Almost shyly, Nica does flick their eyes up to meet his then and they're so hard to read, swamp of complicated emotions leaking out over their red tinged edges, *like tears like a never ending stream of sorrow of anguish what is it what's wrong what the hell happened with you,* as they all but whisper, "I-I can *do it. Trust. Me.*"

And Etienne is admittedly something of a control freak, *wants to make sure they can really do it wants to make sure they really do mean it,* but he said this was all about trusting one another and it is, so he nods, promising them just as softly, "Okay...I will."

And it's not exactly an, *I'm sorry,* but maybe it doesn't have to be, and Etienne can tell almost right away that he's forgiven.

✦✦ 415 ✦✦

It's there in the soft way Nica looks at him, not in pity, *but in understanding,* a gentle whispering of, *you get it you know you've worn these shoes too,* and they don't really say anything else of consequence, just step closer, a little past him, inclining their head shakily at his improvised sigil, but it's all in their voice, "W-What'cha workin' on?"

Which is half of what they wanted to say, and Etienne is more than happy to take the unasked for request of the rest, *it's okay we're okay can we stop talking about this can we move on,* turns around to survey his work too, "Recursive energy loop. Not really a *uh, super* official thing? B-But it should do in a pinch. The theory is, I'll feed it a flicker of my power an' it'll keep spinnin' it around for- well, *probably indefinitely,* but it'll hopefully make it seem like m'workin' on that sendforth ritual or somethin' of the sort."

"Oh yeah?" Nica hums, and Etienne's proud of the fact that he doesn't jump, because in between one inhale and its accompanying exhale, there is an unexpected warm weight pressing hesitantly against his arm, and he may act all cool about it, but he still ends up tripping over his tongue a bit, "Y-Yeah, it should um, *s-should* be enough of a draw that the tordu u-uh, focuses its attention on this spot? Keepin' it distracted enough that we can slip outta here easier-"

"*Wait-* y-you found a *new way out* then?" Nica accidentally interrupts with, whips to look up at him in wide eyed shock and waffling his left hand side to side, Etienne leans delicately back into the pressure along his right, *"Kinda sorta?* I'm not sure how much you uh, *overheard?* But we're goin' with our original plan, *kinda-* the one with the entire room of bloodstone? Just...*change of location.* Apparently Carter an' them poured a new foundation last week or so which means that we have...well you get it."

Etienne doesn't bother finishing the thought once he sees that *spark* flash in Nica's eyes, *understanding elation giddy overflowing hope can do the reaction can make what he needs ~~don't have to watch him die,~~* disbelieving laugh tumbling out of their mouth as their head cranes around him to look across the room, "For real? *Like-* l-like you're not fuckin' with me we can actually- *Christ alive,*

What Goes Bump In The Night

why the *hell* didn't that stupid fuckhead say anythin' before now then?"

"I believe in callin' him a *'stupid fuckhead'*, you've just answered your own question." Etienne mutters dryly and Nica swings back around to stare up at him, hard gust of air shooting out of their nose as they snort in amusement, which comes again as it quickens into giggles and then outright cackles. They hunch over and lightly knock their forehead against his upper arm, laughter growing muffled by the cotton of his shirt sleeve but is no less pleasant for it, and it brings a smile of his own to Etienne's lips as he shrugs them off gently.

"Ya'know, I kinda like it when you're a dick to someone that's not me. Is that mean? *I feel like that's a lil'mean.*" Nica muses and with a sharp bark of laughter, Etienne steps over towards his sigil and shakily crouches down, tossing airy over his shoulder, "Oh that's not *mean*. You haven't heard me *mean*, but get a couple glasses of bourbon in me, an' I'll tell you some stories from city council meetin's that'll have you rollin' on the floor in no time. *Guarantee.*"

"Yeah? Sounds like a date then." Nica jokes as they crouch down next to him, head cocked while they watch him reach out for the first ring of clean chalk glyphs, "You said they poured a new foundation though, didn't you? Which I'm assumin' means the basement. Which, and again, *I'm assumin'*, means we are *not* doing your ritual in this room you said we can't leave or we'd get killed...*to go to the basement.* Correct?"

"Correct." Etienne agrees and arches all of his fingers steeply over his neat lines, lets power flow in controlled amounts from him to the sigil, and is happy to see it light up a vivid maroon, hears Nica make an interested noise before they mutter, *"Wonderful.* This sounds *just* like the plot of a shit horror movie, ya'know. Like- *'oh the only way to save the day is if you leave the saferoom and venture out into the spooky, p-pitch black, monster infested basement'-"*

"Well the theory is it won't be monster infested if this sigil works, since the tordu will be too distracted tryin' to break in here an' kill what it thinks is me that it won't-"

✦✦✦ 417 ✦✦✦

"R-Right right right right- but I-like- *still*. It's the *b-basement*. *You're never supposed to go into the basement.* That's like- *horror movie s-survival one'o'one*, someone *a-always* gets killed in the basement...you know it's been statistically proven that the blonde d-dies first in like- *most* scary movies? Like, *across the board.* I had to read this article on it for m-my film an' media class, but like, m-messed up, huh?"

Nica's not really doing a good job at masking the nerves that lace through each and every word, anxious *scared* tremble in their voice Etienne can hear clear as day, and he can't say he's too surprised. Not that he thinks Nica is a coward or anything for it, *far from it*, because really, all things considered, they've held it together surprisingly well despite their undoubtedly mounting fear, but there are cracks forming and it's honestly not that unexpected of a reaction.

This entire night goes well beyond what most humans would be comfortable dealing with, *the inky shadows the stench of blood bodies littering the floor an abyssal nightmare creature shrieking its heads off a scant few feet away,* but, if Etienne's remembering right, he's pretty sure Nica's also very afraid of the dark on their own. It seems like so long ago, but he remembers that night outside Audubon, where he...*mocked them for it,* an unkindness he never should've given them and something which seems like it was a lifetime past, but he knows it wasn't, *not really.*

So much has happened since then, and now really isn't the time to be reflecting on it, but Etienne knows he probably should after this is all over. Once their lives aren't on the line, he'll have a nice long think about all the things he's said and done, *both back before the thought of neon colored windbreakers made him smile and then after the point where they did,* but for now, there is a scared Nica and no room in his heart for *doubting himself or his choices.*

And in the moment, he has such a *strong urge* to take this fear from them, to make sure they feel safe, *protected secure cared for,* he's a little taken aback at the intensity of the feeling, worried he comes across as too harsh when he goes to reassure them.

What Goes Bump In The Night

"You're not going to die, Nica. Not first. Not last. *Not at all. I'll make sure of it.*" Energy starts to build at the tips of Etienne's fingers, and even this little amount *burns* as he calls his magic up from the depths, but he cuts it off before it becomes too difficult to bear.

Flicking his fingers in a quick burst, Etienne sends a sliver of raw magic into the heart of the activated sigil, watches as it catches in the innermost loop and begins to churn, glances over at where Nica is beside him and somehow isn't surprised to find them already staring back.

They still look terrified, already pale face drawn ever paler, really makes all their freckles stand out starkly, like an inverted image of the night's sky, and for once, their eyes don't shy away, stay locked onto his in a desperate plea for help, for reassurance, *for something.*

"Hey, it's gonna be okay. I'm not gonna let anythin' hurt you, you have my word on that." Etienne promises as maroon light chases itself around and around in the depths of Nica's eyes, bounces off the bump of their nose, *caresses the slope of a cheek,* "I know it's hard to ask this from you, but don't be scared. You're safe as long as you're with me, so if you're strugglin' to trust in anything, trust in *that.* Trust that m'gonna make sure nothin' gets you."

Nica's eyes dart all around his face then, unsure of where to rest *unsure of whether to believe him or not,* and their tongue darts out briefly in a pink flash before their teeth start gnawing at their lower lip, "H-How can you be so *s-sure?* It's- things go *w-wrong- acci-dents happen- c-can't control it all-* s-so *how* can you be so s-sure nothin' bad'll happen *to m-me? T-To you?* Who's to say w-we won't step out that door an' immediately get *got?*"

Valid questions, *valid fears,* but rocking back onto his heels, Etienne begins the arduous task of getting to his feet.

"*Because-* that's what I do. I told you before. *I'm a Boudreaux.* An' that's what we're here to do, *defend the defenseless.*" He says with conviction, ignoring the way his stiff joints ache and how the blood loss makes him so dizzy, braces a scabbed over palm

✦✦ 419 ✦✦

against his thigh as he pushes himself all the way upright, "That's my purpose, *that's the entire reason I was born,* and I'm *not* about to go an' disgrace my birthright again. I've already lost too many lives tonight, m'not about to lose another."

Etienne holds out a hand for them, *left hand this time remember how they shied away with their right,* and answers them more honest than he thinks he's ever answered anything, "I can't do this without you, Nica. The plan isn't shit without the two of us an' I know that no matter how scared you may be, you're not gonna let these people down. You said it yourself- *you're a Caldwell...*you don't leave anyone behind either."

We're the same we're the same Mothers of the Night Above but we're the same in this, pounds through his head *through his heart,* and he flexes his fingers just a little, begging them to meet him halfway, "I can't imagine what all this must be like for you, *all the stress you must be under,* b-but I trust you. M'trustin' you to do your part because I know you can do it, so now trust in *me* to do *mine.* I can do this. I *can* keep you safe...*I won't let you fall.*"

It's hard to describe the charge that cracks between them both, but Nica jolts, Etienne twitches, *they each felt it,* and slowly, *hesitantly an inch at a time,* Nica reaches out for him with a shaking hand, their smooth palm gently brushing past his cut up one, his fingers trying to be careful where they wrap once more over Nica's burnt wrist, and it's barely a puff of breath as they look up at him with maroon burning bright in their eyes and whisper, *"O-Okay."*

Etienne goes to help them up then, and even though Nica ends up doing most of the work actually getting themself off the floor, he thinks they appreciate the gesture nonetheless, thumb sweeping soft but quick over his arm in something like thanks.

He flexes his fingers back in kind and their lips quirk up with a small smile, an expression he finds himself mirroring, both of them swaying closer together, *world narrowing heart rate picking up you kinda wanna,* until someone else in the room starts coughing and Etienne remembers very suddenly where he is at the same time Nica seems to as well, and they both stumble apart, talking fast

What Goes Bump In The Night

over one another-

"M-Mo çé ariyin d- *I-I just-* sorry, a-are you good now? You bon? *V-Vou good, fuck-* you good to um, *you good to-*"

"Yeah! *Y-Yeah yup mmhm yeah,* I- totally yeah so much good *fine* I'm- I mean- yeah sorry, m'good I'm-"

"Good! Good, good to hear that, that's- *really good that's-*"

"Y-Yep! *F-For sure-* I'm good, *y-you're good,* let's uh, let's get- w-why don't you tell me what the plan-?"

"Oh- *yeah!* Y-Yeah, sure of course so um, I was thinkin' that..."

Etienne has never been more grateful to talk about concrete and malignant spirits before, and, face on fire, runs quick through what he'd been working on while he was sketching out his recursive energy loop.

The plan is still largely the same, they're just going to have to relocate to the basement to do the sendforth ritual, and after making sure he repacked the supplies he took out earlier, Etienne walks Nica through his rough sketch of the process. Step one is already in progress- *distract tordu with fake sendforth ritual,* the little recursion loop he's got going on the one side of the room should do in a pinch, and then after it's sufficiently ensconced, step two would be- *sneak out of here and make way to basement,* a task *neither* of them is looking forward to but is largely unavoidable.

Step three gets a little more nebulous, but boils down to- *Nica preps for cool alchemy shit,* which segways nicely into step three point five- *you keep the tordu from killing both of you while Nica does cool alchemy shit,* and assuming they're still alive after that, on from there to step four, five, *and* six- *you do cool magic shit, tordu gets trapped hurrah, blasto huge ass hole in wall to drag everyone to safety-*

And *boom,* there you have it.

Mission accomplished.

✦✦ 421 ✦✦

"Sounds very uh, *technical.*" Nica quips with a roll of their eyes, trying to seem all cocky and sure, but their fingers dance a nervous staccato against their arm, something that sounds vaguely like rain drumming against a tin roof, "Are you *s-sure* that torpo thing is gonna fall for your loop-de-loop though? *Like-* n-not tryin' to doubt you or anything but it just- i-it just seemed really hellbent on killin' us all earlier, so s'it *really* gonna be distracted by that lil'blinkin' thing over there?"

They gesture at the softly thrumming sigil behind him in question, and Etienne half turns to look at it, which him doing so somehow coincides *perfectly* with this loud thud that reverberates through the room just over his shoulder, moaning and wailing much louder now as the Aratus ward groans under the invigorated assault from the tordu, and he looks back at Nica with a smug little grin.

It takes every ounce of willpower Etienne has not to say *I told you so,* especially once Nica mutters, "Don't you *fuckin'* start-"

"*Me? I* don't know *what* you're talkin' about, I haven't said *a single word.*" Etienne drawls through an overly delighted grin, traipses past Nica and grunts as he's elbowed none too softly in the side, though the sharp jab is mellowed out by a giggly snort, "You didn't have to. S'written all over your *stupid cat bastard face.*"

"Ouch, that one hurt, Caldwell. Really truly."

"Well tough it up then, spooks, you're an adult. You can take a hit."

Etienne begs to differ, was about to whine back in the way he *knows* irritates Oliver and Katie, *no I'm not I don't wanna can't you do it for me,* but forgets what he was going to say entirely when a shadowy figure lurches in front of their path. He instinctually throws an arm out, stepping quick in front of Nica, mind whirring fast trying to figure out how to deal with this new threat when he realizes it's *not* actually some ghoul or creature of the night, but rather something *much* more mundane and *much more irritating,* and drops his arm with a heavy sigh, *"Carter-"*

What Goes Bump In The Night

"Is this some kinda *joke* to you?" The foreman snaps, and Etienne is so taken aback by the random accusation, he can't come up with anything to say at first, leaves what Carter apparently assumes is a telling silence considering he seethes, *"What the hell's wrong with you?* Are you even takin' this *seriously?* Y'all've been over there, *titterin' like schoolgirls,* w-while the rest of us are coughin' an' dyin' and that- *thing,* is still wailin' out there trying to-!"

"Okay first off it's called *gallows humor,* and it's how we're *coping*- and secondly, we're literally going to go take care of the situation right now, you...*oh what was it*...ah, yes. *You dense motherfucker.*" Etienne enunciates in a bored sounding deadpan, nailing beat for beat the way Carter snapped at him earlier, and the man must recognize it, clicks his mouth shut with a hollow sound. He stands frozen for a beat or two in front of them, hands clenching and unclenching at his side, like he can't decide what he wants to do next, *like he's not sure where to go from here,* and Etienne regards him warily, not sure where this is going either.

Eventually though, after some internal debate, Carter's shoulders sag noticeably, and he doesn't exactly move out of their way, but Etienne still takes that to mean he's done letting his last little bit of steam off, goes to step around him and mutters, *"Okaaay then*...well, for the *last time,* you really shouldn't be on your feet. Go sit down an' we'll be back to get you in a few-"

"M'sorry..."

Etienne actually stumbles forward like he's been struck on the back of the head, whips around and very nearly smacks right into a wide eyed Nica as he says incredulous over their head, "W-What'd you just *say to me-?"*

"I said, I'm...*sorry.*" Carter bites out dejectedly, like each syllable *pains* him to say it, and one dragging step at a time, he slowly turns to face a gob smacked Etienne, "Listen, m'never gonna like you, an' I'm never gonna like your order, and I have the *right* to speak out 'bout that. The way you people do things is fucked up, an' I will *never* be in support of it...but I...I-I shouldn't've said what I did to you. And I apologize."

✦✦ 423 ✦✦

"I- *w-what?*" Etienne stammers, too dumfounded to really process the words being spoken at him, and clearly not liking his reaction, Carter defaults to his fallback setting whenever Etienne seems to be concerned, *anger.*

"For the love of- don't you know w-what an *apology is?* G-Goin' on to me about propriety an' human decency an' all that *bullshit-* but then when a man looks *y-you* in the eyes an' says he's *sorry you c-can't even-!*"

"I *know* what an *apology is-* I just-" Etienne shakes his head, chains on his hat clinking softly like they're the whispers from equally as surprised bystanders, "I just never thought I'd hear one...*from you,* of *all* people, after everythin' you said, and you *uh,* y-you said *a lot...*"

"And I never thought you'd save my life after...a-after everythin' I said either." Carter murmurs astonishingly subdued, coughs roughly into the crook of his elbow and then looks back up at Etienne with a deep kind of begrudging respect in his eyes, "M'not an idiot, I know when a-a debt is owed, an' I-I know if you get my guys outta here, I'll owe you an even *bigger one*...I just don't know how I'll ever be able to repay it. An' I *don't* wanna owe you *shit.*"

The first thing that leaps to Etienne's tongue is the insistence that Carter doesn't owe him anything, actually, that there's no repayment needed for someone just doing the right thing, but then he thinks about it, and realizes there is something he'd ask of the man.

"Well..." Etienne starts, rolling the words around his mouth to get a feel for them before he starts laying them out slowly, one at a time with careful hands, "There is one thing you could do, an' it's no small thing but...*learn. Listen.* Hear the voices of the Occult an' *try* to understand where we're comin' from. We're not some faceless monsters of the night...we're here to *help you. To protect you.* To keep the balance between mundane and arcane and bring *order.*"

There's a beat or two of quiet, in which Etienne is painfully aware of the tordu digging at that one Aratus ward, each drag of it's gnarled, *broken hands* feeling like it's pushing up against his skin

What Goes Bump In The Night

from the inside, and he's about to cut his losses with Carter, *tell him to forget it move on- you need to forget it move on you have more important things to be doing,* when the man sneers and shakes his head.

"I-Is that what you call it? *Bringin' order?*" Carter murmurs, and even though he's not acting as combative as he has been at other times tonight, there's still that *raging seething* fire at the core of him, *"Pah-* order, huh? An' I guess the price for that is o-our kids? You claim to care about us so much an' yet y'all go and deliberately break up families? T-Take babies from their mothers? *S'not right-"*

"See that's what I mean. You've got it twisted. Children are *chosen* to be a part of the coven, they're not *taken*. It's a high honor to receive a Night Mother's blessing." Etienne corrects gently, thinks of the markings under his own eyes, *the ones he feels so deeply proud of.*

The aspect of claiming is something he's had to explain a lot before, because, *for whatever reason,* it always seems to be a concept some humans struggle to grasp, and it's no surprise that Carter is one of them, the man scoffing bitterly, "An *honor?* That's really what you're- yeah...o-okay. *Sure.* Ya'know...there are...*a-a lotta words,* I'd use to describe that day Shyann was *'chosen', the day where I-I had to try an' console my sister while she cried over her lost child...*but *honor* ain't one of them."

And he doesn't want to, but Etienne feels the pull of something unpleasant squirming in his gut at that.

A niggling sort of guilt tugging at him, whispering things he doesn't have the patience to hear, but it's gone almost as soon as it cropped up, *crushed* beneath the understanding that this is the way things are and that they're all better off for it.

Carter just...*isn't getting that.*

He doesn't understand what it's like for witches, how nothing feels more right for them than being with their own kind, that it's not exactly something they can just *stop being* or *stop doing,* but is something so fundamentally a part of who they are, there is *never*

✦✦ 425 ✦✦

any going back.

Which is a lot of nuance to explain in not that much time.

And he really shouldn't be taking the time for this anyway, *he doesn't have it,* but still, Etienne can't shake the feeling that he *has* to do this, *has to make Carter understand that he is wrong,* "I'm...*sorry,* you feel that way, but you've got to know this is honestly what's best for your niece. She'll be happier with her coven, amongst her *own kind,* rather than with humans who don't even understand what it is that she *needs.*"

"What she *needs.* Is her *family.*" Carter grits out and Etienne can't stop himself from rolling his eyes, "And she has it. Her coven will care for her an' love her more than you could *possibly understand.* She will lead a life of *purpose* and *fulfillment,* will be doted on, *looked after...*don't you want that for her? For her to be with people that know her *an' love her unconditionally?*"

To him, it's an easy enough answer.

He thinks about his own family, *his own coven house,* how he grew up knowing *every fiber of his being* was seen and understood *and loved,* and can't imagine a better life than the one he's led. This is the way it goes, how things are supposed to be done, *witches raise witches humans raise humans,* and it's *fair* that way, but he doesn't think Carter is getting it, watches a whole host of riotous emotions play across the man's face before something finally gives and then it's all gone, nothing left besides a blank, exhausted apathy.

"We're not- y-you don't- *just*...whatever. Get my crew outta here as soon as you can." Carter shakes his head with a tired, rattling exhale, and turns on his heel, tottering off back towards the center of the room, barely there whisper slipping out of his mouth as he goes, "...*we would've loved her t-too ya'know.*"

And somehow, his dismissal of the entire thing leaves Etienne feeling worse than anything else has all night. The sensation of something hot and bubbly starts to ooze across his skin then, rolling up the back of his neck and puddling deep in the divots of his eye sockets, *yanks loose his aorta collapses his ventricles,* and

✦✦ 426 ✦✦

What Goes Bump In The Night

Etienne refuses to name the feeling even though he knows what it's called.

~~Shame.~~

~~Guilt.~~

~~Wrongdoing.~~

You're not getting it, he wants to shout at Carter's sloped back, *you're not getting it you're not getting it she's happier she's better there with them with us,* a frantic desperation building under his lungs that he doesn't understand but that he wants to make Carter *understand,* to *prove they know what's best, she's one of us magic in her blood power in her lungs where else does she go nowhere else she belongs don't get to mourn don't get to miss don't get to long for what's not yours you don't get to have her you dON'T-*

It is suddenly such an all consuming need to explain this to him, *make him see make him see he's wrong you're right make him see,* that Etienne unthinkingly steps after the man, would probably have kept trying to argue his position until Carter acknowledged he was right, until he agreed, *until he gave in,* but Nica grabs him around the elbow and pulls him up short, "Hey- *what're you doin'? Leave'im.* We don't have time to deal with his shit."

"But I just...*o-one second...*" Etienne mutters, only half paying attention, spends a second longer staring after where Carter went, crouched down low talking to a few haggard looking members of his crew, and still can't shake off that feeling of desperate need. What is he not understanding, *what is he not getting humans get to raise humans witches should get to raise witches it's fair it's how it's supposed to be so why does he act like you did something bad like he's the victim like you're in the wr-* and Nica has to tug him a few times to fully pull him out of his own head.

"Etienne-"

"Y-Yes, right, *sorry.* I'm coming." He assures, and with one last lingering look he can't control, Etienne firmly turns his back on Carter. He shoots Nica an apologetic look then, knows their time is

✦✦ 427 ✦✦

valuable and he shouldn't be wasting it, and they give him a flicker of a smile in return, an expression that could only barely be called a *grin* over a *grimace*.

There's something in it though, the shadow of some other emotion, but Etienne can't figure out what it is before it's gone, and so he just chalks it up to lingering nerves for what they're about to do. It makes sense that Nica would still be anxious over the plan anyway. For all his insisting that things are going to be fine, Etienne really doesn't know if they will be or not, can't truthfully control every aspect of this dangerous situation, and Nica isn't blind to that reality either.

But, *even so,* despite that obviously concerned look, *the way their fingers pick at one another,* Nica follows along after him as he makes his way towards the door, steps unfaltering, and it's honestly amazing how willing they are to go through with this anyway. Etienne is finally able to really appreciate how brave they are then, knew they had the capacity for it in the heat of the moment, but this slow kinda deliberateness is the truest test of someone's character and unsurprisingly, *just like their classes,* Nica is passing it with flying colors as well.

"We'll be done before you know it, an' then this'll all be nothin' but a bad dream." Etienne promises, hovering just up against the door to try and pinpoint *exactly* where the tordu is and gauge how focused it is on his recursion loop, "In an' out. Fast, simple, *done.* We just gotta keep *reeeal quiet* an' we shouldn't have *aaaany* problems...simply lay low and keep your mind neutral. If you don't believe you're a threat, it won't either, *an' we'll slip right on by.*"

"Y-You make it seem so *easy.*" Nica murmurs shaky and thankfully, it sounds like the tordu is still in the same spot, clawing futilely at the brunt of an Aratus ward on the other side of the room. If Etienne is remembering the layout of the building correctly, that would put it a little ways down the hall from them, almost tucked around the corner into the main atrium where this all started. Which isn't a *ton* of space between them and the abomination, *maybe a scant two dozen feet,* but it's the most Etienne is going to be able to weasel free given the circumstances.

What Goes Bump In The Night

He hopes it's enough, but the time for hoping and wishing and wanting is drawing to a close, *I suppose* and *I think,* needing to be traded out for *I'm sure* and *I know.*

Soon, it'll be the time for doing, *for action,* and Etienne looks back at Nica, like he has done so many times tonight, and maybe he'll never get used to still finding them there, forever surprised they haven't run yet, but it means more to him than they'll probably ever know that they haven't.

That they're still here with him.

Etienne wants to tell them that, *he wants to tell them a lot of things,* make sure they understand that he knows he was wrong about them, but none of it matters unless it's spoken in the light of day freed from this place, so he bites his tongue for now, asking instead, "Where are we meetin' Monday?"

And he doesn't ask because he doesn't know the answer, he *asks* because there's honestly nothing else left to say.

They've done everything they possibly could to work the odds out into their favor, have to trust in each other if not in themselves now and make that leap of faith, take the chance *accept the risks,* see if they plummet completely to an early grave or not. Etienne isn't exactly pessimistic over their chances, but he's not about to fill their heads with false optimisms either, knows the task ahead is dangerous no matter how careful they are.

Putting your life on the line is a lot to ask of somebody, he is very much aware of that, and maybe if it was someone else, they'd have backed down at this point, but Nica isn't *like* anybody else, steps up so they're shoulder to shoulder and looks him dead in the eye as they recite unerringly, "Monday. Amandine's. *Three-thirty sharp.*"

Even in the near darkness there's something *special* about that look, *about their eyes,* and sure, heterochromia is rare enough on its own, but Etienne can't recall the last time he looked at someone dead on and *knew* they were a fighter, saw resolve burning so bright in a pair of irises, it might as well be its own flame.

✦✦ 429 ✦✦

"Monday, Amandine's, *three-thirty sharp.*" Etienne parrots back quietly, *a promise of his own,* and wonders if Nica has fire to spare.

And with one final entreating thought to the Night Mothers, *please watch over us please guide my hand please get them all home safe,* Etienne wraps his fingers around the doorknob, double checks he has his spellbook for the last time, and then, *without any other reason to stall,* slowly begins to ease the door open.

He blocks the gap with his own body in case something immediately comes rushing in, but the way seems clear so he slips out first, gingerly skating a tendril of magic along the aether. No longer under the protective glow of the Aratus wards, that familiar, pervasive, *sickening cold* feeling bites at him instantly, and a sharp jolt of, *DEATH and ROT and RUINATION and A G O N Y,* cracks into him as it bleeds in undulating waves off the tordu.

Repeating Sabine's mantra to him from all those years ago, *still as glass still as glass keep your mind mirror smooth and still as glass,* Etienne dares to probe deeper, doesn't want to alert the tordu to the fact that something is amiss, but wants to get a handle on its current state.

He can't exactly read the minds of spirits, but he can get a sense for their intentions through the aether, and when he reaches out now, he's hit with buffeting wave of *anger* after *anger,* so *much torment and suffering,* it makes him a little sick to the stomach.

Get them kILL THEM RIP them APART make them feel this mAKE THEM FEEL THIS MAKE THEM MAKE THEM hate this hate HERE hate being hate THEM hate us hate uS HATE US HATE HATE H A T E B E I N G A L I V E, the maelstrom wails, a dozen voices all screaming slightly out of sync but warped together as one, and, not as reluctantly as you might imagine, Etienne does feel a sharp stab of sympathy for the abomination.

It may be a terrifying monstrosity now, but it wasn't always like this. It used to be people, *still is to some degree,* and they never wanted this for themselves. They had no control over their fates, died under miserable circumstances and never knew their anguish

What Goes Bump In The Night

would lead them here, *trapped,* for almost a century. Which, is bad enough on its own, but then they were provoked and fed and *tormented* to the point that, they figured it was better to suffer in eternity together rather than carry this burden alone.

And his heart breaks for these spirits, *it really does it kills him to know how this has to end for them once mother knows,* but he can't give in to his tenderhearted nature, *he just can't,* or it'll get everyone in here killed. Etienne knows he's something of a bleeding heart, but he has to be an *exorcist* right now, not a *wayfarer,* and while he's kinda supposed to be a little bit of everything as scion, *exorcist summoner wayfarer archivist,* this situation calls for a firmer hand, *a little more unbending of a will.*

It demands the resolve to do what needs to be done and to not second guess that decision.

They're too far gone to be saved anyway, he reminds himself as he draws that coil of magic back in a little closer, *there's nothing more you can do for them,* and with a grimace, he pushes out his sympathies and tender compassions.

A light poke comes to his back then and Etienne knows without having to be told what Nica's asking, *everything alright what's the hold up you okay,* and being careful to not let too much flicker across his mind, he nods his head slowly and deliberately.

Thankfully, the tordu doesn't appear to have noticed that anything has changed, is still trying to breach the Aratus ward where the recursion loop is going, and stepping further out into the hall, Etienne beckons Nica to follow him with a few crooking fingers.

It's still black as pitch out here since all the lights got burned out, and while he *could* make a guide light, Etienne worries if even that brief pop of magic will be enough to draw the tordu's attention or not. He figures it's better not to risk it. Besides, Etienne is fairly confident he knows the way, at least until they get to the basement, and maybe once they start down that way, he can signal to Nica that they should pull their phone out and use it as a light if things are still hairy.

✦✦ 431 ✦✦

At the moment though, Etienne is hesitant to communicate anything like that with the tordu literally *right* around the corner, but his eyes have started adjusting and he can pick his way over the floor well enough, and the moment he starts out the door is when he sees all the marks.

They're long, *deep,* thick troughs of splintering wood and crumbling plaster marring the floor and walls, rent open by the broken, claw like fingernails of the tordu as it attempted to get past his wards. Etienne looks at them with a sour taste in his mouth, *the destruction they caused,* and has the brief flash of those marks raking across a body.

Of course, he has experience with that, has his own arm for reference, the flesh puckered and nearly stripped from the bone, *knows the dark color blood gets when too much of it is spilling free has felt it soaking into his shirt sleeve that's why we wear it's practical,* and with those little scraps at its disposal, his brain more than happily builds a possibility for him.

Should he fail-

There's himself with three deep gouges slashed across his stomach, hands slippery and too red *red red,* fingers desperately trying to keep his pale pink insides on the *inside.* There's Reggie, *chunks missing from his face as he gazes at you hollow,* teeth dipped in burgundy and grinning a ghoulish smile despite him not having lips anymore. *There's Nica,* metal fist clenching and unclenching, what used to be a dozen different colors all one shade of *carmine slicked magenta white points of their ribs curled up out of their chest like the shriveled legs of a dead bug help me why didn't you help me-*

Etienne's heart stutters and without meaning to, so do his feet, toe of his boot getting caught on the rough edge of some broken part of the floor, and he goes stumbling forwards. *His heart stops.* He can see it in his mind, he's going to go crashing down onto his knees, make a *ton of noise* that's impossible to ignore, the tordu is going to come shrieking over here and reintroduce itself and *kill them all Etienne you idiot-*

What Goes Bump In The Night

And the only reason *none* of that happens is because something stops him before he can, fists itself in the material of his shirt and yanks him back *hard.*

He doesn't need to look to know it's Nica, just clamps his mouth shut tight so he doesn't make that involuntary gasp he was going to make, and waits, hardly daring to breathe. It seems like it's quiet for *forever.* Etienne can't tell if he's just imagining things because of panic or if it really has grown that silent, tries to hear past the furious pounding in his head and only comes back with crackling static and the understanding that his lack of coordination might've just killed them both.

After what feels like an eternity but is realistically only a few seconds, there's a low echoing moan and Nica slowly unfists their hand from his shirt, hanging on just long enough to make sure Etienne has found his balance again. They kinda slap him across the shoulder blades once they're sure he's not about to fall on his face, and Etienne does look back then with an apologetic wince, is met with an evolving array of facial expressions from Nica that quite clearly convey, *what the fuck dude.*

Sorry, he mouths, pointing down at his feet next with an awkward shrug, *clumsy,* which is sort of the understatement of the year, but he doesn't really think he's got enough time to explain the extent of what it's like living with two left feet.

Nica rolls their entire head at that though, because apparently, their eyes alone just aren't enough this time, and without turning around, reaches behind them to softly shut the door to the old classroom. It latches in place with nary a click, and they motion for him to lead on, which Etienne makes sure he does *very carefully.*

One cautious step at a time, he picks his way down the dark corridor, trying to balance being both mindful on where he's stepping and also picking his pace up, doesn't want to be out here, *essentially unprotected,* for any longer than they have to be.

His spellbook bumps against his hip as he moves, a comforting weight *and* a gentle reminder that he is anything but defenseless,

✦✦ 433 ✦✦

and he tries to ground himself in the solid heft of it. *You can do this you are strong you have a plan just stick to it,* he repeats in his mind like a warding spell, but Etienne isn't entirely delusional, knows he couldn't survive another round of one on one with the tordu. Sometimes though, it's the *idea* that does more than acknowledging the reality, like the more sure he is of himself, *the more he believes he can do this,* the more likely it is that they'll have a positive outcome.

Which sounds delusional in and of itself, but is supposed to be a *'helpful'* holdover from Cynin and small glass vials and a plush armchair he sank too far into for his own comfort. Etienne never put much stock in the whole *verbal affirmations thing,* could only stand in front of a mirror for so long avoiding his own eye contact while he said, *I am capable I am smart I am enough,* before he felt like an idiot. For some reason though, that kind of thinking feels like it fits into this situation better than it ever did back in his bathroom at Maisette, and maybe Etienne is *just* desperate enough to indulge the strategies of his old therapist like he never cared to before.

You can do this you are strong you have a plan, cycles by again and maybe it's because there's real stakes at play here, or maybe it's because he knows his magic feeds off his emotions and if he's telling himself he *can't* do it, why they hell would his magic *ever* follow through, but Etienne actually finds his lingering nerves dissipating.

He *has* to do this, so what other choice is there other than that he *does do it?* And there is a certain amount of comfort in *inevitability,* makes him feel like he's standing on more stable ground as he slinks down the dilapidated hallway, mind still as glass and reflecting back nothing save for what looks into it, but underneath, a steady eddy of, *you're capable you can do this believe in yourself,* swirls past in a current strong like the ocean's tides.

And you know what, Etienne *can* do this.

He is the scion of House Boudreaux, he *is* the son of Matriarch Catherine Amélie, and he's *going* to get everyone still trapped in this building *out alive.*

✦✦ 434 ✦✦

What Goes Bump In The Night

Feeling some shade of confidence again is refreshing. It adds pep to his step, dulls the aching pulse of the laceration running down his arm, and makes the bleak corridor before him appear less than so.

Etienne hasn't been this sure of himself since that first cold prickle ran down his spine, at the beginning of the night, where he assumed this wasn't anything and he'd have it taken care of before dawn broke, and it is...*something* of a surprise when *disquiet* slimes so unexpectedly soon into his mind like an oil slick.

At first, he just assumes it's his own anxieties coming back for another round of kicking him until he's down, but his pulse remains calm and his hands aren't shaking and Etienne is something of an expert when it comes to his own neurotic breakdowns, knows immediately this isn't from *him*. He touches at it, trying to figure out where it's coming from, and *malaise* coats his thoughts and suspicions, reeks like grave rot and burns like a winter storm, and there can only be one source.

The tordu.

It unnerves him from the get-go even though it's barely anything, a puff of an exhale of hardly a breath, just the featherlike slide of its reaching mind, *cold* and *damp*, as it caresses across the surface of his own consciousness. Etienne doesn't quit walking, but he stops paying as much attention to what's in front of him as opposed to *what's behind him*, keeps the waters of his mind calm despite the film slowly coating everything. He's hesitant to poke at it again, is concerned that'll just more firmly draw the tordu's attention where he *really* doesn't want it, and thinks that, *maybe*, if he ignores it, *pretends it's not there*, the ooze of its thoughts will slide right back out just like how it slid in to shadow his mind.

Like a cloud moving to block the sun, give it time, *and it'll just pass on its own.* That is not, however, what happens.

There aren't words at first. It's just the reaching, far shores of the abomination's collective consciousness, but as it drips more and more into Etienne's mind, each rolling slosh of its thoughts leaves snippets and pieces behind. *Who are...don't want...leave here,* sighs through his ears in phantom whispers, the overlapping voices of the spirits warped and muddied as they rush in and out of his mind, *can't feel...where are...don't leave...*

Etienne valiantly pretends like he doesn't hear any of it, would plug his ears if that would help in the slightest, and keeps his eyes fixed straight ahead, *mind trained with them,* just letting the ever increasing thoughts from the tordu slop around his skull like it'd be empty otherwise, *cold...it hurts...where is...don't feel...can't leave...who are...you...are...know...you...know you...knoW YOU-*

Interest suddenly blooms through Etienne's mind like a poisonous flower, and for all the things the tordu's been mumbling, he's tried to just let them pass through without thinking about any too much, but that last thought snags in him like a fishhook. Ripples dance across the waters of his consciousness and he fights to settle it. *Still as glass still as glass keep your mind mirror smooth and still as glass you're not here there's nothing here you don't know us move on,* he pushes back against those questing thoughts gently but insistent, a firm bulwark that ends up doing very little as scores of rotting fingers prickle at the top.

KNow you KNOW YOU you are...same HURT...same PAIN...SAME RUINATION, a dozen or so voices mutter, all slightly off from the others so it creates a distorted echo as the tordu starts hauling more of its mind forwards, *know YOU KNOW you one was two is not really one same it's the same WE'RE THE SAME.* Etienne has no idea what it's talking about, can't pull sense from this stream of nonsense the tordu is subjecting him to, but it sounds almost hysterical with relief or some sick sense of...*gratitude?* Like it's found great comfort in a kinship Etienne can't understand and doesn't care to, thoughts growing more erratic and forceful as they clamber over his walls and completely trample through the sanctity of his mind.

Parts together parts apart parts apart together in pieces and parts, the collective consciousness of the tordu babbles like an insane thing, and Etienne tenses as he feels *attention* fixate on him, *in pieces TOGETHER aparts LOST in pieces in parts ONCE*

What Goes Bump In The Night

TOGETHER ONCE LOST, muscles drawing taught when he gets the sensation of *eyes* burning into his back, magic crackling painfully to life at the spectral hands pawing at him, *mentally clawing over him,* the sonorous voice of power in his core hissing *get back GET BACK GET BACK don't touch HIM get BACK-*

One plus ONE IS two IS ONE you are to WE ARE TO you are again together apart PARTS TOGETHER, howls through his mind in complete disregard to his warning, cacophony of voices manic with frantic glee and the elation of some discovery that can only be born of pure madness, *us is we is YOU IS ME one plus one IS TWO IS ONE KNOW YOU KNOW YOU KN O W Y O U,* and Etienne gets ready to blast the thing with whatever he has left when it goes for him, can feel the intention to grab, to *maim, to possess-* hanging in the air like an executioner's blade waiting to fall, readies himself for an attack and then at the last second the-!

...sensation moves on.

It passes him over.

Drifts free from his mind like a stray leaf sailing by.

What in the-

He is confused and relieved for all of a second, has the mental impression of hands clambering over him, *of all those eyes turning away not you not you...not interested in you,* and doesn't know what to make of it when the tordu heaves the bulk of its consciousness away from his, *like it's using him as a stepladder as a boost like it's trying to get to something else,* until he hears a soft intake of breath and remembers he's not alone.

Mothers of the Night...*he's not alone-*

Etienne spins on his heel and finds Nica a few paces behind him, unharmed for now, but frozen in place and as white as a sheet. Their hands are fisted and twisted up in the front of their windbreaker, legs shaking so bad, it's making all of them tremble. Mismatched eyes frantically jump to his, blown wide by unrelenting *panic* and unsettling *fear,* and it's clear that, even though

✦✦ 437 ✦✦

Nica doesn't have as strong a connection as Etienne does to the paranormal, *they're still feeling something see yoU know yOu want yOU,* and it's *scaring them.*

"E...*E-Etienne-*" Nica whispers hoarse and desperate, terrified tears thick in their voice and further down the hall, something seems to moan low in response, *slick slide of decomposing flesh against old boards wet slap of a palm against a wall aRe you coMing kNoW yOu shouLD wanT yoU hEre,* and Nica flinches like they heard it too, all but begging him, "H-Help. *M-Me-*"

Problem is he doesn't *know* how to help them, never considered this when they were coming up with plans, *that Nica would be a target,* not when it could have him, *thought it would come for you first why isn't it coming for you first,* but that is clearly not the case. Do they stay quiet? Hope if they don't react it'll simply grow bored and move on? Or should they fight. Should Etienne call up what magic he has left and make his stand while Nica continues on to the basement, hoping he'll be right on their heels?

Or do they just run-

An inquisitive wail echoes down the hallway before Etienne can make a decision, cold chill seeping out along with it, frosts the air and numbs his fingers *makes both their panicking breaths puff white,* and he doesn't know if he should be reaching for his spellbook or one of Nica's hands, *doesn't know what's right,* and ends up watching like the world is falling out below his feet as a lumpy, misshapen head drags itself into the open mouth at the opposite end of the corridor.

It moans in question, distorted voices bubbling up like sludge in Etienne's ears, *wAnt you neEd YOU come HERE-*

Oh...*oh fuck-*

"*E- Etienne-*" Nica whispers again, more urgent this time, and they haven't turned around to look, *probably can't,* keep their panicked eyes trained on him, but seem to understand the peril they're in anyway, flinching every time the tordu groans, the same looping thoughts echoing through both of their skulls, *whO aRe yoU you*

✦✦ 438 ✦✦

What Goes Bump In The Night

arE kNow yOu wANt you neED yoU kNoW yOU COME HERE-

One of them has to do *something,* and with the way Nica is practically shaking apart in front of him, Etienne supposes it falls solely on his shoulders, *the witch in training the would-be exorcist.* And he's meant to trust his gut because of that, *is supposed to trust his judgment calls,* but his mind is in a dozen directions and his heart is in his throat and everything is happening way too fast and yet also *way too slow,* and Etienne worries he's going to freeze like he did earlier, *is going to show his true colors as the coward he really is-*

And then the tordu drags itself more firmly into the hall, one broken to hell hand wrapping over the side of the doorway and crunching old plaster, dozen mouths hanging agape and wheezing harshly, and the two of them get hit with another wave of *crushing and CRUNCHING and COMPRESSING one is TWO is ONE AGAIN wANt yOu NEED you C O M E H E R E,* and everything snaps into startling focus like pieces of a puzzle cracking together.

Etienne doesn't hesitate.

He lurches forwards, snags one of Nica's trembling hands and pulls them towards him, *pushing them past him,* his magic flaring to life like a beacon right as the tordu howls in mindless rage and he fights to scream over it, *"RUN!"*

Both their shoes scuff wildly against the floor, muscles bunching and expanding rapidly as they take off sprinting down the shadowed hallway, the entire building shaking around them as the tordu thunders after in pursuit. Etienne can't think, it's all a racing blur of darkness and more blackness and the frozen damp breath of a monster panting over the back of his neck. He let go of Nica almost as soon as he grabbed them but makes sure they stay ahead of him now, just so that if either one of them gets hit, his back will be the one that takes the brunt of the blow instead of theirs.

Nica gets to the stairwell first and misses a few treads with how fast they go flying down it, Etienne hot on their heels and the tordu *even hotter on his.*

✦✦ 439 ✦✦

The abomination screeches in tormented joy at having almost caught up to its quarry, frozen spittle striking the back of Etienne's neck and he's got to get this thing away from them, pulls his spellbook into his hands and flips to his sigil page on muscle memory alone. He can see the layout crystal clear in his mind, blindly reaches for what he's pretty sure is a repulsion sigil and spins on the balls of his feet to cast it, hoping the tordu isn't *right* behind him.

The tordu is right behind him.

It's just as foul as he unfortunately remembers, translucent rotting skin and dark craterous eyes, saliva hanging stringy between cracked teeth that clack together like rattling train trestles while it bears down on him. Etienne needs clear space for the spell to land, and there really isn't anywhere he's standing at the top of the stairs, so he does the most logical thing he can think of and throws himself back, *down the stairwell,* activating the sigil in midair.

Power blooms painfully from his fingers, feels like liquid fire racing through his veins, but now that he's no longer occupying those scant few feet, there's enough room for him to flick the spell into being, maroon lines cracking across the floorboards like fractaling lightning. The repulsion sigil balloons to life, a glowing dome of softly pulsating reddish light that thrums with a steady beat of energy, and the tordu slams full tilt into it, brute forces itself about halfway through before it gets snagged.

It screams its outrage, fists alternating as it beats at the undulating waves of crackling force pushing it back, and it may be pissed over the whole situation but Etienne is *proud.*

He's surprised beyond measure that his magic is still managing to hold that thing back, honestly, didn't think he put much power into the sigil, is trying to conserve what he can, *is trying to avoid burnout,* and sure it feels like a knife to the heart every time the tordu punches it, and *yeah,* the sigil *is* cracking, but all in all its keeping together when he really didn't expect it to.

And Etienne can't help grinning like a fool about it...which *would* be an apt description actually, considering he just flung himself

What Goes Bump In The Night

down a flight of stairs, and now that he doesn't have a spell to cast, he's starting to realize that might not have been the best call.

Well fuck, Etienne thinks idly while he falls backwards through the air, starts trying to twist so he at least won't land on his ass and shatter his tailbone, when he crashes into something a lot sooner than expected. He winces instinctually, expecting on principle for it to hurt, and blinks his eyes wide in shock once it doesn't. Whatever he hit moves with him but it's also stable enough that it keeps him from falling over, pair of hands gripping his waist before arms follow, wrapping securely around him to help keep him steady, and then it's no longer a mystery.

Warmth blooms across his back for a brief moment as he's held to a sturdy chest, *comfort relief you're here you're here you got my back,* but it's gone all too soon. Etienne is spun around once he's found his footing, Nica's ghastly pale face and shaking hands checking him over for injury, which is really sweet and he sincerely appreciates it, but literally could not matter in the slightest right now. A sharp, splintering pain explodes through his chest, and Etienne grimaces, snaps a quick look behind him, sees the light wavering as the tordu hauls itself backwards out of the sigil's radius, and grabs for Nica again.

"Come on!" He shouts, pulling them towards the next flight of stairs that'll take them to the basement proper, and they clatter down the newer looking treads hand in hand.

Etienne has no idea what to expect going down here. Basements aren't super common in this part of the country and there's no telling what state this one is in, could be even nastier and more detritus filled than the rest of the building. What he ends up finding is a mostly clean but messy warren of half framed out walls, patched up brick supporting pillars that have clearly seen better days, and clusters of dangerous looking construction equipment.

Light filters in orange and grainy from the little half moon windows dotted along the side of the building that faces the street, paradoxically makes it harder to see since it just casts all the shadows darker by comparison.

◆✦◆ 441 ◆✦◆

And it's kinda something of a nightmare.

There's too much to trip over or smack your head into, *little nooks and crannies to find yourself stuck in with death breathing down your neck,* and Etienne starts violently swearing in the privacy of his own brain. Outwardly though, he at least tries to keep his composure, and spins in a circle with his mind jumping from thought to thought, Nica's hand still firmly clasped in one of his. He assumes they're going to need a minute to prep for the reaction, has watched them before twisting the pieces and parts of their prosthesis, adjusting dials and tile sets depending on what they were wanting to do, and knows getting all that ready takes *time.*

And with the tordu yanking its way free of the sigil right over their heads, they don't have many seconds to spare, which means Etienne has got to buy some for them.

He has a few ideas on how to do that, how to throw himself into the line of fire, shifting the tordu's *confusing* attention and ire off Nica, to back where it should be, *on him,* but he's got to find someplace for Nica to hide first. Etienne twists again, and there, close by where the two of them are standing, a slight dip in the half formed walls that might be a utility room one day but is a decent tucked away spot for now.

It's not much in terms of protection, just a few scant inches of sheet rock and two-by-fours, but it gets Nica out of the center of the room and still leaves them in view of the staircase so they can flee if need be.

Something pulls in Etienne's chest at the thought though, sharp pain under his ribs that digs into all the softest parts of his heart, but he can't tell if it's from the tordu shaking free of the repulsion sigil or the image of Nica leaving him down here to *die.* Either way, he doesn't have time to dwell on it, slips his hand free from Nica's and places both of his on their shoulders, walking them back towards the little alcove, "Listen- I need you to stay put an' just focus on your reaction okay? I'll stall as long as I can but, *just- try an' be quick-"*

✦✦✦ 442 ✦✦✦

What Goes Bump In The Night

Nica was letting themself be moved back but they dig their heels in now, throwing their weight forwards so Etienne might as well be pushing on a brick wall for all the good that's doing. They glare up at him, probably less convincing than they're wanting, fear making the expression brittle, and he can hear it too in their voice when they snap, "Are you o-out of your mind? I'm not gonna- I-I can't just- s-stand around, while that thing is a-after me-!"

"It won't be for long, but it's not gonna so much as *touch you*. I said it earlier- *I won't let anythin' hurt you*." Etienne defends hotly, winces at the tearing sensation that rips through his body, feels a release of power next that soothes his fraying nerves and knows then his sigil has broken, "I don't have time to argue about this with you. Just focus on your reaction an' let me do my damn job, I'll make sure you're safe."

"But w-what about *you?* You *also* told me earlier there's n-no *way* you can handle that thing on your own, so what makes you think you can do it *n-now?*" Nica argues anyway, somehow always finding the time for it, and Etienne doesn't miss the way their breath fogs as they speak. A freezing shiver darts down his spine next, all the hair on the back of his neck standing at attention, and the temperature in the basement plummets as something swells against the aether like a boil about to burst.

Fuck- it's remembered how to phase, and he throws a harried look to the left, back towards the stairs, *where this thing is about to descend from the floor above like an apocalyptical omen.* Nica must follow his eyes, because Etienne can feel them jolt under his hands, *like they're sensing it too like they understand what's about to happen,* and everything is happening so fast and he's not really thinking about what he's doing, *he just does it,* slides his hand up to cup the back of Nica's neck, gripping them firmly as he turns their head back to face his.

"*Hey,* I need you to *trust me.* I know I've given you no reason to do so, have made an' *absolute fool of myself* tonight an' many others, but...*just- trust me* when I say m'gonna keep you safe." The back of Nica's neck is damp with sweat, their hair coarse where it drags past his fingers, and Etienne feels their pulse hammering

✦✦ 443 ✦✦

away under his thumb, *like a rushing river like driving rain like the thundering beat of his own heart,* absentmindedly strokes down the length of that artery and back up, "Stay here, focus on your reaction. Don't pay attention to anything else that's happenin'. I don't care what you hear or *think you hear,* let me handle it. *Let me take care of this.*"

There are different words hiding under that last set he breathes, but they are too raw and too impulsive and he's too coward to make them true, uses what lame strength he has in comparison and shoves Nica in the direction of the alcove.

Surprisingly, they trip backwards into the tiny space, eyes wide and trained on him, flesh hand gripping the side of their neck where his just was like a lifeline, and it's more desperate than joking when Nica wheezes, *"P-Please* be careful- E-Etienne, *I'm serious.* Just-*please don't do a-anything stupid-"*

And Etienne doesn't respond because he's not in the habit of making promises he doesn't intend to keep, already has his spell-book open and doesn't hesitate casting his last repulsion sigil on the ground between Nica's feet. His magic yanks and protests lividly as it's pulled from his chest, *too much too much have to stop can't keep hauling us up and out it's too much,* but it is a comfort to see maroon wrapping around Nica like a loving embrace. He's hoping that'll be enough of a deterrent for the tordu, making Nica more of an annoyance to get to rather than...say...*him,* especially once Etienne does what he's planning on doing.

Mothers help him, but this is such a *fucking stupid idea,* and not in the way that it's not going to work. It'll probably work too well actually, and all Etienne can hope for is not getting eviscerated immediately, rocks up on his toes and feels his pulse somewhere near the back of his throat. Part of him doesn't want to do this, knows the hurt he's going to cause and is already regretting it, but there isn't any other option.

The tordu is intent on Nica, its desires to *possess consume own-*still bleeding sickly across the veil, and he absolutely cannot let that happen, *has* to make himself the focal point of the abomina-

What Goes Bump In The Night

tion's ire by any means necessary.

Even if that means doing one of the most idiotic things he could possibly do.

Chapter 20

Right about then is when the aether pulls taught at the other end of the room, like a steel ball dropped onto a sheet of stretchy rubber, and feeling out where the tordu is isn't an *exact* science, Etienne can't pinpoint it precisely, but it should be close enough now to hear him, so he sucks in a big gust of air, *and hopes he didn't just sink the last nail into his coffin.*

"*HEY!*" He shouts, planting his feet and gathering the power that remains to him, sends it snapping from him in a crackling burst of snarling spitting *energy,* a threat display and a challenge to fight all rolled into one, "You know what? *I was wrong earlier!* You *do* deserve to be trapped here! In fact- I'm *happy you're trapped here!* You're out of the way and *forgotten* in a moldering hell like all *useless things should be!*"

Instantly, it's like a hundred eyes all violently snap to where he's standing, disquieted *anger* trembling through the air in the same way glass shakes whenever you knock too hard into it, and shifting onto the balls of his feet, Etienne keeps talking, *snide and mean and intentionally mocking,* "What? Didn't like hearin' that? *Well it's true, you miserable sack of rotting flesh-* no one missed you, no one even cared enough to remember where you *died.* That's why you came back in the first place, isn't it? *So desperate to have someone know you were here.*"

A low moan echoes and pitches from everywhere and nowhere, Etienne's breath fogging intensely as thin whisps of frost start creeping along the edges of brick columns and old iron pipes, *malice infusing the air like incense,* but the thing hasn't crawled free from the aether to kill him yet, so he's not done, thinks he knows what'll break it though and works his jaw back and forth before spitting out words that nearly break *him.*

What Goes Bump In The Night

"Well...I hate to be the bearer of bad news, but no one's *ever* gonna remember you. You'll fade into the nothing of reality and there won't be so much as a crumb of your consciousness left. I'll make sure of it. I will *rend you from this plane of existence with a snap of my fingers."* Etienne does snap his fingers then for emphasis, feels the electrical field in the room jump in fright and then a slow building, *inescapable freezing rage,* swelling against reality, and he bounces on his toes, *getting ready to run.*

"You can try an' stop me all you want, *it won't make a difference.* I'm more powerful an' *more important than you ever were,* so this is nothing to me. *You,* are nothing to me." *Not true not true Mothers of the Night you don't mean it,* but it's working, furious hatred un-like any he's ever felt bubbles under the surface of reality, scalding his mind with its freezing malaise a cacophony of voices shrieking *be quiet be quiet bE QUIET BE QUIET STOP IT STOP S T O P,* "No one mourned for you! *No one came for you!* You were forgotten and you will *continue* to be forgotten! Wiped from this plane like *you never even MATTERED AT ALL-!"*

Every single one of his hairs stand on end, each scrap of air in his lungs freezes solid, and call it fight or flight or primal instincts or what have you, but something in Etienne screams at him to dodge to the left and he does so without another thought. A whip fast blur goes streaking past on his right a second later, leathery arm slamming into the floor with enough force it sends massive cracks running through the entire concrete slab, rattles his eyeballs in his skull, and he knows another is coming, twists on the balls of his feet and *runs.*

And with the shriek of a thousand sorrows, *the mangled roar of a hundred burning souls,* the tordu launches the rest of its body free from the aether and gives chase like an out of control train.

Etienne's mind works fast, trying to account for the most likely spot the creature will strike next, *back back it's going to be your back,* and slips in between gaps of some two-by-fours looking for cover. He's barely wiggled through the opening before he hears the crackling splinter of wood exploding behind him, followed by the thundering crash of something large *barreling* through that

✦✦ 447 ✦✦

section of wall next.

Wood chips strike the nape of his neck, *frozen damp panting of a dozen yawning maws wafting across your skin ruffling your hair get H I M KILL H I M pull the FLESH FROM HIS BONES fuck it's too close-*

Out of the corner of his eye though, Etienne sees a dark, blocky shape, *a support pillar,* and pivots sharply on the toes of his boots.

He's thinking since he's smaller and can more easily maneuver, he's gonna be able to duck behind that brick column before the tordu has a chance to course correct, can picture it steaming off and smashing through drywall in its blind fury, which would hopefully put some much needed space between the two.

But Etienne never makes it that far.

Because that same uncomfortable prickling from a moment ago rushes up his spine again, and he hits the floor without entirely being aware of *why,* rolling forward on his arms right as everything shakes and an explosive shower of stone cascades down around him. Rocking up onto his feet in one smooth move, Etienne swipes his hat from the floor and gets half a look at the now obliterated column, *the one the tordu's arm is currently stuck in,* and has the passing thought of that being his torso instead, jerks around to face the tordu with panic simmering at the edges of his mind.

The abomination howls at him, *dead eyes on fire,* and yanks its warped arm free from the rubble, makes like it's going to strike *him* this time, but he claps his shaking hands together, *power igniting under his skin,* and quickly draws them apart to form a crackling net of raw electricity.

It's not an actual spell or anything, *you don't have many of those left and there's no time to go rooting around for one,* but it still makes his body *ache* as he calls his magic up, burns in his veins like intentionally digging fingers into a fresh wound. Reality undulates a bit as he flings the snapping net at the tordu, whatever that lump of energy is supposed to be striking the abomination dead on as its arm comes barreling towards him. The not spell

What Goes Bump In The Night

expands on impact, ensnaring the tordu in a staticky web of jumping, constricting lightning, halting its momentum probably a few feet before Etienne was going to be paste across the floor.

The tordu shrieks upon being hit, thrashes and strains against the maroon bonds that dig into its spectral flesh like barbed wire, but it stays tangled for now and Etienne should be taking this opportunity to run, *really needs to be taking the chance to run,* but he can't quite get his legs to cooperate, is stuck swaying on the spot for a moment longer than he wants.

A sudden wave of fatigue hits him and hits him hard, payback from his body for delving further into his magic than he should have, and sickly heat sweeps through him like the sticky winds of summer. *You're burning yourself up,* some part of his mind ominously whispers, and it may be a warning or it may just be simple fact, *Etienne can't tell,* feels like he's running a fever though as he frantically tries to communicate to his rubbery limbs that they need to be backing away from this thing.

NOW

But his mind is hot mush and his legs might as well be springs for how little they help in moving him anywhere, and all the while, the tordu rips through his pathetic excuse for magic like it's the morning of Yule and it's desperate to see what it got.

Lighting surges through the tordu's form as it pulls at the zapping web encasing it, and maybe earlier in the night, those bolts would've destabilized its connection to this plane, but all it causes now is a brief flicker, a barely there strobing across its body that doesn't stop that *monstrosity* in the slightest.

To be fair, Etienne wasn't expecting his gobbledygook to have done much, *was a lousy attempt at magic by a desperate spellcaster,* but the tordu also wasn't super vexed by his latest repulsion sigil either. It may have gotten stopped for a moment, but ultimately, ripped through that thing in under a minute, and it makes him concerned seeing *just* how ineffective his magic is now. He starts to worry about later, once Nica does their reaction, *when he has to*

✦✦ 449 ✦✦

perform his bootleg sending on when it all comes down to him will he even be able do it can he do it or will he just fuck everything up like before with the dragon with his grandfather's sigil like the crew members he let die ~~like always~~

Etienne shakes his head harshly.

No, he will not sow the seeds of his own destruction, forces the doubts from his mind and the pain from his body, reminds himself of who he is and *why* he's down here and that a little burnout never killed anyone.

Well...

Whatever, that's a worry for future Etienne, ~~if he ever gets there,~~ and until then, what matters the most is continuing to be a good distraction and holding out for maybe five minutes more.

Which, *he can do that,* turns to run before the tordu manages to free itself entirely but overestimated his legs' willingness to bear his weight, has to catch himself on a nearby beam or risk falling to his knees.

C'mon Boudreaux that was just pathetic you can do better than that, a snide challenging voice snips through his ears while the world spins, cadence of it goading but not necessarily hateful, sounds half like indigo markings out in the middle of a scorching hot courtyard and half like jabbing fingers and eyes that don't match and *'fraid you're gonna lose hot shot-*

"Not a chance." Etienne mutters under his breath, digs his fingers into splintery wood and pushes himself off, uses the momentum to find his footing as he stumble runs his way through this maze of a basement, tordu ripping his tangle of magic apart and giving chase after him once more.

Running for your life is never much fun, but it's especially not fun when you can barely see where you're going and have to keep ducking awkwardly to avoid hitting your head on low set doorframes. Every time Etienne slides under a support beam in between sections of framed out walls, and *doesn't* come up smashing his

What Goes Bump In The Night

head into a metal pipe, is considered a win in his books, and *Mothers of the Night,* does he desperately need every little advantage he can get right now.

Etienne may be something of a klutz, but he's not exactly unathletic, has to be in some form of fitness to survive the horrors he's expected to face on a nightly basis.

So, he goes on runs and sometimes lifts weights and generally prepares himself to not get killed instantly, *does a halfway decent job he thinks,* but working to stay ahead of the tordu is absolutely wrecking him.

Each shuddering inhale Etienne takes never seems to have enough oxygen in it, and yet, catches and *burns* in his lungs like he thinks the Gagnon's magic must do for them, slowly asphyxiating him with the curling smoke of his own exhaustion. His limbs are shaking, *his body is tired,* muscles overtaxed and needing a break, but he has to keep pushing them for more *more more,* literally running himself ragged in an attempt to keep the lead he's steadily losing.

He's not going to last long like this, and it's impossible to tell how much time has passed, *feel like everything is stretching forward indefinitely a hell of your own making,* but surely Nica is almost done with their reaction by now, surely they're *close* at the very least, *surely he's not going to be running for an eternity surely he won't die down here* ~~surely they didn't leave you to-~~

And Etienne tries not to think like that. He tries to be positive, *he tries to be rational quick smart one step ahead,* but no matter what he tries to be, *no matter where he seems to turn how fast he changes directions,* the tordu is always right behind him.

The floor jumps under his boots with every pounding, wet slap of its massive, *gnarled* hands striking concrete, the abomination using its arms to propel itself forwards like a grotesque pair of legs and slam through whatever obstacle Etienne darts behind like it's not even there. Sawdust and the fine powder of rock debris suffuse the air, rest thick on his tongue and threaten to dredge up nasty sounding coughs, but Etienne can't spare the loss of air for it, swallows everything back down even if it makes his chest hurt worse.

The debris cloud soon becomes more of a problem than just choking him on its grit though. It reduces his already limited visibility to a scant *foot* in front of him, and Etienne may as well be truly running blind then. He was sort of keeping a mental map of the basement's floorplan, *stairs there blocked off room to the right duck head here,* but that's completely worthless to him once he can no longer orient himself.

Where do I go where do I go, is a constant circulating scream in his mind as he starts hesitating before openings, can't remember if he's already gone that way and the cover is all destroyed, or worrying if it could possibly lead to a dead end. And he's pausing for only the briefest seconds, *literally a millisecond of time,* but that's the margin of error that sets good exorcists apart from dead exorcists, and in any other circumstance, his indecision for which path to take would probably lead to the tordu overtaking him already.

It's technically faster than he is, could catch up with him in a heartbeat if it *thought to do so,* but it's not thinking at the moment. It's just chasing him in a pure mindless *rage,* has been flying past him and getting half trapped in crumbling obstacles instead of remembering to phase through them, all logical thought *completely* eclipsed by the frantic need to separate Etienne's limbs from his body.

So right now, that's his only saving grace, the fact that whatever intellect the tordu had has been robbed from it, its entire focus narrowed down to a senseless swirl of- *kill him kill him kILL HIM KILL HIM RIP HIM APART SEVER HIS HEAD FROM HIS BODY MAKE HIM SUFFER LIKE WE SUFFER TAKE HIS BONES FOR AN ETERNITY SPREAD HIS ENTRAILS ACROSS THE W A L L S LET HIS BLOOD SOAK AND S T A I N THE F L O O R S KILL HIM KILL HIM KILL H I M-*

Which blasts through Etienne's brain like a freezing hurricane, threatening to swamp everything he knows and drown out all that

What Goes Bump In The Night

he is, and he doesn't have enough presence of mind to fix his mental shields, is stuck listening to the enraged thoughts of the tordu on full blast while he runs for his life.

And it's somewhere in this dark, filthy scrabble through the bowels of a decommissioned hospital that more than anger starts to bleed through this unwanted connection.

It comes softly at first, maybe little more than a trickle. A feeling that's cool as opposed to *cold,* water in counterpoint to all the ice, leaks in through the gaps of his shields and floods down into the empty spaces behind his ribs, *into his heart,* and like a flower reluctantly blooming in the face of its first frost, is an agony unlike anything Etienne has ever felt.

Why why why, are the first laps of it, little droplets that strike hollow against his bones and leave *regret* in their wake, *why me hands limp against sheets why them chests limp against sheets why us heads limp under sheets,* deep despair next that rises over his feet, up past his knees, swirls in hopeless eddies around his fingers, *didn't know open beds to open graves didn't know open throat open chest open eyes closed eyes closed chest closed throat goodnight d-didn't know d-didn't k-know d- didn't think didn't w-want wanted to stay wanted to l-live thought we'd see them aga-*

A monstrous scream echoes past, low and guttural, but it sounds more pained than it does angry, *more hurt than it wants to cause hurt,* and words are hard to form when there's so many of you and yet there's only one of you, but memories aren't, go flickering through Etienne's mind like burned out rolls of film.

Tiny coins of light race across the kitchen entire house smells like cherries hear a gaggle of little feet running towards you chipper voices excitedly laughing of course you remembered how could you ever forget your own daughter's – hands shake as you try and smooth hair back from her face she's so scared don't be scared sweetie but they won't let you touch her THEY WON'T LET YOU TOUCH HER try to reach for her anyway try to grab her ANYWAY your baby your darling but she's gone and then so are-

✦✦ 453 ✦✦

Flowers in your back pocket oh you are so nervous to be here you cannot let anyone know you are here this is such a bad idea you're not the same moonless night and magnolias on the breeze window over your head creaks open hair tumbling free and the warm gold of their markings – blood flies out of your mouth everything hurts try and remember flowers and stolen kisses under the shade of their hat they don't know you're here you can't tell them you are never gonna get a chance you were in-

Sunlight warm against your back wood handle of the hammer rough in your hand shingles laid out in neat rows can't even tell a storm tore them off it's gotta be perfect though it's gonna be great so excited to meet so excited for him to come pen pals a country apart finally getting the chance to – it's just a cold it's just a cold Christ alive it has to just be a cold but you've seen the papers you've read the headlines your feet have turned black you can't keep air in your lungs need to write a letter have to let him know can't hold the pen you can't-

And there's more than that, hundreds of memories that go shuttering past in brief glimpses and snatches of heartache, showing people once loved, places once adored, *lives once lived,* all taken too soon but remembered in agonizing memorial by the creature chasing him, *by the people it used to be.*

Etienne can't process everything it's hurling at him, *he's only one man,* but each new wave that crashes over his head feels like it takes a chunk out of his heart, the *emotions* contained in those snapshots getting caught under his skin and branding themselves there for an eternity. It's easy to forget the tordu was people, still is, in a roundabout way, and *Mothers,* does it tear him to shreds having that brutal reminder thrust in his face, that these were people who suffered for no good reason, *died miserably,* and have then been forced to spend their afterlife suffering as well.

It just...it shouldn't've happened to them.

This should not have happened to them, and he's aware a lot of shit happens in life to people that should not happen to them, but if someone from the construction crew had just *done what*

✦✦ 454 ✦✦

What Goes Bump In The Night

they were fucking supposed to, Etienne could've *helped.* He could've done *something worthwhile.* Could've given the spirits the long fought for peace they deserved, finally help lay them to rest properly and not- *a-and not drive them further into this hell,* his actions more or less helping them along into the state they're now in.

This, *monument* to mortal suffering, and the worst part is, *the fucking worst part is,* that in between the suffocating sorrow and mindless rage, *he can tell it believes him.*

Everything he said to intentionally draw it out.

All of the nasty words and disparaging taunts that were intentionally crafted to cause harm.

Each wound he purposefully inflicted trying to get a reaction, it believes every single one to be the truth, doesn't want to, *but it does.*

That's the thing with insecurities, *with doubts,* they're harbors for things you're terrified are true about yourself, about the world, *about the ones who supposedly care for you,* and Etienne played a cruel game going after them, spoke into being these spirits' truest nightmare.

That they were forgotten.

That they were abandoned by the ones they loved the most.

And it doesn't matter that some of them might've had proper burials or that someone came for them in the end, because even though their bodies were removed, their souls never went with, and to them, that's proof enough they didn't matter.

To them, being left behind like they were, was a fate worse than their original deaths.

W H Y, howls through his mind in an animalistic sob at the same time as a guttural roar shakes the foundations under his feet, *we were good kind decent we fought we tried we struggled didn't wanna go didn't wanna GO you left us you forgot uS YOU NEVER CARED*

✦✦ 455 ✦✦

ABOUT US you loved us you left us you left us we loved you LeFT us we loved you LEFT US we lo YOU LEFT US Y O U L E F T U S HATE YOU H-HATE YOU H A T E Y O U-

Something strikes the ground so harshly, Etienne can hear the sharp cracking sound of shattering concrete and tries to keep his foot from catching in the crevice that splinters open in front of him. The toe of his boot gets wedged in the gap though, and he goes flailing forwards, only barely manages to catch himself on a nearby doorframe.

It stops his fall, but ultimately fucks him over in the long term, because even though he's hanging on to it for no more than a second, is literally pushing himself right back off as soon as he hits it, the loss of momentum brings all of the snarling aches in his body back to the forefront of his mind and suddenly moving, let alone *running,* seems an insurmountable task.

There is a stich in his side that feels like an axe head is being repeatedly driven into the column of his torso, a constricting force around his ribs that makes breathing a punishment not a relief.

His head *swims,* his throat *burns,* and the best Etienne can manage is a lame sprint that decays into a staggered jog, barely gets him anywhere before a crushing force is wrapping around his calf. The touch is freezing, it burns him through the material of his pants, grip just shy of snapping his leg bones like toothpicks as it yanks him back, and Etienne goes unwillingly, slams against the ground with a painful thud while he's drug backwards.

Maybe he screams, he doesn't really know.

Everything's gone white static and the frantic tumbling of his own heart in his ears, endless roar of *HATE YOU HATE YOU HATE YOU* that's bellowing inside and outside his head while that grip grows ever tighter and *tighter,* hauling him towards where he really doesn't want to be. It's going to kill him, *it's going to kill him,* and Etienne tries kicking that massive hand off but it's like kicking at frozen mud, *it won't budge it's like a shackle.*

He calls for his magic next but it scorches his hands and black-

What Goes Bump In The Night

ens his bones, *something ignites in his chest every panicked inhale breathing that flame to life can't do it can't do it we're going to burn you alive STOP*, and his power slinks back away in a nervous tide.

We won't we can't don't ask us to hurt you, it wails, knows it'll kill him if it answers his call but is also aware he's as good as dead if it doesn't. It's a catch twenty-two, and while an argument can be made on the merits of going down putting up as much of a fight as you can, it violates one of the chief laws of reality Etienne's magic persists under, *never turn back on your caster.* Which is the exact same exploit he made use of earlier when he purposefully detonated that ward and launched the tordu away from him, but now, his magic's reluctance to hurt him is going to be what signs his death certificate.

Etienne tries again and again to get it to spark anyway, urging it on, *telling it he doesn't care if it ends up killing him,* but as far as his magic is concerned, there is no winning scenario here. Either way you cut it, *he doesn't make it out alive,* so it refuses to be the one that lands the killing blow, coils around him instead and settles in close, at least staying with him until the end.

Sorry sorry sorry our son our child failed you we're sorry so sorry can't help you can't hurt you we're sorry, something that is him and isn't him hushes, *it's over it's done come with us come to us lay your aching head to rest,* but Etienne won't go, digs his nails in against the smooth slick of brand new concrete looking for something, *anything,* to grab onto. He's grabbing at nothing though, can't find a sliver or a gap to sink his fingers into for purchase, *tries anyway can't ever let go,* and leaves broken pieces of black chipped nails and blood behind in a messy scrawl of *I was here I was here don't forget me I was here I tried I did my best but you fell you lost this is it it's over it's done stop fighting give-*

No.

NO-

It's not over, *it's not done,* and if Etienne can't get out of this, *if he is dying,* he's not doing it on his stomach, *meek and desperate*

✦ 457 ✦

and coddled, ravaged senselessly by an abomination he can't even *see.* No, he's going to turn and look this thing in its eyes, face to its *many fucking faces,* and die like a Boudreaux is supposed to die, with his boot kicking in rotted teeth and a middle finger of lightning shot straight up its thrice cursed ass.

He's not going to lay down and *accept it,* and it may be his birthright to protect others, *it may be his bloodcurse to die in their name,* but fuck it, he's at least picking how he goes out and his magic better get on board right the fuck now. Etienne knows it's doing what it's doing because it loves him, understands that this power is a precious gift that was *given* to him, and he respects what it is more than anyone could *possibly understand,* but at the end of the day, it *was given* to *him.*

It is *his* power to control and shape, *he* is the one that's supposed to decide what kind of witch he's going to be, and Etienne's kinda been in a rut recently where he's felt completely unmoored and without direction, but he's not feeling that way now.

He knows who he is.

This is still his life for however long it lasts, *his destiny no matter how cut short,* and he's *choosing* how he wants it to end.

Sorry Nica I hope you get out okay on your own, Etienne thinks, twisting his body in one sharp jerk that screws up the hip socket of the leg being pulled, but puts him in view of the tordu looming above him. His eyes find the nearest ghastly pair boring into him, and everything seems to slow down to a crawl. Pure malice leaks in black streams out of the monster's hollow eye sockets, milky white spittle flying free from its screaming, *gaping mouths,* and Etienne has half a thought that maybe he should be afraid, or at least despaired, but he's not.

If anything, *he's angry,* and not at the tordu, *not even with himself for once,* but rather at every single choice that has led to this exact fucking moment.

Tonight's tragedy was completely preventable.

◆✦◆ 458 ◆✦◆

What Goes Bump In The Night

No one here had to suffer like they have been tonight, *not the spirits not the crew not him and Nica,* but they did and they will continue to do so, and he's so fucking pissed off about it. If given the chance, Etienne could've had this all taken care of in a few hours, would have been *more than happy* to do so, but thanks to negligence and *bloody fucking stupid mistrust,* he's going to likely be dying an entirely avoidable death and it's *not fair.*

And yeah, *sure,* he said it himself, *some things in life just aren't fair,* but what a way to go out, eviscerated by the hands of tormented souls that never wanted to hurt anyone, *have only ever been hurt themselves in turn,* and who could've been saved if given the chance they deserved.

Mothers of the Night- what a load of *bull, it's so stupid they never even had to end up here,* and he's got to stop thinking about it, it gets him nowhere and there's no point spending his last few seconds skirting along the edge of *madness.* So taking what could be his last breath, Etienne hisses air in sharp through his teeth and starts drawing on his magic. It resists and clings to his bones like swamp muck just as he knew it would, but this time, he counters, *yanks harder,* and in a reversal of roles, *he* floods his consciousness through *it.*

Etienne can count on one hand the number of times he's entered the bright flashing collection of sentience that makes up his power, and it's not been very many for many good reasons, feels like dipping your face completely under a sea of stars instead of just walking atop it.

Because there is nothing.

And there is *e v e r y t h i n g*

Energy bombards him, goes whizzing past in a thousand whispering tails of comets, swelling and collapsing like solar flares, empty spaces that sink for miles and form hands and heads that bend in loops and swirls, turning to him inquisitively, and they seem confused to see him, keep shying away from his request to *come fight stand on your feet back me up listen* but he won't let

✦✦✦ 459 ✦✦✦

them continue to hide, sinks his hands down into their infinity and doesn't ask again.

He demands.

You are mine and I am yours, Etienne intones, fingers encased in *absence* and elbows slowly submerging all the way into *abyss, I was given to you and you were given to me you are mine I am yours we are each other's,* there's a presence that flickers across his skin suddenly, delicate, lacelike, *too unknowable for all that it pretends it may be known,* and he grabs onto it, doesn't let go no matter how much it feels like he's just *inhaled a bolt of lightning,* grits his teeth and hopes he makes it out the other side, *but I am your son I am your host I am your scion you picked me you chose me and you will. Listen. To. Me-*

Light suddenly flares around him in a fractal network of a thousand galaxies, harsh and inviting and figures a century tall tower on the horizon, eyes blazing like the sun bodies glowing powerfully like the moon, a horrible beautiful low humming whine emitting from their very beings, and he's never seen anything like this *he's not even sure what he's looking at,* but as Etienne stumbles to his feet, they sink to their knees, ringing him in a circle older than time and speaking with voices lost to the ages when they bow their heads to him, *for him, in difference to their-*

So it was done so shall it be your command is our will

as you speak so it will be wrought...

An untold amount of hands reach out for him, alighting over his shoulders, crowning the top of his head, an infinite smattering of glowing arms that branch off Etienne's body like a thousand spokes on a wheel, *like the never ending points of a beaming star,* and this shallow surface of a much deeper pool that he stands upon shakes and trembles as They tell him,

You take what is freely given you return freely what is asked

worth in the bearer and worth in the buried

What Goes Bump In The Night

you shall have what you seek gwéiníath...

And Etienne slips, *he sinks,* pushed down into the sea beneath him by the countless hands upon him, *is pulled up from the bottom of the ocean by the countless hands upon him,* is flying and drowning and is lost somewhere in between, can't catch his breath *doesn't know if there's even air to find,* descends into a spinning network of undulating light he's never supposed to know and ascends through things he didn't know were possible to be, *he rises, he falls,* and he feels himself getting pulled apart as Their voices cascade in unending ripples,

There is much you don't know there is much you never will

a contract bound not in blood but in something far stronger

the ties of the universe intent will a reflection of the soul

do you know

have you seen

what it means to carry power under your breast...

He is being unmade *he is being reborn, this was a bad idea this was a bad idea this is why they always tell you not to reach too deep he is lost,* but from across the universe he's being pushed into, *out of,* there's this hiccupping sensation, like a stone being skipped across the surface far above him, *like something hopping across the sea floor far below him,* and each staccato touch of it brings a surge of power that's not him and *not Them* but it's not *not* enough of either and They turn Their monstrous infinity towards it,

Ah...a weadhíath...

such a curious anomaly...

Etienne doesn't know what They call it but he thinks he knows *it,* reaches out a hand towards those silver bright rings of electric blue, wants to remember, *wants to be known again thinks he sees the arm that threw the stone the hands that made the ripples each one a cry of the same word thinks he'd know that voice anywhere,*

✦✦ 461 ✦✦

and They hum the way a star would explode for an eternity,

It can barely reach this place but you still hear it don't you...

can you see how it calls for you gwéiniath like how you called for us

do you yearn for it the way we yearn for you...

Yes no maybe he has no idea, but the incredible pressure that had been dragging him under draws lax all of a sudden, and Etienne doesn't so much as kick for the surface as he shoots for it, sea of stars and hard answers pulsing past in sickening spirals, vertigo warping his sense of direction so that it almost feels like he's being pulled inside out, and the whisper of a warning or a truth he doesn't want to taste flows up after him like a streaking comet vomiting free from his own mouth,

Beware how often you choose to answer those that call you

paths are hard wrought things that rarely change

a will shackled is a will brought to heel gwéiniath

be mindful of what you give parts of yourself to

for seldom

are they

returned

e n t a c t-

Etienne thinks he comes gasping awake from a dream, *a memory a past life feels like he's been gone for centuries for his entire existence,* but no, he's still right where he last remembers being, here on his back, *trapped in hell,* being reeled in closer to obliteration while the knobs of his spine drag harshly across the concrete floor.

There's so much in him now and it's attempting to find places to go, *parts and starlight and quickly fading memories beware gwéiniath,* and while he's struggling to put it all back together, *to*

✦✦ 462 ✦✦

What Goes Bump In The Night

put himself back together, the tordu howls and gets ready to kill him.

Etienne remembers that same sound paralyzing him before.

He remembers the way it made him cringe back in fright, *made him angry,* but now, it seems flatter somehow. It bounces around his skull, *rattles his teeth,* but doesn't get stuck or lodged anywhere, and Etienne forgets about it almost as quickly as it came, collapsing echo of its wail washing over him like a wave.

Cresting past the top of his head and then it's just gone, swept away into surf why are you doing this

Another sharp tug, a bump to the head, and he finds himself pulled about level with the abomination's many sets of eyes. They glow sickly white in the ghastly black hollows of its sockets, entire form of the tordu heaving as it struggles to be what it is and feel what it's feeling, and all Etienne knows in that moment is pity's kinder twin. His heart doesn't break for the creature, but it goes out to it, and for the second time that night, he is aware of the difficult compassion that comes when you find love for something that hurt you.

Blood down his arm and dead at his feet, didn't want to do it know you didn't want to so then why are you

And as insane as it sounds, Etienne does love the tordu.

Because it was people, *because it still is void beyond they will always be people to him,* and his entire purpose in life is supposed to be protecting them but he knows there's a limit. A point in which the scales tip and it's no longer about the individual, *the needs of the many gaçon we're responsible for an entire city,* and it's never sat right with him. *Mothers of the Night,* he understands the principle of it, *the utilitarianism of it,* but how is Etienne supposed to look himself in the eye and say sacrificing the suffering is justifiable.

It's not and it never will be to him, you didn't ask for this you didn't want this there has to be another way

✦✦ 463 ✦✦

He blinks bleary eyed up at the creature, seeing spinning galaxies and infinities and the never ending shape of his coven as it spirals ever on and *on, beginning to end it's a circle it's a connection life begets death,* and watches distantly while the tordu raises it's other tumorous arm, like it's going to be coming down on his chest, *snapping his ribs into splinters maybe ripping his neck clean off his body death begets life,* and an aching wave of, *I don't want to hurt you,* pulses between them both.

"Then don't-" Etienne mouths, not sure if his words are meant for himself or the monster and in the air something stirs, in the space between spaces atoms begin to shiver, *a stone skips across the ocean hands clap together fingers draw apart resonating molecules pulsating their own song know you,* and with a pressure drop like an incoming storm, the floor ripples under his hands.

Etienne's never physically touched alchemy before.

He's felt it move past his mind many times from across the room, the slips and trickles of energy that skate along the underside of reality and nettle at him like briars, and, *on occasion,* has even curiously touched at the finished thing. Sneakily running his hands over patched up columns, or picking at compounds that have gone from being one to another when he knew Nica wasn't paying attention, looking for a hint, *a flicker,* of that power he heard calling to him in his heart like a siren's song, but he always came up empty handed.

There was never anything left of the whispers Etienne felt along the back of his neck, *the wisps of something other he knew in him and his family his coven the call of the beyond,* and alchemy felt... *hollow,* to him, because of that, like a house with no furniture or picture frames with nothing in them.

A basic structure and little else.

It doesn't feel like that now.

Now, it races right under him like a storm wall, *straight through him like a speeding bullet,* the apex of the reaction passing directly over where he's got *both* palms, *the most sensitive part of any caster,*

✦✦ 464 ✦✦

What Goes Bump In The Night

pressed flat to the floor, and the sensation that cracks through him is mind-bendingly disorienting. Etienne had gotten a shadow of intent from one of Nica's reactions earlier in the night, the first time he'd ever felt a suggestion of conscious will from it, but, as teal light surges past now, he becomes swamped with a compulsion so strong, it's hard to *think* of anything else.

Barreling through Etienne's mind like a category five hurricane is the want- no, *need need NEED,* for him to bend, *to change to make himself into something completely different,* break apart and reorganize everything he is on a molecular level and rebuild it just like he's being *ordered too.*

Not asked, not told.

Ordered.

There is no room for arguments against a tone like that.

No space to try and wiggle your way free. Just a seemingly never ending wave that decimates everything in its path, forcefully smashing apart elemental bonds as it executes the sheer intensity of its *will.* It is demanding, it is arresting, *it steals all the air from his lungs bow bend heel to me,* and carried with it are blueprints that miraculously means this wave of power leaves not absolute destruction in its wake, but rather something completely new.

Like a star exploding, *like the formation of a galaxy.*

Like something breathing to life.

In a pulse, the rough grit of porous concrete under his hands is replaced with the smooth waxy glide of stone, *of bloodstone,* and *Mothers of the Night,* the way it *immediately sings to him,* it's like a balm to everything that hurts and a sharp jolt of pain to everything that's tender, and Etienne is left with the sensation of fading thunder in his head and lightning crackling to life under his skin and a thousand whispering voices telling him if he's doing this ritual after all he needs to do it *now-*

With a twist and a jerk, Etienne pries his trapped leg from the confuse slackened grip of the tordu and urges his shaking limbs to push himself up, *up,* right into the maw of the proverbial beast, and he swears he's been here before, *dark of another night closing over him jaws of another monster looming over you too weak to stand on your own you're going to fall,* but fuck that night and *fuck* those memories.

He won't give in again.

He won't he won't *he won't,* grits his teeth and claws his way up and the second he stands, a dozen roving eyes all retrain on him. Etienne meets every single one dead on, does not feel fear as he's bathed in their eerie white light, does not falter when he's met with the sight of an endless tunnel of black that calls itself a throat, nor does he flinch when a roar belches out, reeking of death and decomposing offal and promising the same to him.

No, Etienne stands tall, and in the way the memory of a dream comes to you, he thinks he feels hands coming to rest upon him once more, *like starlight like spokes on a wheel like an unbroken chain.*

Do you know what it means to carry power, echoes through his ears from that place outside of time, and it does not refer to the magic he was gifted.

It means the strength with which Etienne holds himself up despite it all. It *means* the ironclad way he sets his spine and the purpose he drags his shoulders back with. *It means* that his resolve to see something through is the strongest weapon he could possibly wield, and he's less than a foot away from rank, decomposing flesh when he *finally* understands that unequivocally, *he's strong enough to do this,* brings his hands together, flings them apart, and without any prep or supplies or even a chalk outline, he summons the largest sendforth sigil he thinks he's ever seen.

Hot air blasts up from his feet as the sigil slides smooth and effortless into existence, practically dripping off Etienne's fingertips easier than any other magic he's spent hours agonizing over, and with it, *light* explodes into being.

What Goes Bump In The Night

Glowing lines arc and crack over the now mottled red green floor, fissure out like the interwoven net of a lightning storm, instantly starting to resonate with the bloodstone and it makes the most beautiful music.

High pitched frequencies dip and swell as his magic comes burning out of his hands, echoing through the bloodstone in a way that sounds like echoing bells in a church steeple, and it compounds, reverberating back and forth until the entire room is alive with the sound of magic singing to itself.

If there are words, Etienne doesn't know them, struggles enough keeping his feet planted with the sheer amount of force that's coming whipping off this sigil, power building under him at an alarming rate.

Which, to be fair, *was* the plan, but Etienne might've underestimated how difficult it would be to control a sigil of this size being fueled by so much bloodstone. He barely twitches a finger, wanting to redirect a line, and the entire thing pulsates with energy *violently,* responding to his order with quadruple the amount of output than he necessarily wanted.

Trying to control this sigil is like what Etienne imagines attempting to steer a comet would be like, *lots of power lots of force not a lot of fine control,* and he bites his cheek against a surge of energy that threatens to buck him from the equation. The wind really picks up then too, buffets him with coils of rising heat that threaten to swipe the hat from his head and knock him clear off his feet.

Etienne has to dig his soles into the slippery stone under them trying to find his balance, really fighting to stay in control.

It's a precarious situation to be in.

Magic is dangerous, and no matter how it loves him, how well he commands it, that doesn't change the volatile nature of it, *how quickly it can spiral out of control,* but slowly flexing his hands out flat, Etienne keeps his mind calm and breathes in deep.

He can do this, he just needs to stay focused.

◆✦◆ 467 ◆✦◆

Reworking his stance a bit, Etienne leans into the winds and lets them prop him up as he crooks his fingers the barest amount, and lightning cracks to life. He directs it to spiral closer, *tighter,* towards its trapped quarry, and with an answering rumble of displaced air, it's more than happy to obey.

The tordu shrieks as electricity seethes around it, a steadily growing cyclone of power that's centered directly on its writhing form, and it howls senselessly, thrashing against the glyphs constraining it. They throb a stronger maroon in warning, strangle the amalgamation further and pieces of the tordu almost seem to shatter off under the pressure as it's pushed out of reality. More and more chunks start to crack away the harder it struggles and it's...actually working, *their plan is working,* and an inch at a time, the tordu is slowly being worked back into the aether, will soon be forced from existence entirely.

And that's great! That's awesome, *it's amazing,* something is finally going right but it...doesn't...*feel right,* necessarily, not with the sounds the tordu is making, those screams of anguish and pain as it's getting torn apart by the storm encircling it, rent from this world one bloody chunk at a time. It's less than half driven from the fringes of this plane and already, it's not looking too great, is ragged and splintering in places and yet the tordu clings on frantically, *like hands gripping the edge of a doorframe body glitching spastically can't make me,* absolutely *refusing* to go where Etienne is working on shoving it.

Please stop fighting please just fucking work with me you're only hurting yourself more, he thinks furiously, doesn't know if it can hear him let alone understand, but he's still getting bits and snatches of *its* thoughts every now and again, and *Mothers,* does it really not want to be sent back to the aether.

No no NO NO n O NOnoNO STOP won't CAN'T D ON T NO NO NO S T O P S TOP, breaks through his mind in bursts of crackling static, anything else that comes through unintelligible from how many different voices are all screaming over one another at once. It's an impossible mishmash to decipher, but Etienne can at least tell every soul sucked into being the tordu is vehemently against

◆✦◆ 468 ◆✦◆

What Goes Bump In The Night

the idea of being ejected from the mortal plane. Which twists his heart up something ugly in his chest, but what other choice does he have here?

Let it kill him?

Arching his fingers more purposefully this time, Etienne sends another guttering hiccup of magic from himself that's weak at first, but amplifies through the bloodstone until it's an explosive shock-wave of power. The glyphs all spin faster in response, *glow brighter,* and the new force the sigil generates drags on the tordu like a set of lead weights about its neck.

The creature staggers, form crumpling inwards as it's being forced to fold out of reality, and more ragged, weeping cracks appear across its body. Translucent flesh begins peeling back in strips and reveals decomposing muscle underneath, a disgusting display that only worsens as the sigil keeps trying to pull it further and further into the aether, *and the tordu screams and screams and s c r e a m s.*

It sounds just like a human would.

Etienne almost can't stand to look at it, feels so wrong doing this, and even though the tordu doesn't bleed, black globs of torment leak faster out of its eye sockets, spill down its spasming form before fizzling from existence like an evaporating oil slick, and it might as well be weeping blood.

S TO P, the creature begs desperately, *STOP GOD PleAse sTOP,* deformed hands made up of a dozen smaller limbs twitching erratic in the way a bug dies, *DON't cAn't plEAS E DON'T MAKE st OP STOP S T O P P L E A S E G O D S T O P-*

Chewing harshly on the inside of his cheek, Etienne tries to prop his mental shields back up so he doesn't have to *listen to this,* but he pauses, because the thought comes to him of how is that any better. How is it *any better* to shut the panicked thoughts of the tordu out, *to be willfully ignorant to another's suffering-* better for him maybe, in the short term, but it won't erase the guilt, *it won't negate the fact that he feels like this is wrong.*

✦✦ 469 ✦✦

P leA SE, the tordu's dozens of voices sob, *PL easE DON'T,* sickening crunch as another part of it is sucked back out of reality, and what remains of it in the physical plane *howls, S T OP STOP g OD p LEA se STOP dOn't WAN nA g O DON'T fo R GET Hu rtS iT HURTS pLeasE GOD it HURTS MAKE IT STOP M A KE IT S TOP-*

This is...*wrong, t-this is wrong,* and Etienne's mind again tries to remind him he has *no other choice,* but it finally just sounds like an excuse. Life is full of choices, *he knows that he's been taught that since he was a boy,* and there's a thousand others he could've made, *a dozen different pathways,* and yet he chose this one, he *chose* to do this- *is choosing to do this,* and his magic waivers in response.

I don't want to do this, Etienne thinks, forcing himself to look at the way the tordu is collapsing in front of him, sobbing and howling and bleeding itself raw, *making* himself understand that *he's* the one putting it through that. *I don't want to be doing this,* he thinks again, and a soft protest comes to him, sounding like mother, *like Gilbert like everything in the tomes he's assigned,* telling him he *has* to do this, but Etienne doesn't *have* to do anything.

His decisions are his own, the path he walks is his own, *this magic he was given is his own,* and if he doesn't like the way it's turning out to be, then *he* has the power to change that, is the only one that can.

One day mother will step down and Etienne will have to step up, and he can't lead his coven or the Council of Night plagued by indecision, with no idea of where he stands. And his mother and all the Boudreaux atriarchs that came before her may help shape his idea of self, but ultimately, the decision for what kind of patriarch he's going to be, *what kind of witch,* rests solely in Etienne's own hands.

His fingers twitch and the power bubbling under the sendforth sigil swells violently in exaggeration, coming quickly to a crescendo of bright, *searing* light and the earsplitting thrumming that still doesn't manage to drown out the tortured noises of the tordu as it's ripped piece by piece from this plane. *NO nO no NOnONo*

What Goes Bump In The Night

DON'T WaNNA GO CA N'T bE FOrG OT TEN, the thing wails, its myriad of voices splitting apart into raw static that can only convey unspeakable *pain* and unfathomable *anguish,* and all Etienne has to do is crook his fingers one last time and it'd be over.

He would push it the rest of the way through and then they could escape, leaving the tordu to fight and claw and yank itself back to the physical plane.

Because it *is* going to come back here no matter what he does.

It will continue to suffer, it will keep fighting to be known, and then, *at the pinnacle of its misery,* mother will destroy it- *cracks his heart in two rips the lungs straight from his chest please no they're just people* -but there's nothing else to be done, *this is the only thing he can do there's no way to save a tordu he's just one man there's no other choice he has to do-*

Black tar dribbles down across broken, smashed together faces, parts around open mouths contorted in screams of torment that get worse as the sigil pulses, *sucking them in further,* crunching squelching rip and more pieces get completely unmade, leaving behind even greater of a mangled mess than where they started, and he's going to have to keep doing that *he's going to have to put it through more condemn them to absolute suffering destroying what humanity they have left and he...h-he-*

Etienne can't do it.

He *can't* be what subjects these tormented souls to even more pain.

A sendforth ritual is supposed to be a joyous thing.

It's supposed to be about granting trapped spirits peace, *helping them find release,* but that's not what this is and he can't keep pretending it is. Etienne refuses to continue whatever torture it is that he's doing, can't let his magic be an instrument of harm and woe, *that's not their way that's not the kind of man he wants to be,* and in an instant, his magic goes from *pushing* the tordu out of existence to *pulling it back in.*

✦ 471 ✦

The sigil still hums wildly under his feet but it changes its pitch, strobing and jittering as Etienne's intent cuts new searing lines of light through the bloodstone. None of it is done by his conscious thought. This isn't anything he's ever learned or practiced. They're hitting uncharted waters and his magic is exacting a will of its own in tune to his, helping shape the spell into something that'll do what he wants it to do but it's unlike anything Etienne's ever seen before.

Follow where you lead point the way we'll cut a path, the lightning sizzles as it crackles past his ears, *at your command at your beck at your call follow you anywhere,* warm baking heat rising with it, winds swirling faster, *tighter,* as the sigil pulses in time to his own beating heart, *our son our child picked you chose you know you always our Patriarch-*

Etienne inhales sharply and his magic almost seems to laugh a bit at him, leaps from his skin in a dancing arc to the tordu's, sinking down beneath the surface of that ghastly flesh with a great spark of maroon.

Unlike earlier, it's not trying to push the tordu away or repel it though, but is rather seeking splits, *cracks,* for it to seep down into, lights the tordu up from the inside out like lightning surging behind thunderheads.

The sensation in Etienne's mind goes from one of palms pushing flat against something to fingers digging into crevices, acting like wedges trying to force sealed objects back apart, and at the intrusion, the tordu begins thrashing once more.

Now that the sigil is no longer pulling it from this plane, the amalgamation has more leeway, tries swinging a decaying arm at Etienne but it falls flat, broken tendons flopping around uselessly. That doesn't stop it from trying again with its other arm, grunting in agony as that one messily falls apart too, and Etienne shouts over the rising wind, *"STOP IT! I'm trying to HELP YOU!"*

Or at least, *that's what he hopes he's doing,* is having to put a lot of blind faith in his magic and trust it's the right call, but when

What Goes Bump In The Night

he doesn't know what he's doing on a technical level, that trust is easier said than given. What it's come down to is basically a battle of head over heart and perhaps foolishly, Etienne has gone with his heart. Logic tells him this is a stupid decision to have made, that he *knows* empirically tordu *cannot* be re-separated without incurring great losses on the casters involved, but there's just-*something under his sternum* that's urging him on, *telling him this is the correct path.*

And Etienne has to trust in that, *has to trust in himself,* arches his fingers up steeper and slowly draws them together, like he's trying to pull out all the separate pieces and parts he knows the tordu is made up from and liquid *fire* races through his veins, sends his pulse tumbling into double- *triple time,* and he sucks in a shaky breath through his teeth.

"I want to help you! I-I know you're in pain. I know you've been hurt, *I know I've hurt you,* and there's nothin' I can say to that besides *I'm sorry!*" Etienne yells past the turbulent currents and zapping electricity, *hopes to the Mothers it hears him,* but this is what he's good at, isn't it, *putting all that he is into everything he's trying to give,* "I never should've said what I did. I never should'a put you through more than you've already been through! You are not forgotten, *you are not overlooked!* I was wrong to act like you were. I see you, I remember you, *I mourn for you-*"

The tordu wails gutturally in response, tossing its massive, mis-shapen head, *hates to hear it craves to hear it can't believe what he's saying ~~but it wants to~~,* and ever so softly, *ever so faintly,* Etienne feels something give the barest amount under his hands.

"I've seen your suffering! I've felt your misery! And you shouldn't have had to go through any of it! I'm sorry you died the way you did! *I'm sorry your afterlife's been this way,* but let me *help fix it!*" Etienne winces at the bolt of aching lightning that shoots down the length of his spine, feels it feather out along his back and then his hands start shaking and he fights to keep them steady, *"I-I mean it!* I want to help- *I care about you.* I care about what happens to you, an' I know this pain is tearing you apart on the inside, so let me take it from you...let me help lead you to rest."

✦✦ 473 ✦✦

Come on come on come on, he's chanting to himself internally, can't shake the mental image of a clock hand ticking ever faster towards the minute mark and isn't optimistic about what happens once it reaches that line. He's so close though, *Etienne can feel it,* his magic wound down deep in the tordu where it's trying to break it back apart, and it's fracturing ever so slightly, but the creature's bonds are strong.

Shared pain unites all of their spirits and they're reluctant to let it go, but Etienne starts to wonder if maybe a *different* shared experience could be the key he's looking for. Something that's stronger than grief and even more central than all their resentment combined. He thinks he might have an idea for what that could be, and so, in what's perhaps the second stupidest thing he's done today... Etienne plunges the entirety of his mind into the disintegrating consciousness of the tordu.

It's a bit like stepping into the ocean of energy that lives under his bones, complete disorientation as he plummets through a frothing surge of *who am I who are you what's it matter hate it all.* Disjointed images and searing hot feelings go streaking past him like supersonic debris, and Etienne struggles to get his bearings quickly, because this isn't his magic and it's *not* happy to see him and the atmosphere turns *dark,* cloudy thoughts seething towards him as a hundred rotting eyes all open and spin to face where he's standing, deep ominous hiss of, *Y O U-*

Shadows coalesce and slowly puddle together in front of him, the malignant warped core of the tordu beginning to rear itself up, dead eyes glowing in warning as it threatens to crest over his head like a cancerous wave and drown him out *YOU IT'S YOU HATE YOU KILL Y O U SMOTHER YOU RIP O U T Y O U R S O U L SHOULD NEVER HAVE COME will make you regret will MaKe YoU SufFER LIKE WE HAVE like you WILL KNOW pain KNOW ruination KNOW D A M N A T I O N-*

But it never gets the chance to.

Because Etienne is an exorcist, because he wields his *will* like a weapon, because even though this place isn't his to command, *he*

What Goes Bump In The Night

makes it so, floods his own memories and emotions down through all the cracks and crevices, and an explosion of color lights up where they stand in this dingy hell.

Brightly painted buildings suddenly trundle past the trolley's windows, polished wood is cool under his hands and Spanish moss hangs down out of trees where leafy green ferns sprout up in between their roots. Window baskets are choked thick with flowers and small bells ring out over teahouse doors, black and white tiles under his clicking bootheels and sunlight filtering past open shutters. People call out to one another in French, in English, in Spanish, *in a little mixture of them all,* clutter the streets with their colorful voices and overhead, dark wrought iron lanterns are coiled through with climbing ivy while their flames gutter ever on.

Everything inside the tordu's consciousness comes to a dead stop.

Whatever it was getting ready to do is completely abandoned as its flickering collection of minds stares arrested at all the scenes reeling past, *feeling the sun on their skin the wind blowing back across the Mississippi,* and a soft, broken sound escapes them.

It's been almost a hundred years since any of them have seen their home, and a lot changes in that time, *a century of progress a century of storms a century they lost.* The cars probably look alien to them, people's clothes foreign in design, technology now a mindboggling concept they can't even possibly begin to understand, but a lot of the buildings survived. Most of the trees are still there, just more grown, and sure, people have come and gone, *lived and died,* but the essence is the same.

The living breathing soul of New Orleans remains.

And Etienne shows them that, how the city comes alive for Mardi Gras, for Litha, *for a thousand other reasons,* how the people proudly decorate in greens and golds and purples and intricate fleurs-de-lis, repair their windows and roofs after a storm has blown through, *the way they look out for one another care for their city,* how they sing their songs and congregate around newly sealed tombs like it's a party instead of a funeral.

Not to mourn, but to celebrate a *life*.

"Don't you see..." Etienne whispers, watching as the towering figure in front of him starts to hunch over, bringing its collection of faces closer to the memories that swirl past in giddy spirals, "Don't you see how much more there is?"

Another soft, *begging desperate anguished,* noise, and he shows them the city lights at night from broomstick, how the streets glow gold and the stars race with him far above. He takes them to the French Quarter, where things are still old and dense and quieter, where it's all wooden signs above ancient doors and gilt letters in shopfront windows. He stands with them in a parade thick street, confetti raining down over their heads while the bands play and people dance heedlessly in the road, laughing and singing and *living-*

Something wet drips onto the back of Etienne's hand and he takes them a step in further, *closer,* opening the doors to Maisette's sunny parlor, leaves shaking gently outside the large windows where he sits in between the twins, pointy knees tucked up to his chest while Oliver reads them a story and Katie is pressed like a fire against his side. Through an archway and mother is laughing in the kitchen over a tray of cookies, pots and pans flying past her as she drags a smear of green frosting across his cheek, a messy swipe of her own already decorating the bridge of her nose and he mirrors her when she sticks a tongue out at him.

More drops of water strike him and they're coming *faster,* racing down past him in thin streams that thicken when Etienne chases a smaller Abel and Felix through the house, their giggling turning into screams of delight as they round a corner and a monster with bright orange hair and a foxy grin pops out. He turns on his heel then to run and he's rolling over on his bed, making room for a blur of white and navy that flops down next to him, heads resting together while their feet kick at one another and they complain about everyone and *everything,* schoolbags spread over the floor in a messy heap.

What Goes Bump In The Night

There's water pouring from everywhere now and it pools around his feet, swamping over the toes of his boots and it's a never ending susurration, sounds like the swishing of fabric as he's spun across the dancefloor, hand caught and locked with Sabine's and the warmth that radiates back is the same as when mother kisses him on the forehead, gentle brush of her fingers carding through his hair like the way Katie's hands slide off him slow after a hug *blonde head tucked into the crook of your neck freckled cheeks mismatched eyes big crinkling grin never laughed so hard never smiled so much hey Etienne-*

"There is more to you than you have convinced yourself there is." He says, and a sound echoes across time and space, *half a laugh sort of a sob a desperate breath of fresh air,* waterfalls cascading by like streams of pure silver, *like moonlight,* and the air is cleaner for it, less stagnant, the colors of Etienne's memories catching in the glistening streams and refracting back a kaleidoscope of being.

Dim light in bars glasses clinking together heat along your side Cheshire grins and dark eyes you once thought were your own can't imagine a life without them, broom handle warm under your hands night air cold against your face and you all whoop loudly as you race down empty fall streets leaves dancing under you, standing shoulder to shoulder with mother try to emulate the way she orates as you speak on your family's behalf and the smile she gives you when you finish thrives under your skin in your heart for days,

And you love them, all the people in your life all the big moments and all the small, little things that wedge in the gaps and get caught half forgotten under your nails, like good cups of tea simple pleasure of the sun warm on your back your favorite type of clouds gliding across the sky and that's it isn't it, that's the answer, what everything is all about what it all comes back to what it means to be-

We'd forgotten, ripples through the air, rings of sound that travel outwards like the rings Etienne's shoes make as he starts forwards, *we'd forgotten what it was like,* and that dark mass is still in front of him, *still hunched,* but it's coming apart now. Huge murky globs slough off, splash wetly to the ground and it's less like a disintegration or fragmentation, more like melting, *like a release,* and the

✦✧✦ 477 ✦✧✦

water under him turns dark before it runs clean, a score of voices hushing softly, *we'd forgotten how it felt...*

Thousands of images dance through the water, rippling like auroras, *old streetcars older streets young trees and young boys playing ball under them a girl with ribbons in her hair the laughing gold marked face of a lover unopened letters and excitement waiting on the kitchen table warm meals jazz on the radio a good pipe wispy paper thin clouds in the sky dancing the night away hands so many hands holding caressing waving spelling out I love you,* and with a great heaving shudder, the last of the grime and grit fall away, Etienne coming to a stop right in front of what remains.

We'd forgotten what it meant...

He holds out a hand in offer.

...to be human-

They take it.

Energy comes roaring up from the sigil, sends Etienne skidding back as he's whipped by a gale of winds, his magic coiling sharply and driving home like a lance, *shattering glittery crack like breaking glass,* and then fissures of light open up around him. They pulse in time to the rapid music of the spinning sigil, grow and expand as this mindscape he's in starts falling apart one chunk at a time, the pieces it was made from getting whisked away into the beyond.

Squinting against the searing light, Etienne ducks behind the crook of an arm and can just barely make out this collection of figures standing across the sigil from him. They anxiously bob back and forth as wind pulls and tugs at their forms, and he lowers his arm involuntarily, shocked to see...*people* standing there, and not just corpses, but *actual* human beings. Ones with bright eyes and filled in cheeks and wonderment on their faces as they stare at healthy looking hands, and there's a deep sort of contented relief settling under his ribs.

A woman looks up at him then, and they're probably close to the same age, wavy curls framing a heart shaped face and full cheeks

What Goes Bump In The Night

that bunch up into a shy smile when she waves at him awkwardly. Etienne waves back, kinda gestures at the sigil next in a, *well are you gonna,* gesture, and the woman's mouth drops open into a small o. She shuffles closer to the lip of it, squinting against the glaring light as the winds whip her hair around, and hesitantly glances once more at Etienne.

Go on, he mouths, doesn't think he'd be heard over the winds even if he screamed as loud as he could, *you'll be fine,* and she nods, steps right into the column of light and the last thing Etienne sees of her is a beaming smile as she's whirled away.

The others hesitantly follow her lead, some of them making eye contact with him before they go and a few looking too embarrassed to. He doesn't begrudge them for it, knows he'd be beyond awkward if he spent most of an evening trying to kill a guy only for him to save you in the end, but still, he stays long enough to see the majority of them off.

Each time a soul departs though, the light grows stronger, *the winds build in speed coiling faster sharper more dangerous,* and it gets increasingly difficult for Etienne to keep his balance.

Through the near blinding glow coming off the sigil, he can make out the few faces left, *men women people of all ages looking back at you with the most heartfelt gratitude can't tell you what this means,* and they see him struggling to stay, roll their heads, motion at him to *go,* and with a reluctant nod, Etienne finally does.

He lets go of his connection, *getting caught up in the winds too bound for somewhere else though,* and everything starts to fade out, but not before hands chase up and after him, hold on to him just long enough to make sure two words are pressed reverently into his palms.

Thank you

Etienne comes slamming back into his own mind like he just came slingshotting in off the bad end of a hurricane, stumbles on unsteady feet while the sigil starts to wind down, high pitched whining evening out into a more mellow hum before fading entirely.

The silence it leaves in its wake is strangely explosive, like the ringing in your ears after a bomb's gone off, and with nothing left hanging over his head, *no monster of ill intent trying to kill him no trapped souls needing guidance,* he's been given *way* too much space to be aware of himself again. Etienne runs his tongue over dry teeth, feeling...*cooked,* and also completely at peace, tastes metal in his mouth and smells something burning *hair or skin maybe,* head rolling around in a woozy arc that doesn't really seem to have a stop or starting point?

Mothers, he doesn't feel *great,* like he has a high grade fever or something, and he keeps trying to get his bearings but it's super disorienting to have gone from *blinding white searing light* to seemingly *absolute darkness,* leaves Etienne feeling like he's floating in a void of his own design. His magic's gone quiet too, shrunk way far away from him same as the ocean during low tide, and the absence of it is something like having his entire head wrapped double layers in cotton.

Things trickle to him *slow,* and Etienne's pretty sure there was some sort of, *pressingly urgent task,* that followed dealing with the tordu, but for the life of him, he can't seem to remember *what* it was he needed to do.

A crumbling *creaking* sound pulls sluggishly on his attention though, and his eyes drift lazily up, watching with incomprehension as pieces of debris rain down from this massive hole that now exists over his head. In the darkness, it's really easy to spot the faint flickering of embers burning through old floorboards and then even further up, *way way waaaaay up there,* the glow of the moon, beaming down at him like an accusatory eye that's caught him red handed.

Huh

That's...*interesting,* guess all the energy backlog in the sigil released when he did the...and then it all discharged vertically so... burned a hole straight through to the-

What Goes Bump In The Night

"O-Oops..." Etienne mumbles under his breath, wonders if maybe he should apologize to the moon for destroying the building a bit, because that seems like a normal thing to do right now, but dark fingers start to wiggle across his vision and then looking up gets to be too difficult.

Blinking as hard as he can doesn't remove the spots from his vision, and Etienne is in the process of trying to rub the grit out of his eyes, *if only he could get his fucking hand up there Mothers why is it filled with lead,* when something, *someone,* calls his name hesitantly and he turns to it like compasses do towards the north pole.

Helpless involuntary completely at the whim of, swings in a wide arc and makes his eyes focus and there, standing in the darkness, like a beacon of hope *a sigh of relief,* is his friend, *is his friend Nica. Alive.* Hurt a bit, *burned wrist blood smeared across their face red staining the front of their jacket debris in their hair eyes wild,* but *alive.*

Etienne feels tension he didn't even know he was holding drain out of him instantly and a massive weight lifts from his shoulders.

They're alive...t-they're alive you did it they made it you kept your promise you did it you...you did uh...

They look like they've seen a ghost though, *like they're currently looking at one,* stand there stock still with a kind of terrified amazement in their eyes that bleeds their face white, *er, whiter,* almost as white as the blotches of skin across their right cheek. Nica's mouth opens, *it shuts,* it looks like they're struggling to *breathe talk think be here,* and they're still scared, Etienne realizes, *sees them shaking now,* great shudders that run up the length of their body.

And he wants to help put their mind at ease, right?

Because the danger is gone and Nica is safe and Etienne *needs* them to know that, so he smiles at them gently, *seems to forget there's blood in his mouth,* knocks the brim of his hat up and smoothly readjusts his bolo tie, *although...not really because he*

◆✦◆ 481 ◆✦◆

kinda can't control his arms, and says with reassuring confidence, "See? Told'ya I could handle it!"

Except, all Etienne really gets out in a weak garble is a barely understandable, *see told'ya,* before the power gets cut to his brain and it's *knees crumpling legs folding vertigo swoop like a pistol whip lights out idiot,* and the last coherent thought he has before his head meets unforgiving concrete is, *fuck this is going to hurt.*

But strangely, it never does.

Chapter 21

His dreams are the slow slide of a paint smeared hand across a window, *blurry disoriented random blobs of color,* and Etienne muzzily floats across the warm sea of them. He's not really aware of what's going on in anything he dreams, just fades in and out of what look like Monet paintings, placidly enjoying the way color bleeds up the length of his arm and then back down, for some reason, parting along this one black seam running across his left forearm.

There's not a matching line on his right, skin smooth and mottled a thousand different shades of pastel from fingertips up, so he turns back to that winding absence of color on his left, curiosity peaked.

Etienne tries rotating his arm to get a better look at it, but just ends up spinning around it like a fixed point through space, lands somewhere emerald green and glimmering, like sunlight shining down through water. Ripples shake their way across bare toes and trace up his calves, and he sighs dreamily. It's really warm here, *like thick piles of blankets and warm patches of sun and a heavy head settling into the crook of your neck,* and Etienne's tempted to keep drifting, *floating on his back through the cosmos for an eternity,* but his interest is fatally hooked by this snaking black line.

Since he can't look at it that easily, touching seems like the next most useful sense, though getting at it is a kind of difficult task he was not prepared for.

His limbs feel impossibly like lead filled rubber, heavy and *way too bendy,* and getting them motivated to move becomes such a herculean chore, that Etienne is half tempted to let it go, *to just keep floating,* but sheer stubbornness wins out in the end.

Knew you wouldn't give up that easy spooks, something pops and fizzes in his ears like electric blue sparklers, *teasing lighthearted hand punching way too hard into your shoulder oh don't cry you can take a hit,* and he rocks his head into the sensation, feeling it curl around him like an old friend.

Go on, it urges him, *see what there is to find,* and Etienne hums sleepily, watches as the sound turns into golden bubbles while his right hand begins the trek towards his other arm, scaling the mountain of his side and inching across the flat plane of his stomach. Once he actually makes contact, the skin of his left forearm feels stiff, *numb,* almost like there's a barrier in between his questing fingers and the dark river that cuts a path through his flesh.

He pokes and prods at it for a minute, but nothing gives, and so Etienne does what anyone who is lacking some sense and overburdened with curiosity would do- wraps his fingers around his arm and *squeezes.*

Hard.

Lightning arcs out from the area and tints the sky an entire loathsome red, pain rippling with it in fiery bands that drip through his bloodstream, *flash bright in the air,* revealing a monstrous black shape that looms on his horizon.

Etienne has never let go of something faster, but the discomfort and the figure remain. He tries to scrabble backwards on his hands, *get away,* but it's like he's suddenly stuck in bog muck, *can't move your legs can't move your arms you're trapped can't moVE you have to get out of here can'T MOVE you have to run CAN'T MOVE,* and the panic that causes just makes him struggle harder. He tries to push himself up, but putting any sort of pressure on his left arm is a mistake, sends bolts of crackling lighting through his eyes and in each shuddering burst, he's assaulted by grimy black corridors that stretch for miles, *the stench of blood,* unrelenting *fear* curling its claws under the doorjamb.

His dreams change then, grow darker, *uglier,* fester into nightmares, and suddenly a never ending hallway is expanding out in

What Goes Bump In The Night

front of him and he's being forced to stand on legs that don't wanna bear his weight. Lights flicker on one at a time over his head, throw long shadows across the detritus strewn floor as they make their way down the hall, and at some point, they illuminate this hulking form that had been hiding in the darkness.

It doesn't move, it doesn't have eyes, *but it's looking at him,* and Etienne is paralyzed over what to do, *doesn't want to be here keeps telling himself to wake up,* but he can't and he wonders if he *is* actually asleep at all.

Maybe he's awake.

Maybe this is real, and he never left, that rotting hell he now can't remember escaping, *maybe he's still there. Trapped. For an eternity.* And the thought alone makes the whole world spin, pulse drumming up under his ears louder and *louder,* sounds like fists banging on a door *like monstrous palms beating against the floor chasing you into the night gotta be faster or it'll-*

Etienne swallows past this fist sized lump in his throat- *around his throat can't breathe something's choking you,* knows any second now that thing is going to start coming after him *and he'll have to run,* but his legs are already shaking and his head feels woozy, is *pounding* like someone is hammering away at it from *inside his skull.* He has to stay focused though, he has to stay on top of his game, or people are going to die, and he can't let that happen, *he can't be that great of a failure,* blinks his eyes once and now the hallway is lined with shadowed portraits of all his ancestors passed.

Disgraceful, they sneer, lips wrinkled watching the way he shakes and struggles to stand, *no descendant of ours is this weak this pathetic,* and Etienne averts his gaze from their coldly painted eyes in shame, looks down the length of the hall, *at the thing waiting for him the thing that wants to kill him c o n s u m e him the one he can't escape his destiny-*

Do you fear it, they hiss, and he tries to shake his head *no,* but the bones of his neck grind together like some force is keeping them locked in place and he blinks.

Do you want to run from it, they scoff, *condescension* bleeding from their words and old blood starts to ooze from their eyes, running down the slopes of cheeks like a curse, and Etienne feels something drip off his own chin and he blinks.

Do you wish to escape it, they whisper like the *grave, cold endless final the abyss staring back like an unblinking eye,* and it feels like an inevitability that he's ended up here, *can't seem to get out of here,* but this is not where he wanted to die and he has to tell them that, *maybe they'll let him out but you work your throat you try and turn your head you can't they won't let you they never will they're never giving you up you're going to die here-*

He blinks.

And the hallway is clear in front of him.

Etienne breathes harshly into the startling silence and feels something frozen and moist puff onto the back of his neck. All the hair raises along his arms and he doesn't want to look but he already is, stares back and up at the hulking, dribbling shape behind him.

It's a horror.

It's a nightmare.

It's a blackened mishmash of warped together fears, *you'll never be good enough you're going to die an early death,* anxieties, *can you handle this supposed to be born to handle this don't know if you can,* doubts, *you're never going to be what they want you to be you'll always be a disappointment you weren't made for this-*

Do you know, centuries worth of decaying mouths wheeze, rotting eyes in a hundred colors spinning around in collapsing sockets, *have you seen,* deep splinter like cuts opening up here and there, slice through fragile flesh, *what it means to carry power,* black maroon blood weeping to the surface and it's the same color *it's the same color staining their hands staining the delicate skin under their eyes painting their tombs do you know where this leads do*

What Goes Bump In The Night

you know what it takes can you pay the cost gwéiníath do you even want to-

Etienne takes off running.

He feels like he's moving in slow motion but everything is whipping past him at breakneck speeds, floor moving so fast under his feet he can barely keep up, slipping and tripping down this grime coated hallway while the thing *pursues.*

The slap of its palms striking the ground rattles *everything,* including the teeth in his gums, a choppily building crescendo that hammers faster and faster along to the frantic beating of Etienne's heart. It's like a storm out of control, barreling towards him with all the unhinged power of a train completely off its tracks, sound of its running palms so loud, he's half convinced they're going to reawake the dead.

Lights start exploding behind him, the bright sharp high notes to this symphony of disaster, and Etienne keeps trying to stay ahead of that incoming wave of darkness, *knows it's coming,* but it soon envelopes him like an unforgiving shroud.

Ahead of him, bulbs continue to shatter, and there is nothing worse than watching those lights go out one at a time. *No no no no no,* Etienne pants desperately, stretching a hand out, thinks someone should be ahead of him, that maybe they can reach back and grab him, pull him out of the night and into the warmth of salvation.

They should be there, *they should be there waiting for him,* he knows it, *he remembers,* he just has to run a little further, a little harder, and they'll be there, *they promised you they'd be there always at your back at your side look down and surprised they're still here I'm a ~~Caldwell~~ we don't leave people behind they'll be there they'll be-*

But no one reaches back for him, *his hand flails for nothing he is alone they left him down here they left him to die* and those lights get further and further away, and the sound of the creature gets *louder and louder,* roaring all around him, *it's in his head it's going*

◆✦◆ 487 ◆✦◆

to burst his eardrums hands banging against the floor the walls the inside of his skull let us out LET US OUT shattering pain around his ankle yanking him back yanking him

d

o

w

n

straight to the middle of the bottom of nowhere and melted skin drips off his arm in pale ropes pale like snow can't see everything's too bright a thousand unblinking eyes half of them blue half of them hazel all of them empty one plus one is two is one wake up blonde hair soaked in blood matted into clumps sticks here and there out of rotting flesh waKE uP a dozen instances of the same face melted together hey Etienne parts together parts apart WAKE UP it took them it got them didn't save them YOU FAILED you did this you did this YOU DID THIS PARTS APART TOGETHER IN PIECES AND PARTS WAKE UP

WAKE UP

WAKE UP

W A K E U P-

Etienne jolts awake with a painful inhale, *heart hammering,* woodenly pulls his face out of the pillow he was smashing it into and half props himself up on his right arm, blinking blearily at his surroundings. Dark floral wallpaper arches over his head, decorating the inside walls of this ornate alcove that the bed is tucked back into, band posters and other concert paraphernalia tacked up on the underside in a messy collage of macabre colors.

Around his legs is a rumpled tangle of white linen sheets, down comforter scrunched up on the other side of the bed like it'd been hurled off sometime in the night, and it's kinda hard to see the rest of the room since he's lying on his stomach, but Etienne twists a

What Goes Bump In The Night

fraction before a stiff pain in his back makes him stop.

In that brief moment though, he saw light slipping in softly past curtains drawn taught across the windows, dark teal walls that make the whole room feel like it's suspended far underwater, bits and bobs crammed onto bookshelves and plants set on any space left, leaves waving gently, and he can relax back into the cushy mattress under him, knows he's in his room and that where he just came from was only a nightmare.

And *fuck, but what a nightmare.*

His heart is still drumming away unhappily under his ribs, and Etienne hangs his head, letting the shakes rattle out of him so then maybe its frantic beat will calm. He snuffles his face against his pillow, pushing sweat damp hair out of his eyes, and normally, he'd use one of his hands for the task, but both his arms feel like deadweight now that he's more awake.

Right is doing marginally better than left though, was at least able to prop him up a moment ago, but it's shaking where he's tucked it back under his pillow and then his other forearm has started burning faintly, so that's fun.

Etienne slowly tries to flex the fingers on that hand, just wants to gauge where things are at and immediately regrets it, groans as he buries his face completely back into the pillow.

He works on breathing evenly while he waits for the pain to subside, counting internally, *one two three one two fucking shit that hurts three one two,* but that dull, low burning fire continues to swirl up through his muscles and nerves. Involuntarily, Etienne's legs squirm through his tangle of bedsheets and accidentally drag to life a whole new host of hurts that throb in his lower back, across the sides of his chest, *up around the front of his throat,* and yeah *okay, fuck consciousness,* he should probably just stop moving and hope he falls back asleep because this is-

A sudden loud banging makes him jackknife upright, forces him back to dark corridors and freezing terrors *and running for his life* as he clumsily spins around to face the noise, *scared over what*

✦✦ 489 ✦✦

he's going to find about what came crawling out of the dark to take him back there, but his room is *blessedly* empty even though the hammering persists. Etienne squints into the half gloom, aches temporarily forgotten while he tries to figure out what's going on, *if he's having another nightmare or not does he need to run,* but the longer he listens, the more the thudding sounds less like flesh slapping old floorboards so much as it sounds like...*wood striking wood.*

Which is a confusing mystery for all of five seconds until a creaky little voice shouts from outside his door, "Èy, *boy!* You hearin' me? I've been callin' for you! You can't sleep all day now, komprenn? S'already past noon an' I know you kabris need your rest but *there's compa- èy!* Pester off Mai! What're you...*me? I'm* the one that's pester-? *Mmm mmm, non madame,* you did *not just say that to me, you kolèksyon a punaises-!"*

And Etienne collapses exhausted back against his pillows while Gran Mémé starts arguing with Maisette vehemently in French, slaps a leaden hand across his eyes and rubs his fingers in, *hard.*

Well...at least it's not a tordu?

Though, dealing with his great-grandmother at the moment is not exactly high on the list of wants Etienne currently has *either.*

He is so tired, and he loves his Mémé, *really he does,* but it sounds like she's been up here before trying to get him for something, and *Mothers,* it's bad, but he wishes she would just *leave him alone already.* Normally, he doesn't mind doing anything she needs, *running errands changing out her pillows helping her find whatever she's lost,* but right now, Etienne's just...*so tapped out,* can't really remember a time he's been *this* injured and *this exhausted* coming off an assignment.

Part of him just wants to try and go back to sleep anyway, see if she'll lose interest on her own, and then he can get some more rest like his drooping eyelids are *desperately* encouraging him to do, but with the racket she's making, he doesn't think he's going to be able to relax much until she's gone.

What Goes Bump In The Night

"Etien-! Oh don't *shush me,* you blasted *creature-!"* Mémé fusses again way too loudly, and Etienne drags his hand down off his face to rest lightly on his chest, fingers drumming against his collarbones while he thinks.

If she's still up here bothering him about whatever, there must not be anyone else home, and since Maisette hasn't dealt with it yet either, whatever it is Mémé needs must require a corporeal body to get done.

Or she's just being obstinate and won't let the house help, which has happened before, but however you choose to cut it, Mémé has apparently decided that Etienne is the person she needs, and once she's got something stuck in her craw, she is not easily deterred onto a different path.

Honestly, it might just be easier to see what it is she wants and get her calmed down, then he can deal with it from there, so with a sigh, Etienne rocks his head back and says to the canopy over him, "You can let her in."

The frame kinda creaks inwards, like a set of concerned eyebrows drawing together, curtains swaying up in an, *are you sure,* gesture, and he waves them on, "Yes m'sure...but thank you for tryin' to let me sleep though, 'ppreciate it."

Etienne runs a knuckle along the gilded headboard behind him and smiles when the blankets shuffle up higher, not quite tucking under his chin, but definitely bundling closer. The comforter also wiggles itself back into place, a nice heavy weight across his feet as his bedroom door swings open on its own, and Etienne tries to prop himself up some, *wants to look halfway respectable,* but his left arm twinges *bad* and he's forced back into a tired slump.

Still, he does the best that he can, picks his head up and puts a pleasant expression on his face, and with a tottering lurch, Gran Mémé's chair waddles a little ways into his room, her perched atop its scarlet cushions like a reigning dowager.

"Oooh! There you are shéri, I've been callin' for you, ya'know?" She says with a sunny smile, readjusting her half moon spectacles

✦✦✦ 491 ✦✦✦

where they've slipped down her nose, cane balanced across her knees like a riding crop, "You sleep like the dead you do, you know that?"

"Yes ma'am, *sorry,* I uh...I-I had kinda a late night last night." Etienne explains tentatively, surprised to see her so seemingly coherent. Today must be one of her ever scarcer good days, and leaning forward over her blanket clad lap, Mémé wags a hand at him, "Don't worry about that apology now, your maman told me you were gonna be restin' this mornin' anyway, an' I figured while she was out, I should keep an eye on you in her stead-"

Mothers of the Night-

Did she...*seriously just wake you up to see if you needed anything for the love of fucking-* no, *no,* he can't be irritated about that since it is such a- *kind and thoughtful gesture...is in no way super annoying,* and nodding his head like her reasoning makes *perfect* sense, Etienne is going to tell her that, *thanks Gran Mémé but I'm good just need to rest,* emphasis on the *rest,* when she finishes her thought, "-so I won't keep you long, shéri, but I just wanted to let you know your friends are here."

"My friends?" Etienne mutters in confusion, more bamboozled than he should be by that simple statement, and cupping a hand around an ear, Gran Mémé raps one side of her cane against an armrest of her chair and fusses, "*What?* Speak up boy, you know I can't hear you when you're mumblin' like that-"

"My friends! What friends? Who's *here?"* Etienne asks louder, trying to figure out who the hell would be visiting him randomly in the middle of the day like this. Sabine does normally swing by after every near death event to act fake concerned over Etienne's health, *because he's too emotionally stunted to actually admit how sick with worry he's been,* but he should still be at work, no way Renee would excuse him from his duties for the day over something like this.

Besides him though, there's only been one other time where anyone else came to see him, and that was after Etienne had shat-

What Goes Bump In The Night

tered a leg not too far into his apprenticeship. He's definitely more banged up now than he was then, but being exhausted and cut up is way less exciting than a fractured limb, there's no cast to sign for starters, plus, he and his friends are all adults now.

No one is surprised when they hear through the grapevine that Etienne's gone and landed himself in bed for a day or two, he's a Boudreaux, that's just what happens now.

While he's been lost in thought, Etienne's been waiting for Gran Mémé to answer his question, and he doesn't want to pressure her, but it's been a good minute or two and she still hasn't said anything. She's just smiling at him softly expectant, so he figures she didn't hear him on the second repetition either, *really* makes sure to project this time when he asks, *"Mémé-!* Who is *at the door!* Who did you *talk to?"*

"Hm? Oh I don't know." She shakes her head and nearly knocks her glasses off her nose, "It's some girl an' her sister. They look just alike, ya'know? I think they're classmates of yours, the one said somethin' about a club. Are you in a club, my boy? Is it chess? My Éleutaire *loves* his chess, he was captain of the chess team back at the academy, is that the club you're thinkin' of joinin'? Oh, he'd be so happy to have someone play with him mô lamou, *so happy."*

Alright. So maybe she's not as lucid as Etienne previously thought, and he collapses back against the bed, tiredly rubbing at his eyes and seriously doubting the fact that someone is even *at* the door, "I- okay, thank you, Mémé. Could you um, would you mind telling my *friends* that I uh...*appreciate,* them stoppin' by, but I'm just a little too tired to visit right now?"

"Of course my boy, of course. That's what *I* said in the first place, but that girl is too damn stubborn for her own good. I'll see them off. You just worry about gettin' your rest now, ya hear?" Mémé says, patting her lap forcefully for emphasis and takes her cane in hand next, rapping it against the arms of her chair as she whistles, "Alon, Général! Back downstairs we go! We've got girls to shoo off an' tea to make! I'll bring you a cup mô shè, peppermint is good for the sinuses it is. You want cream an' honey?"

✦✦ 493 ✦✦

"No, Mémé, you really don't have to, I-I'm fine, *seriously! I just want to sleep-!*"

"Would you quit your shoutin'! You'll wake the whole house! I'll just fix your tea like I know you like Éli, don't you worry." She hums over her shoulder and before he can get another word in edgewise, her chair heaves itself back to its feet and goes clunking out of his room, Gran Mémé muttering to herself while she's swayed back and forth, "Such curious company you keep, Éli, *such curious company*...never seen a hand shine like that...*hehe, like a new nickel*...that used to buy you a *whooole* nickelodeon back in my day, mm hmm..."

The door obligingly swings shut on her absentminded ramblings and Etienne lets out a long sigh, thumping his head back into his pillows. So...he's probably got about thirty minutes before she's back up here banging on his door, hot tea in hand, though that's assuming she remembers to *make* tea in the first place, and honestly, given their recent conversation, he's not too optimistic about that. He doesn't even *want* the blasted tea anyway, *he just wants to sleep,* can feel fatigue weighing on him like lead weights, but with the way his shit luck works, Etienne just *knows* that as soon as he drifts off, Mémé will unintentionally wake him back up anyway.

Ugh

Well, half an hour is still half an hour and his eyelids are already drooping, so he figures, *fuck it,* might as well get what rest he can, *while he can.*

Etienne wriggles his aching body into a slightly more comfortable position, though comfort is really an evasive concept at the moment all things considered, and tries to be careful about how he drapes his throbbing left arm over his stomach. It's wrapped neatly in gauze from palm to the crook of his elbow, so Etienne can't see it, but the way his skin is sticking and pulling makes him think he ended up with stitches after all.

Another addition to the collection, he thinks drowsily, fingers dancing featherlight over the area where he's sure to have a gnarly

What Goes Bump In The Night

looking scar, and already knows Sabine's going to have an aneurysm. He always does whenever Etienne turns back up with stories and stitches, but that's a worry for another day...probably this evening actually, as soon as Sabine gets off work, but generically, it's a problem for future Etienne to deal with.

The aftermath of near death experiences are one of the rare occurrences where he does *not* relish the visit with his best friend, and letting out a long sigh, the kind that empties all the air from his lungs, Etienne takes the premature stress he was already holding on to and lets it go.

Whatever...he's gonna have to get over that eventually, Etienne shifts a bit, pulling the pressure off his right hip which is still a little tender from where he twisted himself around it last night, *s'not like it's avoidable...gotta deal with this shit the rest of our lives,* humming happily when the blankets bundle themselves up closer, their warmth and weight filling his head with static, and his eyes grow heavier, his breaths more even, *can't run from it...can't run from it s'our fates...our birthrights...his an' mine him an' me... together always...back to back...hand in...hand...*

Etienne quickly starts to drift off, lulled back into the welcoming arms of sleep, and of course it's only then, after he's gotten comfortable, where he's luridly thinking of best friends and long nights and confused great-grandmothers, *about Big Band music playing over crunchy nickelodeons tea he didn't ask for and hands passing it to him made out of...shiny metal...ones that could...hold you gently and catch you out of midair...that glow brighter than the sun and stubborn bastard eye like the dawn eye like willow bark never seen anything like that like you fingers crushing rocks and dusting over yours carefully metal plating rippling like dragon scales hey Etienne-*

And a terrible thought comes to him.

About who could be on his front porch.

He sits bolt upright in bed.

There's no way that...*no,* he's just being paranoid, there's no

✦✦ 495 ✦✦

reason for them to be here, *absolutely none they wouldn't...but they could,* and if they *did,* that would mean that- *Gran Mémé,* his dear beloved great-grandmother with degenerative mental conditions, who they *never let answer the door for fear of what's going to come out of her mouth,* is downstairs, *talking to- those girls classmates of yours said something about a club you're in together or a...program hi I'm his Arcane Diversity partner too damn stubborn hand like a new nickel I'll just go see them off got to get rid of oh fuck-*

And what are the odds, *what are the fucking odds* that anyone else in this city would be here to see him and be stubborn as anything *and have a metal arm prosthesis-*

Oh fuck. *Oh fuck oh fuck oh fuck oh fuck-!*

"Maisette!" Etienne calls desperate, half hunched over his bent knees while he stares up at the crossbeams of his canopy bed in slowly simmering panic, asking now like he couldn't when Gran Mémé was in the room, "Please, *p-please,* tell me no one's *actually* at the door? *Like- please tell me she's just confused an' nobody's here-"*

And with the awkward clack of a few wooden struts, the dark fabric of the canopy crumples inwards like an anxious set of brows, quick shake side to side translating out as *no, no she's not confused,* meaning Mémé is *right, didn't imagine it didn't dream it up someone is at the door,* here right now, *asking for him,* and Etienne's hands fist in his blankets as he hisses strangled, *"Well is it at least a witch?"*

Please say yes please say yes please just bob up and down, chants in his mind like the most desperate pray he's ever offered up, and he *hopes, beyond measure,* that he is wrong and it's just Sabine's stupid ass outside waiting to give him a lecture, but with another hesitant shake of inky fabric, *another no,* Etienne is out of his bed like a *shot.*

He scrabbles gracelessly off the end and vaults the small settee backed up to the footboard, tripping across his room in a flail of

What Goes Bump In The Night

limbs while he yells, *"Pants pants pants! I don't give a shi- shoot what kind! Just pants!"*

A dark blur comes flying at him from inside his wardrobe and Etienne grabs it clumsily, shaking out the pair of pajamas, gets them tugged up over his boxers as fast as he can, and before he can ask for a shirt next, he catches one with his face.

"Thanks!" He calls muffled, stumbling out his door while pulling his head free from the collar. Etienne rushes down the hallway in a frantic thudding of heels on carpet, unsuccessfully works on getting his arms through the sleeve holes of the old band shirt, and valiantly ignores the protesting scream that is his stitched up left forearm.

Paintings titter and arch their eyebrows as he careens past, likely getting a kick out of seeing him so discombobulated, and Etienne's still kinda only half dressed when he trips into the banister at the top of the stairs. He shakes dark hair out of his eyes and looks down into the foyer, gaze spinning past richly colored carpets and the clawed feet of furniture until it lands on where Gran Mémé is sitting atop her chair, *talking to someone outside the open front door.*

Etienne catches a sliver of ruby red past her figure, *a glimpse of ashy blonde flash of silver no hat in sight fuck has he never hated being right more,* and then he's practically falling headfirst down the stairs, pulse roaring in his ears and underscoring a single noted symphony of, *crap crap crap CRAP CRAP-!*

"I got it I got it I GOT IT!" He yells, finally situating his shirt as he comes skittering to a stop at Gran Mémé's side, trying desperately to shoulder her out of the way, voice obnoxiously loud in the *hopes that she fucking hears him, "Thank you Gran Mémé!* B-But I got it! *You can go sit down er-* well, I-I'll just- *bring you some tea in a minute, that sound good? WOULD YOU LIKE TH-!"*

"Blast it, boy! Would you quit your *yellin'?* I'm right here!" Mémé fusses and jabs him in the side with her cane, nearly knocks him on his ass but blessedly the coat rack catches him before he can

◆✦◆ 497 ◆✦◆

go crashing to the floor, "Also, fix your balance! What sort of witch trips over his own feet like you do? *Tsk*, two left feet an' no sense in your head, *Mères de la Nwit*, you're lucky you've never fallen down those stairs an' broken your fool *neck!*"

Funnily enough, right now *Etienne wishes he had fallen down the stairs and broken his fool neck*, stares mortified at the front door's threshold and the shuffling toes of Nica's sneakers and feels his entire face bleed a vibrant *crimson*, tips of his ears *on fire*.

Mothers, he should've just stayed in his *fucking room*.

Apparently satisfied that she's quite literally *embarrassed him to death*, Mémé whistles and smacks the side of her chair then, getting it to move back a bit so it's no longer hulking in the doorway, "Well, now that my laze-about grandson is here, I suppose I'll leave you kids to your chit chattin'. Such a pleasure meetin' you, Niki, you're quite an articulate young g-"

"I- thank you, ma'am, b-but it's um, *it's a-actually*, uh, Nica? And um, I-I'm not- that is- *ah, i-it's just-*"

"That's nice dear, *that's very nice*, always good to meet more of uh...hm, *oh what's his*...ki çé ça...*oh! Esteban*, darlin', can you try an' keep it down? I wanna listen to my shows an' sometimes you really wake snakes, my boy." Mémé chuckles, turning to pat at his cheek roughly and shake him a bit, nearly puts his eye out in the process because she probably thought his face was going to be higher than it is at the moment.

Etienne grunts and tips his chin back to reposition her hand, attempting to preserve the structural integrity of his eyeball, and has the brief need to correct her on a...*lot of things*. Like how his name isn't Esteban and the fact that Nica isn't a girl and that *she's* the one that *keeps asking him to speak up*, but really, it doesn't matter whatever wrong name Mémé called him or what she almost said to Nica, there's no point arguing. She's not having a very clear day and pressing any issue is just going to confuse her further, *make her more distressed*, so honestly the best thing to do is just agree with whatever she said and let it go.

What Goes Bump In The Night

Plus it gets her out of here faster anyway, and that's really all that matters.

"Yes, ma'am, of course. Sorry. Enjoy your show. We're just gonna be out here, but let Maisette know if you need me for anythin' an' I'll be right in, okay?" Etienne says evenly, clear and loud but not *too loud,* and is reward with a sunny smile and another jarring pat to the face before she takes her hand back, "Atta boy. *That's a good boy,* your maman raised a good one, *wé li fait, mm hm..."*

And without any more preamble, Gran Mémé kicks at the leg of her chair to get it moving, huffing at *General Bonaparte to march like you mean it you little nightmare,* singing softly under her breath as it goes lumbering off towards the back parlor. She rounds a corner, voice fading, and thankfully is now out of earshot *and* line of sight, and Etienne doesn't waste any time scrambling to his feet, hissing under his breath to Maisette in French, *"Don't let her back out here!"*

The curtains salute him as he slips out the front door, and after closing it solidly behind him, Etienne collapses back against its glossy black surface, face twisting into an expression of pure mortification when he looks up at Nica, *"Mothers of the Night-!* I-I am *so sorry-* I didn't know that you were- I-I've been sleepin' all day or I would've been down here to meet you instead of *her,* but she's the only other one home right now. I know it's not, *like- an excuse,* but she's like a hundred and *two,* an' has dementia really bad, she didn't mean- *i-it's not like-"*

"Nah, *hey, chill-* s'fine, don't worry about it. *Seriously.* My mammaw is the same way." Nica allows in what Etienne considers to be a very *charitable tone,* flesh hand kneading at the back of their neck as they nod towards the house, "Least she's not doin' it on purpose to try an' guilt trip me into bein' something I'm *not,* because- *'that's just the natural state of things, Addie, you got men an' you got women, you can't be neither',* but anyway...u-um, yeah-"

An extremely awkward silence follows this statement wherein Etienne doesn't know *what* to say and Nica looks like they really wish they hadn't said *anything.*

✦✦✦ 499 ✦✦✦

Their expression is one of immediate regret, *eyes pinching closed hands diving for shelter in the front pocket of their hoodie fuck should not have said that,* and Etienne remembers them mentioning once they're not great at knowing social cues, is going to attempt a conversational rescue with a nice easy, *so what brings you to my neck of the woods,* when Nica beats him to it.

Or, that's probably what they're *trying* to do, except they course correct a little *too* hard and it ends up coming out as something a hair short of disastrous.

"So you're alive, *that's neat-* I-I mean-! *Not neat, n-neat is not the word I should-* but it's not *not* neat that you survived- *made it out didn't d-die-* because I really thought you *were gonna die,* b-but you didn't!" Nica rambles, hands clearly picking at each other in the pocket of their red Hermes University hoodie, a color very similar to the shade their face is going, "Honestly I'm surprised you're standing. I thought you'd be like, *i-in a coma for sure,* 'cause that thing *fucked you up.* Like I saw you get drug off and it was like, *welp, guess we're all gonna die now,* b-but then we didn't! Because you um, b-because you didn't get...*murdered...s-somehow...*"

They trail off, eyes firmly fixed on one of the porch's support columns, lips tucked back over their teeth so their mouth gets pressed into this long, thin line, and maybe it's because he's still so tired, or his hurts are really hurting now that he's been on his feet for a minute, but the way Nica's talking about him stings more than it probably should.

It's all, *'surprised'* this, and, *'didn't think you could do it'* that, and once Etienne's got it in his head that they actually had no faith in him last night, *that's suddenly the only thing he can hear,* how Nica assumed he was *lying* about protecting them. *They probably figured you'd fuck it up in the end,* something nasty whispers to him from the dark corners of his mind, *that's all you're good at anyways disgrace of a son disgrace of a witch you brought that dragon down on their head why would anyone assume you're capable of anything after that,* and it yanks sharply on his heart.

His arms shuffle closer in response, a facsimile of a hug or maybe

What Goes Bump In The Night

a painful embrace, *like the truth that they never even believed in you for a moment why would they what good have you ever been got people killed your ancestors are right to scorn you what kind of Boudreaux loses- shut UP SHUT UP-* and it's involuntary, the way he dives to hide his insecurities and panic behind a shield of scornful snobbery.

"Gee- thanks for the *vote of confidence. Really means a lot."* Etienne drawls and can feel his mouth twist up into an ugly sneer, chooses to focus on that and the acid it steeps into his tone rather than the way his throat gets scratchy, *like it only does when he's about to cry,* "Well if you just came by to pluck at my inadequacies, I'd rather save it for Monday. That way, you can lay them *allll* out in your assignment report for the program liaison, paint the- *perfect picture for the city of how I nearly got us all killed-!"*

"N-NO! *No t-that's not what I-!"* Nica yelps, eyes instantly snapping to his, hands clumsily shooting out of their pocket to wave frantically, "I-I didn't *mean-* that came out w-wrong- *incorrect not right b-bad choice-* I should've said- I-I just meant I was worried about you, *I've b-been so w-worried about you-* the whole time *t-the entire night!* I didn't sleep- *I c-couldn't sleep-"*

"-I just- I kept hearin' it over an' *over again, that scream, y-your scream,* when it g-grabbed you, a-an' I was...*so scared."* Nica's voice gets really ragged then and their skin and bone hand comes up to rub jointly at their eyes, at the imposing dark bags under them, *ones that look way worse than usual the entire night they said,* "I don't think you're incapable, you're- *h-holy shit,* you're *incredible,* I-I've never seen *anyone- you're just- amazing.* You asked me to trust you an' I did- *I-I do,* still- b-but, *bad shit happens.* People *d-die. Horrifically.* And I-I was *s-so scared that was gonna be you, Etienne, I w-was so scared it was gonna be you-"*

Nica lets out a huge gust of breath that sounds a little shaky, jitters up and down on their toes in something like a nervous tick, and their left hand migrates to find its home on the back of their neck, right crawling to hide in a pants pocket as they sigh, *"M'sorry.* I...I-I shouldn't've come here without hearin' back from you first. I just thought- *was w-worried didn't know if you-* I...*I don't know*

✦✦✦ 501 ✦✦✦

what I thought. I wasn't thinking, I guess, sorry."

Awkwardly shuffling back a pace or two, Nica hikes a thumb over their shoulder and stares somewhere in the vicinity of Etienne's right ear, "I should...*go*. Um, s-sorry again for gettin' you woken up. I'll just- *you j-just get some rest,* and I'll see you Monday? *Unless you're not feelin' up to it which*- totally understandable, just let me know, but I'll uh...I-I'll see'ya around...hope you have a good weekend."

They turn to go and Etienne is hit with the understanding of several things at once.

Primarily it's that he's an *idiot,* which nothing really new there hello Mister *'I Threw Myself Down The Stairs Because I Couldn't Think Of Anything Better',* and secondly it's how he's really got to stop assuming the only thing people see in him is worthlessness. That's something he's always struggled with, *the ~~fact~~ lie that he's never been worth anything and everyone else knows it,* but that's a shackled weight of his own making, a burden no one but him should have to bear.

Etienne can't keep passing it off and demanding the people around him carry it, *can't keep taking his frustrations and fears out on others,* but despite knowing this, he realizes now he's been doing it *anyway,* and that's his mistake. He thought he'd been doing better, but it feels like it's happening more and more often lately, like he's backsliding to where he was four years ago, and maybe mother was right, *maybe he does need to go back and see Cynin.*

The thought does not bring him peace though, if anything, it makes his pulse skitter faster, a nervous tumble of *I can't I can't I can't go back there and fail again I can't have someone else so thoroughly rooted in my mind,* so Etienne cuts a deal with himself.

Going forwards from now, he really, *sincerely* works on trying to fix shit on his own, wants at least *a chance* to prove to himself he has the ability to do it, *that he's capable of change,* but, if he's still struggling in a few months, *or void beyond,* if it gets *worse,* then he

✦✦ 502 ✦✦

What Goes Bump In The Night

will be an adult and...*go ask for the help he needs.*

Which does not leave a pleasant taste in his mouth but rarely does medicine taste pleasing on the pallet, and Etienne supposes this is the first drop of it, lurches after Nica and snags them with a hand in the crook of their elbow.

"Wait." He says, doesn't have to try hard to reel them in and he doesn't think that will ever stop being a comfort, how readily Nica turns back for him, "Don't go. It's really kind you comin' by to check on me, an'...you're right, to have been worried about me? I know it must've'nt been real pretty walkin' out of there. I'm sorry you had to see any of that, *go through what you did,* an' I'm sorry for-"

-failing you, he almost confesses, bites it off at the last second but it's still right there on the tip of his tongue, *the continued self-dep-recation – I'm sorry for letting you down for not being enough for nearly costing you your life I'm sorry I'm a failure and a fuckup...I'm sorry I'm good for nothing,* and they run rancid down his throat when Etienne swallows them all back.

You did what you could you saved who you could, he says, *forcing* himself to believe it, *no it wasn't perfect no you're not perfect,* takes a small steadying inhale, *and that's okay what in life is without flaw,* lets it out, *lets it go takes a step away from the black muck clinging at his ankles,* and pivots elegantly into, "I'm sorry for snappin' at you. I...I-I know I say that a lot, an' I'm workin' on it, *promise,* but I just...I just let my um, *m-my insecurities,* win a lot of the time? A-And I'm sorry for that. I'm really tryin' to be better about it, but that's not an excuse, so...*sorry.*"

Mothers of the Night, he feels *sick to his stomach, heart racing sweaty palms lightheaded inducing nausea why did you admit that,* but he just breathes through it and tells himself it's going to be okay, because who better to say this to?

Etienne's not naive enough to think everyone around him isn't struggling with *something,* it's the human condition, an inescapable system of imperfections, but they all seem like they're handling it better than he does. Mother has more duties and responsibilities

✦✦ 503 ✦✦

than he can wrap his brain around, but she's never dropped the ball on any of them, and then Sabine is under a suffocating amount of pressure, and Etienne knows it eats at him, but he still continues to outperform any LeBlanc that's come before him and likely any that'll come after.

And it's intimidating talking to them about his own problems, because Etienne knows they love him, *sometimes knows they don't think less of him,* but it's hard always feeling like you're the subject of scrutiny. Like a bug under a microscope, and there's, *oh I've got some issues I'm working through,* but then there's also, *I'm not really sure my head was put on right,* and with Etienne, *it's always the latter,* and it's so hard to have a conversation when you and the person you're talking to are facing the wrong directions.

Which is why he's trying not to be sick across the front porch now, kneejerk fear of, *don't let them see don't let them know don't show them how backwards you are,* pounding in his ears but Etienne doesn't think it matters here, *not with them,* thinks they already know what it's like to be a bug, *is pretty sure Nica's head wasn't put on correctly either.*

"Oh." They say soft, *barely a word,* just an exhalation that's free of judgment and isn't weighed down by heavy things like pity, and something leaden feels like it's cut loose from Etienne's chest, "Um, t-thanks? *I mean-* t-thank you. *Really.* I uh, I get how it could've sounded like I was...*doubting you,* but I wasn't. Words are hard. *I-I'm kinda bad at them.* But I didn't mean to make you feel self-conscious, I really didn't...*I was just worried.*"

"I know." Etienne sighs heavy, and lets his hand fall away from their arm to steady himself on a nearby post, allowing with a rueful shrug of the shoulders, "I'm...kinda bad at lettin' people worry about me."

Mouth quirking back and forth, Nica nods slowly, fingers incessantly fiddling with the fraying ends of their hoodie sleeves as their eyes jump up and down his body, "I get that, I...*yeah.* M'not gonna press, but...you okay, though? I don't know what's the last thing you remember but you um, y-you kinda passed out from blood

What Goes Bump In The Night

loss? An' the paramedics were...*kiiiindaaa* freaking out over you..."

Ah.

Yes.

Etienne does remember something to that effect when he thinks back to last night, but not much beyond it. Everything is a vivid reel of, *oh shit oh shit run faster dodge that don't die SEARING LIGHT oh fuck,* up until a certain point where it gets kinda crinkly and that's probably about when he lost consciousness. He can't really recall another instance where he passed out while in the field like that, usually is better equipped *and* better prepared, but all things considered, he honestly doesn't think he got out half bad.

A lot of the injuries he sustained were mostly just annoying and not immediately life threatening, and whoever saw to him last night did a bang-up job with their pharmaceutical magic anyway. The cuts on his hands are all completely gone, skin still raw and tender but overwise smooth and blemish free. His arm needed stitches, and yeah it'll scar, but it's not splinted so that means none of the bones were broken, which, after already dealing with a broken leg once, Etienne is not eager to revisit the whole cast situation.

Mostly, he's just extremely sore and bruised and in need of another ten hour nap, and shifting the weight off his aching hip, Etienne waffles a hand back and forth, "Eh? I mean I lived, *obviously,* an' I will continue to do so, but s'just gonna be an...*uncomfortable,* kind of livin' until the rest of this gets healed up...how about you? You doin' alright? How's the wrist?"

"Oh they gave me some stuff for that an' it's completely healed, but otherwise, *you know,* can't really complain...I've definitely had worse." Nica brings their metal hand up and wiggles their fingers in a little rolling tinkle, clearly making light of their prosthesis and what must have been a difficult amputation, but recognizing this as something he's *supposed* to find funny, Etienne lets a crooked grin tug his lips up.

He's always been fond of dark humor, *only recently been fond of*

✦✦ 505 ✦✦

Nica, and this is a delightful combination that Etienne hasn't realized he could enjoy. Nica's made jokes in a similar vein before, but the two of them hadn't known each other well, *kinda didn't like one another either,* and Etienne was never sure if he was allowed to laugh or not. Half the time, he was more worried that he'd been being insensitive, and this was Nica's way of conveying that, so he always default resorted to the comfort of *panic* and profusely apologizing.

Now though, he can see that huffing a laugh out of his nose was the correct call, quick flash of a smile darting up Nica's mouth, not quite enough to settle into a dimple, but pleased none the less.

It feels like such a relief to be talking like this without the threat of imminent death hanging over their heads, but the jaunty mood does sober a touch when Nica shuffles their feet closer together, eyes darting away as they ask hesitantly, "H-Hey, do you, *um,* d-do you have a minute to talk? *I-I won't stay long!* I just...w-wanted to talk to you real quick s'all..."

A couple things pop up fast in Etienne's mind like the poisonous flowers in Au Delà, *something's wrong you messed up somewhere what're they mad about what did you do,* but he stomps them back down for being the useless, involuntary anxieties they are. *Calm down it's not anything you're just being nervous and irrational,* he thinks, nodding to Nica before hobbling over to one of the cushioned benches sitting along the front porch, "Yeah sure, I don't have anythin' else to be doin'."

Etienne flops down with less coordination than usual, limbs stiff and not happy with him about the whole verticality thing, and quicker than he can think to grab for one, a pillow fluffs itself and wiggles behind his back.

"Thank you." He says out of habit and feels an answering flicker of gratitude, *of course of course our child,* but Nica gives him a weird look as they tentatively sit down near him, "Uh, for what?"

"Oh no, not you. Maisette." Etienne reshuffles a bit, trying to get comfortable, *fails that,* and doesn't think his answer is warranted

What Goes Bump In The Night

more of an explanation until Nica asks him a baffled, *"Who?"*

"What do you mean *who? Does your *coven not-* o-oh. Right."* Etienne stumbles to a stop, forgetting for a moment the vastly different lives they lead and then is wary about actually explaining, knows what people have said in the past about coven houses, *creepy weird unnatural it's alive it can think it's a threat to us to the rest of the world,* but this isn't some idiot on the street.

This is Nica, *his friend,* who is incredibly smart and pragmatic, has already put up with a lot more disturbing magical entities than this, *Gertie raccoon terrors the tordu,* and so surely they'll be able to handle a house possessed by a fathomless entity that exists outside of time and space, who's true consciousness is shrouded in so much knowable mystery, that not even Etienne and his family truly understand its whims or intentions, but what they *do* know is that it likes to make them soup when they're sick and that it keeps the floors heated in the winter...

So there's that.

Maybe he should omit some of what comes before that-

Clearing his throat, Etienne gestures in the general direction of the porch and says hesitantly, "Uh, Maisette is our house. It cooks and cleans an' takes care of us."

There.

A nice, short, simple answer that leaves out the- *unfathomable cosmic entity existentialism,* and like the *obliging* eldritch construct it is, Maisette ruffles all the floorboards on the porch from one end to another, a decorative strut from up near the trim temporarily cracking off to wave back and forth at the two of them.

And that's cute right? Like- *that's friendly and not a weird thing for a house to do, right?*

...oh who is he kidding, that's not something any other house does and he is so worried for a second that Nica's gonna freak out.

Typically, humans aren't real fond of coming across things that have sentience when they don't think that said thing *should* have sentience. It freaks them out, *makes them feel small,* and Nica may be as understanding as can be, *may be masking their horror really well,* but they're still *human.*

And he knows what humans are *like, distrust in their eyes anger in their voices freaks jinxflingers monsters get out of our city protest lines back to burning pyres pitchforks and torches and heathens savages godless people never should've trusted you never should've let you live-* or, he knows what they *can* be like, and the possibility of Nica being the same makes him *scared.*

Etienne is terrified of them judging him, *scared of them hating him afraid of the pins on their bag of seeing their face in an angry crowd wood handle of a protest sign melting into that of a weapon,* and that type of assumption is mistake number one for him to think, but mistake two is Etienne basing his assumptions off how a *typical* human would react to meeting Maisette.

Because that is very much *not the case* in this particular instance.

Instead of cringing back in fright, Nica shoots to basically the very edge of the bench, leaning over to watch wide eyed and fascinated as the floorboards settle back into place, lips parting in absolute fascination.

"Holy shit." They whisper, hunching forward until they can press fingertips against oak planks, voice slightly muffled by their bent in half posture while they ramble a mile a minute, "Like- I figured it was charmed once I got here since like, *ya'know,* shit moves on its own an' stuff, b-but I never thought it was *conscious.* And it *is* conscious right? Is that a *spell?* Like- c-can y'all just- *infuse inanimate objects with life?* Oh my God...think of the *philosophical implications of that-"*

"Ah, *no,* it's not a spell." Etienne says, cautious about what he's revealing, *all the dark corners and winding branches of the unknown of the dark night and full moon and glittering beyond he was born from,* can't shake the deep fear under his bones that no matter the

What Goes Bump In The Night

human, *no matter how curious,* they will judge him for it in the end, "The coven houses aren't...like the notebooks or anythin' else the Laferriere create, we don't *make them-* well, I-I mean my ancestors did *build* Maisette's physical structure, but we didn't make *it.*"

He worries that was a little too revealing, and pieces of the bench's armrest kinda crack apart then and curl over the back of his band, shine of black lacquered wood standing out stark against his olive complexion, and it's probably the only thing that keeps him from flinching when Nica says, "Ah so it's...it's like a separate thing then, or- *no,* m-more like...*a wellspring*...ooooh, it's where your magic comes from, isn't it."

And the sole reason that statement is not pitched up like a question is because they already know the answer, *are just seeking confirmation,* and Etienne shouldn't be, and *isn't* surprised, that Nica put two and two together after everything, *knows they're too damn smart for their own good.*

How witches get access to their powers isn't *exactly* a secret, but it's not something they all really wanna advertise either, want to protect their houses just as much as their houses want to protect them. It's a rule of thumb that's a product from centuries of persecution and decades of mistrust, but in this case, the proverbial cat is already out of the bag, so Etienne doesn't see a point in lying, looks out across the front lawn at where the grass has already started to yellow, and murmurs a quiet, "Yeah."

Something squirms up in his chest at the immediate silence that follows, and his unoccupied hand picks restlessly at the cotton of his pajama pants. He tries not to be too anxious about it, *wants to think Nica is an exception to the absolute he knows,* but he's also desperate to know what they're thinking, needs a window inside their head so he can watch all their thoughts dart past with ease.

Like- are they second guessing everything they know about him?

Deciding that, *woah maybe this is actually a little too much, a little too weird I can't do this anymore.* Do they see where Carter is coming from? *Incorrect as he may be,* he's still human, *he's still closer to being what Nica is than Etienne will ever be,* and there's comfort in kinship, but is it enough to drive them away? B-But can Etienne even claim that they're close enough for any separation to be noticeable, like, is there even really a connection between the two of them? *Or is he just making the whole thing up are they even friends don't think you ever asked were they ever don't think you ever will-*

A cold touch at his elbow shocks him out of his spiral, and Etienne does jump this time, eyes snapping down expecting nothing nice, *a ghost a specter the undead clawing hand of your demise chasing you into the night beware,* and not a-

...small bottle of orange juice?

"Here." There's a metallic hand connected to it by the very tip, but when Etienne doesn't immediately take it, the hand sets the bottle down before retreating quickly.

Etienne just blinks at it.

What in the...*why* do they have...*what-?*

Looking up from the forlorn OJ lying next to him, Etienne stares in bewilderment at Nica, who refuses to look back at him and whose hands are now currently burrowed deeply in the front pocket of their hoodie, hair shaken to cover as much of their face as they can. One of their ears sticks out past the tangle of blonde anyway, freckled tip dusted a light red that's probably the same color as their face, and gesturing sloppily with their elbow, Nica wags at the bottle's general direction and stammers, "It um- t-they give that out in the ER to like, *h-help with shock-? Blood loss fainting l-low blood sugar-* and I wanted- *j-just thought maybe-* um, y-ya'know, orange juice-"

Alright.

Okay, so he's following the line of logic, *he thinks,* but there's still a lot of questions that can be asked here like, *why* did Nica give this to him now when he's clearly not in imminent danger of passing out, and also, how *long* have they had that juice on them.

◆✦◆ 510 ◆✦◆

What Goes Bump In The Night

In the end, Etienne just decides to go with the most obvious in his opinion, which is a horribly confused, "Do you...just- *carry* orange juice around with *you*? Like- *on hand?* Just on the off chance that someone *has low blood sugar?*"

"*No.*" Nica huffs at his incredulous tone, shoulders hunching up while their shoes nervously scuff at the floorboards, chin tucking closer to their chest as they mutter, "I don't- I-I'm not like- *a soccer coach*...I just...I-I brought it for *you*, because of *last night*, b-because I thought it might...*help you feel better...I dunno, it sounds stupid now-*"

And oh that's...*oh.*

"*Oh.*" Etienne says like an idiot, eyes snapping back down to the little plastic bottle sitting by his thigh.

There's a cartoon of a smiling orange on it giving him a thumbs up, beads of condensation gathering along the sides of the bottle, and he swipes his fingers through the dew, feeling how cold it is against his skin.

It must have literally just come out of the fridge not too long ago, *hell,* maybe Nica even bought it on their way here, *just to make sure it'd stay cold,* and there's something about this small kindness, *the fact that they were thinking about him worrying about him even still,* that feels like it knocks Etienne straight on his ass.

Taken out by fruit juice I'm sure that's a family first, he thinks mildly irrationally, and the breath catches in his lungs when he picks it up with his injured arm before passing it off to the other, can't rid himself of the sensation that the bottle is heavier than it has any right to be.

Like it means more than it is.

Orange juice or olive branch-

"I won't tell anyone, ya'know." Nica says out of the blue, apropos of nothing, and Etienne's brain is still seizing over orange juice so that's what he almost spits out in confusion, but he's saved the

✦✦ 511 ✦✦

mortification by Nica continuing, "About where your magic comes from? I can tell you didn't wanna tell me an' I'm...*sorry for askin'*. I didn't know it was a secret, though...I suppose there's a *lot* I don't know."

They laugh humorlessly and it turns into a sigh as they tuck hair behind their ear, shyly turning to half look at him, eyes settling unsure somewhere to the side of Etienne's face, "Um, that's what I wanted to talk to you about actually, *er-* I-I guess it would've been better to say I have a favor- *question p-proposition* -to ask? B-But either way, I think I need to apologize to you first...if you'll let me, that is."

"*Why?*" Etienne croaks, and there's a million things he could be asking that for and he doesn't even know which one it is, *why are you doing this why have you always been so nice to me why do you always know me better than most why do you even care,* and maybe Nica hears all his unasked questions in that single word, *maybe they don't,* eyes drifting to his as they answer them all anyway, "Because I *want* to, because you matter, because I...I don't wanna live with the regret of you not knowin' that."

And suddenly they're not sitting on Maisette's front porch anymore but are back crouched on the dirty ground, bloodied and scared and Nica is basically telling him, *I don't think I'm gonna live long enough to see my regrets attended to,* and Etienne is stuck thinking about his own. Which, in this moment, is not him despairing about being a letdown of a son, but rather how he never even gave Nica one chance, came into their whole arrangement already hating them on principle alone.

He sits there and he thinks about how the first thing they ever gave him was an apology and all he offered in return were insults and a thinly veiled, *go fuck yourself.* How Nica kept trying to meet him halfway with kindness and Etienne just kept spitting in their face, so determined to dislike them, he couldn't even see all the ways he *did* like them up until recently.

And it's been almost two months of this, of Etienne generally being the most miserable person to be around and Nica trying their

What Goes Bump In The Night

best to likely not punch him in the face for it, and the *guilt* that washes through him now that he can finally see it is humbling, to say the least.

He was a dick, *he was so absolutely a dick and so very in the wrong,* and he thought it last night but he knows it even better now.

Nica's not the only one that has an apology to give.

"I...think I owe you one too..." Etienne finds himself murmuring, thumbnail running along the plastic grooves of the bottle cap in his hands, and to him, it's clear what he's talking about, but maybe he should've clarified, because in a hilarious parody of events, Nica blurts out, "A-An ...*orange. Juice?*"

And the laugh that tumbles free from Etienne's chest hurts his ribs like you *would not fucking believe,* but it feels too good to stop, and he doesn't think he could even if he wanted to, wraps an arm around his midsection to try and protect his bruises, "Ah, *fucuuudge hah, n-no.* Not an o-orange juice! J-Just an apology. *I owe you an apology,* n-need to- *hah* -tell you *m'sorry-*"

"What? *Why?*" Nica demands, sounding way harsher than they likely intend, but the incredulous tone does work on sobering Etienne up, and he coughs the last of the giggles out of his throat, glances over at scrunched confused bi-colored eyes and thinks he should try to be like Nica for once.

Humble, self-reflective, strong enough to be vulnerable and brave enough to not take it back.

He swallows rough.

That's a lot to ask of himself all at once, especially when he's only good at a few of those things on their own, *not all linked together,* but looking at Nica, at the way they stare at him in seemingly honest confusion, like they have *no idea* why he would apologize to them, Etienne knows he *needs to.*

"Because...I was horrible to you an' I never should have been. Like I know we butt heads, a-an' if m'bein' honest, I...*do really like*

✦✦ 513 ✦✦

the way you tell it to me straight, b-but the hostility I treated you with from the start was so...*unwarranted.*" His fingers pick uselessly at the plastic bottle in his hands, rotating it around like it's a puzzle cube and if he solves it, it'll give him the exact words he needs, "I acted like you were never worth *what you are,* which is countlessly more than anything I could ever ascribe to you, but still, I shouldn't have said what I did...*I never should've said you're worthless...*"

Etienne really hopes he's doing this right, because it doesn't hurt to say what he is even though he thinks it's supposed to, and yeah, he does feel guilty for his past actions, but it's a deserved feeling. He won't shy away from it, and he's not trying to self-flagellate, it's just good to understand he was in the wrong and let himself feel that before moving on. Etienne can't change what was done in the past, *all the stupid crap he said,* but what he *can* do, is use this feeling as motivation to change how things are going forwards.

To be better.

Kinder.

Treating Nica like an equal and not an enemy.

And maybe it would've been obvious from the start if he wasn't so blind to see it, but once the thought crosses his mind, it's like a bell being struck inside his head, an assertion clamoring forth in a clear ringing truth he can't ignore, that Nica is not his enemy.

They never have been.

Gripping the orange juice bottle like a lifeline, *like a hand stretching back reaching out for you checking you for injury keeping you safe burning eyes stubborn chin not leaving you here alone,* Etienne says with as much earnest conviction as he can, "I need to apologize to you because you're a good person, *a kind person,* an' you never deserved to be treated like that. I need to apologize because I *want* to. *Because you matter...*because I don't wanna regret not telling you that I was *wrong.* I was so wrong, Nica...about *you...*a-about a lot of things, an' I am *so, unbelievably, sorry.*"

What Goes Bump In The Night

And Etienne doesn't really have a super concrete expectation for where things are going to go after that, but it's not necessarily Nica just staring at him blankly like he up and said all of that in French, and who knows, *maybe he panicked and did.*

It wouldn't be the most moronic thing he's ever done, but before he can try and correct himself, Nica's lower lip moves like they're about to say something, *later he looks back and sees it's actually more of a tremble,* and that's really the only prelude for these thick streams of tears that start rolling down their face.

Fuck

"Oh- *no no no!* Shit- *I-I mean shoot-* don't cry! I'm sorry! I-I didn't mean to make you cry, I- *f-fu*...please don't cry. I don't hate you or anythin', *promise!*" Etienne stammers, lurching forward in an aborted attempt to do...*something,* but he's not sure he's welcome so he's stuck halfway across the bench, wringing his hands, "Was it somethin' I said? *Mères de la Nwit, of course it was somethin' I said moron-* I'm so sorry! I didn't mean to make you upset, I-I was just tryin' to apologize b-but I *totally* get if what I said was upsettin' o-or out *of line an' that's on me I should've been more careful w-with my words a-an'-!*"

Nica waves their hands frantically in a, *cut it out,* motion, and Etienne dutifully snaps his mouth shut, feels like his chest is caving in on itself when Nica brings their hands up to their face next. They messily try to wipe their eyes clear, but their shoulders keep hitching and more tears keep leaking out and feeling like he wants to compress himself out of this dimension, Etienne drags his legs up onto the bench one agonizing heave at a time.

He folds in half over them, ignoring the way his arm and spine protest, mumbling dejected into his kneecaps, "*Sorry*...I should've just kept my stupid mouth shut. I didn't mean to hurt you, well... *more than I already have.*"

"*N-No!* N-No it's not- *i-it's not you.* M'just a- a-a *c-crier-*" Nica hiccups, palms of both hands pressing into their cheeks, fingers wrapping over their ears to scratch through their own hair in an

❖✦❖ 515 ❖✦❖

attempt to get themself calmed down, "Y-You didn't do anythin' wrong- w-well- I mean- m'not g-gonna lie, *you were a-a dick,* like, you w-were so mean to me an' it did hurt, *a l-lot-* b-but I wasn't nice to y-you *either.* And it's um, i-it's been better recently? *I-I think?* But I just...I-I still never thought you'd *a-apologize for it.*"

Etienne tries not to let that get to him as much as it does, but he's bad at taking things too personally and overthinking himself to death, and he absolutely *hates* hearing how little Nica thought of him as a person. It's deserved though. Whatever poor opinion Nica had, *or has,* of him is entirely Etienne's own doing, and he absolutely cannot take his growing resentment out on them, flexes his hands against his biceps and lets off the static that had been building up.

You did this you sowed this you have to take whatever they give you with a stiff upper lip, he reminds himself in the same stern tone he coaches his magic back into line with, and once he's sure he's not gonna come across like a pissy baby, Etienne nods his head, "That's fair. I...there's no excuse for my actions, an' the only explanation I can give is one of prejudice...which is...*also,* inherently in the wrong. The most meaningful thing I can offer is my most sincere apologies, but I understand if you can't forgive me."

"*S-So formal-*" Nica huffs wetly, wiping at their eyes one last time before they shake their hair back from their face, turning to peek at him with a red rimmed eye and the smallest of smiles, "Of course I forgive you. It means...*s-so much,* to hear you say all that but I...I-I haven't been mad 'bout that for a while, not since I figured out you were actually a good person at least."

Relief courses through Etienne upon hearing that he's forgiven, but his curiosity is also stoked, and he cocks his head, wondering what he could've *possibly* done to change Nica's rotten opinion of him.

"Oh yeah? When was that?" Etienne asks, running back through his memories of the last few months, trying to think about what it could be. It had to have been something recent, *hell it might've been last night actually,* because there's not a single thing he can

What Goes Bump In The Night

think of between now and August that redeems him even a little bit, besides saving them all yesterday he supposes.

So imagine his shock when Nica exhales shaky, looking down at their lap where their hands are moving to wrap around the crooks of their elbows, fingers flexing harshly, "U-Um...that day you took me to get my notebook? And my uh, *o-old name,* came up, b-but you never said *anything.* You never asked, o-or made some sort of comment- *j-joke remark jab-* you just...y-you just *helped me change it.* You d-didn't even *l-like me,* b-but you *helped me change it.* I...m'sorry m'cryin' again but- i-it just *meant a lot t-to me-*"

Nica's chin tucks closer to their chest as tears go falling past, little droplets landing dark maroon on the edge of their hoodie, and Etienne leans closer out of instinct, hand curling over their metal forearm in comfort. There isn't a single time before now where he can recall having touched their prosthesis, remembers more the fact that Nica goes *out* of their way to avoid touching him, *or anyone,* with it, and even though it's covered with the fleecy material of their hoodie, it's something of a jarring sensation.

His fingers wrap over interlocking metal plates, squeeze once gently like he'd do with anyone else, *I'm here I'm here you're not alone I'm here,* and even though he *knows,* his brain is still not prepared for the unrelenting strength of metal as opposed to the soft give of flesh under his touch.

It's an arresting realization, but it's not off-putting, and once Etienne knows what to expect, it's no longer strange to feel the ridges and dips of whatever plate his fingers are running over, "Hey you're okay, Nica, *you're okay.* I'm really glad that meant somethin' to you. I- honestly it's the least I coulda done like, *just-basic human decency,* b-but I'm happy it made you feel uh, s-seen an' respected? You deserve to be called whatever you like, an' we were friends so of course I-"

"W-Were *we?*" Nica snuffles, interrupting him, and only then does Etienne realize what he said, deep color spreading across his face as Nica turns to look at him, cheeks blotchy red and eyes glassy from their crying, "Were we f-friends *then?* I-I didn't think

✦✦ 517 ✦✦

we were, a-an' I don't think- *I mean-* a-are we even friends *n-now?"*

"Do you want to be?" Etienne deflects with his own question, thinks he can taste rejection in the air and wishes he could back-pedal harder than this, but he already said it, *it's out there he can't take it back,* so all he can do is sit here like an idiot and wait for Nica to wince and say, *of course not why would I ever be friends with you you're an asshole a dickhead a freak you almost got me killed twice who would ever want to be around-*

"Yes. I- *y-yeah,* yeah I do." Nica wipes at their nose with their other arm, dropping it down across their belly to grip at their metal bicep, eyes awkwardly darting away and then back up, the most unsure question he's ever heard curling out of their mouth, "D-d-do *you?"*

And his answer is almost immediate, knows it would've been last night, *nodding off in their arms looking for their hand in the dark their shoulder to lean up on wanna go get coffee wanna go get drinks just wanna spend time with you of course I do,* but now, *in the harsh light of day,* there aren't any shadows for him to push the things he can't ignore back into.

Nica is an alchemist, *a usurper.*

Etienne is the scion of House Boudreaux, *he has duties to his line he can't forsake.*

He has a family that expects him to behave a certain way, a mother that is *actively* trying to get Hermes shut down and the practice of alchemy outlawed in the parish, if not the entire *state.* What the hell is he supposed to do in the face of that? Turn his back on them, *go against her wishes?* Fat chance of that. Etienne's family *is his life,* and not only is Catherine his *mother,* someone he loves and respects with all his heart, but she's also his *matriarch,* and you *do not* work against the interests of your atriarch.

That leads to all sorts of dark paths outside the tenets, trespasses against their very creed, and it only ever ends in the same place, with a knife pressed against your jugular instead of your palm *you do not disobey your atriarch you do not defy your order*, but...

What Goes Bump In The Night

Etienne's going to be an atriarch someday too, so where does that line get drawn?

When does it become other people's duty to listen to *him*, to follow his ideas and wishes? Is it when he's sworn in fifteen years from now? Sooner? *Later?* Or will his decisions never be his own until mother dies?

If it's the latter, then why is he constantly put under pressure to already carry himself like the patriarch he's *not*, when he's stuck with no power and no authority and all the crushing expectations of being a leader no one listens to?

It hardly seems fair, and maybe that's the point of it, *maybe it's to teach him humility,* but Etienne feels like he's swallowed enough humility to last a lifetime, *or...at least a good chunk of it,* so then what's his answer.

Does what he think is right matter or not?

And maybe the answer is easier to divine than he believes it is, *maybe it's the same one he gives his magic,* where there are lines he still needs to stay behind but he retains the ability to define their shape, *holds the right to curve them how he wants and make it his own.*

Maybe Etienne is destined to walk this direction, *never disobey your order never work against your atriarch,* but maybe he doesn't have to take the road they set him on, maybe he can *choose* a new path to forge instead, one that still leads him to the same ending destination, *won't betray the Council won't betray his mother uphold the tenets safeguard the covens be the witch you want to be,* but it's the one that he chooses for himself.

Mother will always be his mother, and she will continue to be his matriarch for a decade or more, but she's raising him to be the leader that steps up after her, and if he's never willing to take a stand for the things he thinks matters, then what kind of leader is he ever going to be?

Etienne is twenty years old now, almost twenty-one.

✦✦ 519 ✦✦

He's halfway through his apprenticeship and he's aware that he doesn't know *everything,* but he knows enough to make an informed decision like this.

Alchemy isn't going anywhere, *it's just not,* as much as his mother and all the other atriarchs wish it would just crawl back into whatever crevice of a mind it sprung from, there's no forcing knowledge like that to be forgotten once it's known. The city is also never going to abandon Hermes, it generates enough money and prestige to be useful still, *drives patents brings in grants turns eyes all over the country back to New Orleans,* and so they will never stop pushing for greater cooperation between the Occult and the college.

And, *as much as he once would've been loath to admit,* Etienne can understand their insistence for a closer partnership, has gotten the *barest* inkling of what him and Nica are capable of, *the floor changing seamlessly under his feet power rushing up through his legs building his magic into a massive echoing crescendo never felt energy like this never seen your magic react like that,* and he already wants more, wants to know what they could accomplish together if given the chance.

There's so much room for growth, *for change for opportunities and possibilities,* and that's the whole mantra of his coven isn't it, *the house of change of new beginnings hellos and farewells and new dawns don't shy away from goodbyes and the sun,* and it makes sense that it should start here.

It makes sense that it should start with him.

This won't be an easy thing to go forward with though, *Etienne knows that,* knows who he is and how many eyes are constantly trained on him, and he *knows* people will talk because don't they always. It's not like it's expressly against any rules or laws for him and Nica to be friends, well...*at least not officially,* and as long as he has his say, it never will be. Etienne understands mother has her own way she's wanting to fight against the recent opposition, but he's gonna be an atriarch someday too, and he's got ideas of his own.

✦✦ 520 ✦✦

What Goes Bump In The Night

Like, how instead of spending all this time and resources working towards a future that is never going to be feasible, *one where alchemy is unmade and they once more have no opposition,* they could instead turn towards more practical goals, like extending an open palm rather than a clenched fist.

Befriend the college administration, *win the alchemists over to their side,* show them they have more to gain by working together than against one another, and the city council loses a very key bargaining chip, would have no choice but to bend to their demands. Of course it won't be as simple as that, requires making space for alchemy in a way that sends Etienne's head spinning for a loop, and that's just his own personal struggle with the idea of a more equal footing, it doesn't even take into account how others will react.

There will be pushback, *there will be dissent,* from both the Council of Night *and* Hermes, but Etienne can feel it down under his bones, tripping along in the shuddering chambers of his heart, *this is the correct decision to make.*

This is the path he needs to set them on.

And it starts here, *it starts today,* on an unexceptional Friday in October, when he's sitting on his front porch in cartoon skull pajama pants and there's a grinning orange giving him a thumbs up, *this* is the first step down this way he is making for himself, *for all of them,* towards a better tomorrow, and it begins with only a few simple words.

"Yes...yes, I do. I want to be friends." Etienne says, and they feel just as weighty as the words he said on his fifteenth birthday, when he knelt before the Mother of his house and bled the first of his blood in Her name, and there's no knife and no statue here, but his words still feel just as irrevocable.

Just as permanent.

Binding.

~~*Beware gwéiniath*~~

If there are any lingering doubts, he never knows them, forgets there could be anything else but the way Nica smiles at him, *unsure to shy to happy to wonderous,* a rising expression that lights up their entire face and crinkles their eyes into twin crescents of shining, heady joy.

It's the brightest sunrise he's ever seen.

Epilogue

They end up sitting and talking for much longer than the original minute Nica asked for.

The conversation wanders here, it pokes its head into there, sunlight dances across the front yard while ratty sneakers scuff against Maisette's floorboards, and Nica winds out that apology they owed him and caps it with the question they said they needed to ask him.

I'm sorry, it starts in a soft but earnest hush, *you were right,* Nica admits, fidgeting with the metallic joints of their fingers, *wasn't my place never should have made excuses never should have played it off,* rhythmic swinging of their foot a metronome of penance, *I should have listened to you I should've backed you up,* hazel eye cutting to his like a guilt ridden magnet, *I'm sorry I'm ignorant I'm sorry I didn't know that I didn't ask...but I want to listen I want to learn...I wanted to ask,* and out it sails in a summer soft country drawl-

Would you teach me would you show me would you let me know?

And Etienne is so stunned for a minute he doesn't know how to answer, can't think of a time where someone asked him anything about his heritage and it was born of a genuine desire to *understand* rather than morbid, *mocking* curiosity.

It's more common than you'd think, *that condescending interest,* because while some people just hate them flat out right, don't care to learn or budge in their convictions, *Carter the protesters that haunt your dreams the man that shot Gerome,* there is a startling majority that regard him and his family like a slightly amusing carnival freakshow.

A salacious source of gossip.

Etienne doesn't use a computer often, but he's still seen the garish blinking blogs online, has read the newspaper gossip columns that are just *dripping* with condemnation, ignores the prying questions that get flung at him on the street or when he's just trying to go about his day, *the cameras aimed at his face- hey hey hey is it true is what they say true do you really dig up graves for their bones or perform blood sacrifices under new moons stealing babies and defiling tombs is it true?*

He knows what people *think* they know about him, *about his family about his culture blood drinking savages out in the bayous not based on any real covens but those are your markings under that actor's eyes,* and it seems like everyone has an opinion or some idea of how things are, but no one's ever honestly asked him about it simply because they wanted to *know, because they wanted to do better.*

Except for now.

Except for Nica.

"I- what do you *want to know?"* Etienne eventually lands on, picking at the disintegrating paper label on the orange juice bottle, and Nica shrugs, eyes trained on where a trolley goes trundling down the street, "Whatever you can tell me. I know it won't be everythin', *a-an' I respect that,* but I just...t-there's so much online and I don't know what's true and what *isn't.* I don't wanna be wrong again...*I don't wanna hurt you like that again...*"

And oh, *oh that does something to Etienne's heart,* makes it a little melted and a little soft in his chest, like it could come pouring out from behind the gaps in his ribs if he's not careful. *Mothers of the Night,* is he ever fond of Nica Caldwell, adores their candor and self-reflection and humility, and now that he's allowed himself this closeness, he can freely admit that. He likes their personality, he's *fond* of their mannerisms, *he's going to enjoy being their friend,* and Etienne leans back into the feeling, *lets that warmth envelope him.*

"Thank you, I...I-I really appreciate that. *Genuinely."* He smiles at

What Goes Bump In The Night

them kindly even though their gaze is resolutely trained far ahead, studies the curve of their profile instead and his eyes hook on the paler patches of skin that decorate the right side of their face, little blotches across their cheek that flow under their chin, *down their neck like a waterfall,* "Being a witch though...that's...not exactly somethin' I can really explain in an hour, o-or even a *day.* There's just so much to it, an' I don't think you want the entire *hundred hour* history lecture."

Etienne's trying to make light, trying to give Nica an out, and it's not that he doesn't appreciate their gesture, *he does so much Mothers he thinks it touches him all the way down at the sinews,* but he also doesn't think they meant it when they said *everything.* Hyperbole is what it is though, and witch history is long and complicated and their culture equally more so, all of it bound up in the dancing tide of energy and entities that made them who they are.

It's a lot, and he can recognize that even though he *grew up with it,* but without missing a beat, Nica turns to look at him, chin propped up on the metal ridge of their shoulder while they say like it should be obvious, "Well if that's how long it takes. I got time. I wanna hear whatever it is you have to say, Etienne."

Light shifts across the front porch then and makes the white paint illuminate, that gentle glow catching in Nica's eyes, cupping the soft curve of their cheek, *makes all these little wayward hairs shine like the sun,* and starting and stopping, jumping and rolling, squishing sideways and inverting all together, Etienne's heart does a bunch of weird shit he has no explanation for and all he can do is nod, somewhere at the back of his brain thinking he liked it better when Nica *didn't* look at him so much.

What is this what is this, trips and jolts under his bones, *calm down act normal why are you being like this,* slimy nerves crawling up his throat and nettling at his fingers and he can't seem to swallow it back down, *what's wrong with you what's wrong with you,* and he doesn't know, *he doesn't know,* and the sun creeps across the porch, *falls off Nica he makes himself look away.*

And he can breathe again.

✦✦✦ 525 ✦✦✦

In one two, *out one two,* and they move on.

Wind ruffles past and they talk about a lot of things, the birds call to one another and they talk about nothing. It's back to being hot today and Etienne gets irritated enough he rolls up the dark hems of his pajama pants, crosses his leg over a knee, and Nica asks about the huge suckered scar winding around his right calf so Etienne tells them about the only time he's broken a bone.

"*Yeeeaaah,* the Gagnon try an' keep the marémeb in Au Delà from gettin' *too big,* but they're good at hidin'. *Even the big ones.*" Etienne mumbles, cheek resting in his hand while he twists his leg, showcasing the gnarly rope of sucker marks that dance up his skin in paler rings of missing flesh, "Didn't even know what was happenin' at first, just misstepped an' then I was whippin' across the bayou at a hundred miles an hour. Snapped my tibia in half like it was a wishbone."

Nica must also overheat because they push the sleeves of their hoodie up, and Etienne's eyes snap right to their prosthesis, admiring the clever puzzle like way the joints and plates fit together, and he doesn't want to be weird about it, but he's as fascinated as he's always been, awkwardly rocks back and forth until Nica shoots him a look and then one of the few questions he'll let himself ask comes tumbling out.

Who made it? It's beautiful.

"Oh, uh, t-thanks? Um, me an' my uncle did. T-Technically just him that first time. I um...I-I couldn't really do uh, *alchemy,* with only one arm so he made the first prototype." Nica says, using their other hand to hike their right sleeve higher, exposing more plating, more intricately carved metal that they rotate as easily as anyone else moves a part of their body, "We've both done a lotta work since then. Lots of different versions, lots of trial- *tests- e-experiments* -and error. A-An' it's not *perfect*...but it'll do."

More lurks under that statement than Nica would willingly reveal it seems, but Etienne knows better than to pry, learned his lesson once about stepping off the path into waters you can't clearly see

What Goes Bump In The Night

the bottom of. So, *blessing of blessings,* he manages to keep his mouth shut for once like he's been trying to learn to be better at, only telling Nica they've got one of the cleverest minds he knows and leaving it there.

Which, what he assumed to just be a simple fact ends up being so much more, and it's honestly amazing to see someone turn that *exact* shade of fire engine red in response before murmuring a nearly silent, incredibly bashful *thanks.*

Etienne says *you're welcome* around a small laugh, Nica tucks hair behind their red ear, the hot bugs sing to fill the warm silence and Maisette seems to settle closer around them both.

The subject shifts to school and the breeze blows sweetly through the windchimes, talk of assignments and hated tests smoothing out into discussion of movies and shows and the sun starts to burnish the tops of the trees a sunny gold, conversation sliding into things they like and spots they know and places they want to take each other, and Etienne forgets they were only supposed to be here a minute, *that it's been much longer than that.*

He forgets, *he's forgotten,* but he knows he's already gotten Nica on the hook for Amandine's – *everything there is amazing you really should try their chai I don't think it's that bitter more spicy really* – Nica wants to bring him by this tea place they found that serves something he's never heard of before – *it's called boba and stop making that face it's really good and yeah a lot of their stuff is sweet but they have matcha and I figured if anyone liked the taste of grass it'd be you-*

Etienne once again has to defend his tea preference, once again Nica tells him he's wrong *and an idiot,* they get into an argument that could never be called serious, drift closer the harder they laugh, Etienne can't open his stupid orange juice because of some way his left arm flexes and it nearly puts him on the floor it hurts so bad, but after Nica is done freaking out over him, *has been assured he's not dying,* they crack the seal for him without any comment.

Though they do sit there with a fucking- *smug-ass smirk* on

✦✦ 527 ✦✦

their face while he drinks his shitty OJ and Etienne hates them so much, *is so glad they came over,* because hanging out on Maisette's porch fucking around has been a million times better for him than grumpily trying to sleep would have been. He honestly hasn't noticed any of his aches and pains until just now, wiggles his bare toes against warm wood and wonders if maybe he should invite Nica in so they can watch a movie or something, *wonders if they like old horror or maybe a good slasher,* but a familiar chiming sinks that idea fast.

Etienne tries not to be too disappointed as Nica starts the frantic song and dance that is trying to find their phone, hopes it isn't but knows it probably is, *the sound of an alarm that means they have to go,* and sure enough, when Nica eventually hauls it out of a back pocket, their entire face falls.

"Fuck-! Shit! W-What do you *mean it's past four thirty alre-* oh my God, I've got a fuckin' tutoring session in like, *twenty minutes-"* They hiss, scrambling to their feet and start spinning in a circle looking for something, "Did I bring anythin'- *do I h-have anythin' else-* phone, check. Keys, check. W-Wallet- *coin purse* -check, bbbbackpaaaack? No...no? Nope. *Shit fuck shit-* okay gotta go by the dorm then but that's an added- e-extra- *additional fifteen-* aaaauuugghhHHH! I'm gonna be so *laaaaaaateeeeeee-!"*

Nica whines as they bounce around on their toes in a nervous circle, giving Etienne the most hangdog look as they slip a small tie off their wrist, impressively pulling their hair back with only their skin and bone fingers, "Shit, I'm so sorry I'm just cuttin' an' runnin', I-I was really enjoying chattin' but I got this thing all the way back on campus an' m'already gonna be hella- i-incredibly- r-really stupid late a-an' I just-! *I'm really sorry!"*

"Éy, don't worry about it, I understand. An' I appreciate you takin' the time to come check on me in the first place, thanks for the blood sugar juice." Etienne waggles his mostly empty bottle at them, and then because he's not a *heathen,* he pushes himself to his feet to see Nica off.

It takes him a second longer than he normally would to get up-

What Goes Bump In The Night

right, legs shaking ominously once Etienne settles his weight back on his heels, but Maisette scoots the bench closer for him to use as a subtle prop.

Thanks, he hushes through their bond, feels an answering gliding touch that rumbles through his heart like loving, distant thunder, and shoving off from an armrest, he uses the momentum to take a few wooden steps towards Nica.

They glance over at him when he hobbles closer and he knows they need to get going, but there's this idea that's been scuttling around his brain since last night, *before everything went to shit,* and it's not really a big deal, *except for it is it really is,* but Etienne *wants to* and he anxiously scratches through his hair, looking at anything that's not Nica as he stumbles out, "Well I guess I'll... see you Monday, then? Unless um, *well,* I'll probably be busy this weekend but we uh, w-we should...grab drinks o-or somethin'? *Sometime maybe?* I-If you want! *That is...*"

Oh real smooth Boudreaux that's gonna make them wanna spend time with you for suuuure, and he winces, knows that was awkward as hell, but asking Nica to hang out is surprisingly a much more nerve wracking experience than he was expecting.

Up until today, any interaction they've had has been within the parameters of the diversity program, *was mandated by the city... compulsory,* and there was a lot to hide behind with that, *I'm just doing this because they're making me I don't have to talk to you I don't have to try and get you to like me I don't care what you think of me-* and that's where the anxiety is coming in.

Etienne is usually pretty good with people, likes talking to and getting to know them, but he's stupidly worried all of a sudden that he's forgotten how to do that, can't help but feel like as soon as Nica and him are in a place and it's not *required* for them to be there together, he's not going to have a *clue* of what to say or do.

Like what if it gets awkward and quiet and Etienne runs out of normal things to say. What the fuck is he supposed to talk about then?

✦✦ 529 ✦✦

Almost everything in his life involves death and decomposition and unholy nightmares, and he's definitively learned by now most people do *not* find those charming or amusing bar stories. He could always fall back to just asking Nica about themself, *wants to know wants to hear,* but then the fear there is Nica realizing he's not actually all that smart, *struggles with math can't mix a potion to save his life,* and Etienne knows he'd never be able to follow along the second they started talking about their coursework.

And there's so much more waiting in line after those, a dozen more anxieties that pop up one after another, all clamoring for his attention in a nasty little symphony of nerves, *you're weird they won't like you you're too different the both of you are too different,* but they're summarily crushed by the way Nica's face lights up, *gets a little red across the cheeks,* wide shy smile unfurling across their lips and boom, there it is.

Dimple.

"O-Oh! Y-You mean like- *yeah,* y-yeah I'd like- *love* -that! That'd be- *um,* I uh, I-I can't actually drink because of uh, *medication?* B-But tea an' coffee are cool! *O-Or hot depends on how you like it-* but liquids are neat, I like drinking them, I um, I- *yeah.*" Nica rambles around their grin, goes to habitually tuck hair back behind their ear before realizing they already put it up, "I- I really gotta get goin' but um, I-I'll text you later? Er, write you, I guess, since, ya'know- *notebook.* B-But yeah! I'll uh, I'll talk to you later an' we can get something planned? I-If you want?"

"Yeah I- t-that sounds good. I'd like that." Etienne says with a warm smile of his own, wraps an arm around a porch column to steady his balance while he tries stretching his legs out one at a time, winces as something pulls funny, *"Ack-* I'll uh, I'll see ya later, have a good tutoring session."

"You too! *I mean-* you h-have a good weekend too!" Nica exclaims, clattering down Maisette's front steps, stuffs their hands in their pockets and then draws up short not even halfway down the path, spinning back around in a flurry, "Oh! *Fuck-* I-I almost forgot- here, *catch!"*

✦✦ 530 ✦✦

What Goes Bump In The Night

They lob something small at him unprompted and Etienne can't *fathom* why Nica thinks he has the hand eye coordination to catch something that little, *let alone the foot coordination to not fall down the stairs trying,* but thankfully Maisette manages to get it for him. A section of trim breaks off and shoots forwards, snagging the flying object out of midair before coiling down and offering it to Etienne with a gentle shake.

Nestled in the center of glossy white crown molding is a chunk of dark blue green stone, smatterings of vibrant oranges and reds cutting through the duller background color like snapping coils of nebulas. Its edges are rougher, more of a natural stone look than a polished one, but Etienne would still recognize it anywhere in any shape, even if it didn't hum gently to him once he picks it up.

Bloodstone.

His fingers curl protectively over the uneven shape of it, eyes darting to where Nica waves exuberantly on his front walk, edging backwards as they call, "To replace the one I blew up! Don't worry- I made it have a clasp an' everythin' so you can stick it on your hat! I gotta run though, so- *bye!* H-Have a good weekend!"

Etienne barely gets his hand up in a farewell wave before Nica's out the front gate and jogging down the sidewalk, stays leaned up against the porch's column though until they're completely out of sight, swallowed up by the heavy hanging limbs of moss laden trees and the haze of a soon to be setting sun.

He turns his attention back to the bloodstone brooch in his palm once they're gone, flips it over and sure enough, there is a shining golden pin clasp on the back. Unlike his last one though, the fastening isn't just attached to the stone, but is literally coming *out of* the stone, like it's all a single solid piece rather than two separate objects. Etienne thumbs at the juncture between what's probably brass and the stone itself, can't find any lip or ridge so it really has to be one thing, and knows the only way to get something like this is through alchemy.

Nica made this for me...specifically, he thinks, turning it back

✦✦ 531 ✦✦

over and admiring the way the colors blend together, swirled like watercolors and oil slicks and galaxies far away, tiny inclusions of iron catching in the light and shining like stars. It's stunning, way more beautiful than the one he used to have, and Etienne curls it protectively to his chest, looks up at his empty yard glowing in the early evening sun and doesn't think he'd be able to hand this one over so easily.

The door opens for him when he turns to go back inside, dark wood and creamy walled interior of Maisette quiet around him, light seeping through the windows to cast everything a warm shade, soft in its silence and peacefully still, but it won't stay that way for long.

Abel and Felix are probably done with their after-school activities and are likely almost home with Gilbert, mother should be finished up at the offices downtown and then she'll be back, maybe beating Oliver home or maybe not if he's caught up with something else. Katie and Atha will be later, *one more so than the other,* but they'll still be in time for dinner, everyone sitting down to eat and catch up before the night rotation starts and then those who have assignments are out again, likely until dawn breaks or just shortly before.

It's a short window they have, crazy and hectic in its brevity, but Etienne adores those few hours they manage to steal every day where the whole family can be together, grins now thinking about the story *he'll* have to tell around the table tonight.

None of them are gonna believe you for a second, and they honestly probably won't at first, but here he is, alive and mostly in one piece, though he's certainly been better off, body a little stiff after sitting for that long. Apparently he's hobbling so bad, Maisette jokingly shakes a bin of spare canes at him and Etienne barks out a laugh, crinkles his lip at the jangling box and snarks, "Oh piss *off.* Mémé was right, you are nothin' but a glorified collection of thumbtacks."

The bin's feet clatter against the floor and it sounds something like a hitching laugh, and with a fond shake of his head, Etienne

What Goes Bump In The Night

steps up to the coat rack, crooks his fingers so the thing will lean down for him. His hat sits alone on one of the numerous prongs, looking fairly decent considering all that went down last night, but the crow feathers are knocked slightly askew, no longer held in place by the brooch he used to have.

Stretching up on his toes, Etienne flips open the pin on the piece of bloodstone in his hands, works it through the old holes punched through his hatband, and gets it fitted snuggly in place.

He readjusts it a bit, but it doesn't need much to look good, deep red clouds of the stone picking up the maroon in the gilded ribbon Etienne has wound around the base of his hat. He takes a step back, head cocked to the side to make sure it's even, and likes the way it looks, something about it seeming slightly ethereal nestled back against the black felt and shiny gold chains.

Honestly, as he's heading back upstairs to finally change out of his pajamas, *put on something more respectable,* Etienne can't help but think it looks better than his old one ever did.

Like it was the one that was always supposed to be there.

Acknowledgements

Thank you to my friends and family, without your support, I'm not sure this book would have happened. Thank you specifically to my husband, who has been so kind and unwaveringly encouraging, it has given me the opportunity to pursue my dreams to an extent I never thought possible. Thank you also to my two editors, Gracie and Clarity, for catching all my spelling errors...and grammar errors...*and isnts*...I can't thank you enough for that, and for listening to all my unhinged, long winded rambles. And lastly, thank you to Link, my couch companion and book formatting emotional support dog, without you, I would have actually descended into madness.

About the author

Hellen is a small, independent author from the southeastern United States. She has exactly one cat, one dog, and one husband, all of whom are very confsed about the amount of time she spends making faces at her laptop. Outside of writing, Knight enjoys hiking, creating art, and replaying Dragon Age: Inquisition ad nauseum.

To stay up to date on the latest news, and to find things such as; social media/discord links, marketable trinkets for your perusal, whimsical apparel designs, etc., please scan the QR code or visit the link below.

https://linktr.ee/hellenknight